EMILY LEARNS THE TRUTH

Emily stood quite still and looked up at Ellen's broad, red face—as still as if she had been suddenly turned to stone. She was as stunned as if Ellen had struck her a physical blow.

"I'm telling you this because I think it's high time you was told," Ellen said. "I've been at your pa for months to tell you, but he's kept putting it off and off. When the doctor told me last night that the end might come any time now, I just made up my mind that *I'd* do what was right. Laws-a-massy, child, don't look like that! You'll be looked after. Your ma's people will see to that—on account of the Murray pride, if for no other reason. You'll have a good home—better'n you've ever had here. For mercy's sake, Emily Byrd Starr, don't stand there staring like that! You ain't the first child that's been left an orphan and you won't be the last."

Emily
of New Moon

L. M. Montgomery

Published by
Dell Laurel-Leaf
an imprint of
Random House Children's Books
a division of Random House, Inc.
New York

J. B. Lippincott edition published 1923

"Emily of New Moon," "Emily," and "L. M. Montgomery" are trademarks of the Heirs of L. M. Montgomery, Inc., and are used under license by Bantam Books.

Visit us on the Web! www.randomhouse.com/teens

Educators and librarians, for a variety of teaching tools, visit us at www.randomhouse.com/teachers

ISBN: 0-553-23370-X

Reprinted by arrangement with HarperCollins Publishers, Inc.

RL: 7.0

Printed in the United States of America

First Dell Laurel-Leaf Edition March 2003

40   39

OPM

To
Mr. George Boyd Macmillan
Alloa, Scotland
in recognition of
a long and stimulating friendship

Contents

1 The House in the Hollow   1
2 A Watch in the Night   8
3 A Hop out of Kin   19
4 A Family Conclave   32
5 Diamond Cut Diamond   42
6 New Moon   50
7 The Book of Yesterday   61
8 Trial by Fire   76
9 A Special Providence   88
10 Growing Pains   101
11 Ilse   109
12 The Tansy Patch   117
13 A Daughter of Eve   132
14 Fancy Fed   141
15 Various Tragedies   148
16 Check for Miss Brownell   160
17 Living Epistles   173
18 Father Cassidy   186
19 Friends Again   204
20 By Aërial Post   208
21 "Romantic but not Comfortable"   219
22 Wyther Grange   230
23 Deals with Ghosts   238

24 A Different Kind of Happiness   248
25 "She Couldn't Have Done It"   255
26 On the Bay Shore   261
27 The Vow of Emily   272
28 A Weaver of Dreams   291
29 Sacrilege   304
30 When the Curtain Lifted   314
31 Emily's Great Moment   328

1
The House in the Hollow

The house in the hollow was "a mile from anywhere"—so Maywood people said. It was situated in a grassy little dale, looking as if it had never been built like other houses but had grown up there like a big, brown mushroom. It was reached by a long, green lane and almost hidden from view by an encircling growth of young birches. No other house could be seen from it although the village was just over the hill. Ellen Greene said it was the lonesomest place in the world and vowed that she wouldn't stay there a day if it wasn't that she pitied the child.

Emily didn't know she was being pitied and didn't know what lonesomeness meant. She had plenty of company. There was Father—and Mike—and Saucy Sal. The Wind Woman was always around; and there were the trees—Adam-and-Eve, and the Rooster Pine, and all the friendly lady-birches.

And there was "the flash," too. She never knew when it might come, and the possibility of it kept her a-thrill and expectant.

Emily had slipped away in the chilly twilight for a walk. She remembered that walk very vividly all her life—perhaps because of a certain eerie beauty that was in it—perhaps because "the flash" came for the first time in weeks—more likely because of what happened after she came back from it.

It had been a dull, cold day in early May, threatening to rain but never raining. Father had lain on the sittingroom lounge all day. He had coughed a good

1

deal and he had not talked much to Emily, which was a very unusual thing for him. Most of the time he lay with his hands clasped under his head and his large, sunken, dark-blue eyes fixed dreamily and unseeingly on the cloudy sky that was visible between the boughs of the two big spruces in the front yard—Adam-and-Eve, they always called those spruces, because of a whimsical resemblance Emily had traced between their position, with reference to a small apple-tree between them, and that of Adam and Eve and the Tree of Knowledge in an old-fashioned picture in one of Ellen Greene's books. The Tree of Knowledge looked exactly like the squat little apple-tree, and Adam and Eve stood up on either side as stiffly and rigidly as did the spruces.

Emily wondered what Father was thinking of, but she never bothered him with questions when his cough was bad. She only wished she had somebody to talk to. Ellen Greene wouldn't talk that day either. She did nothing but grunt, and grunts meant that Ellen was disturbed about something. She had grunted last night after the doctor had whispered to her in the kitchen, and she had grunted when she gave Emily a bedtime snack of bread and molasses. Emily did not like bread and molasses, but she ate it because she did not want to hurt Ellen's feelings. It was not often that Ellen allowed her anything to eat before going to bed, and when she did it meant that for some reason or other she wanted to confer a special favor.

Emily expected the grunting attack would wear off over night, as it generally did; but it had not, so no company was to be found in Ellen. Not that there was a great deal to be found at any time. Douglas Starr had once, in a fit of exasperation, told Emily that "Ellen Greene was a fat, lazy old thing of no importance," and Emily, whenever she looked at Ellen after that, thought the description fitted her to a hair.

So Emily had curled herself up in the ragged, comfortable old wing-chair and read *The Pilgrim's Progress* all the afternoon. Emily loved *The Pilgrim's Progress*. Many a time had she walked the straight and narrow path with *Christian* and *Christiana*—although she never liked *Christiana*'s adventures half as well as *Christian*'s. For one thing, there was always such a crowd with *Christiana*. She had not half the fascination of that solitary, intrepid figure who faced all alone the shadows of the Dark Valley and the encounter with Apollyon. Darkness and hobgoblins were nothing when you had plenty of company. But to be *alone*—ah, Emily shivered with the delicious horror if it!

When Ellen announced that supper was ready Douglas Starr told Emily to go out to it.

"I don't want anything tonight. I'll just lie here and rest. And when you come in again we'll have a real talk, Elfkin."

He smiled up at her his old, beautiful smile, with the love behind it, that Emily always found so sweet. She ate her supper quite happily—though it wasn't a good supper. The bread was soggy and her egg was underdone, but for a wonder she was allowed to have both Saucy Sal and Mike sitting, one on each side of her, and Ellen only grunted when Emily fed them wee bits of bread and butter.

Mike had such a cute way of sitting up on his haunches and catching the bits in his paws, and Saucy Sal had *her* trick of touching Emily's ankle with an almost human touch when her turn was too long in coming. Emily loved them both, but Mike was her favourite. He was a handsome, dark-grey cat with huge owl-like eyes, and he was so soft and fat and fluffy. Sal was always thin; no amount of feeding put any flesh on her bones. Emily liked her, but never cared to cuddle or stroke her because of her thinness. Yet there was a sort of weird beauty about her that appealed to Emily. She was grey-and-white—very white and very sleek, with a long, pointed face, very long ears and very green eyes. She was a redoubtable fighter, and strange cats were vanquished in one round.

The fearless little spitfire would even attack dogs and rout them utterly.

Emily loved her pussies. She had brought them up herself, as she proudly said. They had been given to her when they were kittens by her Sunday School teacher.

"A *living* present is so nice," she told Ellen, "because it keeps on getting nicer all the time."

But she worried considerably because Saucy Sal didn't have kittens.

"I don't know why she doesn't," she complained to Ellen Greene. "Most cats seem to have more kittens than they know what to do with."

After supper Emily went in and found that her father had fallen asleep. She was very glad of this; she knew he had not slept much for two nights; but she was a little disappointed that they were not going to have that "real talk." "Real" talks with Father were always such delightful things. But next best would be a walk— a lovely all-by-your-lonesome walk through the grey evening of the young spring. It was so long since she had had a walk.

"You put on your hood and mind you scoot back if it starts to rain," warned Ellen. "*You* can't monkey with colds the way some kids can."

"Why can't I?" Emily asked rather indignantly. Why must *she* be debarred from "monkeying with colds" if other children could? It wasn't fair.

But Ellen only grunted. Emily muttered under her breath for her own satisfaction, "You are a fat old thing of no importance!" and slipped upstairs to get her hood—rather reluctantly, for she loved to run bareheaded. She put the faded blue hood on over her long, heavy braid of glossy, jet-black hair, and smiled chummily at her reflection in the little greenish glass. The smile began at the corners of her lips and spread over her face in a slow, subtle, very wonderful way, as Douglas Starr often thought. It was her dead mother's smile—the thing that had caught and held him long ago when he had first seen Juliet Murray. It seemed to be Emily's only physical inheritance from her mother. In all else, he thought, she was like the Starrs—in her large, purplish-grey eyes with their very long lashes and black brows, in her high, white forehead—too high for beauty—in the delicate modeling of her pale oval face and sensitive mouth, in the little ears that were pointed just a wee bit to show that she was kin to tribes of elfland.

"I'm going for a walk with the Wind Woman, dear," said Emily. "I wish I could take you too. Do you *ever* get out of that room, I wonder. The Wind Woman is going to be out in the fields to-night. She is tall and misty, with thin, grey, silky clothes blowing all about her—and wings like a bat's—only you can see through them—and shining eyes like stars looking through her long, loose hair. She can fly—but to-night she will walk with me all over the fields. She's a *great* friend of mine—the Wind Woman is. I've known her ever since I was six. We're *old*, *old* friends—but not quite so old as you and I, little Emily-in-the-glass. We've been friends *always*, haven't we?"

With a blown kiss to little Emily-in-the-glass, Emily-out-of-the-glass was off.

The Wind Woman was waiting for her outside—ruffling the little spears of striped grass that were sticking up stiffly in the bed under the sitting-room window—tossing the big boughs of Adam-and-Eve—whispering among the misty green branches of the birches—teasing the "Rooster Pine" behind the house—it really did look like an enormous, ridiculous rooster, with a huge, bunchy tail and a head thrown back to crow.

It was so long since Emily had been out for a walk that she was half crazy with the joy of it. The winter had been so stormy and the snow so deep that she was never allowed out; April had been a month of rain and wind; so on this May evening she felt like a released prisoner. Where should she go? Down the brook—or over the fields to the spruce barrens? Emily chose the latter.

She loved the spruce barrens, away at the further end of the long, sloping pasture. That was a place where magic was made. She came more fully into her fairy birthright there than in any other place. Nobody who saw Emily skimming over the bare field would have envied her. She was little and pale and poorly clad; sometimes she shivered in her thin jacket; yet a queen might have gladly given a crown for her visions—her dreams of wonder. The brown, frosted grasses under her feet were velvet piles. The old, mossy, gnarled half-dead spruce-tree, under which she paused for a moment to look up into the sky, was a marble column in a palace of the gods; the far dusky hills were the ramparts of a city of wonder. And for companions she had all the fairies of the countryside—for she could believe in them here—the fairies of the white clover and satin catkins, the little green folk of the grass, the elves of the young fir-trees, sprites of wind and wild fern and thistledown. Anything might happen there—everything might come true.

And the barrens were such a splendid place in which to play hide and seek with the Wind Woman. She was so very *real* there; if you could just spring quickly enough around a little cluster of spruces—only you never could—you would *see* her as well as feel her and hear her. There she was—that *was* the sweep of her grey cloak—no, she was laughing up in the very top of the taller trees—and the chase was on again—till, all at once, it seemed as if the Wind Woman were gone—and the evening was bathed in a wonderful silence—and there was a sudden rift in the curdled clouds westward, and a lovely, pale, pinky-green lake of sky with a new moon in it.

Emily stood and looked at it with clasped hands and her little black head upturned. She must go home and write down a description of it in the yellow account book, where the last thing written had been, "Mike's

Biograffy." It would hurt her with its beauty until she wrote it down. Then she would read it to Father. She must not forget how the tips of the trees on the hill came out like fine black lace across the edge of the pinky-green sky.

And then, for one glorious, supreme moment, came "the flash."

Emily called it that, although she felt that the name didn't exactly describe it. It couldn't be described—not even to Father, who always seemed a little puzzled by it. Emily never spoke of it to any one else.

It had always seemed to Emily, ever since she could remember, that she was very, very near to a world of wonderful beauty. Between it and herself hung only a thin curtain; she could never draw the curtain aside—but sometimes, just for a moment, a wind fluttered it and then it was as if she caught a glimpse of the enchanting realm beyond—only a glimpse—and heard a note of unearthly music.

This moment came rarely—went swiftly, leaving her breathless with the inexpressible delight of it. She could never recall it—never summon it—never pretend it; but the wonder of it stayed with her for days. It never came twice with the same thing. To-night the dark boughs against that far-off sky had given it. It had come with a high, wild note of wind in the night, with a shadow wave over a ripe field, with a greybird lighting on her window-sill in a storm, with the singing of "Holy, holy, holy" in church, with a glimpse of the kitchen fire when she had come home on a dark autumn night, with the spirit-like blue of ice palms on a twilit pane, with a felicitous new word when she was writing down a "description" of something. And always when the flash came to her Emily felt that life was a wonderful, mysterious thing of persistent beauty.

She scuttled back to the house in the hollow, through the gathering twilight, all agog to get home and write down her "description" before the memory picture of what she had seen grew a little blurred. She knew just how she would begin it—the sentence seemed to shape itself in her mind: "The hill called to me and something in me called back to it."

She found Ellen Greene waiting for her on the sunken front-doorstep. Emily was so full of happiness that she loved everything at that moment, even fat things of no importance. She flung her arms around Ellen's knees and hugged them. Ellen looked down gloomily into the rapt little face, where excitement had kindled a faint wild-rose flush, and said, with a ponderous sigh:

"Do you know that your pa has only a week or two more to live?"

2
A Watch in the Night

Emily stood quite still and looked up at Ellen's broad, red face—as still as if she had been suddenly turned to stone. She felt as if she had. She was as stunned as if Ellen had struck her a physical blow. The colour faded out of her little face and her pupils dilated until they swallowed up the irises and turned her eyes into pools of blackness. The effect was so startling that even Ellen Greene felt uncomfortable.

"I'm telling you this because I think it's high time you was told," she said. "I've been at your pa for months to tell you, but he's kept putting it off and off. I says to him, says I, 'You know how hard she takes things, and if you drop off suddent some day it'll most kill her if she hasn't been prepared. It's your duty to prepare her,' and he says, says he, 'There's time enough yet, Ellen.' But he's never said a word, and when the doctor told me last night that the end might come any time now, I just made up my mind that I'd do what was right and drop a hint to prepare you. Laws-a-massy, child, don't look like that! You'll be looked after. Your ma's people will see to that—on account of the Murray pride, if for no other reason. They won't let one of their own blood starve or go to strangers—even if they have always hated your pa like p'isen. You'll have a good home—better'n you've ever had here. You needn't worry a mite. As for your pa, you ought to be thankful to see him at rest. He's been dying by inches for the last five years. He's kept it from you, but he's been a great sufferer. Folks say his heart broke when your ma died—it came on him so suddent-like—she was only sick three days. That's why I want you to know what's coming, so's you won't be all upset when it happens. For mercy's sake, Emily Byrd Starr, don't stand there staring like that! You give me the creeps! You ain't the first child that's been left an orphan and you won't be the last. Try and be sensible. And don't go pestering your pa about what I've told you, mind that. Come you in now, out of the damp, and I'll give you a cooky 'fore you go to bed."

Ellen stepped down as if to take the child's hand. The power of motion returned to Emily—she must scream if Ellen even touched her *now*. With one sudden, sharp, bitter little cry she avoided Ellen's hand, darted through the door and fled up the dark staircase.

Ellen shook her head and waddled back to her kitchen. "Anyhow, I've done *my* duty," she reflected. "He'd have just kept saying 'time enough' and put it off till he was dead and then there'd have been no managing her. She'll have time now to get used to it, and she'll brace up in a day or two. I will say for her she's got spunk—which is lucky, from all I've heard of the Murrays. They won't find it easy to overcrow *her*. She's got a streak of their pride, too, and that'll help her through. I wish I dared send some of the Murrays word that he's dying, but I don't dast go that far. There's no telling what *he*'d do. Well, I've stuck on here to the last and I ain't sorry. Not many women would 'a' done it, living as they do here. It's a shame the way that child's been brought up—never even sent to school. Well, I've told him often enough what I've thought of it—it ain't on *my* conscience, that's one comfort. Here, you Sal-thing, you git out! Where's Mike, too?''

Ellen could not find Mike for the very good reason that he was upstairs with Emily, held tightly in her arms, as she sat in the darkness on her little cot bed. Amid her agony and desolation there was a certain comfort in the feel of his soft fur and round velvety head.

Emily was not crying; she stared straight into the darkness, trying to face the awful thing Ellen had told her. She did not doubt it—something told her it was true. Why couldn't she die, too? She couldn't go on living without Father.

"If I was God I wouldn't let things like this happen," she said.

She felt it was very wicked of her to say such a thing—Ellen had told her once that it was the wickedest thing any one could do to find fault with God. But she didn't care. Perhaps if she were wicked enough God would strike her dead and then she and Father could keep on being together.

But nothing happened—only Mike got tired of being held so tightly and squirmed away. She was all alone now, with this terrible burning pain that seemed all over her and yet was not of the body. She could never get rid of it. She couldn't help it by writing about it in the old yellow account book. She had written there about her Sunday School teacher going away, and of being hungry when she went to bed, and Ellen telling her she must be half crazy to talk of Wind Women and flashes; and after she had written down all about them these things hadn't hurt her any more. But this couldn't be written about. She could not even go to Father for comfort, as she had gone when she burned her hand so badly, picking up the red-hot poker by mistake. Father had held her in his arms all that night and told her stories and helped her to bear the pain. But Father, so Ellen had said, was going to die in a week or two. Emily felt as if Ellen had told her this years and years ago. It surely couldn't be less than an hour since she had been playing with the Wind Woman in the barrens and looking at the new moon in the pinky-green sky.

"The flash will never come again—it can't," she thought.

But Emily had inherited certain things from her fine old ancestors—the power to fight—to suffer—to pity—to love very deeply—to rejoice—to endure. These things were all in her and looked out at you through her purplish-grey eyes. Her heritage of endurance came to her aid now and bore her up. She must not let Father know what Ellen had told her—it might hurt him. She must keep it all to herself and *love* Father, oh, so much, in the little while she could yet have him.

She heard him cough in the room below: she must be in bed when he came up; she undressed as swiftly as her cold fingers permitted and crept into the little cot bed which stood across the open window. The voices of the gentle spring night called to her all unheeded—unheard the Wind Woman whistled by the eaves. For the fairies dwell only in the kingdom of Happiness; having no souls they cannot enter the kingdom of Sorrow.

She lay there cold and tearless and motionless when her father came into the room. How very slowly he walked—how very slowly he took off his clothes. How was it she had never noticed these things before? But he was not coughing at all. Oh, what if Ellen were mistaken?—what if—a wild hope shot through her aching heart. She gave a little gasp.

Douglas Starr came over to her bed. She felt his dear nearness as he sat down on the chair beside her, in his old red dressing-gown. Oh, how she loved him! There was no other Father like him in all the world—there never could have been—so tender, so understanding, so wonderful! They had always been such chums—

they had loved each other so much—it couldn't be that they were to be separated.

"Winkums, are you asleep?"

"No," whispered Emily.

"Are you sleepy, small dear?"

"No—no—not sleepy."

Douglas Starr took her hand and held it tightly.

"Then we'll have our talk, honey. I can't sleep either. I want to tell you something."

"Oh—I know it—I know it!" burst out Emily. "Oh, Father, I know it! Ellen told me."

Douglas Starr was silent for a moment. Then he said under his breath, "The old fool—the *fat* old fool!"—as if Ellen's fatness was an added aggravation of her folly. Again, for the last time, Emily hoped. Perhaps it was all a dreadful mistake—just some more of Ellen's fat foolishness.

"It—it isn't true, is it, Father?" she whispered.

"Emily, child," said her father, "I can't lift you up—I haven't the strength—but climb up and sit on my knee—in the old way."

Emily slipped out of bed and got on her father's knee. He wrapped the old dressing-gown about her and held her close with his face against hers.

"Dear little child—little beloved Emilykin, it is quite true," he said, "I meant to tell you myself to-night. And now that old absurdity of an Ellen has told you—brutally, I suppose—and hurt you dreadfully. She has the brain of a hen and the sensibility of a cow. May jackals sit on her grandmother's grave! *I* wouldn't have hurt you, dear."

Emily fought something down that wanted to choke her.

"Father, I can't—I can't bear it."

"Yes, you can and will. You will live because there is something for you to do, I think. You have my gift—along with something I never had. You will succeed where I failed, Emily. I haven't been able to do much for you, sweetheart, but I've done what I could. I've taught you something, I think—in spite of Ellen Greene. Emily, do you remember your mother?"

"Just a little—here and there—like lovely bits of dreams."

"You were only four when she died. I've never talked much to you about her—I couldn't. But I'm going to tell you all about her to-night. It doesn't hurt me to talk of her now—I'll see her so soon again. You don't look like her, Emily—only when you smile. For the rest, you're like your namesake, my mother. When you were born I wanted to call you Juliet, too. But your mother wouldn't. She said if we called you Juliet then I'd soon take to calling her 'Mother' to distinguish between you, and she couldn't endure *that*. She said her Aunt Nancy had once said to her, 'The first time your husband calls you "Mother" the romance of life is over.' So we called you after my mother—*her* maiden name was Emily Byrd. Your mother thought Emily the prettiest name in the world,—it was quaint and arch and delightful, she said. Emily, your mother was the sweetest woman ever made."

His voice trembled and Emily snuggled close.

"I met her twelve years ago, when I was sub-editor of the *Enterprise* up in Charlottetown and she was in her last year at Queen's. She was tall and fair and blue-eyed. She looked a little like your Aunt Laura, but Laura was never so pretty. Their eyes were very much alike—and their voices. She was one of the Murrays from Blair Water. I've never told you much about your mother's people, Emily. They live up on the old north shore at Blair Water on New Moon Farm—always have lived there since the first Murray came out from the Old Country in 1790. The ship he came on was called the *New Moon* and he named his farm after her."

"It's a nice name—the new moon is such a pretty thing," said Emily, interested for a moment.

"There's been a Murray ever since at New Moon Farm. They're a proud family—the Murray pride is a byword along the north shore, Emily. Well, they had some things to be proud of, that cannot be denied—but they carried it too far. Folks call them 'the chosen people' up there.

"They increased and multiplied and scattered all over, but the old stock at New Moon Farm is pretty well run out. Only your Aunts, Elizabeth and Laura, live there now, and their cousin, Jimmy Murray. They never married—could not find any one good enough for a Murray, so it used to be said. Your Uncle Oliver and your Uncle Wallace live in Summerside, your Aunt Ruth in Shrewsbury and your Great-Aunt Nancy at Priest Pond."

"Priest Pond—that's an *interesting* name—not a pretty name like New Moon and Blair Water—but interesting," said Emily. Feeling Father's arm around her the horror had momentarily shrunk away. For just a little while she ceased to believe it.

Douglas Starr tucked the dressing-gown a little more closely around her, kissed her black head, and went on.

"Elizabeth and Laura and Wallace and Oliver and Ruth were old Archibald Murray's children. His first wife was their mother. When he was sixty he married again—a young slip of a girl—who died when your mother was born. Juliet was twenty years younger than her half-family, as she used to call them. She was very pretty and charming and they all loved and petted her and were very proud of her. When she fell in love with me, a poor young journalist, with nothing in the world but his pen and his ambition, there was a family earthquake. The Murray pride couldn't tolerate the thing at all. I won't rake it all up—but things were said I could never forget or forgive. Your mother married me, Emily—and the New Moon people would have nothing more to do with her. Can you believe that, in spite of it, she was never sorry for marrying me?"

Emily put up her hand and patted her father's hollow cheek.

"*Of course* she wouldn't be sorry. *Of course* she'd

rather have you than all the Murrays of any kind of a moon."

Father laughed a little—and there was just a note of triumph in his laugh.

"Yes, she seemed to feel that way about it. And we were so happy—oh, Emilykin, there never were two happier people in the world. You were the child of that happiness. I remember the night you were born in the little house in Charlottetown. It was in May and a west wind was blowing silvery clouds over the moon. There was a star or two here and there. In our tiny garden—everything we had was small except our love and our happiness—it was dark and blossomy. I walked up and down the path between the beds of violets your mother had planted—and prayed. The pale east was just beginning to glow like a rosy pearl when some one came and told me I had a little daughter. I went in—and your mother, white and weak, smiled just that dear, slow, wonderful smile I loved, and said, 'We've—got—the only—baby—of any importance—in—the world, dear. Just—think—of that!'"

"I wish people could remember from the very moment they're born," said Emily. "It would be so very interesting."

"I dare say we'd have a lot of uncomfortable memories," said her father, laughing a little. "It can't be very pleasant getting used to living—no pleasanter than getting used to stopping it. But you didn't seem to find it hard, for you were a good wee kidlet, Emily. We had four more happy years and then—do you remember the time your mother died, Emily?"

"I remember the funeral, Father—I remember it *distinctly*. You were standing in the middle of a room, holding me in your arms, and Mother was lying just before us in a long, black box. And you were crying—and I couldn't think why—and I wondered why Mother looked so white and wouldn't open her eyes. And I leaned down and touched her cheek—and oh, it was so cold. It made me shiver. And somebody in the room said, 'Poor little thing!' and I was frightened and put my face down on your shoulder.''

"Yes, I recall that. Your mother died very suddenly. I don't think we'll talk about it. The Murrays all came to her funeral. The Murrays have certain traditions and they live up to them very strictly. One of them is that nothing but candles shall be burned for light at New Moon—and another is that no quarrel must be carried past the grave. They came when she was dead—they would have come when she was ill if they had known, I will say that much for them. And they behaved very well—oh, very well indeed. They were not the Murrays of New Moon for nothing. Your Aunt Elizabeth wore her best black satin dress to the funeral. For any funeral but a Murray's the second best one would have done; and they made no serious objection when I said your mother would be buried in the Starr plot in Charlottetown cemetery. They would have liked to take her back to the old Murray burying-ground in Blair Water—they had their own private burying-ground, you know—no indiscriminate graveyard for *them*. But your Uncle Wallace handsomely admitted that a woman should belong to her husband's family in death as in life. And then they offered to take you and bring you up—to 'give you your mother's place.' I refused to let them have you—then. Did I do right, Emily?''

"Yes—yes—yes!" whispered Emily, with a hug at every "yes."

"I told Oliver Murray—it was he who spoke to me about you—that as long as I lived I would not be parted from my child. He said, 'If you ever change your mind, let us know.' But I did not change my mind—not even three years later when my doctor told me I must give up work. 'If you don't, I give you a year,' he said, 'if you do, and live out-of-doors all you can, I give you three—or possibly four.' He was a good prophet. I came out here and we've had four lovely years together, haven't we, small dear one?''

"Yes—oh, yes!"

"Those years and what I've taught you in them are the only legacy I can leave you, Emily. We've been living on a tiny income I have from a life interest that was left me in an old uncle's estate—an uncle who died before I was married. The estate goes to a charity now, and this little house is only a rented one. From a worldly point of view I've certainly been a failure. But your mother's people will care for you—I know that. The Murray pride will guarantee so much, if nothing else. And they can't help loving you. Perhaps I should have sent for them before—perhaps I ought to do it yet. But I have pride of a kind, too—the Starrs are not entirely traditionless—and the Murrays said some very bitter things to me when I married your mother. Will I send to New Moon and ask them to come, Emily?"

"No!" said Emily, almost fiercely.

She did not want any one to come between her and Father for the few precious days left. The thought was horrible to her. It would be bad enough if they had to come—afterwards. But she would not mind anything much—then.

"We'll stay together to the very end, then, little Emily-child. We won't be parted for a minute. And I want you to be brave. You mustn't be afraid of *any-thing*, Emily. Death isn't terrible. The universe is full of love—and spring comes everywhere—and in death you open and shut a door. There are beautiful things on the other side of the door. I'll find your mother there—I've doubted many things, but I've never doubted *that*. Sometimes I've been afraid that she would get so far ahead of me in the ways of eternity that I'd never catch up. But I feel *now* that she's waiting for me. And we'll wait for you—we won't hurry—we'll loiter and linger till you catch up with us."

"I wish you—could take me right through the door with you," whispered Emily.

"After a little while you won't wish that. You have yet to learn how kind time is. And life has something for you—I feel it. Go forward to meet it fearlessly, dear.

I know you don't feel like that just now—but you will remember my words by and by."

"I feel just now," said Emily, who couldn't bear to hide anything from Father, "that I don't like God any more."

Douglas Starr laughed—the laugh Emily liked best. It was such a dear laugh—she caught her breath over the dearness of it. She felt his arms tightening round her.

"Yes, you do, honey. You can't help liking God. He is Love itself, you know. You mustn't mix Him up with Ellen Greene's God, of course."

Emily didn't know exactly what Father meant. But all at once she found that she wasn't afraid any longer—and the bitterness had gone out of her sorrow, and the unbearable pain out of her heart. She felt as if love was all about her and around her, breathed out from some great, invisible, hovering Tenderness. One couldn't be afraid or bitter where love was—and love was everywhere. Father was going through the door—no, he was going to lift a curtain—she liked *that* thought better, because a curtain wasn't as hard and fast as a door—and he would slip into that world of which the flash had given her glimpses. He would be there in its beauty—never very far away from her. She could bear anything if she could only feel that Father wasn't very far away from her—just beyond that wavering curtain.

Douglas Starr held her until she fell asleep; and then in spite of his weakness he managed to lay her down in her little bed.

"She will love deeply—she will suffer terribly—she will have glorious moments to compensate—as I have had. As her mother's people deal with her, so may God deal with them," he murmured brokenly.

3
A Hop out of Kin

Douglas Starr lived two weeks more. In after years when the pain had gone out of their recollection, Emily thought they were the most precious of her memories. They were beautiful weeks—beautiful and not sad. And one night, when he was lying on the couch in the sitting-room, with Emily beside him in the old wing-chair, he went past the curtain—went so quietly and easily that Emily did not know he was gone until she suddenly felt the strange *stillness* of the room—there was no breathing in it but her own.

"Father—Father!" she cried. Then she screamed for Ellen.

Ellen Greene told the Murrays when they came that Emily had behaved real well, when you took everything into account. To be sure, she had cried all night and hadn't slept a wink; none of the Maywood people who came flocking kindly in to help could comfort her; but when morning came her tears were all shed. She was pale and quiet and docile.

"That's right, now," said Ellen, "that's what comes of being properly prepared. Your pa was so mad at me for warning you that he wasn't rightly civil to me since—and him a dying man. But I don't hold any grudge against him. *I* did my duty. Mrs. Hubbard's fixing up a black dress for you and it'll be ready by supper time. Your ma's people will be here tonight, so they've telegraphed, and I'm bound they'll find you looking respectable. They're well off and they'll provide for you. Your pa hasn't left a cent but there ain't any debts, I'll say *that* for him. Have you been in to see the body?"

"Don't call him *that*," cried Emily, wincing. It was horrible to hear Father called *that*.

"Why not? If you ain't the queerest child! He makes a better looking corpse than I thought he would, what with being so wasted and all. He was always a pretty man, though too thin."

"Ellen Greene," said Emily suddenly, "if you say any more of—those things—about Father, I will put the black curse on you!"

Ellen Greene stared.

"I don't know what on earth you mean. But that's no way to talk to me, after all I've done for you. You'd better not let the Murrays hear you talking like that or they won't want much to do with you. The black curse indeed! Well, here's gratitude!"

Emily's eyes smarted. She was just a lonely, solitary little creature and she felt very friendless. But she was not at all remorseful for what she had said to Ellen and she was not going to pretend she was.

"Come you here and help me wash these dishes," ordered Ellen. "It'll do you good to have something to take up your mind and then you won't be after putting curses on people who have worked their fingers to the bone for you."

Emily, with an eloquent glance at Ellen's hands, went and got the dish towel.

"Your hands are fat and pudgy," she said. "The bones don't show at all."

"Never mind sassing back! It's awful, with your poor pa dead in there. But if your Aunt Ruth takes you she'll soon cure you of that."

"Is Aunt Ruth going to take me?"

"I don't know, but she ought to. She's a widow with no chick or child, and well-to-do."

"I don't think I want Aunt Ruth to take me," said Emily deliberately, after a moment's reflection.

"Well, *you* won't have the choosing likely. You ought

to be thankful to get a home anywhere. Remember you're not of much importance."

"I am important to myself," cried Emily proudly.

"It'll be some chore to bring *you* up," muttered Ellen. "Your Aunt Ruth is the one to do it, in my opinion. *She* won't stand no nonsense. A fine woman she is and the neatest housekeeper on P. E. Island. You could eat off her floor."

"I don't want to eat off her floor. I don't care if a floor is dirty as long as the tablecloth is clean."

"Well, her tablecloths are clean too, I reckon. She's got an elegant house in Shrewsbury with bow windows and wooden lace all round the roof. It's very stylish. It would be a fine home for you. She'd learn you some sense and do you a world of good."

"I don't want to learn sense and be done a world of good to," cried Emily with a quivering lip. "I—I want somebody to love me."

"Well, you've got to behave yourself if you want people to like you. You're not to blame so much—your pa has spoiled you. I told him so often enough, but he just laughed. I hope he ain't sorry for it now. The fact is, Emily Starr, you're queer, and folks don't care for queer children."

"How am I queer?" demanded Emily.

"You talk queer—and you act queer—and at times you look queer. And you're too old for your age—though that ain't *your* fault. It comes of never mixing with other children. I've always threaped at your father to send you to school—learning at home ain't the same thing—but he wouldn't listen to me, of course. I don't say but what you are as far along in book learning as you need to be, but what you want is to learn how to be like other children. In one way it would be a good thing if your Uncle Oliver would take you, for he's got a big family. But he's not as well off as the rest, so it ain't likely he will. Your Uncle Wallace might, seeing as he reckons himself the head of the family. He's only got a grown-up daughter. But his wife's delicate—or fancies she is."

"I wish Aunt Laura would take me," said Emily. She remembered that Father had said Aunt Laura was something like her mother.

"Aunt Laura! *She* won't have no say in it—Elizabeth's boss at New Moon. Jimmy Murray runs the farm, but he ain't quite all there, I'm told—"

"What part of him isn't there?" asked Emily curiously.

"Laws, it's something about his mind, child. He's a bit simple—some accident or other when he was a youngster, I've heard. It addled his head, kind of. Elizabeth was mixed up in it some way—I've never heard the rights of it. I don't reckon the New Moon people will want to be bothered with you. They're awful set in their ways. You take my advice and try to please your Aunt Ruth. Be polite—and well-behaved—mebbe she'll take a fancy to you. There, that's all the dishes. You'd better go upstairs and be out of the way."

"Can I take Mike and Saucy Sal?" asked Emily.

"No, you can't."

"They'd be company for me," pleaded Emily.

"Company or no company, you can't have them. They're outside and they'll stay outside. I ain't going to have them tracking all over the house. The floor's been scrubbed."

"Why didn't you scrub the floor when Father was alive?" asked Emily. "He liked things to be clean. You hardly ever scrubbed it then. Why do you do it now?"

"Listen to her! Was I to be always scrubbing floors with my rheumatiz? Get off upstairs and you'd better lie down awhile."

"I'm going upstairs, but I'm not going to lie down," said Emily. "I've got a lot of thinking to do."

"There's one thing I'd advise you to do," said Ellen, determined to lose no chance of doing her duty, "and that is to kneel down and pray to God to make you a good and respectful and grateful child."

Emily paused at the foot of the stairs and looked back.

"Father said I wasn't to have anything to do with your God," she said gravely.

Ellen gasped foolishly, but could not think of any reply to this heathenish statement. She appealed to the universe.

"Did any one ever hear the like!"

"I know what *your* God is like." said Emily. "I saw His picture in that Adam-and-Eve book of yours. He has whiskers and wears a nightgown. I don't like Him. But I like Father's God."

"And what is your father's God like, if I may ask?" demanded Ellen sarcastically.

Emily hadn't any idea what Father's God was like, but she was determined not to be posed by Ellen.

"He is clear as the moon, fair as the sun, and terrible as an army with banner," she said triumphantly.

"Well, you're bound to have the last word, but the Murrays will teach you what's what," said Ellen, giving up the argument. "They're strict Presbyterians and won't hold by any of your father's awful notions. Get off upstairs."

Emily went up to the south room, feeling very desolate.

"There isn't anybody in the world who loves me now," she said, as she curled up on her bed by the window. But she was determined she would not cry. The Murrays, who had hated her father, should not see her crying. She felt that she detested them all—except perhaps Aunt Laura. How very big and empty the world had suddenly become. Nothing was interesting any more. It did not matter that the little squat apple-tree between Adam-and-Eve had become a thing of rose-and-snow beauty—that the hills beyond the hollow were of green silk, purple-misted—that the daffodils were out in the garden—that the birches were hung all over with golden tassels—that the Wind Woman was blowing white young clouds across the sky. None of these things had any charm or consolation for her now. In her inexperience she believed they never would have again.

"But I promised Father I'd be brave," she whispered, clenching her little fists, "and I will. And I *won't* let the Murrays see I'm afraid of them—I won't *be* afraid of them!"

When the far-off whistle of the afternoon train blew beyond the hills, Emily's heart began to beat. She clasped her hands and lifted her face.

"Please help me, Father's God—*not* Ellen's God," she said. "Help me to be brave and not cry before the Murrays."

Soon after there was the sound of wheels below—and voices—loud, decided voices. Then Ellen came puffing up the stairs with the black dress—a sleazy thing of cheap merino.

"Mrs. Hubbard just got it done in time, thanks be. I wouldn't 'a' had the Murrays see you not in black for the world. They can't say I haven't done my duty. They're all here—the New Moon people and Oliver and his wife, your Aunt Addie, and Wallace and his wife, your Aunt Eva, and Aunt Ruth—Mrs. Dutton, *her* name is. There, you're ready now. Come along."

"Can't I put my Venetian beads on?" asked Emily.

"Did ever any mortal! Venetian beads with a mourning dress! Shame on you! Is this a time to be thinking of vanity?"

"It isn't vanity!" cried Emily. "Father gave me those beads last Christmas—and I want to show the Murrays that I've got *something!*"

"No more of your nonsense! Come along, I say! Mind your manners—there's a good deal depends on the impression you make on them."

Emily walked rigidly downstairs before Ellen and into the parlour. Eight people were sitting around it—and she instantly felt the critical gaze of sixteen stranger eyes. She looked very pale and plain in her black dress; the purple shadows left by weeping made her large eyes look too large and hollow. She was desperately afraid, and she knew it—but she would not let the Murrays see it. She held up her head and faced the ordeal before her gallantly.

"This," said Ellen, turning her around by the shoulder, "is your Uncle Wallace."

Emily shuddered and put out a cold hand. She did not like Uncle Wallace—she knew that at once—he was black and grim and ugly, with frowning, bristly brows and a stern, unpitying mouth. He had big pouches under his eyes, and carefully-trimmed black side-whiskers. Emily decided then and there that she did not admire side-whiskers.

"How do you do, Emily?" he said coldly—and just as coldly he bent forward and kissed her cheek.

A sudden wave of indignation swept over Emily's soul. How *dared* he kiss her—he had hated her father and disowned her mother! She would have none of his kisses! Flash-quick, she snatched her handkerchief from her pocket and wiped her outraged cheek.

"Well—*well!*" exclaimed a disagreeable voice from the other side of the room.

Uncle Wallace looked as if he would like to say a great many things but couldn't think of them. Ellen, with a grunt of despair, propelled Emily to the next sitter.

"Your Aunt Eva," she said.

Aunt Eva was sitting huddled up in a shawl. She had the fretful face of the imaginary invalid. She shook hands with Emily and said nothing. Neither did Emily.

"Your Uncle Oliver," announced Ellen.

Emily rather liked Uncle Oliver's appearance. He was big and fat and rosy and jolly-looking. She thought she would not mind so much if *he* kissed her, in spite of his bristly white moustache. But Uncle Oliver had learned Uncle Wallace's lesson.

"I'll give you a quarter for a kiss," he whispered genially. A joke was Uncle Oliver's idea of being kind and sympathetic, but Emily did not know this, and resented it.

"I don't *sell* my kisses," she said, lifting her head as haughtily as any Murray of them all could do.

Uncle Oliver chuckled and seemed infinitely amused and not a bit offended. But Emily heard a sniff across the room.

Aunt Addie was next. She was as fat and rosy and jolly-looking as her husband and she gave Emily's cold hand a nice, gentle squeeze.

"How are you, dear?" she said.

That "dear" touched Emily and thawed her a trifle. But the next in turn froze her up instantly again. It was Aunt Ruth—Emily knew it was Aunt Ruth before Ellen said so, and she knew it was Aunt Ruth who had "well—welled" and sniffed. She knew the cold, grey eyes, the prim, dull brown hair, the short, stout figure, the thin, pinched, merciless mouth.

Aunt Ruth held out the tips of her fingers, but Emily did not take them.

"Shake hands with your Aunt," said Ellen in an angry whisper.

"She does not want to shake hands with me," said Emily, distinctly, "and so I am not going to do it."

Aunt Ruth folded her scorned hands back on her black silk lap.

"You are a very ill-bred child," she said; "But of course it was only what was to be expected."

Emily felt a sudden compunction. Had she cast a reflection on her father by her behaviour? Perhaps after all she should have shaken hands with Aunt Ruth. But it was too late now—Ellen had already jerked her on.

"This is your Cousin, Mr. James Murray," said Ellen, in the disgusted tone of one who gives up something as a bad job and is only anxious to be done with it.

"Cousin Jimmy—Cousin Jimmy," said that individual. Emily looked steadily at him, and liked him at once without any reservations.

He had a little, rosy, elfish face with a forked grey beard; his hair curled over his head in a most un-Murray-like mop of glossy brown; and his large, brown eyes were as kind and frank as a child's. He gave Emily a hearty handshake, though he looked askance at the lady across from him while doing it.

"Hello, pussy!" he said.

Emily began to smile at him, but her smile was, as always, so slow in developing that Ellen had whisked her on before it was in full flower, and it was Aunt Laura who got the benefit of it. Aunt Laura started and paled.

"Juliet's smile!" she said, half under her breath. And again Aunt Ruth sniffed.

Aunt Laura did not look like any one else in the room. She was almost pretty, with her delicate features and the heavy coils of pale, sleek, fair hair, faintly greyed, pinned closely all around her head. But it was her eyes that won Emily. They were such round blue, *blue* eyes. One never quite got over the shock of their blueness. And when she spoke it was in a beautiful, soft voice.

"You poor, dear, little child," she said, and put her arm around Emily for a gentle hug.

Emily returned the hug and had a narrow escape then from letting the Murrays see her cry. All that saved her was the fact that Ellen suddenly pushed her on into the corner by the window.

"And this is your Aunt Elizabeth."

Yes, this was Aunt Elizabeth. No doubt about that—and she had on a stiff, black satin dress, so stiff and rich that Emily felt sure it must be her very best. This pleased Emily. Whatever Aunt Elizabeth thought of her father, at least she had paid him the respect of her best dress. And Aunt Elizabeth was quite fine looking in a tall, thin, austere style, with clear-cut features and a massive coronet of iron-grey hair under her black lace cap. But her eyes, though steel-blue, were as cold as Aunt Ruth's, and her long thin mouth was compressed severely. Under her cool, appraising glance Emily retreated into herself and shut the door of her soul. She would have liked to please Aunt Elizabeth—who was "boss" at New Moon—but she felt she could not do it.

Aunt Elizabeth shook hands and said nothing—the truth being that she did not know exactly what to say. Elizabeth Murray would not have felt "put about" before King or Governor-General. The Murray pride would have carried her through there; but she did feel disturbed in the presence of this alien, level-gazing child who had already shown that she was anything but meek and humble. Though Elizabeth Murray would never have admitted it, she did not want to be snubbed as Wallace and Ruth had been.

"Go and sit on the sofa," ordered Ellen.

Emily sat on the sofa with her eyes cast down, a slight, black, indomitable little figure. She folded her hands on her lap and crossed her ankles. They should see she had manners.

Ellen had retreated to the kitchen, thanking her stars that *that* was over. Emily did not like Ellen but she felt deserted when Ellen had gone. She was alone now before the bar of Murray opinion. She would have given anything to be out of the room. Yet in the back of her mind a design was forming of writing all about it in the old account book. It would be interesting. She could describe them all—she knew she could. She had the very word for Aunt Ruth's eyes—"stone-grey." They were just like stones—as hard and cold and relentless. Then a pang tore through her heart. Father could never again read what she wrote in the account book.

Still—she felt that she would rather like to write it all out. How could she best describe Aunt Laura's eyes? They were such beautiful eyes—just to call them "blue" meant nothing—hundreds of people had blue eyes—oh, she had it—"wells of blue"—that was the very thing.

And then the flash came!

It was the first time since the dreadful night when Ellen had met her on the doorstep. She had thought it could never come again—and now in this most unlikely place and time it *had* come—she had seen, with other eyes than those of sense, the wonderful world behind the veil. Courage and hope flooded her cold little soul like a wave of rosy light. She lifted her head and looked about her undauntedly—"brazenly" Aunt Ruth afterwards declared.

Yes, she *would* write them all out in the account book—describe every last one of them—sweet Aunt Laura, nice Cousin Jimmy, grim old Uncle Wallace, and moonfaced Uncle Oliver, stately Aunt Elizabeth and detestable Aunt Ruth.

"She's a delicate-looking child," said Aunt Eva, suddenly, in her fretful, colourless voice.

"Well, what else could you expect?" said Aunt Addie, with a sigh that seemed to Emily to hold some dire significance. "She's too pale—if she had a little colour she wouldn't be bad-looking."

"I don't know who she looks like," said Uncle Oliver, staring at Emily.

"She is not a Murray, that is plain to be seen," said Aunt Elizabeth, decidedly and disapprovingly.

"They are talking about me just as if I wasn't here," thought Emily, her heart swelling with indignation over the indecency of it.

"I wouldn't call her a Starr either," said Uncle Oliver. "Seems to me she's more like the Byrds—she's got her grandmother's hair and eyes."

"She's got old George Byrd's nose," said Aunt Ruth, in a tone that left no doubt as to her opinion of George's nose.

"She's got her father's forehead," said Aunt Eva, also disapprovingly.

"She has her mother's smile," said Aunt Laura, but in such a low tone that nobody heard her.

"And Juliet's long lashes—hadn't Juliet very long lashes?" said Aunt Addie.

Emily had reached the limit of her endurance.

"You make me feel as if I was made up of scraps and patches!" she burst out indignantly.

The Murrays stared at her. Perhaps they felt some compunction—for, after all, none of them were ogres and all were human, more or less. Apparently nobody could think of anything to say, but the shocked silence was broken by a chuckle from Cousin Jimmy—a low chuckle, full of mirth and free from malice.

"That's right, puss," he said. "Stand up to them—take your own part."

"Jimmy!" said Aunt Ruth.

Jimmy subsided.

Aunt Ruth looked at Emily.

"When I was a little girl," she said, "I never spoke until I was spoken to."

"But if nobody ever spoke until they were spoken to there would be no conversation," said Emily argumentatively.

"I never answered back," Aunt Ruth went on severely. "In those days little girls were trained properly. We were polite and respectful to our elders. We were taught our place and we kept it."

"I don't believe you ever had much fun," said Emily—and then gasped in horror. She hadn't meant to say that out loud—she had only meant to *think* it. But she had such an old habit of thinking aloud to Father.

"Fun!" said Aunt Ruth, in a shocked tone. "I did not think of fun when I was a little girl."

"No, I know," said Emily gravely. Her voice and manner were perfectly respectful, for she was anxious to atone for her involuntary lapse. Yet Aunt Ruth looked as if she would like to box her ears. This child was *pitying* her—insulting her by being sorry for *her*—because of her prim, impeccable childhood. It was unendurable—especially in a Starr. And that abominable Jimmy was chuckling again! Elizabeth should suppress him!

Fortunately Ellen Greene appeared at this juncture and announced supper.

"You've got to wait," she whispered to Emily. "There ain't room for you at the table."

Emily was glad. She knew she could not eat a bite under the Murray eyes. Her aunts and uncles filed out stiffly without looking at her—all except Aunt Laura, who turned at the door and blew her a tiny, furtive kiss. Before Emily could respond Ellen Greene had shut the door.

Emily was left all alone in the room that was filling with twilight shadows. The pride that had sustained her in the presence of the Murrays suddenly failed her and she knew that tears were coming. She went straight to the closed door at the end of the parlour, opened it, and went in. Her father's coffin stood in the centre of the small room which had been a bedroom. It was heaped with flowers—the Murrays had done the proper thing in that as in all else. The great anchor of white roses Uncle Wallace had brought stood up aggressively on the small table at the head. Emily could not see her father's face for Aunt Ruth's heavily-fragrant pillow of white hyacinths lying on the glass, and she dared not move it. But she curled herself up on the floor and laid her cheek against the polished side of the casket. They found her there asleep when they came in after supper. Aunt Laura lifted her up and said,

"I'm going to take the poor child up to bed—she's worn right out."

Emily opened her eyes and looked drowsily about her.

"Can I have Mike?" she said.

"Who is Mike?"

"My cat—my big grey cat."

"A cat!" exclaimed Aunt Elizabeth in a shocked tone. "You must not have a cat in your bedroom!"

"Why not—for once?" pleaded Laura.

"Certainly not!" said Aunt Elizabeth. "A cat is a most unwholesome thing in a sleeping apartment. I'm surprised at you, Laura! Take the child up to bed and see that there are plenty of bedclothes. It's a cold night— but let me hear no more talk of sleeping with cats."

"Mike is a clean cat," said Emily. "He washes himself—every day."

"Take her up to bed, Laura!" said Aunt Elizabeth, ignoring Emily.

Aunt Laura yielded meekly. She carried Emily upstairs, helped her undress, and tucked her into bed. Emily was very sleepy. But before she was wholly asleep she felt something, soft and warm and purry and companionable, snuggling down by her shoulder. Aunt Laura had sneaked down, found Mike and brought him up to her. Aunt Elizabeth never knew and Ellen Greene dared not say a word in protest—for was not Laura a Murray of New Moon?

4
A Family Conclave

Emily wakened at daylight the next morning. Through her low, uncurtained window the splendour of the sunrise was coming in, and one faint, white star was still lingering in the crystal-green sky over the Rooster Pine. A fresh sweet wind of dawn was blowing around the eaves. Ellen Greene was sleeping in the big bed and snoring soundly. Except for that the little house was very still. It was the chance for which Emily had waited.

Very carefully she slipped from her bed, tiptoed across the room and opened the door. Mike uncoiled himself from the mat on the middle of the floor and followed her, rubbing his warm sides against her chilly little ankles. Almost guiltily she crept down the bare, dark staircase. How the steps creaked—surely it would waken everybody! But nobody appeared and Emily got down and slipped into the parlour, drawing a long breath of relief as she closed the door. She almost ran across the room to the other door.

Aunt Ruth's floral pillow still covered the glass of the casket. Emily, with a tightening of the lips that gave her face an odd resemblance to Aunt Elizabeth, lifted up the pillow and set it on the floor.

"Oh, Father—Father!" she whispered, putting her hand to her throat to keep something down. She stood there, a little shivering, white-clad figure, and looked at her father. This was to be her good-bye; she must say it when they were alone together—she would not say it before the Murrays.

Father looked so beautiful. All the lines of pain had vanished—his face looked almost like a boy's except for the silver hair above it. And he was smiling—such a nice, whimsical, wise little smile, as if he had suddenly discovered something lovely and unexpected and surprising. She had seen many nice smiles on his face in life but never one just like this.

"Father, I didn't cry before them," she whispered. "I'm sure I didn't disgrace the Starrs. Not shaking hands with Aunt Ruth wasn't disgracing the Starrs, was it? Because she didn't really want me to—oh, Father, I don't think any of them like me, unless perhaps Aunt Laura does a little. And I'm going to cry a little bit now, Father, because I can't keep it back *all* the time."

She laid her face on the cold glass and sobbed bitterly but briefly. She must say good-bye before any one found her. Raising her head she looked long and earnestly at the beloved face.

"Good-bye, dearest darling," she whispered chokingly.

Dashing away her blinding tears she replaced Aunt Ruth's pillow, hiding her father's face from her forever. Then she slipped out, intent on speedily regaining her room. At the door she almost fell over Cousin Jimmy, who was sitting on a chair before it, swathed in a huge, checked dressing-gown, and nursing Mike.

"S-s-h!" he whispered, patting her on the shoulde

"*I* heard you coming down and followed you. *I* knew what you wanted. I've been sitting here to keep them out if any of them came after you. Here, take this and hurry back to your bed, small pussy."

"This" was a roll of peppermint lozenges. Emily clutched it and fled, overcome with shame at being seen by Cousin Jimmy in her nightgown. She hated peppermints and never ate them, but the fact of Cousin Jimmy Murray's kindness in giving them to her sent a thrill of delight to her heart. And he called her "small pussy," too,—she liked that. She had thought nobody would ever call her nice pet names again. Father had had so many of them for her—"sweetheart" and "darling" and "Emily-child" and "dear wee kidlet" and "honey" and "elfkin." He had a pet name for every mood and she had loved them all. As for Cousin Jimmy, he was nice. Whatever part of him was missing it wasn't his heart. She felt so grateful to him that after she was safely in her bed again she forced herself to eat one of the lozenges, though it took all her grit to worry it down.

The funeral was held that forenoon. For once the lonesome little house in the hollow was filled. The coffin was taken into the parlour and the Murrays as mourners sat stiffly and decorously all round it, Emily among them, pale and prim in her black dress. She sat between Aunt Elizabeth and Uncle Wallace and dared not move a muscle. No other Starr was present. Her father had no near living relatives. The Maywood people came and looked at his dead face with a freedom and insolent curiosity they would never have presumed on in life. Emily hated to have them looking at her father like that. They had no right—they hadn't been friendly to him while he was alive—they had said harsh things of him—Ellen Greene had sometimes repeated them. Every glance that fell on him hurt Emily; but she sat still and gave no outward sign. Aunt Ruth said afterwards that she had never seen a child so absolutely devoid of all natural feeling.

When the service was over the Murrays rose and marched around the coffin for a dutiful look of farewell. Aunt Elizabeth took Emily's hand and tried to draw her along with them but Emily pulled it back and shook her head. She had said her good-bye already. Aunt Elizabeth seemed for a moment to be on the point of insisting; then she grimly swept onward, alone, looking every inch a Murray. No scene must be made at a funeral.

Douglas Starr was to be taken to Charlottetown for burial beside his wife. The Murrays were all going but Emily was not to go. She watched the funeral procession as it wound up the long, grassy hill, through the light grey rain that was beginning to fall. Emily was glad it was raining; many a time she had heard Ellen Greene say that happy was the corpse the rain fell on; and it was easier to see Father go away in that soft, kind, grey mist than through sparkling, laughing sunshine.

"Well, I must say the funeral went off fine," said Ellen Greene at her shoulder. "Everything's been done regardless. If your father was looking down from heaven at it, Emily, I'm sure he'd be pleased."

"He isn't in heaven," said Emily.

"Good gracious! Of all the children!" Ellen could say no more.

"He isn't there *yet*. He's only on the way. He said he'd wait around and go slow until I died, too, so that I could catch up with him. I hope I'll die soon."

"That's a wicked, wicked thing to wish," rebuked Ellen.

When the last buggy had disappeared Emily went back to the sitting-room, got a book out of the bookcase, and buried herself in the wing-chair. The women who were tidying up were glad she was quiet and out of the way.

"It's well she can read," said Mrs. Hubbard gloomily. "Some little girls couldn't be so composed—Jennie Hood just screamed and shrieked after they carried her mother out—the Hoods are all such a *feeling* people."

Emily was not reading. She was thinking. She knew the Murrays would be back in the afternoon; and she knew her fate would probably be settled then. "We'll talk the matter over when we come back," she had heard Uncle Wallace saying that morning after breakfast. Some instinct told her just what "the matter" was; and she would have given one of her pointed ears to hear the discussion with the other. But she knew very well she would be sent out of the way. So she was not surprised when Ellen came to her in the twilight and said:

"You'd better go upstairs, Emily. Your aunts and uncles are coming in here to talk over the business."

"Can't I help you get supper?" asked Emily, who thought that if she were going and coming around the kitchen she might catch a word or two.

"No. You'd be more bother than help. March, now."

Ellen waddled out to the kitchen, without waiting to see if Emily marched. Emily got up reluctantly. How could she sleep to-night if she did not know what was going to happen to her? And she felt quite sure she would not be told till morning, if then.

Her eyes fell on the oblong table in the centre of the room. Its cloth was of generous proportions, falling in heavy folds to the floor. There was a flash of black stockings across the rug, a sudden disturbance of drapery and then—silence. Emily, on the floor under the table, arranged her legs comfortably and sat triumphant. She would hear what was decided and nobody would be any the wiser.

She had never been told that it was not considered strictly honourable to eavesdrop, no occasion for such instruction ever having arisen in her life with her father; and she considered that it was a bit of pure luck that she had thought of hiding under the table. She could even see dimly through the cloth. Her heart beat so loudly in her excitement that she was afraid they would hear it; there was no other sound save the soft, faraway singing of frogs through the rain, that sounded through the open window.

In they came; down they sat around the room; Emily held her breath; for a few minutes nobody spoke, though Aunt Eva sighed long and heavily. Then Uncle Wallace cleared his throat and said,

"Well, what is to be done with the child?"

Nobody was in a hurry to answer. Emily thought they would *never* speak. Finally Aunt Eva said with a whine,

"She's such a difficult child—so odd. *I* can't understand her at all."

"I think," said Aunt Laura timidly, "that she has what one might call an artistic temperament."

"She's a spoiled child," said Aunt Ruth very decidedly. "There's work ahead to straighten out *her* manners, if you ask me."

(The little listener under the table turned her head and shot a scornful glance at Aunt Ruth through the tablecloth. "*I* think that your own manners have a slight curve." Emily did not dare even to murmur the words under her breath, but she shaped them with her mouth; this was a great relief and satisfaction.)

"I agree with you," said Aunt Eva, "and I for one do not feel equal to the task."

(Emily understood that this meant Uncle Wallace didn't mean to take her and she rejoiced thereat.)

"The truth is," said Uncle Wallace, "Aunt Nancy ought to take her. She has more of this world's goods than any of us."

"Aunt Nancy would never dream of taking her and you know it well enough!" said Uncle Oliver. "Besides, she's entirely too old to have the bringing up of a child—her and that old witch Caroline. Upon my soul, I don't believe either of them is human. I would like to take Emily—but I feel that I can hardly do it. I've a large family to provide for."

"She'll not likely live long to bother any one," said

Aunt Elizabeth crisply. "She'll probably die of consumption same as her father did."

("I won't—I won't!" exclaimed Emily—at least she *thought* it with such vim that it almost seemed that she exclaimed it. She forgot that she had wanted to die soon, so that she could overtake Father. She wanted to live now, just to put the Murrays in the wrong. "I haven't *any* intention of dying. I'm going to live—for ages—and be a famous *authoress*—you'll just see if I don't, Aunt Elizabeth Murray!")

"She *is* a weedy looking child," acknowledged Uncle Wallace.

(Emily relieved her outraged feelings by making a face at Uncle Wallace through the tablecloth. "If I ever possess a pig I am going to name it after *you*," she thought—and then felt quite satisfied with her revenge.)

"Somebody has to look after her as long as she's alive though, you know," said Uncle Oliver.

("It would serve you all right if I *did* die and you suffered terrible remorse for it all the rest of your lives," Emily thought. Then in the pause that happened to follow, she dramatically pictured out her funeral, selected her pall-bearers, and tried to choose the hymn verse that she wanted engraved on her tombstone. But before she could settle this Uncle Wallace began again.)

"Well, we are not getting anywhere. We have to look after the child—"

("I *wish* you wouldn't call me '*the child*,'" thought Emily bitterly.)

"— and some of us must give her a home. Juliet's daughter must not be left to the mercy of strangers. Personally, I feel that Eva's health is not equal to the care and training of a child—"

"Of *such* a child," said Aunt Eva.

(Emily stuck her tongue out at Aunt Eva.)

"Poor little soul," said Aunt Laura gently.

(Something frozen in Emily's heart melted at that moment. She was pitifully pleased over being called "poor little soul" so tenderly.)

"I do not think you need pity her overmuch, Laura," said Uncle Wallace decidedly. "It is evident that she has very little feeling. I have not seen her shed a tear since we came here."

"Did you notice that she would not even take a last look at her father?" said Aunt Elizabeth.

Cousin Jimmy suddenly whistled at the ceiling.

"She feels so much that she has to hide it," said Aunt Laura.

Uncle Wallace snorted.

"Don't you think *we* might take her, Elizabeth?" Laura went on timidly.

Aunt Elizabeth stirred restlessly.

"I don't suppose she'd be contented at New Moon, with three old people like us."

("I would—I would!" thought Emily.)

"Ruth, what about you?" said Uncle Wallace. "You're all alone in that big house. It would be a good thing for you to have some company."

"I don't like her," said Aunt Ruth sharply. "She is as sly as a snake."

("I'm *not!*" thought Emily.)

"With wise and careful training many of her faults may be cured," said Uncle Wallace, pompously.

("I don't *want* them cured!" Emily was getting angrier and angrier all the time under the table. "I like *my* faults better than I do *your*—your—" she fumbled mentally for a word—then triumphantly recalled a phrase of her father's—"your *abominable* virtues!")

"I doubt it," said Aunt Ruth, in a biting tone. "What's bred in the bone comes out in the flesh. As for Douglas Starr, I think that it was perfectly disgraceful for him to die and leave that child without a cent."

"Did he do it on purpose?" asked Cousin Jimmy blandly. It was the first time he had spoken.

"He was a miserable failure," snapped Aunt Ruth.

"He wasn't—he wasn't!" screamed Emily, suddenly sticking her head out under the tablecloth, between the end legs of the table.

For a moment the Murrays sat as silent and motionless as if her outburst had turned them to stone. Then Aunt Ruth rose, stalked to the table, and lifted the cloth, behind which Emily had retired in dismay, realising what she had done.

"Get up and come out of that, Em'ly Starr!" said Aunt Ruth.

"Em'ly Starr" got up and came out. She was not specially frightened—she was too angry to be that. Her eyes had gone black and her cheeks crimson.

"What a little beauty—what a regular little beauty!" said Cousin Jimmy. But nobody heard him. Aunt Ruth had the floor.

"You shameless little eavesdropper!" she said. "There's the Starr blood coming out—a Murray would never have done such a thing. You ought to be whipped!"

"Father wasn't a failure!" cried Emily, choking with anger. "You had no right to call him a failure. Nobody who was loved as much as he was could be a failure. I don't believe anybody *ever* loved you. So it's *you* that's a failure. And I'm *not* going to die of consumption."

"Do you realize what a shameful thing you've been guilty of?" demanded Aunt Ruth, cold with anger.

"I wanted to hear what was going to become of me," cried Emily. "I didn't know it was such a dreadful thing to do—I didn't know you were going to say such horrid things about me."

"Listeners never hear any good of themselves," said Aunt Elizabeth impressively. "Your mother would *never* have done that, Emily."

The bravado all went out of poor Emily. She felt guilty and miserable—oh, so miserable. She hadn't known—but it seemed she had committed a terrible sin.

"Go upstairs," said Aunt Ruth.

Emily went, without a protest. But before going she looked around the room.

"While I was under the table," she said, "I made a

face at Uncle Wallace and stuck my tongue out at Aunt Eva."

She said it sorrowfully, desiring to make a clean breast of her transgressions; but so easily do we misunderstand each other that the Murrays actually thought that she was indulging in a piece of gratuitous impertinence. When the door had closed behind her they all—except Aunt Laura and Cousin Jimmy—shook their heads and groaned.

Emily went upstairs in a state of bitter humiliation. She felt that she had done something that gave the Murrays the right to despise her, and they thought it was the Starr coming out in her—and she had not even found out what her fate was to be.

She looked dismally at little Emily-in-the-glass.

"I didn't know—I didn't know," she whispered. "But I'll know after this," she added with sudden vim, "and I'll never, *never* do it again."

For a moment she thought she would throw herself on her bed and cry. She *couldn't* bear all the pain and shame that were burning in her heart. Then her eyes fell on the old yellow account book on her little table. A minute later Emily was curled up on her bed, Turk-fashion, writing eagerly in the old book with her little stubby lead pencil. As her fingers flew over the faded lines her cheeks flushed and her eyes shone. She forgot the Murrays although she was writing about them—she forgot her humiliation—although she was describing what had happened; for an hour she wrote steadily by the wretched light of her smoky little lamp, never pausing, save now and then, to gaze out of the window into the dim beauty of the misty night, while she hunted through her consciousness for a certain word she wanted; when she found it she gave a happy sigh and fell to again.

When she heard the Murrays coming upstairs she put her book away. She had finished; she had written a description of the whole occurrence and of that conclave ring of Murrays, and she had wound up by a pathetic description of her own deathbed, with the Murrays standing around imploring her forgiveness. At first she depicted Aunt Ruth as doing it on her knees in an agony of remorseful sobs. Then she suspended her pencil—"Aunt Ruth couldn't *ever* feel as bad as *that* over anything," she thought—and drew her pencil through the line.

In the writing, pain and humiliation had passed away. She only felt tired and rather happy. It *had* been fun, finding words to fit Uncle Wallace and what exquisite satisfaction it had been to describe Aunt Ruth as "a dumpy little woman."

"I wonder what my uncles and aunts would say if they knew what I *really* think of them," she murmured as she got into bed.

5
Diamond Cut Diamond

Emily, who had been pointedly ignored by the Murrays at breakfast, was called into the parlour when the meal was over.

They were all there—the whole phalanx of them—and it occurred to Emily as she looked at Uncle Wallace, sitting in the spring sunshine, that she had not just found the exact word after all to express his peculiar quality of grim-ness.

Aunt Elizabeth stood unsmilingly by the table with slips of paper in her hand.

"Emily," she said, "last night we could not decide who should take you. I may say that none of us feel very much like doing so, for you have behaved very badly in many respects—"

"Oh, Elizabeth,—" protested Laura. "She—she is our sister's child."

Elizabeth lifted a hand regally.

"*I* am doing this, Laura. Have the goodness not to interrupt me. As I was saying, Emily, we could not decide as to who should have the care of you. So we have agreed to Cousin Jimmy's suggestion that we settle the matter by lot. I have our names here, written on these slips of paper. You will draw one and the one whose name is on it will give you a home."

Aunt Elizabeth held out the slips of paper. Emily trembled so violently that at first she could not draw one. This was terrible—it seemed as if she must blindly settle her own fate.

"Draw," said Aunt Elizabeth.

Emily set her teeth, threw back her head with the air of one who challenges destiny, and drew. Aunt Elizabeth took the slip from the little shaking hand and held it up. On it was her own name—"Elizabeth Murray." Laura Murray suddenly put her handkerchief to her eyes.

"Well, that's settled," said Uncle Wallace, getting up with an air or relief. "And if I'm going to catch that train I've got to hurry. Of course, as far as the matter of expense goes, Elizabeth, I'll do my share."

"We are not paupers at New Moon," said Aunt Elizabeth rather coldly. "Since it has fallen to me to take her, I shall do all that is necessary, Wallace. I do not shirk my duty."

"*I* am her duty," thought Emily. "Father said nobody ever liked a duty. So Aunt Elizabeth will never like me."

"You've got more of the Murray pride than all the rest of us put together, Elizabeth," laughed Uncle Wallace.

They all followed him out—all except Aunt Laura. She came up to Emily, standing alone in the middle of the room, and drew her into her arms.

"I'm so glad, Emily—I'm so glad," she whispered.

"Don't fret, dear child. I love you already—and New Moon is a nice place, Emily."

"It has—a pretty name," said Emily, struggling for self-control. "I've—always hoped—I could go with you, Aunt Laura. I think I am going to cry—but it's not because I'm sorry I'm going there. My manners are *not* as bad as you may think, Aunt Laura—and I wouldn't have listened last night if I'd known it was wrong."

"Of course you wouldn't," said Aunt Laura.

"But I'm not a Murray, you know."

Then Aunt Laura said a queer thing—for a Murray.

"Thank heaven for that!" said Aunt Laura.

Cousin Jimmy followed Emily out and overtook her in the little hall. Looking carefully around to ensure privacy, he whispered,

"Your Aunt Laura is a great hand at making an apple turnover, pussy."

Emily thought apple turnover sounded nice, though she did not know what it was. She whispered back a question which she would never have dared ask Aunt Elizabeth or even Aunt Laura.

"Cousin Jimmy, when they make a cake at New Moon, will they let me scrape out the mixing-bowl and eat the scrapings?"

"Laura will—Elizabeth won't," whispered Cousin Jimmy solemnly.

"And put my feet in the oven when they get cold? And have a cooky before I go to bed?"

"Answer same as before," said Cousin Jimmy. "*I'll* recite my poetry to you. It's very few people I do that for. I've composed a thousand poems. They're not written down—I carry them here." Cousin Jimmy tapped his forehead.

"Is it very hard to write poetry?" asked Emily, looking with new respect at Cousin Jimmy.

"Easy as rolling off a log if you can find enough rhymes," said Cousin Jimmy.

They all went away that morning except the New Moon people. Aunt Elizabeth announced that they would stay until the next day to pack up and take Emily with them.

"Most of the furniture belongs to the house," she said, "so it won't take us long to get ready. There are only Douglas Starr's books and his few personal belongings to pack."

"How shall I carry my cats?" asked Emily anxiously.

Aunt Elizabeth stared.

"Cats! You'll take no cats, miss."

"Oh, I must take Mike and Saucy Sal!" cried Emily wildly. "I can't leave them behind. I can't live without a cat."

"Nonsense! There are barn cats at New Moon, but they are never allowed in the house."

"Don't you like cats?" asked Emily wonderingly.

"No, I do *not*."

"Don't you like the *feel* of a nice, soft, fat cat?" persisted Emily.

"No; I would as soon touch a snake."

"There's a lovely old wax doll of your mother's up there," said Aunt Laura. "I'll dress it up for you."

"I don't like dolls—they can't talk," exclaimed Emily.

"Neither can cats."

"Oh, can't they! Mike and Saucy Sal can. Oh, I *must* take them. Oh, *please*, Aunt Elizabeth. I *love* those cats. And they're the only things left in the world that love me. Please!"

"What's a cat more or less on two hundred acres?" said Cousin Jimmy, pulling his forked beard. "Take 'em along, Elizabeth."

Aunt Elizabeth considered for a moment. She couldn't understand why anybody should want a cat. Aunt Elizabeth was one of those people who never do understand anything unless it is told them in plain language and hammered into their heads. And *then* they understand it only with their brains and not with their hearts.

"You may take *one* of your cats," she said at last, with the air of a person making a great concession.

"One—and no more. No, don't argue. You may as well learn first as last, Emily, that when *I* say a thing I mean it. That's enough, Jimmy."

Cousin Jimmy bit off something he had tried to say, stuck his hands in his pockets, and whistled at the ceiling.

"When she won't, she won't—Murray like. We're all born with that kink in us, small pussy, and you'll have to put up with it—more by token that you're full of it yourself, you know. Talk about your not being Murray! The Starr is only skin deep with you."

"It isn't—I'm *all* Starr—I *want* to be," cried Emily. "And, oh, how can I choose between Mike and Saucy Sal?"

This was indeed a problem. Emily wrestled with it all day, her heart bursting. She liked Mike best—there was no doubt of that; but she *couldn't* leave Saucy Sal to Ellen's tender mercies. Ellen had always hated Sal; but she rather liked Mike and she would be good to him. Ellen was going back to her own little house in Maywood village and she wanted a cat. At last in the evening, Emily made her bitter decision. She would take Saucy Sal.

"Better take the Tom," said Cousin Jimmy. "Not so much bother with kittens you know, Emily."

"Jimmy!" said Aunt Elizabeth sternly. Emily wondered over the sternness. Why weren't kittens to be spoken of? But she didn't like to hear Mike called "the Tom." It sounded insulting, someway.

And she didn't like the bustle and commotion of packing up. She longed for the old quiet and the sweet, remembered talks with her father. She felt as if he had been thrust far away from her by this influx of Murrays.

"What's this?" said Aunt Elizabeth suddenly, pausing for a moment in her packing. Emily looked up and saw with dismay that Aunt Elizabeth had in her hands the old account book—that she was opening it—that she was *reading* in it. Emily sprang across the floor and snatched the book.

"You mustn't read that, Aunt Elizabeth," she cried indignantly, "that's mine,—my own *private property.*"

"Hoity-toity, Miss Starr," said Aunt Elizabeth, staring at her, "let me tell you that I have a right to read your books. I am responsible for you now. I am not going to have anything hidden or underhanded, understand that. You have evidently something there that you are ashamed to have seen and I mean to see it. Give me that book."

"I'm *not* ashamed of it," cried Emily, backing away, hugging her precious book to her breast. "But I won't let you—or *anybody*—see it."

Aunt Elizabeth followed.

"Emily Starr, do you hear what I say? Give me that book—at *once.*"

"No—no!" Emily turned and ran. She would *never* let Aunt Elizabeth see that book. She fled to the kitchen stove—she whisked off a cover—she crammed the book into the glowing fire. It caught and blazed merrily. Emily watched it in agony. It seemed as if part of herself were burning there. But Aunt Elizabeth should never see it—see all the little things she had written and read to Father—all her fancies about the Wind Woman, and Emily-in-the-glass—all her little cat dialogues—all the things she had said in it last night about the Murrays. She watched the leaves shrivel and shudder, as if they were sentient things, and then turn black. A line of white writing came out vividly on one. "Aunt Elizabeth is very cold and *hawty.*" What if Aunt Elizabeth had seen *that?* What if she were seeing it now! Emily glanced apprehensively over her shoulder. No, Aunt Elizabeth had gone back to the room and shut the door with what, in anybody but a Murray, would have been called a bang. The account book was a little heap of white film on the glowing coals. Emily sat down by the stove and cried. She felt as if she had lost something incalculably precious. It was terrible to think that all those dear things were gone. She could never write them again—not just the same; and if she could she wouldn't dare—she would never dare to write *anything* again, if Aunt Elizabeth must see everything. Father never insisted on seeing them. She liked to read them to *him*—but if she hadn't wanted to do it he would never have made her. Suddenly Emily, with tears glistening on her cheeks, wrote a line in an imaginary account book.

"Aunt Elizabeth is cold and hawty; and she is *not fair.*"

Next morning, while Cousin Jimmy was tying the boxes at the back of the double-seated buggy, and Aunt Elizabeth was giving Ellen her final instructions, Emily said good-bye to everything—to the Rooster Pine and Adam-and-Eve—"they'll miss me so when I'm gone; there won't be any one here to love them," she said wistfully—to the spider crack in the kitchen window— to the old wing-chair—to the bed of striped grass—to the silver birch-ladies. Then she went upstairs to the window of her own old room. That little window had always seemed to Emily to open on a world of wonder. In the burned account book there had been one piece of which she was especially proud. "A deskripshun of the vew from my Window." She had sat there and dreamed; at night she used to kneel there and say her little prayers. Sometimes the stars shone through it— sometimes the rain beat against it—sometimes the little greybirds and swallows visited it—sometimes airy fragrances floated in from apple and lilac blossom— sometimes the Wind Woman laughed and sighed and sang and whistled round it—Emily had heard her there in the dark nights and in wild, white winter storms. She did not say good-bye to the Wind Woman, for she knew the Wind Woman would be at New Moon, too; but she said good-bye to the little window and the green hill she had loved, and to her fairy-haunted barrens and to little Emily-in-the-glass. There might be another Emily-in-the-glass at New Moon, but she wouldn't be the same one. And she unpinned from the wall and stowed away in her pocket the picture of the ball dress she had cut from a fashion sheet. It was such a wonderful dress—all white lace and wreaths of rose-buds, with a long, long, train of lace flounces that must reach clear across a room. Emily had pictured herself a thousand times wearing that dress, sweeping, a queen of beauty, across a ballroom floor.

Downstairs they were waiting for her. Emily said good-bye to Ellen Greene rather indifferently—she had never liked Ellen Greene at any time, and since the night Ellen had told her her father was going to die she had hated and feared her.

Ellen amazed Emily by bursting into tears and hug-ging her—begging her not to forget her—asking her to write to her—calling her "my blessed child."

"I am not your blessed child," said Emily, "but I will write to you. And will you be very good to Mike?"

"I b'lieve you feel worse over leaving that cat than you do over leaving me," sniffed Ellen.

"Why, of course I do," said Emily, amazed that there could be any question about it.

It took all her resolution not to cry when she bade farewell to Mike, who was curled up on the sun-warm grass at the back door.

"Maybe I'll see you again sometime," she whispered as she hugged him. "I'm sure *good* pussy cats go to heaven."

Then they were off in the double-seated buggy with its fringed canopy, always affected by the Murrays of New Moon. Emily had never driven in anything so splendid before. She had never had many drives. Once or twice her father had borrowed Mr. Hubbard's old buckboard and grey pony and driven to Charlottetown. The buckboard was rattly and the pony slow, but Father had talked to her all the way and made the road a wonder.

Cousin Jimmy and Aunt Elizabeth sat in front, the latter very imposing in black lace bonnet and mantle.

Aunt Laura and Emily occupied the seat behind, with Saucy Sal between them in a basket, shrieking piteously.

Emily glanced back as they drove up the grassy lane, and thought the little, old, brown house in the hollow had a broken-hearted look. She longed to run back and comfort it. In spite of her resolution, the tears came into her eyes; but Aunt Laura put a kid-gloved hand across Sal's basket and caught Emily's in a close, understanding squeeze.

"Oh, I just love you, Aunt Laura," whispered Emily.

And Aunt Laura's eyes were very, very blue and deep and kind.

6
New Moon

Emily found the drive through the blossomy June world pleasant. Nobody talked much; even Saucy Sal had subsided into the silence of despair; now and then Cousin Jimmy made a remark, more to himself, as it seemed, than to anybody else. Sometimes Aunt Elizabeth answered it, sometimes not. She always spoke crisply and used no unnecessary words.

They stopped in Charlottetown and had dinner. Emily, who had had no appetite since her father's death, could not eat the roast beef which the boarding-house waitress put before her. Whereupon Aunt Elizabeth whispered mysteriously to the waitress, who went away and presently returned with a plateful of delicate, cold chicken—fine white slices, beautifully trimmed with lettuce frills.

"Can you eat *that?*" said Aunt Elizabeth sternly, as to a culprit at the bar.

"I'll—try," whispered Emily.

She was too frightened just then to say more, but by the time she had forced down some of the chicken she had made up her small mind that a certain matter must be put right.

"Aunt Elizabeth," she said.

"Hey, what?" said Aunt Elizabeth, directing her steel-blue eyes straight at her niece's troubled ones.

"I would like you to understand," said Emily, speaking very primly and precisely so that she would be sure to get things right, "that it was not because I did not like the roast beef I did not eat it. I was not hungry at all; and I just et some of the chicken to oblige you, not because I liked it any better."

"Children should eat what is put before them and never turn up their noses at good, wholesome food," said Aunt Elizabeth severely. So Emily felt that Aunt Elizabeth had not understood after all and she was unhappy about it.

After dinner Aunt Elizabeth announced to Aunt Laura that they would do some shopping.

"We must get some things for the child," she said.

"Oh, please don't call me 'the child,'" exclaimed Emily. "It makes me feel as if I didn't belong anywhere. Don't you like my name, Aunt Elizabeth? Mother thought it so pretty. And I don't need any 'things.' I have two whole sets of underclothes—only one is patched—"

"S-s-sh!" said Cousin Jimmy, gently kicking Emily's shins under the table.

Cousin Jimmy only meant that she would better let Aunt Elizabeth buy "things" for her when she was in the humour for it; but Emily thought he was rebuking her for mentioning such matters as underclothes and subsided in scarlet conviction. Aunt Elizabeth went on talking to Laura as if she had not heard.

"She must not wear that cheap black dress in Blair Water. You could sift oatmeal through it. It is nonsense expecting a child of ten to wear black at all. I shall get her a nice white dress with black sash for good, and some black-and-white-check gingham for school. Jimmy, we'll leave the child with you. Look after her."

Cousin Jimmy's method of looking after her was to take her to a restaurant down street and fill her up with ice-cream. Emily had never had many chances at ice-cream and she needed no urging, even with lack of appetite, to eat two saucerfuls. Cousin Jimmy eyed her with satisfaction.

"No use my getting anything for you that Elizabeth could see," he said. "But she can't see what is inside of you. Make the most of your chance, for goodness alone knows when you'll get any more."

"Do you never have ice-cream at New Moon?"

Cousin Jimmy shook his head.

"Your Aunt Elizabeth doesn't like new-fangled things. In the house, we belong to fifty years ago, but on the farm she has to give way. In the house—candles; in the dairy, her grandmother's big pans to set the milk in. But, pussy, New Moon is a pretty good place after all. You'll like it some day."

"Are there any fairies there?" asked Emily, wistfully.

"The woods are full of em," said Cousin Jimmy. "And so are the columbines in the old orchard. We grow columbines there on purpose for the fairies."

Emily sighed. Since she was eight she had known there were no fairies anywhere nowadays; yet she hadn't quite given up the hope that one or two might linger in old-fashioned, out-of-the-way spots. And where so likely as at New Moon?

"Really-truly fairies?" she questioned.

"Why, you know, if a fairy was really-truly it wouldn't *be* a fairy," said Uncle Jimmy seriously. "Could it, now?"

Before Emily could think this out the aunts returned and soon they were all on the road again. It was sunset when they came to Blair Water—a rosy sunset that flooded the long, sandy sea-coast with colour and brought red road and fir-darkened hill out in fleeting clearness of outline. Emily looked about her on her new environment and found it good. She saw a big house peering whitely through a veil of tall old trees—no mushroom growth of yesterday's birches but trees that had loved and been loved by three generations—a glimpse of silver water glistening through the dark spruces—that was the Blair Water itself, she knew—and a tall, golden-white church spire shooting up above the maple woods in the valley below. But it was none of these that brought her the flash—*that* came with the sudden glimpse of the dear, friendly, little dormer window peeping through vines on the roof—and right over it, in the opalescent sky, a real new moon, golden and slender. Emily was tingling all over with it as Cousin Jimmy lifted her from the buggy and carried her into the kitchen.

She sat on a long wooden bench that was satin-smooth with age and scrubbing, and watched Aunt Elizabeth lighting candles here and there, in great, shining, brass candlesticks—on the shelf between the windows, on the high dresser where the row of blue and white plates began to wink her a friendly welcome, on the long table in the corner. And as she lighted them, elvish "rabbits' candles" flashed up amid the trees outside the windows.

Emily had never seen a kitchen like this before. It had dark wooden walls and low ceiling, with black rafters crossing it, from which hung hams and sides of bacon and bunches of herbs and new socks and mittens, and many other things, the names and uses of which Emily could not imagine. The sanded floor was spotlessly white, but the boards had been scrubbed away through the years until the knots in them stuck up all over in funny little bosses, and in front of the stove they had sagged, making a queer, shallow little hollow. In one corner of the ceiling was a large square hole which looked black and spookish in the candle-light, and made her feel creepy. *Something* might pop down out of a hole like that if one hadn't behaved just right, you know. And candles cast such queer wavering shadows. Emily didn't know whether she liked the New Moon kitchen or not. It was an interesting place—and she rather thought she would like to describe it in the old account book, if it hadn't been burned—but Emily suddenly found herself trembling on the verge of tears.

"Cold?" said Aunt Laura kindly. "These June evenings are chilly yet. Come into the sitting-room—Jimmy has kindled a fire in the stove there."

Emily, fighting desperately for self-control, went into the sitting-room. It was much more cheerful than the kitchen. The floor was covered with gay-striped homespun, the table had a bright crimson cloth, the walls were hung with pretty, diamond-patterned paper, the curtains were of wonderful pale-red damask with a design of white ferns scattered all over them. They looked very rich and imposing and Murray-like. Emily had never seen such curtains before. But best of all were the friendly gleams and flickers from the jolly hardwood fire in the open stove that mellowed the ghostly candlelight with something warm and rosy-golden. Emily toasted her toes before it and felt reviving interest in her surroundings. What lovely little leaded glass doors closed the china closets on either side of the high, black, polished mantel! What a funny, delightful shadow the carved ornament on the sideboard cast on the wall behind it—just like a negro's side-face, Emily decided. What mysteries might lurk behind the chintz-lined glass doors of the bookcase! Books were Emily's friends wherever she found them. She flew over to the bookcase and opened the door. But before she could see more than the backs of rather ponderous volumes, Aunt Elizabeth came in, with a mug of milk and a plate whereon lay two little oatmeal cakes.

"Emily," said Aunt Elizabeth sternly, "shut that door. Remember that after this you are not to meddle with things that don't belong to you."

"I thought books belonged to everybody," said Emily.

"Ours don't," said Aunt Elizabeth, contriving to convey the impression that New Moon books were in a class by themselves. "Here is your supper, Emily. We are all so tired that we are just having a lunch. Eat it and then we will go to bed."

Emily drank the milk and worried down the oatcakes, still gazing about her. How pretty the wallpaper was, with the garland of roses inside the gilt diamond! Emily wondered if she could "see it in the air." She tried—yes, she could—there it hung, a yard from her eyes, a little fairy pattern, suspended in mid-air like a screen. Emily had discovered that she possessed this odd knack when she was six. By a certain movement of the muscles of her eyes, which she could never describe, she could produce a tiny replica of the wallpaper in the air before her—could hold it there and look at it as long as she liked—could shift it back and forth, to any distance she chose, making it larger or smaller as it went farther away or came nearer. It was one of her secret joys when she went into a new room anywhere to "see the paper in the air." And this New Moon paper made the prettiest fairy paper she had ever seen.

"What are you staring at nothing in that queer way for?" demanded Aunt Elizabeth, suddenly returning.

Emily shrank into herself. She couldn't explain to Aunt Elizabeth—Aunt Elizabeth would be like Ellen Greene and say she was "crazy."

"I—I wasn't staring at nothing."

"Don't contradict. I say you were," retorted Aunt Elizabeth. "Don't do it again. It gives your face an unnatural expression. Come now—we will go upstairs. You are to sleep with me."

Emily gave a gasp of dismay. She had hoped it might be with Aunt Laura. Sleeping with Aunt Elizabeth seemed a very formidable thing. But she dared not protest. They went up to Aunt Elizabeth's big, sombre bedroom where there was dark, grim wallpaper that could never be transformed into a fairy curtain, a high black bureau, topped with a tiny swing-mirror, so far above her that there could be no Emily-in-the-glass, tightly closed windows with dark-green curtains, a high bedstead with a dark-green canopy, and a huge, fat, smothering featherbed, with high, hard pillows.

Emily stood still, gazing about her.

"Why don't you get undressed?" asked Aunt Elizabeth.

"I—I don't like to undress before you," faltered Emily.

Aunt Elizabeth looked at Emily through her cold, spectacled eyes.

"Take off your clothes, *at once*," she said.

Emily obeyed, tingling with anger and shame. It was abominable—taking off her clothes while Aunt Elizabeth stood and watched her. The outrage of it was unspeakable. It was even harder to say her prayers before Aunt Elizabeth. Emily felt that it was not much good to pray under such circumstances. Father's God seemed very far away and she suspected that Aunt Elizabeth's was too much like Ellen Greene's.

"Get into bed," said Aunt Elizabeth, turning down the clothes.

Emily glanced at the shrouded window.

"Aren't you going to open the window, Aunt Elizabeth?"

Aunt Elizabeth looked at Emily as if the latter had suggested removing the roof.

"Open the window—and let in the night air!" she exclaimed. "Certainly not!"

"Father and I always had our window open," cried Emily.

"No wonder he died of consumption," said Aunt Elizabeth. "Night air is poison."

"What air is there at night but night air?" asked Emily.

"Emily," said Aunt Elizabeth icily, "get—into—bed."

Emily got in.

But it was utterly impossible to sleep, lying there in that engulfing bed that seemed to swallow her up, with that cloud of blackness above her and not a gleam of light anywhere—and Aunt Elizabeth lying beside her, long and stiff and bony.

"I feel as if I was in bed with a griffin," thought Emily. "Oh—oh—oh—I'm going to cry—I know I am."

Desperately and vainly she strove to keep the tears back—they *would* come. She felt utterly alone and lonely—there in that darkness, with an alien, hostile world all around her—for it seemed hostile now. And there was such a strange, mysterious, mournful sound in the air—far away, yet clear. It was the murmur of the sea, but Emily did not know that and it frightened her. Oh, for her little bed at home—oh, for Father's soft breathing in the room—oh, for the dancing friendliness of well-known stars shining down through her open window! She *must* go back—she couldn't stay here— she would never be happy here! But there wasn't any "back" to go to—no home—no father—. A great sob burst from her—another followed and then another. It was no use to clench her hands and set her teeth—and chew the inside of her cheeks—nature conquered pride and determination and had her way.

"What are you crying for?" asked Aunt Elizabeth.

To tell the truth Aunt Elizabeth felt quite as uncomfortable and disjointed as Emily did. She was not used to a bedfellow; she didn't want to sleep with Emily any more than Emily wanted to sleep with her. But she considered it quite impossible that the child should be put off by herself in one of the big, lonely New Moon rooms; and Laura was a poor sleeper, easily disturbed; children always kicked, Elizabeth Murray had heard. So there was nothing to do but take Emily in with her; and when she had sacrificed comfort and inclination to do her unwelcome duty this ungrateful and unsatisfactory child was not contented.

"I asked you what you were crying for, Emily?" she repeated.

"I'm—homesick, I guess," sobbed Emily.

Aunt Elizabeth was annoyed.

"A nice home you had to be homesick for," she said sharply.

"It—it wasn't as elegant—as New Moon," sobbed Emily, "but—*Father* was there. I guess I'm Fathersick, Aunt Elizabeth. Didn't you feel awfully lonely when *your* father died?"

Elizabeth Murray involuntarily remembered the ashamed, smothered feeling of relief when old Archibald Murray had died—the handsome, intolerant, autocratic old man who had ruled his family with a rod of iron all his life and had made existence at New Moon miserable with the petulant tyranny of the five years of invalidism that had closed his career. The surviving Murrays had behaved impeccably, and wept decorously, and printed a long and flattering obituary. But had one genuine feeling of regret followed Archibald Murray to his tomb? Elizabeth did not like the memory and was angry with Emily for evoking it.

"I was resigned to the will of Providence," she said coldly. "Emily, you must understand right now that you are to be grateful and obedient and show your appreciation of what is being done for you. I won't have tears and repining. What would you have done if you had no friends to take you in? Answer me that."

"I suppose I would have starved to death," admitted Emily—instantly beholding a dramatic vision of herself lying dead, looking exactly like the pictures she had seen in one of Ellen Greene's missionary magazines depicting the victims of an Indian famine.

"Not exactly—but you would have been sent to some orphanage where you would have been half-starved, probably. You little know what you have escaped. You have come to a good home where you will be cared for and educated properly."

Emily did not altogether like the sound of being "educated properly." But she said humbly,

"I know it was very good of you to bring me to New Moon, Aunt Elizabeth. And I won't bother you long, you know. I'll soon be grown-up and able to earn my own living. What do you think is the earliest age a person can be called grown-up, Aunt Elizabeth?"

"You needn't think about that," said Aunt Elizabeth shortly. "The Murray women have never been under any necessity for earning their own living. All we require of you is to be a good and contented child and to conduct yourself with becoming prudence and modesty."

This sounded terribly hard.

"I *will* be," said Emily, suddenly determining to be heroic, like the girl in the stories she had read. "Perhaps it won't be so very hard after all, Aunt Elizabeth,"—Emily happened at this point to recall a speech she had heard her father use once, and thought this a good opportunity to work it in—"because, you know, God is good and the devil might be worse."

Poor Aunt Elizabeth! To have a speech like that fired at her in the darkness of the night from that unwelcome little interloper into her orderly life and peaceful bed! Was it any wonder that for a moment or so she was too paralyzed to reply! Then she exclaimed in tones of horror,

"Emily, *never* say that again."

"All right," said Emily meekly. "But," she added defiantly under her breath, "I'll go on thinking it."

"And now," said Aunt Elizabeth, "I want to say that I am not in the habit of talking all night if you are. I tell you to go to sleep, and I *expect* you to obey me. Good-night."

The tone of Aunt Elizabeth's good-night would have spoiled the best night in the world. But Emily lay very still and sobbed no more, though the noiseless tears trickled down her cheeks in the darkness for some time. She lay so still that Aunt Elizabeth imagined she was asleep and went to sleep herself.

"I wonder if anybody in the world is awake but me," thought Emily, feeling a sickening loneliness. "If I only had Saucy Sal here! She isn't so cuddly as Mike but she'd be better than nothing. I wonder where she is. I wonder if they gave her any supper."

Aunt Elizabeth had handed Sal's basket to Cousin Jimmy with an impatient, "Here—look to this cat," and Jimmy had carried it off. Where had he put it? Perhaps Saucy Sal would get out and go home—Emily had heard cats always went back home. She wished *she* could get out and go home—she pictured herself and her cat running eagerly along the dark, starlit roads to the little house in the hollow—back to the birches and Adam-and-Eve and Mike, and the old wing-chair and her dear little cot and the open window where the Wind Woman sang to her and at dawn one could see the blue of the mist on the homeland hills.

"Will it ever be morning?" thought Emily. "Perhaps things won't be so bad in the morning."

And then—she heard the Wind Woman at the window— she heard the little, low, whispering murmur of the June night breeze—cooing, friendly, lovesome.

"Oh, you're out there, are you, dearest one?" she whispered, stretching out her arms. "Oh, I'm so glad to hear you. You're such company, Wind Woman. I'm not lonesome any more. And the flash came, too! I was afraid it might never come at New Moon."

Her soul suddenly escaped from the bondage of Aunt Elizabeth's stuffy feather-bed and gloomy canopy and sealed windows. She was out in the open with the Wind Woman and the other gipsies of the night—the fireflies, the moths, the brooks, the clouds. Far and wide she wandered in enchanted reverie until she coasted the shore of dreams and fell soundly asleep on the fat, hard pillow, while the Wind Woman sang softly and luringly in the vines that clustered over New Moon.

7
The Book of Yesterday

That first Saturday and Sunday at New Moon always stood out in Emily's memory as a very wonderful time, so crowded was it with new and generally delightful impressions. If it be true that we "count time by heart throbs" Emily lived two years in it instead of two days. Everything was fascinating from the moment she came down the long, polished staircase into the square hall that was filled with a soft, rosy light coming through the red glass panes of the front door. Emily gazed through the panes delightedly. What a strange, fascinating, red world she beheld, with a weird red sky that looked, she thought, as if it belonged to the Day of Judgment.

There was a certain charm about the old house which Emily felt keenly and responded to, although she was too young to understand it. It was a house which aforetime had had vivid brides and mothers and wives, and the atmosphere of their loves and lives still hung around it, not yet banished by the old-maidishness of the régime of Elizabeth and Laura.

"Why—I'm going to *love* New Moon," thought Emily, quite amazed at the idea.

Aunt Laura was setting the breakfast table in the kitchen, which seemed quite bright and jolly in the glow of morning sunshine. Even the black hole in the ceiling had ceased to be spookish and become only a commonplace entrance to the kitchen loft. And on the red-sandstone doorstep Saucy Sal was sitting, preening her fur as contentedly as if she had lived at New Moon all her life. Emily did not know it, but Sal had already drunk deep the delight of battle with her peers that morning and taught the barn cats their place once and for all. Cousin Jimmy's big yellow Tom had got a fearful drubbing, and was minus several bits of his anatomy, while a stuck-up, black lady-cat, who fancied herself considerably, had made up her mind that if that grey-and-white, narrow-faced interloper from goodness knew where was going to stay at New Moon, *she* was not.

Emily gathered Sal up in her arms and kissed her joyously, to the horror of Aunt Elizabeth, who was coming across the platform from the cook-house with a plate of sizzling bacon in her hands.

"Don't ever let me see you kissing a cat again," she ordered.

"Oh, all right," agreed Emily cheerfully. "I'll only kiss her when you don't see me after this."

"I don't want any of your pertness, miss. You are not to kiss cats at all."

"But, Aunt Elizabeth, I didn't kiss her on her mouth, *of course*. I just kissed her between her ears. It's nice— won't you just try it for once and see for yourself?"

"That will do, Emily. You have said quite enough." And Aunt Elizabeth sailed on into the kitchen majestically, leaving Emily momentarily wretched. She felt that she had offended Aunt Elizabeth, and she hadn't the least notion why or how.

But the scene before her was too interesting to worry long over Aunt Elizabeth. Delicious smells were coming from the cook-house—a little, slant-roofed building at the corner where the big cooking-stove was placed in summer. It was thickly overgrown with hop vines, as most of the New Moon buildings were. To the right was the "new" orchard, very wonderful now in blossom, but a rather commonplace spot after all, since Cousin Jimmy cultivated it in most up-to-date fashion and had grain growing in the wide spaces between the straight rows of trees that looked all alike. But on the other side of the barn lane, just behind the well, was the "old orchard," where Cousin Jimmy said the columbines grew and which seemed to be a delightful place where trees had come up at their own sweet will, and grown into individual shapes and sizes, where blue-eyed ivy twined about their roots and wild-briar roses rioted over the grey paling fence. Straight ahead, closing the vista between the orchards, was a little slope covered with huge white birches, among which were the big New Moon barns, and beyond the new orchard a little, lovable red road looped lightly up and up, over a hill, until it seemed to touch the vivid blue of the sky.

Cousin Jimmy came down from the barns, carrying brimming pails of milk, and Emily ran with him to the dairy behind the cook-house. Such a delightful spot she had never seen or imagined. It was a snow-white little building in a clump of tall balm-of-gileads. Its grey roof was dotted over with cushions of moss like fat green-velvet mice. You went down six sandstone steps, with ferns crowding about them, and opened a white door with a glass panel in it, and went down three more steps. And then you were in a clean, earthy-smelling, damp, cool place with an earthen floor and windows screened by the delicate emerald of young hop-vines, and broad wooden shelves all around, whereon stood wide, shallow pans of glossy brown ware, full of milk coated over with cream so rich that it was positively yellow.

Aunt Laura was waiting for them and she strained the milk into empty pans and then skimmed some of the full ones. Emily thought skimming was a lovely occupation and longed to try her hand at it. She also longed to sit right down and write a description of that dear dairy; but alas, there was no account book; still, she could write it in her head. She squatted down on a little three-legged stool in a dim corner and proceeded to do it, sitting so still that Jimmy and Laura forgot her and went away and later had to hunt for her a quarter of an hour. This delayed breakfast and made Aunt Elizabeth very cross. But Emily had found just the right sentence to define the clear yet dim green light that filled the dairy and was so happy over it that she didn't mind Aunt Elizabeth's black looks a bit.

After breakfast Aunt Elizabeth informed Emily that henceforth it would be one of her duties to drive the cows to pasture every morning.

"Jimmy has no hired man just now and it will save him a few minutes."

"And don't be afraid," added Aunt Laura, "the cows know the way so well they'll go of themselves. You have only to follow and shut the gates."

"I'm not afraid," said Emily.

But she was. She knew nothing about cows; still, she was determined that the Murrays should not suspect a Starr was scared. So, her heart beating like a triphammer, she sallied valiantly forth and found that what Aunt Laura had said was true and cows were not such ferocious animals after all. They went gravely on ahead and she had only to follow, through the old orchard and then through the scrub maple growth beyond, along a twisted ferny path where the Wind Woman was purring and peeping around the maple clumps.

Emily loitered by the pasture gate until her eager eyes had taken in all the geography of the landscape. The old pasture ran before her in a succession of little green bosoms right down to the famous Blair Water—an almost perfectly round pond, with grassy, sloping, treeless margins. Beyond it was the Blair Water valley, filled with homesteads, and further out the great sweep of the white-capped gulf. It seemed to Emily's eyes a charming land of green shadows and blue waters. Down in one corner of the pasture, walled off by an old stone dyke, was the little private graveyard where the dead-and-gone Murrays were buried. Emily wanted to go and explore it, but was afraid to trust herself in the pasture.

"I'll go as soon as I get better acquainted with the cows," she resolved.

Off to the right, on the crest of a steep little hill, covered with young birches and firs, was a house that puzzled and intrigued Emily. It was grey and weather-worn, but it didn't look old. It had never been finished; the roof was shingled but the sides were not, and the windows were boarded over. Why had it never been finished? And it was meant to be such a pretty little house—a house you could love—a house where there would be nice chairs and cozy fires and bookcases and lovely, fat, purry cats and unexpected corners; then and there she named it the Disappointed House, and many an hour thereafter did she spend finishing that house, furnishing it as it should be furnished, and inventing the proper people and animals to live in it.

To the left of the pasture field was another house of a quite different type—a big, old house, tangled over with vines, flat-roofed, with mansard windows, and a general air of indifference and neglect about it. A large, untidy lawn, overgrown with unpruned shrubs and trees, straggled right down to the pond, where enormous willows drooped over the water. Emily decided that she would ask Cousin Jimmy about these houses when she got a good chance.

She felt that, before she went back, she must slip along the pasture fence and explore a certain path which she saw entering the grove of spruce and maple further down. She did—and found that it led straight into Fairyland,—along the bank of a wide, lovely brook—a wild, dear, little path with lady-ferns beckoning and blowing along it, the shyest of elfin June-bells under the firs, and little whims of loveliness at every curve. She breathed in the tang of fir-balsam and saw the shimmer of gossamers high up in the boughs, and everywhere the frolic of elfin lights and shadows. Here and there the young maple branches interlaced as if to make a screen for dryad faces—Emily knew all about dryads, thanks to her father—and the great sheets of moss under the trees were meet for Titania's couch.

"This is one of the places where dreams grow," said Emily happily.

She wished the path might go on forever, but presently it veered away from the brook, and when she had scrambled over a mossy, old board fence she found herself in the "front-garden" of New Moon, where Cousin Jimmy was pruning some spirea bushes.

"Oh, Cousin Jimmy, I've found the dearest little road," said Emily breathlessly.

"Coming up through Lofty John's bush?"

"Isn't it our bush?" asked Emily, rather disappointed.

"No, but it ought to be. Fifty years ago Uncle Archibald sold that jog of land to Lofty John's father—old Mike Sullivan. He built a little house down near the pond and lived there till he quarrelled with Uncle Archibald—which wasn't long, of course. Then he moved his house across the road—and Lofty John lives there now. Elizabeth has tried to buy the land back from him—she's offered him far more than it's worth—but Lofty John won't sell—just for spite, seeing that he has a good farm of his own and this piece isn't much good to him. He only pastures a few young cattle on it through the summer, and what was cleared is all growing up with scrub maple. It's a thorn in Elizabeth's side and likely to be as long as Lofty John nurses his spite."

"Why is he called Lofty John?"

"Because he's a high and lofty fellow. But never mind him. I want to show you round my garden, Emily. It's mine. Elizabeth bosses the farm; but she lets me run the garden—to make up for pushing me into the well."

"*Did* she do that?"

"Yes. She didn't mean to, of course. We were just children—I was here on a visit—and the men were putting a new hood on the well and cleaning it. It was open—and we were playing tag around it. I made Elizabeth mad—forget what I said—'twasn't *hard* to make her mad, you understand—and she made to give me a bang on the head. I saw it coming—and stepped back to get out of the way—and down I went, head first. Don't remember anything more about it. There was nothing but mud at the bottom—but my head struck the stones at the side. I was took up for dead—my head all cut up. Poor Elizabeth was—'' Cousin Jimmy shook his head, as if to intimate that it was impossible to describe how or what poor Elizabeth was. "I got about after a while, though—pretty near as good as new. Folks say I've never been quite right since—but they only say that because I'm a poet, and because nothing ever worries me. Poets are so scarce in Blair Water folks don't understand them, and most people worry so much, they think you're not right if you don't worry."

"Won't you recite some of your poetry to me, Cousin Jimmy?" asked Emily eagerly.

"When the spirit moves me I will. It's no use to ask me when the spirit don't move me."

"But how am I to know when the spirit moves you, Cousin Jimmy?"

"I'll begin of my own accord to recite my compositions. But I'll tell you this—the spirit generally moves me when I'm boiling the pigs' potatoes in the fall. Remember that and be around."

"Why don't you write your poetry down?"

"Paper's too scarce at New Moon. Elizabeth has some pet economies and writing paper of any kind is one of them."

"But haven't you any money of your own, Cousin Jimmy?"

"Oh, Elizabeth pays me good wages. But she puts all my money in the bank and just doles out a few dollars to me once in a while. She says I'm not fit to be trusted with money. When I came here to work for her she paid me my wages at the end of the month and I started for Shrewsbury to put it in the bank. Met a tramp on the road—a poor, forlorn creature without a cent. I gave *him* the money. Why not? *I* had a good home and a steady job and clothes enough to do me for years. I s'pose it was the foolishest thing I ever did—and the nicest. But Elizabeth never got over it. *She's* managed my money ever since. But come you now, and I'll show you my garden before I have to go and sow turnips."

The garden was a beautiful place, well worthy Cousin Jimmy's pride. It seemed like a garden where no frost could wither or rough wind blow—a garden remembering a hundred vanished summers. There was a high hedge of clipped spruce all around it, spaced at intervals by tall lombardies. The north side was closed in by a thick grove of spruce against which a long row of peonies grew, their great red blossoms splendid against its darkness. One big spruce grew in the center of the garden and underneath it was a stone bench, made of flat shore stones worn smooth by long polish of wind and wave. In the southeast corner was an enormous clump of lilacs, trimmed into the semblance of one large drooping-boughed tree, gloried over with purple. An old summer house, covered with vines, filled the southwest corner. And in the northwest corner there was a sun-dial of grey stone, placed just where the broad red walk that was bordered with striped grass, and picked out with pink conchs, ran off into Lofty John's bush. Emily had never seen a sundial before and hung over it enraptured.

"Your great-great grandfather, Hugh Murray, had that brought out from the Old Country," said Cousin Jimmy. "There isn't as fine a one in the Maritime Provinces. And Uncle George Murray brought those conchs from the Indies. He was a sea-captain."

Emily looked about her with delight. The garden was lovely and the house quite splendid to her childish eyes. It had a big front porch with Grecian columns. These were thought very elegant in Blair Water, and went far to justify the Murray pride. A schoolmaster had said they gave the house a classical air. To be sure, the classical effect was just now rather smothered in hop vines that rioted over the whole porch and hung in pale-green festoons above the rows of potted scarlet geraniums that flanked the steps.

Emily's heart swelled with pride.

"It's a noble house," she said.

"And what about my garden?" demanded Cousin Jimmy jealously.

"It's fit for a queen," said Emily, gravely and sincerely.

Cousin Jimmy nodded, well pleased, and then a strange sound crept into his voice and an odd look into his eyes.

"There is a spell woven round this garden. The blight shall spare it and the green worm pass it by. Drought dares not invade it and the rain comes here gently."

Emily took an involuntary step backward—she almost felt like running away. But now Cousin Jimmy was himself again.

"Isn't this grass about the sun-dial like green velvet? I've taken some pains with it, I can tell you. You make yourself at home in this garden." Cousin Jimmy made a splendid gesture. "I confer the freedom of it upon you. Good-luck to you, and may you find the Lost Diamond."

"The Lost Diamond?" said Emily wonderingly. What fascinating thing was this?

"Never hear the story? I'll tell it tomorrow—Sunday's lazy day at New Moon. I must get off to my turnips now or I'll have Elizabeth out looking at me. She won't say anything—she'll just *look*. Ever seen the real Murray look?"

"I guess I saw it when Aunt Ruth pulled me out from under the table," said Emily ruefully.

"No—no. That was the Ruth Dutton look—spite and malice and all uncharitableness. I hate Ruth Dutton. She laughs at my poetry—not that she ever hears any of it. The spirit never moves when Ruth is around. Dunno where they got her. Elizabeth is a crank but she's sound as a nut, and Laura's a saint. But Ruth's worm-eaten. As for the Murray look, you'll know it when you see it. It's as well-known as the Murray pride. We're a darn queer lot—but we're the finest people ever happened. I'll tell you all about us tomorrow."

Cousin Jimmy kept his promise while the aunts were away at church. It had been decided in family conclave that Emily was not to go to church that day.

"She has nothing suitable to wear," said Aunt Elizabeth. "By next Sunday we will have her white dress ready."

Emily was disappointed that she was not to go to church. She had always found church very interesting on the rare occasions when she got there. It had been too far at Maywood for her father to walk but sometimes Ellen Greene's brother had taken her and Ellen.

"Do you think, Aunt Elizabeth," she said wistfully, "that God would be much offended if I wore my black dress to church? Of course it's cheap—I think Ellen Greene paid for it herself—but it covers me all up."

"Little girls who do not understand things should hold their tongues," said Aunt Elizabeth. "I do not choose that Blair Water people should see my niece in such a dress as that wretched black merino. And if Ellen Greene paid for it we must repay her. You should have told us that before we came away from Maywood. No, you are not going to church to-day. You can wear the black dress to school to-morrow. We can cover it up with an apron."

Emily resigned herself with a sigh of disappointment to staying home; but it was very pleasant after all. Cousin Jimmy took her for a walk to the pond, showed her the graveyard and opened the book of yesterday for her.

"Why are all the Murrays buried here?" asked Emily. "Is it really because they are too good to be buried with common people?"

"No—no, pussy. We don't carry our pride as far as *that*. When old Hugh Murray settled at New Moon there was nothing much but woods for miles and no graveyards nearer than Charlottetown. That's why the old Murrays were buried here—and later on we kept it up because we wanted to lie with our own, here on the green, green banks of the old Blair Water."

"That sounds like a line out of a poem, Cousin Jimmy," said Emily.

"So it is—out of one of my poems."

"I kind of like the idea of a 'sclusive burying-ground like this," said Emily decidedly, looking around her approvingly at the velvet grass sloping down to the fairy-blue pond, the neat walks, the well-kept graves.

Cousin Jimmy chuckled.

"And yet they say you ain't a Murray," he said. "Murray and Byrd and Starr—and a dash of Shipley to boot, or Cousin Jimmy Murray is much mistaken."

"Shipley?"

"Yes—Hugh Murray's wife—your great-great-grandmother—was a Shipley—an Englishwoman. Ever hear of how the Murrays came to New Moon?"

"No."

"They were bound for Quebec—hadn't any notion of coming to P. E. I. They had a long rough voyage and water got scarce, so the captain of the *New Moon* put in here to get some. Mary Murray had nearly died of seasickness coming out—never seemed to get her sea-legs—so the captain, being sorry for her, told her she could go ashore with the men and feel solid ground under her for an hour or so. Very gladly she went and when she got to shore she said, 'Here I stay.' And stay she did; nothing could budge her; old Hugh—he was young Hugh then, of course—coaxed and stormed and raged and argued—and even cried, I've been told—but Mary wouldn't be moved. In the end he gave in and had his belongings landed and stayed, too. So that is how the Murrays came to P. E. Island."

"I'm glad it happened like that," said Emily.

"So was old Hugh in the long run. And yet it rankled, Emily—it rankled. He never forgave his wife with a whole heart. Her grave is over there in the corner—that one with the flat red stone. Go you and look at what he had put on it."

Emily ran curiously over. The big flat stone was inscribed with one of the long, discursive epitaphs of an older day. But beneath the epitaph was no scriptural verse or pious psalm. Clear and distinct, in spite of age and lichen, ran the line, "Here I stay."

"*That's* how he got even with her," said Cousin Jimmy. "He was a good husband to her—and she was a good wife and bore him a fine family—and he never was the same after her death. But that rankled in him until it had to come out."

Emily gave a little shiver. Somehow, the idea of that grim old ancestor with his undying grudge against his nearest and dearest was rather terrifying.

"I'm glad I'm only *half* Murray," she said to herself. Aloud—"Father told me it was a Murray tradition not to carry spite past the grave."

"So 'tis now—but it took its rise from this very thing. His family were so horrified at it, you see. It made considerable of a scandal. Some folks twisted it round to mean that old Hugh didn't believe in the resurrection, and there was talk of the session taking it up, but after a while the talk died away."

Emily skipped over to another lichen-grown stone.

"Elizabeth Burnley—who was she, Cousin Jimmy?"

"Old William Murray's wife. He was Hugh's brother, and came out here five years after Hugh did. His wife was a great beauty and had been a belle in the Old Country. She didn't like the P. E. Island woods. She was homesick, Emily—scandalous homesick. For weeks after she came here she wouldn't take off her bonnet—just walked the floor in it, demanding to be taken back home."

"Didn't she take it off when she went to bed?" asked Emily.

"Dunno if she did go to bed. Anyway, William wouldn't take her back home so in time she took off her bonnet and resigned herself. Her daughter married Hugh's son, so Elizabeth was just great-great-grandmother."

Emily looked down at the sunken green grave and wondered if any homesick dreams haunted Elizabeth Burnley's slumber of a hundred years.

"It's dreadful to be homesick—*I* know," she thought sympathetically.

"Little Stephen Murray is buried over there," said Cousin Jimmy. "His was the first marble stone in the burying-ground. He was your grandfather's brother—died when he was twelve. He has," said Cousin Jimmy solemnly, "become a Murray tradition."

"Why?"

"He was so beautiful and clever and good. He hadn't a fault—so of course he couldn't live. They say there never was such a handsome child in the connection. And lovable—everybody loved him. He has been dead for ninety years—not a Murray living to-day ever saw him—and yet we talk about him at family gatherings—he's more real than lots of living people. So you see, Emily, he must have been an extraordinary child—but it ended in that—" Cousin Jimmy waved his hand towards the grassy grave and the white, prim headstone.

"I wonder," thought Emily, "if any one will remember *me* ninety years after I'm dead."

"This old yard is nearly full," reflected Cousin Jimmy. "There's just room in yonder corner for Elizabeth and Laura—and me. None for you, Emily."

"I don't want to be buried here," flashed Emily. "I think it's splendid to have a graveyard like this in the family—but *I* am going to be buried in Charlottetown graveyard with Father and Mother. But there's one thing worries me, Cousin Jimmy, do *you* think I'm likely to die of consumption?"

Cousin Jimmy looked judicially down into her eyes.

"No," he said, "no, Miss Puss. You've got enough life in *you* to carry you far. You aren't meant for death."

"I feel that, too," said Emily, nodding. "And now,

Cousin Jimmy, *why* is that house over there disappointed?"

"Which one?—oh, Fred Clifford's house. Fred Clifford began to build that house thirty years ago. He was to be married and his lady picked out the plan. And when the house was just as far along as you see she jilted him, Emily—right in the face of day she jilted him. Never another nail was driven in the house. Fred went out to British Columbia. He's living there yet— married and happy. But he won't sell that lot to any one—so I reckon he feels the sting yet."

"I'm so sorry for that house. I *wish* it had been finished. It *wants* to be—even yet it *wants* to be."

"Well, I reckon it never will. Fred had a bit of Shipley in him, too, you see. One of old Hugh's girls was his grandmother. And Doctor Burnley up there in the big grey house has more than a bit."

"Is he a relation of ours, too, Cousin Jimmy?"

"Forty-second cousin. Way back he had a cousin of Mary Shipley's for a great-something. That was in the Old Country—his forebears came out here after we did. He's a good doctor but an odd stick—odder by far than I am, Emily, and yet nobody ever says he's not all there. Can you account for that? *He* doesn't believe in God—and *I* am not such a fool as that"

"Not in *any* God?"

"Not in any God. He's an infidel, Emily. And he's bringing his little girl up the same way, which *I* think is a shame, Emily," said Cousin Jimmy confidentially.

"Doesn't her mother teach her things?"

"Her mother is—dead," answered Cousin Jimmy, with a little odd hesitation. "Dead these ten years," he added in a firmer tone. "Ilse Burnley is a great girl— hair like daffodils and eyes like yellow diamonds."

"Oh, Cousin Jimmy, you promised you'd tell me about the Lost Diamond," cried Emily eagerly.

"To be sure—to be sure. Well, it's there—somewhere in or about the old summer-house, Emily. Fifty years ago Edward Murray and his wife came here from

Kingsport for a visit. A great lady she was, and wearing silks and diamonds like a queen, though no beauty. She had a ring on with a stone in it that cost two hundred pounds, Emily. That was a big lot of money to be wearing on one wee woman-finger, wasn't it? It sparkled on her white hand as she held her dress going up the steps of the summer house; but when she came down the steps it was gone."

"And was it *never* found?" asked Emily breathlessly.

"Never—and for no lack of searching. Edward Murray wanted to have the house pulled down—but Uncle Archibald wouldn't hear of it—because he had built it for his bride. The two brothers quarrelled over it and were never good friends again. Everybody in the connection has taken a spell hunting for the diamond. Most folks think it fell out of the summer house among the flowers or shrubs. But I know better, Emily. I know Miriam Murray's diamond is somewhere about that old house yet. On moonlit nights, Emily, I've seen it glinting—glinting and beckoning. But never in the same place—and when you go to it—it's gone, and you see it laughing at you from somewhere else."

Again there was that eerie, indefinable something in Cousin Jimmy's voice or look that gave Emily a sudden crinkly feeling in her spine. But she loved the way he talked to her, as if she were grown-up; and she loved the beautiful land around her; and, in spite of the ache for her father and the house in the hollow which persisted all the time and hurt her so much at night that her pillow was wet with secret tears, she was beginning to be a little glad again in sunset and bird song and early white stars, in moonlit nights and singing winds. She knew life was going to be wonderful here—wonderful and interesting, what with outdoor cook-houses and cream-girdled dairies and pond paths and sun-dials, and Lost Diamonds, and Disappointed Houses and men who didn't believe in *any* God—not even Ellen Greene's God. Emily hoped she would soon see Dr. Burnley. She was very curious to see what an infidel looked like. And she had already quite made up her mind that she would find the Lost Diamond.

8
Trial by Fire

Aunt Elizabeth drove Emily to school the next morning. Aunt Laura had thought that, since there was only a month before vacation, it was not worth while for Emily to "start school." But Aunt Elizabeth did not yet feel comfortable with a small niece skipping around New Moon, poking into everything insatiably, and was resolved that Emily must go to school to get her out of the way. Emily herself, always avid for new experiences, was quite keen to go, but for all that she was seething with rebellion as they drove along. Aunt Elizabeth had produced a terrible gingham apron and an equally terrible gingham sunbonnet from somewhere in the New Moon garret, and made Emily put them on. The apron was a long sack-like garment, high in the neck, with *sleeves*. Those sleeves were the crowning indignity. Emily had never seen any little girl wearing an apron with sleeves. She rebelled to the point of tears over wearing it, but Aunt Elizabeth was not going to have any nonsense. Emily saw the Murray look then; and when she saw it she buttoned her rebellious feelings tightly up in her soul and let Aunt Elizabeth put the apron on her.

"It was one of your mother's aprons when she was a little girl, Emily," said Aunt Laura comfortingly, and rather sentimentally.

"Then," said Emily, uncomforted and unsentimental,

"I don't wonder she ran away with Father when she grew up."

Aunt Elizabeth finished buttoning the apron and gave Emily a none too gentle push away from her.

"Put on your sunbonnet," she ordered.

"Oh, please, Aunt Elizabeth, don't make me wear that horrid thing."

Aunt Elizabeth, wasting no further words, picked up the bonnet and tied it on Emily's head. Emily had to yield. But from the depths of the sunbonnet issued a voice, defiant though tremulous.

"Anyway, Aunt Elizabeth, you can't boss God," it said.

Aunt Elizabeth was too cross to speak all the way to the schoolhouse. She introduced Emily to Miss Brownell, and drove away. School was already "in," so Emily hung her sunbonnet on the porch nail and went to the desk Miss Brownell assigned her. She had already made up her mind that she did not like Miss Brownell and never would like her.

Miss Brownell had the reputation in Blair Water of being a fine teacher—due mainly to the fact that she was a strict disciplinarian and kept excellent "order." She was a thin, middle-aged person with a colourless face, prominent teeth, most of which she showed when she laughed, and cold, watchful grey eyes—colder even than Aunt Ruth's. Emily felt as if those merciless agate eyes saw clean through her to the core of her sensitive little soul. Emily could be fearless enough on occasion; but in the presence of a nature which she instinctively felt to be hostile to hers she shrank away in something that was more repulsion than fear.

She was a target for curious glances all the morning. The Blair Water school was large and there were at least twenty little girls of about her own age. Emily looked back curiously at them all and thought the way they whispered to each other behind hands and books when they looked at her very ill-mannered. She felt suddenly unhappy and homesick and lonesome—she wanted her father and her old home and the dear things she loved.

"The New Moon girl is crying," whispered a black-eyed girl across the aisle. And then came a cruel little giggle.

"What is the matter with you, Emily?" said Miss Brownell suddenly and accusingly.

Emily was silent. She could not tell Miss Brownell what was the matter with her—especially when Miss Brownell used such a tone.

"When I ask one of my pupils a question, Emily, I am accustomed to having an answer. Why are you crying?"

There was another giggle from across the aisle. Emily lifted miserable eyes and in her extremity fell back on a phrase of her father's.

"It is a matter that concerns only myself," she said.

A red spot suddenly appeared in Miss Brownell's sallow cheek. Her eyes gleamed with cold fire.

"You will remain in during recess as a punishment for your impertinence," she said—but she left Emily alone the rest of the day.

Emily did not in the least mind staying in at recess, for, acutely sensitive to her environment as she was, she realized that, for some reason she could not fathom, the atmosphere of the school was antagonistic. The glances cast at her were not only curious but ill-natured. She did not want to go out to the playground with those girls. She did not want to go to school in Blair Water. But she would not cry any more. She sat erect and kept her eyes on her book. Suddenly a soft, malignant hiss came across the aisle.

"Miss Pridey—Miss Pridey!"

Emily looked across at the girl. Large, steady, purplish-grey eyes gazed into beady, twinkling, black ones—gazed unquailingly—with something in them that cowed and compelled. The black eyes wavered and fell, their owner covering her retreat with another giggle and toss of her short braid of hair.

"I can master *her*," thought Emily, with a thrill of triumph.

But there is strength in numbers and at noon hour Emily found herself standing alone on the playground facing a crowd of unfriendly faces. Children can be the most cruel creatures alive. They have the herd instinct of prejudice against any outsider, and they are merciless in its indulgence. Emily was a stranger and one of the proud Murrays—two counts against her. And there was about her, small and ginghamed and sunbonneted as she was, a certain reserve and dignity and fineness that they resented. And they resented the level way she looked at them, with that disdainful face under cloudy black hair, instead of being shy and drooping as became an interloper on probation.

"You are a proud one," said Black-eyes. "Oh, my, you may have buttoned boots, but you are living on charity."

Emily had not wanted to put on the buttoned boots. She wanted to go barefoot as she had always done in summer. But Aunt Elizabeth had told her that no child from New Moon had ever gone barefoot to school.

"Oh, just look at the baby apron," laughed another girl, with a head of chestnut curls.

Now Emily flushed. This was indeed the vulnerable point in her armour. Delighted at her success in drawing blood the curled one tried again.

"Is that your grandmother's sunbonnet?"

There was a chorus of giggles.

"Oh, she wears a sunbonnet to save her complexion," said a bigger girl. "That's the Murray pride. The Murrays are rotten with pride, my mother says."

"You're awful ugly," said a fat, squat little miss, nearly as broad as she was long. "Your ears look like a cat's."

"You needn't be so proud," said Black-eyes. "Your kitchen ceiling isn't plastered even."

"And your Cousin Jimmy is an idiot," said Chestnut-curls.

"He isn't!" cried Emily. "He has more sense than any of you. You can say what you like about me but you are not going to *insult my family*. If you say one more word about them I'll look you over with the evil eye."

Nobody understood what this threat meant, but that made it all the more effective. It produced a brief silence. Then the baiting began again in a different form.

"Can you sing?" asked a thin, freckled girl, who yet contrived to be very pretty in spite of thinness and freckles.

"No," said Emily.

"Can you dance?"

"No."

"Can you sew?"

"No."

"Can you cook?"

"No."

"Can you knit lace?"

"No."

"Can you crochet?"

"No."

"Then what *can* you do?" said the freckled-one in a contemptuous tone.

"I can write poetry," said Emily, without in the least meaning to say it. But at that instant she knew she *could* write poetry. And with this queer unreasonable conviction came—the flash! Right there, surrounded by hostility and suspicion, fighting alone for her standing, without backing or advantage, came the wonderful moment when soul seemed to cast aside the bonds of flesh and spring upward to the stars. The rapture and delight on Emily's face amazed and enraged her foes. They thought it a manifestation of Murray pride in an uncommon accomplishment.

"You lie," said Black-eyes bluntly.

"A Starr does not lie," retorted Emily. The flash was gone, but its uplift remained. She looked them all over with a cool detachment that quelled them temporarily.

"Why don't you like me?" she asked directly.

There was no reply. Emily looked straight at Chestnut-curls and repeated her question. Chestnut-curls felt herself compelled to answer it.

"Because you ain't a bit like us," she muttered.

"I wouldn't want to be," said Emily scornfully.

"Oh, my, you are one of the Chosen People," mocked Black-eyes.

"Of course I am," retorted Emily.

She walked away to the schoolhouse, conqueror in that battle.

But the forces against her were not so easily cowed. There was much whispering and plotting after she had gone in, a conference with some of the boys, and a handing over of bedizened pencils and chews of gum for value received.

An agreeable sense of victory and the afterglow of the flash carried Emily through the afternoon in spite of the fact that Miss Brownell ridiculed her for her mistakes in spelling. Miss Brownell was very fond of ridiculing her pupils. All the girls in the class giggled except one who had not been there in the morning and was consequently at the tail. Emily had been wondering who she was. She was as unlike the rest of the girls as Emily herself, but in a totally different style. She was tall, oddly dressed in an overlong dress of faded, striped print, and barefooted. Her thick hair, cut short, fluffed out all around her head in a bushy wave that seemed to be of brilliant spun gold; and her glowing eyes were of a brown so light and translucent as to be almost amber. Her mouth was large, and she had a saucy, pronounced chin. Pretty she might not be called, but her face was so vivid and mobile that Emily could not drag her fascinated eyes from it. And she was the only girl in class who did not, sometime through the lesson, get a barb of sarcasm from Miss Brownell, though she made as many mistakes as the rest of them.

At recess one of the girls came up to Emily with a box in her hand. Emily knew that she was Rhoda Stuart and thought her very pretty and sweet. Rhoda had been in the crowd around her at the noon hour but she had not said anything. She was dressed in a crispy pink gingham; she had smooth, lustrous braids of sugar-brown hair, big blue eyes, a rose-bud mouth, doll-like features and a sweet voice. If Miss Brownell could be said to have a favourite it was Rhoda Stuart, and she seemed generally popular in her own set and much petted by the older girls.

"Here is a present for you," she said sweetly.

Emily took the box unsuspectingly. Rhoda's smile would have disarmed any suspicion. For a moment Emily was happily anticipant as she removed the cover. Then with a shriek she flung the box from her, and stood pale and trembling from head to foot. There was a snake in the box—whether dead or alive she did not know and did not care. For any snake Emily had a horror and repulsion she could not overcome. The very sight of one almost paralyzed her.

A chorus of giggles ran around the porch.

"Before I'd be so scared of an old dead snake!" scoffed Black-eyes.

"Can you write poetry about *that?*" giggled Chestnut-curls.

"I *hate* you—I hate you!" cried Emily. "You are mean, hateful girls!"

"Calling names isn't ladylike," said the Freckled-one. "I thought a Murray would be too grand for that."

"If you come to school to-morrow, *Miss* Starr," said Black-eyes deliberately, "we are going to take that snake and put it around your neck."

"Let me see you do it!" cried a clear, ringing voice. Into their midst with a bound came the girl with amber eyes and short hair. "Just let me *see* you do it, Jennie Strang!"

"This isn't any of your business, Ilse Burnley," muttered Jennie, sullenly.

"Oh, isn't it? Don't you sass me, Piggy-eyes." Ilse walked up to the retreating Jennie and shook a sunburned fist in her face. "If I catch you teasing Emily Starr tomorrow with that snake again I'll take *it* by the tail and *you* by *your* tail, and slash you across the face with it. Mind that, Piggy-eyes. Now you go and pick up that precious snake of yours and throw it down on the ash pile."

Jennie actually went and did it. Ilse faced the others.

"Clear out, all of you, and leave the New Moon girl alone after this," she said. "If I hear of any more meddling and sneaking I'll slit your throats, and rip out your hearts and tear your eyes out. Yes, and I'll cut off your ears and wear them pinned on my dress!"

Cowed by these ferocious threats, or by something in Ilse's personality, Emily's persecutors drifted away. Ilse turned to Emily.

"Don't mind them," she said contemptuously. "They're jealous of you, that's all—jealous because you live at New Moon and ride in a fringed-top buggy and wear buttoned boots. You smack their mugs if they give you any more of their jaw."

Ilse vaulted the fence and tore off into the maple bush without another glance at Emily. Only Rhoda Stuart remained.

"Emily, I'm awful sorry," she said, rolling her big blue eyes appealingly. "I didn't know there was a snake in that box, cross my heart I didn't. The girls just told me it was a present for you. You're not mad at me, are you? Because I like you."

Emily had been "mad" and hurt and outraged. But this little bit of friendliness melted her instantly. In a moment she and Rhoda had their arms around each other, parading across the playground.

"I'm going to ask Miss Brownell to let you sit with me," said Rhoda. "I used to sit with Annie Gregg but she's moved away. You'd like to sit with me, wouldn't you?"

"I'd love it," said Emily warmly. She was as happy as she had been miserable. Here was the friend of her dreams. Already she worshipped Rhoda.

"We *ought* to sit together," said Rhoda importantly.

"We belong to the two best families in Blair Water. Do you know that if my father had his rights he would be on the throne of England?"

"England!" said Emily, too amazed to be anything but an echo.

"Yes. We are descended from the kings of Scotland," said Rhoda. "So of course we don't 'sociate with everybody. My father keeps store and I'm taking music lessons. Is your Aunt Elizabeth going to give you music lessons?"

"I don't know."

"She ought to. She is very rich, isn't she?"

"I don't know," said Emily again. She wished Rhoda would not ask such questions. Emily thought it was hardly good manners. But surely a descendant of the Stuart kings ought to know the rules of breeding, if anybody did.

"She's got an awful temper, hasn't she?" asked Rhoda.

"No, she hasn't!" cried Emily.

"Well, she nearly killed your Cousin Jimmy in one of her rages," said Rhoda. "That's true—Mother told me. Why doesn't your Aunt Laura get married? Has she got a beau? What wages does your Aunt Elizabeth pay your Cousin Jimmy?"

"I don't know."

"Well," said Rhoda, rather disappointedly. "I suppose you haven't been at New Moon long enough to find things out. But it must be very different from what you've been used to, I guess. Your father was as poor as a church mouse, wasn't he?"

"My father was a very, *very* rich man," said Emily deliberately.

Rhoda stared.

"I thought he hadn't a cent."

"Neither he had. But people can be rich without money."

"I don't see how. But anyhow, *you'll* be rich some day—your Aunt Elizabeth will likely leave you all her money, Mother says. So I don't care if you *are* living on charity—I love you and I'm going to stick up for you. Have you got a beau, Emily?"

"No," cried Emily, blushing violently and quite scandalized at the idea. "Why, I'm only eleven."

"Oh, everybody in our class has a beau. Mine is Teddy Kent. I shook hands with him after I'd counted nine stars for nine nights without missing a night. If you do that the first boy you shake hands with afterwards is to be your beau. But it's awful hard to do. It took me all winter. Teddy wasn't in school to-day—he's been sick all June. He's the best-looking boy in Blair Water. You'll have to have a beau, too, Emily."

"I won't," declared Emily angrily. "I don't know a thing about beaux and I won't have one."

Rhoda tossed her head.

"Oh, I s'pose you think there's nobody good enough for you, living at New Moon. Well, you won't be able to play Clap-in-and-clap-out if you haven't a beau."

Emily knew nothing of the mysteries of Clap-in-and-clap-out, and didn't care. Anyway, she wasn't going to have a beau and she repeated this in such decided tones that Rhoda deemed it wise to drop the subject.

Emily was rather glad when the bell rang. Miss Brownell granted Rhoda's request quite graciously and Emily transferred her goods and chattels to Rhoda's seat. Rhoda whispered a good deal during the last hour and Emily got scolded for it but did not mind.

"I'm going to have a birthday party the first week in July, and I'm going to invite you, if your aunts will let you come. I'm not going to have Ilse Burnley though."

"Don't you like her?"

"No. She's an awful tomboy. And then her father is an infidel. And so's she. She always spells 'God' with a little 'g' in her dictation. Miss Brownell scolds her for it but she does it right along. Miss Brownell won't whip *her* because she's setting her cap for Dr. Burnley. But Ma says she won't get him because he hates women. *I* don't think it's proper to 'sociate with such people. Ilse is an awful wild queer girl and has an awful temper. So has her father. She doesn't chum with anybody. Isn't it ridic'lus the way she wears her hair? *You* ought to have a bang, Emily. They're all the rage and you'd look well with one because you've such a high forehead. It would make a real beauty of you. My, but you have lovely hair, and your hands are just lovely. All the Murrays have pretty hands. And you have the *sweetest* eyes, Emily."

Emily had never received so many compliments in her life. Rhoda laid flattery on with a trowel. Her head was quite turned and she went home from school determined to ask Aunt Elizabeth to cut her hair in a bang. If it would make a beauty of her it must be compassed somehow. And she would also ask Aunt Elizabeth if she might wear her Venetian beads to school next day.

"The other girls may *respect* me more then," she thought.

She was alone from the crossroads, where she had parted company with Rhoda, and she reviewed the events of the day with a feeling that, after all, she had kept the Starr flag flying, except for a temporary reverse in the matter of the snake. School was very different from what she had expected it to be, but that was the way in life, she had heard Ellen Greene say, and you just had to make the best of it. Rhoda was a darling; and there was something about Ilse Burnley that one liked; and as for the rest of the girls Emily got square with them by pretending she saw them all being hanged in a row for frightening her to death with a snake, and felt no more resentment towards them, although some of the things that had been said to her rankled bitterly in her heart for many a day. She had no father to tell them to, and no account book to write them out in, so she could not exorcise them.

She had no speedy chance to ask for a bang, for there was company at New Moon and her aunts were busy getting ready an elaborate supper. But when the preserves were brought on Emily snatched the opportunity of a lull in the older conversation.

"Aunt Elizabeth," she said, "can I have a bang?"

Aunt Elizabeth looked her disdain.

"No," she said, "I do not approve of bangs. Of all the silly fashions that have come in now-a-days, bangs are the silliest."

"Oh, Aunt Elizabeth, *do* let me have a bang. It would make a beauty of me,—Rhoda says so."

"It would take a good deal more than a bang to do that, Emily. We will not have bangs at New Moon—except on the Molly cows. *They* are the only creatures that should wear bangs."

Aunt Elizabeth smiled triumphantly around the table—Aunt Elizabeth *did* smile sometimes when she thought she had silenced some small person by exquisite ridicule. Emily understood that it was no use to hope for bangs. Loveliness did not lie that way for her. It was mean of Aunt Elizabeth—mean. She heaved a sigh of disappointment and dismissed the idea for the present. There was something else she wanted to know.

"Why doesn't Ilse Burnley's father believe in God?" she asked.

"'Cause of the trick her mother played him," said Mr. Slade, with a chuckle. Mr. Slade was a fat, jollylooking old man with bushy hair and whiskers. He had already said some things Emily could not understand and which had seemed greatly to embarrass his very lady-like wife.

"What trick did Ilse's mother play?" asked Emily, all agog with interest.

Now Aunt Laura looked at Aunt Elizabeth and Aunt Elizabeth looked at Aunt Laura. Then the latter said:

"Run out and feed the chickens, Emily."

Emily rose with dignity.

"You might just as well tell me that Ilse's mother isn't to be talked about and I would obey you. I understand *perfectly* what you mean," she said as she left the table.

9
A Special Providence

Emily was sure on that first day at school that she would never like it. She must go, she knew, in order to get an education and be ready to earn her own living; but it would always be what Ellen Greene solemnly called "a cross." Consequently Emily felt quite astonished when, after going to school a few days, it dawned upon her that she was liking it. To be sure, Miss Brownell did not improve on acquaintance; but the other girls no longer tormented her—indeed, to her amazement, they seemed suddenly to forget all that had happened and hailed her as one of themselves. She was admitted to the fellowship of the pack and, although in some occasional tiff she got a dig about baby aprons and Murray pride, there was no more hostility, veiled or open. Besides, Emily was quite able to give "digs" herself, as she learned more about the girls and their weak points, and she could give them with such merciless lucidity and irony that the others soon learned not to provoke them. Chestnut-curls, whose name was Grace Wells, and the Freckled-one, whose name was Carrie King, and Jennie Strang became quite chummy with her, and Jennie sent chews of gum and tissue thumb-papers across the aisle instead of giggles. Emily allowed them all to enter the outer court of her temple of friendship but only Rhoda was admitted to the inner shrine. As for Ilse Burnley, she did not appear after that first day. Ilse, so Rhoda said, came to school or not, just as she liked. Her father never bothered about her. Emily always felt a certain hankering to know more of Ilse, but it did not seem likely to be gratified.

Emily was insensibly becoming happy again. Already she felt as if she belonged to this old cradle of her family. She thought a great deal about the old Murrays; she liked to picture them revisiting the glimpses of New Moon—Great-grandmother rubbing up her candle-sticks and making cheeses; Great-aunt Miriam stealing about looking for her lost treasure; homesick Great-great-aunt Elizabeth stalking about in her bonnet; Captain George, the dashing, bronzed sea-captain, coming home with the spotted shells of the Indies; Stephen, the beloved of all, smiling from its windows; her own mother dreaming of Father—they all seemed as real to her as if she had known them in life.

She still had terrible hours when she was overwhelmed by grief for her father and when all the splendours of New Moon could not stifle the longing for the shabby little house in the hollow where they had loved each other so. Then Emily fled to some secret corner and cried her heart out, emerging with red eyes that always seemed to annoy Aunt Elizabeth. Aunt Elizabeth had become used to having Emily at New Moon but she had not drawn any nearer to the child. This hurt Emily always; but Aunt Laura and Cousin Jimmy loved her and she had Saucy Sal and Rhoda, fields creamy with clover, soft dark trees against amber skies, and the madcap music the Wind Woman made in the firs behind the barns when she blew straight up from the gulf; her days became vivid and interesting, full of little pleasures and delights, like tiny, opening, golden buds on the tree of life. If she could only have had her old yellow account book, or some equivalent, she could have been fully content. She missed it next to her father, and its enforced burning was something for which she held Aunt Elizabeth responsible and for which she felt she could never wholly forgive her. It did not seem possible to get any substitute. As Cousin Jimmy had said, writing paper of any kind was scarce at New Moon. Letters were seldom written, and when they were a sheet of note-paper sufficed. Emily dared not ask Aunt Elizabeth for any. There were times when she felt she would burst if she couldn't write out some of the things that came to her. She found a certain safety valve in writing on her slate in school; but these scribblings had to be rubbed off sooner or later—which left Emily with a sense of loss—and there was always the danger that Miss Brownell would see them. That, Emily felt, would be unendurable. No stranger eyes must behold these sacred productions. Sometimes she let Rhoda read them, though Rhoda rasped her by giggling over her finest flights. Emily thought Rhoda as near perfection as a human being could be, but giggling was her fault.

But there is a destiny which shapes the ends of young misses who are born with the itch for writing tingling in their baby fingertips, and in the fulness of time this destiny gave to Emily the desire of her heart— gave it to her, too, on the very day when she most needed it. That was the day, the ill-starred day, when Miss Brownell elected to show the fifth class, by example as well as precept, how the *Bugle Song* should be read.

Standing on the platform Miss Brownell, who was not devoid of a superficial, elocutionary knack, read those three wonderful verses. Emily, who should have been doing a sum in long division, dropped her pencil and listened entranced. She had never heard the *Bugle Song* before—but now she heard it—and *saw* it—the rose-red splendour falling on those storied, snowy summits and ruined castles—the lights that never were on land or sea streaming over the lakes—she heard the wild echoes flying through the purple valleys and the misty passes—the mere sound of the words seemed to make an exquisite echo in her soul—and when Miss Brownell came to "Horns of elf-land faintly blowing" Emily trembled with delight. She was snatched out of herself. She forgot everything but the magic of that unequalled line—she sprang from her seat, knocking her slate to the floor with a clatter, she rushed up the aisle, she caught Miss Brownell's arm.

"Oh, teacher," she cried with passionate earnestness, "read that line over again—oh, read that line over again!"

Miss Brownell, thus suddenly halted in her elocutionary display, looked down into a rapt, uplifted face where great purplish-grey eyes were shining with the radiance of a divine vision—and Miss Brownell was angry. Angry with this breach of her strict discipline—angry with this unseenly display of interest in a third class atom whose attention should have been focused on long division. Miss Brownell shut her book and shut her lips and gave Emily a resounding slap on her face.

"Go right back to your seat and mind your own business, Emily Starr," said Miss Brownell, her cold eyes malignant with her fury.

Emily, thus dashed to earth, moved back to her seat in a daze. Her smitten cheek was crimson, but the wound was in her heart. One moment ago in the seventh heaven—and now *this*—pain, humiliation, misunderstanding! She could not bear it. What had she done to deserve it? She had never been slapped in her life before. The degradation and the injustice ate into her soul. She could not cry—this was "a grief too deep for tears"—she went home from school in a suppressed anguish of bitterness and shame and resentment—an anguish that had no outlet, for she dared not tell her story at New Moon. Aunt Elizabeth, she felt sure, would say that Miss Brownell had done quite right, and even Aunt Laura, kind and sweet as she was, would not understand. She would be grieved because Emily had misbehaved in school and had had to be punished.

"Oh, if I could only tell Father all about it!" thought Emily.

She could not eat any supper—she did not think she would ever be able to eat again. And oh, how she hated that unjust, horrid Miss Brownell! She could never forgive her—never! If there were only some way in which she could get square with Miss Brownell! Emily, sitting small and pale and quiet at the New Moon supper table, was a seething volcano of wounded feeling and misery and pride—ay, pride! Worse even than the injustice was the sting of humiliation over this thing that had happened. She, Emily Byrd Starr, on whom no hand had ever before been ungently laid, had been slapped like a naughty baby before the whole school. Who could endure this and live?

Then destiny stepped in and drew Aunt Laura to the sitting-room bookcase to look in its lower compartment for a certain letter she wanted to see. She took Emily with her to show her a curious old snuff-box that had belonged to Hugh Murray, and in rummaging for it lifted out a big, flat bundle of dusty paper—paper of a deep pink colour in oddly long and narrow sheets.

"It's time these old letter-bills were burned," she said. "What a pile of them! They've been here gathering dust for years and they are no earthly good. Father once kept the post-office here at New Moon, you know, Emily. The mail came only three times a week then, and each day there was one of these long red 'letter-bills,' as they were called. Mother always kept them, though when once used they were of no further use. But I'm going to burn them right away."

"Oh, Aunt Laura," gasped Emily, so torn between desire and fear that she could hardly speak. "Oh, don't do that—give them to me—*please* give them to me."

"Why, child, what ever do you want of them?"

"Oh, Aunty, they have such lovely blank backs for writing on. Please, Aunt Laura, it would be a *sin* to burn those letter-bills."

"You can have them, dear. Only you'd better not let Elizabeth see them."

"I won't—I won't," breathed Emily.

She gathered her precious booty into her arms and fairly ran upstairs—and then upstairs again into the garret, where she already had her "favourite haunt," in which her uncomfortable habit of thinking of things thousands of miles away could not vex Aunt Elizabeth. This was the quiet corner of the dormer window, where shadows always moved about, softly and swingingly, and beautiful mosaics patterned the bare floor. From it one could see over the tree-tops right down to the Blair Water. The walls were hung around with great bundles of soft fluffy rolls, all ready for spinning, and hanks of untwisted yarn. Sometimes Aunt Laura spun on the great wheel at the other end of the garret and Emily loved the whirr of it.

In the recess of the dormer window she crouched—breathlessly she selected a letter-bill and extracted a lead pencil from her pocket. An old sheet of cardboard served as a desk; she began to write feverishly.

"Dear Father"—and then she poured out her tale of the day—of her rapture and her pain—writing heedlessly and intently until the sunset faded into dim, star-litten twilight. The chickens went unfed—Cousin Jimmy had to go himself for the cows—Saucy Sal got no new milk—Aunt Laura had to wash the dishes—what mattered it? Emily, in the delightful throes of literary composition, was lost to all worldly things.

When she had covered the backs of four letter-bills she could see to write no more. But she had emptied out her soul and it was once more free from evil passions. She even felt curiously indifferent to Miss Brownell. Emily folded up her letter-bills and wrote clearly across the packet,

> *Mr. Douglas Starr,*
> *On the Road to Heaven.*

Then she stepped softly across to an old, worn-out sofa in a far corner and knelt down, stowing away her letter and her "letter-bills" snugly on a little shelf formed by a board nailed across it underneath. Emily had discovered this one day when playing in the garret and had noted it as a lovely hiding-place for secret documents. Nobody would ever come across them there. She had writing paper enough to last for months—there must be hundreds of those jolly old letter-bills.

"Oh," cried Emily, dancing down the garret stairs, "I feel as if I was made out of star-dust."

Thereafter few evenings passed on which Emily did not steal up to the garret and write a letter, long or short, to her father. The bitterness died out of her grief. Writing to him seemed to bring him so near; and she told him everything, with a certain honesty of confession that was characteristic of her—her triumphs, her failures, her joys, her sorrows, everything went down on the letter-bills of a Government which had not been so economical of paper as it afterwards became. There was fully half a yard of paper in each bill and Emily wrote a small hand and made the most of every inch.

"I like New Moon. It's so *stately* and *splendid* here," she told her father. "And it seems as if we must be very aristokratik when we have a sun dyal I can't help feeling proud of it all. I am afraid I have too much pride and so I ask God every night to take *most* of it away but not quite all. It is very easy to get a repputation for pride in Blair Water school. If you walk straight and hold your head up you are a proud one. Rhoda is proud, too, because her father ought to be King of England. I wonder how Queen Victoria would feel if she knew that. It's very wonderful to have a friend who would be a princess if every one had their rites. I love Rhoda with all my heart. She is so sweet and kind. But I don't like her giggles. And when I told her I could see the school wallpaper small in the air she said You lie. It hurt me awfully to have my dearest friend say that to me. And it hurt me worse when I woke up in the night and thought about it. I had to stay awake ever so long, too, because I was tired lying on one side and I was afraid to turn over because Aunt Elizabeth would think I was figitting.

"I didn't dare tell Rhoda about the Wind Woman because I suppose that really is a kind of lie, though she seems so real to me. I hear her now singing up on the roof around the big chimneys. I have no Emily-in-the-glass here. The looking-glasses are all too high up in the rooms I've been in. I've never been in the look-out. It is always locked. It was Mother's room and Cousin Jimmy says her father locked it up after she ran away with you and Aunt Elizabeth keeps it locked still out of respect to his memory, though Cousin Jimmy says Aunt Elizabeth used to fight with her father something scandalus when he was alive though no outsider knew of it because of the Murray pride. I feel that way myself. When Rhoda asked me if Aunt Elizabeth burned candles because she was old-fashioned I answered hawtily no, it was a Murray tradishun. Cousin Jimmy has told me all the tradishuns of the Murrays. Saucy Sal is very well and bosses the barns but still she will not have kittens and I can't understand it. I asked Aunt Elizabeth about it and she said nice little girls didn't talk about such things but I cannot see why kittens are impropper. When Aunt Elizabeth is away Aunt Laura and I smuggle Sal into the house but when Aunt Elizabeth comes back I always feel gilty and wish I hadn't. *But the next time I do it again.* I think that very strange. I never hear about dear Mike. I wrote Ellen Greene and asked about him and she replyed and never mentioned Mike but told me all about her roomatism. As if I cared about her roomatism.

"Rhoda is going to have a birthday party and she is going to invite me. I am so excited. You know I never was to a party before. I think about it a great deal and picture it out. Rhoda is not going to invite all the girls but only a favered few. I hope Aunt Elizabeth will let me ware my white dress and good hat. Oh, Father, I pinned that lovely picture of the lace ball dress up on the wall of Aunt Elizabeth's room, just like I had it at home and Aunt Elizabeth took it down and burned it and skolded me for making pin marks in the paper. I said Aunt Elizabeth you should not have burned that picture. I wanted to have it when I grow up to have a dress made like it for balls. And Aunt Elizabeth said Do you expect to attend many balls if I may ask and I said Yes when I am rich and famus and Aunt Elizabeth said Yes when the moon is made of green cheese.

"I saw Dr. Burnley yesterday when he came over to buy some eggs from Aunt Elizabeth. I was disappointed because he looks just like other people. I thought a man who didn't believe in God would look queer in some way. He did not sware either and I was sorry for I have never heard any one sware and I am very angshus to. He has big yellow eyes like Ilse and a loud voice and Rhoda says when he gets mad you can hear him yelling all over Blair Water. There is some mistery about Ilse's mother which I cannot fathum. Dr. Burnley and Ilse live alone. Rhoda says Dr. Burnley says he will have no devils of women in that house. That speech is wikked but striking. Old Mrs. Simms goes over and cooks dinner and supper for them and then vamooses and they get their own breakfast. The doctor sweeps out the house now and then and Ilse never does anything but run wild. The doctor never smiles so Rhoda says. He must be like King Henry the Second.

"I would like to get akwanted with Ilse. She isn't as sweet as Rhoda but I like her looks, too. But she doesn't come to school much and Rhoda says I mustn't have any chum but her or she will cry her eyes out. Rhoda loves me as much as I love her. We are both going to pray that we may live together all our lives and die the same day.

"Aunt Elizabeth always puts up my school dinner for me. She won't give me anything but plain bread and butter but she cuts good thick slices and the butter is thick too and never has the horrid taste Ellen Greene's butter used to have. And Aunt Laura slips in a cooky or an apple turnover when Aunt Elizabeth's back is turned. Aunt Elizabeth says apple turnovers are not helthy for me. Why is it that the nicest things never are helthy, Father? Ellen Greene used to say that too.

"My teacher's name is Miss Brownell. I don't like the

cut of her jib. (That is a naughtical frays that Cousin Jimmy uses. I know frays is not spelled right but there is no dixonary at New Moon but that is the sound of it.) She is too sarkastik and she likes to make you rediklus. Then she laughs at you in a disagreable, snorting way. But I forgave her for slapping me and I took a boquet to her to school next day to make up. She receeved it very coldly and let it fade on her desk. In a story she would have wepped on my neck. I don't know whether it is any use forgiving people or not. Yes, it is, it makes you feel more comfortable yourself. You never had to ware baby aprons and sunbonnets because you were a boy so you can't understand how I feel about it. And the aprons are made of such good stuff that they will never ware out and it will be years before I grow out of them. But I have a white dress for church with a black silk sash and a white legorn hat with black bows and black kid slippers, and I feel very elegant in them. I wish I could have a bang but Aunt Elizabeth will not hear of it. Rhoda told me I had beautiful eyes. I wish she hadn't. I have always suspected my eyes were beautiful but I was not sure. Now that I know they are I'm afraid I'll always be wondering if people notis it. I have to go to bed at half past eight and I don't like it but I sit up in bed and look out of the window till it gets dark, so I get square with Aunt Elizabeth that way, and I listen to the sound the sea makes. I like it now though it always makes me feel sorrowful, but it's a kind of a nice sorrow. I have to sleep with Aunt Elizabeth and I don't like that either because if I move ever so little she says I figit but she admits that I don't kick. And she won't let me put the window up. She doesn't like fresh air or light in the house. The parlour is dark as a toomb. I went in one day and rolled up all the blinds and Aunt Elizabeth was horrifyed and called me a little hussy and gave me the Murray look. You would suppose I had committed a crime. I felt so insulted that I came up to the garret and wrote a deskription of myself being drowned on a letter-bill and then I felt better. Aunt Elizabeth said I was never to go into the parlour again without permission but I don't want to. I am afraid of the parlour. All the walls are hung over with pictures of our ancestors and there is not one goodlooking person among them except Grand-father Murray who looks handsome but very cross. The spare room is upstairs and is just as gloomy as the parlour. Aunt Elizabeth only lets distingwished people sleep there. I like the kitchen in daytime, and the garret and the cookhouse and the sitting-room and the hall because of the lovely red front door and I love the dairy, but I don't like the other New Moon rooms. Oh, I forgot the cellar cubbord. I love to go down there and look at the beautiful rows of jam and jelly pots. Cousin Jimmy says it is a New Moon tradishun that the jam pots must never be empty. What a lot of tradishuns New Moon has. It is a very spashus house, and the trees are lovely. I have named the three lombardys at the garden gate the Three Princesses and I have named the old summer house Emily's Bower, and the big apple tree by the old orchard gate the Praying Tree because it holds up its long boughs exactly as Mr. Dare holds up his arms in church where he prays.

"Aunt Elizabeth has given me the little right hand top burow drawer to keep my things in.

"Oh, Father dear, I have made a great diskoverry. I wish I had made it when you were alive for I think you'd have liked to know. *I can write poetry.* Perhaps I could have written it long ago if I'd tried. But after that first day in school I felt I was bound in honnour to try and it is so easy. There is a little curly black-covered book in Aunt Elizabeth's bookcase called Thompson's Seasons and I decided I would write a poem on a season and the first three lines are,

Now Autumn comes ripe with the peech and pear,
The sportsman's horn is heard throughout the land,
And the poor partridge fluttering falls dead.

"Of course there are no peeches in P. E. Island and I never heard a sportsman's horn here either, but you don't have to stick too close to facts in poetry. I filled a whole letter-bill with it and then I ran and read it to Aunt Laura. I thought she would be overjoyed to find she had a niece who could write poetry but she took it very coolly and said it didn't sound much like poetry. It's blank verse I cried. *Very* blank said Aunt Elizabeth sarcastically though I hadn't asked *her* opinion. But I think I will write ryming poetry after this so that there will be no mistake about it and I intend to be a poetess when I grow up and become famus. I hope also that I will be silph-like. A poetess should be silph-like. Cousin Jimmy makes poetry too. He had made over 1000 pieces but he never writes any down but carries them in his head. I offered to give him some of my letter-bills—for he is very kind to me—but he said he was too old to learn new habits. I haven't heard any of his poetry yet because the spirit hasn't moved him but I am very angshus to and I am sorry they don't fatten the pigs till the fall. I like Cousin Jimmy more and more all the time, except when he takes his queer spells of looking and talking. Then he fritens me but they never last long. I have read a good many of the books in the New Moon bookcase. A history of the reformation in France, very relijus and sad. A little fat book deskribing the months in England and the afoursaid Thompson's Seasons. I like to read them because they have so many pretty words in them, but I don't like the feel of them. The paper is so rough and thick it makes me creepy. Travels in Spain, very fassinating, with lovely smooth shiny paper, a missionary book on the Paciffic Islands, pictures very interesting because of the way the heathen chiefs arange their hair. After they became Christians they cut it off which I think was a pity. Mrs. Hemans Poems. I am passhunately fond of poetry, also of stories about desert islands. Rob Roy, a novel, but I only read a little of it when Aunt Elizabeth said I must stop because I must not read novels. Aunt

Laura says to read it on the sly. I don't see why it wouldn't be all right to obey Aunt Laura but I have a queer feeling about it and I haven't yet. A lovely Tiger-book, full of pictures and stories of tigers that make me feel so nice and shivery. The Royal Road, also relijus but some fun in it so very good for Sundays. Reuben and Grace, a story but not a novel, because Reuben and Grace are brother and sister and there is no getting married. Little Katy and Jolly Jim, same as above but not so exciting and traggic. Nature's Mighty Wonders which is good and improving. Alice in Wonderland, which is perfectly lovely, and the Memoirs of Anzonetta B. Peters who was converted at seven and died at twelve. When anybody asked her a question she answered with a hym verse. That is after she was converted. Before that she spoke English. Aunt Elizabeth told me I ought to try to be like Anzonetta. I think I might be an Alice under more faverable circumstances but I am sure I can never be as good as Anzonetta was and I don't believe I want to be because she never had any fun. She got sick as soon as she was converted and suffered aggonies for years. Besides I am sure that if I talked hyms to people it would exite ridicule. I tried it once. Aunt Laura asked me the other day if I would like blue stripes better than red in my next winter's stockings and I ansered just as Anzonetta did when asked a similar question, only different, about a sack,

> Jesus Thy blood and rightchusness
> My beauty are, my glorious dress.

And Aunt Laura said was I crazy and Aunt Elizabeth said I was ireverent. So I know it wouldn't work. Besides, Anzonetta couldn't eat anything for years having ulsers in her stomach and I am pretty fond of good eating.

"Old Mr. Wales on the Derry Pond Road is dying of

canser. Jennie Strang says his wife has her morning all ready.

"I wrote a biograffy of Saucy Sal to-day and a deskripshun of the road in Lofty John's bush. I will pin them to this letter so you can read them too. Good night my beloved Father.

"Your most obedient humble servant,

"Emily B. Starr.

"P. S. I think Aunt Laura loves me. I like to be loved, Father dear.

"E. B. S."

10
Growing Pains

There was a great deal of suppressed excitement in school during the last week in June, the cause thereof being Rhoda Stuart's birthday party, which was to take place early in July. The amount of heart burning was incredible. Who was to be invited? That was the great question. There were some who knew they wouldn't and some who knew they would; but there were more who were in truly horrible suspense. Everybody paid court to Emily because she was Rhoda's dearest friend and might conceivably have some voice in the selection of guests. Jennie Strang even went as far as bluntly to offer Emily a beautiful white box with a gorgeous picture of Queen Victoria on the cover, to keep her pencils in, if she would procure her an invitation. Emily refused the bribe and said grandly that she could not interfere in such a delicate matter. Emily really did put on some airs about it. *She* was sure of her invitation. Rhoda had told her about the party weeks before and had talked it all over with her. It was to be a very grand affair—a birthday cake covered with pink icing and adorned with ten tall pink candles—ice-cream and oranges—and written invitations on pink, gilt-edged notepaper *sent through the post-office*—this last being an added touch of exclusiveness. Emily dreamed about that party day and night and had her present all ready for Rhoda—a pretty hair ribbon which Aunt Laura had brought from Shrewsbury.

On the first Sunday in July Emily found herself sitting beside Jennie Strang in Sunday School for the opening exercises. Generally she and Rhoda sat together, but now Rhoda was sitting three seats ahead with a strange little girl—a very gay and gorgeous little girl, dressed in blue silk, with a large, flower-wreathed leghorn hat on her elaborately curled hair, white lace-work stockings on her pudgy legs and a bang that came clean down to her eyes. Not all her fine feathers could make a really fine bird of her, however; she was not in the least pretty and her expression was cross and contemptuous.

"Who is the girl sitting with Rhoda?" whispered Emily.

"Oh, she's Muriel Porter," answered Jennie. "She's a towny, you know. She's come out to spend her vacation with her aunt, Jane Beatty. I hate her. If I was her I'd never *dream* of wearing blue with a skin as dark as hers. But the Porters are rich and Muriel thinks she's a wonder. They say Rhoda and her have been *awful thick* since she came out—Rhoda's always chasing after anybody she thinks is up in the world."

Emily stiffened up. She was not going to listen to disparaging remarks about her friends. Jennie felt the stiffening and changed her note.

"Anyway, I'm *glad* I'm not invited to Rhoda's old party. I wouldn't *want* to go when Muriel Porter will be there, putting on her airs."

"How do you know you are not invited?" wondered Emily.

"Why, the invitations went out yesterday. Didn't you get yours?"

"No—o—o."

"Did you get your mail?"

"Yes—Cousin Jimmy got it."

"Well, maybe Mrs. Beecher forgot to give it to him. Likely you'll get it to-morrow."

Emily agreed that it was likely. But a queer cold sensation of dismay had invaded her being, which was not removed by the fact that after Sunday School Rhoda strutted away with Muriel Porter without a glance at any one else. On Monday Emily herself went to the post-office, but there was no pink envelope for her. She cried herself to sleep that night, but did not quite give up hope until Tuesday had passed. Then she faced the terrible truth—that she—she, Emily Byrd Starr, of New Moon—had not been invited to Rhoda's party. The thing was incredible. There *must* be a mistake somewhere. Had Cousin Jimmy lost the invitation on the road home? Had Rhoda's grown-up sister who wrote the invitations overlooked her name? Had,— Emily's unhappy doubts were forever resolved into bitter certainty by Jennie, who joined her as she left the post-office. There was a malicious light in Jennie's beady eyes. Jennie liked Emily quite well by now, in spite of their passage-at-arms on the day of their first meeting, but she liked to see her pride humbled for all that.

"So you're not invited to Rhoda's party after all."

"No," admitted Emily.

It was a very bitter moment for her. The Murray pride was sorely wrung—and, beneath the Murray pride, something else had been grievously wounded but was not yet quite dead.

"Well, I call it dirt mean," said Jennie, quite honestly sympathetic in spite of her secret satisfaction. "After all the fuss she's made over you, too! But that's Rhoda Stuart all over. Deceitful is no name for *her.*"

"I don't think she's deceitful," said Emily, loyal to

the last ditch. "I believe there's some mistake about my not being invited."

Jennie stared.

"Then you don't know the reason? Why, Beth Beatty told me the whole story. Muriel Porter hates you and she just up and told Rhoda that she would not go to her party if you were invited. And Rhoda was so crazy to have a town girl there that she promised she wouldn't invite you."

"Muriel Porter doesn't know me," gasped Emily. "How can she hate me?"

Jennie grinned impishly.

"*I* can tell you. She's *dead stuck* on Fred Stuart and Fred knows it and he teased her by praising *you* up to her—told her you were the sweetest girl in Blair Water and he meant to have you for *his* girl when you were a little older. And Muriel was so mad and jealous she made Rhoda leave you out. *I* wouldn't care if I was you. A Murray of New Moon is away above such trash. As for Rhoda not being deceitful, I can tell you she *is*. Why, she told you that she didn't know that snake was in the box, when it was her thought of doing it in the first place."

Emily was too crushed to reply. She was glad that Jennie had to switch off down her own lane and leave her alone. She hurried home, afraid that she could not keep the tears back until she got there. Disappointment about the party—humiliation over the insult—all were swallowed up in the anguish of a faith betrayed and a trust outraged. Her love of Rhoda was quite dead now and Emily smarted to the core of her soul with the pain of the blow that had killed it. It was a child's tragedy—and all the more bitter for that, since there was no one to understand. Aunt Elizabeth told her that birthday parties were all nonsense and that the Stuarts were not a family that the Murrays had ever associated with. And even Aunt Laura, though she petted and comforted, did not realize how deep and grievous the hurt had been—so deep and grievous that Emily could not even write about it to her father, and had no outlet for the violence of emotion that racked her being.

The next Sunday Rhoda was alone in Sunday School, Muriel Porter having been suddenly summoned back to town by her father's illness; and Rhoda looked sweetly towards Emily. But Emily sailed past her with a head held very high and scorn on every lineament. She would *never* have anything to do with Rhoda Stuart again—she couldn't. She despised Rhoda more than ever for trying to get back with her, now that the town girl for whom she had sacrificed her was gone. It was not for Rhoda she mourned—it was for the friendship that had been so dear to her. Rhoda *had* been dear and sweet on the surface at least, and Emily had found intense happiness in their companionship. Now it was gone and she could never, *never* love or trust anybody again. *There* lay the sting.

It poisoned everything. Emily was of a nature which, even as a child, did not readily recover from or forget such a blow. She moped about New Moon, lost her appetite and grew thin. She hated to go to Sunday School because she thought the other girls exulted in her humiliation and her estrangement from Rhoda. Some slight feeling of the kind there was, perhaps, but Emily morbidly exaggerated it. If two girls whispered or giggled together she thought she was being discussed and laughed at. If one of them walked home with her she thought it was out of condescending pity because she was friendless. For a month Emily was the most unhappy little being in Blair Water.

"I think I must have been put under a curse at birth," she reflected disconsolately.

Aunt Elizabeth had a more prosaic idea to account for Emily's languor and lack of appetite. She had come to the conclusion that Emily's heavy masses of hair "took from her strength" and that she would be much stronger and better if it were cut off. With Aunt Elizabeth to decide was to act. One morning she coolly informed Emily that her hair was to be "shingled."

Emily could not believe her ears.

"You don't mean that you are going to cut off my hair, Aunt Elizabeth," she exclaimed.

"Yes, I mean exactly that," said Aunt Elizabeth firmly. "You have entirely too much hair especially for hot weather. I feel sure that is why you have been so miserable lately. Now, I don't want any crying."

But Emily could not keep the tears back.

"Don't cut it *all* off," she pleaded. "Just cut a good big bang. Lots of the girls have their hair banged clean from the crown of their heads. That would take half my hair off and the rest won't take too much strength."

"There will be no bangs here," said Aunt Elizabeth. "I've told you so often enough. I'm going to shingle your hair close all over your head for the hot weather. You'll be thankful to me some day for it."

Emily felt anything but thankful just then.

"It's my one beauty," she sobbed, "it and my lashes. I suppose you want to cut off my lashes too."

Aunt Elizabeth *did* distrust those long, upcurled fringes of Emily's, which were an inheritance from the girlish stepmother, and too un-Murray-like to be approved; but she had no designs against them. The hair must go, however, and she curtly bade Emily wait there, without any fuss, until she got the scissors.

Emily waited—quite hopelessly. She must lose her lovely hair—the hair her father had been so proud of. It might grow again in time—if Aunt Elizabeth let it—but that would take years, and meanwhile what a fright she would be! Aunt Laura and Cousin Jimmy were out; she had no one to back her up; this horrible thing must happen.

Aunt Elizabeth returned with the scissors; they clicked suggestively as she opened them; that click, as if by magic, seemed to loosen something—some strange formidable power in Emily's soul. She turned deliberately around and faced her aunt. She felt her brows drawing together in an unaccustomed way—she felt an uprush as from unknown depths of some irresistible surge of energy.

"Aunt Elizabeth," she said, looking straight at the lady with the scissors, *"my hair is not going to be cut off. Let me hear no more of this."*

An amazing thing happened to Aunt Elizabeth. She turned pale—she laid the scissors down—she looked aghast for one moment at the transformed or possessed child before her—and then for the first time in her life Elizabeth Murray turned tail and fled—literally fled—to the kitchen.

"What is the matter, Elizabeth?" cried Laura, coming in from the cook-house.

"I saw—Father—looking from her face," gasped Elizabeth, trembling. "And she said, 'Let me hear no more of this,'—just as *he* always said it—his very words."

Emily overheard her and ran to the sideboard mirror. She had had, while she was speaking, an uncanny feeling of wearing somebody else's face instead of her own. It was vanishing now—but Emily caught a glimpse of it as it left—the Murray look, she supposed. No wonder it had frightened Aunt Elizabeth—it frightened herself—she was glad that it had gone. She shivered —she fled to her garret retreat and cried; but somehow, she knew that her hair would not be cut.

Nor was it; Aunt Elizabeth never referred to the matter again. But several days passed before she meddled much with Emily.

It was a rather curious fact that from that day Emily ceased to grieve over her lost friend. The matter had suddenly become of small importance. It was as if it had happened so long ago that nothing, save the mere emotionless memory of it, remained. Emily speedily regained appetite and animation, resumed her letters to her father and found that life tasted good again, marred only by a mysterious prescience that Aunt Elizabeth had it in for her in regard to her defeat in the matter of her hair and would get even sooner or later.

Aunt Elizabeth "got even" within the week. Emily was to go on an errand to the shop. It was a broiling day and she had been allowed to go barefooted at

home; but now she must put on boots and stockings.
Emily rebelled—it was too hot—it was too dusty—she
couldn't walk that long half-mile in buttoned boots.
Aunt Elizabeth was inexorable. No Murray must be
seen barefooted away from home—and on they went.
But the minute Emily was outside the New Moon gate
she deliberately sat down, took them off, stowed them
in a hole in the dyke, and pranced away barefooted.

She did her errand and returned with an untroubled
conscience. How beautiful the world was—how softly
blue was the great, round Blair Water—how glorious
that miracle of buttercups in the wet field below Lofty
John's bush! At sight of it Emily stood stock still and
composed a verse of poetry.

> "Buttercup, flower of the yellow dye,
>   I see thy cheerful face
> Greeting and nodding everywhere
>   Careless of time and place.
>
> "In boggy field or public road
>   Or cultured garden's pale
> You sport your petals satin-soft,
>   And down within the vale."

So far, so good. But Emily wanted another verse to
round the poem off properly and the divine afflatus
seemed gone. She walked dreamily home, and by the
time she reached New Moon she had got her verse and
was reciting it to herself with an agreeable sense of
completion.

> "You cast your loveliness around
>   Where'er you chance to be,
> And you shall always, buttercup,
>   Be a flower dear to me."

Emily felt very proud. This was her third poem and
undoubtedly her best. Nobody could say *it* was very

blank. She must hurry up to the garret and write it on a letter-bill. But Aunt Elizabeth was confronting her on the steps.

"Emily, where are your boots and stockings?"

Emily came back from cloudland with a disagreeable jolt. She had forgotten all about boots and stockings.

"In the hole by the gate," she said flatly.

"You went to the store barefooted?"

"Yes."

"After I had told you not to?"

This seemed to Emily a superfluous question and she did not answer it. But Aunt Elizabeth's turn had come.

11
Ilse

Emily was locked in the spare-room and told that she must stay there until bedtime. She had pleaded against such a punishment in vain. She had tried to give the Murray look but it seemed that—in her case at any rate—it did not come at will.

"Oh, don't shut me up alone there, Aunt Elizabeth," she implored. "I know I was naughty—but don't put me in the spare-room."

Aunt Elizabeth was inexorable. She knew that it was a cruel thing to shut an over-sensitive child like Emily in that gloomy room. But she thought she was doing her duty. She did not realize and would not have for a moment believed that she was really wreaking her own smothered resentment with Emily for her defeat and fright on the day of the threatened hair-cutting. Aunt Elizabeth believed she had been stampeded on that occasion by a chance family resemblance coming out under stress, and she was ashamed of it. The Murray pride had smarted under that humbling, and the smart ceased to annoy her only when she turned the key of the spare-room on the white-faced culprit.

Emily, looking very small and lost and lonely, her eyes full of such fear as should have no place in a child's eyes, shrank close against the door of the spare-room. It was better that way. She could not imagine things behind her then. And the room was so big and dim that a dreadful number of things could be imagined in it. Its bigness and dimness filled her with a terror against which she could not strive. Ever since she could remember she had had a horror of being shut up alone in semi-darkness. She was not frightened of twilight out-of-doors, but this shadowy, walled gloom made of the spare-room a place of dread.

The window was hung with heavy, dark-green material, reinforced by drawn slat-blinds. The big canopied bed, jutting out from the wall into the middle of the floor, was high and rigid and curtained also with dark draperies. *Anything* might jump at her out of such a bed. What if some great black hand should suddenly reach out of it—reach right across the floor—and pluck at her? The walls, like those of the parlour, were adorned with pictures of departed relatives. There *was* such a large collection of dead Murrays. The glasses of their frames gave out weird reflections of the spectral threads of light struggling through the slat blinds. Worst of all, right across the room from her, high up on the top of the black wardrobe, was a huge, stuffed white Arctic owl, staring at her with uncanny eyes. Emily shrieked aloud when she saw it, and then cowered down in her corner aghast at the sound she had made in the great, silent, echoing room. She wished that something *would* jump out of the bed and put an end to her.

"I wonder what Aunt Elizabeth would feel like if I was found here *dead*," she thought, vindictively.

In spite of her fright she began to dramatize it and felt Aunt Elizabeth's remorse so keenly that she decided only to be unconscious and come back to life when everybody was sufficiently scared and penitent. But people *had* died in this room—dozens of them. According to Cousin Jimmy it was a New Moon tradition that when any member of the family was near death he or she was promptly removed to the spare-room, to die amid surroundings of proper grandeur. Emily could *see* them dying, in that terrible bed. She felt that she was going to scream again, but she fought the impulse down. A Starr must not be a coward. Oh, that owl! Suppose, when she looked away from it and then looked back she would find that it had silently hopped down from the wardrobe and was coming towards her. Emily dared not look at it for fear that was just what had happened. *Didn't* the bed curtains stir and waver! She felt beads of cold perspiration on her forehead.

Then something did happen. A beam of sunlight struck through a small break in one of the slats of the blind and fell directly athwart the picture of Grandfather Murray hanging over the mantel-piece. It was a crayon "enlargement" copied from the old daguerreotype in the parlour below. In that gleam of light his face seemed veritably to leap out of the gloom at Emily with its grim frown strangely exaggerated. Emily's nerve gave way completely. In an ungovernable spasm of panic she rushed madly across the room to the window, dashed the curtains aside, and caught up the slat blind. A blessed flood of sunshine burst in. Outside was a wholesome, friendly, human world. And, of all wonders, there, leaning right against the window-sill was a ladder! For a moment Emily almost believed that a miracle had been worked for her escape.

Cousin Jimmy had tripped that morning over the ladder, lying lost among the burdocks under the balm-of-gileads behind the dairy. It was very rotten and he decided it was time it was disposed of. He had shouldered it up against the house so that he would be sure to see it on his return from the hayfield.

In less time than it takes to write of it Emily had got

the window up, climbed out on the sill, and backed down the ladder. She was too intent on escaping from that horrible room to be conscious of the shakiness of the rotten rungs. When she reached the ground she bolted through the balm-of-gileads and over the fence into Lofty John's bush, nor did she stop running till she reached the path by the brook.

Then she paused for breath, exultant. She was full of a fearful joy with an elfin delight running through it. Sweet was the wind of freedom that was blowing over the ferns. She had escaped from the spare-room and its ghosts—she had got the better of mean old Aunt Elizabeth.

"I feel as if I was a little bird that had just got out of a cage," she told herself; and then she danced with joy of it all along her fairy path to the very end, where she found Ilse Burnley huddled up on the top of a fence panel, her pale-gold head making a spot of brilliance against the dark young firs that crowded around her. Emily had not seen her since that first day of school and again she thought she had never seen or pretended anybody just like Ilse.

"Well, Emily of New Moon," said Ilse, "where are you running to?"

"I'm running away," said Emily frankly. "I was bad—at least, I was a little bad—and Aunt Elizabeth locked me in the spare-room. I hadn't been bad enough for *that*—it wasn't fair—so I got out of the window and down the ladder."

"You little cuss! I didn't think you'd gimp enough for that," said Ilse.

Emily gasped. It seemed very dreadful to be called a little cuss. But Ilse had said it quite admiringly.

"I don't think it was gimp," said Emily, too honest to take a compliment she didn't deserve. "I was too scared to stay in that room."

"Well, where are you going now?" asked Ilse. "You'll have to go somewhere—you can't stay outdoors. There's a thunderstorm coming up."

So there was. Emily did not like thunderstorms. And her conscience smote her.

"Oh," she said, "do you suppose God is bringing up that storm to punish me because I've run away?"

"No," said Ilse scornfully. "If there is any God he wouldn't make such a fuss over nothing."

"Oh, Ilse, don't you believe there is a God?"

"I don't know. Father says there isn't. But in that case how did things happen? Some days I believe there's a God and some days I don't. You'd better come home with me. There's nobody there. I was so dodgastedly lonesome I took to the bush."

Ilse sprang down and held out her sunburned paw to Emily. Emily took it and they ran together over Lofty John's pasture to the old Burnley house which looked like a huge grey cat basking in the warm late sunshine, that had not yet been swallowed up by the menacing thunderheads. Inside, it was full of furniture that must have been quite splendid once; but the disorder was dreadful and the dust lay thickly over everything. Nothing was in the right place apparently, and Aunt Laura would certainly have fainted with horror if she had seen the kitchen. But it was a good place to play. You didn't have to be careful not to mess things up. Ilse and Emily had a glorious game of hide and seek all over the house until the thunder got so heavy and the lightning so bright that Emily felt she must huddle on the sofa and nurse her courage.

"Aren't you ever afraid of thunder?" she asked Ilse.

"No, I ain't afraid of anything except the devil," said Ilse.

"I thought you didn't believe in the devil either—Rhoda said you didn't."

"Oh, there's a devil all right, Father says. It's only God he doesn't believe in. And if there *is* a devil and no God to keep him in order, is it any wonder I'm scared of him? Look here, Emily Byrd Starr, I like you—heaps. I've always liked you. I knew you'd soon be good and sick of that little, white-livered, lying sneak of a Rhoda Stuart. *I* never tell lies. Father told me once he'd kill me if he ever caught me telling a lie. I want you for *my* chum. I'd go to school regular if I could sit with you."

"All right," said Emily off-handedly. No more senti-mental Rhodian vows of eternal devotion for her. *That* phase was over.

"And you'll tell me things—nobody ever tells me things. And let *me* tell *you* things—I haven't anybody to tell things to," said Ilse. "And you won't be ashamed of me because my clothes are always queer and because I don't believe in God?"

"No. But if you knew Father's God you'd believe in *Him*."

"I wouldn't. Besides, there's only one God if there is any at all."

"I don't know," said Emily perplexedly. "No, it can't be like that. Ellen Greene's God isn't a bit like Father's, and neither is Aunt Elizabeth's. I don't think I'd *like* Aunt Elizabeth's, but He is a *dignified* God at least, and Ellen's isn't. And I'm sure Aunt Laura's is another one still—nice and kind but not wonderful like Father's."

"Well never mind—I don't like talking about God," said Ilse uncomfortably.

"*I* do," said Emily. "I think God is a very interesting subject, and I'm going to pray for you, Ilse, that you can believe in Father's God."

"Don't you dast!" shouted Ilse, who for some myste-rious reason did not like the idea. "I won't be prayed for!"

"Don't you ever pray yourself, Ilse?"

"Oh, now and then—when I feel lonesome at night— or when I'm in a scrape. But I don't want any one else to pray for me. If I catch you doing it, Emily Starr, I'll tear your eyes out. And don't you go sneaking and praying for me behind my back either."

"All right, I won't," said Emily sharply, mortified at the failure of her well-meant offer. "I'll pray for every single soul I know, but I'll leave you out."

For a moment Ilse looked as if she didn't like this either. Then she laughed and gave Emily a volcanic hug.

"Well, anyway, please like me. Nobody likes me, you know."

"Your father *must* like you, Ilse."

"He doesn't," said Ilse positively. "Father doesn't care a hoot about me. I think there's times when he hates the sight of me. I wish he *did* like me because he can be awful nice when he likes any one. Do you know what I'm going to be when I grow up? I'm going to be an elo-cu-tion-ist."

"What's that?"

"A woman who recites at concerts. I can do it dandy. What are you going to be?"

"A poetess."

"Golly!" said Ilse, apparently overcome. "I don't believe *you* can write poetry," she added.

"I can so, too," cried Emily. "I've written three pieces—'Autumn' and 'Lines to Rhoda'—only I burned *that*—and 'An Address to a Buttercup.' I composed it to-day and it is my—my masterpiece."

"Let's hear it," ordered Ilse.

Nothing loth, Emily proudly repeated her lines. Somehow she did not mind letting Ilse hear them.

"Emily Byrd Starr, you *didn't* make that out of your own head?"

"I did."

"Cross your heart?"

"Cross my heart."

"Well"—Ilse drew a long breath—"I guess you *are* a poetess all right."

It was a very proud moment for Emily—one of the great moments of life, in fact. Her world had conceded her standing. But now other things had to be thought of. The storm was over and the sun had set. It was twilight—it would soon be dark. She must get home and back into the spare-room before her absence was discovered. It was dreadful to think of going back but she must do it lest a worse thing come upon her at Aunt Elizabeth's hands. Just now, under the inspiration of Ilse's personality, she was full of Dutch courage. Besides, it would soon be her bedtime and she would be let out. She trotted home through Lofty John's bush, that was full of the wandering, mysterious lamps of the fireflies, dodged cautiously through the balm-of-gileads—and stopped short in dismay. The ladder was gone!

Emily went around to the kitchen door, feeling that she was going straight to her doom. But for once the way of the transgressor was made sinfully easy. Aunt Laura was alone in the kitchen.

"Emily dear, where on earth did you come from?" she exclaimed. "I was just going up to let you out. Elizabeth said I might—she's gone to prayer-meeting."

Aunt Laura did not say that she had tiptoed several times to the spare-room door and had been racked with anxiety over the silence behind it. Was the child unconscious from fright? Not even while the thunderstorm was going on would relentless Elizabeth allow that door to be opened. And here was Miss Emily walking unconcernedly in out of the twilight after all this agony. For a moment even Aunt Laura was annoyed. But when she heard Emily's tale her only feeling was thankfulness that Juliet's child had not broken her neck on that rotten ladder.

Emily felt that she had got off better than she deserved. She knew Aunt Laura would keep the secret; and Aunt Laura let her give Saucy Sal a whole cupful of strippings, and gave her a big plummy cooky and put her to bed with kisses.

"You oughtn't to be so good to me because I *was* bad to-day," Emily said, between delicious mouthfuls. "I suppose I disgraced the Murrays going barefoot."

"If I were you I'd hide my boots every time I went out of the gate," said Aunt Laura. "But I wouldn't forget to put them on before I came back. What Elizabeth doesn't know will never hurt her."

Emily reflected over this until she had finished her cooky. Then she said,

"That would be nice, but I don't mean to do it any more. I guess I must obey Aunt Elizabeth because she's the head of the family."

"Where do you get such notions?" said Aunt Laura.

"Out of my head. Aunt Laura, Ilse Burnley and I are going to be chums. I like her—I've always felt I'd like her if I had a chance. I don't believe I can ever *love* any girl again, but I *like* her."

"Poor Ilse!" said Aunt Laura, sighing.

"Yes, her father doesn't like her. Isn't it dreadful?" said Emily. "Why doesn't he?"

"He does—really. He only thinks he doesn't."

"But *why* does he think it?"

"You are too young to understand, Emily."

Emily hated to be told she was too young to understand. She felt that she could understand perfectly well if only people would take the trouble to explain things to her and not be so mysterious.

"I wish I could pray for her. It wouldn't be fair, though, when I know how she feels about it. But I've always asked God to bless all my friends so she'll be in *that* and maybe some good will come of it. Is 'golly' a proper word to say, Aunt Laura?"

"No—no!"

"I'm sorry for that," said Emily, seriously, "because it's very striking."

12
The Tansy Patch

Emily and Ilse had a splendid fortnight of fun before their first fight. It was really quite a terrible fight, arising out of a simple argument as to whether they would or would not have a parlour in the playhouse they were building in Lofty John's bush. Emily wanted a parlour and Ilse didn't. Ilse lost her temper at once, and went into a true Burnley tantrum. She was very fluent in her rages and the volley of abusive "dictionary words" which she hurled at Emily would have staggered most of the Blair Water girls. But Emily was too much at home with words to be floored so easily; she grew angry too, but in the cool, dignified, Murray way which was more exasperating than violence. When Ilse had to pause for breath in her diatribes, Emily, sitting on a big stone with her knees crossed, her eyes black and her cheeks crimson, interjected little sarcastic retorts that infuriated Ilse still further. Ilse was crimson, too, and her eyes were pools of scintillating, tawny fire. They were both so pretty in their fury that it was almost a pity they couldn't have been angry all the time.

"You needn't suppose, you little puling, snivelling chit, that you are going to boss *me*, just because you live at New Moon," shrieked Ilse, as an ultimatum, stamping her foot.

"I'm not going to boss you—I'm not going to associate with you ever again," retorted Emily, disdainfully.

"I'm glad to be rid of you—you proud, stuck-up, conceited, top-lofty *biped*," cried Ilse. "Never you speak to me again. And don't you go about Blair Water saying things about me, either."

This was unbearable to a girl who *never* "said things" about her friends or once-friends.

"I'm not going to *say* things about you," said Emily deliberately. "I am just going to *think* them."

This was far more aggravating than speech and Emily knew it. Ilse was driven quite frantic by it. Who knew what unearthly things Emily might be thinking about her any time she took the notion to? Ilse had already discovered what a fertile invention Emily had.

"Do you suppose I care what you think, you insignificant serpent? Why, you haven't *any* sense."

"I've got something then that's far better," said Emily, with a maddening superior smile. "Something that *you* can *never* have, Ilse Burnley."

Ilse doubled her fists as if she would like to demolish Emily by physical force.

"If I couldn't write better poetry than you, I'd hang myself," she derided.

"I'll lend you a dime to buy a rope," said Emily.

Ilse glared at her, vanquished.

"You go to the devil!" she said.

Emily got up and went, not to the devil, but back to New Moon. Ilse relieved *her* feelings by knocking the boards of their china closet down, and kicking their "moss gardens" to pieces, and departed also.

Emily felt exceedingly badly. Here was another friendship destroyed—a friendship, too, that had been very delightful and satisfying. Ilse *had* been a splendid chum—there was no doubt about that. After Emily had cooled down she went to the dormer window and cried.

"Wretched, wretched me!" she sobbed, dramatically, but very sincerely.

Yet the bitterness of her break with Rhoda was not present. *This* quarrel was fair and open and above-board. She had not been stabbed in the back. But of course she and Ilse would never be chums again. You couldn't be chums with a person who called you a chit and a biped, and a serpent, and told you to go to the devil. The thing was impossible. And besides, Ilse could *never* forgive *her*—for Emily was honest enough to admit to herself that she had been very aggravating, too.

Yet, when Emily went to the play house next morning, bent on retrieving her share of broken dishes and boards, there was Ilse, skipping around, hard at work, with all the shelves back in place, the moss garden re-made, and a beautiful parlour laid out and connected with the living-room by a spruce arch.

"Hello, you. Here's your parlour and I hope you'll be satisfied now," she said gaily. "What's kept you so long? I thought you were never coming."

This rather posed Emily after her tragic night, wherein she had buried her second friendship and wept over its grave. She was not prepared for so speedy a resurrection. As far as Ilse was concerned it seemed as if no quarrel had ever taken place.

"Why, that was *yesterday*," she said in amazement, when Emily, rather distantly, referred to it. Yesterday and to-day were two entirely different things in Ilse's philosophy. Emily accepted it—she found she had to. Ilse, it transpired, could no more help flying into tantrums now and then than she could help being jolly and affectionate between them. What amazed Emily, in whom things were bound to rankle for a time, was the way in which Ilse appeared to forget a quarrel the moment it was over. To be called a serpent and a crocodile one minute and hugged and darling-ed the next was somewhat disconcerting until time and experience took the edge off it.

"Aren't I nice enough between times to make up for it?" demanded Ilse. "Dot Payne never flies into tempers, but would you like *her* for a chum?"

"No, she's too stupid," admitted Emily.

"And Rhoda Stuart is never out of temper, but you got enough of *her*. Do you think I'd ever treat you as she did?"

No, Emily had no doubt on this point. Whatever Ilse was or was not, she was loyal and true.

And certainly Rhoda Stuart and Dot Payne compared to Ilse were "as moonlight unto sunlight and as water unto wine"—or would have been if Emily had as yet known anything more of her Tennyson than the *Bugle Song*.

"You can't have everything," said Ilse. "I've got Dad's temper and that's all there is to it. Wait till you see *him* in one of his rages."

Emily had not seen this so far. She had often been

down in the Burnley's house but on the few occasions when Dr. Burnley had been home he had ignored her save for a curt nod. He was a busy man, for, whatever his shortcomings were, his skill was unquestioned and the bounds of his practice extended far. By the sickbed he was as gentle and sympathetic as he was brusque and sarcastic away from it. As long as you were ill there was nothing Dr. Burnley would not do for you; once you were well he had apparently no further use for you. He had been absorbed all through July trying to save Teddy Kent's life up at the Tansy Patch. Teddy was out of danger now and able to be up, but his improvement was not speedy enough to satisfy Dr. Burnley. One day he held up Emily and Ilse, who were heading through the lawn to the pond, with fishing-hooks and a can of fat, abominable worms—the latter manipulated solely by Ilse—and ordered them to betake themselves up to the Tansy Patch and play with Teddy Kent.

"He's lonesome and moping. Go and cheer him up," said the doctor.

Ilse was rather loth to go. She liked Teddy, but it seemed she did not like his mother. Emily was secretly not averse. She had seen Teddy Kent but once, at Sunday School the day before he was taken seriously ill, and she had liked his looks. It had seemed that he liked hers, too, for she caught him staring shyly at her over the intervening pews several times. He was very handsome, Emily decided. She liked his thick, dark-brown hair and his black-browed blue eyes, and for the first time it occurred to her that it might be rather nice to have a boy playmate, too. Not a "beau" of course. Emily hated the school jargon that called a boy your "beau" if he happened to give you a pencil or an apple and picked you out frequently for his partner in the games.

"Teddy's nice but his mother is queer," Ilse told her on their way to the Tansy Patch. "She never goes out anywhere—not even to church—but I guess it's because of the scar on her face. They're not Blair Water people—they've only been living at the Tansy Patch since last fall. They're poor and proud and not many people visit them. But Teddy is awfully nice, so if his mother gives us some black looks we needn't mind."

Mrs. Kent gave them no black looks, though her reception was rather distant. Perhaps she, too, had received some orders from the doctor. She was a tiny creature, with enormous masses of dull, soft, silky, fawn hair, dark, mournful eyes, and a broad scar running slantwise across her pale face. Without the scar she must have been pretty, and she had a voice as soft and uncertain as the wind in the tansy. Emily, with her instinctive faculty of sizing up people she met, felt that Mrs. Kent was not a happy woman.

The Tansy Patch was east of the Disappointed House, between the Blair Water and the sand-dunes. Most people considered it a bare, lonely, neglected place, but Emily thought it was fascinating. The little clap-boarded house topped a small hill, over which tansy grew in a hard, flaunting, aromatic luxuriance, rising steeply and abruptly from a main road. A straggling rail fence, almost smothered in wild rosebushes, bounded the domain, and a sagging, ill-used little gate gave ingress from the road. Stones were let into the side of the hill for steps up to the front door. Behind the house was a tumbledown little barn, and a field of flowering buckwheat, creamy green, sloping down to the Blair Water. In front was a crazy veranda around which a brilliant band of red poppies held up their enchanted cups.

Teddy was unfeignedly glad to see them, and they had a happy afternoon together. There was some colour in Teddy's clear olive skin when it ended and his dark-blue eyes were brighter. Mrs. Kent took in these signs greedily and asked the girls to come back, with an eagerness that was yet not cordiality. But they had found the Tansy Patch a charming place and were glad to go again. For the rest of the vacation there was hardly a day when they did not go up to it—preferably

in the long, smoky, delicious August evenings when
the white moths sailed over the tansy plantation and
the golden twilight faded into dusk and purple over
the green slopes beyond and fireflies lighted their gob-
lin torches by the pond. Sometimes they played games
in the tansy patch, when Teddy and Emily somehow
generally found themselves on the same side and then
no more than a match for agile, quick-witted Ilse;
sometimes Teddy took them to the barn loft and showed
them his little collection of drawings. Both girls thought
them very wonderful without knowing in the least
how wonderful they really were. It seemed like magic
to see Teddy take a pencil and bit of paper and with a
few quick strokes of his slim brown fingers bring out a
sketch of Ilse or Emily or Smoke or Buttercup, that
looked ready to speak—or meow.

Smoke and Buttercup were the Tansy Patch cats.
Buttercup was a chubby, yellow, delightful creature
hardly out of kittenhood. Smoke was a big Maltese and
an aristocrat from the tip of his nose to the tip of his
tail. There was no doubt whatever that he belonged to
the cat caste of Vere de Vere. He had emerald eyes and
a coat of plush. The only white thing about him was an
adorable dicky.

Emily thought of all the pleasant hours spent at the
Tansy Patch the pleasantest were those, when, tired
with play, they all three sat on the crazy veranda steps
in the mystery and enchantment of the borderland
'tween light and dark when the little clump of spruce
behind the barn looked like beautiful, dark, phantom
trees. The clouds of the west faded into grey and a
great round yellow moon rose over the fields to be
reflected brokenly in the pond, where the Wind Woman was making wonderful, woven lights and shadows.

Mrs. Kent never joined them, though Emily had a
creepy conviction that she was watching them stealthi-
ly from behind the kitchen blind. Teddy and Ilse sang
school ditties, and Ilse recited, and Emily told stories;
or they sat in happy silence, each anchored in some

secret port of dreams, while the cats chased each other madly over the hill and through the tansy, tearing round and round the house like possessed creatures. They would spring up at the children with sudden pounces and spring as suddenly away. Their eyes gleamed like jewels, their tails swayed like plumes. They were palpitating with nervous, stealthy life.

"Oh, isn't it good to be alive—like this?" Emily said once. "Wouldn't it be dreadful if one had never lived?"

Still, existence was not wholly unclouded—Aunt Elizabeth took care of that. Aunt Elizabeth only permitted the visits to the Tansy Patch under protest, and because Dr. Burnley had ordered them.

"Aunt Elizabeth does not aprove of Teddy," Emily wrote in one of her letters to her father—which epistles were steadily multiplying on the old garret sofa shelf. "The first time I asked her if I might go and play with Teddy she looked at me *severely* and said, Who is this Teddy person. We do not know anything about these Kents. Remember, Emily, the Murrays do not associate with every one. I said I am a Starr—I am not a Murray, you said so yourself. Dear Father I did not mean to be impertnent but Aunt Elizabeth said I was and would not speak to me the rest of the day. She seemed to think that was a very bad punishment but I did not mind it much only it is rather unpleasant to have your own family preserve a disdaneful silence towards you. But since then she lets me go to the Tansy Patch because Dr. Burnley came and told her to. Dr. Burnley has a *strange inflewence* over Aunt Elizabeth. I do not understand it. Rhoda said once that Aunt Elizabeth hoped Dr. Burnley and Aunt Laura would make a match of it—which, you know means get married—but that is not so. Mrs. Thomas Anderson was here one afternoon to tea. (Mrs. Thomas Anderson is a big fat woman and her grandmother was a Murray and there is nothing else to say about *her*.) She asked Aunt Elizabeth if she thought Dr. Burnley would marry again and Aunt Elizabeth said no, he would not and she did not think it right for people to marry a second time. Mrs. Anderson said Sometimes I have thought he would take Laura. Aunt Elizabeth just swept her a hawty glance. There is no use in denying it, there are times when I am very proud of Aunt Elizabeth, even if I do not like her.

"Teddy is a very nice boy, Father. I think you would aprove of him. Should there be two p's in aprove? He can make splendid pictures and he is going to be a famus artist some day, and then he is going to paint my portrate. He keeps his pictures in the barn loft because his mother doesn't like to see them. He can whistle just like a bird. The Tansy Patch is a *very quante* place—espesially at night. I love the twilight there. We always have such fun in the twilight. The Wind Woman makes herself small in the tansy just like a tiny, tiny fairy and the cats are so queer and creepy and delightful then. They belong to Mrs. Kent and Teddy is afraid to pet them much for fear she will drown them. She drowned a kitten once because she thought he liked it better than her. But he didn't because Teddy is *very much attatched* to his mother. He washes the dishes for her and helps her in all the house work. Ilse says the boys in school call him sissy for that but I think it is noble and manley of him. Teddy wishes she would let him have a dog but she wont. I have thought Aunt Elizabeth was tirannical but Mrs. Kent is far worse in some ways. But then she loves Teddy and Aunt Elizabeth does not love me.

"But Mrs. Kent doesn't like Ilse or me. She never says so but we *feel* it. She never asks us to stay to tea—and we've always been so polite to her. I believe she is jellus of us because Teddy likes us. Teddy gave me the sweetest picture of the Blair Water he had painted on a big white cowhawk shell but he said I mustn't let his mother know about it because she would cry. Mrs. Kent is a very misterious person, very like some people you read of in books. I like misterious people but not too close. Her eyes always look hungry though she has plenty to eat. She never goes anywhere because she has a scar on her face where she was burned with a lamp exploding. It made my blood run cold, dear Father. How thankful I am that Aunt Elizabeth only burns candles. Some of the Murray tradishuns are very sensible. Mrs. Kent is very relijus—what she calls relijus. She prays even in the middle of the day. Teddy says that before he was born into this world he lived in another one where there were two suns, one red and one blue. The days were red and the nights blue. I don't know where he got the idea but it sounds atractive to me. And he says the brooks run honey instead of water. But what did you do when you were thirsty, I said. Oh, we were never thirsty there. But I think I would *like* to be thirsty because then cold water tastes so good. *I* would like to live in the moon. It must be such a nice silvery place.

"Ilse says Teddy ought to like her best because there is more fun in her than in me but that is not true. There is just as much fun in me when my conshence doesn't bother me. I guess Ilse wants Teddy to like her best but she is not a jellus girl.

"I am glad to say that Aunt Elizabeth and Aunt Laura both aprove of my friendship with Ilse. It is so seldom they aprove of the same thing. I am getting used to fighting with Ilse now and don't mind it much. Besides I can fight pretty well myself when my blood is up. We fight about once a week but we make up right away and Ilse says things would be dull if there was never a row. I would like it better without rows but you can never tell what will make Ilse mad. She never gets mad twice over the same thing. She calls me dreadful names. Yesterday she called me a lousy lizard and a toothless viper. But somehow I didn't mind it much because I knew I wasn't lousy or toothless and she knew it too. I don't call names because that is unladylike but I smile and that makes Ilse far madder than if I skowled and stamped as she does, and that is why I do it. Aunt Laura says I must be careful not to pick up the words Ilse uses and try to set her a good example because the poor child has no one to look after her propperly. I wish I could use some of her words because they are so striking. She gets them from her father. I think my aunts are too perticular. One night when the Rev. Mr. Dare was here to tea I used the word bull in my conversashun. I said Ilse and I were afraid to go through Mr. James Lee's pasture where the old well was because he had a cross bull there. After Mr. Dare had gone Aunt Elizabeth gave me an awful skolding and told me I was never to use *that word* again. But she had been talking of tigers at tea—in connexshun with missionaries—and I can't understand why it is more disgraceful to talk about bulls than tigers. Of course bulls are feroshus animals but so are tigers. But Aunt Elizabeth says I am always disgracing them when they have company. When Mrs. Lockwood was here from Shrewsbury last week they were talking about Mrs. Foster Beck, who is a bride, and I said Dr. Burnley thought she was devilishly pretty. Aunt Elizabeth said EMILY in an awful tone. She was pale with rath. Dr. Burnley said it, I cryed, I am only kwoting. And Dr. Burnley did say it the day I stayed to dinner with Ilse and Dr. Jameson was there from Shrewsbury. I saw Dr. Burnley in one of his rages that afternoon over something Mrs. Simms had done in his office. It was a groosome sight. His big yellow eyes blazed and he tore about and kicked over a chair and threw a mat at the wall and fired a vase out of the window and said *terrible things*. I sat on the sofa and stared at him like one fassinated. It was so interesting I was sorry when he cooled down which he soon did because he is like Ilse and never stays mad long. He never gets mad at Ilse though. Ilse says she wishes he would—it would be better than being taken no notis of. She is as much of an orfan as I am, poor child. Last Sunday she went to church with her old faded blue dress on. There was a tare right in front of it. Aunt Laura wepped when she came home and then spoke to Mrs. Simms about it

because she did not dare speak to Dr. Burnley. Mrs.
Simms was cross and said it was not her place to look
after Ilses close but she said she had got Dr. Burnley to
get Ilse a nice sprigged muslin dress and Ilse had got
egg stane on it, and when Mrs. Simms skolded her for
being so careless Ilse flew into a rage and went upstairs
and tore the muslin dress to pieces, and Mrs. Simms
said she wasn't going to bother her head again about a
child like that and there was nothing for her to ware
but her old blue but Mrs. Simms didn't know it was
tore. So I sneaked Ilses dress over to New Moon and
Aunt Laura mended it neetly and hid the tare with a
pocket. Ilse said she tore up her muslin dress one of
the days she didn't believe in God and didn't care what
she did. Ilse found a mouse in her bed one night and
she just shook it out and jumped in. Oh, how brave. I
could never be as brave as that. It is not true that Dr.
Burnley never smiles. I have seen him do it but not
often. He just smiles with his lips but not his eyes and
it makes me feel uncomfortable. Mostly he laughs in a
horrid sarkastic way like *Jolly Jim's* uncle.

"We had barley soup for dinner that day—very watery.

"Aunt Laura is giving me five cents a week for
washing the dishes. I can only spend one cent of it and
the other four have to be put in the toad bank in the
sitting-room on the mantel. The toad is made of brass
and sits on top of the bank and you put the cents in his
mouth one at a time. He swallows them and they drop
into the bank. It's very fassinating (I should not write
fassinating again because you told me I must not use
the same word too often but I cant think of any other
that deskribes my feelings so well). The toad bank is
Aunt Laura's but she said I could use it. I just hugged
her. Of course I never hug Aunt Elizabeth. She is too
rijid and bony. She does not aprove of Aunt Laura
paying me for washing dishes. I tremble to think what
she would say if she knew Cousin Jimmy gave me a
whole dollar on the sly last week.

"I wish he had not given me so much. It worrys me.

It is an awful responsibility. It will be so diffikult to spend it wisely also without Aunt Elizabeth finding out about it. I hope I shall never have a million dollars. I am sure it would crush me utterly. I keep my dollar hid on the shelf with my letters and I put it in an old envelope and wrote on it Cousin Jimmy Murray gave me this so that if I died suddenly and Aunt Elizabeth found it she would know I came by it honestly.

"Now that the days are getting cool Aunt Elizabeth makes me wear my thick flannel petticoat. I hate it. It makes me so bunchy. But Aunt Elizabeth says I must wear it because you died of consumption. I wish close could be both graceful and helthy. I read the story of Red Riding Hood to-day. I think the wolf was the most interesting caracter in it. Red Riding Hood was a stupid little thing so easily fooled.

"I wrote two poems yesterday. One was short and entitelled Lines Adressed to a blue-eyed-grass flower gathered in the Old Orchard. Here it is.

> Sweet little flower thy modest face
> Is ever lifted tords the sky
> And a reflexshun of its face
> Is caught within thine own blue eye.
> The meadow queens are tall and fair
> The columbines are lovely too
> But the poor talent I possess
> Shall laurel thee my flower of blue.

"The other poem was long and I wrote it on a letter-bill. It is called The Monark of the Forest. The Monark is the big birch in Lofty John's bush. I love that bush so much it hurts. Do you understand that kind of hurting. Ilse likes it too and we play there most of the time when we are not at the Tansy Patch. We have three paths in it. We call them the To-day Road, the Yesterday Road and the To-morrow Road. The To-day Road is by the brook and we call it that because it is lovely now. The Yesterday Road is out in the stumps where Lofty John cut some trees down and we call it that because it used to be lovely. The To-morrow Road is just a tiny path in the maple clearing and we call it that because it is going to be lovely some day, when the maples grow bigger. But oh Father dear I haven't forgotten the dear old trees down home. I always think of them after I go to bed. But I am happy here. It isn't wrong to be happy, is it Father. Aunt Elizabeth says I got over being homesick very quick but I am often homesick *inside*. I have got akwanted with Lofty John. Ilse is a great friend of his and often goes there to watch him working in his carpenter shop. He says he has made enough ladders to get to heaven without the priest but that is just his joke. He is really a very devowt Catholic and goes to the chapel at White Cross every Sunday. I go with Ilse though perhaps I ought not to when he is an enemy of my family. He is of stately baring and refined manners—very sivil to me but I don't always like him. When I ask him a serius question he always winks over my head when he ansers. That is insulting. Of course I never ask any questions on relijus subjects but Ilse does. She likes him but she says he would burn us all at the stake if he had the power. She asked him right out if he wouldn't and he winked at me and said Oh, we wouldn't burn nice pretty little Protestants like you. We would only burn the old ugly ones. That was a frivellus reply. Mrs. Lofty John is a nice woman and not at all proud. She looks just like a little rosy rinkled apple.

"On rainy days we play at Ilse's. We can slide down the bannisters and do what we like. Nobody cares only when the doctor is home we have to be quiet because he cant bear any noise in the house except what he makes himself. The roof is flat and we can get out on it through a door in the garret ceiling. It is very exiting to be up on the roof of a house. We had a yelling contest there the other night to see which could yell the loudest. To my surprise I found I could. You never can tell what you can do till you try. But too many people heard us and Aunt Elizabeth was very angry. She asked me what made me do such a thing. That is an okward question because often I cant tell what makes me do things. Sometimes I do them just to find out what I feel like doing them. And sometimes I do them because I want to have some exiting things to tell my grandchildren. Is it improper to talk about having grandchildren. I have discovered that it is impropper to talk about haveing children. One evening when people were here Aunt Laura said to me quite kindly What are you thinking so ernestly about, Emily, and I said I am picking names for my children. I mean to have ten. And after the company had gone Aunt Elizabeth said to Aunt Laura *icilly* I think it will be better in the future Laura if you do *not* ask that child what she is thinking of. If Aunt Laura doesnt I shall be sorry because when I have an intresting thought I like to tell it.

"School begins again next week. Ilse is going to ask Miss Brownell if I can sit with her. I intend to act as if Rhoda was not there at all. Teddy is going too. Dr. Burnley says he is well enough to go though his mother doesnt like the idea. Teddy says she never likes to have him go to school but she is glad that he hates Miss Brownell. Aunt Laura says the right way to end a letter to a dear friend is yours affeckshunately.

"So I am yours very affeckshunately.
                                    "*Emily Byrd Starr.*"

"P. S. Because *you* are my *very dearest friend still*, Father. Ilse says she loves me best of anything in the world and her red leather boots that Mrs. Simms gave her next."

13
A Daughter of Eve

New Moon was noted for its apples and on that first autumn of Emily's life there both the "old" and the "new" orchards bore a bumper crop. In the new were the titled and pedigreed apples; and in the old the seedlings, unknown to catalogues, that yet had a flavour wildly sweet and all their own. There was no taboo on any apple and Emily was free to eat all she wanted of each and every kind,—the only prohibition being that she must not take any to bed with her. Aunt Elizabeth, very properly, did not want her bed messed up with apple seeds; and Aunt Laura had a horror of any one eating apples in the dark lest they might eat an apple worm into the bargain. Emily, therefore, should have been able fully to satisfy her appetite for apples at home; but there is a certain odd kink in human nature by reason of which the flavour of the apples belonging to somebody else is always vastly superior to our own—as the crafty serpent of Eden very well knew. Emily, like most people, possessed this kink, and consequently thought that nowhere were there such delicious apples as those belonging to Lofty John. He was in the habit of keeping a long row of apples on one of the beams in his workshop and it was understood that she and Ilse might help themselves freely whenever they visited that charming, dusty, shaving-carpeted spot. Three varieties of Lofty John's apples were their especial favourites—the "scabby apples," that looked as if they had leprosy but were of unsurpassed deliciousness under their queerly blotched skins; the "little red apples," scarcely bigger than a crab, deep crimson all over and glossy as satin, that had such a sweet, nutty flavour; and the big green "sweet apples" that children usually thought the best of all. Emily considered that day wasted whose low descending sun had not beheld her munching one of Lofty John's big green sweets.

In the back of her mind Emily knew quite well that she should not be going to Lofty John's at all. To be sure, she had never been forbidden to go—simply because it had never occurred to her aunts that an inmate of New Moon could so forget the beloved old family feud between the houses of Murray and Sullivan belonging to two generations back. It was an inheritance that any proper Murray would live up to as a matter of course. But when Emily was off with that wild little Ishmaelite of an Ilse, traditions lost their power under the allurement of Lofty John's "reds" and "scabs."

She wandered rather lonesomely into his workshop one September evening at twilight. She had been alone since she came from school; her aunts and Cousin Jimmy had gone to Shrewsbury, promising to be back by sunset. Ilse was away also, her father, prodded thereto by Mrs. Simms, having taken her to Charlottetown to get her a winter coat. Emily liked being alone very well at first. She felt quite important over being in charge of New Moon. She ate the supper Aunt Laura had left on the cook-house dresser for her and she went into the dairy and skimmed six lovely big pans of milk. She had no business at all to do this but she had always hankered to do it and this was too good a chance to be missed. She did it beautifully and nobody ever knew—each aunt supposing the other had done it—and so she was never scolded for it. This does not point any particular moral, of course; in a proper yarn Emily should either have been found out and punished for disobedience or been driven by an uneasy conscience to confess; but I am sorry—or ought to be—to have to state that Emily's conscience never worried her about the matter at all. Still, she was doomed to suffer enough that night from an entirely different cause, to balance all her little peccadillos.

By the time the cream was skimmed and poured into the big stone crock and well stirred—Emily didn't forget *that*, either—it was after sunset and still nobody had come home. Emily didn't like the idea of going alone into the big, dusky, echoing house; so she hied her to Lofty John's shop, which she found unoccupied, though the plane halted midway on a board indicated that Lofty John had been working there quite recently and would probably return. Emily sat down on a round section of a huge log and looked around to see what she could get to eat. There was a row of "reds" and "scabs" clean across the side of the shop but no "sweet" among them; and Emily felt that what she needed just then was a "sweet" and nothing else.

Then she spied one—a huge one—the biggest "sweet" Emily had ever seen, all by itself on one of the steps of the stair leading up to the loft. She climbed up, possessed herself of it and ate it out of hand. She was gnawing happily at the core when Lofty John came in. He nodded to her with a seemingly careless glance around.

"Just been in to get my supper," he said. "The wife's away so I had to get it myself."

He fell to planing in silence. Emily sat on the stairs, counting the seeds of the big "sweet"—you told your fortunes by the seeds—listening to the Wind Woman whistling elfishly through a knot hole in the loft, and composing a "Deskripshun of Lofty John's Carpenter Shop By Lantern Light," to be written later on a letter-bill. She was lost in a mental hunt for an accurate phrase to picture the absurd elongated shadow of Lofty John's nose on the opposite wall when Lofty John whirled about, so suddenly that the shadow of his nose shot upward like a huge spear to the ceiling, and demanded in a startled voice,

"What's become av that big sweet apple that was on that stair?"

"Why—I—I et it," stammered Emily.

Lofty John dropped his plane, threw up his hands, and looked at Emily with a horrified face.

"The saints preserve us, child! Ye never et that apple—don't tell me ye've gone and et *that* apple!"

"Yes, I did," said Emily uncomfortably. "I didn't think it was any harm—I—"

"Harm! Listen to her, will you? That apple was poisoned for the rats! They've been plaguing me life out here and I had me mind made up to finish their fun. And now you've et the apple—it would kill a dozen av ye in a brace of shakes."

Lofty John saw a white face and a gingham apron flash through the workshop and out into the dark. Emily's first wild impulse was to get home at once—before she dropped dead. She tore across the field through the bush and the garden and dashed into the house. It was still silent and dark—nobody was home yet. Emily gave a bitter little shriek of despair—when they came they would find her stiff and cold, black in the face likely, everything in this dear world ended for her forever, all because she had eaten an apple which she thought she was perfectly welcome to eat. It wasn't fair—she didn't want to die.

But she must. She only hoped desperately that some one would come before she was dead. It would be so terrible to die there all alone in that great, big, empty New Moon. She dared not try to go anywhere for help. It was too dark now and she would likely drop dead on the way. To die out there—alone—in the dark—oh, that would be too dreadful. It did not occur to her that anything could be done for her; she thought if you once swallowed poison that was the end of you.

With hands shaking in panic she got a candle lighted. It wasn't quite so bad then—you *could* face things in the light. And Emily, pale, terrified, alone, was already deciding that this must be faced bravely. She must not shame the Starrs and the Murrays. She clenched her cold hands and tried to stop trembling. How long would it be before she died, she wondered. Lofty John had said the apple would kill her in a "brace of shakes." What did that mean? How long was a brace of shakes? Would it hurt her to die? She had a vague idea that poison did hurt you awfully. Oh; and just a little while ago she had been so happy! She had thought she was going to live for years and write great poems and be famous like Mrs. Hemans. She had had a fight with Ilse the night before and hadn't made it up yet—never could make it up now. And Ilse would feel so terribly. She must write her a note and forgive her. Was there time for that much? Oh, how cold her hands were! Perhaps that meant she was dying already. She had heard or read that your hands turned cold when you were dying. She wondered if her face was turning black. She grasped her candle and hurried up the stairs to the spare-room. There was a looking-glass there— the only one in the house hung low enough for her to see her reflection if she tipped the bottom of it back. Ordinarily Emily would have been frightened to death at the mere thought of going into that spare-room by dim, flickering candlelight. But the one great terror had swallowed up all lesser ones. She looked at her reflection, amid the sleek, black flow of her hair, in the upward-striking light on the dark background of the shadowy room. Oh, she was pale as the dead already. Yes, that was a dying face—there could be no doubt of it.

Something rose up in Emily and took possession of her—some inheritance from the good old stock behind her. She ceased to tremble—she accepted her fate— with bitter regret, but calmly.

"I don't want to die but since I have to I'll die as becomes a Murray," she said. She had read a similar sentence in a book and it came pat to the moment. And now she must hurry. That letter to Ilse must be written. Emily went to Aunt Elizabeth's room first, to assure herself that her right-hand top bureau drawer was quite tidy; then she flitted up the garret stairs to her dormer corner. The great place was full of lurking, pouncing shadows that crowded about the little island of faint candlelight, but they had no terrors for Emily now.

"And to think I was feeling so bad to-day because my petticoat was bunchy," she thought, as she got one of her dear letter-bills—the last she would ever write on. There was no need to write to Father—she would see him soon—but Ilse must have her letter—dear, loving, jolly, hot-tempered Ilse, who, just the day before had shrieked insulting epithets after her and who would be haunted by remorse all her life for it.

"Dearest Ilse," wrote Emily, her hand shaking a little but her lips firmly set. "I am going to die. I have been poisoned by an apple Lofty John had put for rats. I will never see you again, but I am writing this to tell you I love you and you are not to feel bad because you called me a skunk and a bloodthirsty mink yesterday. I forgive you, so do not worry over it. And I am sorry I told you that you were beneath contemt because I didn't mean a word of it. I leave you all my share of the broken dishes in our playhouse and please tell Teddy good-bye for me. He will never be able to teach me how to put worms on a fish-hook now. I promised him I would learn because I did not want him to think I was a coward but I am glad I did not for I know what the worm feels like now. I do not feel sick yet but I dont know what the simptoms of poisoning are and Lofty John said there was enough to kill a dozen of me so I cant have long to live. If Aunt Elizabeth is willing you can have my necklace of Venetian beads. It is the only valuable possession I have. Don't let anybody do anything to Lofty John because he did not mean to poison me and it was all my own fault for being so greedy. Perhaps people will think he did it on purpose because I am a Protestant but I feel sure he did not and please tell him not to be hawnted by remorse. I think I feel a pain in my stomach now so I guess that the end draws ni. Fare well and remember her who died so young.

> "Your own devoted,
> "*Emily.*"

As Emily folded up her letter-bill she heard the sound of wheels in the yard below. A moment later Elizabeth and Laura Murray were confronted in the kitchen by a tragic-faced little creature, grasping a guttering candle in one hand and a red letter-bill in the other.

"Emily, what is the matter?" cried Aunt Laura.

"I'm dying," said Emily solemnly. "I et an apple Lofty John had poisoned for rats. I have only a few minutes to live, Aunt Laura."

Laura Murray dropped down on the black bench with her hand at her heart. Elizabeth turned as pale as Emily herself.

"Emily, is this some play-acting of yours?" she demanded sternly.

"No," cried Emily, quite indignantly. "It's the truth. Do you suppose a dying person would be play-acting? And oh, Aunt Elizabeth, please will you give this letter to Ilse—and please forgive me for being naughty—though I wasn't always naughty when you thought I was—and don't let any one see me after I'm dead if I turn black—especially Rhoda Stuart."

By this time Aunt Elizabeth was herself again.

"How long ago is it since you ate that apple, Emily?"

"About an hour."

"If you'd eaten a poisoned apple an hour ago you'd be dead or sick by now—"

"Oh," cried Emily transformed in a second. A wild, sweet hope sprang up in her heart—was there a chance for her after all? Then she added despairingly, "But I felt another pain in my stomach just as I came downstairs."

"Laura," said Aunt Elizabeth, "take this child out to the cook-house and give her a good dose of mustard and water at once. It will do no harm and *may* do some good, if there's anything in this yarn of hers. I'm going down to the doctor's—he may be back—but I'll see Lofty John on the way."

Aunt Elizabeth went out—and Aunt Elizabeth went out very quickly—if it had been any one else it might have been said she ran. As for Emily—well, Aunt Laura gave her that emetic in short order and two minutes later Emily had no doubt at all that she was dying then and there—and the sooner the better. When Aunt Elizabeth returned Emily was lying on the sofa in the kitchen, as white as the pillow under her head, and as limp as a faded lily.

"Wasn't the doctor home?" cried Aunt Laura desperately.

"I don't know—there's no need of the doctor. I didn't think there was from the first. It was just one of Lofty John's jokes. He thought he'd give Emily a fright—just for fun—*his* idea of fun. March you off to bed, Miss Emily. You deserve all you've got for going over there to Lofty John's at all and I don't pity you a particle. I haven't had such a turn for years."

"I *did* have a pain in my stomach," wailed Emily, in whom fright and mustard-and-water combined had temporarily extinguished all spirit.

"Any one who eats apples from dawn to dark must expect a few pains in her stomach. You won't have any more to-night, I reckon—the mustard will remedy that. Take your candle and go."

"Well," said Emily, getting unsteadily to her feet, "I *hate* that dod-gasted Lofty John."

"Emily!" said both aunts together.

"He *deserves* it," said Emily vindictively.

"Oh, Emily—that dreadful word you used!" Aunt Laura seemed curiously upset about something.

"Why, what's the matter with dod-gasted?" said Emily, quite mystified. "Cousin Jimmy uses it often, when things vex him. He used it to-day—he said that dod-gasted heifer had broken out of the graveyard pasture again."

"Emily," said Aunt Elizabeth, with the air of one impaling herself on the easiest horn of a dilemma, "your Cousin Jimmy is a man—and men sometimes use expressions, in the heat of anger, that are not proper for little girls."

"But what *is* the matter with dod-gasted?" persisted Emily. "It isn't a swear word, is it? And if it isn't, why can't I use it?"

"It isn't a—ladylike word," said Aunt Laura.

"Well, then, I won't use it any more," said Emily resignedly, "but Lofty John *is* dod-gasted."

Aunt Laura laughed so much after Emily had gone upstairs that Aunt Elizabeth told her a woman of her age should have more sense.

"Elizabeth, you *know* it was funny," protested Laura.

Emily being safely out of sight, Elizabeth permitted herself a somewhat grim smile.

"I told Lofty John a few plain truths—he'll not go telling children they're poisoned again in a hurry. I left him fairly dancing with rage."

Worn out, Emily fell asleep as soon as she was in bed, but an hour later she awakened. Aunt Elizabeth had not yet come to bed so the blind was still up and Emily saw a dear, friendly star winking down at her. Far away the sea moaned alluringly. Oh, it was nice just to be alone and to be alive. Life tasted good to her again—"tasted like more," as Cousin Jimmie said. She could have a chance to write more letter-bills, and poetry—Emily already saw a yard of verses entitled "Thoughts of One Doomed to Sudden Death"—and play with Ilse and Teddy—scour the barns with Saucy Sal, watch Aunt Laura skim cream in the dairy and help cousin Jimmy garden,—read books in Emily's Bower and trot along the To-day Road—but *not* visit Lofty John's workshop. She determined that she would never have anything to do with Lofty John again after his diabolical cruelty. She felt so indignant with him for frightening her—after they had been such good friends, too—that she could not go to sleep until she had composed an account of her death by poison, of Lofty John being tried for her murder and condemned to death, and of his being hanged on a gibbet as lofty as himself, Emily being present at the dreadful scene, in spite of the fact that she was dead by his act. When she had finally cut him down and buried him with obloquy—the tears streaming down her face out of sympathy for Mrs. Lofty John—she forgave him. Very likely he was not dod-gasted after all.

She wrote it all down on a letter-bill in the garret the next day.

14
Fancy Fed

In October Cousin Jimmy began to boil the pigs' potatoes—unromantic name for a most romantic occupation—or so it appeared to Emily, whose love of the beautiful and picturesque was satisfied as it had never yet been on those long, cool, starry twilights of the waning year at New Moon.

There was a clump of spruce-trees in a corner of the old orchard, and under them an immense iron pot was hung over a circle of large stones—a pot so big that an ox could have been comfortably stewed in it. Emily thought it must have come down from the days of fairy tales and been some giant's porridge pot; but Cousin Jimmy told her that it was only a hundred years old and old Hugh Murray had had it sent out from England.

"We've used it ever since to boil the potatoes for the New Moon pigs," he said. "Blair Water folks think it old-fashioned; they've all got boiler-houses now, with built-in boilers; but as long as Elizabeth's boss at New Moon we'll use this.''

Emily was sure no built-in boiler could have the charm of the big pot. She helped Cousin Jimmie fill it full of potatoes after she came from school; then, when supper was over, Cousin Jimmy lighted the fire under it and puttered about it all the evening. Sometimes he poked the fire—Emily loved that part of the performance—sending glorious streams of rosy sparks upward into the darkness; sometimes he stirred the potatoes with a long pole, looking, with his queer, forked grey beard and belted ''jumper,'' just like some old gnome or troll of northland story mixing the contents of a magical caldron; and sometimes he sat beside Emily on the grey granite boulder near the pot and recited his poetry for her. Emily liked this best of all, for Cousin Jimmy's poetry was surprisingly good—at least in spots—and Cousin Jimmy had ''fit audience though few'' in this slender little maiden with her pale eager face and rapt eyes.

They were an odd couple and they were perfectly happy together. Blair Water people thought Cousin Jimmy a failure and a mental weakling. But he dwelt in an ideal world of which none of them knew anything. He had recited his poems a hundred times thus, as he boiled the pigs' potatoes; the ghosts of a score of autumns haunted the clump of spruces for him. He was an odd, ridiculous figure enough, bent and wrinkled and unkempt, gesticulating awkwardly as he recited. But it was his hour; he was no longer ''simple Jimmy Murray'' but a prince in his own realm. For a little while he was strong and young and splendid and beautiful, accredited master of song to a listening, enraptured world. None of his prosperous, sensible Blair Water neighbours ever lived through such an hour. He would not have exchanged places with one of them. Emily, listening to him, felt vaguely that if it had not been for that unlucky push into the New Moon well, this queer little man beside her might have stood in the presence of kings.

But Elizabeth *had* pushed him into the New Moon well and as a consequence he boiled pigs' potatoes and recited to Emily—Emily, who wrote poetry too, and loved these evenings so much that she could not sleep after she went to bed until she had composed a minute description of them. The flash came almost every evening over something or other. The Wind Woman swooped or purred in the tossing boughs above them—Emily had never been so near to seeing her; the sharp air was full of the pleasant tang of the burning spruce cones Cousin Jimmy shovelled under the pot; Emily's furry kitten, Mike II, frisked and scampered about like a small, charming demon of the night; the fire glowed with beautiful redness and allure through the gloom; there were nice whispery sounds everywhere; the "great big dark" lay spread around them full of mysteries that daylight never revealed; and over all a purple sky powdered with stars.

Ilse and Teddy came, too, on some evenings. Emily always knew when Teddy was coming, for when he reached the old orchard he whistled his "call"—the one he used just for her—a funny, dear little call, like three clear bird notes, the first just medium pitch, the second higher, the third dropping away into lowness and sweetness long-drawn-out—like the echoes in the *Bugle Song* that went clearer and further in their dying. That call always had an odd effect on Emily; it seemed to her that it fairly drew the heart out of her body—and she *had* to follow it. She thought Teddy could have whistled her clear across the world with those three magic notes. Whenever she heard it she ran quickly through the orchard and told Teddy whether Cousin Jimmy wanted him or not, because it was only on certain nights that Cousin Jimmy wanted anybody but her. He would never recite his poetry to Ilse or Teddy; but he told them fairy stories, and tales about the old dead-and-gone Murrays in the pond graveyard that were as queer, sometimes, as the fairy stories; and Ilse would recite too, doing better there than she ever did anywhere else; and sometimes Teddy lay sprawled out on the ground beside the big pot and drew pictures by the light of the fire—pictures of Cousin Jimmy stirring the potatoes—pictures of Ilse and Emily dancing hand in hand around it like two small witches, pictures of Mike's cunning, little, whiskered face peering around the old boulder, pictures of weird, vague faces crowding in the darkness outside their enchanted circle. They had very wonderful evenings there, those four children.

"Oh, don't you like the world at night, Ilse?" Emily once said rapturously.

Ilse glanced happily around her—poor little neglected Ilse, who found in Emily's companionship what she had hungered for all her short life and who was, even now, being led by love into something of her rightful heritage.

"Yes," she said. "And I always believe there *is* a God when I'm here like this."

Then the potatoes were done—and Cousin Jimmy gave each of them one before he mixed in the bran; they broke them in pieces on plates of birch-bark, sprinkled them with salt which Emily had cached in a small box under the roots of the biggest spruce, and ate them with gusto. No banquet of gods was ever as delicious as those potatoes. Then finally came Aunt Laura's kind, silvery voice calling through the frosty dark; Ilse and Teddy scampered homewards; and Emily captured Mike II and shut him up safely for the night in the New Moon dog-house which had held no dog for years, but was still carefully preserved and white-washed every spring. Emily's heart would have broken if anything had happened to Mike II.

"Old Kelly," the tin pedlar, had given him to her. Old Kelly had come round through Blair Water every fortnight from May to November for thirty years, perched on the seat of a bright red pedlar's wagon and behind a dusty, ambling, red pony of that peculiar gait and

appearance pertaining to the ponies of country pedlars—
a certain placid, unhasting leanness as of a nag that has
encountered troubles of his own and has lived them
down by sheer patience and staying power. From the
bright red wagon proceeded a certain metallic rumbling
and clinking as it bowled along, and two huge nests of
tin pans on its flat, rope-encircled roof flashed back the
sunlight so dazzlingly that Old Kelly seemed the beam-
ing sun of a little planetary system all his own. A new
broom, sticking up aggressively at each of the four
corners gave the wagon a resemblance to a triumphal
chariot. Emily hankered secretly for a ride in Old
Kelly's wagon. She thought it must be very delightful.

Old Kelly and she were great friends. She liked his
red, clean-shaven face under his plug hat, his nice,
twinkly, blue eyes, his brush of upstanding, sandy hair,
and his comical pursed-up mouth, the shape of which
was partly due to nature and partly to much whistling.
He always had a little three-cornered paper bag of
"lemon drops" for her, or a candy stick of many
colours, which he smuggled into her pocket when
Aunt Elizabeth wasn't looking. And he never forgot to
tell her that he supposed she'd soon be thinking of
getting married—for Old Kelly thought that the surest
way to please a female creature of any age was to tease
her about getting married.

One day, instead of candy, he produced a plump
grey kitten from the back drawer of his wagon and told
her it was for her. Emily received the gift rapturously,
but after Old Kelly had rattled and clattered away Aunt
Elizabeth told her they did not want any more cats at
New Moon.

"Oh, please let me keep it, Aunt Elizabeth," Emily
begged. "It won't be a bit of bother to you. *I* have had
experience in bringing up cats. And I'm so lonesome
for a kitten. Saucy Sal is getting so wild running with
the barn cats that I can't 'sociate with her like I used to
do—and she never was nice to cuddle. *Please*, Aunt
Elizabeth."

Aunt Elizabeth would not and did not please. She was in a very bad humour that day, anyhow,—nobody knew just why. In such a mood she was entirely unreasonable. She would not listen to anybody—Laura and Cousin Jimmy had to hold their tongues, and Cousin Jimmy was bidden to take the grey kitten down to the Blair Water and drown it. Emily burst into tears over this cruel command, and this aggravated Aunt Elizabeth still further. She was so cross that Cousin Jimmy dared not smuggle the kitten up to the barn as he had at first planned to do.

"Take that beast down to the pond and throw it in and come back and tell me you've done it," said Elizabeth angrily. "I mean to be obeyed—New Moon is not going to be made a dumping-ground for Old Jock Kelly's superfluous cats."

Cousin Jimmy did as he was told and Emily would not eat any dinner. After dinner she stole mournfully away through the old orchard down the pasture to the pond. Just why she went she could not have told, but she felt that go she must. When she reached the bank of the little creek where Lofty John's brook ran into Blair Water, she heard piteous shrieks; and there, marooned on a tiny islet of sere marsh grass in the creek, was an unhappy little beast, its soaking fur plastered against its sides, shivering and trembling in the wind of the sharp autumnal day. The old oat-bag in which Cousin Jimmy had imprisoned it was floating out into the pond.

Emily did not stop to think, or look for a board, or count the consequences. She plunged in the creek up to her knees, she waded out to the clump of grass and caught the kitten up. She was so hot with indignation that she did not feel the cold of the water or the chill of the wind as she ran back to New Moon. A suffering or tortured animal always filled her with such a surge of sympathy that it lifted her clean out of herself. She burst into the cook-house where Aunt Elizabeth was frying doughnuts.

"Aunt Elizabeth," she cried, "the kitten wasn't drowned after all—and I *am* going to keep it."

"You're not," said Aunt Elizabeth.

Emily looked her aunt in the face. Again she felt that odd sensation that had come when Aunt Elizabeth brought the scissors to cut her hair.

"Aunt Elizabeth, this poor little kitten is cold and starving, and oh, so miserable. It has been suffering for hours. It shall *not* be drowned again."

Archibald Murray's look was on her face and Archibald Murray's tone was in her voice. This happened only when the deeps of her being were stirred by some peculiarly poignant emotion. Just now she was in an agony of pity and anger.

When Elizabeth Murray saw her father looking at her out of Emily's little white face, she surrendered without a struggle, rage at herself as she might afterwards for her weakness. It was her one vulnerable point. The thing might not have been so uncanny if Emily had resembled the Murrays. But to see the Murray look suddenly superimposed like a mask over alien features, was such a shock to her nerves that she could not stand up against it. A ghost from the grave could not have cowed her more speedily.

She turned her back on Emily in silence but Emily knew that she had won her second victory. The grey kitten stayed at New Moon and waxed fat and lovable, and Aunt Elizabeth never took the slightest notice of its existence, save to sweep it out of the house when Emily was not about. But it was weeks before Emily was really forgiven and she felt uncomfortable enough over it. Aunt Elizabeth could be a not ungenerous conqueror but she was very disagreeable in defeat. It was really just as well that Emily could not summon the Murray look at will.

15
Various Tragedies

Emily, obedient to Aunt Elizabeth's command, had eliminated the word "bull" from her vocabulary. But to ignore the existence of bulls was not to do away with them—and specifically with Mr. James Lee's English bull, who inhabited the big windy pasture west of Blair Water and who bore a dreadful reputation. He was certainly an awesome looking creature and Emily sometimes had fearful dreams of being chased by him and being unable to move. And one sharp November day these dreams came true.

There was a certain well at the far end of the pasture concerning which Emily felt a curiosity, because Cousin Jimmy had told her a dreadful tale about it. The well had been dug sixty years ago by two brothers who lived in a little house which was built down near the shore. It was a very deep well, which was considered a curious thing in that low-lying land near pond and sea; the brothers had gone ninety feet before they found a spring. Then the sides of the well had been stoned up—but the work never went further. Thomas and Silas Lee had quarrelled over some trivial difference of opinion as to what kind of a hood should be put over it; and in the heat of his anger Silas had struck Thomas on the head with his hammer and killed him.

The well-house was never built. Silas Lee was sent to prison for manslaughter and died there. The farm passed to another brother—Mr. James Lee's father—who moved the house to the other end of it and planked the well over. Cousin Jimmie added that Tom

Lee's ghost was supposed to haunt the scene of his tragic death but he couldn't vouch for that, though he had written a poem on it. A very eerie poem it was, too, and made Emily's blood run cold with a fearful joy when he recited it to her one misty night by the big potato pot. Ever since she had wanted to see the old well.

Her chance came one Saturday when she was prowling alone in the old graveyard. Beyond it lay the Lee pasture and there was apparently not a sign of a bull in or about it. Emily decided to pay a visit to the old well and went skimming down the field against the sweep of the north wind racing across the gulf. The Wind Woman was a giantess that day and a mighty swirl she was stirring up along the shore; but as Emily drew near the big sanddunes they made a little harbour of calmness around the old well.

Emily coolly lifted up one of the planks, knelt on the others and peered down. Fortunately the planks were strong and comparatively new—otherwise the small maiden of New Moon might have explored the well more thoroughly than she desired to do. As it was, she could see little of it; huge ferns grew thickly out of the crevices among the stones of its sides and reached across it, shutting out the view of its gloomy depths. Rather disappointed, Emily replaced the plank and started homeward. She had not gone ten steps before she stopped. Mr. James Lee's bull was coming straight towards her and was less than twenty yards away.

The shore fence was not far behind Emily, and she might possibly have reached it in time had she run. But she was incapable of running; as she wrote that night in her letter to her father she was "parralised" with terror and could no more move than she could in her dreams of this very occurrence. It is quite conceivable that a dreadful thing might have happened then and there had not a certain boy been sitting on the shore fence. He had been sitting there unnoticed all the time

Emily had been peering into the well; now he sprang down.

Emily saw, or sensed, a sturdy body dashing past her. The owner thereof ran to within ten feet of the bull, hurled a stone squarely into the monster's hairy face, then sped off at right angles towards the side fence. The bull, thus insulted, turned with a menacing rumble and lumbered off after this intruder.

"Run now!" screamed the boy over his shoulder to Emily.

Emily did not run. Terrified as she was, there was something in her that would not let her run until she saw whether her gallant rescuer made good his escape. He reached his fence in the nick of time. Then and not till then Emily ran too, and scrambled over the shore fence just as the bull started back across the pasture, evidently determined to catch somebody. Trembling, she made her way through the spiky grass of the sand-hills and met the boy at the corner. They stood and looked at each other for a moment.

The boy was a stranger to Emily. He had a cheery, impudent, clean-cut face, with keen, grey eyes and plenty of tawny curls. He wore as few clothes as decency permitted and had only the pretence of a hat. Emily liked him; there was nothing of Teddy's subtle charm in him but he had a certain forceful attraction of his own and he had just saved her from a terrible death.

"Thank you," said Emily shyly, looking up at him with great grey eyes that looked blue under her long lashes. It was a very effective look which lost nothing of effectiveness from being wholly unconscious. Nobody had as yet told Emily how very winsome that shy, sudden, up-glance of hers was.

"Isn't he a rip-snorter?" said the boy easily. He thrust his hands into his ragged pockets and stared at Emily so fixedly that she dropped her eyes in confusion— thereby doing further damage with those demure lids and silken fringes.

"He's dreadful," she said with a shudder. "And I was so scared."

"Were you now? And me thinking you were full of grit to be standing there like that looking at him cool as a cucumber. What's it like to be afraid?"

"Weren't *you* ever afraid?' asked Emily.

"No—don't know what it's like," said the boy carelessly, and a bit boastfully. "What's your name?"

"Emily Byrd Starr."

"Live round here?"

"I live at New Moon."

"Where Simple Jimmy Murray lives?"

"He *isn't* simple," cried Emily indignantly.

"Oh, all right. I don't know him. But I'm going to. I'm going to hire with him for chore boy for the winter."

"I didn't know," said Emily, surprised. "Are you really?"

"Yep. I didn't know it myself till just this minute. He was asking Aunt Tom about me last week but I didn't mean to hire out then. Now I guess I will. Want to know my name?"

"Of course."

"Perry Miller. I live with my old beast of an Aunt Tom down at Stovepipe Town. Dad was a sea-captain and I uster sail with him when he was alive—sailed everywhere. Go to school?"

"Yes."

"I don't—never did. Aunt Tom lives so far away. Anyhow, I didn't think I'd like it. Guess I'll go now, though."

"Can't you read?" asked Emily wonderingly.

"Yes—some—and figger. Dad learned me some when he was alive. I hain't bothered with it since—I'd ruther be down round the harbour. Great fun there. But if I make up my mind to go to school I'll learn like thunder. I s'pose you're awful clever."

"No—not very. Father said I was a genius, but Aunt Elizabeth says I'm just queer."

"What's a genius?"

"I'm not sure. Sometimes it's a person who writes poetry. *I* write poetry."

Perry stared at her.

"Golly. I'll write poetry too, then."

"I don't believe *you* could write poetry," said Emily—a little disdainfully, it must be admitted. "Teddy can't—and he's *very* clever."

"Who's Teddy?"

"A friend of mine." There was just a trace of stiffness in Emily's voice.

"Then," said Perry, folding his arms across his breast and scowling, "I'm going to punch this friend of yours' head for him."

"You're not," cried Emily. She was very indignant and quite forgot for the moment that Perry had rescued her from the bull. She tossed her own head and started homeward. Perry turned too.

"May as well go up and see Jimmy Murray about hiring 'fore I go home," he said. "Don't be mad, now. If you don't want anybody's head punched I won't punch it. Only you've gotter like me, too."

"Why, of course I'll like you," said Emily, as if there could be no question about it. She smiled her slow, blossoming smile at Perry and thereby reduced him to hopeless bondage.

Two days later Perry Miller was installed as chore boy at New Moon and in a fortnight's time Emily felt as if he must have been there always.

"Aunt Elizabeth didn't want Cousin Jimmy to hire him," she wrote to her father, "because he was one of the boys who did a dreadful thing one night last fall. They changed all the horses that were tied to the fence one Sunday night when preaching was going on and when folks came out the confushun was awful. Aunt Elizabeth said it wouldn't be safe to have him round the place. But Cousin Jimmy said it was awful hard to get a chore boy and that we ode Perry something for saving my life from the bull. So Aunt Elizabeth gave in and lets him sit at the table with us but he has to stay in the kitchen in the evenings. The rest of us are in the sitting-room, but I am allowed to go out and help Perry with his lessons. He can only have one candle and the light is very dim. It keeps us snuffing it all the time. It is great fun to snuff candles. Perry is head of his class in school already. He is only in the third book allthough he is nearly twelve. Miss Brownell said something sarkastik to him the first day in school and he just threw back his head and laughed loud and long. Miss Brownell gave him a whipping for it but she has never been sarkastik to him again. She does not like to be laughed at I can see. Perry isn't afraid of anything. I thought he might not go to school any more when she whipped him but he says a little thing like that isn't going to keep him from getting an educashun since he has made up his mind to it. He is very determined.

"Aunt Elizabeth is determined too. But she says Perry is stubborn. I am teaching Perry grammar. He says he wants to learn to speak properly. I told him he should not call his Aunt Tom an old beast but he said he had to because she wasn't a young beast. He says the place he lives in is called Stovepipe Town because the houses have no chimneys, only pipes sticking out of the roof, but he would live in a manshun some day. Aunt Elizabeth says I ought not to be so friendly with a hired boy. But he is a nice boy though his manners are crood. Aunt Laura says they are crood. I don't know what it means but I guess it means he always says what he thinks right out and eats beans with his knife. I like Perry but in a different way from Teddy. Isn't it funny, dear Father, how many kinds of ways of liking there are? I don't think Ilse likes him. She makes fun of his ignerance and turns up her nose at him because his close are patched though her own close are queer enough. Teddy doesnt like him much and he drew such a funny picture of Perry hanging by his heels from a gallos. The face looked like Perrys and still it didn't. Cousin Jimmy said it was a carrycachure and laughed at it but I dared not show it to Perry for fear he would punch Teddys head. I showed it to Ilse and she got mad and tore it in two. I cant imagine why.

"Perry says he can recite as well as Ilse and could draw pictures too if he put his mind to it. I can see he doesnt like to think anybody can do anything he cant. But he cant see the wallpaper in the air like I can though he tries until I fear he will strane his eyes. He can make better speeches than any of us. He says he used to mean to be a sailor like his father but now he thinks he will be a lawyer when he grows up and go to parlament. Teddy is going to be an artist if his mother will let him, and Ilse is going to be a concert reciter— there is another name but I don't know how it is spelled—and I am going to be a poetess. I think we are a tallented crowd. Perhaps that is a vane thing to say, dear Father.

"A very terrible thing happened the day before yesterday. On Saturday morning we were at family prayers, all kneeling quite solemn around the kitchen. I just looked at Perry once and he made such a funny face at me that I laughed right out loud before I could help it. (*That* was not the terrible thing.) Aunt Elizabeth was *very* angry. I would not tell that it was Perry made me laugh because I was afraid he might be sent away if I did. So Aunt Elizabeth said I was to be punished and I was not let go to Jennie Strangs party in the afternoon. (It was a dreadful disappointment but *it* was not the terrible thing either.) Perry was away with Cousin Jimmy all day and when he came home at night he said to me, very feerce, Who has been making you cry. I said I had been crying—a little but not much—because I was not let go to the party because I had laughed at prayers. And Perry marched right up to Aunt Elizabeth and told her it was all his fault that I laughed. Aunt Elizabeth said I should not have laughed anyhow, but Aunt Laura was *greevously* upset and said my punishment had been far too severe; and she said that she would let me ware her pearl ring to school Monday to make up for it. I was enraptured for it is a lovely ring and no other girl has one. As soon as roll call was over Monday morning I put up my hand to ask Miss Brownell a question but really to show off my ring. That was wikked pride and I was punished. At recess Cora Lee, one of the big girls in the sixth class came and asked me to let her ware the ring for a while. I didnt want to but she said if I didnt she would get all the girls in my class to send me to coventry (which is a dreadful thing, dear Father, and makes you feel like an outcast). So I let her and she kept it on till the afternoon recess and then she came and told me she had lost it in the brook. (This was the terrible thing). Oh, Father dear, I was nearly wild. I dared not go home and face Aunt Laura. I had promised her I would be so careful of the ring. I thought I might earn money to get her another ring but when I figgered it out on my slate I knew I would have to wash dishes for twenty years to do it. I wepped in my despare. Perry saw me and after school he marched up to Cora Lee and said You fork over that ring or I'll tell Miss Brownell about it. And Cora Lee forked it over, very meek and said I was going to give it to her anyhow. I was just playing a joke and Perry said, Dont you play any more jokes on Emily or I'll joke you. It is very comforting to have such a champeen! I tremble to think what it would have been like if I had had to go home and tell Aunt Laura I had lost her ring. But it was crewel of Cora Lee to tell me she had lost it when she had not and harrow up my mind so. I could not be so crewel to an orfan girl.

"When I got home I looked in the glass to see if my hair had turned white. I am told that sometimes happens. But it hadnt.

"Perry knows more geograffy than any of us because he has been nearly everywhere in the world with his father. He tells me such fassinating stories after his lessons are done. He talks till the candle is burned to the last inch and then he uses that to go to bed with up the black hole into the kitchen loft because Aunt Elizabeth will not let him have more than one candle a night.

"Ilse and I had a fight yesterday about which we'd rather be Joan of Arc or Frances Willard. We didn't begin it as a fight but just as an argewment but it ended that way. *I* would rather be Frances Willard because she is alive.

"We had the first snow yesterday. I made a poem on it. This is it.

> *Along the snow the sunbeams glide*
> *Earth is a peerless, gleaming bride,*
> *Dripping with diamonds, clad in traling white,*
> *No bride was ever half so fair and bright.*

"I read it to Perry and he said he could make poetry just as good and he said right off,

> *Mike has made a long row*
> *Of tracks across the snow.*

Now isnt that as good as yours. I didnt think it was because you could say it just as well in prose. But when you talk of peerless gleaming brides in prose it sounds funny. Mike *did* make a row of little tracks right across the barn field and they looked so pretty, but not so pretty as the mice tracks in some flour Cousin Jimmy spilled on the granary floor. They are the dearest little things. They *look* like poetry.

"I am sorry winter has come because Ilse and I cant play in our house in Lofty Johns bush any more till spring or outside at the Tansy Patch. Sometimes we play indoors at the Tansy Patch but Mrs. Kent makes us feel queer. She sits and watches us all the time. So we dont go only when Teddy coaxes very hard. And the pigs have been killed, poor things, so Cousin Jimmy doesnt boil for them any more. But there is one consolashun I do not have to ware a sunbonnet to school now. Aunt Laura made me such a pretty red hood with ribbons on it at which Aunt Elizabeth looked skornfully saying it was extravagant. I like school here better every day but I cant like Miss Brownell. She isnt fair. She told us she would give the one who wrote the best composishun a pink ribbon to wear from Friday night to Monday. I wrote The Brooks Story about the brook in Lofty John's bush—all its advenshures and thoughts—and Miss Brownell said I must have copyed it and Rhoda Stuart got the ribbon. Aunt Elizabeth said You waste enough time writing trash I think you might have won that ribbon. She was mortifyed (I think) because I had disgraced New Moon by not getting it but I did not tell her what had happened. Teddy says a *good sport* never whines over losing. I want to be a good sport. Rhoda is so hateful to me now. She says she is surprised that a New Moon girl should have a hired boy for a bow. That is very silly because Perry is not my bow. Perry told her she had more gab than sense. That was not polite but it is true. One day in class Rhoda said the moon was situated east of Canada. Perry laughed right out and Miss Brownell made him stay in at recess but she never said anything to Rhoda for saying such a ridikulus thing. But the meanest thing Rhoda said was that she had forgiven me for the way I had used her. That made my blood boil when I hadnt done anything to be forgiven for. The idea.

"We have begun to eat the big beef ham that hung in the southwest corner of the kitchen.

"The other Wednesday night Perry and I helped Cousin Jimmy pick a road through the turnips in the first cellar. We have to go through it to the second cellar because the outside hatch is banked up now. It was great fun. We had a candle stuck up in a hole in the wall and it made such lovely shadows and we could eat all the apples we wanted from the big barrel in the corner and the spirit moved Cousin Jimmy to recite some of his poetry as he threw the turnips.

"I am reading The Alhambra. It belongs to our book case. Aunt Elizabeth does not like to say it isnt fit for me to read because it was one of her fathers books, but I dont believe she aproves because she knits very furiusly and looks black at me over her glasses. Teddy lent me Hans Andersons stories. I love them—only I always think of a different end for the Ice Maiden and save Rudy.

"They say Mrs. John Killegrew has swallowed her wedding-ring. I wonder what she did that for.

"Cousin Jimmy says there is to be an eklips of the sun in December. I hope it wont interfear with Christmas.

"My hands are chapped. Aunt Laura rubs mutton tallow on them every night when I go to bed. It is hard to write poetry with chapped hands. I wonder if Mrs. Hemans ever had chapped hands. It does not mention anything like that in her biograffy.

"Jimmy Ball has to be a minister when he grows up. His mother told Aunt Laura that she consekrated him to it in his cradle. I wonder how she did it.

"We have brekfast by candlelight now and I like it.

"Ilse was up here Sunday afternoon and we went up in the garret and talked about God, because that is proper on Sundays. We have to be very careful what we do on Sundays. It is a traddishun of New Moon to keep Sundays very holy. Grandfather Murray was very strikt. Cousin Jimmy told me a story about him. They always cut the wood for Sunday on Saturday night, but one time they forgot and there was no wood on Sunday to cook the dinner, so Grandfather Murray said you must not cut wood on Sundays, boys, but just break a little with the back of the axe. Ilse is very curious about God although she doesnt believe in Him most of the time and doesnt like to talk about Him but still wants to find out about Him. She says she thinks she might like Him if she knew Him. She spells his name with a Capital G now because it is best to be on the safe side. *I* think God is just like my flash, only *it* lasts only a second and He lasts always. We talked so long we got hungry and I went down to the sitting-room cubbord and got two donuts. I forgot Aunt Elizabeth had told me I could not have donuts between meals. It was not stealing it was just forgetting. But Ilse got mad at the last and said I was a she jakobite (whatever that is) and a thief and that no Christian would steal donuts from her poor old aunt. So I went and confessed to Aunt Elizabeth and she said I was not to have a donut at supper. It was hard to see the others eating them. I thought Perry et his very quick but after supper he bekoned me out doors and gave me half his donut which he had kept for me. He had rapped it in his hangkerchief which was not very clean but I et it because I did not want to hurt his feelings.

"Aunt Laura says Ilse has a nice smile. I wonder if I have a nice smile. I looked at the glass in Ilse's room and smiled but it did not seem to me very nice.

"Now the nights have got cold Aunt Elizabeth always puts a gin jar full of hot water in the bed. I like to put my toes against it. That is all we use the gin jar for nowadays. But Grandfather Murray used to keep real gin in it.

"Now that the snow has come Cousin Jimmy cant work in his garden any more and he is very lonesome. I think the garden is just as pretty in winter as in summer. There are such pretty dimples and baby hills where the snow has covered up the flower beds. And in the evenings it is all pink and rosy at sunset and by moonlight it is like dreamland. I like to look out of the sitting-room window at it and watch the rabbits candles floting in the air above it and wonder what all the little roots and seeds are thinking of down under the snow. And it gives me a lovely creepy feeling to look at it through the red glass in the front door.

"There is a beautiful fringe of isikles along the cookhouse roof. But there will be much more beautiful things in heaven. I was reading about Anzonetta today and it made me feel relijus. Good night, my dearest of fathers.

                                        "Emily.

*   *   *

"P. S. That doesnt mean that I have any other Father.
It is just a way of saying *very very* dear.

"E. B. S."

16
Check for Miss Brownell

Emily and Ilse were sitting out on the side bench of
Blair Water school writing poetry on their slates—at
least, Emily was writing poetry and Ilse was reading it
as she wrote and occasionally suggesting a rhyme
when Emily was momentarily stuck for one. It may as
well be admitted here and now that they had no
business whatever to be doing this. They should have
been "doing sums," as Miss Brownell supposed they
were. But Emily never did sums when she took it into
her black head to write poetry, and Ilse hated arithmetic on general principles. Miss Brownell was hearing
the geography class at the other side of the room, the
pleasant sunshine was showering in over them through
the big window, and everything seemed propitious for
a flight with the muses. Emily began to write a poem
about the view from the school window.

It was quite a long time since she had been allowed
to sit out on the side bench. This was a boon reserved
for those pupils who had found favour in Miss Brownell's
cold eyes—and Emily had never been one of those. But
this afternoon Ilse had asked for both herself and
Emily, and Miss Brownell had let both go, not being
able to think of any valid reason for permitting Ilse and
refusing Emily—as she would have liked to do, for she
had one of those petty natures which never forget or
forgive any offence. Emily, on her first day of school,
had, so Miss Brownell believed, been guilty of imperti-

nence and defiance—and successful defiance at that. This rankled in Miss Brownell's mind still and Emily felt its venom in a score of subtle ways. She never received any commendation—she was a target for Miss Brownell's sarcasm continually—and the small favours that other girls received never came her way. So this opportunity to sit on the side bench was a pleasing novelty.

There were points about sitting on the side bench. You could see all over the school without turning your head—and Miss Brownell could not sneak up behind you and look over your shoulder to see what you were up to; but in Emily's eyes the finest thing about it was that you could look right down into the "school bush," and watch the old spruces where the Wind Woman played, the long grey-green trails of moss hanging from the branches, like banners of Elfland, the little red squirrels running along the fence, and the wonderful white aisles of snow where splashes of sunlight fell like pools of golden wine; and there was one little opening in the trees through which you could see right over the Blair Water valley to the sand-hills and the gulf beyond. To-day the sand-hills were softly rounded and gleaming white under the snow, but beyond them the gulf was darkly, deeply blue with dazzling white masses of ice like baby icebergs, floating about in it. Just to look at it thrilled Emily with a delight that was unutterable but which she yet must try to utter. She began her poem. Fractions were utterly forgotten—what had numerators and denominators to do with those curving bosoms of white snow—that heavenly blue—those crossed dark fir tips against the pearly skies—those ethereal woodland aisles of pearl and gold? Emily was lost to her world—so lost that she did not know the geography class had scattered to their respective seats and that Miss Brownell, catching sight of Emily's entranced gaze sky-wards as she searched for a rhyme, was stepping softly towards her. Ilse was drawing a picture on her slate and did not see her or she would have warned Emily. The latter suddenly felt her slate drawn out of her hand and heard Miss Brownell saying:

"I suppose you have finished those sums, Emily?"

Emily had not finished even one sum—she had only covered her slate with verses—verses that Miss Brownell must not see—*must not* see! Emily sprang to her feet and clutched wildly after her slate. But Miss Brownell, with a smile of malicious enjoyment on her thin lips, held it beyond her reach.

"What is this? It does not look—excactly—like fractions. 'Lines on the View—v-e-w—from the Window of Blair Water School.' Really, children, we seem to have a budding poet among us."

The words were harmless enough, but—oh, the hateful sneer that ran through the tone—the contempt, the mockery that was in it! It seared Emily's soul like a whiplash. Nothing was more terrible to her than the thought of having her beloved "poems" read by stranger eyes—cold, unsympathetic, derisive, stranger eyes.

"Please—please, Miss Brownell," she stammered miserably, "don't read it—I'll rub it off—I'll do my sums right away. Only please don't read it. It—it isn't anything."

Miss Brownell laughed cruelly.

"You are too modest, Emily. It is a whole slateful of—*poetry*—think of that, children—*poetry*. We have a pupil in this school who can write—*poetry*. And she does not want us to read this—*poetry*. I am afraid Emily is selfish. I am sure we should all enjoy this—*poetry*."

Emily cringed every time Miss Brownell said "*poetry*," with that jeering emphasis and that hateful pause before it. Many of the children giggled, partly because they enjoyed seeing a "Murray of New Moon" grilled, partly because they realized that Miss Brownell expected them to giggle. Rhoda Stuart giggled louder than any one else; but Jennie Strang, who had tormented Emily on her first day at school, refused to giggle and scowled blackly at Miss Brownell instead.

Miss Brownell held up the slate and read Emily's poem aloud, in a sing-song nasal voice, with absurd intonations and gestures that made it seem a very ridiculous thing. The lines Emily had thought the finest seemed the most ridiculous. The other pupils laughed more than ever and Emily felt that the bitterness of the moment could never go out of her heart. The little fancies that had been so beautiful when they came to her as she wrote were shattered and bruised now, like torn and mangled butterflies—"vistas in some fairy dream," chanted Miss Brownell, shutting her eyes and wagging her head from side to side. The giggles became shouts of laughter.

"Oh," thought Emily, clenching her hands, "I wish—I wish the bears that ate the naughty children in the Bible would come and eat *you*."

There were no nice, retributive bears in the school bush, however, and Miss Brownell read the whole "poem" through. She was enjoying herself hugely. To ridicule a pupil always gave her pleasure and when that pupil was Emily of New Moon, in whose heart and soul she had always sensed something fundamentally different from her own, the pleasure was exquisite.

When she reached the end she handed the slate back to the crimson-cheeked Emily.

"Take your—*poetry*, Emily," she said.

Emily snatched the slate. No slate "rag" was handy but Emily gave the palm of her hand a fierce lick and one side of the slate was wiped off. Another lick—and the rest of the poem went. It had been disgraced—degraded—it must be blotted out of existence. To the end of her life Emily never forgot the pain and humiliation of that experience.

Miss Brownell laughed again.

"What a pity to obliterate such—*poetry*, Emily," she said. "Suppose you do those sums now. They are not—*poetry*, but I am in this school to teach arithmetic and I am not here to teach the art of writing—*poetry*. Go to your own seat. Yes, Rhoda?"

For Rhoda Stuart was holding up her hand and snapping her fingers.

"Please, Miss Brownell," she said, with distinct triumph in her tones, "Emily Starr has a whole bunch of poetry in her desk. She was reading it to Ilse Burnley this morning while you thought they were learning history."

Perry Miller turned around and a delightful missile, compounded of chewed paper and known as a "spit pill," flew across the room and struck Rhoda squarely in the face. But Miss Brownell was already at Emily's desk, having reached it one jump before Emily herself.

"Don't touch them—you have no *right!*" gasped Emily frantically.

But Miss Brownell had the "bunch of poetry" in her hands. She turned and walked up to the platform. Emily followed. Those poems were very dear to her. She had composed them during the various stormy recesses when it had been impossible to play out of doors and written them down on disreputable scraps of paper borrowed from her mates. She had meant to take them home that very evening and copy them on letter-bills. And now this horrible woman was going to read them to the whole jeering, giggling school.

But Miss Brownell realized that the time was too short for that. She had to content herself with reading over the titles, with some appropriate comments.

Meanwhile Perry Miller was relieving his feelings by bombarding Rhoda Stuart with spit pills, so craftily timed that Rhoda had no idea from what quarter of the room they were coming and so could not "tell" on any one. They greatly interfered with her enjoyment of Emily's scrape, however. As for Teddy Kent, who did not wage war with spit pills but preferred subtler methods of revenge, he was busy drawing something on a sheet of paper. Rhoda found the sheet on her desk the next morning; on it was depicted a small, scrawny monkey, hanging by its tail from a branch; and the face of the monkey was as the face of Rhoda Stuart. Whereat Rhoda Stuart waxed wroth, but for the sake of her own vanity tore the sketch to tatters and kept silence regarding it. She did not know that Teddy had made a similar sketch, with Miss Brownell figuring as a vampirish-looking bat, and thrust it into Emily's hand as they left school.

"'The Lost Dimond—a Romantic Tale,'" read Miss Brownell. "'Lines on a Birch Tree'—looks to me more like lines on a very dirty piece of paper, Emily—'Lines Written on a Sundial in our Garden'—ditto—'Lines to my Favourite Cat'—another romantic *tail*, I presume—'Ode to Ilse'—'Thy neck is of a wondrous pearly sheen'—hardly that, I should say. Ilse's neck is very sunburned—'A Deskripshun of Our Parlour,' 'The Violets Spell'—I hope the violet *spells* better than you do, Emily—'The Disappointed House'—

> "'Lilies lifted up white cups
> For the bees to dr—r—i—i—ink.'"

"I didn't write it that way!" cried tortured Emily.

"'Lines to a Piece of Brokade in Aunt Laura's Burow Drawer,' 'Farewell on Leaving Home,' 'Lines to a Spruce Tree'—'It keeps off heat and sun and glare, Tis a goodly tree I ween'—are you quite sure that you know what 'ween' means, Emily?—'Poem on Mr. Tom Bennet's Field'—'Poem on the Vew from Aunt Elizabeth's Window' —you are strong on 'v-e-w-s,' Emily—'Epitaff on a Drowned Kitten,' 'Meditashuns at the tomb of my great great grandmother'—poor lady—'To my Northern Birds'—'Lines composed on the bank of Blair Water gazing at the stars'—h'm—h'm—

> "'Crusted with uncounted gems,
> Those stars so distant, cold and true,'

Don't try to pass those lines off as your own, Emily. You couldn't have written them."

"I did—I did!" Emily was white with sense of outrage. "And I've written lots far better."

Miss Brownell suddenly crumpled the ragged little papers up in her hand.

"We have wasted enough time over this trash," she said. "Go to your seat, Emily."

She moved towards the stove. For a moment Emily did not realize her purpose. Then, as Miss Brownell opened the stove door, Emily understood and bounded forward. She caught at the papers and tore them from Miss Brownell's hand before the latter could tighten her grasp.

"You *shall not* burn them—you shall not have them," gasped Emily. She crammed the poems into the pocket of her "baby apron" and faced Miss Brownell in a kind of calm rage. The Murray look was on her face—and although Miss Brownell was not so violently affected by it as Aunt Elizabeth had been, it nevertheless gave her an unpleasant sensation, as of having roused forces with which she dared not tamper further. This tormented child looked quite capable of flying at her, tooth and claw.

"Give me those papers, Emily,"—but she said it rather uncertainly.

"I will not," said Emily stormily. "They are mine. You have no right to them. I wrote them at recesses—I didn't break any rules. You"—Emily looked defiantly into Miss Brownell's cold eyes—"You are an unjust, tyrannical *person*."

Miss Brownell turned to her desk.

"I am coming up to New Moon to-night to tell your Aunt Elizabeth of this," she said.

Emily was at first too much excited over saving her precious poetry to pay much heed to this threat. But as her excitement ebbed cold dread flowed in. She knew she had an unpleasant time ahead of her. But at all events they should not get her poems—not one of them, no matter what they did to *her*. As soon as she got home from school she flew to the garret and secreted them on the shelf of the old sofa.

She wanted terribly to cry but she would not. Miss Brownell was coming and Miss Brownell should *not* see her with red eyes. But her heart burned within

her. Some sacred temple of her being had been desecrated and shamed. And more was yet to come, she
felt wretchedly sure. Aunt Elizabeth was certain to
side with Miss Brownell. Emily shrank from the impending ordeal with all the dread of a sensitive, fine
strung nature facing humiliation. She would not have
been afraid of justice; but she knew at the bar of Aunt
Elizabeth and Miss Brownell she would not have
justice.

"And I can't write Father about it," she thought, her
little breast heaving. The shame of it all was too deep
and intimate to be written out, and so she could find
no relief for her pain.

They did not have supper at New Moon in winter
time until Cousin Jimmy had finished his chores and
was ready to stay in for the night. So Emily was left
undisturbed in the garret.

From the dormer window she looked down on a
dreamland scene that would ordinarily have delighted
her. There was a red sunset behind the white, distant hills, shining through the dark trees like a great
fire; there was a delicate blue tracery of bare branch
shadows all over the crusted garden; there was a
pale, ethereal alpen-glow all over the southeastern
sky; and presently there was a little, lovely new
moon in the silvery arch over Lofty John's bush. But
Emily found no pleasure in any of them.

Presently she saw Miss Brownell coming up the lane,
under the white arms of the birches, with her mannish
stride.

"If my father was alive," said Emily, looking down at
her, "you would go away from this place with a flea in
your ear."

The minutes passed, each seeming very long to
Emily. At last Aunt Laura came up.

"Your Aunt Elizabeth wants you to come down to
the kitchen, Emily."

Aunt Laura's voice was kind and sad. Emily fought
down a sob. She hated to have Aunt Laura think she

had been naughty, but she could not trust herself to explain. Aunt Laura would sympathize and sympathy would break her down. She went silently down the two long flights of stairs before Aunt Laura and out to the kitchen.

The supper table was set and the candles were lighted. The big black-raftered kitchen looked spookish and weird, as it always did by candlelight. Aunt Elizabeth sat rigidly by the table and her face was very hard. Miss Brownell sat in the rocking-chair, her pale eyes glittering with triumphant malice. There seemed something baleful and poisonous in her very glance. Also, her nose was very red—which did not add to her charm.

Cousin Jimmy, in his grey jumper, was perched on the edge of the wood-box, whistling at the ceiling, and looking more gnome-like than ever. Perry was nowhere to be seen. Emily was sorry for this. The presence of Perry, who was on her side, would have been a great moral support.

"I am sorry to say, Emily, that I have been hearing some very bad things about your behaviour in school today," said Aunt Elizabeth.

"No, I don't think you are sorry," said Emily, gravely.

Now that the crisis had come she found herself able to confront it coolly—nay, more, to take a curious interest in it under all her secret fear and shame, as if some part of her had detached itself from the rest and was interestedly absorbing impressions and analyzing motives and describing settings. She felt that when she wrote about this scene later on she must not forget to describe the odd shadows the candle under Aunt Elizabeth's nose cast upward on her face, producing a rather skeletonic effect. As for Miss Brownell, could *she* ever have been a baby—a dimpled, fat, laughing baby? The thing was unbelievable.

"Don't speak impertinently to *me*," said Aunt Elizabeth.

"You see," said Miss Brownell, significantly.

"I don't mean to be impertinent, but you are *not* sorry," persisted Emily. "You are angry because you think I have disgraced New Moon, but you are a little glad that you have got some one to agree with you that I'm bad."

"What a *grateful* child," said Miss Brownell—flashing her eyes up at the ceiling—where they encountered a surprising sight. Perry Miller's head—and no more of him—was stuck down out of the "black hole" and on Perry Miller's upside-down face was a most disrespectful and impish grimace. Face and head disappeared in a flash, leaving Miss Brownell staring foolishly at the ceiling.

"You have been behaving disgracefully in school," said Aunt Elizabeth, who had not seen this by-play. "I am ashamed of you."

"It was not as bad as that, Aunt Elizabeth," said Emily steadily. "You see it was this way—"

"I don't want to hear anything more about it," said Aunt Elizabeth.

"But you must," cried Emily. "It isn't fair to listen only to *her* side. I was a little bad—but not so bad as she says—"

"Not another word! I have heard the whole story," said Aunt Elizabeth grimly.

"You heard a pack of lies," said Perry, suddenly sticking his head down through the black hole again.

Everybody jumped—even Aunt Elizabeth, who at once became angrier than ever because she *had* jumped.

"Perry Miller, come down out of that loft instantly!" she commanded.

"Can't," said Perry laconically.

"At once, I say!"

"Can't," repeated Perry, winking audaciously at Miss Brownell.

"Perry Miller, come down! I *will* be obeyed. I am mistress here *yet*."

"Oh, all right," said Perry cheerfully. "If I must."

He swung himself down until his toes touched the

ladder. Aunt Laura gave a little shriek. Everybody else seemed to be stricken dumb.

"I've just got my wet duds off," Perry was saying cheerfully, waving his legs about to get a foothold on the ladder while he hung to the sides of the black hole with his elbows. "Fell into the brook when I was watering the cows. Was going to put on dry ones—but just as you say—"

"Jimmy," implored poor Elizabeth Murray, surrendering at discretion. *She* could not cope with the situation.

"Perry, get back into that loft and get your clothes on this minute!" ordered Cousin Jimmy.

The bare legs shot up and disappeared. There was a chuckle as mirthful and malicious as an owl's beyond the black hole. Aunt Elizabeth gave a convulsive gasp of relief and turned to Emily. She was determined to regain ascendancy and Emily must be thoroughly humbled.

"Emily, kneel down here before Miss Brownell and ask her pardon for your conduct to-day," she said.

Into Emily's pale cheek came a scarlet protest. She could not do this—she would ask pardon of Miss Brownell but not on her knees. To kneel to this cruel woman who had hurt her so—she could not—would not do it. Her whole nature rose up in protest against such a humiliation.

"Kneel down," repeated Aunt Elizabeth.

Miss Brownell looked pleased and expectant. It would be very satisfying to see this child who had defied her kneeling before her as a penitent. Never again, Miss Brownell felt, would Emily be able to look levelly at her with those dauntless eyes that bespoke a soul untamable and free, no matter what punishment might be inflicted upon body or mind. The memory of this moment would always be with Emily—she could never forget that she had knelt in abasement. Emily felt this as clearly as Miss Brownell did and remained stubbornly on her feet.

"Aunt Elizabeth, *please* let me tell my side of the story," she pleaded.

"I have heard all I wish to hear of the matter. You will do as I say, Emily, or you will be outcast in this house until you do. No one will talk to you—play with you—eat with you—have anything to do with you until you have obeyed me."

Emily shuddered. *That* was a punishment she could not face. To be cut off from her world—she knew it would bring her to terms before long. She might as well yield at once—but, oh, the bitterness, the shame of it!

"A human being should not kneel to any one but God," said Cousin Jimmy, unexpectedly, still staring at the ceiling.

A sudden strange change came over Elizabeth Murray's proud, angry face. She stood very still, looking at Cousin Jimmy—stood so long that Miss Brownell made a motion of petulant impatience.

"Emily," said Aunt Elizabeth in a different tone," I was wrong—I shall not ask you to kneel. But you must apologize to your teacher—and I shall punish you later on."

Emily put her hands behind her and looked straight into Miss Brownell's eyes again.

"I am sorry for anything I did to-day that was wrong," she said, "and I ask your pardon for it."

Miss Brownell got on her feet. She felt herself cheated of a legitimate triumph. Whatever Emily's punishment would be she would not have the satisfaction of seeing it. She could have shaken "simple Jimmy Murray" with a right good will. But it would hardly do to show all she felt. Elizabeth Murray was not a trustee but she was the heaviest ratepayer in New Moon and had great influence with the School Board.

"I shall excuse your conduct if you behave your-self in future, Emily," she said coldly. "*I* feel that I have only done my duty in putting the matter before your aunt. No, thank you, Miss Murray, I cannot stay to supper—I want to get home before it is too dark."

"God speed all travellers," said Perry cheerfully, climbing down his ladder—this time with his clothes on.

Aunt Elizabeth ignored him—she was not going to have a scene with a hired boy before Miss Brownell. The latter switched herself out and Aunt Elizabeth looked at Emily.

"You will eat your supper alone to-night, Emily, in the pantry—you will have bread and milk only. And you will not speak one word to anyone until to-morrow morning."

"But you won't forbid me to think?" said Emily anxiously.

Aunt Elizabeth made no reply but sat haughtily down at the supper table. Emily went into the pantry and ate her bread and milk, with the odour of the delicious suasages the others were eating for savour. Emily liked sausages, and New Moon sausages were the last word in sausages. Elizabeth Burnley had brought the recipe out from the Old Country and its secret was carefully guarded. And Emily was hungry. But she had escaped the unbearable, and things might be worse. It suddenly occurred to her that she would write an epic poem in imitation of *The Lay Of The Last Minstrel.* Cousin Jimmy had read *The Lay* to her last Saturday. She would begin the first canto right off. When Laura Murray came into the pantry, Emily, her bread and milk only half eaten, was leaning her elbows on the dresser, gazing into space, with faintly moving lips and the light that never was on land or sea in her young eyes. Even the aroma of sausages was forgotten—was she not drinking from a fount of Castaly?

"Emily," said Aunt Laura, shutting the door, and looking very lovingly upon Emily out of her kind blue eyes, "you can talk to *me* all you want to. I don't like

Miss Brownell and I don't think you were altogether in the wrong—although of course you shouldn't be writing poetry when you have sums to do. And there are some ginger cookies in that box."

"I don't want to talk to any one, dear Aunt Laura— I'm too happy," said Emily dreamily. "I'm composing an epic—it is to be called *The White Lady*, and I've got twenty lines of it made already—and two of them are thrilling. The heroine wants to go into a convent and her father warns her that if she does she will never be able to

> *Come back to the life you gave*
> *With all its pleasures to the grave.*

Oh, Aunt Laura, when I composed those lines the flash came to me. And ginger cookies are nothing to me any more."

Aunt Laura smiled again.

"Not just now perhaps, dear. But when the moment of inspiration has passed it will do no harm to remember that the cookies in the box have not been counted and that they are as much mine as Elizabeth's."

17
Living Epistles

"Dear Father:

"O, I have such an exiting thing to tell you. I have been the heroin of an adventure. One day last week Ilse asked me if I would go and stay all night with her because her father was away and wouldn't be home till very late and Ilse said she wasn't fritened but very lonesome. So I asked Aunt Elizabeth if I could. I hardly dared hope, dear Father, that she would let me, for she doesn't aprove of little girls being away from home at night but to my surprise she said I could go very kindly. And then I heard her say in the pantry to Aunt Laura It is a shame the way the doctor leaves that poor child so much alone at nights. It is *wikked* of him. And Aunt Laura said The poor man is warped. You know he was not a bit like that before his wife— and then just as it was getting intresting Aunt Elizabeth gave Aunt Laura a nudge and said s-s-s-h, little pitchers have big ears. I knew she meant me though my ears are not big, only pointed. I do wish I could find out what Ilse's mother did. It worrys me after I go to bed. I lie awake for ever so long thinking about it. Ilse has no idea. Once she asked her father and he told her (in a *voice of thunder*) never to mention *that woman* to him again. And there is something else that worrys me too. I keep thinking of Silas Lee who killed his brother at the old well. How dreadful the poor man must have felt. And what is it to be warped.

"I went over to Ilses and we played in the garret. I like playing there because we dont have to be careful and tidy like we do in our garret. Ilses garret is very untidy and cant have been dusted for years. The rag room is worse than the rest. It is boarded off at one end of the garret and it is full of old close and bags of rags and broken furniture. I dont like the smell of it. The kitchen chimney goes up through it and things hang round it (or did). For all this is in the past now, dear Father.

"When we got tired playing we sat down on an old chest and talked. This is splendid in daytime I said but it must be awful queer at night. Mice, said Ilse,—and spiders and gosts. I dont believe in gosts I said skornfully. There isnt any such thing. (But maybe there is for all that, dear Father.) I believe this garret is hawnted, said Ilse. They say garrets always are. Nonsense I said. You know dear Father it would not do for a New Moon person to believe in gosts. But I felt very queer. Its easy to talk said Ilse beginning to be mad (though I wasnt trying to run down her garret) but you wouldnt stay here alone at night. I wouldnt mind it a bit I said. Then I dare you to do it said Ilse. I dare you to come up here at bedtime and sleep here all night. Then I saw I was in an awful skrape Father dear. It is a foolish thing to bost. I knew not what to do. It was dreadful to think of sleeping alone in that garret but if I didnt Ilse would always cast it up to me whenever we fought and worse than that she would tell Teddy and he would think me a coward. So I said proudly Ill do it Ilse Burnley and I'm not afraid to either. (But oh I was—inside.) The mice will run over you said Ilse. O I wouldn't be you for the world. It was mean of Ilse to make things worse than they were. But I could feel she admired me too and that helped me a great deal. We dragged an old feather bed out of the rag room and Ilse gave me a pillow and half her close. It was dark by this time and Ilse wouldn't go up into the garret again. So I said my prayers very carefully and then I took a lamp and started up. I am so used to candles now that the lamp made me nervus. Ilse said I looked scared to death. My knees shook dear Father but for the honnor of the Starrs (and the Murrays too) I went on. I had undressed in Ilses room, so I got right into bed and blew out the lamp. But I couldnt go to sleep for a long time. The moonlight made the garret look weerd. I dont know exactly what weerd means but I feel the garret was it. The bags and old close hanging from the beams looked like creatures. I thought I need not be fritened. The angels are here. But then I felt as if I would be as much fritened of angels as of anything else. And I could hear rats and mice scrambling over things. I thought What if a rat was to run over me, and then I thought that next day I would write out a descripshon of the garret by moonlight and my feelings. At last I heard the doctor driving in and then I heard him knocking round in the kitchen and I felt better and before very long I went to sleep and I dreamed a dreadful dream. I dreamed the door of the rag room opened and a big newspaper came out and chased me all around the garret. And then it went on fire and I could smell the smoke plain as plain and it was just on me when I skreamed and woke up. I was sitting right up in bed and the newspaper was gone but I could smell smoke still. I looked at the rag room door and smoke was coming out under it and I saw firelight through the cracks of the boards. I just yelled at the top of my voice and tore down to Ilses room and she rushed across the hall and woke her father. He said dam but he got right up and then all three of us kept running up and down the garret stairs with pails of water and we made an awful mess but we got the fire out. It was just the bags of wool that had been hanging close to the chimney that had caught fire. When all was over the doctor wiped the persperation from his manly brow and said That was a close call. A few minutes later would have been too late. I put on a fire when I came in to make a cup of tea and I suppose those bags must have caught fire from a spark. I see theres a hole here where the plaster has tumbled out. I must have this whole place cleaned out. How in the world did you come to diskover the fire, Emily. I was sleeping in the garret I said. Sleeping in the garret said the doctor, what in—what the—*what* were you doing there. Ilse dared me I said. She said Id be too scared to stay there and I said I wouldnt. I fell asleep and woke up and smelled smoke. You little devil, said the doctor. I suppose it was a dreadful thing to be called a devil but the doctor looked at me so admiringly that I felt as if he was paying me a complement. He has queer ways of talking. Ilse says the only time he ever said a kind thing to her was once when she had a sore throat he called her "a poor little animal" and looked as if he was sorry for her. I feel sure Ilse feels dreadfully bad because her father doesnt like her though she pretends she does not care. But oh dear Father there is more to tell. Yesterday the Shrewsbury *Weekly Times* came and in the Blair Notes it told all about the fire at the doctors and said it had been fortunately diskovered in time by Miss Emily Starr. I cant tell you what I felt like when I saw my name in the paper. I felt *famus*. And I never was called Miss in ernest before.

"Last Saturday Aunt Elizabeth and Aunt Laura went to Shrewsbury for the day and left Cousin Jimmy and me to keep house. We had such fun and Cousin Jimmy let me skim all the milk pans. But after dinner unexpected company came and there was no cake in the house. That was a dreadful thing. It never happened before in the annels of New Moon. Aunt Elizabeth had toothache all day yesterday and Aunt Laura was away at Priest Pond visiting Great Aunt Nancy, so no cake was made. I prayed about it and then I went to work and made a cake by Aunt Laura's receet and it turned out all right. Cousin Jimmy helped me set the table and get supper, and I poured the tea and never slopped any over in the saucers. You would have been proud of me Father. Mrs. Lewis took a second piece of cake and said I would know Elizabeth Murrays cake if I found it in central Africa. I said not a word for the honnor of the family. But I felt very proud. I had saved the Murrays from disgrace. When Aunt Elizabeth came home and heard the tale she looked grim and tasted a piece that was left and then she said Well, you have got *some* Murray in you anyway. That is the first time Aunt Elizabeth has ever praised me. She had three teeth out so they will not ache any more. I am glad for her sake. Before I went to bed I got the cook book and picked out all the things Id like to make. Queen Pudding, Seafoam Sauce, Blackeyed Susans, Pigs In Blankets. They sound just lovely.

"I can see such beautiful fluffy white clouds over Lofty Johns bush. I wish I could sore up and drop right into them. I cant believe they would be wet and messy like Teddy says. Teddy cut my initials and his together on the Monark of The Forest but somebody has cut them out. I don't know whether it was Perry or Ilse.

"Miss Brownell hardly ever gives me good deportment marks now and Aunt Elizabeth is much displeased on Friday nights but Aunt Laura understands. I wrote an account of the afternoon when Miss Brownell made fun of my poems and put it in an old envelope and wrote Aunt Elizabeths name on it and put it among my papers. If I die of consumption Aunt Elizabeth will find it and know the rites of it and mourn that she was so unjust to me. But I don't think I will die because Im getting much fatter and Ilse told me she heard her father tell Aunt Laura I would be handsome if I had more color. Is it wrong to want to be handsome, dearest Father. Aunt Elizabeth says it is and when I said to her Wouldn't *you* like to be handsome, Aunt Elizabeth, she seemed anoyed about something.

"Miss Brownell has had a spite at Perry ever since that evening and treats him very mean but he is meek and says he wont kick up any fuss in school because he wants to learn and get ahead. He keeps saying his rymes are as good as mine and I know they are not and it exassperates me. If I do not pay attention all the time in school Miss Brownell says I suppose you are composing—poetry Emily and then everybody laughs. No not everybody. I must not exagerate. Teddy and Perry and Ilse and Jennie never laugh. It is funny that I like Jennie so well now and I hated her so that first day in school. Her eyes are not piggy after all. They are small but they are jolly and twinkly. She is quite poplar in school. I do hate Frank Barker. He took my new reader and wrote in a big sprawly way all over the front page

> *Steal not this book for fear of shame*
> *For on it is the owners name*
> *And when you die the Lord will say*
> *Where is that book you stole away*
> *And when you say you do not know*
> *The Lord will say go down below.*

*　　*　　*

"That is not a refined poem and besides it is not the rite way to speak about God. I tore out the leaf and burned it and Aunt Elizabeth was angry and even when I explained why her rath was not apeased. Ilse says she is going to call God Alla after this. I think it is a nicer name myself. It is so soft and doesn't sound so stern. But I fear its not relijus enough.

"May 20.

"Yesterday was my birthday dear Father. It will soon be a year since I came to New Moon. I feel as if I had always lived here. I have grown two inches. Cousin Jimmy measured me by a mark on the dairy door. My birthday was very nice. Aunt Laura made a lovely cake and gave me a beautiful new white pettycoat with an embroidered flounce. She had run a blue ribbon through it but Aunt Elizabeth made her pull it out. And Aunt Laura also gave me that piece of pink satin brokade in her burow drawer. I have longed for it ever since I saw it but never hoped to possess it. Ilse asked me what I meant to do with it but I dont mean to do anything with it. Only keep it up here in the garret with my treasures and look at it, because it is beautiful. Aunt Elizabeth gave me a dixonary. That was a useful present. I feel I ought to like it. You will soon notice an improovement in my spelling, I hope. The only trouble is when I am writing something interesting I get so exited it is just awful to have to stop and hunt up a word to see how it is spelled. I looked up ween in it and Miss Brownell was right. I did not know what it really meant. It rymed so well with sheen and I thought it meant to behold or see but it means to think. Cousin Jimmy gave me a big thick blank book. I am so proud of it. It will be so nice to write pieces in. But I will still use the letter-bills to write to you, dear Father, because I can fold each one up by itself and adress it like a real letter. Teddy gave me a picture of myself. He painted it in water colors and called it The Smiling Girl. I look as if I was listening to something that made me very happy. Ilse says it flatters me. It does make me better looking than I am but not any better looking than I would be if I could have a bang. Teddy says he is going to paint a real big picture of me when he grows up. Perry walked all the way to Shrewsbury to get me a necklace of pearl beads and lost it. He had no more money so he went home to Stovepipe Town and got a young hen from his Aunt Tom and gave me that. He is a very persistent boy. I am to have all the eggs the hen lays to sell the pedler for myself. Ilse gave me a box of candy. I am only going to eat one piece a day to make it last a long time. I wanted Ilse to eat some but she said she wouldnt because it would be mean to help eat a present you had given and I insisted and then we fought over it and Ilse said I was a caterwawling quadruped (which was ridiklus) and didn't know enough to come in when it rained. And I said I knew enough to have some manners at least. Ilse got so mad she went home but she cooled off soon and came back for supper.

"It is raining tonight and it sounds like fairies feet dancing over the garret roof. If it had not rained Teddy was going to come down and help me look for the Lost Dimond. Wouldnt it be splendid if we could find it.

"Cousin Jimmy is fixing up the garden. He lets me help him and I have a little flower bed of my own. I always run out first thing every morning to see how much the things have grown since yesterday. Spring is such a happyfying time isnt it, Father. The little Blue People are all out round the summer house. That is what Cousin Jimmy calls the violets and I think it is lovely. He has names like that for all the flowers. The roses are the Queens and the June lilies are the Snow Ladies and the tulips are the Gay Folk and the daffodils are the Golden Ones and the China Asters are My Pink Friends.

"Mike II is here with me, sitting on the window-sill. Mike is a smee cat. Smee is not in the dictionary. It is a word I invented myself. I could not think of any

English word which just describes Mike II so I made this up. It means sleek and glossy and soft and fluffy all in one and something else besides that I cant express.

"Aunt Laura is teaching me to sew. She says I must learn to make a hem on muslin that can't be seen (tradishun). I hope she will teach me how to make point lace some day. All the Murrays of New Moon have been noted for making point lace (I mean all the women Murrays). None of the girls in school can make point lace. Aunt Laura says she will make me a point lace hangkerchief when I get married. All the New Moon brides had point lace hangkerchiefs except my mother who ran away. But you didn't mind her not having one did you Father. Aunt Laura talks a good bit about my mother to me but not when Aunt Elizabeth is around. Aunt Elizabeth never mentions her name. Aunt Laura wants to show me Mothers room but she has never been able to find the key yet because Aunt Elizabeth keeps it hid. Aunt Laura says Aunt Elizabeth loved my mother very much. You would think she would love her daughter some wouldnt you. But she doesnt. She is just bringing me up as a duty.

"JUNE 1.

"Dear Father:

"Th ... has been a very important day. I wrote my first letter, I mean the first letter that was really to go in the mail. It was to Great-Aunt Nancy who lives at Priest Pond and is very old. She wrote Aunt Elizabeth and said I might write now and then to a poor old woman. My heart was touched and I wanted to. Aunt Elizabeth said We might as well let her. And she said to me You must be careful to write a nice letter and I will read it over when it is written. If you make a good impression on Aunt Nancy she may do something for you. I wrote the letter very carefully but it didn't sound a bit like me when it was finished. I couldn't write a good letter when I knew Aunt Elizabeth was going to read it. I felt paralyzed.

"JUNE 7.

"Dear Father, my letter did not make a good impression on Great-Aunt Nancy. She did not answer it but she wrote Aunt Elizabeth that I must be a very stupid child to write such a stupid letter. I feel insulted because I am not stupid. Perry says he feels like going to Priest Pond and knocking the daylights out of Great-Aunt Nancy. I told him he must not talk like that about my family, and anyhow I dont see how knocking the daylights out of Great-Aunt Nancy would make her change her opinion about me being stupid. (I wonder what daylights are and how you knock them out of people.)

"I have three cantos of *The White Lady* finished. I have the heroin imured in a convent and I dont know how to get her out because I am not a Catholic. I suppose it would have been better if I had a Protestant heroin but there were no Protestants in the days of shivalry. I might have asked Lofty John last year but this year I cant because Ive never spoken to him since he played that horrid joke on me about the apple. When I meet him on the road I look straight ahead just as lofty as he does. I have called my pig after him to get square. Cousin Jimmy has given me a little pig for my own. When it is sold I am to have the money. I mean to give some for missionaries and put the rest in the bank to go to my educashun. And I thought if I ever had a pig I would call it Uncle Wallace. But now it does not seem to me propper to call pigs after your uncles even if you dont like them.

"Teddy and Perry and Ilse and I play we are living in the days of shivalry and Ilse and I are distressed damsels reskued by galant knites. Teddy made a splendid suit of armor out of old barrel staves and then Perry made a better one out of old tin boilers hammered flat with a broken saucepan for a helmit. Sometimes we play at the Tansy Patch. I have a queer feeling that Teddys mother hates me this summer. Last summer she just didn't like me. Smoke and Buttercup are not there now. They disappeared misteriously in the winter. Teddy says he feels sure his mother poisoned them because she thought he was getting too fond of them. Teddy is teaching me to whistle but Aunt Laura says it is unladylike. So many jolly things seem to be unladylike. Sometimes I almost wish my aunts were infidels like Dr. Burnly. *He* never bothers whether Ilse is unladylike or not. But no, it would not be good manners to be an infidel. It would not be a New Moon tradishun.

"Today I taught Perry that he must not eat with his knife. He wants to learn all the *rules of etiket.* And I am helping him learn a recitation for school examination day. I wanted Ilse to do it but she was mad because he asked me first and she wouldnt. But she should because she is a far better reciter than I am. I am too nervus.

"JUNE 14.

"Dear Father, we have composition in school now and I learned today that you put in things like this " " when you write anything anybody has said. I didnt know that before. I must go over all my letters to you and put them in. And after a question you must put a mark like this ? and when a letter is left out a postroffe which is a comma up in the air. Miss Brownell is sarkastic but she *does* teach you things. I am putting that down because I want to be fair even if I do hate her. And she is interesting although she is not nice. I have written a descripshun of her on a letter-bill. I like writing about people I don't like better than about those I do like. Aunt Laura is nicer to live with than Aunt Elizabeth, but Aunt Elizabeth is nicer to write about. I can deskribe *her* fawlts but I feel wikked and ungrateful if I say anything that is not complementary about dear Aunt Laura. Aunt Elizabeth has locked your books away and says I'm not to have them till I'm grown up. Just as if I wouldn't be careful of them, dear Father. She says I wouldn't because she found that when I was reading one of them I put a tiny pencil dot under every beautiful word. It didn't hurt the book a bit, dear Father. Some of the words were dingles, pearled, musk, dappled, intervales, glen, bosky, piping, shimmer, crisp, beechen, ivory. I think those are all lovely words, Father.

"Aunt Laura lets me read her copy of A Pilgrims Progress on Sundays. I call the big hill in the road to White Cross the Delectable Mountain because it is such a beautiful one.

"Teddy lent me 3 books of poetry. One of them was Tennyson and I have learned The Bugle Song off by heart so I will always have it. One was Mrs. Browning. She is lovely. I would like to meet her. I suppose I will when I die but that may be a long time away. The other was just one poem called Sohrab and Rustum. After I went to bed I cried over it. Aunt Elizabeth said "what are you sniffling about?" I wasn't sniffling—I was weeping sore. She made me tell her and then she said "You must be crazy." But I couldn't go to sleep until I had thought out a different end for it—a happy one.

"JUNE 25.

"Dear Father:

"There has been a dark shadow over this day. I dropped my cent in church. It made a dreadful noise. I felt as if everybody looked at me. Aunt Elizabeth was much annoyed. Perry dropped his too soon after. He told me after church he did it on purpose because he thought it would make me feel better but it didn't because I was afraid the people would think it was me dropping mine again. Boys do such queer things. I hope the minister did not hear because I am beginning to like him. I never liked him much before last Tuesday. His family are all boys and I suppose he doesn't understand little girls very well. Then he called at New Moon. Aunt Laura and Aunt Elizabeth were both away and I was in the kitchen alone. Mr. Dare came in and sat down on Saucy Sal who was asleep in the rocking-chair. He was comfortable but Saucy Sal wasn't. He didn't sit on her stomach. If he had I suppose he would have killed her. He just sat on her legs and tail. Sal yowled but Mr. Dare is a little deaf and didn't hear her and I was too shy to tell him. But Cousin Jimmy came in just as he was asking me if I knew my catechism and said "Catechism, is it? Lawful heart, man, listen to that poor dum beast. Get up if you're a Christian." So Mr. Dare got up and said, "Dear me, this is very remarkable. I thought I felt something moving."

"I thought I would write this to you, dear Father, because it struck me as humerus.

"When Mr. Dare finished asking me questions I thought it was my turn and I would ask him some about some things I've wanted to know for years. I asked him if he thought God was very perticular about every little thing I did and if he thought my cats would go to heaven. He said he hoped I never did wrong things and that animals had no souls. And I asked him why we shouldn't put new wine in old bottles. Aunt Elizabeth does with her dandelion wine and the old bottles do just as well as new ones. He explained quite kindly that the Bible bottles were made of skins and got rotten when they were old. It made it quite clear to me. Then I told him I was worried because I knew I ought to love God better than anything but there were things I loved better than God. He said "What things?" and I said flowers and stars and the Wind Woman and the Three Princesses and things like that. And he smiled and said "But they are just a part of God, Emily—every beautiful thing is." And all at once I liked him ever so much and didn't feel shy with him any more. He preeched a sermon on heaven last Sunday. It seemed like a dull place. I think it must be more exiting than that. I wonder what I will do when I go to heaven since I cant sing. I wonder if they will let me write poetry. But I think church is interesting. Aunt Elizabeth and Aunt Laura always read their Bibles before the servis begins but I like to stare around and see everybody and wonder what they are thinking of. It's so nice to hear the silk dresses swishing up the isles. Bustles are very fashionable now but Aunt Elizabeth will not wear them. I think Aunt Elizabeth *would* look funny with a bustle. Aunt Laura wears a very little one.

"Your lovingest daughter,
"*Emily B. Starr.*

"P. S. Dear Father, it is lovely to write to you. But O, I never get an answer back.
"*E. B. S.*"

18
Father Cassidy

Consternation reigned at New Moon. Everybody was desperately unhappy. Aunt Laura cried. Aunt Elizabeth was so cantankerous that there was no living with her. Cousin Jimmy went about as one distracted and Emily gave up worrying about Ilse's mother and Silas Lee's remorseful ghost after she went to bed, and worried over this new trouble. For it had all originated in her disregard of New Moon tradition in making calls on Lofty John, and Aunt Elizabeth did not mince matters in telling her so. If she, Emily Byrd Starr, had never gone to Lofty John's she would never have eaten the Big Sweet apple, and if she had never eaten the Big Sweet apple Lofty John would not have played a joke on her and if he had not played a joke on her Aunt Elizabeth would never have gone and said bitter, Murray-like things to him; and if Aunt Elizabeth had never said bitter Murray-like things to him Lofty John would not have become offended and revengeful; and if Lofty

John had not become offended and revengeful he would never have taken it into his lofty head to cut down the beautiful grove to the north of New Moon.

For this was exactly where this house-that-Jack-built progression had landed them all. Lofty John had announced publicly in the Blair Water blacksmith shop that he was going to cut down the bush as soon as harvest was over—every last tree and sapling was to be laid low. The news was promptly carried to New Moon and upset the inhabitants thereof as they had not been upset for years. In their eyes it was nothing short of a catastrophe.

Elizabeth and Laura could hardly bring themselves to believe it. The thing was incredible. That big, thick, protecting bush of spruce and hardwood had *always* been there; it belonged to New Moon *morally*; even Lofty John Sullivan would not *dare* to cut it down. But Lofty John had an uncomfortable reputation for doing what he said he would do; that was a part of his loftiness; and if he did—if he did—

"New Moon will be ruined," wailed poor Aunt Laura. "It will look *dreadful—all* its beauty will go—and we will be left open to the north wind and the sea storms— we have always been so warm and sheltered here. And Jimmy's garden will be ruined too."

"This is what comes of bringing Emily here," said Aunt Elizabeth.

It was a cruel thing to say, even when all allowances were made,—cruel and unjust, since her own sharp tongue and Murray sarcasm had had quite as much to do with it as Emily. But she said it and it pierced Emily to the heart with a pang that left a scar for years. Poor Emily did not feel as if she needed any additional anguish. She was already feeling so wretched that she could not eat or sleep. Elizabeth Murray, angry and unhappy as she was, slept soundly at nights; but beside her in the darkness, afraid to move or turn, lay a slender little creature whose tears, stealing silently down her cheeks, could not ease her breaking heart.

For Emily thought her heart *was* breaking; she couldn't go on living and suffering like this. Nobody could.

Emily had lived long enough at New Moon for it to get pretty thoroughly into her blood. Perhaps it had even been born there. At any rate, when she came to it she fitted into its atmosphere as a hand into a glove. She loved it as well as if she had lived there all her short life—loved every stick and stone and tree and blade of grass about it—every nail in the old kitchen floor, every cushion of green moss on the dairy roof, every pink and white columbine that grew in the old orchard, every "tradition" of its history. To think of its beauty being in a large measure reft from it was agony to her. And to think of Cousin Jimmy's garden being ruined! Emily loved that garden almost as much as he did; why, it was the pride of Cousin Jimmy's life that he could grow these plants and shrubs that would winter nowhere else in P. E. Island; if the northern shelter were removed they would die. And to think of that beautiful bush itself being cut down—the Today Road and the Yesterday Road and the Tomorrow Road being swept out of existence—the stately Monarch of the Forest discrowned—the little playhouse where she and Ilse had such glorious hours destroyed—the whole lovely, ferny, intimate place torn out of her life at one fell swoop.

Oh, Lofty John had chosen and timed his vengeance well!

When would the blow fall? Every morning Emily listened miserably as she stood on the sandstone door-step of the kitchen, for the sound of axe blows on the clear September air. Every evening when she returned from school she dreaded to see that the work of de-struction had begun. She pined and fretted. There were times when it seemed to her she couldn't bear her life any longer. Every day Aunt Elizabeth said some-thing imputing the whole blame to her and the child grew morbidly sensitive about it. Almost she wished

Lofty John would begin and be done with it. If Emily had ever heard the classic story of Damocles she would have heartily sympathized with him. If she had had any hope that it would do any good she would have swallowed Murray pride and Starr pride and every other kind of pride and gone on her knees to Lofty John to entreat him to hold his revengeful hand. But she believed it would not. Lofty John had left no doubt in anybody's mind as to his bitter determination in the matter. There was much talk about it in Blair Water and some were very well pleased at this blow to New Moon pride and prestige, and some held that it was low and unclean behaviour on Lofty John's part, and all agreed that this was what they had prophesied all along as bound to happen some day when the old Murray-Sullivan feud of three generations should have come to its inevitable head. The only surprising thing was that Lofty John hadn't done it long ago. He had always hated Elizabeth Murray since their schooldays, when her tongue had not spared him.

One day by the banks of Blair Water Emily sat down and wept. She had been sent to trim the dead blossoms off the rosebushes on Grandmother Murray's grave; having finished her task she had not the heart to go back to the house where Aunt Elizabeth was making everybody miserable because she was herself so unhappy. Perry had reported that Lofty John had stated the day before at the blacksmith's that he was going to begin cutting down the big bush on Monday morning.

"I *can't* bear it," sobbed Emily to the rosebushes.

A few late roses nodded at her; the Wind Woman combed and waved and stirred the long green grasses on the graves where proud Murrays, men and women, slept calmly, unstirred by old feuds and passions; the September sunlight shone beyond on old harvest fields mellowly bright and serene, and very softly against its green, shrub-hung bank, purred and lapped the blue Blair Water.

"I don't see why God doesn't *stop* Lofty John," said

Emily passionately. Surely the New Moon Murrays had a right to expect that much from Providence.

Teddy came whistling down the pasture, the notes of his tune blowing across the Blair Water like elfin drops of sound, vaulted the graveyard fence and perched his lean, graceful body irreverently on the "Here I stay" of Great-Grandmother Murray's flat tombstone.

"What's the matter?" he said.

"Everything's the matter," said Emily, a little crossly. Teddy had no business to be looking so cheerful. She was used to more sympathy from Teddy and it aggravated her not to find it. "Don't you know Lofty John is going to begin cutting down the bush Monday?"

Teddy nodded.

"Yep. Ilse told me. But look here, Emily, I've thought of something. Lofty John wouldn't dare cut down that bush if the priest told him not to, would he?"

"Why?"

"Because the Catholics have to do just what their priests tell them to, haven't they?"

"I don't know—I don't know anything about them. *We* are Presbyterians."

Emily gave her head a little toss. Mrs. Kent was known to be an "English Church" woman and though Teddy went to the Presbyterian Sunday School, that fact gave him scanty standing among bred-in-the-bone Presbyterian circles.

"If your Aunt Elizabeth went to Father Cassidy at White Cross and asked him to stop Lofty John, maybe he'd do it," persisted Teddy.

"Aunt Elizabeth would never do that," said Emily positively. "I'm sure of it. She's too proud."

"Not even to save the bush?"

"Not even for that."

"Then I guess nothing can be done," said Teddy rather crest-fallen. "Look here—see what I've made. This is a picture of Lofty John in purgatory, with three little devils sticking red-hot pitch forks into him. I copied some of it out of one of mother's books—Dante's

Infernal, I think it was—but I put Lofty John in place of the man in the book. You can have it."

"I don't want it." Emily uncoiled her legs and got up. She was past the stage when inflicting imaginary torments on Lofty John could comfort her. She had already slain him in several agonizing ways during her night vigils. But an idea had come to her—a daring, breathless idea. "I must go home now, Teddy—it's supper time."

Teddy pocketed his despised sketch—which was really a wonderful bit of work if either of them had had the sense to know it; the expression of anguish in Lofty John's face as a merry little devil touched him up with a pitchfork would have been the despair of many a trained artist. He went home wishing he could help Emily; it was all wrong that a creature like Emily—with soft purple-gray eyes and a smile that made you think of all sorts of wonderful things you couldn't put into words—should be unhappy. Teddy felt so worried about it that he added a few more devils to his sketch of Lofty John in purgatory and lengthened the prongs of their pitchforks quite considerably.

Emily went home with a determined twist to her mouth. She ate as much supper as she could—which wasn't much, for Aunt Elizabeth's face would have destroyed her appetite if she had had any—and then sneaked out of the house by the front door. Cousin Jimmy was working in his garden but he did not call her. Cousin Jimmy was always very sorrowful now. Emily stood a moment on the Grecian porch and looked at Lofty John's bush—green-bosomed, waving, all lovely. Would it be a desecrated waste of stumps by Monday night? Goaded by the thought Emily cast fear and hesitation to the winds and started briskly off down the lane. When she reached the gate she turned to the left on the long red road of mystery that ran up the Delectable Mountain. She had never been on that road before; it ran straight to White Cross; Emily was going to the parish house there to interview Father Cassidy. It was two miles to White Cross and Emily walked it all too soon—not because it was a beautiful road of wind and wild fern, haunted by little rabbits—but because she dreaded what awaited her at the end. She had been trying to think what she should say—how she should say it; but her invention failed her. She had no acquaintance with Catholic priests, and couldn't imagine how you should talk to them at all. They were even more mysterious and unknowable than ministers. Suppose Father Cassidy should be dreadfully angry at her daring to come there and ask a favour. Perhaps it *was* a dreadful thing to do from every point of view. And very likely it would do no good. Very likely Father Cassidy would refuse to interfere with Lofty John, who was a good Catholic, while she was, in his opinion, a heretic. But for any chance, even the faintest, of averting the calamity impending over New Moon, Emily would have faced the entire Sacred College. Horribly frightened, miserably nervous as she was, the idea of turning back never occurred to her. She was only sorry that she hadn't put on her Venetian beads. They might have impressed Father Cassidy.

Although Emily had never been to White Cross she knew the parish house when she saw it—a fine, tree-embowered residence near the big white chapel with the flashing gilt cross on its spire and the four gilt angels, one on each of the little spires at the corners. Emily thought them very beautiful as they gleamed in the light of the lowering sun, and wished they could have some on the plain white church at Blair Water. She couldn't understand why Catholics should have all the angels. But there was not time to puzzle over this, for the door was opening and the trim little maid was looking a question.

"Is—Father Cassidy—at—home?" asked Emily, rather jerkily.

"Yes."

"Can—I—see—him?"

"Come in," said the little maid. Evidently there was

no difficulty about seeing Father Cassidy—no mysterious ceremonies such as Emily had half expected, even if she were allowed to see him at all. She was shown into a book-lined room and left there, while the maid went to call Father Cassidy, who, she said, was working in the garden. *That* sounded quite natural and encouraging. If Father Cassidy worked in a garden, he could not be so very terrible.

Emily looked about her curiously. She was in a very pretty room—with cosy chairs, and pictures and flowers. Nothing alarming or uncanny about it—except a huge black cat who was sitting on the top of one of the bookcases. It was really an enormous creature. Emily adored cats and had always felt at home with any of them. But she had never seen such a cat as this. What with its size and its insolent, gold-hued eyes, set like living jewels in its black velvet face, it did not seem to belong to the same species as nice, cuddly, respectable kittens at all. Mr. Dare would never have had such a beast about his manse. All Emily's dread of Father Cassidy returned.

And then in came Father Cassidy, with the friendliest smile in the world. Emily took him in with her level glance as was her habit—or gift—and never again in the world was she the least bit afraid of Father Cassidy. He was big and broad-shouldered, with brown eyes and brown hair; and his very face was so deeply tanned from his inveterate habit of going about bareheaded in merciless sunshine, that it was brown, too. Emily thought he looked just like a big nut—a big, brown, wholesome nut.

Father Cassidy looked at her as he shook hands; Emily had one of her visitations of beauty just then. Excitement had brought a wildrose hue to her face, the sunlight brought out the watered-silk gloss of her black hair; her eyes were softly dark and limpid; but it was at her ears Father Cassidy suddenly bent to look. Emily had a moment of agonized wonder if they were clean.

"She's got pointed ears," said Father Cassidy, in a

thrilling whisper. "Pointed ears! I *knew* she came straight from fairyland the minute I saw her. Sit down, Elf—if elves do sit—sit down and give me the latest news av Titania's court."

Emily's foot was now on her native heath. Father Cassidy talked her language, and he talked it in such a mellow, throaty voice, slurring his "ofs" ever so softly as became a proper Irishman. But she shook her head a little sadly. With the burden of her errand on her soul she could not play the part of ambassadress from Elfland.

"I'm only Emily Starr of New Moon," she said; and then gasped hurriedly, because there must be no deception—no sailing under false colours, "and I'm a Protestant."

"And a very nice little Protestant you are," said Father Cassidy. "But for sure I'm a bit disappointed. I'm used to Protestants—the woods hereabouts being full av them—but it's a hundred years since the last elf called on me."

Emily stared. Surely Father Cassidy wasn't a hundred years old. He didn't look more than fifty. Perhaps, though, Catholic priests did live longer than other people. She didn't know exactly what to say so she said, a bit lamely.

"I see you have a cat."

"Wrong." Father Cassidy shook his head and groaned dismally. "A cat has me."

Emily gave up trying to understand Father Cassidy. He was nice but ununderstandable. She let it go at that. And she must get on with her errand.

"You are a kind of minister, aren't you?" she asked timidly. She didn't know whether Father Cassidy would like being called a minister.

"Kind av," he agreed amiably. "And you see ministers and priests can't do their own swaring. They have to keep cats to do it for them. I never knew any cat that could sware as genteelly and effectively as the B'y."

"Is that what you call him?" asked Emily, looking at

the black cat in some awe. It seemed hardly safe to discuss him right before his face.

"That's what he calls himself. My mother doesn't like him because he steals the cream. Now, *I* don't mind his doing that; no, it's his way av licking his jaws after it that I can't stand. Oh, B'y, we've a fairy calling on us. Be excited for once, I implore you—there's a duck av a cat."

The B'y refused to be excited. He winked an insolent eye at Emily.

"Have you any idea what goes on in the head av a cat, elf?"

What queer questions Father Cassidy asked. Yet Emily thought she would like his questions if she were not so worried. Suddenly Father Cassidy leaned across the table and said,

"Now, just what's bothering you?"

"I'm so unhappy," said Emily piteously.

"So are lots av other people. Everybody is unhappy by spells. But creatures who have pointed ears shouldn't be unhappy. It's only mortals who should be that."

"Oh, please—please—" Emily wondered what she should call him. Would it offend him if a Protestant called him "Father"? But she had to risk it—"please, Father Cassidy, I'm in such trouble and I've come to ask a *great favour* of you."

Emily told him the whole tale from beginning to end—the old Murray-Sullivan feud, her erstwhile friendship with Lofty John, the Big Sweet apple, the unhappy consequence, and Lofty John's threatened revenge. The B'y and Father Cassidy listened with equal gravity until she had finished. Then the B'y winked at her, but Father Cassidy put his long brown fingers together.

"Humph," he said.

("That's the first time," reflected Emily, "that I've ever heard anyone outside of a book say 'Humph.'")

"Humph," said Father Cassidy again. "And you want me to put a stop to this nefarious deed?"

"If you can," said Emily. "Oh, it would be so splendid if you could. Will you—will you?"

Father Cassidy fitted his fingers still more carefully together.

"I'm afraid I can hardly invoke the power av the keys to prevent Lofty John from disposing as he wishes av his own lawful property, you know, elf."

Emily didn't understand the allusion to the keys but she did understand that Father Cassidy was declining to bring the lever of the Church to bear on Lofty John. There was no hope, then. She could not keep the tears of disappointment out of her eyes.

"Oh, come now, darling, don't cry," implored Father Cassidy. "Elves never cry—they can't. It would break my heart to discover you weren't av the Green Folk. You may call yourself av New Moon and av any religion you like, but the fact remains that you belong to the Golden Age and the old gods. That's why I must save your precious bit av greenwood for you."

Emily stared.

"I think it can be done," Father Cassidy went on. "I think if I go to Lofty John and have a heart-to-heart talk with him I can make him see reason. Lofty John and I are very good friends. He's a reasonable creature, if you know how to take him—which means to flatter his vanity judiciously. I'll put it to him, not as priest to parishioner, but as man to man, that no decent Irishman carries on a feud with women and that no sensible person is going to destroy for nothing but a grudge those fine old trees that have taken half a century to grow and can never be replaced. Why the man who cuts down such a tree except when it is really necessary should be hanged as high as Haman on a gallows made from the wood av it."

(Emily thought she would write that last sentence of Father Cassidy's down in Cousin Jimmy's blank book when she got home.)

"But I won't say *that* to Lofty John," concluded Father Cassidy. "Yes, Emily av New Moon, I think we can consider it a settled thing that your bush will not be cut down."

Suddenly Emily felt very happy. Somehow she had entire confidence in Father Cassidy. She was sure he would twist Lofty John around his little finger.

"Oh, I can never thank you enough!" she said earnestly.

"That's true, so don't waste breath trying. And now tell me things. Are there any more av you? And how long have you been yourself?"

"I'm twelve years old—I haven't any brothers or sisters. And I *think* I'd better be going home."

"Not till you've had a bite av lunch."

"Oh, thank you, I've had my supper."

"Two hours ago and a two-mile walk since. Don't tell me. I'm sorry I haven't any nectar and ambrosia on hand—such food as elves eat—and not even a saucer av moonshine—but my mother makes the best plum cake av any woman in P. E. Island. And we keep a cream cow. Wait here a bit. Don't be afraid av the B'y. He eats tender little Protestants sometimes, but he never meddles with leprechauns."

When Father Cassidy came back his mother came with him, carrying a tray. Emily had expected to see her big and brown too, but she was the tiniest woman imaginable, with snow-white, silky hair, mild blue eyes, and pink cheeks.

"Isn't she the sweetest thing in the way av mothers?" asked Father Cassidy. "I keep her to look at. Av course—" Father Cassidy dropped his voice to a pig's whisper— "there's something odd about her. I've known that woman to stop right in the middle av housecleaning, and go off and spend an afternoon in the woods. Like yourself, I'm thinking she has some truck with fairies."

Mrs. Cassidy smiled, kissed Emily, said she must go out and finish her preserving, and trotted off.

"Now you sit right down here, Elf, and be human for ten minutes and we'll have a friendly snack."

Emily *was* hungry—a nice comfortable feeling she hadn't experienced for a fortnight. Mrs. Cassidy's plum cake was all her reverend son claimed, and the cream cow seemed to be no myth.

"What do you think av me now?" asked Father Cassidy suddenly, finding Emily's eyes fixed on him speculatively.

Emily blushed. She had been wondering if she dared ask another favour of Father Cassidy.

"I think you are awfully good," she said.

"I *am* awfully good," agreed Father Cassidy. "I'm so good that I'll do what you want me to do—for I feel there's something else you want me to do."

"I'm in a scrape and I've been in it all summer. You see"—Emily was very sober—"I am a poetess."

"Holy Mike! That *is* serious. I don't know if I can do much for you. How long have you been that way?"

"Are you making fun of me?" asked Emily gravely.

Father Cassidy swallowed something besides plum cake.

"The saints forbid! It's only that I'm rather overcome. To be after entertaining a lady av New Moon—and an elf—and a poetess all in one is a bit too much for a humble praste like meself. Have another slice av cake and tell me all about it."

"It's like this—I'm writing an epic."

Father Cassidy suddenly leaned over and gave Emily's wrist a little pinch.

"I just wanted to see if you were real," he explained. "Yes—yes, you're writing an epic—go on. I think I've got my second wind now."

"I began it last spring. I called it *The White Lady* first but now I've changed it to *The Child of the Sea*. Don't you think that's a better title?"

"Much better."

"I've got three cantos done, and I can't get any further because there's something I don't know and can't find out. I've been so worried about it."

"What is it?"

"My epic," said Emily, diligently devouring plum cake, "is about a very beautiful high-born girl who was stolen away from her real parents when she was a baby and brought up in a woodcutter's hut."

"One av of the seven original plots in the world," murmured Father Cassidy.

"What?"

"Nothing. Just a bad habit av thinking aloud. Go on."

"She had a lover of high degree but his family did not want him to marry her because she was only a woodcutter's daughter—"

"Another of the seven plots—excuse me."

"—so they sent him away to the Holy land on a crusade and word came back that he was killed and then Editha—her name was Editha—went into a convent—"

Emily paused for a bite of plum cake and Father Cassidy took up the strain.

"And now her lover comes back very much alive, though covered with Paynim scars, and the secret av her birth is discovered through the dying confession av the old nurse and the birthmark on her arm."

"How did you know?" gasped Emily in amazement.

"Oh, I guessed it—I'm a good guesser. But where's your bother in all this?"

"I don't know how to get her out of the convent," confessed Emily. "I thought perhaps you would know how it could be done."

Again Father Cassidy fitted his fingers.

"Let us see, now. It's no light matter you've undertaken, young lady. How stands the case? *Editha* has taken the veil, not because she has a religious vocation but because she imagines her heart is broken. The Catholic Church does not release its nuns from their vows because they happen to think they've made a little mistake av that sort. No, no,—we must have a better reason. Is this Editha the sole child av her real parents?"

"Yes."

"Oh, then the way is clear. If she had had any brothers or sisters you would have had to kill them off, which is a messy thing to do. Well, then, she is the sole daughter and heiress av a noble family who have for years been at deadly feud with another noble family— the family av the lover. Do you know what a feud is?"

"Of course," said Emily disdainfully. "And I've got all that in the poem already."

"So much the better. This feud has rent the kingdom in twain and can only be healed by an alliance between Capulet and Montague."

"Those aren't their names."

"No matter. This, then, is a national affair, with far-reaching issues, therefore an appeal to the Supreme Pontiff is quite in order. What you want," Father Cassidy nodded solemnly, "is a dispensation from Rome."

"Dispensation is a hard word to work into a poem," said Emily.

"Undoubtedly. But young ladies who *will* write epic poems and who *will* lay the scenes thereof amid times and manners av hundreds av years ago, and *will* choose heroines av a religion quite unknown to them, *must* expect to run up against a few snags."

"Oh, I think I'll be able to work it in," said Emily cheerfully. "And I'm so much obliged to you. You don't know what a relief it is to my mind. I'll finish the poem right up now in a few weeks. I haven't done a thing at it all summer. But then of course I've been busy. Ilse Burnley and I have been making a new language."

"Making a—new—excuse me. *Did* you say *language*?"

"Yes."

"What's the matter with English? Isn't it good enough for you, you incomprehensible little being?"

"Oh, yes. *That* isn't why we're making a new one. You see in the spring, Cousin Jimmy got a lot of French boys to help plant the potatoes. I had to help too, and Ilse came to keep me company. And it was so annoying to hear those boys talking French when we couldn't understand a word of it. They did it just to make us mad. Such jabbering! So Ilse and I just made up our minds we'd invent a new language that *they* couldn't understand. We're getting on fine and when the potato picking time comes we'll be able to talk to each other and those boys won't be able to understand a word we're saying. Oh, it will be great fun!"

"I haven't a doubt. But two girls who will go to all the trouble av inventing a new language just to get square with some poor little French boys—you're beyond me," said Father Cassidy, helplessly. "Goodness knows what you'll be doing when you grow up. You'll be Red Revolutionists. I tremble for Canada."

"Oh, it isn't a trouble—it's fun. And all the girls in school are just wild because they hear us talking in it and can't make it out. We can talk secrets right before them."

"Human nature being what it is, I can see where the fun comes in all right. Let's hear a sample av your language."

"Nat millan O ste dolman bote ta Shrewsbury fernas ta poo litanos," said Emily glibly. "That means, 'Next summer I am going to Shrewsbury woods to pick strawberries.' I yelled that across the playground to Ilse the other day at recess and oh, how everybody stared."

"Staring, is it? I should say so. My own poor old eyes are all but dropping out av me head. Let's hear a bit more av it."

"Mo tral li dead seb ad li mo trene. Mo bertral seb mo bertrene das sten dead e ting setra. *That* means 'My father is dead and so is my mother. My grandfather and grandmother have been dead a long time.' We haven't invented a word for 'dead' yet. I think I will soon be able to write my poems in our language and then Aunt Elizabeth will not be able to read them if she finds them."

"Have you written any other poetry besides your epic?"

"Oh, yes—but just short pieces—dozens of them."

"H'm. Would you be so kind as to let me hear one av them?"

Emily was greatly flattered. And she did not mind letting Father Cassidy hear her precious stuff.

"I'll recite my last poem," she said, clearing her throat importantly. "It's called *Evening Dreams*."

Father Cassidy listened attentively. After the first verse a change came over his big brown face, and he began patting his fingertips together. When Emily finished she hung down her lashes and waited tremblingly. What if Father Cassidy said it was no good? No, he wouldn't be so impolite—but if he bantered her as he had done about her epic—she would know what *that* meant.

Father Cassidy did not speak all at once. The prolonged suspense was terrible to Emily. She was afraid he could not praise and did not want to hurt her feelings by dispraise. All at once her "Evening Dreams" seemed trash and she wondered how she could ever have been silly enough to repeat it to Father Cassidy.

Of course, it *was* trash. Father Cassidy knew that well enough. All the same, for a child like this—and rhyme and rhythm were flawless—and there was one line—just one line—"the light of faintly golden stars" —for the sake of that line Father Cassidy suddenly said,

"Keep on,—keep on writing poetry."

"You mean?"—Emily was breathless.

"I mean you'll be able to do something by and by. Something—I don't know how much—but keep on— keep on."

Emily was so happy she wanted to cry. It was the first word of commendation she had ever received except from her father—and a father might have too high an opinion of one. *This* was different. To the end of her struggle for recognition Emily never forgot Father Cassidy's "Keep on" and the tone in which he said it.

"Aunt Elizabeth scolds me for writing poetry," she

said wistfully. "She says people will think I'm as simple as Cousin Jimmy."

"The path of genius never did run smooth. But have another piece av cake—do, just to show there's something human about you."

"Ve, merry ti. O del re dolman cosey aman ri sen ritter. *That* means, 'No, thank you. I must be going home before it gets dark.'"

"I'll drive you home."

"Oh, no, no. It's very kind of you"—the English language was quite good enough for Emily now. "But I'd rather *walk*. It's—it's—such good exercise."

"Meaning," said Father Cassidy with a twinkle in his eye, "that we must keep it from the old lady. Goodbye, and may you always see a happy face in your looking-glass!"

Emily was too happy to be tired on the way home. There seemed to be a bubble of joy in her heart—a shimmering, prismatic bubble. When she came to the top of the big hill and looked across to New Moon, her eyes were satisfied and loving. How beautiful it was, lying embowered in the twilight of the old trees; the tips of the loftiest spruces came out in purple silhouette against the northwestern sky of rose and amber; down behind it the Blair Water dreamed in silver; the Wind Woman had folded her misty bat-wings in a valley of sunset and stillness lay over the world like a blessing. Emily felt sure everything would be all right. Father Cassidy would manage it in some way.

And he had told her to "keep on."

19
Friends Again

Emily listened very anxiously on Monday morning, but "no sound of axe, no ponderous hammer rang" in Lofty John's bush. That evening on her way home from school, Lofty John himself overtook her in his buggy and for the first time since the night of the apple stopped and accosted her.

"Will ya take a lift, Miss Emily av New Moon?" he said affably.

Emily climbed in, feeling a little bit foolish. But Lofty John looked quite friendly as he clucked to his horse.

"So you've clean wiled the heart out av Father Cassidy's body," he said. "'The sweetest scrap av a girl I've iver seen,' says he to me. Sure an' ye might lave the poor prastes alone."

Emily looked at Lofty John out of the corner of her eye. He did not seem angry.

"Ye've put *me* in a nice tight fix av it," he went on. "I'm as proud as any New Moon Murray av ye all and your Aunt Elizabeth said a number av things that got under my skin. I've many an old score to settle with her. So I thought I'd get square by cutting av the bush down. And you had to go and quare me wid me praste bekase av it and now I make no doubt I'll not be after daring to cut a stick av kindling to warm me shivering carcase without asking lave av the Pope."

"Oh, Mr. Sullivan, are you going to leave the bush alone?" said Emily breathlessly.

"It all rests with yourself, Miss Emily av New Moon. Ye can't be after expecting a Lofty John to be too humble. I didn't come by the name bekase av me makeness."

"What do you want me to do?"

"First, then, I'm wanting you to let bygones be bygones in that matter av the apple. And be token av the same come over and talk to me now and then as ye did last summer. Sure now, and I've missed ye—ye and that spit-fire av an Ilse who's never come aither bekase she thinks I mistrated you."

"I'll come of course," said Emily doubtfully, "if only Aunt Elizabeth will let me."

"Tell her if she don't the bush'll be cut down—ivery last stick av it. That'll fetch her. And there's wan more thing. Ye must ask me rale make and polite to do ye the favour av not cutting down the bush. If ye do it pretty enough sure niver a tree will I touch. But if ye don't down they go, praste or no praste," concluded Lofty John.

Emily summoned all her wiles to her aid. She clasped her hands, she looked up through her lashes at Lofty John, she smiled as slowly and seductively as she knew how—and Emily had considerable native knowledge of that sort. "Please, Mr. Lofty John," she coaxed, "won't you leave me the dear bush I love?"

Lofty John swept off his crumpled old felt hat. "To be sure an' I will. A proper Irishman always does what a lady asks him. Sure an' it's been the ruin av us. We're at the mercy av the petticoats. If ye'd come and said that to me afore ye'd have had no need av your walk to White Cross. But mind ye keep the rest av the bargin. The reds are ripe and the scabs soon will be—and all the rats have gone to glory."

Emily flew into the New Moon kitchen like a slim whirlwind.

"Aunt Elizabeth, Lofty John isn't going to cut down the bush—he told me he wouldn't—but I have to go and see him sometimes—if you don't object."

"I suppose it wouldn't make much difference to you if I did," said Aunt Elizabeth. But her voice was not so sharp as usual. She would not confess how much Emily's announcement relieved her; but it mellowed her attitude considerably. "There's a letter here for you. I want to know what it means."

Emily took the letter. It was the first time she had ever received a real letter through the mail and she tingled with the delight of it. It was addressed in a heavy black hand to "Miss Emily Starr, New Moon, Blair Water." But—

"You opened it!" she cried indignantly.

"Of course I did. You are not going to receive letters I am not to see, Miss. What I want to know is—how comes Father Cassidy to be writing you—and writing such nonsense?"

"I went to see him Saturday," confessed Emily, realizing that the cat was out of the bag. "And I asked him if he couldn't prevent Lofty John from cutting down the bush."

"Emily—Byrd—Starr!"

"I *told* him I was a Protestant," cried Emily. "He understands all about it. And he was just like anybody else. I like him *better* than Mr. Dare."

Aunt Elizabeth did not say much more. There did not seem to be much she *could* say. Besides the bush wasn't going to be cut down. The bringer of good news is forgiven much. She contented herself with glaring at Emily—who was too happy and excited to mind glares. She carried her letter off to the garret dormer and gloated over the stamp and the superscription a bit before she took out the enclosure.

"Dear Pearl of Emilys," wrote Father Cassidy. "I've seen our lofty friend and I feel sure your green outpost of fairyland will be saved for your moonlit revels. I know you *do* dance there by light o' moon when mortals are snoring. I think you'll have to go through the form of asking Mr. Sullivan to spare those trees, but you'll find him quite reasonable. It's all in the knowing how and the time of the moon. How goes the epic and the language? I hope you'll have no trouble in freeing the *Child of The Sea* from her vows. Continue to be the friend of all good elves, and of

> "Your admiring friend,
> "James Cassidy.

"P.S. The B'y sends respects. What word have you for 'cat' in your language? Sure and you can't get anything cattier than 'cat' can you, now?"

Lofty John spread the story of Emily's appeal to Father Cassidy far and wide, enjoying it as a good joke on himself. Rhoda Stuart said she always knew Emily Starr was a bold thing and Miss Brownell said she would be surprised at *nothing* Emily Starr would do, and Dr. Burnley called her a Little Devil more admiringly than ever, and Perry said she had pluck and Teddy took credit for suggesting it, and Aunt Elizabeth endured, and Aunt Laura thought it might have been worse. But Cousin Jimmy made Emily feel very happy.

"It would have spoiled the garden and broken my heart, Emily," he told her. "You're a little darling girl to have prevented it."

One day a month later, when Aunt Elizabeth had taken Emily to Shrewsbury to fit her out with a winter coat, they met Father Cassidy in a store. Aunt Elizabeth bowed with great stateliness, but Emily put out a slender paw.

"What about the dispensation from Rome?" whispered Father Cassidy.

One Emily was quite horrified lest Aunt Elizabeth should overhear and think she was having sly dealings with the Pope, such as no good Presbyterian half-Murray of New Moon should have. The other Emily thrilled to her toes with the dramatic delight of a secret understanding of mystery and intrigue. She nodded gravely, her eyes eloquent with satisfaction.

"I got it without any trouble," she whispered back.

"Fine," said Father Cassidy. "I wish you good luck, and I wish it hard. Good-bye."

"Farewell," said Emily, thinking it a word more in keeping with dark secrets than good-bye. She tasted the flavour of that half-stolen interview all the way home, and felt quite as if she were living in an epic herself. She did not see Father Cassidy again for years— he was soon afterwards removed to another parish; but she always thought of him as a very agreeable and understanding person.

20
By Aerial Post

"Dearest Father:

"My heart is very sore to night. Mike died this morning. Cousin Jimmy says he must have been poisoned. Oh, Father dear, I felt so bad. He was such a lovely cat. I cried and cried and cried. Aunt Elizabeth was disgusted. She said, "You did not make half so much fuss when your father died." What a crewel speech. Aunt Laura was nicer but when she said, "Don't cry dear. I will get you another kitten," I saw she didn't understand either. I don't want another kitten. If I had *millions* of kittens they wouldn't make up for Mike.

"Ilse and I buried him in Lofty John's bush. I am so thankful the ground wasn't frozen yet. Aunt Laura gave me a shoe box for a coffin, and some pink tissue paper to wrap his poor little body in. And we put a stone over the grave and I said "Blessed are the dead who die in the Lord." When I told Aunt Laura about it she was horrified and said, "Oh, Emily, that was a dreadful thing. You should not have said that over a cat." And Cousin Jimmy said, "Don't you think, Laura, that an innocent little dum creature has a share in God?

Emily loved him and all love is part of God." And Aunt Laura said, "Maybe you are right, Jimmy. But I am thankful Elizabeth did not hear her."

"Cousin Jimmy may not be all there, but what is there is very nice.

"But oh, Father, I am so lonesome for Mike tonight. Last night he was here playing with me, so cunning and pretty and *smee*, and now he is cold and dead in Lofty John's bush.

"DECEMBER 18.

"Dear Father:

"I am here in the garret. The Wind Woman is very sorry about something tonight. She is sying so sadly around the window. And yet the first time I heard her tonight the flash came—I felt as if I had just seen something that happened long, long ago—something so lovely that it hurt me.

"Cousin Jimmy says there will be a snow storm tonight. I am glad. I like to hear a storm at night. It's so cozy to snuggle down among the blankets and feel it can't get at you. Only when I snuggle Aunt Elizabeth says I skwirm. The idea of any one not knowing the difference between snuggling and skwirming.

"I am glad we will have snow for Christmas. The Murray dinner is to be at New Moon this year. It is our turn. Last year it was at Uncle Oliver's but Cousin Jimmy had grippe and couldn't go so I stayed home with him. I will be right in the thick of it this year and it exites me. I will write you all about it after it is over, dearest.

"I want to tell you something, Father. I am ashamed of it, but I think I'll feel better if I tell you all about it. Last Saturday Ella Lee had a birthday party and I was invited. Aunt Elizabeth let me put on my new blue cashmere dress. It is a very pretty dress. Aunt Elizabeth wanted to get a dark brown but Aunt Laura insisted on blue. I looked at myself in my glass and I remembered that Ilse had told me her father told her I would be handsome if I had more colour. So I pinched my cheeks to make them red. I looked ever so much nicer but it didn't last. Then I took an old red velvet flower that had once been in Aunt Laura's bonnet and wet it and then rubbed the red on my cheeks. I went to the party and the girls all *looked* at me but nobody said anything, only Rhoda Stuart giggled and giggled. I meant to come home and wash the red off before Aunt Elizabeth saw me. But she took a notion to call for me on her way home from the store. She did not say anything there but when we got home she said, "What have you been doing to your face, Emily?" I told her and I expected an awful scolding, but all she said was, "Don't you know that you have made yourself *cheap*?" I did know it, too. I had felt that all along although I couldn't think of the right word for it before. "I will never do such a thing again, Aunt Elizabeth," I said. "You'd better not," she said. "Go and wash your face this instant." I did and I was not half so pretty but I felt ever so much better. Strange to relate, dear Father, I heard Aunt Elizabeth laughing about it in the pantry to Aunt Laura afterwards. You never can tell what will make Aunt Elizabeth laugh. I am sure it was ever so much funnier when Saucy Sal followed me to prayer meeting last Wednesday night, but Aunt Elizabeth never laughed a bit then. I don't often go to prayer meeting but Aunt Laura couldn't go that night so Aunt Elizabeth took me because she doesn't like to go alone. I didn't know Sal was following us till just as we got to the church I saw her. I shooed her away but after we went in I suppose Sal sneaked in when someone opened the door and got upstairs into the galery. And just as soon as Mr. Dare began to pray Sal began to yowl. It sounded awful up in that big empty galery. I felt so gilty and miserable. I did not need to paint my face. It was just burning red and Aunt Elizabeth's eyes glittered feendishly. Mr. Dare prayed a long time. He is deaf, so he did not hear Sal any more than when he sat on her. But everyone else did and the boys giggled. After the prayer Mr. Morris went up to the galery and chased Sal out. We could hear her skrambling over the seats and Mr. Morris after her. I was wild for fear he'd hurt her. I ment to spank her myself with a shingle next day but I did not want her to be kicked. After a long time he got her out of the galery and she tore down the stairs and into the church, up one isle and down the other two or three times as fast as she could go and Mr. Morris after her with a broom. It is awfully funny to think of it now but I did not think it so funny at the time I was so ashamed and so afraid Sal would be hurt.

"Mr. Morris chased her out at last. When he sat down I made a face at him behind my hymn book. Coming home Aunt Elizabeth said, "I hope you have disgraced us enough tonight, Emily Starr. I shall never take you to prayer meeting again." I am sorry I disgraced the Murrays but I don't see how I was to blame and anyway I don't like prayer meeting because it is dull.

"But it wasn't dull that night, dear Father.

"Do you notice how my spelling is improved? I have thought of such a good plan. I write my letter first and then I look up all the words I'm not sure of and correct them. Sometimes though I think a word is all right when it isn't.

"Ilse and I have given up our language. We fought over the verbs. Ilse didn't want to have any tenses for the verbs. She just wanted to have a different word altogether for every tense. I said if I was going to make a language it was going to be a proper one and Ilse got mad and said she had enough bother with grammer in English and I could go and make my old language by myself. But that is no fun so I let it go too. I was sorry because it was very interesting and it was such fun to puzzle the other girls in school. We weren't able to get square with the French boys after all for Ilse had sore throat all through potato picking time and couldn't come over. It seems to me that life is full of disappointments.

"We had examinations in school this week. I did pretty well in all except arithmetic. Miss Brownell explained something about the questions but I was busy composing a story in my mind and did not hear her so I got poor marks. The story is called *Madge MacPherson's Secret*. I am going to buy four sheets of foolscap with my egg money and sew them into a book and write the story in it. I can do what I like with my egg money. I think maybe I'll write novels when I grow up as well as poetry. But Aunt Elizabeth won't let me read any novels so how can I find out how to write them? Another thing that worries me, if I do grow up and write a wonderful poem, perhaps people won't see how wonderful it is.

"Cousin Jimmy says that a man in Priest Pond says the end of the world is coming soon. I hope it won't come till I've seen everything in it.

"Poor Elder McKay has the mumps.

"I was over sleeping with Ilse the other night because her father was away. Ilse says her prayers now and she said she'd bet me anything she could pray longer than me. I said she couldn't and I prayed ever so long about everything I could think of and when I couldn't think of anything more I thought at first I'd begin over again. Then I thought, "No, that would not be honerable. A Starr must be honerable." So I got up and said "You win" and Ilse never answered. I went around the bed and there she was asleep on her knees. When I woke her up she said we'd have to call the bet off because she could have gone on praying for ever so long if she hadn't fell asleep.

"After we got into bed I told her a lot of things I wished afterwards I hadn't. Secrets.

"The other day in history class Miss Brownell read that Sir Walter Raleigh had to lie in the Tower for fourteen years. Perry said "Wouldn't they let him get up sometimes?" Then Miss Brownell punished him for impertinence, but Perry was in earnest. Ilse was mad at Miss Brownell for whipping Perry and mad at Perry for

.asking such a fool question as if he didn't know anything. But Perry says he is going to write a history book
some day that won't have such puzzling things in it.

"I am finishing the Disappointed House in my mind.
I'm furnishing the rooms like flowers. I'll have a rose
room all pink and a lily room all white and silver and a
pansy room, blue and gold. I wish the Disappointed
House could have a Christmas. It never has any
Christmasses.

"Oh, Father, I've just thought of something nice.
When I grow up and write a great novel and make lots
of money, I will buy the Disappointed House and finish
it. Then it won't be Disappointed any more.

"Ilse's Sunday School teacher, Miss Willeson, gave
her a Bible for learning 200 verses. But when she took
it home her father laid it on the floor and kicked it out
in the yard. Mrs. Simms says a judgment will come on
him but nothing has happened yet. The poor man is
warped. That is why he did such a wicked thing.

"Aunt Laura took me to old Mrs. Mason's funeral last
Wednesday. I like funerals. They are so dramatic.

"My pig died last week. It was a *great finanshul loss* to
me. Aunt Elizabeth says Cousin Jimmy fed it too well. I
suppose I should not have called it after Lofty John.

"We have maps to draw in school now. Rhoda Stuart
always gets the most marks. Miss Brownell doesn't
know that Rhoda just puts the map up against a
window pane and the paper over it and copies it off. I
like drawing maps. Norway and Sweden look like a
tiger with mountains for stripes and Ireland looks like a
little dog with its back turned on England, and its paws
held up against its breast, and Africa looks like a big
pork ham. Australia is a lovely map to draw.

"Ilse is getting on real well in school now. She says
she isn't going to have me beating her. She can learn
like the dickins, as Perry says, when she tries, and she
has won the silver metal for Queen's County. The
W.C.T.U. in Charlottetown gave it for the best reciter.
They had the contest in Shrewsbury and Aunt Laura

took Ilse because Dr. Burnley wouldn't and Ilse won it. Aunt Laura told Dr. Burnley when he was here one day that he ought to give Ilse a good education. He said "I'm not going to waste money educating any she-thing." And he looked black as a thunder cloud. Oh, I wish Dr. Burnley would love Isle. I'm so glad *you* loved *me*, Father.

"Dec. 22.

"Dear Father: We had our school examination today. It was a great occasion. Almost everybody was there except Dr. Burnley and Aunt Elizabeth. All the girls wore their best dresses but me. I knew Ilse had nothing to wear but her shabby old last winter's plaid that is too short for her, so to keep her from feeling bad, I put on my old brown dress, too. Aunt Elizabeth did not want to let me do it at first because New Moon Murrays should be well dressed but when I explained about Ilse she looked at Aunt Laura and then said I might.

"Rhoda Stuart made fun of Ilse and me but I heaped coals of fire on her head. (That is what is called a figure of speech.) She got stuck in her recitation. She had left the book home and nobody else knew the piece but me. At first I looked at her triumphantly. But then a queer feeling came into me and I thought "What would I feel like if I was stuck before a big crowd of people like this? And besides the honour of the school is at stake," so I whispered it to her because I was quite close. She got through the rest all right. The strange thing is, dear Father, that now I don't feel any more as if I hated her. I feel quite kindly to her and it is much nicer. It is uncomfortable to hate people.

"Dec. 28.

"Dear Father:
Christmas is over. It was pretty nice. I never saw so many good things cooked all at once. Uncle Wallace and Aunt Eva and Uncle Oliver and Aunt Addie and

Aunt Ruth were here. Uncle Oliver didn't bring any of his children and I was much disappointed. We had Dr. Burnley and Ilse too. Everyone was dressed up. Aunt Elizabeth wore her black satin dress with a pointed lace collar and cap. She looked quite handsome and I was proud of her. You like your relations to look well even if you don't like *them*. Aunt Laura wore her brown silk and Aunt Ruth had on a grey dress. Aunt Eva was *very* elegant. Her dress had a train. But it smelled of moth balls.

"I had on my blue cashmere and wore my hair tied with blue ribbons, and Aunt Laura let me wear mother's blue silk sash with the pink daisies on it that she had when she was a little girl at New Moon. Aunt Ruth sniffed when she saw me. She said, "You have grown a good deal, Em'ly. I hope you are a better girl."

"But she *didn't* hope it (really). I saw that quite plain. Then she told me my bootlace was untyed.

"She looks better," said Uncle Oliver. "I wouldn't wonder if she grew up into a strong, healthy girl after all."

"Aunt Eva sighed and shook her head. Uncle Wallace didn't say anything but shook hands with me. His hand was as cold as a fish. When we went out to the sitting room for dinner I stepped on Aunt Eva's train and I could hear some stitches rip somewhere. Aunt Eva pushed me away and Aunt Ruth said, "What a very awkward child you are, Emily." I stepped behind Aunt Ruth and stuck out my tongue at her. Uncle Oliver makes a noise eating his soup. We had all the good silver spoons out. Cousin Jimmy carved the turkeys and he gave me two slices of the breast because he knows I like the white meat best. Aunt Ruth said "When I was a little girl the wing was good enough for me," and Cousin Jimmy put *another* white slice on my plate. Aunt Ruth didn't say anything more then till the carving was done, and then she said, "I saw your school teacher in Shrewsbury last Saturday, Em'ly, and she did not give me a very good account of you. If you were *my* daughter I would expect a different report."

"I am very glad I am not your daughter," I said in my mind. I didn't say it out loud of course but Aunt Ruth said, "Please do not look so sulky when I speak to you, Em'ly." And Uncle Wallace said, "It is a pity she has such an unattractive expression."

"*You* are conceited and domineering and stingy," I said, still in my mind. "I heard Dr. Burnley say you were."

"I see there is an ink-stain on her finger," said Aunt Ruth. (I had been writing a poem before dinner.)

"And then a most surprising thing happened. Relations are always surprising you. Aunt Elizabeth spoke up and said, "*I do wish, Ruth, that you and Wallace would leave that child alone.*" I could hardly believe my ears. Aunt Ruth looked annoyed but she *did* leave me alone after that and only sniffed when Cousin Jimmy slipped a bit more white meat on my plate.

"After that the dinner was nice. And when they got as far as the pudding they all began to talk and it was splendid to listen to. They told stories and jokes about the Murrays. Even Uncle Wallace laughed and Aunt Ruth told some things about Great-Aunt Nancy. They were sarcastic but they were interesting. Aunt Elizabeth opened Grandfather Murray's desk and took out an old poem that had been written to Aunt Nancy *by a lover* when she was young and Uncle Oliver read it. Great-Aunt Nancy must have been very beautiful. I wonder if anyone will ever write a poem to me. If I could have a bang somebody might. I said, "Was Great Aunt Nancy really as pretty as that?" and Uncle Oliver said, "They say she was 70 years ago" and Uncle Wallace said, "She hangs on well—she'll see the century mark yet," and Uncle Oliver said, "Oh, she's got so in the habit of living she'll never die."

"Dr. Burnley told a story I didn't understand. Uncle Wallace hawhawed right out and Uncle Oliver put his napkin up to his face. Aunt Addie and Aunt Eva looked at each other sidewise and then at their plates and smiled a little bit. Aunt Ruth seemed offended and Aunt Elizabeth looked *coldly* at Dr. Burnley and said, "I think you forget that there are children present." Dr. Burnley said, "I beg your pardon, Elizabeth," *very* politely. He can speak with a *grand air* when he likes. He is very handsome when he is dressed up and shaved. Ilse says she is proud of him even if he hates her.

"After dinner was over the presents were given. That is a Murray tradishun. We never have stockings or trees but a big bran pie is passed all around with the presents buried in it and ribbons hanging out with names on them. It was fun. My relations all gave me useful presents except Aunt Laura. She gave me a bottle of perfume. I love it. I love nice smells. Aunt Elizabeth does not approve of perfumes. She gave me a new apron but I am thankful to say not a baby one. Aunt Ruth gave me a New Testament and said "Em'ly, I hope you will read a portion of that every day until you have read it through," and I said, "Why Aunt Ruth, I've read the whole New Testament a dozen times (and so I have) I *love* Revelations." (And I *do*. When I read the verse "and the twelve gates were twelve pearls" I just *saw* them and the flash came.) "The Bible is not to be read as a story book," Aunt Ruth said coldly. Uncle Wallace and Aunt Eva gave me a pair of black mits and Uncle Oliver and Aunt Addie gave me a whole dollar in nice new silver dimes and Cousin Jimmy gave me a hair ribbon. Perry had left a silk bookmark for me. He had to go home to spend Christmas day with his Aunt Tom at Stovepipe Town but I saved a lot of nuts and raisins for him. I gave him and Teddy handkerchiefs (Teddy's was a *little* the nicest) and I gave Ilse a hair ribbon. I bought them myself out of my egg money. (I will not have any more egg money for a long time because my hen has stopped laying.) Everybody was happy and once Uncle Wallace smiled right at me. I did not think him so ugly when he smiled.

"After dinner Ilse and I played games in the kitchen and Cousin Jimmy helped us make taffy. We had a big supper but nobody could eat much because they had had such a dinner. Aunt Eva's head ached and Aunt Ruth said she didn't see why Elizabeth made the sausages so rich. But the rest were good humored and Aunt Laura kept things pleasant. She is good at making things pleasant. And after it was all over Uncle Wallace said (this is another Murray tradishun) "Let us think for a few moments of those who have gone before." I liked the way he said it—very solemnly and kind. It was one of the times when I am glad the blood of the Murrays flows in my vains. And I thought of *you*, darling Father, and Mother and poor little Mike and Great-great-Grandmother Murray, and of my old account book that Aunt Elizabeth burned, because it seemed just like a person to me. And then we all joined hands and sung "For Auld Lang Syne" before they went home. I didn't feel like a stranger among the Murrays any more. Aunt Laura and I stood out on the porch to watch them go. Aunt Laura put her arm around me and said, "Your mother and I used to stand like this long ago, Emily, to watch the Christmas guests go away." The snow creaked and the bells rang back through the trees and the frost on the pighouse roof sparkled in the moonlight. And it was all so lovely (the bells and the frost and the big shining white night) that *the flash* came and that was best of all."

21
"Romantic but not Comfortable"

A certain thing happened at New Moon because Teddy Kent paid Ilse Burnley a compliment one day and Emily Starr didn't altogether like it. Empires have been overturned for the same reason.

Teddy was skating on Blair Water and taking Ilse and Emily out in turns for "slides." Neither Ilse nor Emily had skates. Nobody was sufficiently interested in Ilse to buy skates for her, and as for Emily, Aunt Elizabeth did not approve of girls skating. New Moon girls had never skated. Aunt Laura had a revolutionary idea that skating would be good exercise for Emily and would, moreover, prevent her from wearing out the soles of her boots sliding. But neither of these arguments was sufficient to convince Aunt Elizabeth, in spite of the thrifty streak that came to her from the Burnleys. The latter, however, caused her to issue an edict that Emily was not to "slide." Emily took this very hardly. She moped about in a woe-begone fashion and she wrote to her father, "I *hate* Aunt Elizabeth. She is so unjust. She never plays fair." But one day Dr. Burnley stuck his head in at the door of the New Moon kitchen and said gruffly, "What's this I hear about you not letting Emily slide, Elizabeth?"

"She wears out the soles of her boots," said Elizabeth.

"Boots be—" the doctor remembered that ladies were present just in time. "Let the creature slide all she wants to. She ought to be in the open air all the time. She ought"—the doctor stared at Elizabeth ferociously— "she ought to sleep out of doors."

Elizabeth trembled lest the doctor should go on to insist on this unheard-of proceeding. She knew he had absurd ideas about the proper treatment of consumptives and those who might become such. She was glad to appease him by letting Emily stay out-of-doors in daytime and do what seemed good to her, if only he would say no more about staying out all night too.

"He is much more concerned about Emily than he is about his own child," she said bitterly to Laura.

"Ilse is too healthy," said Aunt Laura with a smile. "If she were a delicate child Allan might forgive her for—for being her mother's daughter."

"S—s—h," said Aunt Elizabeth. But she "s—s—s—h'd" too late. Emily, coming into the kitchen, had heard Aunt Laura and puzzled over what she had said all day in school. Why had Ilse to be forgiven for being her mother's daughter? Everybody was her mother's daughter, wasn't she? Wherein did the crime consist? Emily worried over it so much that she was inattentive to her lessons and Miss Brownell raked her fore and aft with sarcasm.

It is time we got back to Blair Water where Teddy was just bringing Emily in from a glorious spin clear round the great circle of ice. Ilse was waiting for her turn, on the bank. Her golden cloud of hair aureoled her face and fell in a shimmering wave over her forehead under the faded, little red tam she wore. Ilse's clothes were always faded. The stinging kiss of the wind had crimsoned her cheeks and her eyes were glowing like amber pools with fire in their hearts. Teddy's artistic perception saw her beauty and rejoiced in it.

"Isn't Ilse handsome?" he said.

Emily was not jealous. It never hurt her to hear Ilse praised. But somehow she did not like this. Teddy was looking at Ilse altogether *too* admiringly. It was all, Emily believed, due to that shimmering fringe on Ilse's white brows.

"If *I* had a bang Teddy might think me handsome

too," she thought resentfully. "Of course, black hair isn't as pretty as gold. But my forehead is too high—everybody says so. And I *did* look nice in Teddy's picture because he drew some curls over it."

The matter rankled. Emily thought of it as she went home over the sheen of the crusted snow-field slanting to the light of the winter sunset, and she could not eat her supper because she did not have a bang. All her long hidden yearning for a bang seemed to come to a head at once. She knew there was no use in coaxing Aunt Elizabeth for one. But when she was getting ready for bed that night she stood on a chair so that she could see little Emily-in-the-glass, then lifted the curling ends of her long braid and laid them over her forehead. The effect, in Emily's eyes at least, was very alluring. She suddenly thought—what if she cut a bang herself? It would take only a minute. And once done what could Aunt Elizabeth do? She would be very angry and doubtless inflict some kind of punishment. But the bang would be there—at least until it grew out long.

Emily, her lips set, went for the scissors. She unbraided her hair and parted the front tresses. Snip—snip—went the scissors. Glistening locks fell at her feet. In a minute Emily had her long-desired bang. Straight across her brows fell the lustrous, softly curving fringe. It changed the whole character of her face. It made it arch, provocative, elusive. For one brief moment Emily gazed at her reflection in triumph.

And then—sheer terror seized her. Oh, what had she done? How angry Aunt Elizabeth would be! Conscience suddenly awoke and added its pang also. She had been wicked. It was wicked to cut a bang when Aunt Elizabeth had forbidden it. Aunt Elizabeth had given her a home at New Moon—hadn't Rhoda Stuart that very day in school twitted her again with "living on charity"? And she was repaying her by disobedience and ingratitude. A Starr should not have done that. In a panic of fear and remorse Emily snatched the scissors and cut the bang off—cut it close against the hair line. Worse and worse! Emily beheld the result in dismay. Any one could see that a bang *had* been cut, so Aunt Elizabeth's anger was still to face. And she had made a terrible fright of herself. Emily burst into tears, snatched up the fallen locks and crammed them into the waste-basket, blew out her candle and sprang into bed, just as Aunt Elizabeth came in.

Emily burrowed face downward in the pillows, and pretended to be asleep. She was afraid Aunt Elizabeth would ask her some question and insist on her looking up while she answered it. That was a Murray tradition—you looked people in the face when you spoke to them. But Aunt Elizabeth undressed in silence and came to bed. The room was in darkness—thick darkness. Emily sighed and turned over. There was a hot gin-jar in the bed, she knew, and her feet were cold. But she did not think she ought to have the privilege of the gin-jar. She was too wicked—too ungrateful.

"*Do* stop squirming," said Aunt Elizabeth.

Emily squirmed no more—physically at least. Mentally she continued to squirm. She could not sleep. Her feet or her conscience—or both—kept her awake. And fear, also. She dreaded the morning. Aunt Elizabeth would see then what had happened. If it were only over—if the revelation were only over. Emily forgot and squirmed.

"What makes you so restless tonight?" demanded Aunt Elizabeth, in high displeasure. "Are you taking a cold?"

"No, ma'am."

"Then go to sleep. I can't bear such wriggling. One might as well have an eel in bed—O—W!"

Aunt Elizabeth, in squirming a bit herself, had put her own foot against Emily's icy ones.

"Goodness, child, your feet are like snow. Here, put them on the gin-jar."

Aunt Elizabeth pushed the gin-jar over against Emily's feet. How lovely and warm and comforting it was!

Emily worked her toes against it like a cat. But she suddenly knew she could not wait for morning.

"Aunt Elizabeth, I've got something to confess."

Aunt Elizabeth was tired and sleepy and did not want confessions just then. In no very gracious tone she said,

"What have you been doing?"

"I—I cut a bang, Aunt Elizabeth."

"A bang?"

Aunt Elizabeth sat up in bed.

"But I cut it off again," cried Emily hurriedly. "Right off—close to my head."

Aunt Elizabeth got out of bed, lit a candle, and looked Emily over.

"Well you *have* made a sight of yourself," she said grimly. "I never saw any one as ugly as you are this minute. And you have behaved in a most underhanded fashion."

This was one of the times Emily felt compelled to agree with Aunt Elizabeth.

"I'm sorry," she said, lifting pleading eyes.

"You will eat your supper in the pantry for a week," said Aunt Elizabeth. "And you will not go to Uncle Oliver's next week when I go. I had promised to take you. But I shall take no one who looks as you do anywhere with me."

This was hard. Emily had looked forward to that visit to Uncle Oliver's. But on the whole she was relieved. The worst was over and her feet were getting warm. But there was one thing yet. She might as well unburden her heart completely while she was at it.

"There's another thing I feel I ought to tell you."

Aunt Elizabeth got into bed again with a grunt. Emily took it for permission.

"Aunt Elizabeth, you remember that book I found in Dr. Burnley's bookcase and brought home and asked you if I could read it? It was called 'The History of Henry Esmond.' You looked at it and said you had no objections to my reading history. So I read it. But, Aunt

Elizabeth, it wasn't history—it was a novel. And I *knew it when I brought it home.*"

"You know that I have forbidden you to read novels, Emily Starr. They are wicked books and have ruined many souls."

"It was very dull," pleaded Emily, as if dullness and wickedness were quite incompatible. "And it made me feel unhappy. Everybody seemed to be in love with the wrong person. I have made up my mind, Aunt Elizabeth, that I will never fall in love. It makes too much trouble."

"Don't talk of things you can't understand, and that are not fit for children to think about. This is the result of reading novels. I shall tell Dr. Burnley to lock his bookcase up."

"Oh, don't do that, Aunt Elizabeth," exclaimed Emily. "There are no more novels in it. But I'm reading such an interesting book over there. It tells about everything that's inside of you. I've got as far along as the liver and its diseases. The pictures are so interesting. Please let me finish it.

This was worse than novels. Aunt Elizabeth was truly horrified. Things that were inside of you were not to be read about.

"Have you no shame, Emily Starr? If you have not I am ashamed for you. Little girls do not read books like that."

"But, Aunt Elizabeth, why not? I *have* a liver, haven't I—and heart and lungs—and stomach—and—"

"That will do, Emily. Not another word."

Emily went to sleep unhappily. She wished she had never said a word about 'Esmond.' And she knew she would never have a chance to finish that other fascinating book. Nor had she. Dr. Burnley's bookcase was locked thereafter and the doctor gruffly ordered her and Ilse to keep out of his office. He was in a very bad humour about it for he had words with Elizabeth Murray over the matter.

Emily was not allowed to forget her bang. She was twitted and teased in school about it and Aunt Elizabeth looked at it whenever she looked at Emily and the contempt in her eyes burned Emily like a flame. Nevertheless, as the mistreated hair grew out and began to curl in soft little ringlets, Emily found consolation. The bang was tacitly permitted, and she felt that her looks were greatly improved thereby. Of course, as soon as it grew long enough she knew Aunt Elizabeth would make her brush it back. But for the time being she took comfort in her added beauty.

The bang was just about at its best when the letter came from Great-Aunt Nancy.

It was written to Aunt Laura—Great-Aunt Nancy and Aunt Elizabeth were not over-fond of each other—and in it Great-Aunt Nancy said, "If you have a photograph of that child Emily send it along. I don't want to see *her*; she's stupid—I know she's stupid. But I want to see what Juliet's child looks like. Also the child of that fascinating young man, Douglas Starr. He *was* fascinating. What fools you all were to make such a fuss about Juliet running away with him. If you and Elizabeth had *both* run away with somebody in your running days it would have been better for you."

This letter was not shown to Emily. Aunt Elizabeth and Aunt Laura had a long secret consultation and then Emily was told that she was to be taken to Shrewsbury to have her picture taken for Aunt Nancy. Emily was much excited over this. She was dressed in her blue cashmere and Aunt Laura put a point lace collar on it and hung her Venetian beads over it. And new buttoned boots were got for the occasion.

"I'm so glad this has happened while I still have my bang," thought Emily happily.

But in the photographer's dressing-room, Aunt Elizabeth grimly proceeded to brush back her bang and pin it with hairpins.

"Oh, please, Aunt Elizabeth, let me have it down," Emily begged. "Just for the picture. After this I'll brush it back."

Aunt Elizabeth was inexorable. The bang was brushed

back and the photograph taken. When Aunt Elizabeth saw the finished result she was satisfied.

"She looks sulky; but she is neat; and there is a resemblance to the Murrays I never noticed before," she told Aunt Laura. "That will please Aunt Nancy. She is very clannish under all her oddness."

Emily would have liked to throw every one of the photographs in the fire. She hated them. They made her look hideous. Her face seemed to be *all* forehead. If they sent Aunt Nancy that Aunt Nancy would think her stupider than ever. When Aunt Elizabeth did the photograph up in cardboard and told Emily to take it to the office Emily already knew what she meant to do. She went straight to the garret and took out of her box the water-colour Teddy had made of her. It was just the same size as the photograph. Emily removed the latter from its wrappings, spurning it aside with her foot.

"That isn't *me*," she said. "I looked sulky because I felt sulky about the bang. But I hardly ever look sulky, so it isn't fair."

She wrapped Teddy's sketch up in the cardboard and then sat down and wrote a letter.

"DEAR GREAT-AUNT NANCY:

"Aunt Elizabeth had my picture taken to send you but I don't like it because it makes me look too ugly and I am putting another picture in instead. An *artist friend* made it for me. It is just like me when I'm smiling and have a bang. I am only *lending* it to you, not *giving* it, because I valew it very highly.

> "Your obedient grand niece,
> "EMILY BYRD STARR.

"P.S. I am not so stupid as you think.
"E. B. S.

"P.S. No. 2. I am not stupid *at all*."

*   *   *

Emily put her letter in with the picture—thereby unconsciously cheating the post-office—and slipped out of the house to mail it. Once it was safely in the post-office she drew a breath of relief. She found the walk home very enjoyable. It was a bland day in early April and spring was looking at you round the corners. The Wind Woman was laughing and whistling over the wet sweet fields; freebooting crows held conferences in the tree tops; little pools of sunshine lay in the mossy hollows; the sea was a blaze of sapphire beyond the golden dunes; the maples in Lofty John's bush were talking about red buds. Everything Emily had ever read of dream and myth and legend seemed a part of the charm of that bush. She was filled to her finger-tips with a rapture of living.

"Oh, I smell spring!" she cried as she danced along the brook path.

Then she began to compose a poem on it. Everybody who has ever lived in the world and could string two rhymes together has written a poem on spring. It is the most be-rhymed subject in the world—and always will be, because it is poetry incarnate itself. You can never be a real poet if you haven't made at least one poem about spring.

Emily was wondering whether she would have elves dancing on the brookside by moonlight, or pixies sleeping in a bed of ferns in her poem, when something confronted her at a bend in the path which was neither elf nor pixy, but seemed odd and weird enough to belong to some of the tribes of Little People. Was it a witch? Or an elderly fay of evil intentions—the bad fairy of all christening tales?

"I'm the b'y's Aunt Tom," said the appearance, seeing that Emily was too amazed to do anything but stand and stare.

"Oh!" Emily gasped in relief. She was no longer frightened. But what a *very* peculiar looking lady Perry's Aunt Tom was. Old—so old that it seemed quite impossible that she could ever have been young; a bright red hood over crone-like, fluttering grey locks; a little face seamed by a thousand fine, criss-cross wrinkles; a long nose with a knob on the end of it; little twinkling, eager, grey eyes under bristly brows; a ragged man's coat covering her from neck to feet; a basket in one hand and a black knobby stick in the other.

"Staring wasn't thought good breeding in my time," said Aunt Tom.

"Oh!" said Emily again. "Excuse me— How do you do!" she added, with a vague grasp after her manners.

"Polite—and not too proud," said Aunt Tom, peering curiously at her. "I've been up to the big house with a pair of socks for the b'y but 'twas yourself I wanted to see."

"Me?" said Emily blankly.

"Yis. The b'y has been talking a bit of you and a plan kem into my head. Thinks I to myself it's no bad notion. But I'll make sure before I waste my bit o' money. Emily Byrd Starr is your name and Murray is your nature. If I give the b'y an eddication will ye marry him when ye grow up?"

"Me!" said Emily again. It seemed to be all she could say. Was she dreaming? She *must* be.

"Yis—you. You're half Murray and it'll be a great step up f'r the b'y. He's smart and he'll be a rich man some day and boss the country. But divil a cent will I spend on him unless you promise."

"Aunt Elizabeth wouldn't let me," cried Emily, too frightened of this odd old body to refuse on her own account.

"If you've got any Murray in you you'll do your own choosing," said Aunt Tom, thrusting her face so close to Emily's that her bushy eyebrows tickled Emily's nose. "Say you'll marry the b'y and to college he goes."

Emily seemed to be rendered speechless. She could think of nothing to say—oh, if she could *only* wake up! She could not even run.

"Say it!" insisted Aunt Tom, thumping her stick sharply on a stone in the path.

Emily was so horrified that she might have said something—anything—to escape. But at this moment Perry bounded out of the spruce copse, his face white with rage, and seized his Aunt Tom most disrespectfully by the shoulder.

"You go home!" he said furiously.

"Now, b'y dear," quavered Aunt Tom deprecatingly. "I was only trying to do you a good turn. I was asking her to marry ye after a bit an—"

"I'll do my own asking!" Perry was angrier than ever. "You've likely spoiled everything. Go home—go home, I say!"

Aunt Tom hobbled off muttering, "Then I'll know better than to waste me bit o' money. No Murray, no money, me b'y."

When she had disappeared down the brook path Perry turned to Emily. From white he had gone very red.

"Don't mind her—she's cracked," he said. "Of course, when I grow up I mean to ask you to marry me but—"

"I couldn't—Aunt Elizabeth—"

"Oh, she will then. I'm going to be premier of Canada some day."

"But I wouldn't want—I'm sure I wouldn't—"

"You will when you grow up. Ilse is better looking of course, and I don't know why I like you best but I do."

"Don't you ever talk to me like this again!" commanded Emily, beginning to recover her dignity.

"Oh, I won't—not till we grow up. I'm as ashamed of it as you are," said Perry with a sheepish grin. "Only I had to say something after Aunt Tom butted in like that. I ain't to blame for it so don't you hold it against me. But just you remember that I'm going to ask you some day. And I believe Teddy Kent is too."

Emily was walking haughtily away but she turned at this to say coolly over her shoulder,

"If he does I'll marry him."

"If you do I'll knock his head off," shouted Perry in a prompt rage.

But Emily walked steadily on home and went to the garret to think things over.

"It has been romantic but not comfortable," was her conclusion. And that particular poem on spring was never finished.

22
Wyther Grange

No reply or acknowledgement came from Great-Aunt Nancy Priest regarding Emily's picture. Aunt Elizabeth and Aunt Laura, knowing Great-Aunt Nancy's ways tolerably well, were not surprised at this, but Emily felt rather worried over it. Perhaps Great-Aunt Nancy did not approve of what she had done; or perhaps she still thought her too stupid to bother with.

Emily did not like to lie under the imputation of stupidity. She wrote a scathing epistle to Great-Aunt Nancy on a letter-bill in which she did not mince her opinions as to that ancient lady's knowledge of the rules of epistolary etiquette; the letter was folded up and stowed away on the little shelf under the sofa but it served its purpose in blowing off steam and Emily had ceased to think about the matter when a letter came from Great-Aunt Nancy in July.

Elizabeth and Laura talked the matter over in the cookhouse, forgetful or ignorant of the fact that Emily was sitting on the kitchen doorstep just outside. Emily was imagining herself attending a drawing-room of Queen Victoria. Robed in white, with ostrich plumes, veil, and court train, she had just bent to kiss the Queen's hand when Aunt Elizabeth's voice shattered her dream as a pebble thrown into a pool scatters the fairy reflection.

"What is your opinion, Laura," Aunt Elizabeth was saying, "of letting Emily visit Aunt Nancy?"

Emily pricked up her ears. What was in the wind now?

"From her letter she seems very anxious to have the child," said Laura.

Elizabeth sniffed.

"A whim—a whim. You know what her whims are. Likely by the time Emily got there she'd be quite over it and have no use for her."

"Yes, but on the other hand if we don't let her go she will be dreadfully offended and never forgive us—or Emily. Emily should have her chance."

"I don't know that her chance is worth much. If Aunt Nancy really has any money beyond her annuity—and that's what neither you nor I nor any living soul knows, unless it's Caroline—she'll likely leave it all to some of the Priests—Leslie Priest's a favourite of hers, I understand. Aunt Nancy always liked her husband's family better than her own, even though she's always slurring at them. Still—she *might* take a fancy to Emily—they're both so odd they might suit each other—but you know the way she talks—she and that abominable old Caroline."

"Emily is too young to understand," said Aunt Laura.

"I understand more than you think," cried Emily indignantly.

Aunt Elizabeth jerked open the cook-house door.

"Emily Starr, haven't you learned by this time not to listen?"

"I wasn't listening. I thought you knew I was sitting here—I can't help my ears *hearing*. Why didn't you *whisper*? When you whisper I know you're talking secrets and I don't try to hear them. Am I going to Great-Aunt Nancy's for a visit?"

"We haven't decided," said Aunt Elizabeth coldly, and that was all the satisfaction Emily got for a week. She hardly knew herself whether she wanted to go or not. Aunt Elizabeth had begun making cheese—New

Moon was noted for its cheeses—and Emily found the whole process absorbing, from the time the rennet was put in the warm new milk till the white curds were packed away in the hoop and put under the press in the old orchard, with the big, round, grey "cheese" stone to weight it down as it had weighed down New Moon cheeses for a hundred years. And then she and Ilse and Teddy and Perry were absorbed heart and soul in "playing out" the "Midsummer Night's Dream" in Lofty John's bush and it was very fascinating. When they entered Lofty John's bush they went out of the realm of daylight and things known into the realm of twilight and mystery and enchantment. Teddy had painted wonderful scenery on old boards and pieces of sails, which Perry had got at the Harbor. Ilse had fashioned delightful fairy wings from tissue paper and tinsel, and Perry had made an ass's head for *Bottom* out of an old calf-skin that was very realistic. Emily had toiled happily for many weeks copying out the different parts and adapting them to circumstances. She had "cut" the play after a fashion that would have harrowed Shakespeare's soul but after all the result was quite pretty and coherent. It did not worry them that four small actors had to take six times as many parts. Emily was *Titania* and *Hermia* and a job lot of fairies besides, Ilse was *Hippolyta* and *Helena*, plus some more fairies, and the boys were anything that the dialogue required. Aunt Elizabeth knew nothing of it all; she would promptly have put a stop to the whole thing, for she thought play-acting exceedingly wicked; but Aunt Laura was privy to the plot, and Cousin Jimmy and Lofty John had already attended a moonlight rehearsal.

To go away and leave all this, even for a time, would be a hard wrench, but on the other hand Emily had a burning curiosity to see Great-Aunt Nancy and Wyther Grange, her quaint, old house at Priest Pond with the famous stone dogs on the gateposts. On the whole, she thought she would like to go; and when she saw Aunt Laura doing up her starched white petticoats and

Aunt Elizabeth grimly dusting off a small, black, nail-studded trunk in the garret she knew, before she was told, that the visit to Priest Pond was going to come off; so she took out the letter she had written to Aunt Nancy and added an apologetic postscript.

Ilse chose to be disgruntled because Emily was going for a visit. In reality Ilse felt appalled at the lonely prospect of a month or more without her inseparable chum. No more jolly evenings of play-acting in Lofty John's bush, no more pungent quarrels. Besides, Ilse herself had never been anywhere for a visit in her whole life and she felt sore over this fact.

"*I* wouldn't go to Wyther Grange for anything," said Ilse. "It's haunted."

"'Tisn't."

"Yes! It's haunted by a ghost you can *feel* and *hear* but never *see*. Oh, I wouldn't be *you* for the world! Your Great-Aunt Nancy is an *awful crank* and the old woman who lives with her is a *witch*. She'll put a spell on you. You'll pine away and die."

"I won't—she isn't!"

"*Is!* Why, she makes the stone dogs on the gateposts howl every night if any one comes near the place. They go, 'Wo-or-oo-oo.'"

Ilse was not a born elocutionist for nothing. Her "wo-or-oo-oo" was extremely gruesome. But it was daylight, and Emily was brave as a lion in daylight.

"You're jealous," she said, and walked off.

"I'm not, you blithering centipede," Ilse yelled after her. "Putting on airs because your aunt has stone dogs on her gateposts! Why, I know a woman in Shrewsbury who has dogs on her posts that are ten times stonier than your aunt's!"

But next morning Ilse was over to bid Emily good-bye and entreat her to write every week. Emily was going to drive to Priest Pond with Old Kelly. Aunt Elizabeth was to have driven her but Aunt Elizabeth was not feeling well that day and Aunt Laura could not leave her. Cousin Jimmy had to work at the hay. It looked as if she could not go, and this was rather serious, for Aunt Nancy had been told to expect her that day and Aunt Nancy did not like to be disappointed. If Emily did not turn up at Priest Pond on the day set Great-Aunt Nancy was quite capable of shutting the door in her face when she did appear and telling her to go back home. Nothing less than this conviction would have induced Aunt Elizabeth to fall in with Old Kelly's suggestion that Emily should ride to Priest Pond with him. His home was on the other side of it and he was going straight there.

Emily was quite delighted. She liked Old Kelly and thought that a drive on his fine red wagon would be quite an adventure. Her little black box was hoisted to the roof and tied there and they went clinking and glittering down the New Moon lane in fine style. The tins in the bowels of the wagon behind them rumbled like a young earthquake.

"Get up, my nag, get up," said Old Kelly. "Sure, an' I always like to drive the pretty gurrls. An' when is the wedding to be?"

"Whose wedding?"

"The slyness av her! Your own, av coorse."

"I have no intention of being married—immediately," said Emily, in a very good imitation of Aunt Elizabeth's tone and manner.

"Sure, and ye're a chip av the ould block. Miss Elizabeth herself couldn't have said it better. Get up, my nag, get up."

"I only meant," said Emily, fearing that she had insulted Old Kelly, "that I am too young to be married."

"The younger the better—the less mischief ye'll be after working with them come-hither eyes. Get up, my nag, get up. The baste is tired. So we'll let him go at his own swate will. Here's a bag av swaties for ye. Ould Kelley always trates the ladies. Come now, tell me all about him."

"About who?"—but Emily knew quite well.

"Your beau, av coorse."

"I haven't *any* beau. Mr. Kelly, I wish you wouldn't talk to me about such things."

"Sure, and I won't if 'tis a sore subject. Don't ye be minding if ye haven't got one—there'll be scads av them after a while. And if the right one doesn't know what's good for him, just ye come to Ould Kelly and get some toad ointment."

Toad ointment! It sounded horrible. Emily shivered. But she would rather talk about toad ointment than beaux.

"What is that for?"

"It's a love charm," said Old Kelly mysteriously. "Put a li'l smooch on his eyelids and he's yourn for life with never a squint at any other gurrl."

"It doesn't *sound* very nice," said Emily. "How do you make it?"

"You bile four toads alive till they're good and soft and then mash—"

"Oh, stop, stop!" implored Emily, putting her hands to her ears. "I don't want to hear any more—you couldn't be so cruel!"

"Cruel is it? You were after eating lobsters this day that were biled alive—"

"I don't believe it. I don't. If it's true I'll never, never eat one again. Oh, Mr. Kelly, I thought you were a nice kind man—but those poor toads!"

"Gurrl dear, it was only me joke. An' you won't be nading toad ointment to win your lad's love. Wait you now—I've something in the till behind me for a prisent for you."

Old Kelly fished out a box which he put into Emily's lap. She found a dainty little hairbrush in it.

"Look at the back av it," said Old Kelly. "You'll see something handsome—all the love charm ye'll ever nade."

Emily turned it over. Her own face looked back at her from a little inset mirror surrounded by a scroll of painted roses.

"Oh, Mr. Kelly—how pretty—I mean the roses and

the glass," she cried. "Is it really for me? Oh, thank you, thank you! Now, I can have Emily-in-the-glass whenever I want her. Why, I can carry her round with me. And you were really only in fun about the toads!"

"Av coorse. Get up, my nag, get up. An' so ye're going to visit the ould lady over at Praste Pond? Ever been there?"

"No."

"It's full of Prastes. Ye can't throw a stone but ye hit one. And hit one—hit all. They're as proud and lofty as the Murrays themselves. The only wan I know is Adam Praste—the others hold too high. He's the black shape and quite sociable. But if ye want to see how the world looked on the morning after the flood go into his barnyard on a rainy day. Look a-here, gurrl dear"—Old Kelly lowered his voice mysteriously—"don't ye ever marry a Praste."

"Why not?" asked Emily, who had never thought of marrying a Priest but was immediately curious as to why she shouldn't.

"They're ill to marry—ill to live with. The wives die young. The ould lady of the Grange fought her man out and buried him but she had the Murray luck. I wouldn't trust it too far. The only dacent Praste among them is the wan they call Jarback Praste and he's too ould for you."

"Why do they call him Jarback?"

"Wan av his shoulders is a l'il bit higher than the other. He's got a bit of money and doesn't be after having to work. A book worrum, I'm belaving. Have ye got a bit av cold iron about you?"

"No; why?"

"Ye should have. Old Caroline Praste at the Grange is a witch if ever there was one."

"Why, that's what Ilse said. But there are no such thing as witches really, Mr. Kelly."

"Maybe that's thrue but it's better to be on the safe side. Here, put this horseshoe-nail in your pocket and don't cross her if ye can help it. Ye don't mind if I have a bit av a smoke, do ye?"

Emily did not mind at all. It left her free to follow her own thoughts, which were more agreeable than Old Kelly's talk of toads and witches. The road from Blair Water to Priest Pond was a very lovely one, winding along the gulf shore, crossing fir fringed rivers and inlets, and coming ever and anon on one of the ponds for which that part of the north shore was noted—Blair Water, Derry Pond, Long Pond, Three Ponds where three blue lakelets were strung together like three great sapphires held by a silver thread; and then Priest Pond, the largest of all, almost as round as Blair Water. As they drove down towards it Emily drank the scene in with avid eyes—as soon as possible she must write a description of it; she had packed the Jimmy blank book in her box for just such purposes.

The air seemed to be filled with opal dust over the great pond and the bowery summer homesteads around it. A western sky of smoky red was arched over the big Malvern Bay beyond. Little grey sails were drifting along by the fir-fringed shores. A sequestered side road, fringed thickly with young maples and birches, led down to Wyther Grange. How damp and cool the air was in the hollows! And how the ferns did smell! Emily was sorry when they reached Wyther Grange and climbed in between the gateposts whereon the big stone dogs sat very stonily, looking grim enough in the twilight.

The wide hall door was open and a flood of light streamed out over the lawn. A little old woman was standing in it. Old Kelly seemed suddenly in something of a hurry. He swung Emily and her box to the ground, shook hands hastily and whispered, "Don't lose that bit av a nail. Good-bye. I wish ye a cool head and a warm heart," and was off before the little old woman could reach them.

"So this is Emily of New Moon!" Emily heard a rather shrill, cracked voice saying. She felt a thin, clawlike hand grasp hers and draw her towards the door. There were no witches, Emily knew,—but she thrust her hand into her pocket and touched the horseshoe-nail.

23
Deals with Ghosts

"Your aunt is in the back parlor," said Caroline Priest, "Come this way. Are you tired?"

"No," said Emily, following Caroline and taking her in thoroughly. If Caroline were a witch she was a very small one. She was really no taller than Emily herself. She wore a black silk dress and a little string cap of black net edged with black ruching on her yellowish white hair. Her face was more wrinkled than Emily had ever supposed a face could be and she had the peculiar grey-green eyes which, as Emily afterwards discovered, "ran" in the Priest clan.

"You may be a witch," thought Emily, "but I think I can manage *you*."

They went through the spacious hall, catching glimpses on either side of large, dim, splendid rooms, then through the kitchen end out of it into an odd little back hall. It was long and narrow and dark. On one side was a row of four, square, small-paned windows, on the other were cupboards, reaching from floor to ceiling, with doors of black shining wood. Emily felt like one of the heroines in Gothic romance, wandering at midnight through a subterranean dungeon, with some unholy guide. She had read "The Mysteries of Udolpho" and "The Romance of the Forest" before the taboo had fallen on Dr. Burnley's bookcase. She shivered. It was awful but interesting.

At the end of the hall a flight of steps led up to a door. Beside the steps was an immense black grandfather's clock reaching almost to the ceiling.

"We shut little girls up in that when they're bad," whispered Caroline, nodding at Emily, as she opened the door that led into the back parlour.

"I'll take good care you won't shut *me* up in it," thought Emily.

The back parlour was a pretty, quaint old room where a table was laid for supper. Caroline led Emily through it and knocked at another door, using a quaint old brass knocker that was fashioned like a chessy-cat, with such an irresistible grin that you wanted to grin, too, when you saw it. Somebody said, "Come in," and they went down another four steps—was there ever such a funny house?—into a bedroom. And here at last was Great-Aunt Nancy Priest, sitting in her arm-chair, with her black stick leaning against her knee, and her tiny white hands, still pretty, and sparkling with fine rings, lying on her purple silk apron.

Emily felt a distinct shock of disappointment. After hearing that poem in which Nancy Murray's beauty of nut-brown hair and starry brown eyes and cheek of satin rose had been be-rhymed she had somehow expected Great-Aunt Nancy, in spite of her ninety years, to be beautiful still. But Aunt Nancy was white-haired and yellow-skinned and wrinkled and shrunken, though her brown eyes were still bright and shrewd. Somehow, she looked like an old fairy—an impish, tolerant old fairy, who might turn suddenly malevolent if you rubbed her the wrong way—only fairies never wore long, gold-tasselled earrings that almost touched their shoulders, or white lace caps with purple pansies in them.

"So this is Juliet's girl!" she said, giving Emily one of her sparkling hands. "Don't look so startled, child. I'm not going to kiss you. I never held with inflicting kisses on defenseless creatures simply because they were so unlucky as to be my relatives. Now, who does she look like, Caroline?"

Emily made a mental grimace. Now for another ordeal of comparisons, wherein dead-and-gone noses and eyes and foreheads would be dragged out and fitted on her. She was thoroughly tired of having her looks talked over in every gathering of the clans.

"Not much like the Murrays," said Caroline, peering so closely into her face that Emily involuntarily drew back. "Not so handsome as the Murrays."

"Nor the Starrs either. Her father was a handsome man—so handsome that I'd have run away with him myself if I'd been fifty years younger. There's nothing of Juliet in her that I can see. Juliet was pretty. You are not as good-looking as that picture made you out but I didn't expect you would be. Pictures and epitaphs are never to be trusted. Where's your bang gone, Emily?"

"Aunt Elizabeth combed it back."

"Well, you comb it down again while you're in my house. There's something of your Grandfather Murray about your eye-brows. Your grandfather was a handsome man—and a darned bad-tempered one—almost as bad-tempered as the Priests,—hey, Caroline?"

"If you please, Great-Aunt Nancy," said Emily deliberately, "I don't like to be told I look like other people. I look just like myself."

Aunt Nancy chuckled.

"Spunk, I see. Good. I never cared for meek youngsters. So you're not stupid, eh?"

"No, I'm not."

Great-Aunt Nancy grinned this time. Her false teeth looked uncannily white and young in her old, brown face.

"Good. If you've brains it's better than beauty—brains last, beauty doesn't. Me, for example. Caroline here, now, never had either brains nor beauty, had you, Caroline? Come, let's go to supper. Thank goodness, my stomach has stood by me if my good looks haven't."

Great-Aunt Nancy hobbled, by the aid of her stick, up the steps and over to the table. She sat at one end, Caroline at the other, Emily between, feeling rather uncomfortable. But the ruling passion was still strong in her and she was already composing a description of them for the blank book.

"I wonder if anybody will be sorry when you die," she thought, looking intently at Caroline's wizened old face.

"Come now, tell me," said Aunt Nancy. "If you're not stupid, why did you write me such a stupid letter that first time. Lord, but it was stupid! I read it over to Caroline to punish her whenever she is naughty."

"I couldn't write any other kind of a letter because Aunt Elizabeth said she was going to read it."

"Trust Elizabeth for that. Well, you can write what you like here—and say what you like—and do what you like. Nobody will interfere with you or try to bring you up. I asked you for a visit, not for discipline. Thought likely you'd have enough of that at New Moon. You can have the run of the house and pick a beau to your liking from the Priest boys—not that the young fry are what they were in my time."

"I don't want a beau," retorted Emily. She felt rather disgusted. Old Kelly had ranted about beaux half the way over and here was Aunt Nancy beginning on the same unnecessary subject.

"Don't you tell me," said Aunt Nancy, laughing till her gold tassels shook. "There never was a Murray of New Moon that didn't like a beau. When I was your age I had half a dozen. All the little boys in Blair Water were fighting about me. Caroline here now never had a beau in her life, had you, Caroline?"

"Never wanted one," snapped Caroline.

"Eighty and twelve say the same thing and both lie," said Aunt Nancy. "What's the use of being hypocrites among ourselves? I don't say it isn't well enough when men are about. Caroline, do you notice what a pretty hand Emily has? As pretty as mine when I was young.

And an elbow like a cat's. Cousin Susan Murray had an elbow like that. It's odd—she has more Murray points than Starr points and yet she looks like the Starrs and not like the Murrays. What odd sums in addition we all are—the answer is never what you'd expect. Caroline, what a pity Jarback isn't home. He'd like Emily—I have a feeling he'd like Emily. Jarback's the only Priest that'll ever go to heaven, Emily. Let's have a look at your ankles, puss."

Emily rather unwillingly put out her foot. Aunt Nancy nodded her satisfaction.

"Mary Shipley's ankle. Only one in a generation has it. I had it. The Murray ankles are thick. Even your mother's ankles were thick. Look at that instep, Caroline. Emily, you're not a beauty but if you learn to use your eyes and hands and feet properly you'll pass for one. The men are easily fooled and if the women say you're not 'twill be held for jealousy."

Emily decided that this was a good opportunity to find out something that had puzzled her.

"Old Mr. Kelly said I had come-hither eyes, Aunt Nancy. Have I? And *what* are come-hither eyes?"

"Jock Kelly's an old ass. You haven't come-hither eyes—it wouldn't be a Murray tradish." Aunt Nancy laughed. "The Murrays have keep-your-distance eyes—and so have you—though your lashes contradict them a bit. But sometimes eyes like that—combined with certain other points—are quite as effective as come-hither eyes. Men go by contraries oftener than not—if you tell them to keep off they'll come on. My own Nathaniel now—the only way to get him to do anything was to coax him to do the opposite. Remember, Caroline? Have another cooky, Emily?"

"I haven't had one yet," said Emily, rather resentfully.

Those cookies looked very tempting and she had been wishing they might be passed. She didn't know why Aunt Nancy and Caroline both laughed. Caroline's laugh was unpleasant—a dry, rusty sort of laugh—"no juice in it," Emily decided. She thought she would write in her description that Caroline had a "thin, rattling laugh."

"What do you think of us?" demanded Aunt Nancy. "Come now, what *do* you think of us?"

Emily was dreadfully embarrassed. She had just been thinking of writing that Aunt Nancy looked "withered and shrivelled;" but one couldn't say that—one *couldn't.*

"Tell the truth and shame the devil," said Aunt Nancy.

"That isn't a fair question," cried Emily.

"You think," said Aunt Nancy, grinning, "that I'm a hideous old hag and that Caroline isn't quite human. She isn't. She never was—but you should have seen *me* seventy years ago. I was handsomest of all the handsome Murrays. The men were mad about me. When I married Nat Priest his three brothers could have cut his throat. One cut his own. Oh, I played havoc in my time. All I regret is I can't live it over. 'Twas a grand life while it lasted. I queened it over them. The women hated me, of course—all but Caroline here. You worshipped me, didn't you, Caroline? And you worship me yet, don't you, Caroline? Caroline, I *wish* you didn't have a wart on your nose."

"I wish you had one on your tongue," said Caroline waspishly.

Emily was beginning to feel tired and bewildered. It was interesting—and Aunt Nancy was kind enough in her queer way; but at home Ilse and Perry and Teddy would be foregathering in Lofty John's bush for their evening revel, and Saucy Sal would be sitting on the dairy steps, waiting for Cousin Jimmy to give her the froth. Emily suddenly realized that she was as homesick for New Moon as she had been for Maywood her first night at New Moon.

"The child's tired," said Aunt Nancy. "Take her to bed, Caroline. Put her in the Pink Room."

Emily followed Caroline through the back hall, through the kitchen, through the front hall, up the stairs, down a long hall, through a long side hall. Where on earth was she being taken? Finally they reached a large room. Caroline set down the lamp, and asked Emily if she had a nightgown.

"Of course I have. Do you suppose Aunt Elizabeth would have let me come without one?"

Emily was quite indignant.

"Nancy says you can sleep as long as you like in the morning," said Caroline. "Good-night. Nancy and I sleep in the old wing, of course, and the rest of us sleep well in our graves."

With this cryptic remark Caroline trotted out and shut the door.

Emily sat down on an embroidered ottoman and looked about her. The window curtains were of faded pink brocade and the walls were hung with pink paper decorated with diamonds of rose chains. It made a very pretty fairy paper, as Emily found by cocking her eyes at it. There was a green carpet on the floor, so lavishly splashed with big pink roses that Emily was almost afraid to walk on it. She decided that the room was a very splendid one.

"But I have to sleep here alone, so I must say my prayers very carefully," she reflected.

She undressed rather hastily, blew out the light and got into bed. She covered herself up to her chin and lay there, staring at the high, white ceiling. She had grown so used to Aunt Elizabeth's curtained bed that she felt curiously unsheltered in this low, modern one. But at least the window was wide open—evidently Aunt Nancy did not share Aunt Elizabeth's horror of night air. Through it Emily could see summer fields lying in the magic of a rising yellow moon. But the room was big and ghostly. She felt horribly far away from everybody. She was lonesome—homesick. She thought of Old Kelly and his toad ointment. Perhaps he *did* boil the toads alive after all. This hideous thought tormented her. It was *awful* to think of toads—or anything—being boiled alive. She had never slept alone before. Suddenly she was frightened. How the window rattled. It sounded terribly as if somebody—or *something*—were trying to get in. She thought of Ilse's ghost—a ghost you couldn't *see* but could *hear* and *feel* was something especially spooky in the way of ghosts—she thought of the stone dogs that went "Wo—or—oo—oo" at midnight. A dog *did* begin to howl somewhere. Emily felt a cold perspiration on her brow. *What* had Caroline meant about the rest of them sleeping well in their graves? The floor creaked. Wasn't there somebody—or *something*—tiptoeing round outside the door? Didn't something move in the corner? There were mysterious sounds in the long hall.

"I *won't* be scared," said Emily. "I *won't* think of those things, and tomorrow I'll write down all about how I feel now."

And then—she *did* hear something—right behind the wall at the head of her bed. There was no mistake about it. It was not imagination. She heard distinctly strange uncanny rustles—as if stiff silk dresses were rubbing against each other—as if fluttering wings fanned the air—and there were soft, low, muffled sounds like tiny children's cries or moans. They lasted—they kept on. Now and then they would die away—then start up again.

Emily cowered under the bedclothes, cold with real terror. Before, her fright had been only on the surface—she had *known* there was nothing to fear, even while she feared. Something in her braced her to endure. But *this* was no mistake—no imagination. The rustles and flutterings and cries and moans were all too real. Wyther Grange suddenly became a dreadful, uncanny place. Ilse was right—it *was* haunted. And she was all alone here, with miles of rooms and halls between her and any human being. It was cruel of Aunt Nancy to put her in a haunted room. Aunt Nancy must have known it was haunted—cruel old Aunt Nancy with her ghoulish pride in men who had killed themselves for her. Oh, if she were back in dear New Moon, with Aunt Elizabeth beside her. Aunt Elizabeth was not an ideal bedfellow but she was flesh-and-blood. And if the windows were hermetically sealed they kept out spooks as well as night air.

"Perhaps it won't be so bad if I say my prayers over again," thought Emily.

But even this didn't help much.

To the end of her life Emily never forgot that first horrible night at Wyther Grange. She was so tired that sometimes she dozed fitfully off only to be awakened in a few minutes in panic horror, by the rustling and muffled moans behind her bed. Every ghost and groan, every tortured spirit and bleeding nun of the books she had read came into her mind.

"Aunt Elizabeth was right—novels aren't fit to read," she thought. "Oh, I will die here—of fright—I know I will. I know I'm a coward—I can't be brave."

When morning came the room was bright with sunshine and free from mysterious sounds. Emily got up, dressed and found her way to the old wing. She was pale, with black-ringed eyes, but resolute.

"Well, and how did you sleep?" asked Aunt Nancy graciously.

Emily ignored the question.

"I want to go home today," she said.

Aunt Nancy stared.

"Home? Nonsense! Are you such a homesick baby as that?"

"I'm not homesick—not *very*—but I must go home."

"You can't—there's no one here to take you. You don't expect Caroline can drive you to Blair Water, do you?"

"Then I will walk."

Aunt Nancy thumped her stick angrily on the floor.

"You will stay right here until I'm ready for you to go, Miss Puss. I never tolerate any whims but my own. Caroline knows that, don't you, Caroline? Sit down to your breakfast—and eat—*eat*."

Aunt Nancy glared at Emily.

"I won't stay here," said Emily. "I won't stay another

night in that horrible haunted room. It was cruel of you to put me there. If—'' Emily gave Aunt Nancy glare for glare—"if I was Salome I'd ask for *your* head on a charger."

"Hoity-toity! What nonsense is this about a haunted room? We've no ghosts at Wyther Grange. Have we, Caroline? We don't consider them hygienic."

"You have something *dreadful* in that room—it rustled and moaned and cried all night long right in the wall behind my bed. I won't stay—I won't—."

Emily's tears came in spite of her efforts to repress them. She was so unstrung nervously that she couldn't help crying. It lacked but little of hysterics with her already.

Aunt Nancy looked at Caroline and Caroline looked back at Aunt Nancy.

"We should have told her, Caroline. It's all our fault. I clean forgot—it's so long since any one slept in the Pink Room. No wonder she was frightened. Emily, you poor child, it was a shame. It would serve me right to have my head on a charger, you vindictive scrap. We should have told you."

"Told me—what?"

"About the swallows in the chimney. That was what you heard. The big central chimney goes right up through the walls behind your bed. It is never used now since the fireplaces were built in. The swallows nest there—hundreds of them. They do make an uncanny noise—fluttering and quarrelling as they do."

Emily felt foolish and ashamed—much more ashamed than she needed to feel, for her experience had really been a very trying one, and older folks than she had been woefully frightened o' nights in the Pink Room at Wyther Grange. Nancy Priest *had* put people into that room sometimes expressly to scare them. But to do her justice she really had forgotten in Emily's case and was sorry.

Emily said no more about going home; Caroline and Aunt Nancy were both very kind to her that day; she had a good nap in the afternoon; and when the second night came she went straight to the Pink Room and slept soundly the night through. The rustles and cries were as distinct as ever but swallows and spectres were two entirely different things.

"After all, I think I'll like Wyther Grange," said Emily.

24
A Different Kind of Happiness

"JULY 20th.

"Dear Father:

"I have been a fortnight at Wyther Grange and I have not written to you once. But I thought of you every day. I had to write to Aunt Laura and Ilse and Teddy and Cousin Jimmy and Perry and between times I am having such fun. The first night I was here I did not think I was going to be happy. But I am—only it's a different kind from New Moon happiness.

"Aunt Nancy and Caroline are very good to me and let me do exactly as I like. This is very agreeable. They are very sarcastic to each other. But I think they are a good bit like Ilse and me—they fight quite frequently but love each other very hard between times. I am sure Caroline isn't a witch but I would like to know what she thinks of when she is all alone by herself. Aunt Nancy is not pretty any longer but she is very *aristocratic looking*. She doesn't walk much because of her roomatism, so she sits mostly in her back parlor and reads and knits lace or plays cards with Caroline. I talk to her a great deal because she says it amuses her and I have told her a great many things but I have never told her that I write poetry. If I did I know she would make me recite it to her and I feel she is not the right person to recite your poetry to. And I do not talk about you or Mother to her, though she tries to make me. I told her all about Lofty John and his bush and going to Father Cassidy. She chuckled over that and said she always liked to talk to the Catholic Priests because they were the only men in the world a woman could talk to for more than ten minutes without other women saying she was throwing herself at their heads.

"Aunt Nancy says a great many things like that. She and Caroline talk a great deal to each other about things that happened in the Priest and Murray families. I like to sit and listen. They don't stop just as things are getting interesting the way Aunt Elizabeth and Aunt Laura do. A good many things I don't understand but I will remember them and will find out about them sometime. I have written descriptions of Aunt Nancy and Caroline in my Jimmy-book. I keep the book hid behind the wardrobe in my room because I found Caroline rummidging in my trunk one day. I must not call Aunt Nancy Great-Aunt. She says it makes her feel like Methoosaleh. She tells me all about the men who were in love with her. It seems to me they all behaved pretty much the same. I don't think that was exciting but she says it was. She tells me about all the parties and dances they used to have here long ago. Wyther Grange is bigger than New Moon and the furniture is much handsomer but it is harder to feel acquainted with it.

"There are many interesting things in this house. I love to look at them. There is a Jakobite glass on a stand in the parlor. It was a glass *an old ansester* of the Priests had long ago in Scotland and it has a thistle and a rose on it and they used it to drink Prince Charlie's health with and for *no other purpose*. It is a very *valewable airloom* and Aunt Nancy prizes it highly. And she has a pickled snake in a big glass jar in the china cabinet. It is hideous but fascinating. I shiver when I see it but yet I go to look at it every day. Something seems to drag me to it. Aunt Nancy has a bureau in her room with *glass knobs* and a vase shaped like a green fish sitting up on end and a Chinese draggon with a curly tail, and a case of sweet little stuffed humming birds and a sandglass for boiling eggs by and a framed wreath made out of the hair of all the dead Priests and lots of old dagerrotipes. But the thing I like the best of all is a great silvery shining ball hanging from the lamp in the parlour. It reflects everything like a little fairy world. Aunt Nancy calls it a gazing-ball, and says that when she is dead I am to have it. I wish she hadn't said that because I want the ball so much that I can't help wondering when she will die and that makes me feel wicked. I am to have the chessy-cat door knocker and her gold earrings, too. These are Murray airlooms. Aunt Nancy says the Priest airlooms must go to the Priests. I will like the chessy-cat but I don't want the earrings. I'd rather not have people notice my ears.

I have to sleep alone. I feel frightened but I think if I could get over being frightened I'd like it. I don't mind the swallows now. It's just being alone so far away from any one. But it is lovely to be able to stretch out your legs just as you like and not have anybody scold you for skwirming. And when I wake up in the night and think of a splendid line of poetry (because the things that you think of like that always seem the best) I can get right out of bed and write it right down in my Jimmy-book. I couldn't do that at home and then by morning I'd likely forget it. I thought of such a nice line last night. "Lilies lifted pearly chaluses (a chalus is a kind of cup only more poetical) where bees were drowned in sweetness" and I felt happy because I was sure they were two better lines than any I had composed yet.

"I am allowed to go into the kitchen and help Caroline cook. Caroline is a good cook but sometimes she makes a mistake and this vexes Aunt Nancy because she likes nice things to eat. The other day Caroline made the barley soup far too thick and when Aunt Nancy looked at her plate she said "Lord, is this a dinner or a poltis?"

Caroline said "It is good enough for a Priest and what is good enough for a Priest is good enough for a Murray," and Aunt Nancy said "Woman, the Priests eat of the crumbs that fall from the Murrays' tables," and Caroline was so mad she cried. And Aunt Nancy said to me "Emily, never marry a Priest"—just like Old Kelly, when I have no notion of marrying one of them. I don't like any of them I've seen very much but they seem to me a good deal like other people. Jim is the best of them but impident.

"I like the Wyther Grange breakfasts better than the New Moon breakfasts. We have toast and bacon and marmalade—nicer than porridge.

"Sunday is more amusing here than at New Moon but not so holy. Nice for a change. Aunt Nancy can't go to church or knit lace so she and Caroline play cards all day but she says I must never do it—that she is just a bad example. I love to look at Aunt Nancy's big parlor Bible because there are so many interesting things in it—pieces of dresses and hair and poetry and old tintipes and accounts of deaths and weddings. I found a piece about my own birth and it gave me a queer feeling.

"In the afternoon some of the Priests come to see Aunt Nancy and stay to supper. Leslie Priest always comes. He is Aunt Nancy's faverite neffew, so Jim says. I think that is because he pays her compliments. But I saw him wink at Isaac Priest once when he paid her one. I don't like him. He treats me as if I was a meer child. Aunt Nancy says terrible things to them all but they just laugh. When they go away Aunt Nancy makes fun of them to Caroline. Caroline doesn't like it, because she is a Priest and so she and Aunt Nancy always quarrel Sunday evening and don't speak again till Monday morning.

"I can read all the books in Aunt Nancy's bookcase except the row on the top shelf. I wonder why I can't read them. Aunt Nancy said they were French novels but I just peeped into one and it was English. I wonder if Aunt Nancy tells lies.

"The place I love best is down at bay shore. Some parts of the shore are very steep and there are such nice, woodsy, *unexpected* places all along it. I wander there and compose poetry. I miss Ilse and Teddy and Perry and Saucy Sal a great deal. I had a letter from Ilse today. She wrote me that they couldn't do anything more about the Midsummer Night's Dream till I got back. It is nice to feel so necessary.

"Aunt Nancy doesn't like Aunt Elizabeth. She called her a "tyrant" one day and then she said "Jimmy Murray was a very clever boy. Elizabeth Murray killed his intellect in her temper—and nothing was done to her. If she had killed his body she would have been a murderess. The other was worse, if you ask me." I do not like Aunt Elizabeth at times myself but I felt, dear Father, that I must stand up for *my family* and I said "I do not want to hear such things said of my Aunt Elizabeth."

"And I just gave Aunt Nancy a *look*. She said "Well, Saucebox, my brother Archibald will never be dead as long as you're alive. If you don't want to hear things don't hang around when Caroline and I are talking. I notice there are plenty of things you like to hear."

"This was sarcasm, dear Father, but still I feel Aunt Nancy likes me but perhaps she will not like me very long. Jim Priest says she is fikkle and never liked anyone, even her husband, very long. But after she has been sarcastic to me she always tells Caroline to give me a piece of pie so I don't mind the sarcasm. She lets me have real tea, too. I like it. At New Moon Aunt Elizabeth won't give me anything but cambric tea because it is best for my health. Aunt Nancy says the way to be healthy is to eat just what you want and never think about your stomach. But then she was never threttened with consumption. She says I needn't be a bit frightened of dying of consumption because I have too much ginger in me. That is a comforting thought.

The only time I don't like Aunt Nancy is when she begins talking about the different parts of me and the effect they will have on the men. It makes me feel so silly.

"I will write you oftener after this, dear Father. I feel I have been neglecting you.

"P.S. I am afraid there are some mistakes in spelling in this letter. I forgot to bring my dictionary with me.

"JULY 22.

"Oh, dear Father, I am in a dreadful scrape. I don't know what I am to do. Oh, Father, I have broken Aunt Nancy's Jakobite glass. It seems to me like a dreadful dream.

"I went into the parlor today to look at the pickled snake and just as I was turning away my sleeve caught the Jakobite glass and over it went on the harth and *shivered into fragments*. At first I rushed out and left them there but afterwards I went back and carefully gathered them up and hid them in a box behind the sofa. Aunt Nancy never goes into the parlor now and Caroline not very often and perhaps they may not miss the glass until I go home. But it *haunts* me. I keep thinking of it all the time and I cannot enjoy anything. I know Aunt Nancy will be furious and never forgive me if she finds out. I could not sleep all night for worrying about it. Jim Priest came down to play with me today but he said there was no fun in me and went home. The Priests mostly say what they think. Of course there was no fun in me. How could there be? I wonder if it would do any good to pray about it. I don't feel as if it would be right to pray because I am deceiving Aunt Nancy.

"JULY 24.

"Dear Father, this is a very strange world. Nothing ever turns out just like what you expect. Last night I couldn't sleep again. I was so worried. I thought I was a coward, and doing an underhanded thing and not living up to my tradishuns. At last it got so bad I couldn't stand it. I can bear it when other people have a bad opinion of me but it hurts too much when I have a bad opinion of myself. So I got out of bed and went right back through all those halls to the back parlor. Aunt Nancy was still there all alone playing Solitare. She said what on earth was I out of bed for at such an hour. I just said, short and quick to get the worst over, "I broke your Jakobite glass yesterday and hid the pieces behind the sofa." Then I waited for the *storm to burst*. Aunt Nancy said "What a blessing. I've often wanted to smash it but never had the courage. All the Priest clan are waiting for me to die to get that glass and quarrel over it and I'm tickled to think none of them can have it now and yet can't pick a fuss with me over smashing it. Get off to bed and get your beauty sleep." I said "And aren't you mad at all, Aunt Nancy?" "If it had been a Murray airloom I'd have torn up the turf" Aunt Nancy said. "But I don't care a hoot about the Priest things."

"So I went back to bed, dear Father, and felt very releeved, but not so heroyik.

"I had a letter from Ilse today. She says Saucy Sal has had kittens at last. I feel that I ought to be home to see about them. Likely Aunt Elizabeth will have them all drowned before I get back. I had a letter from Teddy too, not much of a letter but all filled with dear little pictures of Ilse and Perry and the Tansy Patch and Lofty John's bush. They made me feel homesick.

"July 28.

"Oh, Father dear, I have found out all about the mistery of Ilse's mother. It is so terrible I can't write it down even to you. I cannot believe it but Aunt Nancy says it is true. I did not think there could be such terrible things in the world. No, I can't believe it and I won't believe it no matter who says it is true. I *know* Ilse's mother *couldn't* have done anything like that. There must have been a fearful mistake somewhere. I am so unhappy and feel as if I could never be happy any more. Last night I wept on my pillow, like the heroins in Aunt Nancy's books do."

25
"She Couldn't Have Done It"

Great-Aunt Nancy and Caroline Priest were wont to colour their grey days with the remembered crimsons of old, long-past delights and merry-makings, but they went further than this and talked over any number of old family histories before Emily with a total disregard of her youth. Loves, births, deaths, scandals, tragedies—anything that came into their old heads. Nor did they spare details. Aunt Nancy revelled in details. She forgot nothing, and sins and weaknesses that death had covered and time shown mercy to were ruthlessly dragged out and dissected by this ghoulish old lady.

Emily was not quite certain whether she really liked it or not. It *was* fascinating—it fed some dramatic hunger in her—but it made her feel unhappy somehow, as if something very ugly were concealed in the darkness of the pit they opened before her innocent eyes. As Aunt Laura had said, her youth protected her to some extent, but it could not save her from a dreadful understanding of the pitiful story of Ilse's mother on the afternoon when it seemed good to Aunt Nancy to resurrect that tale of anguish and shame.

Emily was curled up on the sofa in the back parlour, reading *The Scottish Chiefs* because it was a breathlessly hot July afternoon—too hot to haunt the bay shore. Emily was feeling very happy. The Wind Woman was ruffling over the big maple grove behind the Grange, turning the leaves until every tree seemed to be covered with strange, pale, silvery blossoms; fragrances drifted in from the garden; the world was lovely; she had had a letter from Aunt Laura saying that one of Saucy Sal's kittens had been saved for her. Emily had felt when Mike II died that she would never want another cat. But now she found she did. Everything suited her very well; she was so happy that she should have sacrificed her dearest possession to the jealous gods if she had known anything about the old pagan belief.

Aunt Nancy was tired of playing solitaire. She pushed the cards away and took up her knitting.

"Emily," she said, "has your Aunt Laura any notion of marrying Dr. Burnley?"

Emily, recalled thus abruptly from the field of Bannockburn, looked bored. Blair Water gossip had often asked or hinted this question; and now it met her in Priest Pond.

"No, I'm sure she hasn't," she said. "Why, Aunt Nancy, Dr. Burnley *hates* women."

Aunt Nancy chuckled.

"Thought perhaps he'd got over that. It's eleven years now since his wife ran away. Few men hold to one idea for anything like eleven years. But Allen Burnley always was stubborn in anything—love or hate. He still loves his wife—and that is why he hates her memory and all other women."

"I never heard the rights of that story," said Caroline. "Who was his wife?"

"Beatrice Mitchell—one of the Shrewsbury Mitchells. She was only eighteen when Allan married her. He was thirty-five. Emily, never you be fool enough to marry a man much older than yourself."

Emily said nothing. *The Scottish Chiefs* was forgotten. Her finger-tips were growing cold as they always did in excitement, her eyes turning black. She felt that she was on the verge of solving the mystery that had so long worried and puzzled her. She was desperately afraid that Aunt Nancy would branch off to something else.

"I've heard she was a great beauty," said Caroline.

Aunt Nancy sniffed.

"Depends on your taste in style. Oh, she was pretty— one of your golden-haired dolls. She had a little birthmark over her left eyebrow—just like a tiny red heart— I never could see anything but that mark when I looked at her. But her flatterers told her it was a beauty spot—'the Ace of Hearts' they called her. Allan was mad about her. She had been a flirt before her marriage. But I *will* say—for justice among women is a rare thing, Caroline—*you*, for instance, are an unjust old hag— that she didn't flirt after marrying—openly, at least. She was a sly puss—always laughing and singing and dancing—no wife for Allan Burnley if you ask me. And he could have had Laura Murray. But between a fool and a sensible woman did a man ever hesitate? The fool wins every time, Caroline. That's why *you* never got a husband. You were too sensible. I got mine by pretending to be a fool. Emily, you remember that. You have brains—hide them. Your ankles will do more for you than your brains ever will."

"Never mind Emily's ankles," said Caroline, keen on a scandal hunt. "Go on about the Burnleys."

"Well, there was a cousin of hers—Leo Mitchell from Shrewsbury. You remember the Mitchells, don't you, Caroline? This Leo was a handsome fellow—a sea-captain. He had been in love with Beatrice, so gossip ran. Some said Beatrice wanted him but that her people made her marry Allan Burnley because he was the better match. Who knows? Gossip lies nine times and tells a half truth the tenth. She pretended to be in love with Allan anyhow, and he believed it. When Leo came home from a voyage and found Beatrice married he took it coolly enough. But he was always over at Blair Water. Beatrice had plenty of excuses. Leo was her cousin—they had been brought up together—they were like brother and sister—she was so lonesome in Blair Water after living in a town—he had no home except with a brother. Allan took it all down—he was so infatuated with her she could have made him believe anything. She and Leo were always together there when Allan was always seeing his patients. Then came the night Leo's vessel—*The Lady of Winds*—was to sail from Blair Harbour for South America. He went—and my lady Beatrice went with him."

A queer little strangled sound came from Emily's corner. If Aunt Nancy or Caroline had looked at her they would have seen that the child was white as the dead, with wide, horror-filled eyes. But they did not look. They knitted and gossiped on, enjoying themselves hugely.

"How did the doctor take it?" asked Caroline.

"Take it—take it—nobody knows. Everybody knows what kind of man he's been ever since, though. He came home that night at dusk. The baby was asleep in its crib and the servant girl was watching it. She told Allan that Mrs. Burnley had gone to the harbour with her cousin for a good-bye walk and would be back at ten. Allan waited for her easily enough—he never doubted her—but she didn't come back. She had never intended to come back. In the morning *The Lady of Winds* was gone—had sailed out of the harbour at dark the night before. Beatrice had gone on board with him—that was all anybody knew. Allan Burnley *said* nothing, beyond forbidding her name ever to be mentioned in his hearing again. But *The Lady of Winds* was lost with all on board off Hatteras and that was the end of that elopement, and the end of Beatrice with her beauty and her laughter and her Ace of Hearts."

"But not the end of the shame and wretchedness she brought to her home," said Caroline shrewishly. "I'd tar and feather such a woman."

"Nonsense—if a man can't look after his wife—if he blinds his own eyes— Mercy on us, child, what is the matter?"

For Emily was standing up, holding out her hands as if pushing some loathly thing from her.

"I don't believe it," she cried, in a high, unnatural voice. "I don't believe Ilse's mother did *that*. She didn't— she couldn't have—not Ilse's *mother*."

"Catch her, Caroline!" cried Aunt Nancy.

But Emily, though the back parlour had whirled about her for a second, had recovered herself.

"Don't touch me!" she cried passionately. "Don't touch me! You—you—you *liked* hearing that story!"

She rushed out of the room. Aunt Nancy looked ashamed for a moment. For the first time it occurred to her that her scandal-loving old tongue had done a black thing. Then she shrugged her shoulders.

"She can't go through life in cotton wool. Might as well learn spades are spades now as ever. I would have thought she'd have heard it all long ago if Blair Water gossip is what it used to be. If she goes home and tells this I'll have the indignant virgins of New Moon coming down on me in holy horror as a corrupter of youth. Caroline, don't you ask me to tell you any more family horrors before my niece, you scandalous old woman. At your age! I'm surprised at you!"

Aunt Nancy and Caroline returned to their knitting and their spicy reminiscences, and upstairs in the Pink Room Emily lay face downwards on her bed and cried for hours. It was so horrible—Ilse's mother had run away and left her little baby. To Emily that was the awful thing—the strange, cruel, heartless thing that Ilse's mother had done. She could not bring herself to believe it—there was some mistake somewhere—there *was*.

"Perhaps she was kidnapped," said Emily, trying desperately to explain it. "She just went on board to look around—and he weighed anchor and carried her off. She *couldn't* have gone away of her own accord and left her dear little baby."

The story haunted Emily in good earnest. She could think of nothing else for days. It took possession of her and worried and gnawed at her with an almost physical pain. She dreaded going back to New Moon and meeting Ilse with this consciousness of a dark secret which she must hide from her. Ilse knew nothing. She had asked Ilse once where her mother was buried and Ilse had said, "Oh, I don't know. At Shrewsbury, I guess—that's where all the Mitchells are buried."

Emily wrung her slim hands together. She was as sensitive to ugliness and pain as she was to beauty and pleasure, and this thing was both hideous and agonizing. Yet she could not keep from thinking about it, day and night. Life at Wyther Grange suddenly went stale. Aunt Nancy and Caroline all at once gave up talking family history, even harmless history, before her. And as it was painful repression for them, they did not encourage her hanging round. Emily began to feel that they were glad when she was out of hearing, so she kept away and spent most of her days wandering on the bay shore. She could not compose any poetry—she could not write in her Jimmy-book—she could not even write to her father. Something seemed to hang between her and her old delights. There was a drop of poison in every cup. Even the filmy shadows on the great bay, the charm of its fir-hung cliffs and its little purple islets that looked like outposts of fairyland, could not bring to her the old "fine, careless rapture." She was afraid she could never be happy again—so intense had been her reaction to her first revelation of the world's sin and sorrow. And under it all, persisted the same incredulity—Ilse's mother *couldn't* have done it—and the same helpless longing to prove she couldn't have done it. But how could it be proved? It couldn't. She had solved one "mystery" but she had stumbled into a darker one—the reason why Beatrice Burnley had never come back on that summer twilight of long ago. For, all the evidence of facts to the contrary notwithstanding, Emily persisted in her secret belief that whatever the reason *was*, it was *not* that she had gone away in *The Lady of Winds* when that doomed ship sailed out into the starlit wonder of the gulf beyond Blair Harbour.

26
On the Bay Shore

"I wonder," thought Emily, "how much longer I have to live."

She had prowled that evening further down the bay shore than she had ever gone before. It was a warm, windy evening; the air was resinous and sweet; the bay a misty turquoise. That part of the shore whereon she found herself seemed as lonely and virgin as if no human foot had ever trodden it, save for a tiny, tricksy path, slender as red thread and bordered by great, green, velvety sheets of moss, that wound in and out of the big firs and scrub spruces. The banks grew steeper and rockier as she went on and finally the little path vanished altogether in a plot of bracken. Emily was just turning to go back when she caught sight of a magnificent spray of farewell summer, growing far out on the edge of the bank. She must get it—she had never seen farewell-summers of so dark and rich a purple. She stepped out to reach them—the treacherous mossy soil gave way under her feet and slid down the steep slope. Emily made a frantic attempt to scramble back but the harder she tried, the faster went the landslide, carrying her with it. In a moment it would pass the slope and go over the brink of the rocks, straight to the boulder-strewn shore thirty feet below. Emily had one dreadful moment of terror and despair; and then she found that the clump of mossy earth which had broken away had held on a narrow ledge of rock, half hanging over it; and she was lying on the clump. It seemed to her that the slightest movement on her part would send it over, straight to the cruel boulders underneath.

She lay very still, trying to think—trying not to be afraid. She was far, far away from any house—nobody could hear her if she screamed. And she did not even dare to scream lest the motion of her body dislodge the fragment on which she lay. How long could she lie there motionless? Night was coming on. Aunt Nancy would grow anxious when the dark fell and would send Caroline to look for her. But Caroline would never find her here. Nobody would ever think of looking here for her, so far away from the Grange, in the spruce barrens of the Lower Bay. To lie there alone all night—to fancy the earth was slipping over—waiting for help that would never come—Emily could hardly restrain a shudder that might have been ruinous.

She had faced death once before, or thought she had, on the night when Lofty John had told her she had eaten a poisoned apple—but this was even harder. To die here, all alone, far away from home! They might never know what had become of her—never find her. The crows or the gulls would pick her eyes out. She dramatized the thing so vividly that she almost screamed with the horror of it. She would just disappear from the world as Ilse's mother had disappeared.

What had become of Ilse's mother? Even in her own desperate plight Emily asked herself that question. And she would never see dear New Moon again and Teddy and the dairy and the Tansy Patch and Lofty John's bush and the mossy old sundial and her precious little heap of manuscripts on the sofa shelf in the garret.

"I must be very brave and patient," she thought. "My only chance is to lie still. And I can pray in my mind—I'm sure God can hear thoughts as well as words. It is nice to think He can hear me if nobody else can. O God—Father's God—please work a miracle and save my life, because I don't think I'm fit to die yet. Excuse my not being on my knees—You can see I can't move. And if I die please don't let Aunt Elizabeth find my letter-bills ever. Please let Aunt Laura find them. And please don't let Caroline move out the wardrobe when she house-cleans because then she would find my Jimmy-book and read what I wrote about her. Please forgive all my sins, especially not being grateful enough and cutting a bang, and please don't let Father be very far away. Amen."

Then, characteristically she thought of a postscript. "And oh, *please* let somebody find out that Ilse's mother didn't do *that*."

She lay very still. The light on the water began to turn warm gold and rose. A great pine on a bluff in front of her overflowed in a crest of dark boughs against the amber splendour behind it—a part of the beauty of the beautiful world that was slipping away from her. The chill of the evening gulf breeze began to creep over her. Once a bit of earth broke off at her side and went down—Emily heard the thud of the little pebbles in it on the boulders below. The portion upon which one of her legs lay was quite loose and pendent also. She knew it might break off, too, at any moment. It would be very dreadful to be there when it got dark. She could see the big spray of farewell-summer that had lured her to her doom, waving unplucked above her, wonderfully purple and lovely.

Then, beside it, she saw a man's face looking down at her!

She heard him say, "My God!" softly to himself. She saw that he was slight and that one shoulder was a trifle higher than the other. This must be Dean Priest— Jarback Priest. Emily dared not call to him. She lay still and her great, grey-purple eyes said, "Save me."

"How can I help you?" said Dean Priest hoarsely, as if to himself. "I cannot reach you—and it looks as if the slightest touch or jar would send that broken earth over the brink. I must go for a rope—and to leave you here alone—like this. Can you wait, child?"

"Yes," breathed Emily. She smiled at him to encourage him—the little soft smile that began a† the corners of her mouth and spread over her face. Dean Priest never forgot that smile—and the steadfast child-eyes looking out through it from the little face that seemed so perilously near the brink.

"I'll be as quick as I can," he said. "I can't go very fast—I'm a bit lame, you see. But don't be frightened—I'll save you. I'll leave my dog to keep you company. Here, Tweed."

He whistled—a great, tawny-gold dog came in sight.

"Sit right there, Tweed, till I come back. Don't stir a paw—don't wag a tail—talk to her only with your eyes."

Tweed sat down obediently and Dean Priest disappeared.

Emily lay there and dramatized the whole incident for her Jimmy-book. She was a little frightened still, but not too frightened to see herself writing it all out the next day. It would be quite a thrilling bit.

She liked to know the big dog was there. She was not so learned in lore of dogs as in lore of cats. But he looked very human and trusty watching her with great kindly eyes. A grey kitten was an adorable thing—but a grey kitten would not have sat there and encouraged her. "I believe," thought Emily, "that a dog is better than a cat when you're in trouble."

It was half an hour before Dean Priest returned.

"Thank God you haven't gone over," he muttered. "I hadn't to go as far as I feared—I found a rope in an empty boat up-shore and took it. And now—if I drop the rope down to you, are you strong enough to hold it while the earth goes and then hang on while I pull you up?"

"I'll try," said Emily.

Dean Priest knotted a loop at the end and slid it down to her. Then he wound the rope around the trunk of a heavy fir.

"Now," he said.

Emily said inwardly, "Dear God, *please*—" and caught

the swaying loop. The next moment the full weight of her body swung from it, for at her first movement the broken soil beneath her slipped down—slipped over. Dean Priest sickened and shivered. Could she cling to the rope while he drew her up?

Then he saw she had got a little knee-hold on the narrow shelf. Carefully he drew on the rope. Emily, full of pluck, helped him by digging her toes into the crumbling bank. In a moment she was within his reach. He grasped her arms and pulled her up beside him into safety. As he lifted her past the farewell-summer Emily reached out her hand and broke off the spray.

"I've got it, anyhow," she said jubilantly. Then she remembered her manners. "I'm much obliged to you. You saved my life. And—and—I think I'll sit down a moment. My legs feel funny and trembly."

Emily sat down, all at once more shaky than she had been through all the danger. Dean Priest leaned against the gnarled old fir. He seemed "trembly" too. He wiped his forehead with his handkerchief. Emily looked curiously at him. She had learned a good deal about him from Aunt Nancy's casual remarks—not always good-natured remarks, for Aunt Nancy did not wholly like him, it seemed. She always called him "Jarback" rather contemptuously, while Caroline scrupulously called him Dean. Emily knew he had been to college, that he was thirty-six years old—which to Emily seemed a venerable age—and well-off; that he had a malformed shoulder and limped slightly; that he cared for nothing save books nor ever had; that he lived with an older brother and travelled a great deal; and that the whole Priest clan stood somewhat in awe of his ironic tongue. Aunt Nancy had called him a "cynic." Emily did not know what a cynic was but it sounded interesting. She looked him over carefully and saw that he had delicate, pale features and tawny-brown hair. His lips were thin and sensitive, with a whimsical curve. She liked his mouth. Had she been older she would have known why—because it connoted strength and tenderness and humour.

In spite of his twisted shoulder there was about him a certain aloof dignity of presence which was characteristic of many of the Priests and which was often mistaken for pride. The green Priest eyes, that were peering and uncanny in Caroline's face and impudent in Jim Priest's, were remarkably dreamy and attractive in his.

"Well, do you think me handsome?" he said, sitting down on another stone and smiling at her. His voice was beautiful—musical and caressing.

Emily blushed. She knew staring was not etiquette, and she did not think him at all handsome, so she was very thankful that he did not press his question, but asked another.

"Do you know who your knightly rescuer is?"

"I think you must be Jar— Mr. Dean Priest." Emily flushed again with vexation. She had come so near to making another terrible hole in her manners.

"Yes, Jarback Priest. You needn't mind the nickname. I've heard it often enough. It's a Priest idea of humour." He laughed rather unpleasantly. "The reason for it is obvious enough, isn't it? I never got anything else at school. How came you to slide over that cliff?"

"I wanted this," said Emily, waving her farewell-summer.

"And you have it! Do you always get what you go after, even with death slipping a thin wedge between? I think you're born lucky. I see the signs. If that big aster lured you into danger it saved you as well, for it was through stepping over to investigate it that I saw you. Its size and colour caught my eye. Otherwise I should have gone on and you—what would have become of you? Whom do you belong to that you are let risk your life on these dangerous banks? What is your name—if you have a name! I begin to doubt you—I see you have pointed ears. Have I been tricked into meddling with fairies, and will I discover presently that twenty years have passed and that I am an old man long since lost to the living world with nothing but the skeleton of my dog for company?"

"I am Emily Byrd Starr of New Moon," said Emily, rather coldly. She was beginning to be sensitive about her ears. Father Cassidy had remarked on them—and now Jarback Priest. Was there really something uncanny about them?

And yet there was a flavour about the said Jarback that she liked—liked decidedly. Emily never was long in doubt about any one she met. In a few minutes she always knew whether she liked, disliked, or was indifferent to them. She had a queer feeling that she had known Jarback Priest for years—perhaps because it had seemed so long when she was lying on that crumbling earth waiting for him to return. He was not handsome but she liked that lean, clever face of his with its magnetic green eyes.

"So you're the young lady visitor at the Grange!" said Dean Priest, in some astonishment. "Then my dear Aunt Nancy should look after you better—my *very* dear Aunt Nancy."

"You don't like Aunt Nancy, I see," said Emily coolly.

"What is the use of liking a lady who won't like me? You have probably discovered by this time that my Lady Aunt detests me."

"Oh, I don't think it's as bad as that," said Emily. "She must have some good opinions about you—she says you're the only Priest who will ever go to heaven."

"She doesn't mean that as a compliment, whatever you in your innocence believe it to be. And you are Douglas Starr's daughter? I knew your father. We were boys together at Queen's Academy—we drifted apart after we left it—he went into journalism, I to McGill. But he was the only friend I had at school—the only boy who would bother himself about Jarback Priest, who was lame and hunchbacked and couldn't play football or hockey. Emily Byrd Starr—Starr should be your first name. You look like a star—you have a radiant sort of personality shining through you—your proper habitat should be the evening sky just after sunset—or the morning sky just before sunrise. Yes. You'd be more at home in the morning sky. I think I shall call you Star."

"Do you mean that you think me pretty?" asked Emily directly.

"Why, it hadn't occurred to me to wonder whether you were pretty or not. Do you think a star should be pretty?"

Emily reflected.

"No," she said finally, "the word doesn't suit a star."

"I perceive you are an artist in words. Of course it doesn't. Stars are prismatic—palpitating—elusive. It is not often we find one made flesh and blood. I think I'll wait for you."

"Oh, I'm ready to go now," said Emily, standing up.

"H'm. That wasn't what I meant. Never mind. Come along, Star—if you don't mind walking a bit slowly. I'll take you back from the wilderness at least—I don't know that I'll venture to Wyther Grange to-night. I don't want Aunt Nancy to take the edge off *you*. And so you don't think me handsome?"

"I didn't say so," cried Emily.

"Not in words. But I can read your thoughts, Star—it won't ever do to think anything you don't want me to know. The gods gave me that gift—when they kept back everything else I wanted. You don't think me handsome but you think me nice. Do you think you are pretty yourself?"

"A little—since Aunt Nancy lets me wear my bang," said Emily frankly.

Jarback Priest made a grimace.

"Don't call it by such a name. It's a worse name even than bustle. Bangs and bustles—they hurt me. I like that black wave breaking on your white brows—but don't call it a bang—ever again."

"It *is* a very ugly word. I never use it in my poetry, of course."

Whereby Dean Priest discovered that Emily wrote

poetry. He also discovered pretty nearly everything else about her in that charming walk back to Priest Pond in the fir-scented dusk, with Tweed walking between them, his nose touching his master's hand softly every now and then, while the robins in the trees above them whistled blithely in the afterlight.

With nine out of ten people Emily was secretive and reserved, but Dean Priest was sealed of her tribe and she divined it instantly. He had a right to the inner sanctuary and she yielded it unquestioningly. She talked to him freely.

Besides, she felt *alive* again—she felt the wonderful thrill of living again, after that dreadful space when she had seemed to hang between life and death. She felt, as she wrote to her father afterwards, "as if a little bird was singing in her heart." And oh, how good the green sod felt under her feet!

She told him all about herself and her doings and beings. Only one thing she did not tell him—her worry over Ilse's mother. *That* she could not speak of to any one. Aunt Nancy need not have been frightened that she would carry tales to New Moon.

"I wrote a whole poem yesterday when it rained and I couldn't get out," she said. "It began,

> *I sit by the western window*
> *That looks on Malvern Bay—"*

"Am I not to hear the whole of it?" asked Dean, who knew perfectly well that Emily was hoping that he would ask it.

Emily delightedly repeated the whole poem. When she came to the two lines she liked best in it,

> *Perhaps in those wooded islands*
> *That gem the proud bay's breast—*

she looked up sidewise at him to see if he admired them. But he was walking with eyes cast down and an absent expression on his face. She felt a little disappointed.

"H'm," he said when she had finished. "You're twelve, didn't you say? When you're ten years older I shouldn't wonder—but let's not think of it."

"Father Cassidy told me to keep on," cried Emily.

"There was no need of it. You *would* keep on anyhow—you have the itch for writing born in you. It's quite incurable. What are you going to do with it?"

"I think I shall be either a great poetess or a distinguished novelist," said Emily reflectively.

"Having only to choose," remarked Dean dryly. "Better be a novelist—I hear it pays better."

"What worries me about writing novels," confided Emily, "is the love talk in them. I'm sure I'll never be able to write it. I've tried," she concluded candidly, "and I can't think of *anything* to say."

"Don't worry about that. *I'll* teach you some day," said Dean.

"Will you—will you really?" Emily was very eager. "I'll be so obliged if you will. I *think* I could manage *everything* else very nicely."

"It's a bargain then—don't forget it. And don't go looking for another teacher, mind. What do you find to do at the Grange besides writing poetry? Are you never lonesome with only those two old survivals?"

"No. I enjoy my own company," said Emily gravely.

"You would. Stars are said to dwell apart, anyhow, sufficient unto themselves—ensphered in their own light. Do you really like Aunt Nancy?"

"Yes, indeed. She is very kind to me. She doesn't make me wear sunbonnets and she lets me go barefooted in the forenoons. But I have to wear my buttoned boots in the afternoons and I hate buttoned boots."

"Naturally. You should be shod with sandals of moonshine and wear a scarf of sea-mist with a few fireflies caught in it over your hair. Star, you don't look like your father, but you suggest him in several ways. Do you look like your mother? I never saw her."

All at once Emily smiled demurely. A real sense of humour was born in her at that moment. Never again was she to feel quite so unmixedly tragic over anything.

"No," she said, "it's only my eyelashes and smile that are like Mother's. But I've got Father's forehead, and Grandma Starr's hair and eyes, and Great-Uncle George's nose, and Aunt Nancy's hands, and Cousin Susan's elbows, and Great-great-Grandmother Murray's ankles, and Grandfather Murray's eyebrows."

Dean Priest laughed.

"A rag-bag—as we all are," he said. "But your soul is your own, and fire-new, I'll swear to that."

"Oh, I'm so glad I like you," said Emily impulsively. "It would be *hateful* to think any one I didn't like had saved my life. I don't mind *your* saving it a bit."

"That's good. Because you see your life belongs to me henceforth. Since I saved it it's mine. Never forget that."

Emily felt an odd sensation of rebellion. She didn't fancy the idea of her life belonging to anybody but herself—not even to anybody she liked as much as she liked Dean Priest. Dean, watching her, saw it and smiled his whimsical smile that always seemed to have so much more in it than mere smiling.

"That doesn't quite suit you? Ah, you see one pays a penalty when one reaches out for something beyond the ordinary. Take your wonderful aster home and keep it as long as you can. It has cost you your freedom."

He was laughing—he was only joking, of course—yet Emily felt as if a cobweb fetter had been flung round her. Yielding to a sudden impulse she flung the big aster on the ground and set her foot on it.

Dean Priest looked on amusedly. His strange eyes were very kindly as he met hers.

"You rare thing—you vivid thing—you starry thing! We are going to be good friends—we *are* good friends. I'm coming up to Wyther Grange to-morrow to see those descriptions you've written of Caroline and my venerable Aunt in your Jimmy-book. I feel sure they're delicious. Here's your path—don't go roaming again so far from civilization. Good-night, my Star of the Morning."

He stood at the crossroad and watched her out of sight.

"What a child!" he muttered. "I'll never forget her eyes as she lay there on the edge of death—the dauntless little soul—and I've never seen a creature who seemed so full of sheer joy in existence. She is Douglas Starr's child—*he* never called me Jarback."

He stooped and picked up the broken aster. Emily's heel had met it squarely and it was badly crushed. But he put it away that night between the leaves of an old volume of *Jane Eyre*, where he had marked a verse—

> *All glorious rose upon my sight*
> *That child of shower and gleam.*

27
The Vow of Emily

In Dean Priest Emily found, for the first time since her father had died, a companion who could fully sympathize. She was always at her best with him, with a delightful feeling of being understood. To love is easy and therefore common—but to *understand*—how rare it is! They roamed wonderlands of fancy together in the magic August days that followed upon Emily's adventure on the bay shore, talked together of exquisite, immortal things, and were at home with "nature's old felicities" of which Wordsworth so happily speaks.

Emily showed him all the poetry and "descriptions" in her "Jimmy-book" and he read them gravely, and, exactly as Father had done, made little criticisms that did not hurt her because she knew they were just. As for Dean Priest, a certain secret well-spring of fancy that had long seemed dry bubbled up in him sparklingly again.

"You make me believe in fairies, whether I will or no," he told her, "and that means youth. As long as you believe in fairies you can't grow old."

"But I can't believe in fairies myself," protested Emily sorrowfully. "I wish I could."

"But *you* are a fairy yourself—or you wouldn't be able to find fairyland. You can't buy a ticket there, you know. Either the fairies themselves give you your passport at your christening—or they don't. That is all there is to it."

"Isn't 'Fairyland' the *loveliest* word?" said Emily dreamily.

"Because it means everything the human heart desires," said Dean.

When he talked to her Emily felt as if she were looking into some enchanted mirror where her own dreams and secret hopes were reflected back to her with added charm. If Dean Priest were a cynic he showed no cynicism to Emily. But in her company he was not a cynic; he had shed his years and become a boy again with a boy's untainted visions. She loved him for the world he opened to her view.

There was such fun in him, too,—such sly, surprising fun. He told her jokes—he made her laugh. He told her strange old tales of forgotten gods who were very beautiful—of court festivals and the bridals of kings. He seemed to have the history of the whole world at his fingers' ends. He described things to her in unforgettable phrases as they walked by the bay shore or sat in the overgrown, shadowy old garden of Wyther Grange. When he spoke of Athens as "the City of the Violet Crown" Emily realized afresh what magic is made when the right words are wedded; and she loved to think of Rome as "the City of the Seven Hills." Dean had been in Rome and Athens—and almost everywhere else.

"I didn't know any one ever talked as you do except in books," she told him.

Dean laughed—with a little note of bitterness that was so often present in his laughter—though less often with Emily than with other people. It was really his laughter that had won Dean his reputation for cynicism. People so often felt that he was laughing *at* them instead of *with* them.

"I've had only books for companions most of my life," he said. "Is it any wonder I talk like them?"

"I'm sure I'll like studying history after this," said Emily; "except Canadian History. I'll never like *it*—it's so dull. Not just at the first, when we belonged to France and there was plenty of fighting, but after that it's nothing but politics."

"The happiest countries, like the happiest women, have no history," said Dean.

"I hope *I'll* have a history," cried Emily. "I want a *thrilling* career."

"We all do, foolish one. Do you know what makes history? Pain—and shame—and rebellion—and bloodshed and heartache. Star, ask yourself how many hearts ached—and broke—to make those crimson and purple pages in history that you find so enthralling. I told you the story of Leonidas and his Spartans the other day. They had mothers, sisters, and sweethearts. If they could have fought a bloodless battle at the polls wouldn't it have been better—if not so dramatic."

"I—can't—*feel*—that way," said Emily confusedly. She was not old enough to think or say, as she would say ten years later, "The heroes of Thermopylae have been an inspiration to humanity for centuries. What squabble around a ballot-box will ever be that?"

"And, like all female creatures, you form your opinions by your feelings. Well, hope for your thrilling career—but remember that if there is to be drama in your life *somebody* must pay the piper in the coin of suffering. If not you—then some one else."

"Oh, no, I wouldn't like *that*."

"Then be content with fewer thrills. What about your tumble over the bank down there? That came near being a tragedy. What if I hadn't found you?"

"But you *did* find me," cried Emily. "I like near escapes—after they're over," she added. "If everybody had always been happy there'd be nothing to read about."

Tweed made a third in their rambles and Emily grew very fond of him, without losing any of her loyalty to the pussy folk.

"I like cats with one part of my mind and dogs with another part," she said.

"I like cats but I never keep one," Dean said. "They're too exacting—they ask too much. Dogs want only love but cats demand worship. They have never got over the Bubastis habit of godship."

Emily understood this—he had told her all about old Egypt and the goddess Pasht—but she did not quite agree with him.

"Kittens don't want to be worshipped," she said. "They just want to be cuddled."

"By their priestesses—yes. If you had been born on the banks of the Nile five thousand years ago, Emily, you would have been a priestess of Pasht—an adorable, slim, brown creature with a fillet of gold around your black hair and bands of silver on those ankles Aunt Nancy admires, with dozens of sacred little godlings frisking around you under the palms of the temple courts."

"Oh," gasped Emily rapturously, "that gave me *the flash*. And," she added wonderingly, "just for a moment it made me *homesick*, too. Why?"

"Why? Because I haven't a doubt you *were* just such a priestess in a former incarnation and my words reminded your soul of it. Do you believe in the doctrine of the transmigration of souls, Star? But of course not—brought up by the true-blue Calvinists of New Moon."

"What does it mean?" asked Emily, and when Dean explained it to her she thought it a very delightful belief but was quite sure Aunt Elizabeth would not approve of it.

"So I won't believe it—yet," she said gravely.

Then it all came to an end quite suddenly. It had been taken for granted by all concerned that Emily was to stay at Wyther Grange until the end of August. But in mid-August Aunt Nancy said suddenly to her one day,

"Go home, Emily. I'm tired of you. I like you very well—you're not stupid and you're passably pretty and you've behaved exceedingly well—tell Elizabeth you do the Murrays credit—but I'm tired of you. Go home."

Emily's feelings were mixed. It hurt her to be told Aunt Nancy was tired of her—it would hurt any one. It rankled in her for several days until she thought of a sharp answer she might have made Aunt Nancy and wrote it down in her Jimmy-book. She felt quite as relieved then as if she had really said it.

And she was sorry to leave Wyther Grange; she had grown to love the old beautiful house, with its flavour of hidden secrets—a flavour that was wholly a trick of its architecture, for there had never been anything in it but the simple tale of births and deaths and marriages and everyday living that most houses have. She was sorry to leave the bay shore and the quaint garden and the gazing-ball and the chessy-cat and the Pink Room bed of freedom; and most of all she was sorry to leave Dean Priest. But on the other hand it was delightful to think of going back to New Moon and all the loved ones there—Teddy and his dear whistle, Ilse and her stimulating comradeship, Perry with his determined reaching up for higher things, Saucy Sal and the new kitten that must be needing proper training now, and the fairy world of the *Midsummer Night's Dream*. Cousin Jimmy's garden would be in its prime of splendour, the

August apples would be ripe. Suddenly, Emily was very ready to go. She packed her little black box jubilantly and found it an excellent chance to work in neatly a certain line from a poem Dean had recently read to her which had captured her fancy.

"'Good-bye, proud world, I'm going home,'" she declaimed feelingly, standing at the top of the long, dark, shining staircase and apostrophizing the row of grim Priest photographs hanging on the wall.

But she was much annoyed over one thing. Aunt Nancy would not give her back the picture Teddy had painted.

"I'm going to keep it," Aunt Nancy said, grinning and shaking her gold tassels. "Some day that picture will be worth something as the early effort of a famous artist."

"I only lent it to you—I told you I only lent it to you," said Emily indignantly.

"I'm an unscrupulous old demon," said Aunt Nancy coolly. "That is what the Priests all call me behind my back. Don't they, Caroline? May as well have the game as the name. I happen to have a fancy for that picture, that's all. I'm going to frame it and hang it here in my parlour. But I'll leave it to you in my will—that and the chessy-cat and the gazing-ball and my gold earrings. Nothing else—I'm not going to leave you a cent of my money—never count on that."

"I don't want it," said Emily loftily. "I'm going to earn heaps of money for myself. But it isn't fair of you to keep my picture. It was given to me."

"I never was fair," said Aunt Nancy. "Was I, Caroline?"

"No," said Caroline shrewishly.

"You see. Now don't make a fuss, Emily. You've been a very good child but I feel that I've done my duty by you for this year. Go back to New Moon and when Elizabeth won't let you do things tell her I always let you. I don't know if it will do any good but try it. Elizabeth, like every one else related to me, is always wondering what I'm going to do with my money."

Cousin Jimmy came over for Emily. How glad she was to see his kind face with its gentle, elfish eyes and forked beard again! But she felt very badly when she turned to Dean.

"If you like I'll kiss you good-bye," she said chokily.

Emily did not like kissing people. She did not really want to kiss Dean but she liked him so much she thought she ought to extend all the courtesies to him.

Dean looked down smiling into her face, so young, so pure, so softly curved.

"No, I don't want you to kiss me—yet. And our first kiss mustn't have the flavour of good-bye. It would be a bad omen. Star O' Morning, I'm sorry you're going. But I'll see you again before long. My oldest sister lives in Blair Water, you know, and I feel a sudden access of brotherly affection towards her. I seem to see myself visiting her very often henceforth. In the meantime remember you have promised to write me every week. And I'll write you."

"Nice fat letters," coaxed Emily. "I love fat letters."

"Fat! They'll be positively corpulent, Star. Now, I'm not even going to *say* good-bye. Let's make a pact, Star. We'll never *say* good-bye to each other. We'll just smile and go."

Emily made a gallant effort—smiled—and went. Aunt Nancy and Caroline returned to the back parlour and their cribbage. Dean Priest whistled for Tweed and went to the bay shore. He was so lonely that he laughed at himself.

Emily and Cousin Jimmy had so much to talk of that the drive home seemed very short.

New Moon was white in the evening sunshine which also lay with exceeding mellowness on the grey old barns. The Three Princesses, shooting up against the silvery sky, were as remote and princessly as ever. The old gulf was singing away down over the fields.

Aunt Laura came running out to meet them, her lovely blue eyes shining with pleasure. Aunt Elizabeth was in the cook-house preparing supper and only shook hands with Emily, but looked a trifle less grim and stately than usual, and she had made Emily's favourite cream-puffs for supper. Perry was hanging about, barefooted and sunburned, to tell her all the gossip of kittens and calves and little pigs and the new foal. Ilse came swooping over, and Emily discovered she had forgotten how vivid Ilse was—how brilliant her amber eyes, how golden her mane of spun-silk hair, looking more golden than ever under the bright blue silk tam Mrs. Simms had bought her in Shrewsbury. As an article of dress, that loud tam made Laura Murray's eyes and sensibilities ache, but its colour certainly did set off Ilse's wonderful hair. She engulfed Emily in a rapturous embrace and quarrelled bitterly with her ten minutes later over the fact that Emily refused to give her Saucy Sal's sole surviving kitten.

"I ought to have it, you doddering hyena," stormed Ilse. "It's as much mine as yours, pig! Our old barn cat is its father."

"Such talk is not decent," said Aunt Elizabeth, pale with horror. "And if you two children are going to quarrel over that kitten I'll have it drowned—remember that."

Ilse was finally appeased by Emily's offering to let her name the kitten and have a half interest in it. Ilse named it Daffodil. Emily did not think this suitable, since, from the fact of Cousin Jimmy referring to it as Little Tommy, she suspected it was of the sterner sex. But rather than again provoke Aunt Elizabeth's wrath by discussing tabooed subjects, she agreed.

"I can call it Daff," she thought. "That sounds more *masculine*."

The kitten was a delicate bit of striped greyness that reminded Emily of her dear lost Mikes. And it smelled so nice—of warmth and clean furriness, with whiffs of the clover hay where Saucy Sal had made her mother-nest.

After supper she heard Teddy's whistle in the old orchard—the same enchanting call. Emily flew out to greet him—after all, there was nobody just like Teddy in the world. They had an ecstatic scamper up to the Tansy Patch to see a new puppy that Dr. Burnley had given Teddy. Mrs. Kent did not seem very glad to see Emily—she was colder and more remote than ever, and she sat and watched the two children playing with the chubby little pup with a smouldering fire in her dark eyes that made Emily vaguely uncomfortable whenever she happened to glance up and encounter it. Never before had she sensed Mrs. Kent's dislike for her so keenly as that night.

"Why doesn't your mother like me?" she asked Teddy bluntly, when they carried little Leo to the barn for the night.

"Because *I* do," said Teddy briefly. "She doesn't like *anything* I like. I'm afraid she'll poison Leo very soon. I—I wish she wasn't so fond of me," he burst out, in the beginning of a revolt against this abnormal jealousy of love, which he felt rather than understood to be a fetter that was becoming galling. "She says she won't let me take up Latin and Algebra this year—you know Miss Brownell said I might—because I'm not to go to college. She says she can't bear to part from me—ever. I don't care about the Latin and stuff—but I want to learn to be an artist—I want to go away some day to the schools where they teach that. She won't let me— she hates my pictures now because she thinks I like them better than her. I *don't*—I love Mother—she's awful sweet and good to me every other way. But she thinks I do—and she's burned some of them. I know she has. They're missing from the barn wall and I can't find them anywhere. If she does anything to Leo— I'll—I'll *hate* her."

"Tell her that," said Emily coolly, with some of the Murray shrewdness coming uppermost in her. "She doesn't know that *you* know she poisoned Smoke and Buttercup. Tell her you know it and that if she does anything to Leo you won't love her any more. She'll be so frightened of your *not* loving her that she won't meddle with Leo—I *know*. Tell her gently—don't hurt her feelings—but *tell* her. It will," concluded Emily, with a killing imitation of Aunt Elizabeth delivering an ultimatum, "be better for all concerned."

"I believe I will," said Teddy, much impressed. "I *can't* have Leo disappear like my cats did—he's the only dog I've ever had and I've always wanted a dog. Oh, Emily, I'm glad you're back!"

It was very nice to be told this—especially by Teddy. Emily went home to New Moon happily. In the old kitchen the candles were lighted and their flames were dancing in the winds of the August night blowing through door and window.

"I suppose you'll not like candles very well, Emily, after being used to lamps at Wyther Grange," said Aunt Laura with a little sigh. It was one of the bitter, small things in Laura Murray's life that Elizabeth's tyranny extended to candles.

Emily looked around her thoughtfully. One candle sputtered and bobbed at her as if greeting her. One, with a long wick, glowed and smouldered like a sulky little demon. One had a tiny flame—a sly, meditative candle. One swayed with a queer fiery grace in the draught from the door. One burned with a steady upright flame like a faithful soul.

"I—don't know—Aunt Laura," she answered slowly. "You can be—friends—with candles. I believe I like the candles best after all."

Aunt Elizabeth, coming in from the cook-house, heard her. Something like pleasure gleamed in her gulf-blue eyes.

"You have some sense in you," she said.

"That's the second compliment she has paid me," thought Emily.

"I think Emily has grown taller since she went to Wyther Grange," Aunt Laura said, looking at her rather wistfully.

Aunt Elizabeth, snuffing the candles, glanced sharply over her glasses.

"I can't see it," she said. "Her dress is just the same length on her."

"I'm sure she has," persisted Laura.

Cousin Jimmy, to settle the dispute, measured Emily by the sitting-room door. She just touched the former mark.

"You see," said Aunt Elizabeth triumphantly, liking to be right even in this small matter.

"She looks—different," said Laura with a sigh.

Laura, after all, was right. Emily *had* grown, taller and older, in soul, if not in body. It was this change which Laura felt, as close and tender affection swiftly feels. The Emily who returned from Wyther Grange was not the Emily who had gone there. She was no longer wholly the child. Aunt Nancy's family histories over which she had pondered, her enduring anguish over the story of Ilse's mother, that terrible hour when she had lain cheek by jowl with death on the cliffs of the bay shore, her association with Dean Priest, all had combined to mature her intelligence and her emotions. When she went to the garret next morning and pulled out her precious little bundle of manuscripts to read them lovingly over she was amazed and rather grieved to find that they were not half so good as she had believed they were. Some of them were positively silly, she thought; she was ashamed of them—so ashamed that she smuggled them down to the cook-house stove and burned them, much to Aunt Elizabeth's annoyance when she came to prepare dinner and found the fire-box all choked up with charred paper.

Emily no longer wondered that Miss Brownell had made fun of them—though this did not mellow her bitterness of remembrance in regard to that lady in any degree. The rest she put back on the sofa shelf, including "The Child of the Sea," which still impressed her as fairly good, though not just the wonderful composition she had once deemed it. She felt that many passages could be re-written to their advantage. Then she immediately began writing a new poem, "On Returning

Home After Weeks' Absence." As everything and everybody connected with New Moon had to be mentioned in this poem it promised to be quite long and to furnish agreeable occupation for spare minutes in many weeks to come. It was very good to be home again.

"There is no place just like dear New Moon," thought Emily.

One thing that marked her return—one of those little household "epochs" that make a keener impression on the memory and imagination than perhaps their real importance warrants—was the fact that she was given a room of her own. Aunt Elizabeth had found her unshared slumber too sweet a thing to be again surrendered. She decided that she could not put up any longer with a squirming bedfellow who asked unearthly questions at any hour of the night she took it into her head to do so.

So, after a long conference with Laura, it was settled that Emily was to have her mother's room—the "lookout" as it was called, though it was not really a lookout. But it occupied the place in New Moon, looking over the front door to the garden, that the real lookouts did in other Blair Water houses, so it went by that name. It had been prepared for Emily's occupancy in her absence and when bedtime came on the first evening of her return Aunt Elizabeth curtly told her that henceforth she was to have her mother's room.

"All to myself?" exclaimed Emily.

"Yes. We will expect you to take care of it yourself and keep it very tidy."

"It has never been slept in since the night before your mother—went away," said Aunt Laura, with a queer sound in her voice—a sound of which Aunt Elizabeth disapproved.

"Your mother," she said, looking coldly at Emily over the flame of the candle—an attitude that gave a rather gruesome effect to her acquiline features—"*ran* away—flouted her family and broke her father's heart.

She was a silly, ungrateful, disobedient girl. I hope *you* will never disgrace your family by such conduct."

"Oh, Aunt Elizabeth," said Emily breathlessly, "when you hold the candle down like that it makes your face look just like a corpse! Oh, it's so interesting."

Aunt Elizabeth turned and led the way upstairs in grim silence. There was no use in wasting perfectly good admonitions on a child like this.

Left alone in her lookout, lighted dimly by the one small candle, Emily gazed about her with keen and thrilling interest. She could not get into bed until she had explored every bit of it. The room was very old-fashioned, like all the New Moon rooms. The walls were papered with a design of slender gilt diamonds enclosing golden stars and hung with worked woollen mottoes and pictures that had been "supplements" in the girlhood of her aunts. One of them, hanging over the head of the bed, represented two guardian angels. In its day this had been much admired but Emily looked at it with distaste.

"I don't like feather wings on angels," she said decidedly. "Angels should have rainbowy wings."

On the floor was a pretty homespun carpet and round braided rugs. There was a high black bedstead with carved posts, a fat feather-bed, and an Irish chain quilt, but, as Emily was glad to see, no curtains. A little table, with funny claw-feet and brass-knobbed drawers, stood by the window, which was curtained with muslin frills; one of the window-panes contorted the landscape funnily, making a hill where no hill was. Emily liked this—she couldn't have told why, but it was really because it gave the pane an individuality of its own. An oval mirror in a tarnished gilt frame hung above the table; Emily was delighted to find she could see herself in it—"all but my boots"—without craning or tipping it. "And it doesn't twist my face or turn my complexion green," she thought happily. Two high-backed, black chairs with horsehair seats, a little wash-stand with a blue basin and pitcher, and a faded ottoman with woollen roses cross-stitched on it, completed the furnishing. On the little mantel were vases full of dried and coloured grasses and a fascinating pot-bellied bottle filled with West Indian shells. On either side were lovable little cupboards with leaded-glass doors like those in the sitting-room. Underneath was a small fireplace.

"I wonder if Aunt Elizabeth will ever let me have a little fire here," thought Emily.

The room was full of that indefinable charm found in all rooms where the pieces of furniture, whether old or new, are well acquainted with each other and the walls and floors are on good terms. Emily felt it all over her as she flitted about examining everything. This was her room—she loved it already—she felt perfectly at home.

"I belong here," she breathed happily.

She felt deliciously *near* to her mother—as if Juliet Starr had suddenly become real to her. It thrilled her to think that her mother had probably crocheted the lace cover on the round pincushion on the table. And that fat, black jar of pot-pourri on the mantel—her mother must have compounded it. When Emily lifted the lid a faint spicy odour floated out. The souls of all the roses that had bloomed through many olden summers at New Moon seemed to be prisoned there in a sort of flower purgatory. Something in the haunting, mystical, elusive odour gave Emily *the flash*—and her room had received its consecration.

There was a picture of her mother hanging over the mantel—a large daguerreotype taken when she was a little girl. Emily looked at it lovingly. She had the picture of her mother which her father had left, taken after their marriage. But when Aunt Elizabeth had brought that from Maywood to New Moon she had hung it in the parlour where Emily seldom saw it. This picture, in her bedroom, of the golden-haired, rose-cheeked girl, was all her own. She could look at it—talk to it at will.

"Oh, Mother," she said, "what did you think of

when you were a little girl here like me? I wish I could have known you *then*. And to think nobody has ever slept here since that last night you did before you ran away with Father. Aunt Elizabeth says you were wicked to do it but *I* don't think you were. It wasn't as if you were running away with a *stranger*. Anyway, I'm glad you *did*, because if you hadn't there wouldn't have been any *me*."

Emily, very glad that there was an Emily, opened her lookout window as high as it would go, got into bed and drifted off to sleep, feeling a happiness that was so deep as to be almost pain as she listened to the sonorous sweep of the night wind among the great trees in Lofty John's bush. When she wrote to her father a few days later she began the letter "Dear Father and Mother."

"And I'll always write the letter to *you* as well as Father after this, Mother. I'm sorry I left you out so long. But you didn't seem *real* till that night I came home. I made the bed beautifully next morning—Aunt Elizabeth didn't find a bit of fault with it—and I dusted *everything*—and when I went out I knelt down and kissed the doorstep. I didn't think Aunt Elizabeth saw me but she did and said had I gone crazy. Why does Aunt Elizabeth think any one is crazy who does something she never does? I said 'No, it's only because I love my room so much' and she sniffed and said 'You'd better love your God.' But so I do, dear Father—and Mother—and I love Him better than ever since I have my dear room. I can see all over the garden from it and into Lofty John's bush and one little bit of the Blair Water through the gap in the trees where the Yesterday Road runs. I like to go to bed early now. I love to lie all alone in my own room and make poetry and think out descriptions of things while I look through the open window at the stars and the nice, big, kind, quiet trees in Lofty John's bush.

"Oh, Father dear and Mother, we are going to have a new teacher. Miss Brownell is not coming back. She is going to be married and Ilse says that when her father heard it he said 'God help the man.' And the new teacher is a Mr. Carpenter. Ilse saw him when he came to see her father about the school—because Dr. Burnley is a trustee this year—and she says he has bushy grey hair and whiskers. He is married, too, and is going to live in that little old house down in the hollow below the school. It seems so funny to think of a teacher having a wife and whiskers.

"I am glad to be home. But I miss Dean and the gazing-ball. Aunt Elizabeth looked very cross when she saw my bang but didn't say anything. Aunt Laura says just to keep quiet and go on wearing it. But I don't feel comfortable going against Aunt Elizabeth so I have combed it all back except a *little* fringe. I don't feel *quite* comfortable about it even yet, but I have to put up with being a little uncomfortable for the sake of my looks. Aunt Laura says bustles are going out of style so I'll never be able to have one but I don't care because I think they're ugly. Rhoda Stuart will be cross because she was just longing to be old enough to wear a bustle. I hope I'll be able to have a gin-jar all to myself when the weather gets cold. There is a row of gin-jars on the high shelf in the cook-house.

"Teddy and I had the nicest *adventure* yesterday evening. We are going to keep it a secret from everybody—partly because it was so nice, and partly because we think we'd get a fearful scolding for one thing we did.

"We went up to the Disappointed House, and we found one of the boards on the windows loose. So we pried it off and crawled in and went all over the house. It is lathed but not plastered, and the shavings are lying all over the floors just as the carpenters left them years ago. It seemed more disappointed than ever. I just felt like crying. There was a dear little fireplace in one room so we went to work and kindled a fire in it with shavings and pieces of boards (this is the thing we would be scolded for, likely) and then sat before it on an old carpenter's bench and talked. We decided that when we grew up we would buy the Disappointed House and live here together. Teddy said he supposed we'd have to get married, but I thought maybe we could find a way to manage without going to all that bother. Teddy will paint pictures and I will write poetry and we will have toast and bacon and marmalade *every morning* for breakfast—just like Wyther Grange—but *never* porridge. And we'll always have lots of nice things to eat in the pantry and I'll make lots of jam and Teddy is always going to help me wash the dishes and we'll hang the gazing-ball from the middle of the ceiling in the fireplace room—because likely Aunt Nancy will be dead by then.

"When the fire burned out we jammed the board into place in the window and came away. Every now and then to-day Teddy would say to me "Toast and bacon and marmalade" in the *most mysterious* tones and Ilse and Perry are wild because they can't find out what he means.

"Cousin Jimmy has got Jimmy Joe Belle to help with the harvest. Jimmy Joe Belle comes from over Derry Pond way. There are a great many French there and when a French girl marries they call her mostly by her husband's first name instead of Mrs. like the English do. If a girl named Mary marries a man named Leon she will always be called Mary Leon after that. But in Jimmy Joe Belle's case, it is the other way and he is called by his wife's name. I asked Cousin Jimmy why, and he said it was because Jimmy Joe was a poor stick of a creature and Belle wore the britches. But still I don't understand. Jimmy Joe wears britches himself—that means trousers—and why should he be called Jimmy Joe Belle instead of her being called Belle Jimmy Joe just because she wears them too! I won't rest till I find out.

"Cousin Jimmy's garden is splendid now. The tiger lilies are out. I am trying to love them because nobody seems to like them at all but deep down in my heart I know I love the late roses best. You just can't help loving the roses best.

"Ilse and I hunted all over the old orchard to-day for a four-leaved clover and couldn't find one. Then I found one in a clump of clover by the dairy steps to-night when I was straining the milk and never thinking of clovers. Cousin Jimmy says that is the way luck always comes, and it is no use to look for it.

"It is lovely to be with Ilse again. We have only fought twice since I came home. I am going to try not to fight with Ilse any more because I don't think it is dignified, although quite interesting. But it is hard not to because even when I keep quiet and don't say a word Ilse thinks that's a way of fighting and gets madder and says worse things than ever. Aunt Elizabeth says it always takes two to make a quarrel but she doesn't know Ilse as I do. Ilse called me a sneaking albatross to-day. I wonder how many animals are left to call me. She never repeats the same one twice. I wish she wouldn't clapper-claw Perry so much. (Clapper-claw is a word I learned from Aunt Nancy. Very striking, I think.) It seems as if she couldn't bear him. He dared Teddy to jump from the henhouse roof across to the pighouse roof. Teddy wouldn't. He said he would try it if it had to be done or would do anybody any good but he wasn't going to do it just to show off. Perry did it and landed safe. If he hadn't he might have broken his neck. Then he bragged about it and said Teddy was afraid and Ilse turned red as a beet and told him to shut up or she would bite his snout off. She can't bear to have anything said against Teddy, but I guess he can take care of himself.

"Ilse can't study for the Entrance either. Her father won't let her. But she says she doesn't care. She says she's going to run away when she gets a little older and study for the stage. That sounds wicked, but interesting.

"I felt very queer and guilty when I saw Ilse first, because I knew about her mother. I don't know why I felt guilty because I had nothing to do with it. The feeling is wearing away a little now but I am so unhappy by spells over it. I wish I could either forget it altogether or find out the rights of it. Because I am sure nobody knows them.

"I had a letter from Dean to-day. He writes lovely letters—just as if I was grown up. He sent me a little poem he had cut out of a paper called *The Fringed Gentian*. He said it made him think of me. It is all lovely but I like the last verse best of all. This is it:

> Then whisper, blossom, in thy sleep
> How I may upward climb
> The Alpine Path, so hard, so steep,
> That leads to heights sublime.
> How I may reach that far-off goal
> Of true and honored fame
> And write upon its shining scroll
> A woman's humble name.

"When I read that *the flash* came, and I took a sheet of paper—I forgot to tell you Cousin Jimmy gave me a little box of paper and envelopes—*on the sly*—and I wrote on it:

> I, Emily Byrd Starr, do solemnly vow this day that I will climb the Alpine Path and write my name on the scroll of fame.

"Then I put it in the envelope and sealed it up and wrote on it *The Vow of Emily Byrd Starr, aged 12 years and 3 months*, and put it away on the sofa shelf in the garret.

"I am writing a murder story now and I am trying to feel how a man would feel who was a murderer. It is creepy, but thrilling. I almost feel as if I *had* murdered somebody.

"Good night, dear Father and Mother.

"Your lovingest daughter,
"Emily.

"P.S. I have been wondering how I'll sign my name when I grow up and print my pieces. I don't know which would be best—Emily Byrd Starr in full or Emily B. Starr, or E. B. Starr, or E. Byrd Starr. Sometimes I think I'll have a *nom-de-plume*—that is, another name you pick for yourself. It's in my dictionary among the "French phrases" at the back. If I did that then I could hear people talking of my pieces right before me, never suspecting, and say just what they really thought of them. That would be interesting but perhaps not always comfortable. I think I'll be,

"*E. Byrd Starr.*"

28
A Weaver of Dreams

It took Emily several weeks to make up her mind whether she liked Mr. Carpenter or not. She knew she did not *dis*like him, not even though his first greeting, shot at her on the opening day of school in a gruff voice, accompanied by a startling lift of his spiky grey brows was, "So you're the girl that writes poetry, eh? Better stick to your needle and duster. Too many fools in the world trying to write poetry and failing. I tried it myself once. Got better sense now."

"You don't keep your nails clean," thought Emily.

But he upset every kind of school tradition so speedily and thoroughly that Ilse, who gloried in upsetting things and hated routine, was the only scholar that liked him from the start. Some never liked him—the Rhoda Stuart type for example—but most of them came to it after they got used to never being used to anything. And Emily finally decided that she liked him tremendously.

Mr. Carpenter was somewhere between forty and fifty—a tall man, with an upstanding shock of bushy grey hair, bristling grey moustache and eyebrows, a truculent beard, bright blue eyes out of which all his wild life had not yet burned the fire, and a long, lean, greyish face, deeply lined. He lived in a little two-roomed house below the school with a shy mouse of a wife. He never talked of his past or offered any explanation of the fact that at his age he had no better profession than teaching a district school for a pittance of salary, but the truth leaked out after a while; for Prince Edward Island is a small province and everybody in it knows something about everybody else. So eventually Blair Water people, and even the school children, understood that Mr. Carpenter had been a brilliant student in his youth and had had his eye on the ministry. But at college he had got in with a "fast set"—Blair Water people nodded heads slowly and whispered the dreadful phrase portentously—and the fast set had ruined him. He "took to drink" and went to the dogs generally. And the upshot of it all was that Francis Carpenter, who had led his class in his first and second years at McGill, and for whom his teachers had predicted a great career, was a country school-teacher at forty-five with no prospect of ever being anything else. Perhaps he was resigned to it—perhaps not. Nobody ever knew, not even the brown mouse of a wife. Nobody in Blair Water cared—he was a good teacher, and that was all that mattered. Even if he did go on occasional "sprees" he always took Saturday for them and was sober enough by Monday. Sober, and especially dignified, wearing a rusty black frock coat which he never put on any other day of the week. He did not invite pity and he did not pose as a tragedy. But sometimes, when Emily looked at his face, bent over the arithmetic problems of Blair Water School, she felt horribly sorry for him without in the least understanding why.

He had an explosive temper which generally burst into flame at least once a day, and then he would storm about wildly for a few minutes, tugging at his beard, imploring heaven to grant him patience, abusing everybody in general and the luckless object of his wrath in particular. But these tempers never lasted long. In a few minutes Mr. Carpenter would be smiling as graciously as a sun bursting through a storm-cloud on the very pupil he had been rating. Nobody seemed to cherish any grudge because of his scoldings. He never said any of the biting things Miss Brownell was wont to say, which rankled and festered for weeks; his hail of words fell alike on just and unjust and rolled off harmlessly.

He could take a joke on himself in perfect good nature. "Do you hear me? Do you hear me, sirrah?" he bellowed to Perry Miller one day. "Of course I hear you," retorted Perry coolly, "they could hear you in Charlottetown." Mr. Carpenter stared for a moment, then broke into a great, jolly laugh.

His methods of teaching were so different from Miss Brownell's that the Blair Water pupils at first felt as if he had stood them on their heads. Miss Brownell had been a martinet for order. Mr. Carpenter never tried to keep order apparently. But somehow he kept the children so busy that they had no time to do mischief. He taught history tempestuously for a month, making his pupils play the different characters and enact the incidents. He never bothered any one to learn dates—but the dates stuck in the memory just the same. If, as Mary Queen of Scots, you were beheaded by the school axe, kneeling blindfolded at the doorstep, with Perry Miller, wearing a mask made out of a piece of Aunt Laura's old black silk, for executioner, wondering what would happen if he brought the axe down *too* hard, you did not forget the year it all happened; and if you fought the battle of Waterloo all over the school playground, and heard Teddy Kent shouting, "Up, Guards

and at 'em!" as he led the last furious charge you
remembered 1815 without half trying to.

Next month history would be thrust aside altogether
and geography would take its place, when school and
playground were mapped out into countries and you
dressed up as the animals inhabiting them or traded in
various commodities over their rivers and cities. When
Rhoda Stuart had cheated you in a bargain in hides,
you remembered that she had bought the cargo from
the Argentine Republic, and when Perry Miller would
not drink any water for a whole hot summer day
because he was crossing the Arabian Desert with a
caravan of camels and could not find an oasis, and then
drank so much that he took terrible cramps and Aunt
Laura had to be up all night with him—you did not
forget where the said desert was. The trustees were
quite scandalized over some of the goings on and felt
sure that the children were having too good a time to
be really learning anything.

If you wanted to learn Latin and French you had to
do it by talking your exercises, not writing them, and
on Friday afternoons all lessons were put aside and Mr.
Carpenter made the children recite poems, make speeches
and declaim passages from Shakespeare and the Bible.
This was the day Ilse loved. Mr. Carpenter pounced on
her gift like a starving dog on a bone and drilled her
without mercy. They had endless fights and Ilse stamped
her foot and called him names while the other pupils
wondered why she was not punished for it but at last
had to give in and do as he willed. Ilse went to school
regularly—something she had never done before. Mr.
Carpenter had told her that if she were absent for a day
without good excuse she could take no part in the
Friday "exercises" and this would have killed her.

One day Mr. Carpenter had picked up Teddy's slate
and found a sketch of himself on it, in one of his
favourite if not exactly beautiful attitudes. Teddy had
labelled it "The Black Death"—half of the pupils of the
school having died that day of the Great Plague, and

having been carried out on stretchers to the Potter's Field by the terrified survivors.

Teddy expected a roar of denunciation, for the day before Garrett Marshall had been ground into figurative pulp on being discovered with the picture of a harmless cow on his slate—at least, Garrett said he meant it for a cow. But now this amazing Mr. Carpenter only drew his beetling brows together, looked earnestly at Teddy's slate, put it down on the desk, looked at Teddy, and said,

"I don't know anything about drawing—I can't help you, but, by gad, I think hereafter you'd better give up those extra arithmetic problems in the afternoon and draw pictures."

Whereupon Garrett Marshall went home and told his father that "old Carpenter" wasn't fair and "made favourites" over Teddy Kent.

Mr. Carpenter went up to the Tansy Patch that evening and saw the sketches in Teddy's old barn-loft studio. Then he went into the house and talked to Mrs. Kent. What he said and what she said nobody ever knew. But Mr. Carpenter went away looking grim, as if he had met an unexpected match. He took great pains with Teddy's general school work after that and procured from somewhere certain elementary text books on drawing which he gave him, telling him not to take them home—a caution Teddy did not require. He knew quite well that if he did they would disappear as mysteriously as his cats had done. He had taken Emily's advice and told his mother he would not love *her* if anything happened to Leo, and Leo flourished and waxed fat and doggy. But Teddy was too gentle at heart and too fond of his mother to make such a threat more than once. He knew she had cried all that night after Mr. Carpenter had been there, and prayed on her knees in her little bedroom most of the next day, and looked at him with bitter, haunting eyes for a week. He wished she were more like other fellows' mothers but they loved each other very much and had dear hours together in the little grey house on the tansy hill. It was only when other people were about that Mrs. Kent was queer and jealous.

"She's always lovely when we're alone," Teddy had told Emily.

As for the other boys, Perry Miller was the only one Mr. Carpenter bothered much with in the way of speeches—and he was as merciless with him as with Ilse. Perry worked hard to please him and practiced his speeches in barn and field—and even by nights in the kitchen loft—until Aunt Elizabeth put a stop to *that*. Emily could not understand why Mr. Carpenter would smile amiably and say, "Very good" when Neddy Gray rattled off a speech glibly, without any expression whatever, and then rage at Perry and denounce him as a dunce and a nincompoop, by gad, because he had failed to give just the proper emphasis on a certain word, or had timed his gesture a fraction of a second too soon.

Neither could she understand why he made red pencil corrections all over her compositions and rated her for split infinitives and too lavish adjectives and strode up and down the aisle and hurled objurgations at her because she didn't know "a good place to stop when she saw it, by gad," and then told Rhoda Stuart and Nan Lee that their compositions were very pretty and gave them back without so much as a mark on them. Yet, in spite of it all, she liked him more and more as time went on and autumn passed and winter came with its beautiful bare-limbed trees, and soft pearl-grey skies that were slashed with rifts of gold in the afternoons, and cleared to a jewelled pageantry of stars over the wide white hills and valleys around New Moon.

Emily shot up so that winter that Aunt Laura had to let down the tucks in her dresses. Aunt Ruth, who had come for a week's visit, said she was outgrowing her strength—consumptive children always did.

"I am *not* consumptive," Emily said. "The Starrs are

tall," she added, with a touch of subtle malice hardly to be looked for in near-thirteen.

Aunt Ruth, who was sensitive in regard to her dumpiness, sniffed.

"It would be well if *that* were the only thing in which you resemble them," she said. "How are you getting on in school?"

"Very well. I am the smartest scholar in my class," answered Emily composedly.

"You conceited child!" said Aunt Ruth.

"I'm *not* conceited." Emily looked scornful indignation. "Mr. Carpenter said it and *he* doesn't flatter. Besides, I can't help seeing it myself."

"Well, it is to be hoped you have some brains, because you haven't much in the way of looks," said Aunt Ruth. "You've no complexion to speak of—and that inky hair around your white face is startling. I see you're going to be a plain girl."

"You wouldn't say that to a grown-up person's face," said Emily with a deliberate gravity which always exasperated Aunt Ruth because she could not understand it in a child. "I don't think it would hurt you to be as polite to me as you are to other people."

"I'm telling you your faults so you may correct them," said Aunt Ruth frigidly.

"It *isn't* my fault that my face is pale and my hair black," protested Emily. "I can't correct that."

"If you were a different girl," said Aunt Ruth, "I would—"

"But I don't *want* to be a different girl," said Emily decidedly. She had no intention of lowering the Starr flag to Aunt Ruth. "I wouldn't want to be anybody but myself even if I am plain. Besides," she added impressively as she turned to go out of the room, "though I may not be very good-looking now, when I go to heaven I believe I'll be very beautiful."

"Some people think Emily quite pretty," said Aunt Laura, but she did not say it until Emily was out of hearing. She was Murray enough for that.

"I don't know where they see it," said Aunt Ruth. "She's vain and pert and says things to be thought smart. You heard her just now. But the thing I dislike most in her is that she is un-childlike—and deep as the sea. Yes, she is, Laura—deep as the sea. You'll find it out to your cost one day if you disregard my warning. She's capable of anything. Sly is no word for it. You and Elizabeth don't keep a tight enough rein over her."

"I've done my best," said Elizabeth stiffly. She herself did think she had been much too lenient with Emily—Laura and Jimmy were two to one—but it nettled her to have Ruth say so.

Uncle Wallace also had an attack of worrying over Emily that winter.

He looked at her one day when he was at New Moon and remarked that she was getting to be a big girl.

"How old are you, Emily?" He asked her that every time he came to New Moon.

"Thirteen in May."

"H'm. What are you going to do with her, Elizabeth?"

"I don't know what you mean," said Aunt Elizabeth coldly—or as coldly as is possible to speak when one is pouring melted tallow into candle-moulds.

"Why, she'll soon be grown up. She can't expect you to provide for her indefinitely"—

"I don't," Emily whispered resentfully under her breath.

"—and it's time we decided what is best to be done for her."

"The Murray women have never had to work out for a living," said Aunt Elizabeth, as if that disposed of the matter.

"Emily is only half Murray," said Wallace. "Besides, times are changing. You and Laura will not live forever, Elizabeth, and when you are gone New Moon goes to Oliver's Andrew. In my opinion Emily should be fitted to support herself if necessary."

Emily did not like Uncle Wallace but she was very grateful to him at that moment. Whatever his motives were he was proposing the very thing she secretly yearned for.

"I would suggest," said Uncle Wallace, "that she be sent to Queen's Academy to get a teacher's license. Teaching is a genteel, lady-like occupation. *I* will do my share in providing for the expense of it."

A blind person might have seen that Uncle Wallace thought this very splendid of himself.

"If you do," thought Emily, "I'll pay every cent back to you as soon as I'm able to earn it."

But Aunt Elizabeth was adamant.

"I do not believe in girls going out into the world," she said. "I don't mean Emily to go to Queen's. I told Mr. Carpenter so when he came to see me about her taking up the Entrance work. He was very rude—schoolteachers knew their place better in my father's time. But I made him understand, I think. I'm rather surprised at *you*, Wallace. You did not send your own daughter out to work."

"*My* daughter had parents to provide for her," retorted Uncle Wallace pompously. "Emily is an orphan. I imagined from what I had heard about her that she would prefer earning her own living to living on charity."

"So I would," cried out Emily. "So I would, Uncle Wallace. Oh, Aunt Elizabeth, please let me study for the Entrance. Please! I'll pay you back every cent you spend on it—I will indeed. I pledge you my word of honour."

"It does not happen to be a question of money," said Aunt Elizabeth in her stateliest manner. "I undertook to provide for you, Emily, and I will do it. When you are older I may send you to the High School in Shrewsbury for a couple of years. I am not decrying education. But you are not going to be a slave to the public—no Murray girl ever was *that*."

Emily realising the uselessness of pleading, went out in the same bitter disappointment she had felt after Mr. Carpenter's visit. Then Aunt Elizabeth looked at Wallace.

"Have you forgotten what came of sending Juliet to Queen's?" she asked significantly.

If Emily was not allowed to take up the Entrance classes, Perry had no one to say him nay and he went at them with the same dogged determination he showed in all other matters. Perry's status at New Moon had changed subtly and steadily. Aunt Elizabeth had ceased to refer scornfully to him as "a hired boy." Even she recognised that though he was still indubitably a hired boy he was not going to remain one, and she no longer objected to Laura's patching up his ragged bits of clothing, or to Emily's helping him with his lessons in the kitchen after supper, nor did she growl when Cousin Jimmy began to pay him a certain small wage—though older boys than Perry were still glad to put in the winter months choring for board and lodging in some comfortable home. If a future premier was in the making at New Moon Aunt Elizabeth wanted to have some small share in the making. It was credible and commendable that a boy should have ambitions. A girl was an entirely different matter. A girl's place was at home.

Emily helped Perry work out algebra problems and heard his lessons in French and Latin. She picked up more thus than Aunt Elizabeth would have approved and more still when the Entrance pupils talked those languages in school. It was quite an easy matter for a girl who had once upon a time invented a language of her own. When George Bates, by way of showing off, asked her one day in French—*his* French, of which Mr. Carpenter had once said doubtfully that perhaps God might understand it—"Have you the ink of my grandmother and the shoebrush of my cousin and the umbrella of my aunt's husband in your desk?" Emily retorted quite as glibly and *quite* as Frenchily, "No, but I have the pen of your father and the cheese of the innkeeper and the towel of your uncle's maidservant in my basket."

To console herself for her disappointment in regard

to the Entrance class Emily wrote more poetry than ever. It was especially delightful to write poetry on a winter evening when the storm winds howled without and heaped the garden and orchard with big ghostly drifts, starred over with rabbits' candles. She also wrote several stories—desperate love affairs wherein she struggled heroically against the difficulties of affectionate dialogue; tales of bandits and pirates—Emily liked these because there was no necessity for bandits and pirates to converse lovingly; tragedies of earls and countesses whose conversation she dearly loved to pepper with scraps of French; and a dozen other subjects she didn't know anything about. She also meditated beginning a novel but decided it would be too hard to get enough paper for it. The letter-bills were all done now and the Jimmy-books were not big enough, though a new one always appeared mysteriously in her school basket when the old one was almost full. Cousin Jimmy seemed to have an uncanny prescience of the proper time—that was part of his Jimmyness.

Then one night, as she lay in her lookout bed and watched a full moon gleaming lustrously from a cloudless sky across the valley, she had a sudden dazzling idea.

She would send her latest poem to the Charlottetown *Enterprise*.

The *Enterprise* had a Poet's Corner where "original" verses were frequently printed. Privately Emily thought her own were quite as good—as probably they were, for most of the *Enterprise* "poems" were sad trash.

Emily was so excited over the idea that she could not sleep for the greater part of the night—and didn't want to. It was glorious to lie there, thrilling in the darkness and picture the whole thing out. She saw her verses in print signed E. Byrd Starr—she saw Aunt Laura's eyes shining with pride—she saw Mr. Carpenter pointing them out to strangers—"the work of a pupil of mine, by gad"—she saw all her schoolmates envying her or admiring, according to type—she saw herself with one foot at least firmly planted on the ladder of fame—one hill at least of the Alpine Path crested, with a new and glorious prospect opening therefrom.

Morning came. Emily went to school, so absent-minded because of her secret that she did badly in everything and was raged at by Mr. Carpenter. But it all slipped off her like the proverbial water off a duck's back. Her body was in Blair Water school but her spirit was in kingdoms empyreal.

As soon as school was out she betook herself to the garret with half a sheet of blue-lined notepaper. Very painstakingly she copied down the poem, being especially careful to dot every *i* and cross every *t*. She wrote it on both sides of the paper, being in blissful ignorance of any taboo thereon. Then she read it aloud delightedly, not omitting the title *Evening Dreams*. There was one line in it she tasted two or three times:

The haunting elfin music of the air.

"I think that line is *very* good," said Emily. "I wonder now how I happened to think of it."

She mailed her poem the next day and lived in a delicious mystic rapture until the following Saturday. When the *Enterprise* came she opened it with tremulous eagerness and ice-cold fingers, and turned to the Poet's Corner. Now for her great moment!

There was not a sign of an Evening Dream about it!

Emily threw down the *Enterprise* and fled to the garret dormer where, face downward on the old hair-cloth sofa, she wept out her bitterness of disappointment. She drained the draught of failure to the very dregs. It was horribly real and tragic to her. She felt exactly as if she had been slapped in the face. She was crushed in the very dust of humiliation and was sure she could never rise again.

How thankful she was that she hadn't told Teddy anything about it—she had been so strongly tempted to, and only refrained because she didn't want to spoil the dramatic surprise of the moment when she would show him the verses with her name signed to them. She *had* told Perry, and Perry was furious when he saw her tear-stained face later on in the dairy, as they strained the milk together. Ordinarily Emily loved this, but to-night the savour had gone out of the world. Even the milky splendour of the still, mild winter evening and the purple bloom over the hillside woods that presaged a thaw could not give her the accustomed soul-thrill.

"I'm going to Charlottetown if I have to walk and I'll bust that *Enterprise* editor's head," said Perry, with the expression which, thirty years later, warned the members of his party to scatter for cover.

"That wouldn't be any use," said Emily drearily. "He didn't think it good enough to print—that is what hurts me so, Perry—he didn't think it any good. Busting his head wouldn't change *that*."

It took her a week to recover from the blow. Then she wrote a story in which the editor of the *Enterprise* played the part of a dark and desperate villain who found lodging eventually behind prison bars. This got the venom out of her system and she forgot all about him in the delight of writing a poem addressed to "Sweet Lady April." But I question if she ever really forgave him—even when she discovered eventually that you must *not* write on both sides of the paper—even when she read over *Evening Dreams* a year later and wondered how she could ever have thought it any good.

This sort of thing was happening frequently now. Every time she read her little hoard of manuscripts over she found some of which the fairy gold had unaccountably turned to withered leaves, fit only for the burning. Emily burned them,—but it hurt her a little. Outgrowing things we love is never a pleasant process.

29
Sacrilege

There had been several clashes between Aunt Elizabeth and Emily that winter and spring. Generally Aunt Elizabeth came out victorious; there was that in her that would not be denied the satisfaction of having her own way even in trifling matters. But once in a while she came up against that curious streak of granite in Emily's composition which was unyielding and unbendable and unbreakable. Mary Murray, of a hundred years agone, had been, so family chronicle ran, a gentle and submissive creature generally; but she had that same streak in her, as her "Here I Stay" abundantly testified. When Aunt Elizabeth tried conclusions with that element in Emily she always got the worst of it. Yet she did not learn wisdom therefrom but pursued her policy of repression all the more rigorously; for it occasionally came home to her, as Laura let down tucks, that Emily was on the verge of beginning to grow up and that various breakers and reefs loomed ahead, ominously magnified in the mist of unseen years. Emily must not be allowed to get out of hand now, lest later on she make shipwreck as her mother had done—or as Elizabeth Murray firmly believed she had done. There were, in short, to be no more elopements from New Moon.

One of the things they fell out about was the fact that Emily, as Aunt Elizabeth discovered one day, was in the habit of using more of her egg money to buy paper than Aunt Elizabeth approved of. What did Emily do with so much paper? They had a fuss over this and eventually Aunt Elizabeth discovered that Emily was writing stories. Emily had been writing stories all winter under Aunt Elizabeth's very nose and Aunt Elizabeth had never suspected it. She had fondly supposed that Emily was writing school compositions. Aunt Elizabeth knew in a vague way that Emily wrote silly rhymes which she called "poetry" but this did not worry her especially. Jimmy made up a lot of similar trash. It was foolish but harmless and Emily would doubtless outgrow it. Jimmy had not outgrown it, to be sure, but then his accident—Elizabeth always went a little sick in soul when she remembered it—had made him more or less a child for life.

But writing stories was a very different thing and Aunt Elizabeth was horrified. Fiction of any kind was an abominable thing. Elizabeth Murray had been trained up in this belief in her youth and in her age she had not departed from it. She honestly thought that it was a wicked and sinful thing in anyone to play cards, dance, or go to the theatre, read or write novels, and in Emily's case there was a worse feature—it was the Starr coming out in her—Douglas Starr especially. No Murray of New Moon had ever been guilty of writing "stories" or of ever wanting to write them. It was an alien growth that must be pruned off ruthlessly. Aunt Elizabeth applied the pruning shears; and found no pliant, snippable root but that same underlying streak of granite. Emily was respectful and reasonable and above-board; she bought no more paper with egg money; but she told Aunt Elizabeth that she could not give up writing stories and she went right on writing them, on pieces of brown wrapping paper and the blank backs of circulars which agricultural machinery firms sent Cousin Jimmy.

"Don't you know that it is wicked to write novels?" demanded Aunt Elizabeth.

"Oh, I'm not writing novels—yet," said Emily. "I can't get enough paper. These are just short stories. And it isn't wicked—Father liked novels."

"Your father—" began Aunt Elizabeth, and stopped. She remembered that Emily had "acted up" before now when anything derogatory was said of her father. But the very fact that she felt mysteriously compelled to stop annoyed Elizabeth, who had said what seemed good to her all her life at New Moon without much regard for other people's feelings.

"You will not write any more of *this stuff*," Aunt Elizabeth contemptuously flourished "The Secret of the Castle" under Emily's nose. "I forbid you—remember, I forbid you."

"Oh, I must write, Aunt Elizabeth," said Emily gravely, folding her slender, beautiful hands on the table and looking straight into Aunt Elizabeth's angry face with the steady, unblinking gaze which Aunt Ruth called unchildlike. "You see, it's this way. It is *in* me. I can't help it. And Father said I was *always* to keep on writing. He said I would be famous some day. Wouldn't you like to have a famous niece, Aunt Elizabeth?"

"I am not going to argue the matter," said Aunt Elizabeth.

"I'm not arguing—only explaining." Emily was exasperatingly respectful. "I just want you to understand how it is that I *have* to go on writing stories, even though I am so very sorry you don't approve."

"If you don't give up this—this worse than nonsense, Emily, I'll—I'll—"

Aunt Elizabeth stopped, not knowing what to say she would do. Emily was too big now to be slapped or shut up; and it was no use to say, as she was tempted to, "I'll sent you away from New Moon," because Elizabeth Murray knew perfectly well she would not send Emily away from New Moon—*could* not send her away, indeed, though this knowledge was as yet only in her feelings and had not been translated into her intellect. She only felt that she was helpless and it angered her; but Emily was mistress of the situation and calmly went on writing stories. If Aunt Elizabeth had asked her to give up crocheting lace or making molasses taffy, or eating Aunt Laura's delicious drop cookies, Emily would have done so wholly and cheerfully, though she loved these things. But to give up writing stories—why, Aunt Elizabeth might as well have asked her to give up breathing. *Why* couldn't she understand? It seemed so simple and indisputable to Emily.

"Teddy can't help making pictures and Ilse can't help reciting and I can't help writing. *Don't* you see, Aunt Elizabeth?"

"I see that you are an ungrateful and disobedient child," said Aunt Elizabeth.

This hurt Emily horribly, but she could not give in; and there continued to be a sense of soreness and disapproval between her and Aunt Elizabeth in all the little details of daily life that poisoned existence more or less for the child, who was so keenly sensitive to her environment and to the feelings with which her kindred regarded her. Emily felt it all the time—except when she was writing her stories. *Then* she forgot everything, roaming in some enchanted country between the sun and moon, where she saw wonderful beings whom she tried to describe and wonderful deeds which she tried to record, coming back to the candle-lit kitchen with a somewhat dazed sense of having been years in No-Man's Land.

She did not even have Aunt Laura to back her up in the matter. Aunt Laura thought Emily ought to yield in such an unimportant matter and please Aunt Elizabeth.

"But it's not unimportant," said Emily despairingly. "It's the most important thing in the world to me, Aunt Laura. Oh, I thought *you* would understand."

"I understand that you like to do it, dear, and I think it's a harmless enough amusement. But it seems to annoy Elizabeth some way and I do think you might give it up on that account. It is not as if it was anything that mattered much—it *is* really a waste of time."

"No—no," said distressed Emily. "Why, some day, Aunt Laura, I'll write real books—and make lots of money," she added, sensing that the businesslike Murrays measured the nature of most things on a cash basis.

Aunt Laura smiled indulgently.

"I'm afraid you'll never grow rich that way, dear. It would be wiser to employ your time preparing yourself for some useful work."

It was maddening to be condescended to like this—maddening that nobody could see that she *had* to write—maddening to have Aunt Laura so sweet and loving and stupid about it.

"Oh," thought Emily bitterly, "if that hateful *Enterprise* editor had printed my piece they'd have believed *then*."

"At any rate," advised Aunt Laura, "don't let Elizabeth *see* you writing them."

But somehow Emily could not take this prudent advice. There *had* been occasions when she had connived with Aunt Laura to hoodwink Aunt Elizabeth on some little matter, but she found she could not do it in this. *This* had to be open and above-board. She *must* write stories—and Aunt Elizabeth *must* know it—that was the way it had to be. She could not be false to herself in this—she could not *pretend* to be false.

She wrote her father all about it—poured out her bitterness and perplexity to him in what, though she did not suspect it at the time, was the last letter she was to write him. There was a great bundle of letters by now on the old sofa shelf in the garret—for Emily had written many letters to her father besides those which have been chronicled in this history. There were a great many paragraphs about Aunt Elizabeth in them, most of them very uncomplimentary and some of them, as Emily herself would have owned when her first bitterness was past, overdrawn and exaggerated. They had been written in moments when her hurt and angry soul demanded some outlet for its emotion and barbed her pen with venom. Emily was mistress of a subtly malicious style when she chose to be. After she had written them the hurt had ceased and she thought no more about them. But they remained.

And one spring day, Aunt Elizabeth, housecleaning in the garret while Emily played happily with Teddy at the Tansy Patch, found the bundle of letters on the sofa shelf, sat down, and read them all.

Elizabeth Murray would never have read any writing belonging to a grown person. But it never occurred to her that there was anything dishonourable in reading the letters wherein Emily, lonely and—sometimes—misunderstood, had poured out her heart to the father she had loved and been loved by, so passionately and understandingly. Aunt Elizabeth thought she had a right to know everything that this pensioner on her bounty did, said, or thought. She read the letters and she found out what Emily thought of her—of her, Elizabeth Murray, autocrat unchallenged, to whom no one had ever dared to say anything uncomplimentary. Such an experience is no pleasanter at sixty than at sixteen. As Elizabeth Murray folded up the last letter her hands trembled—with anger, and something underneath it that was not anger.

"Emily, your Aunt Elizabeth wants to see you in the parlour," said Aunt Laura, when Emily returned from the Tansy Patch, driven home by the thin grey rain that had begun to drift over the greening fields. Her tone—her sorrowful look—warned Emily that mischief was in the wind. Emily had no idea what mischief—she could not recall anything she had done recently that should bring her up before the tribunal Aunt Elizabeth occasionally held in the parlour. It must be serious when it was in the parlour. For reasons best known to herself Aunt Elizabeth held super-serious interviews like this in the parlour. Possibly it was because she felt obscurely that the photographs of the Murrays on the walls gave her a backing she needed when dealing with this hop-out-of-kin; for the same reason Emily detested a trial in the parlour. She always felt on such occasions like a very small mouse surrounded by a circle of grim cats.

Emily skipped across the big hall, pausing, in spite of her alarm, to glance at the charming red world through the crimson glass; then pushed open the parlour door. The room was dim, for only one of the slat blinds was partially raised. Aunt Elizabeth was sitting bolt upright in Grandfather Murray's black horsehair-chair. Emily looked at her stern, angry face first—and then at her lap.

Emily understood.

The first thing she did was to retrieve her precious letters. With the quickness of light she sprang to Aunt Elizabeth, snatched up the bundle and retreated to the door; there she faced Aunt Elizabeth, her face blazing with indignation and outrage. Sacrilege had been committed—the most sacred shrine of her soul had been profaned.

"How dare you?" she said. "How dare you touch *my private papers*, Aunt Elizabeth?"

Aunt Elizabeth had not expected *this*. She had looked for confusion—dismay—shame—fear—for anything but this righteous indignation, as if *she*, forsooth, were the guilty one. She rose.

"Give me those letters, Emily."

"No, I will not," said Emily, white with anger, as she clasped her hands around the bundle. "They are mine and Father's—not yours. You had no right to touch them. I will *never* forgive you!"

This was turning the tables with a vengeance. Aunt Elizabeth was so dumfounded that she hardly knew what to say or do. Worst of all, a most unpleasant doubt of her own conduct suddenly assailed her—driven home perhaps by the intensity and earnestness of Emily's accusation. For the first time in her life it occurred to Elizabeth Murray to wonder if she had done rightly. For the first time in her life she felt ashamed; and the shame made her furious. It was intolerable that *she* should be made to feel ashamed.

For the moment they faced each other, not as aunt and niece, not as child and adult, but as two human beings each with hatred for the other in her heart— Elizabeth Murray, tall and austere and thin-lipped; Emily Starr, white of face, her eyes pools of black flame, her trembling arms hugging her letters.

"So *this* is your gratitude," said Aunt Elizabeth. "You were a penniless orphan—I took you to my home—I have given you shelter and food and education and kindness—and *this* is my thanks."

As yet Emily's tempest of anger and resentment prevented her from feeling the sting of this.

"You did not *want* to take me," she said. "You made me draw lots and you took me because the lot fell to you. You knew some of you had to take me because you were the proud Murrays and couldn't let a relation go to an orphan asylum. Aunt Laura loves me now but you don't. So why should I love you?"

"Ungrateful, thankless child!"

"I'm *not* thankless. I've tried to be good—I've tried to obey you and please you—I do all the chores I can to help pay for my keep. And you had *no business* to read my letters to Father."

"They are disgraceful letters—and must be destroyed," said Aunt Elizabeth.

"No," Emily clasped them tighter. "I'd sooner burn myself. You shall not have them, Aunt Elizabeth."

She felt her brows drawing together—she felt the Murray look on her face—she knew she was conquering.

Elizabeth Murray turned paler, if that were possible. There were times when she could give the Murray look herself; it was not that which dismayed her—it was the uncanny something which seemed to peer out behind the Murray look that always broke her will. She trembled—faltered—yielded.

"Keep your letters," she said bitterly, "and scorn the old woman who opened her home to you."

She went out of the parlour. Emily was left mistress

of the field. And all at once her victory turned to dust and ashes in her mouth.

She went up to her own room, hid her letters in the cupboard over the mantel, and then crept up on her bed, huddling down in a little heap with her face buried in her pillow. She was still sore with a sense of outrage—but underneath another pain was beginning to ache terribly.

Something in her was hurt because she had hurt Elizabeth—for she felt that Aunt Elizabeth, under all her anger, was *hurt*. This surprised Emily. She would have expected Aunt Elizabeth to be angry, of course, but she would never have supposed it would affect her in any other way. Yet she had seen something in Aunt Elizabeth's eyes when she had flung that last stinging sentence at her—something that spoke of bitter hurt.

"Oh! Oh!" gasped Emily. She began to cry chokingly into her pillow. She was so wretched that she could not get out of herself and watch her own suffering with a sort of enjoyment in its drama—set her mind to analyse her feelings—and when Emily was as wretched as that she was very wretched indeed and wholly comfortless. Aunt Elizabeth would not keep her at New Moon after a poisonous quarrel like this. She would send her away, of course. Emily believed this. Nothing was too horrible to believe just then. How could she live away from dear New Moon?

"And I may have to live eighty years," Emily moaned.

But worse even than this was the remembrance of that look in Aunt Elizabeth's eyes.

Her own sense of outrage and sacrilege ebbed away under the remembrance. She thought of all the things she had written her father about Aunt Elizabeth—sharp, bitter things, some of them just, some of them unjust. She began to feel that she should not have written them. It was true enough that Aunt Elizabeth had not loved her—had not wanted to take her to New Moon. But she *had* taken her and though it had been done in duty, not in love, the fact remained. It was no use for her to tell herself that it wasn't as if the letters were written to any one living, to be seen and read by others. While she was under Aunt Elizabeth's roof—while she owed the food she ate and the clothes she wore to Aunt Elizabeth—she should not say, even to her father, harsh things of her. A Starr should not have done it.

"I must go and ask Aunt Elizabeth to forgive me," thought Emily at last, all the passion gone out of her and only regret and repentance left. "I suppose she never will—she'll hate me always now. But I must go."

She turned herself about—and then the door opened and Aunt Elizabeth entered. She came across the room and stood at the side of the bed, looking down at the grieved little face on the pillow—a face that in the dim, rainy twilight, with its tear-stains and black shadowed eyes, looked strangely mature and chiseled.

Elizabeth Murray was still austere and cold. Her voice sounded stern; but she said an amazing thing.

"Emily, I had no right to read your letters. I admit I was wrong. Will you forgive me?"

"Oh!" The word was almost a cry. Aunt Elizabeth had at last discerned the way to conquer Emily. The latter lifted herself up, flung her arms about Aunt Elizabeth, and said chokingly,

"Oh—Aunt Elizabeth—I'm sorry—I'm sorry—I shouldn't have written those things—but I wrote them when I was vexed—and I didn't mean them *all*—truly, I didn't mean the worst of them. Oh, you'll believe *that*, won't you, Aunt Elizabeth?"

"I'd like to believe it, Emily." An odd quiver passed through the tall, rigid form. "I—don't like to think you—*hate* me—my sister's child—little Juliet's child."

"I don't—oh, I don't," sobbed Emily. "And I'll *love* you, Aunt Elizabeth, if you'll let me—if you *want* me to. I didn't think you cared. *Dear* Aunt Elizabeth."

Emily gave Aunt Elizabeth a fierce hug and a passionate kiss on the white, fine-wrinkled cheek. Aunt

Elizabeth kissed her gravely on the brow in return and then said, as if closing the door on the whole incident.

"You'd better wash your face and come down to supper."

But there was yet something to be cleared up.

"Aunt Elizabeth," whispered Emily. "I *can't* burn those letters, you know—they belong to Father. But I'll tell you what I will do. I'll go over them all and put a star by anything I said about you and then I'll add an explanatory footnote saying that I was mistaken."

Emily spent her spare time for several days putting in her "explanatory footnotes," and then her conscience had rest. But when she again tried to write a letter to her father she found that it no longer meant anything to her. The sense of reality—nearness—of close communion had gone. Perhaps she had been outgrowing it gradually, as childhood began to merge into girlhood— perhaps the bitter scene with Aunt Elizabeth had only shaken into dust something out of which the spirit had already departed. But, whatever the explanation, it was not possible to write such letters any more. She missed them terribly but she could not go back to them. A certain door of life was shut behind her and could not be re-opened.

30
When the Curtain Lifted

It would be pleasant to be able to record that after the reconciliation in the lookout Emily and Aunt Elizabeth lived in entire amity and harmony. But the truth was that things went on pretty much the same as before. Emily went softly, and tried to mingle serpent's wisdom and dove's harmlessness in practical proportions, but their points of view were so different that there were bound to be clashes; they did not speak the same language, so there was bound to be misunderstanding.

And yet there was a difference—a very vital difference. Elizabeth Murray had learned an important lesson—that there was not one law of fairness for children and another for grown-ups. She continued to be as autocratic as ever—but she did not do or say to Emily anything she would not have done or said to Laura had occasion called for it.

Emily, on her side, had discovered the fact that, under all her surface coldness and sternness, Aunt Elizabeth really had an affection for her; and it was wonderful what a difference this made. It took the sting out of Aunt Elizabeth's "ways" and words and healed entirely a certain little half-conscious sore spot that had been in Emily's heart ever since the incident of the drawn slips at Maywood.

"I don't believe I'm a duty to Aunt Elizabeth any more," she thought exultantly.

Emily grew rapidly that summer in body, mind, and soul. Life was delightful, growing richer every hour, like an unfolding rose. Forms of beauty filled her imagination and were transferred as best as she could to paper, though they were never so lovely there, and Emily had the heartbreaking moments of the true artist who discovers that

> *"Never on painter's canvas lives*
> *The charm of his fancy's dream."*

Much of her "old stuff" she burned; even the *Child of the Sea* was reduced to ashes. But the little pile of manuscripts in the mantel cupboard of the lookout was growing steadily larger. Emily kept her scribblings there now; the sofa shelf in the garret was desecrated; and, besides, she felt somehow that Aunt Elizabeth would never meddle with her "private papers" again, no matter where they were kept. She did not go now to the garret to read or write or dream; her own dear lookout was the best place for that. She loved that quaint, little old room intensely; it was almost like a living thing to her—a sharer in gladness—a comforter in sorrow.

Ilse was growing, too, blossoming out into strange beauty and brilliance, knowing no law but her own pleasure, recognizing no authority but her own whim. Aunt Laura worried over her.

"She will be a woman so soon—and *who* will look after her? Allan won't."

"I've no patience with Allan," said Aunt Elizabeth grimly. "He is always ready to hector and advise other people. He'd better look at home. He'll come over here and order me to do this or that, or *not* to do it, for Emily; but if I say one word to him about Ilse he blows the roof off. The idea of a man turning against his daughter and neglecting her as he has neglected Ilse simply because her mother wasn't all she ought to be—as if the poor child was to blame for *that*."

"S—s—sh," said Aunt Laura, as Emily crossed the sitting-room on her way upstairs.

Emily smiled sadly to herself. Aunt Laura needn't be "s-s-sh'ing." There was nothing left for her to find out about Ilse's mother—nothing, except the most important thing of all, which neither she nor anybody else living knew. For Emily had never surrendered her conviction that the whole truth about Beatrice Burnley was not known. She often worried about it when she lay curled up in her black walnut bed o'nights, listening to the moan of the gulf and the Wind Woman singing in the trees, and drifted into sleep wishing intensely that she could solve the dark old mystery and dissolve its legend of shame and bitterness.

Emily went rather languidly upstairs to the lookout. She meant to write some more of her story, *The Ghost of the Well*, wherein she was weaving the old legend of the well in the Lee field; but somehow interest was lacking; she put the manuscript back into the mantel cupboard; she read over a letter from Dean Priest which had come that day, one of his fat, jolly, whimsical, delightful letters wherein he had told her that he was coming to stay a month with his sister at Blair Water. She wondered why this announcement did not excite her more. She was tired—her head was aching. Emily couldn't remember ever having had a headache before. Since she could not write she decided to lie down and be *Lady Trevanion* for awhile. Emily was *Lady Trevanion* very often that summer, in one of the dream lives she had begun to build up for herself. *Lady Trevanion* was the wife of an English earl and, besides being a famous novelist, was a member of the British House of Commons—where she always appeared in black velvet with a stately coronet of pearls on her dark hair. She was the only woman in the House and, as this was before the days of the suffragettes, she had to endure many sneers and innuendoes and insults from the ungallant males around her. Emily's favourite dream scene was where she rose to make her first speech—a wonderfully thrilling event. As Emily found it difficult to do justice to the scene in any ideas of her own, she always fell back on "Pitt's reply to Walpole," which she had found in her *Royal Reader*, and declaimed it, with suitable variations. The insolent speaker who had provoked *Lady Trevanion* into speech had sneered at her as a *woman*, and *Lady Trevanion*, a magnificent creature in her velvet and pearls, rose to her feet, amid hushed and dramatic silence, and said,

"The atrocious crime of being a *woman* which the honourable member has, with such spirit and decency, charged upon me, I shall attempt neither to palliate nor deny, but shall content myself with wishing that I may be one of those whose follies cease with their *sex* and *not* one of that number who are ignorant in spite of *manhood* and experience."

(Here she was always interrupted by thunders of applause.)

But the savour was entirely lacking in this scene

today and by the time Emily had reached the line, "But *womanhood*, Sir, is not my only crime"—she gave up in disgust and fell to worrying over Ilse's mother again, mixed up with some uneasy speculations regarding the climax of her story about the ghost of the well, mingled with her unpleasant physical sensations.

Her eyes hurt her when she moved them. She was chilly, although the July day was hot. She was still lying there when Aunt Elizabeth came up to ask why she hadn't gone to bring the cows home from the pasture.

"I—I didn't know it was so late," said Emily confusedly. "I—my head aches, Aunt Elizabeth."

Aunt Elizabeth rolled up the white cotton blind and looked at Emily. She noted her flushed face—she felt her pulse. Then she bade her shortly to stay where she was, went down, and sent Perry for Dr. Burnley.

"Probably she's got the measles," said the doctor as gruffly as usual. Emily was not yet sick enough to be gentle over. "There's an outbreak of them at Derry Pond. Has she had any chance to catch them?"

"Jimmy Joe Bell's two children were here one afternoon about ten days ago. She played with them—she's always playing round with people she's no business to associate with. I haven't heard that they were or have been sick though."

Jimmy Joe Belle, when asked plainly, confessed that his "young ones" had come out with measles the very day after they had been at New Moon. There was therefore not much doubt as to Emily's malady.

"It's a bad kind of measles apparently," the doctor said. "Quite a number of the Derry Pond children have died of it. Mostly French though—the kids would be out of bed when they had no business to be and caught cold. I don't think you need worry about Emily. She might as well have measles and be done with it. Keep her warm and keep the room dark. I'll run over in the morning."

For three or four days nobody was much alarmed.

Measles was a disease everybody had to have. Aunt Elizabeth looked after Emily well and slept on a sofa which had been moved into the lookout. She even left the window open at night. In spite of this—perhaps Aunt Elizabeth thought because of it—Emily grew steadily sicker, and on the fifth day a sharp change for the worse took place. Her fever went up rapidly, delirium set in; Dr. Burnley came, looked anxious, scowled, changed the medicine.

"I'm sent for to a bad case of pneumonia at White Cross," he said, "and I have to go to Charlottetown in the morning to be present at Mrs. Jackwell's operation. I promised her I would go. I'll be back in the evening. Emily is very restless—that high-strung system of hers is evidently very sensitive to fever. What's that nonsense she's talking about the Wind Woman?"

"Oh, I don't know," said Aunt Elizabeth worriedly. "She's always talking nonsense like that, even when she's well. Allan, tell me plainly—is there any danger?"

"There's always danger in this type of measles. I don't like these symptoms—the eruption should be out by now and there's no sign of it. Her fever is very high—but I don't think we need to be alarmed yet. If I thought otherwise I wouldn't go to town. Keep her as quiet as possible—humour her whims if you can—I don't like that mental disturbance. She looks terribly distressed—seems to be worrying over something. Has she had anything on her mind of late?"

"Not that I know of," said Aunt Elizabeth. She had a sudden bitter realisation that she really did not know much about the child's mind. Emily would never have come to her with any of her little troubles and worries.

"Emily, what is bothering you?" asked Dr. Burnley softly—very softly. He took the hot, tossing, little hand gently, oh, so gently, in his big one.

Emily looked up with wild, fever-bright eyes.

"She couldn't have done it—she *couldn't* have done it."

"Of course she couldn't," said the doctor cheerily. "Don't worry—she didn't do it."

His eyes telegraphed, "What does she mean?" to Elizabeth, but Elizabeth shook her head.

"Who are you talking about—dear?" she asked Emily. It was the first time she had called Emily "dear."

But Emily was off on another tack. The well in Mr. Lee's field was open, she declared. Someone would be sure to fall into it. Why didn't Mr. Lee shut it up? Dr. Burnley left Aunt Elizabeth trying to reassure Emily on that point and hurried away to White Cross.

At the door he nearly fell over Perry who was curled up on the sandstone slab, hugging his sunburned legs desperately. "How is Emily?" he demanded, grasping the skirt of the doctor's coat.

"Don't bother me—I'm in a hurry," growled the doctor.

"You tell me how Emily is or I'll hang on to your coat till the seams go," said Perry stubbornly. "I can't get one word of sense out of them old maids. *You* tell me."

"She's a sick child but I'm not seriously alarmed about her yet." The doctor gave his coat another tug—but Perry held on for a last word.

"You've *got* to cure her," he said. "If anything happens to Emily I'll drown myself in the pond—mind that."

He let go so suddenly that Dr. Burnley nearly went headlong on the ground. Then Perry curled up on the doorstep again. He watched there until Laura and Cousin Jimmy had gone to bed and then he sneaked through the house and sat on the stairs, where he could hear any sound in Emily's room. He sat there all night, with his fists clenched, as if keeping guard against an unseen foe.

Elizabeth Murray watched by Emily until two o'clock, and then Laura took her place.

"She has raved a great deal," said Aunt Elizabeth. "I wish I knew what is worrying her—there *is* something, I feel sure. It isn't all mere delirium. She keeps repeating 'She couldn't have done it' in such imploring tones. I wonder oh, Laura, you remember the time I read her letters? Do you think she means me?"

Laura shook her head. She had never seen Elizabeth so moved.

"If the child—doesn't get—better—" said Aunt Elizabeth. She said no more but went quickly out of the room.

Laura sat down by the bed. She was pale and drawn with her own worry and fatigue—for she had not been able to sleep. She loved Emily as her own child and the awful dread that had possessed her heart would not lift for an instant. She sat there and prayed mutely. Emily fell into a troubled slumber which lasted until the gray dawn crept into the lookout. Then she opened her eyes and looked at Aunt Laura—looked through her—looked beyond her.

"I see her coming over the fields," she said in a high, clear voice. "She is coming so gladly—she is singing—she is thinking of her baby—oh, keep her back—keep her back—she doesn't see the well—it's so dark she doesn't see it—oh, she's gone into it—she's gone into it!"

Emily's voice rose in a piercing shriek which penetrated to Aunt Elizabeth's room and brought her flying across the hall in her flannel nightgown.

"What is wrong, Laura?" she gasped.

Laura was trying to soothe Emily, who was struggling to sit up in bed. Her cheeks were crimson and her eyes had still the same far, wild look.

"Emily—Emily, darling, you've just had a bad dream. The old Lee well isn't open—nobody has fallen into it."

"Yes, somebody has," said Emily shrilly. "*She* has—I saw her—I saw her—with the ace of hearts on her forehead. Do you think I don't know her?"

She fell back on her pillow, moaned, and tossed the hands which Laura Murray had loosened in her susprise.

The two ladies of New Moon looked at each other across her bed in dismay—and something like terror.

"Who did you see, Emily?" asked Aunt Elizabeth.

"Ilse's mother—of course. I always knew she didn't do that dreadful thing. She fell into the old well—she's there now—go—go and get her out, Aunt Laura. *Please*."

"Yes—yes, of course we'll get her out, darling," said Aunt Laura, soothingly.

Emily sat up in bed and looked at Aunt Laura again. This time she did not look through her—she looked into her. Laura Murray felt that those burning eyes read her soul.

"You are lying to me," cried Emily. "You don't mean to try to get her out. You are only saying it to put me off. Aunt Elizabeth," she suddenly turned and caught Aunt Elizabeth's hand, "you'll do it for me, won't you? You'll go and get her out of the old well, won't you?"

Elizabeth remembered that Dr. Burnley had said that Emily's whims must be humoured. She was terrified by the child's condition.

"Yes, I'll get her out if she is in there," she said.

Emily released her hand and sank down. The wild glare left her eyes. A great sudden calm fell over her anguished little face.

"I know *you'll* keep your word," she said. "You are very hard—but *you* never lie, Aunt Elizabeth."

Elizabeth Murray went back to her own room and dressed herself with her shaking fingers. A little later, when Emily had fallen into a quiet sleep, Laura went down stairs and heard Elizabeth giving Cousin Jimmy some orders in the kitchen.

"Elizabeth, you don't really mean to have that old well searched?"

"I do," said Elizabeth resolutely. "I know it's nonsense as well as you do. But I had to promise it to quiet her down—and I'll keep my promise. You heard what she said—she believed I wouldn't lie to her. Nor will I. Jimmy, you will go over to James Lee's after breakfast and ask him to come here."

"How has she heard the story?" said Laura.

"I don't know—oh, some one has told her, of course—perhaps that old demon of a Nancy Priest. It doesn't matter who. She *has* heard it and the thing is to keep her quiet. It isn't so much of a job to put ladders in the well and get some one to go down it. The thing that matters is the absurdity of it."

"We'll be laughed at for a pair of fools," protested Laura, whose share of Murray pride was in hot revolt. "And besides, it will open up all the old scandal again."

"No matter. I'll keep my word to the child," said Elizabeth stubbornly.

Allan Burnley came to New Moon at sunset, on his way home from town. He was tired, for he had been going night and day for over a week; he was more worried than he had admitted over Emily; he looked old and rather desolate as he stepped into the New Moon kitchen.

Only Cousin Jimmy was there. Cousin Jimmy did not seem to have much to do, although it was a good hay-day and Jimmy Joe Belle and Perry were hauling in the great fragrant, sun-dried loads. He sat by the western window with a strange expression on his face.

"Hello, Jimmy, where are the girls? And how is Emily?"

"Emily is better," said Cousin Jimmy. "The rash is out and her fever has gone down. I think she's asleep."

"Good. We couldn't afford to lose that little girl, could we, Jimmy?"

"No," said Jimmy. But he did not seem to want to talk about it. "Laura and Elizabeth are in the sitting-room. They want to see you." He paused a minute and then added in an eerie way, "There is nothing hidden that shall not be revealed."

It occurred to Allan Burnley that Jimmy was acting mysteriously. And if Laura and Elizabeth wanted to see him why didn't they come out? It wasn't like them to stand on ceremony in this fashion. He pushed open the sitting-room door impatiently.

Laura Murray was sitting on the sofa, leaning her head on its arm. He could not see her face but he felt that she was crying. Elizabeth was sitting bolt upright on a chair. She wore her second-best black silk and her second-best lace cap. And she, too, had been crying. Dr. Burnley never attached much importance to Laura's tears, easy as those of most women, but that Elizabeth Murray should cry—had he ever seen her cry before?

The thought of Ilse flashed into his mind—his little neglected daughter. Had anything happened to Ilse? In one dreadful moment Allan Burnley paid the price of his treatment of his child.

"What is wrong?" he exclaimed in his gruffest manner.

"Oh, Allan," said Elizabeth Murray. "God forgive us—God forgive us all!"

"It—is—Ilse," said Dr. Burnley, dully.

"No—no—not Ilse."

Then she told him—she told him what had been found at the bottom of the old Lee well—she told him what had been the real fate of the lovely, laughing young wife whose name for twelve bitter years had never crossed his lips.

It was not until the next evening that Emily saw the doctor. She was lying in bed, weak and limp, red as a beet with the measles rash, but quite herself again. Allan Burnley stood by the bed and looked down at her.

"Emily—dear little child—do you know what you have done for me? God knows how you did it."

"I thought you didn't believe in God," said Emily, wonderingly.

"You have given me back my faith in Him, Emily."

"Why, what have I done?"

Dr. Burnley saw that she had no remembrance of her delirium. Laura had told him that she had slept long and soundly after Elizabeth's promise and had awakened with fever gone and the eruption fast coming out. She had asked nothing and they had said nothing.

"When you are better we will tell you all," he said,

smiling down at her. There was something very sorrowful in the smile—and yet something very sweet.

"He is smiling with his eyes as well as his mouth now," thought Emily.

"How—how did she know?" whispered Laura Murray to him when he went down. "I—can't understand it, Allan."

"Nor I. These things are beyond us, Laura," he answered gravely. "I only know this child has given Beatrice back to me, stainless and beloved. It can be explained rationally enough perhaps. Emily has evidently been told about Beatrice and worried over it— her repeated 'she couldn't have done it' shows that. And the tales of the old Lee well naturally made a deep impression on the mind of a sensitive child keenly alive to dramatic values. In her delirium she mixed this all up with the well-known fact of Jimmy's tumble into the New Moon well—and the rest was coincidence. I would have explained it all so myself once—but now—now, Laura, I only say humbly, 'A little child shall lead them.'"

"Our stepmother's mother was a Highland Scotchwoman. They said she had the second sight," said Elizabeth. "I never believed in it—before."

The excitement of Blair Water had died away before Emily was deemed strong enough to hear the story. That which had been found in the old Lee well had been buried in the Mitchell plot at Shrewsbury and a white marble shaft, "Sacred to the memory of Beatrice Burnley, beloved wife of Allan Burnley," had been erected. The sensation caused by Dr. Burnley's presence every Sunday in the old Burnley pew had died away. On the first evening that Emily was allowed to sit up Aunt Laura told her the whole story. Her manner of telling stripped it forever of the taint and innuendo left by Aunt Nancy.

"I *knew* Ilse's mother couldn't have done it," said Emily triumphantly.

"We blame ourselves now for our lack of faith," said

Aunt Laura. "We should have known too—but it *did* seem black against her at the time, Emily. She was a bright, beautiful, merry creature—we thought her close friendship with her cousin natural and harmless. We know now it was so—but all these years since her disappearance we have believed differently. Mr. James Lee remembers clearly that the well was open the night of Beatrice's disappearance. His hired man had taken the old rotten planks off it that evening, intending to put the new ones on at once. Then Robert Greerson's house caught fire and he ran with everybody else to help save it. By the time it was out it was too dark to finish with the well, and the man said nothing about it until the morning. Mr. Lee was angry with him—he said it was a scandalous thing to leave a well uncovered like that. He went right down and put the new planks in place himself. He did not look down in the well—had he looked he could have seen nothing, for the ferns growing out from the sides screened the depths. It was just after harvest. No one was in the field again before the next spring. He never connected Beatrice's disappearance with the open well—he wonders now that he didn't. But you see—dear—there had been much malicious gossip—and Beatrice was *known* to have gone on board *The Lady of Winds*. It was taken for granted she never came off again. But she did—and went to her death in the old Lee field. It was a dreadful ending to her bright young life—but not so dreadful, after all, as what we believed. For twelve years we have wronged the dead. But—Emily—how could you *know*?"

"I—don't—know. When the doctor came in that day I couldn't remember anything—but now it seems to me that I remember something—just as if I'd dreamed it—of *seeing* Ilse's mother coming over the fields, singing. It was dark—and yet I could see the ace of hearts— oh, Aunty, I don't know—I don't like to think of it, some way."

"We won't talk of it again," said Aunt Laura gently.

"It is one of the things best not talked of—one of God's secrets."

"And Ilse—does her father love her now?" asked Emily eagerly.

"Love her! He can't love her enough. It seems as if he were pouring out on her at once all the shut-up love of those twelve years."

"He'll likely spoil her now as much with indulgence as he did before with neglect," said Elizabeth, coming in with Emily's supper in time to hear Laura's reply.

"It will take a lot of love to spoil Ilse," laughed Laura. "She's drinking it up like a thirsty sponge. And she loves him wildly in return. There isn't a trace of grudge in her over his long neglect."

"All the same," said Elizabeth grimly, tucking pillows behind Emily's back with a very gentle hand, oddly in contrast with her severe expression, "he won't get off so easily. Ilse has run wild for twelve years. He won't find it so easy to make her behave properly now—if he ever does."

"Love will do wonders," said Aunt Laura softly. "Of course, Ilse is dying to come and see you, Emily. But she must wait until there is no danger of infection. I told her she might write—but when she found I would have to read it because of your eyes she said she'd wait till you could read it yourself. Evidently"—Laura laughed again—"evidently Ilse has much of importance to tell you."

"I didn't know anybody could be as happy as I am now," said Emily. "And oh, Aunt Elizabeth, it is *so* nice to feel hungry again and to have something to *chew*."

31
Emily's Great Moment

Emily's convalescence was rather slow. Physically she recovered with normal celerity but a certain spiritual and emotional languor persisted for a time. One cannot go down to the depths of hidden things and escape the penalty. Aunt Elizabeth said she "moped." But Emily was too happy and contented to mope. It was just that life seemed to have lost its savour for a time, as if some spring of vital energy had been drained out of it and refilled slowly.

She had, just then, no one to play with. Perry, Ilse and Teddy had all come down with measles the same day. Mrs. Kent at first declared bitterly that Teddy had caught them at New Moon, but all three had contracted them at a Sunday School picnic where Derry Pond children had been. That picnic infected all Blair Water. There was a perfect orgy of measles. Teddy and Ilse were only moderately ill, but Perry, who had insisted on going home to Aunt Tom at the first symptoms, nearly died. Emily was not allowed to know his danger until it had passed, lest it worry her too much. Even Aunt Elizabeth worried over it. She was surprised to discover how much they missed Perry round the place.

It was fortunate for Emily that Dean Priest was in Blair Water during this forlorn time. His companionship was just what she needed and helped her wonderfully on the road to complete recovery. They went for long walks together all over Blair Water, with Tweed woofing around them, and explored places and roads Emily had never seen before. They watched a young moon grow old, night by night; they talked in dim scented chambers of twilight over long red roads of mystery; they followed the lure of hill winds; they saw the stars rise and Dean told her all about them—the great constellations of the old myths. It was a wonderful month; but on the first day of Teddy's convalescence Emily was off to the Tansy Patch for the afternoon and Jarback Priest walked—if he walked at all—alone.

Aunt Elizabeth was extremely polite to him, though she did not like the Priests of Priest Pond overmuch, and never felt quite comfortable under the mocking gleam of "Jarback's" green eyes and the faint derision of his smile, which seemed to make Murray pride and Murray traditions seem much less important than they really were.

"He has the Priest flavour," she told Laura, "though it isn't as strong in him as in most of them. And he's certainly helping Emily—she has begun to spunk up since he came."

Emily continued to "spunk up" and by December, when the measles epidemic was spent and Dean Priest had gone on one of his sudden swoops over to Europe for the autumn, she was ready for school again—a little taller, a little thinner, a little less childlike, with great grey shadowy eyes that had looked into death and read the riddle of a buried thing, and henceforth would hold in them some haunting, elusive remembrance of that world behind the veil. Dean Priest had seen it—Mr. Carpenter saw it when she smiled at him across her desk at school.

"She's left the childhood of her soul behind, though she is still a child in body," he muttered.

One afternoon amid the golden days and hazes of October he asked her gruffly to let him see some of her verses.

"I never meant to encourage you in it," he said. "I don't mean to now. Probably you can't write a line of real poetry and never will. But let me see your stuff. If it's hopelessly bad I'll tell you so. I won't have you wasting years striving for the unattainable—at least I won't have it on my conscience if you do. If there's any promise in it, I'll tell you so just as honestly. And bring some of your stories, too—*they're* trash yet, that's certain, but I'll see if they show just and sufficient cause for going on."

Emily spent a very solemn hour that evening, weighing, choosing, rejecting. To the little bundle of verse she added one of her Jimmy-books which contained, as she thought, her best stories. She went to school next day, so secret and mysterious that Ilse took offense, started in to call her names—and then stopped. Ilse had promised her father that she would try to break herself of the habit of calling names. She was making fairly good headway and her conversation, if less vivid, was beginning to approximate to New Moon standards.

Emily made a sad mess of her lessons that day. She was nervous and frightened. She had a tremendous respect for Mr. Carpenter's opinion. Father Cassidy had told her to keep on—Dean Priest had told her that some day she might really write—but perhaps they were only trying to be encouraging because they liked her and didn't want to hurt her feelings. Emily knew Mr. Carpenter would not do this. No matter if he did like her he would nip her aspirations mercilessly if he thought the root of the matter was not in her. If, on the contrary, he bade her God-speed, she would rest content with that against the world and never lose heart in the face of any future criticism. No wonder the day seemed fraught with tremendous issues to Emily.

When school was out Mr. Carpenter asked her to remain. She was so white and tense that the other pupils thought she must have been found out by Mr. Carpenter in some especially dreadful behaviour and knew she was going to "catch it." Rhoda Stuart flung her a significantly malicious smile from the porch—which Emily never even saw. She was, indeed, at a momentous bar, with Mr. Carpenter as supreme judge, and her whole future career—so she believed—hanging on his verdict.

The pupils disappeared and a mellow sunshiny stillness settled over the old schoolroom. Mr. Carpenter took the little packet she had given him in the morning out of his desk, came down the aisle and sat in the seat before her, facing her. Very deliberately he settled his glasses astride his hooked nose, took out her manuscripts and began to read—or rather to glance over them, flinging scraps of comments, mingled with grunts, sniffs and hoots, at her as he glanced. Emily folded her cold hands on her desk and braced her feet against the legs of it to keep her knees from trembling. This was a very terrible experience. She wished she had never given her verses to Mr. Carpenter. They were no good—of course they were no good. Remember the editor of the *Enterprise*.

"Humph!" said Mr. Carpenter. "*Sunset*—Lord, how many poems have been written on 'Sunset'—

> 'The clouds are massed in splendid state
> At heaven's unbarred western gate
> Where troops of star-eyed spirits wait'—

By gad, what does that mean?"

"I—I—don't know," faltered startled Emily, whose wits had been scattered by the sudden swoop of his spiked glance.

Mr. Carpenter snorted.

"For heaven's sake, girl, don't write what you can't understand yourself. And this—*To Life*—'Life, as thy gift I ask no rainbow joy'—is that sincere? Is it, girl. Stop and think. *Do* you ask 'no rainbow joy' of life?"

He transfixed her with another stare. But Emily was beginning to pick herself up a bit. Nevertheless, she suddenly felt oddly ashamed of the very elevated and unselfish desires expressed in that sonnet.

"No-o," she answered reluctantly. "I *do* want rainbow joy—lots of it."

"Of course you do. We all do. We don't get it—you won't get it—but don't be hypocrite enough to pretend you don't want it, even in a sonnet. *Lines to a Mountain Cascade*— 'On its dark rocks like the whiteness of a veil around a bride'—Where did you see a mountain cascade in Prince Edward Island?"

"Nowhere—there's a picture of one in Dr. Burnley's library."

"*A Wood Stream*—

> *The threading sunbeams quiver,*
> *The bending bushes shiver,*
> *O'er the little shadowy river'*—

There's only one more rhyme that occurs to me and that's 'liver.' Why did you leave it out?"

Emily writhed.

"*Wind Song*—

> *'I have shaken the dew in the meadows*
> *From the clover's creamy gown'*—

Pretty, but weak. *June*—June, for heaven's sake, girl, don't write poetry on June. It's the sickliest subject in the world. It's been written to death."

"No, June is immortal," cried Emily suddenly, a mutinous sparkle replacing the strained look in her eyes. She was not going to let Mr. Carpenter have it all his own way.

But Mr. Carpenter had tossed *June* aside without reading a line of it.

"'I weary of the hungry world'—what do you know of the hungry world?—you in your New Moon seclusion of old trees and old maids—but it *is* hungry. *Ode to Winter*—the seasons are a sort of disease all young poets must have, it seems—ha! 'Spring will not forget' —*that's* a good line—the only good line in it. H'm'm— *Wanderings*—

> *'I've learned the secret of the rune*
> *That the somber pines on the hillside croon'*—

Have you—*have* you learned that secret?"

"I think I've always known it," said Emily dreamily. That flash of unimaginable sweetness that sometimes surprised her had just come and gone.

"*Aim and Endeavor*—too didactic—too didactic. You've no right to try to teach until you're old—and then you won't want to—

> *'Her face was like a star all pale and fair'*—

Were you looking in the glass when you composed that line?"

"No—" indignantly.

" 'When the morning light is shaken like a banner on the hill'—a good line—a good line—

> *'Oh, on such a golden morning*
> *To be living is delight'*—

Too much like a faint echo of Wordsworth. *The Sea in September*—'blue and austerely bright'—'austerely bright'—child, how can you marry the right adjectives like that? *Morning*—'all the secret fears that haunt the night' —what do *you* know of the fears that haunt the night?"

"I know something," said Emily decidedly, remembering her first night at Wyther Grange.

"*To a Dead Day*—

> *'With the chilly calm on her brow*
> *That only the dead may wear'*—

Have you ever *seen* the chilly calm on the brow of the dead, Emily?"

"Yes," said Emily softly, recalling that grey dawn in the old house in the hollow.

"I thought so—otherwise you couldn't have written *that*—and even as it is—how old are you, jade?"

"Thirteen, last May."

"Humph! *Lines to Mrs. George Irving's Infant Son*—you should study the art of titles, Emily—there's a fashion in them as in everything else. Your titles are as out of date as the candles of New Moon—

> *'Soundly he sleeps with his red lips pressed*
> *Like a beautiful blossom close to her breast'*—

The rest isn't worth reading. *September*—is there a month you've missed?—'Windy meadows harvest-deep'—good line. *Blair Water by Moonlight*—gossamer, Emily, nothing but gossamer. *The Garden of New Moon*—

> *'Beguiling laughter and old song*
> *Of merry maids and men'*—

Good line—I suppose New Moon *is* full of ghosts. 'Death's fell minion well fulfilled its part'—that might have passed in Addison's day but not now—not now, Emily—

> *'Your azure dimples are the graves*
> *Where million buried sunbeams play'*—

Atrocious, girl—atrocious. Graves aren't playgrounds. How much would *you* play if you were buried?"

Emily writhed and blushed again. *Why* couldn't she have seen that herself? *Any* goose could have seen it.

> " *'Sail onward, ships—white wings, sail on,*
> *Till past the horizon's purple bar*
> *You drift from sight.—In flush of dawn*
> *Sail on, and 'neath the evening star'*—

Trash—trash—and yet there's a picture in it—

> *'Lap softly, purple waves. I dream,*
> *And dreams are sweet—I'll wake no more'*—

Ah, but you'll have to wake if you want to accomplish anything. Girl, you've used *purple* twice in the same poem.

> *'Buttercups in a golden frenzy'*—

'a golden frenzy'—girl, I *see* the wind shaking the buttercups.

> *'From the purple gates of the west I come'*—

You're too fond of purple, Emily."

"It's such a lovely word," said Emily.

> " *'Dreams that seem too bright to die'*—

Seem but never *are*, Emily—

> *'The luring voice of the echo, fame'*—

So you've heard it, too? It *is* a lure and for most of us only an echo. And that's the last of the lot."

Mr. Carpenter swept the little sheets aside, folded his arms on the desk, and looked over his glasses at Emily.

Emily looked back at him mutely, nervelessly. All the life seemed to have been drained out of her body and concentrated in her eyes.

"Ten good lines out of four hundred, Emily—comparatively good, that is—and all the rest balderdash—balderdash, Emily."

"I—suppose so," said Emily faintly.

Her eyes brimmed with tears—her lips quivered. She could not help it. Pride was hopelessly submerged in the bitterness of her disappointment. She felt exactly like a candle that somebody had blown out.

"What are you crying for?" demanded Mr. Carpenter.

Emily blinked away the tears and tried to laugh.

"I—I'm sorry—you think it's no good—" she said.

Mr. Carpenter gave the desk a mighty thump.

"No good! Didn't I tell you there were ten good lines? Jade, for ten righteous men Sodom had been spared."

"Do you mean—that—after all—" The candle was being relighted again.

"Of course, I mean. If at thirteen you can write ten good lines, at twenty you'll write ten times ten—if the gods are kind. Stop messing over months, though—and don't imagine you're a genius either, if you *have* written ten decent lines. I think there's *something* trying to speak through you—but you'll have to make yourself a fit instrument for it. You've got to work hard and sacrifice—by gad, girl, you've chosen a jealous goddess. And she never lets her votaries go—not even when she shuts her ears forever to their plea. What have you there?"

Emily, her heart thrilling, handed him her Jimmy-book. She was so happy that it shone through her whole being with a positive radiance. She saw her future, wonderful, brilliant—oh, her goddess would listen to *her*—"Emily B. Starr, the distinguished poet" —"E. Byrd Starr, the rising young novelist"—

She was recalled from her enchanting reverie by a chuckle from Mr. Carpenter. Emily wondered a little uneasily what he was laughing at. She didn't think there was anything funny in *that* book. It contained only three or four of her latest stories—*The Butterfly Queen*, a little fairy tale; *The Disappointed House*, wherein she had woven a pretty dream of hopes come true after long years; *The Secret of the Glen*, which, in spite of its title, was a fanciful little dialogue between the Spirit of the Snow, the Spirit of the Grey Rain, the Spirit of Mist, and the Spirit of Moonshine.

"So you think I am not beautiful when I say my prayers?" said Mr. Carpenter.

Emily gasped—realized what had happened—made a frantic grab at her Jimmy-book—missed it. Mr. Carpenter held it up beyond her reach and mocked at her.

She had given him the wrong Jimmy-book! And this one, oh, horrors, what was in it? Or rather, what wasn't in it? Sketches of everyone in Blair Water—and a full—a very full—description of Mr. Carpenter himself. Intent on describing him exactly, she had been as mercilessly lucid as she always was, especially in regard to the odd faces he made on mornings when he opened the school day with a prayer. Thanks to her dramatic knack of word painting, Mr. Carpenter *lived* in that sketch. Emily did not know it, but *he* did—he saw himself as in a glass and the artistry of it pleased him so that he cared for nothing else. Besides, she had drawn his good points quite as clearly as his bad ones. And there were some sentences in it—"He looks as if he knew a great deal that can never be any use to him"—"I think he wears the black coat Mondays because it makes him feel that he hasn't been drunk at all." Who or what had taught the little jade these things? Oh, her goddess would not pass Emily by!

"I'm—sorry," said Emily, crimsom with shame all over her dainty paleness.

"Why, I wouldn't have missed this for all the poetry you've written or ever will write! By gad, it's literature—*literature*—and you're only thirteen. But you don't know what's ahead of you—the stony hills—the steep ascents—the buffets—the discouragements. Stay in the valley if you're wise. Emily, *why* do you want to write? Give me your reason."

"I want to be famous and rich," said Emily coolly.

"Everybody does. Is that all?"

"No. I just *love* to write."

"A better reason—but not enough—not enough. Tell me this—if you knew you would be poor as a church mouse all your life—if you knew you'd never

have a line published—would you still go on writing—
would you?"

"Of course I would," said Emily disdainfully. "Why,
I *have* to write—I can't help it by times—I've just *got*
to."

"Oh—then I'd waste my breath giving advice at all.
If it's *in* you to climb you must—there are those who
must lift their eyes to the hills—they can't breathe
properly in the valleys. God help them if there's some
weakness in them that prevents their climbing. You
don't understand a word I'm saying—yet. But go on—
climb! There, take your book and go home. Thirteen
years from now I will have a claim to distinction in the
fact that Emily Byrd Starr was once a pupil of mine.
Go—go—before I remember what a disrespectful bag-
gage you are to write such stuff about me and be
properly enraged."

Emily went, still a bit scared but oddly exultant
behind her fright. She was so happy that her happiness seemed to irradiate the world with its own
splendour. All the sweet sounds of nature around her
seemed like the broken words of her own delight. Mr.
Carpenter watched her out of sight from the old worn
threshold.

"Wind—and flame—and sea!" he muttered. "Nature
is always taking us by surprise. This child has—what I
have never had and would have made any sacrifice to
have. But 'the gods don't allow us to be in their
debt'—she will pay for it—she will pay."

At sunset Emily sat in the lookout room. It was
flooded with soft splendour. Outside, in sky and trees,
were delicate tintings and aerial sounds. Down in the
garden Daffy was chasing dead leaves along the red
walks. The sight of his sleek, striped sides, the grace of
his movements, gave her pleasure—as did the beautiful, even, glossy furrows of the ploughed fields beyond
the lane, and the first faint white star in the crystal-
green sky.

The wind of the autumn night was blowing trumpets

of fairyland on the hills; and over in Lofty John's bush
was laughter—like the laughter of fauns. Ilse and Perry
and Teddy were waiting there for her—they had made
a tryst for a twilight romp. She would go to them—
presently—not yet. She was so full of rapture that she
must write it out before she went back from her world
of dreams to the world of reality. Once she would have
poured it into a letter to her father. She could no longer
do that. But on the table before her lay a brand-new
Jimmy-book. She pulled it towards her, took up her
pen, and on its first virgin page she wrote.

> NEW MOON,
> BLAIR WATER,
>   P. E. ISLAND.
> October 8th.

I am going to write a dairy, that it may be published
when I die.

LUCY MAUD MONTGOMERY was born on November 30, 1874, in Clifton, Prince Edward Island, Canada. Although few women of that time received a higher education, Maud attended Prince of Wales College in Charlottetown, P.E.I., and then Dalhousie University in Halifax. At seventeen she went to Nova Scotia to work for a newspaper, the Halifax *Chronicle*, and wrote for its evening edition, the *Echo*. But Maud came back to rural Prince Edward Island to teach, and lived with her grandmother at Cavendish. It is this experience, along with the lives of her farmer and fisherfolk neighbors, that came alive when she wrote her "Anne" books, beginning with *Anne of Green Gables* in 1908. First published as a serial for a Sunday school paper, *Anne of Green Gables* quickly became a favorite of readers throughout the world, so much so that L. M. Montgomery published eight novels in all featuring Anne Shirley and her family. Maud Montgomery also wrote the popular *Emily of New Moon* in 1923 followed by two sequels, and *Pat of Silver Bush* in 1933 with its sequel. She and her husband, the Rev. Ewen Macdonald, eventually moved to Ontario. L. M. Montgomery died in Toronto in 1942, but it is her early years of lush green Prince Edward Island that live on in the delightful adventures of the impetuous redhead, the stories Mark Twain called "the sweetest creation of child life yet written."

Anne of Green Gables has been translated into seventeen languages, made into a number of movies, and has had continuing success as a stage play.

The success of these productions inspired *The Road to Avonlea*—enchanting new tales based on characters created by L. M. Montgomery for a television series as well as the new paperback editions.

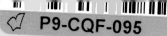

Praise for Monica Ferris's
Needlecraft Mysteries

"Another excellent mystery written by fabulous author Monica Ferris." —Open Book Society

"A comfortable fit for mystery readers who want to spend an enjoyable time with interesting characters."
—*St. Paul Pioneer Press*

"Not just for needleworkers, this is a series that should appeal to anyone who enjoys a good cozy mystery populated by characters who continue to grow and evolve."
—CA Reviews

"Fans will enjoy the needlework lore, the included pattern, and the ongoing adventures." —*Kirkus Reviews*

"Ferris's fans will be charmed." —*Publishers Weekly*

"Ferris's characterizations are top-notch, and the action moves along at a crisp pace." —*Booklist*

"Fans of Margaret Yorke will relate to Betsy's growth and eventual maturity . . . You need not be a needlecrafter to enjoy this . . . Delightful." —Mystery Times

"A true accomplishment . . . The story flows seamlessly and makes for gripping reading." —Mystery Scene

"Filled with great small-town characters . . . A great time . . . Fans of Jessica Fletcher will devour this." —Rendezvous

Knit Your Own Murder

Monica Ferris

BERKLEY PRIME CRIME
New York

BERKLEY PRIME CRIME
Published by Berkley
An imprint of Penguin Random House LLC
375 Hudson Street, New York, New York 10014

ISBN: 9780425270134

Berkley Prime Crime hardcover edition / August 2016
Berkley Prime Crime mass-market edition / July 2017

Printed in the United States of America
1   3   5   7   9   10   8   6   4   2

Cover illustration by Mary Ann Lasher
Cover design by George Long

Acknowledgments

I want to thank Maru Zamora, Alicia Vázquez-De-Ortiz, and Ricardo Ortiz-Nava for language help with the intense quarrel in Spanish that is described in this book.

Dr. Michael Austin of the University of Minnesota's Safety and Environmental Protection Facility was extremely helpful about poisons. He even showed me how, under extraordinary conditions, including coincidence, someone might bypass their safeguards.

Thanks to the Davisson people Allan and Lief, who deal in coins, for selling me an Edward the Confessor early medieval silver penny—and thereby giving me the information I needed to allow Rafael Miguel Antonio de la Valencina Zamora Soto (isn't that a great name?) to add one to his own collection.

Thank you, Bill Staines, for permission to quote the chorus of your song "River (Take Me Along)" in this novel.

And of course, thanks to Diane Davis, the talented needlework artist who created the little knit pattern of Sophie in the back of this book.

Chapter One

♦ ♦ ♦

JOE Mickels sat alone in his big old car. He was a thick-bodied man with a harsh face set on either side with long, old-fashioned sideburns. It was the last Tuesday in March, near the end of winter in Minnesota. The sky was overcast, the sun showing its location by a light spot in the clouds. The temperature was above freezing by two degrees.

Joe was tired; not just physically tired, but spiritually tired. Tired to his bones, tired to his soul. He had worked hard all his life, and what did he have to show for it?

There was the money, of course. Lots of money, actually. Once, that was enough. Every time he worked a deal successfully he got paid, so it became a way of keeping score. It was a game he was good at, and he had played it for a long time, racking up points, until he was so far ahead the numbers had become almost meaningless.

The problem was—and who would have thought it?—

the money itself had also become meaningless. He'd never married, had no children, so there was no one standing by, eager for him to die and leave it to them—so they could blow through it in a couple of years and wind up on welfare. Or to rebel and go all anti-money and declare they didn't want any of it. Or to be grateful for his ability to earn money because they'd inherited that trait themselves. Or to give him grandchildren to tease and love and spoil. There was no one to give a damn.

When he died, his money would dissipate like fog on a sunny morning.

He'd finally thought of a way to leave his mark, a good, solid method. He'd tried and tried and tried to make it happen—and failed. Two days ago he'd failed at what he thought was his last, and best, chance to build the Mickels Building right here in his hometown. A building that would stand for at least a century, maybe two, with his name proudly spread across the lintel. Now it was never going to happen. And he was tired, maybe too tired to care.

Today was his birthday. He was eighty years old. A really big number, eighty. Until two days ago he hadn't felt eighty. Hell, he hadn't even felt seventy. But today he felt every year—every minute—of eighty.

When Joe Mickels was a kid, fifty was old. One foot in the grave, the other on a banana peel was how he would have described it. But nowadays fifty was still middle-aged.

On the other hand, even today eighty was old. The chance to put his permanent mark on the world was almost certainly past. Eighty was summing-up time, not make-your-mark time.

He'd had one last shot at it, a beautiful shot, and almost

succeeded. But he was spread a little thin right now, unable to convert holdings to sufficient cash quickly enough to get that property, to raise his bid past the soaring bids of Maddy O'Leary and Harry Whiteside.

He was almost depressed enough not to be angry.

Almost.

Chapter Two

✦ ✦ ✦

ON Friday afternoon, the Monday Bunch was in session at Crewel World. They had met on Monday earlier that week but were eager to complete a group project and had been meeting two, sometimes three times a week. They were sitting around the big library table in the middle of the shop. The Bunch was a long-standing group of women—and two men—who normally met weekly at the needlework shop to stitch on a wide variety of projects and to gossip. But all seven people in attendance today were knitting, and all were working on toy animals. A heap of excelsior stuffing was in the center of the table.

"I always thought Harry Whiteside would come to a bad end," said Bershada, a handsome black woman. She was casting off the last row of a small Paddington bear she'd been knitting.

"Yes," said Connor, his tone just a little remonstrative, "but murdered? Surely that's a bit harsh."

Harry Whiteside had been found in the kitchen of his fine Wayzata home, his skull broken and his house vandalized.

Bershada responded coolly, "I knew his second wife, poor thing, and helped her pack the day she left him. I thought at the time—that was, what, three years ago?—that he deserved worse."

"I'm surprised she stuck with him as long as she did, knowing what a bast—pardon me—what a hard man he was," said Phil, who was knitting, of all things, a large fruit bat. "But I thought it would be bankruptcy doing him in, not murder. He started small, built slowly, then all of a sudden he's rich. Happened so fast, it seemed bound to fall down around his ears. But he wasn't actually a crook, was he?"

"No," admitted Bershada. "Well, not completely a crook," she amended. "But a lot of people thought they got taken by his methods of doing business." She glanced around the table and added in a quieter voice, "Not excluding our own Maddy O'Leary."

Maddy wasn't exactly one of Crewel World's "own." She was an ardent knitter and did some tatting as well, buying her supplies in the shop. But she didn't come to the weekly gathering of stitchers, and her cruel tongue kept the Monday Bunch from inviting her to do so.

"Hey, Maddy got the better of him over the Water Street property," said Cherie. She was knitting a big macaw whose bright colors were echoed in the bunch of feathers on the natty green hat she wore. "After all, she's the one who wound up with the deed."

"True, but he—and Joe Mickels, don't forget—bid her up well over what she thought she'd have to pay, didn't they?" said Godwin, the store manager, a young-looking thirty-year-old man with a dulcet voice and very swift fingers. He had been showing off by knitting a leopard, a difficult task because of its random pattern of yellow-centered black spots. As he spoke, he was knitting the fortieth, forty-first, and forty-second stitch in the row of forty-five that made up the long tail of the animal.

"I agree Joe Mickels has to take a share of the blame for the high price it sold for," said shop owner Betsy Devonshire, who wasn't sitting at the table but was working on an order for Silk and Ivory floss over at the checkout desk.

Everyone knew Joe Mickels had long harbored a desire to put up a building in Excelsior with his name over the door. At one time he'd thought to build it on the site of Betsy's building, and his ultimately futile attempts to force her out had led to plenty of bad feelings on both sides. He had recently tried to accomplish his goal when the great big car dealership at the top of Water Street had closed and the property had been divided in half and offered for sale. A whole-foods grocery had promptly bought the southwest end, and after an initial shaking out of half a dozen bidders, three people had contended for the northeastern half.

"It's very satisfying to make your dreams come true," said Valentina, who was driving her contractor crazy because she insisted on supervising every element of the reworking of a house she'd inherited. "So I guess I'm feeling a little bad for Mr. Mickels." She was knitting a beautiful ram, complete with horns.

Joe, Maddy, and Harry had taken up cudgels in a bidding war, all the more ferocious for the big egos of the three participants. All three refused to speak on the record about the struggle, but some local folks knew a few interesting details, and enough of them talked about it that many of the people living around Lake Minnetonka were able to follow with amazement as the bids were raised and raised again. Maddy won at the end, but the dust was yet to settle, and the hard feelings lingered.

And now one of the three final bidders, Harry Whiteside, was dead, murdered in his own home.

"You don't suppose—?" said Valentina, and paused. As the newest member of the group, she wasn't sure how far to go in speculating about people.

"Suppose what?" asked Doris, encouragingly.

Valentina shook her head, but Godwin was braver. "That Joe had something to do with Harry's death?" He looked at Valentina, who nodded, then at Betsy, his expression amused. "Maybe trying to get the bidding reopened?"

"Goddy," said Betsy, a little miffed at his flippancy, "Mr. Whiteside was killed by a burglar he interrupted in his home. That is not a matter for joking."

Connor said, "Anyway, if Joe was out to get the bidding reopened, he'd go after Maddy, not Harry." He was finished with his orange-haired orangutan and was stuffing it from the big heap of finely shredded wood chips on the table.

But Godwin was incorrigible. In his most flamboyant tone and gesture, he said, "We don't *know* that. Maybe he decided first to go after his *rival*, so he'd be less obvious. You all just keep watching. If something happens to Maddy, then you'll *know* I'm right." But he made a face to show he was just kidding.

"Pooh," said Emily, who didn't use strong language.

"Ha, finished!" announced Bershada, tossing down her

knitting needles. The Paddington Bear, complete with blue duffel coat and yellow rain hat, lay in a severely collapsed condition across one of her hands. The bear was about eight inches long and without eyes or the black tip of its nose, and its bottom was open. Bershada reached for the excelsior and began to fill the toy, her beautiful, long fingers moving deftly.

"Awwwww," said Emily as the little bear took shape. "How many does that make?"

"Of critters? An even dozen. This is Paddington number five."

"That's amazing!" said Valentina. "I've made six of these rams and thought I was doing well."

"You *are* doing well," said Bershada. "Compared to that ram, this bear is really easy."

"I've only done three toys," said Doris, "so you both are doing well."

Emily said, "I'm glad you're making the bear's coat and hat part of him, Bershada, because otherwise they'd get lost by the second day." She spoke from experience, having three young girls in her household whose ability to remove and lose accessories from their toys held, she was sure, national speed records.

Emily was working on a toy kitten with "tuxedo" markings: It was mostly black with white on its face, chest, and paws. She had a big plastic sewing needle and was using it to fasten the fourth leg to the creature. On the table in front of her was a pair of green glass cat's-eyes with little metal loops on their backs, waiting to be sewn on.

Doris, sitting next to Emily, frowned, sighed, looked

away and back, then snatched up a linen bookmark with an Easter bunny stitched on it and tossed it over the glass eyes. "Well, they were staring at me," she explained as the others looked at her, surprised then amused.

Doris was less than half finished with a lion, her most ambitious project to date. She was using the directions in Sally Muir and Joanna Osborne's delightful *Knit Your Own Zoo* to make the toy, which would be about ten inches long—not counting the tail. At this point the lion's front left limb and both hind limbs were opened out in front of her, their upper ends suspended on separate knitting needles, waiting for her to get that far. She was working on knitting the right front leg onto the right side of the body. There was no head in sight.

"Are you going to have that finished by tomorrow?" asked Godwin. With a contented little sigh he closed his copy of the book in front of him, *Knit Your Own Zoo*. He didn't need instructions on how to stuff his leopard.

"You just mind your own project," advised Doris cheerfully, her fingers moving in the patterns of knit one, purl one. She was not as fast a knitter as Godwin, but neither was she as slow as her husband, Phil, sitting beside her.

He was knitting the second wing on his bat, consulting the pattern he'd photocopied from his wife's copy of the book, then pausing to count the number of stitches on his needle.

Godwin had found a doorbell device that played music whenever anyone opened the door. It sounded like a toy organ and would play anything programmed into it. Godwin hadn't settled on one tune. Today it was playing "Hail to the Chief" and the knitters looked up to see Maddy O'Leary enter, holding a big brown canvas bag in one hand. She was a large woman with masses of gray hair pulled back into an untidy bun, a habitually downturned mouth, and a habit of wearing sturdy wool suits with long skirts.

She turned toward the source of the music, then glanced at the Band-Aid around one of her fingers: a patriotic one in red, white, and blue.

Phil sniggered, and she whirled back to impale him with a glare.

"Ms. O'Leary," said Betsy to distract her. "What can I do for you?"

"I brought some more toys," she said in a strong, unfriendly voice. She walked to the table and upended the bag carelessly. Its contents landed on the excelsior, scattering it onto everyone else's work. Her contribution consisted of four knit dogs: a border collie, a Scottie, a whippet, and a silly-looking flop-eared mutt; and a bald eagle with glaring eyes and folded wings.

"Hey!" exclaimed Phil, hastily lifting his bat and shaking off the wisps of stuffing.

She scowled at the ugly gray-black creature in his hands. "Good heavens, Galvin, who's going to want to bid on that?" she asked.

"Some strange little child is going to beg and beg her mother to get it for her," asserted Phil with happy confidence.

"Humph, I think not!"

"Well, what did they put the pattern in the book for, if they thought no one would want it?" he asked.

"Humph!" she said again. "Betsy, could you write me a

receipt for these toys?" Maddy was generous but business-like. She kept good records of her donations in order to make proper tax deductions.

"Certainly. I can't believe how many contributions you've made to the auction. More than anyone else, did you know that?"

"It's nothing. Got to do something with my hands to keep them busy."

Chapter Three

◆ ◆ ◆

THE Knit Your Own series had been popular from the day two years ago Betsy first put *Knit Your Own Dog* out on one of the box shelves that divided the front of her shop from the back. Beside it she had put a knit boxer her boyfriend, Connor, had completed for her—Betsy wasn't an expert knitter, and the pattern had proved more difficult than she anticipated.

But later she had managed to knit her own rooster—she had an inexplicable fondness for chickens and found the pattern in *Knit Your Own Farm*, the latest in the series. The result was a red-feathered rooster with a typical arrogant look in his eye and a comb tipped dashingly to one side (an unintentional error—but she'd seen many a rooster with the same tilted comb). The rooster had brought on a little rush to buy the farm book, which was very gratifying.

But it was last summer that Bershada Reynolds had

come up with the idea of donating toy animals for an auction to raise funds to repair the elderly little brick building in Excelsior's lakefront park, the Commons. The building contained restrooms on one side and a snack bar on the other. The electrical wiring needed replacement, the tile on the snack bar floor was so badly cracked it was impossible to clean properly, and the restrooms needed new fixtures.

The fund-raiser committee was formed in September; by January donations had faded to a trickle, and the amount raised was insufficient.

Bershada was in Crewel World that August looking at a richly colored cross-stitch pattern leaflet dating back to 1983 of Santa unloading his sack under a tree decorated with apples, pears, and oranges—Betsy had found it in the basement when clearing a shelf. The pattern was on a table of half-price items. Bershada decided to buy it and was going over to select the floss she'd need for it when she saw Betsy putting the new knit rooster beside the boxer.

"Now that is a *chicken*!" she said.

"Isn't it nice?" agreed Betsy.

"You know what? That thing would sell for a lot of money. A lot of the animals in those books would sell very well. We could use the money for the Commons's snack bar repair fund."

"Are you suggesting I turn my needlework shop into a toy store?"

"No, of course not. But we could sell them at garage sales or even open a little shop temporarily. No, on second thought, that would probably cost more money than we'd raise. Hmmm—wait, I know, we could do an auction."

"Who could?" asked Betsy.

"We could—we should! We, the committee to repair the snack bar!"

"An auction?" said Betsy doubtfully.

"Sure! That's what we should do!" Bershada's boyfriend's cousin-in-law was an auctioneer, she said, a bright and funny man, and, even better, an exciting person to watch in action.

Betsy had been to a few auctions and knew how a good auctioneer could stir up the audience, persuading them to spend more than they planned on going in.

"What do you propose to auction off?" asked Betsy.

"What I said: these. Handmade stuffed toys," replied Bershada. She picked up the rooster and gestured at the books with it. "Here are dozens of patterns we can use. Plus, I've got some more at home. I've even got a pattern for a knit sock monkey."

"Are you serious?" Betsy asked.

"You bet I am. We've got some very talented knitters here in town."

"Well," Betsy said, "not a great number. If you're going to do a sale, you need a lot of things to sell. Now over here I've got another animal pattern book, called *Mini Knitted Safari*, by Sachiyo Ishii. Incredibly simple patterns, knit flat and then sewn into shape. Beginning knitters, especially children, love them. You could make a lot of them in a very short time."

"Yes, I've seen that book, but they're so small, I don't think they'd raise a lot of money auctioned one by one."

Another customer had come up behind Bershada. "That's a beautiful rooster," she said. "He's got a real rooster attitude." She raised her head, turned her mouth down, and gave an arrogant sniff. Then, laughing, she reached for a copy of *Knit Your Own Farm*. Paging through, she started making happy noises and nodding at the color photos of the animals: cow, pig, horse, goose with goslings, ram. Then she looked at the several pages of pattern that followed each photograph.

"I like these, but the patterns look kind of hard," she said.

Godwin was immediately at her side. "Oh, you can do these, absolutely, Shar," he said. "I'm thinking of starting a class."

"Well, all right, I'll wait for the class." She put the book back.

But Godwin took it down again and held it out to her. "I'll give you a hint you can use right now."

"A hint? What is it?"

"Write out the pattern. You're not an advanced knitter, but I bet you know most of the abbreviations used in knitting patterns. Like here." He opened the book and quickly searched a pattern. "See?" He pointed to a line in a pattern, K2tog. "It means?"

"Um, knit two together?"

"Right. So take a sheet of paper and write in so many words, knit two together. That's what I mean, go through the pattern you want to knit, writing the instructions. Translate those abbreviations. And also, when it simply says R-E-P, meaning repeat, go back and write out the instructions again—and again, as many times as the repeat calls for. It makes it easier to follow the pattern, plus helps get it clear in your head. I've seen your work, and if you use that method you can absolutely do these, even on your own."

"You think so?"

"Absolutely." He handed the book to her.

"And when you finish one of the animals," said Bershada, in imitation of Godwin's confident tone, "I hope you'll consider donating it to the auction."

And that was the start.

In late February, near the end of the run-up to the auction, Irene Potter came into Crewel World with a large cardboard box. Irene had a lifelong addiction to stitching, and some years back she had begun designing her own needlework patterns. She had an unusual imagination, and her pieces often had eerie, overwrought images. The art world began to take notice, and Irene became famous, which she felt explained her eccentric personality. In Irene's opinion, she had an "artistic temperament." That, she said, was why ordinary people didn't understand her work (though she failed to consider that perhaps her problem was that she didn't understand ordinary people).

"I heard about your wonderful fund-raiser," Irene said, her shiny dark eyes keen, and her graying black curls trembling with excitement, "and I just had to make my own little contribution."

She had put the box on the library table in the center of the room and briskly begun tearing off the tape that held it closed. The box was a cube about fourteen inches on a side. As she tore the last of the tape off, its sides fell open to reveal a terrifying dragon in bright greens and deep purples, with splashes of orange, red, and yellow. It seemed to be made mostly of a combination of knit and crochet laid over a wire form. The scales on its back and sides were outsize and lifted at the edges. It had a long, thin neck that sagged between its hunched shoulders and an unusually large head, which had stiff wires for whiskers. The creature was balanced on its kangaroo-like hind legs, which ended in big, sharply humped nails. The wings were tall and wide, of delicate crochet lace stiffened with starch, but the front claws on the small forepaws were out-of-proportion huge—and a short length of red silk floss hanging on one of them suggested a streamer of blood. The eyes were dull and stupid, and instead of lots of sharp teeth, it had rodent incisors, one of them gold. Its tail was very long, and there was a knot tied in the middle of it, as if it were there to remind the creature of something.

All its contradictions, its combinations of materials—wool and cotton yarns, silk and metallic flosses, thin silver wire, even bits of gold and silver foil—made it an intriguing puzzle to look at.

Then recognition set in. "Why, it's the Jabberwock!" Betsy exclaimed.

Irene looked a little shamefaced. "Is that okay?" she asked. "I did start with the old pen and ink drawing from *Through the Looking Glass*, but I thought I made enough changes that I wouldn't break any copyright laws."

Betsy said, "That doesn't matter, I'm sure it's long out of copyright. Anyway, you could say it's—what's the word?—an homage to the Jabberwock. And you say you want to donate this to the auction? Are you sure?"

"Do you think I shouldn't?"

"I think you should do whatever you want. But your work brings very high prices, so this piece will earn far and away more than anything else up for bids. When people hear an Irene Potter work will be in the auction, I'm sure some will come just for a chance to acquire it. To the auction committee, that's a good thing, a very good thing. But you do realize the money will go into the pot being created to repair the Commons's snack bar? This isn't going to be a sale for you."

This seemed an obvious point, but Betsy knew Irene didn't always understand how the real world worked.

But Irene nodded eagerly. "Yes, yes, I understand. That's why I want to donate it. I like that dear little snack bar, but I no longer go into the restrooms." Her small nose wrinkled. "Sometimes the floor is . . . wet."

Betsy nodded. "You're right, the fixtures are leaking. It's extremely generous of you to offer this wonderful work to the auction so they can make repairs." Betsy walked around to the other side of the table, noting that the creature's knotted tail ended in a tiny bit of red glass shaped like a heart. "This is amazing, Irene. Just wait till the auction committee sees it!"

B ETSY called Bershada about the dragon, and she came in the next morning to see it. "Oh my goodness," she said, awed, and a little alarmed, touching it on one of its raised front claws.

"People are going to come just to bid on this," she agreed. "It's going to change the size and shape of the event. We'll adjust our advertising, of course, and expect to get people who want this piece."

"I wonder if you're not going to have to change the

venue," said Betsy. They'd planned to have the auction just up West Lake Street from her shop. Once a grocery store, now it was an art gallery that rented space for small events. "I've been to that gallery," said Betsy. "It looks as if maybe fifty people could sit down in there. That's adequate for what you initially expected, but you've been telling me how the number of expected attendees has grown. And now this! What if Irene's offering doubles that?"

"I'm sure it will—and from what we're collecting in toys, we underestimated our original number anyhow. I'm going to cancel our reservation, then go over to talk to Kari Beckel, who is facilities director at Mount Calvary. There's an atrium in their church hall that is spectacular—and if that proves too small, they have a full-size gym."

"Very wise," agreed Betsy.

"We were planning on raising a few thousand dollars, but now I'm thinking we should add a zero to that." She frowned and walked around the table, looking at the dragon from all angles. "I don't know whether we should offer Irene's piece first, to clear the room of the collectors, or hold it till last so maybe they'll also bid on the small pieces."

"I suggest last, because a lot of these toys are beautiful, made with lots of invention and talent."

Bershada turned around, eyes brightening. "Girl, you are right! That rooster of yours is amazing, and whoever gave us the feathered serpent deserves a special round of applause. Irene isn't the only talent in the area. So, sure, I'll recommend we offer Irene's Jabberwock last. I'm getting a real good feeling about this fund-raiser."

Chapter Four

◆ ◆ ◆

Now the auction was tomorrow. The Monday Bunch decided that Maddy's entrance with her bag of knitted animals marked the end of its special Friday stitching session. They began putting away their needles and yarn, stacking the finished toys at the end of the table—except Doris, who took her unfinished lion home with her, promising to bring it back in the morning.

Bershada stayed after the others to sweep together the scattered excelsior and put it back in its drawstring bag.

"Maddy—Ms. O'Leary," she called, as Maddy was about to depart, "I want to thank you for changing your mind and agreeing to be honored with the other major donors at the auction tomorrow."

"About that," said Maddy, turning and approaching Bershada, "I've changed my mind again. I'd prefer to just sit in the audience with everyone else."

"Oh, but you can't!" said Bershada. "You agreed to sit with the other six people who are the top knitters donating toys!"

"I know, I know. But I just . . . can't. All those people, staring at me. I just can't." Her usual truculent expression was overridden by something like fear.

And suddenly Betsy gained a new insight into Maddy O'Leary, she of the rude tongue and haughty attitude: She was actually shy.

But Bershada persisted. "They won't be looking at you, they'll be watching Max Irwin in action, calling on people to raise their bids." She made an attempt to imitate an auctioneer's chant. "Hey, now here's a ten, a ten dollar, do I hear twelve, say a twelve, say a twelve!" She waved her arms as if pointing at individuals in a crowd and took a few steps back and forth. "Twelve, I've got twelve dollars—sold!" She continued in her usual tone of voice, "No one will be paying any attention to the seven of you, trust me!"

"Then why ask us to sit there?"

"Because we will introduce you at the start—"

"See?" interrupted Maddy.

"But that will take maybe three minutes, spread over seven people. That's what, ten seconds of focus on you? And remember, as I told you long ago, we're giving each of you a ball of yarn and a pair of knitting needles. You don't have to look back at the audience. You can concentrate on your knitting. I told you that, and you said okay, that you'd just sit there and knit."

Bershada fell silent, and Betsy bit her tongue. Maddy kept drawing a breath to say something, then didn't say it, but finally she tossed her head and said in a hard tone, "Very well, you're right, I did say I'd do it. But I'm not happy about it."

"I understand. And thank you. The amazing number of your contributions will go far to make this auction a success."

"Well, if I'd known you were going to make such a fuss, I wouldn't have given you anything." And on that ungracious note, Maddy turned on her heel and left the shop.

"That was well done!" said Betsy. "She's a difficult person, but you handled her beautifully!"

Godwin asked, "Bershada, are you all in a swivet about the auction tomorrow?" He liked finding and resurrecting old-fashioned terms.

"Swivet?"

"You know, nervous."

"Not now, because I've nailed Maddy to that chair at the front of the room."

"That was a great idea, giving those seven honorees balls of yarn and needles to keep their hands busy during the auction," said Betsy. "You and the rest of the committee are doing a fine job. This is going to be a real success."

"I sure hope so. We've been working hard. Thank you, by the way, for donating the yarn, needles, and little canvas bags to hold them in." Bershada had come up with the idea nearly a month ago, giving Betsy the task of calling the honorees to see what kind of yarn they wanted in their bags.

"The bags say CREWEL WORLD in nice big letters, so I'm calling it an advertising expense," said Betsy with a smile.

"Nevertheless, thank you," repeated Bershada. "Now I've got to run. We're setting up the chairs in the atrium today."

After she left, Godwin said, "Whew-ee, I'm glad I didn't get nominated to that committee! Way too much work!"

Chapter Five

❖ ❖ ❖

BETSY had stayed after closing that Friday. The auction was tomorrow, Saturday, and she had some packing up to do. Over the past few weeks, Betsy had filled two big cardboard boxes with over a hundred knitted animals. She brought them up from the basement to the front of the shop. She had put some of the best ones on display in the shop and was now going around collecting the last of them and putting them with the others in a row in front of the boxes.

The Irene Potter Jabberwock piece had been taken into custody by the auction committee and was never on display in Betsy's shop.

Other stores in town had been collecting toys made of fabric and, in one case, wood. There was a secondary movement afoot for many of the toys' new owners to donate them again to hospitals, day care centers, and charities. Betsy was pleased that Crewel World had outpaced them in donations.

She had just put the last toy, a giraffe, on the table when the door to the shop sounded its music. The door had been left unlocked in anticipation of the arrival of someone from the committee to pick them up. Betsy turned and saw Bershada. With her was a short man of stocky build with a fringe of yellow hair around a bald head. He was wearing white running shoes, pale blue jeans, and a blue blazer over a tan T-shirt, and he was smiling broadly. He looked around the shop with interest, taking in the many spinner racks of floss, the long white cabinet full of needlework books and gadgets, the wall hangings of finished needlework projects, and then returned to Betsy. He was still grinning, prepared to be pleased to meet her.

Bershada said, "Betsy, this is Max Irwin, the auctioneer I've been telling you about."

Betsy put her hand out. "I'm pleased to meet you, Mr. Irwin."

"Max, call me Max," he said, taking her hand in a warm grip. His voice was rough-edged, probably from years of loud and fast talking.

"All right. Max. I hope Bershada has prepared you properly for this auction. It's kind of different from the usual."

Max laughed. "Ma'am, they're all different. No two alike. That's what keeps me going, the variety." He gestured toward Bershada. "This kind lady knows her stuff. She has her eye on the goal and takes dead aim at it. This is going to be a great auction."

Betsy said, "I hope you're right. I guess I'm a little nervous, worried they might end up selling all these beautiful toys for a quarter apiece. People have been working very hard on them."

Bershada said, "Trust Max. That is not going to happen."

"That's right," declared Max, one hand on his chest, elbow out. "Trust me."

"Max wanted an advance look at what we're auctioning off," said Bershada, "so I brought him here."

"All right," said Betsy. She gestured at the toys she'd been picking up, about a dozen of them. They were standing in a row on the library table. "Here are some of the best examples. I've been using them as displays in the shop, both to encourage customers to knit and contribute some, and to sell the books of instruction I have in stock to make them."

Max went to the table and picked up Godwin's leopard. "This is nice, real pretty. I bet it took some talent to make it."

"Yes, it did. My store manager knit it. I'm thinking of bidding on it myself so I can keep it on display next to *Knit Your Own Zoo*, the book he got the pattern from."

Bershada reached around Max to pick up the red rooster. "Oh, I think you should bid on this—it's more of an eye-catcher."

"No, I'm going to knit another one. It'll be easier to talk about it to a customer if I've done two of them."

Max eyed her sideways. "You did this?"

"Yes. I find I have to at least try to work the kinds of patterns I'm selling, so I can answer questions about them. But Godwin's my real expert; he can do just about any kind of needlework."

"Where is this paragon?" asked Max, looking around.

"Gone for the day. He and his partner are going to a concert in Saint Paul, so I let him cut out early."

"Ah," said Max. He picked up a pair of very small penguins. "I don't think these come from the same book as the leopard."

"No, they're from a book called *Mini Knitted Safari*. And there are other books by the same author, too. Quite a few children knitted toys designed by her."

"Maybe we should auction these in lots," he said.

Bershada said, "My son Chaz made a wooden model of the Ark, and I'll finish knitting a figure of Noah tonight. You're right, and there are duplicates of many of these tiny animals, so I'm going to put a group of pairs into one lot with the Ark and Noah."

"Wow, what a great idea!" said Betsy. "Be sure to tell Mount Calvary about that. They might want it for their Sunday school."

"Yes, that's a terrific idea." said Max. "Divide some of the rest of these little bitty ones into lots, so maybe others will get the same idea."

Bershada said to Betsy, "See? I told you he was good!"

Betsy said, "And maybe I can hire Chaz to make me an Ark and sell me the pattern. That should sell more copies of the books—the author has others in addition to that *Safari* one." Betsy was always on the lookout for ways to improve sales.

Chapter Six

❖ ❖ ❖

Mount Calvary Lutheran Church was on the southwest side of Excelsior. The church was relatively new, but not so modern it couldn't be recognized as a church at a glance. It was built in Gothic style, of pale stone, with lots of parking in back and multiple entrances to the large hall.

The atrium was large and beautiful, circular in design, with offices, classrooms, a hallway to the kitchen, and another to the restrooms off it. There were lots of tall windows, and there was a big skylight in its slightly domed ceiling. The floor was light-colored tile, currently covered with padded folding chairs in a crescent pattern, facing a lectern. The lectern was flanked by two pairs of long tables, each pair heaped with toy animals, mostly knit, some crocheted, several made of wood.

On a small, long-legged table by itself was a glass case, and inside it was Irene Potter's strange vision of the Jabberwock. Behind the lectern and tables was a single row of seven folding chairs.

The doors to the hall opened at 1:15 p.m. People filing in for the auction were directed to a desk near the rear of the atrium to sign in and receive a deep yellow cardboard paddle with a bold black number printed on it. Most of the people signing in took a detour to get a closer look at the toys and the dragon before finding their seats.

The auction was scheduled to begin at 2:30 p.m. At 1:30, a musical duo consisting of a husband and wife playing an oboe and a double bass fiddle came in and performed a mix of music as odd as their pairing: some folk, some Renaissance, some original compositions, a couple of Irish jigs. The audience applauded, though more thinly as the hour approached for the auction to begin.

At 2:25 p.m. the duo quit and left the room as a group of two men and five women filed out of one of the hallways near the tables and lectern. The new arrivals were wearing dressy casual clothing—good shirts and blazers for the men, skirts and fancy blouses or sweaters for the women. Maddy O'Leary, in the middle of the row, wore her usual wool suit, this one a purple so dark it was almost black. Each of them carried a small, bright green canvas bag with the CREWEL WORLD logo on it and a pair of bamboo knitting needles poking out the top.

They paused in front of the row of chairs, turned to face the audience, then sat down. The audience, which had fallen silent at their entrance, murmured in bemusement.

Bershada Reynolds came out of the same hallway and stepped up to the lectern. "Ladies and gentlemen," she said, "these seven people"——she half turned and made a wide gesture with one arm——"are responsible for nearly half of the items we are auctioning off here today. In fact, one of them——who does not want me to identify her, thank you, Maddy——knit twenty-six toys all by herself."

The audience burst into applause. Maddy, seated in the middle of the row, kept her head down but blushed furiously.

"Now," continued Bershada, "I would like to introduce you to our auctioneer, Max Irwin."

She got no further.

"Hello, hello, hello, and welcome!" bellowed a man's hoarse voice, and Max came striding out from the same hallway, with his arms wide and a big grin on his face. He was wearing a red T-shirt under a brown blazer, blue jeans, and red high-top canvas shoes. "Wow, what a great turn-out!" he continued, stepping behind the lectern. "Must be three hundred people here."

The audience was slow to quiet down, so he slid the on-off button of the microphone back and forth a few times, making it pop, and suddenly his voice was a deafening roar: "Can you hear me now?" The audience yelled in protest, and he leaped back in mock astonishment. He stepped forward and said in a much quieter voice, "I guess so!"

The audience laughed, its attention fully captured.

"Are you ready for a chance to do some good for Excelsior?" he challenged them.

"Yeah!" replied many voices. "Right on!" said one, and "Bring it!" said another.

"Are you ready for some excitement?" he asked, louder.

"Yeah!" came the reply, also louder.

"Wanna have some *fun*?"

"*Yeah, yeah!*" they replied, at top volume now, and somebody whistled.

"Well, all right, let's get down to it. Let's raise a little money! Here are the rules: My assistant, Frankie—Hey, where is Frankie? Frankie? Frankie! Where are you? Come on out here!"

An extremely attractive young woman wearing tight jeans and an oversize red sweater came out from the hallway making such elaborate apologetic gestures to him and the audience that they laughed.

"Where you been?" he demanded.

She glanced at the audience and came to whisper in his ear.

"Oh," he said, immediately mollified. The audience laughed again. "Okay. You ready to get to work?"

She nodded and smiled at the audience.

"Again, here are the rules: She's gonna hand me one toy at a time! If you want it, you hold up your paddle"—he held up a hand, palm forward—"and call out your bid. We're taking bids in dollar amounts only—no fifty-cent raises! There are people around this room—spotters—who will call my attention to your bid! Somebody else wants it more, hold up your paddle and call out a higher number! Highest bidder gets the toy! At the end of the whole shebang, bring your payment to that nice young lady right over there!" He turned sideways to point with both hands at Bershada, who was standing at the far end of the left-hand table. She held up a notepad and pen in one hand and pointed to a gray cash box in front of her. "You pay her, she'll give you the toy!" he continued. "We take cash, checks, and credit or debit cards! Got it? Everybody ready? Then let's have us an *auction*!"

The audience, roused by his words, cheered and waved their paddles.

His assistant moved swiftly to the table on his right and grabbed a toy. It was a gray felt elephant with a cross-stitched red-patterned blanket on its back, its trunk raised gracefully to its forehead.

"Who's got the money, who's got the money, how much, how much, say ten dollar, ten dollar," he chanted rapidly.

A paddle went up. "Five dollars!" shouted the owner, a man with white hair. A tall, thin man with red hair standing in the aisle nearby pointed at him.

"Five dollar, got five dollar, who'll make it ten, make it ten, five dollar, say ten, say ten," chanted Max.

"Ten!" called a woman near the front.

Max instantly pointed at her. "Ho! Ten dollar, make it fifteen, fifteen dollar, fifteen, I got ten, make it fifteen!"

He was talking so rapidly his audience barely caught one word in three or four—those who had never heard auctioneer chanting before looked around, totally baffled. Then, one by one, they realized they didn't have to hear every word, just the numbers. The lower number was the current bid; the higher what he wanted to hear as a raise. The paddles started coming up faster, in greater numbers, and a kind of fever began to grow among members of the audience.

The elephant went for thirty-five dollars, a wooden camel on wheels went for fifty, and a knit pig for seventy-two. The Noah's Ark went for a hundred and twenty-five.

Chapter Seven

◆ ◆ ◆

IT took Maddy a few minutes to realize that no one was looking at her; everyone was focused on that fast-talking auction man. She pulled the bamboo knitting needles out of the bag and then the ball of dark blue merino wool. Was it darker than she remembered? No matter, it was just something to keep her hands busy while she and the others sat on display.

Ugh, *display*. What an awful label to put on a human being!

Like that strangely beautiful dragon on display in the glass case over there, gorgeous scales and delicate wings— and stupid face. What must Irene have been thinking? And what a peculiar name on the tag leaning against the case: JABBERWOCK, it read. What did that mean? Maddy had somehow never read *Through the Looking Glass*. *Jabberwock*. Perhaps it was an Asian fry pan talking nonsense?

Her lips quirked just a little in amusement. She was fond of elaborate puns.

But never mind, she was becoming too aware of the audience and the gibberish Mr. Irwin was shouting at them. She swiftly cast on twenty-one stitches. She was going to do the plaited basket stitch. It wasn't hard, but it took concentration. The result would be attractive, looking like the yarn was woven, two threads by two threads.

She started by knitting twice, then skipped the next stitch and put the right-hand needle behind the second stitch, knitting it but not taking it off the needle, instead bringing the right-hand needle around to the front and knitting it, then taking both stitches off. She continued like this until the last stitch, which she knitted, then turned to begin the next row. She purled two. Then, as before, she purled the second stitch behind the left needle, brought the needle around to purl the first stitch, then pulled both off.

The noise Max and his audience were making faded as her concentration increased.

It took a few rows for the pattern to become apparent, but there it was, perfect! She felt energized, and ignoring the racket going on in front of her, she fell to her task, her fingers moving deftly. In a short while she had nearly four inches of knitting completed.

Her hands began to move even more swiftly, and she went from warm satisfaction to pride to something like exultation. She could feel her heart beating rapidly, and her hands moved faster and faster.

The auctioneer's rapid chant and the eager shouts of the bidders, which she had been unable to completely ignore, now seemed only to increase her excitement. Her breath came more rapidly, and her head started to ache. She began to make mistakes in her knitting as her concentration faltered. She took a big breath, trying to calm herself, but it didn't work.

Her fingers closed on the yarn, and her heart seemed about to explode in her chest. The pain in her head was unendurable. This was wrong, something was wrong. She tried to stand, to call for help, but all her joints were stiff, and her tongue would not obey. She fell, and darkness came over her.

Chapter Eight

◈ ◈ ◈

MAX'S fast chant and the audience's excited response kept everyone's attention from Maddy's distress. Not until she tried to rise and instead fell to the floor did a few notice and exclaim at her.

"What? What?" Max interrupted himself to look around and see her folded in her wool suit in front of her chair. "Hey, what the devil?" He started for her, then turned back to the audience. "Is there a doctor in the house?"

Meanwhile, Bershada ran to her, stooped, and tried to roll her onto her back. But Maddy was rigid, as if having a seizure. She was not breathing. Bershada was about to call for someone to dial 911 when she saw that more than half the audience had cell phones to their ears. And five people were running toward her. She was not surprised to hear three of them say they were doctors, one say she was an ER nurse, and one declare himself an emergency tech. In less than a minute they had Maddy, now gone limp, flat on her back and were beginning CPR. Bershada got out of their way.

In less than eight minutes a police officer and an emergency crew arrived to the accompaniment of sirens. The techs took over the CPR. They fitted an oxygen mask to Maddy's face, scooped her onto a wheeled stretcher, and took her out.

Bershada conferred with Max while the audience talked among themselves. Finally, Max went to the lectern to bring order to the room.

"All right, all right, let's settle down!" he shouted. "Please, come to order! Come to order!" The audience slowly fell silent. "I am reasonably certain Ms. Maddy will be okay, even though she scared us all half to death just now," he said. "Thanks be to the quick action taken by members of this audience to keep her going until help arrived. Let's give them a hand!" He started to clap and was enthusiastically joined by the audience.

Max let it go on until it just started to fade. "Okay!" he shouted. "All right! Now, are we ready to get back to business?"

"Yeah! Yes! Okay! Carry on!" cheered members of the audience, and the rest applauded.

"We were taking bids on this magnificent leopard. Ho, who's got the money, I got forty, forty, forty, how about fifty, I want fifty, how about fifty, I got forty, you gimme fifty, I got forty, forty—"

"Sixty!" shouted the man who hadn't gotten the elephant.

"Here you go, sixty, sixty, I got sixty, gimme eighty—"

"Eighty!" called a woman dressed all in yellow.

"Eighty-five!" shouted the man.

"Ho! Eighty-five, now I got eighty-five, can I get a hundred, can I get—"

"One hundred!" came the call from the back of the room.

"Whoo!" cheered someone.

"One hundred!" shouted Max. "One hundred, a hundred, a hundred, now looking for a hundred and fifty, one hundred fifty, got a hundred, looking for one hundred fifty—"

"A hundred and fifty!" cried the woman in yellow.

"Yes!" cheered someone.

"One fifty, got one fifty, got one fifty, do I hear two? Two hundred, two hundred, one seventy-five, I got one fifty, one fifty, can I have one seventy five, one seventy five? One fifty, one fifty, lookin' for one seventy-five, one seventy-five."

But he looked in vain. "Can I get one sixty, one sixty, one sixty, I got one fifty, got one fifty, got one fifty, looking for one sixty, one sixty. All in, all done? One fifty, all done?"

"Two hundred!" called the man in the back of the room.

"Two fifty!" the woman in yellow responded instantly.

"Yowser!" shouted someone—the same someone who'd cheered before. It sounded suspiciously like Godwin, sitting in the row facing the audience with the other champion knitters.

"Yo! Two fifty, two fifty, I got two fifty, how about three, do I hear three, three hundred, two fifty, two fifty, two fifty, do I hear two seventy-five, two seventy-five, I got two fifty, two fifty, lookin' for two seventy-five, two fifty, two fifty—" There was a brief pause. "Two fifty, all done, all in? Two fifty, I got two fifty. All in, all done? Sold! Two hundred and fifty dollars! Paddle number forty-seven. Thank you, ladies and gentlemen!"

The audience applauded. Bershada made a note.

Max's assistant picked up the knit fruit bat, saw what it was, and dropped it, pulling her hands up and back in disgust.

"No, no!" called someone. "Let's see it!"

"Yeah, bring it!"

"What is it?" asked someone else.

"Lemme see," ordered Max, and his assistant very gingerly picked it up by one wing, her face reflecting her reluctance.

"Hey, lookit this!" Max shouted, holding it up. He adjusted his grip so each hand was holding a wing and it was spread wide.

"Ewwwww!" went half the audience. The other half laughed, and someone called, "One dollar!"

"Two dollars!" said someone else.

"Seven dollars!" said a third, and they were off. With Max urging them on, Phil's fruit bat sold for seventy-five dollars.

The auction, back in full swing, continued for another hour. At the end, Irene Potter's amazing dragon was brought forward.

"Five hundred!" shouted someone before Max could say anything, and the bidding built swiftly from there until the creature finally topped out at five thousand seven hundred dollars.

Chapter Nine

❖ ❖ ❖

"DEAD?" murmured Betsy. "Oh, but she can't be! They did CPR right away, and the emergency people got here quickly—she can't be dead!"

Betsy was standing in the parking lot beside her car. Jill had seen her, waved to get her attention, and now was standing close to her, talking in a low voice.

"She was dead on the gurney," said Jill. "You know how nowadays they can bring the freshly dead back to life, at least for a little while—well, not in this case. There was no obvious cause, so they'll do an autopsy."

"I thought it was a stroke."

"Did you, Doctor Devonshire?"

Betsy blushed and shrugged. "Just a layman's opinion."

"Probably as good as mine."

A voice called, harsh and alarmed, "Hey! Hey, anyone!" Jill and Betsy whirled to look toward the church hall, where Max was standing shouting at them. "Hey! Is there a doctor still around?"

"What's the matter?" called Jill, starting for him, Betsy on her heels.

"We got a man sick in here!"

Jill went through the door into the hall. Betsy stopped to ask, "Who is it? What do you mean, sick?"

"Sick to his stomach, big headache. He's sitting on the floor. I don't know who it is. He was helping pick up after the auction."

Betsy put her fingers to her lips. Connor had volunteered to stay and help put things away.

A woman, white-haired, thin, short, put her hands on Betsy's shoulders. "Excuse me, let me by, I'm a doctor." She had been one of those who had rushed to help Maddy.

Betsy hastily stepped into the hall. "Sorry," she said, "sorry."

Without replying, the woman hurried by her.

Betsy followed, half afraid of what she was going to discover. To her dismay, it *was* Connor, sitting bent forward on the floor in front of the row of chairs where the honorees had been placed. His face was red, distorted by pain. Jill and another woman were standing nearby, and the woman doctor was kneeling beside him, with one arm around his shoulders and the other taking his pulse. There was a towel across his knees, another under his feet.

As Betsy watched, he picked up the towel from his lap and wiped his face with it. She ran to him. "What's the matter? What happened?" she asked.

"Dunno," said Connor, forcing the words out. "I was

folding the chairs," he gestured to his right, where half the row had been folded and leaned against the wall. "Saw someone's knitting . . ." He stopped to retch, then wiped his mouth with the towel. "God, my head!"

Betsy looked around and saw the knitting, about seven inches of plaited basket weave stitch in dark blue. She recognized the yarn; it was Maddy's. She picked it up. Maddy had been about halfway across a row. The last two or three rows were a mess, hardly recognizable as a pattern.

"Look at this, Jill," she said, holding out the knitting. "I think Maddy did have a stroke."

"Maybe, maybe," said Jill, who was still focused on Connor and the doctor.

Betsy picked up the ball and wound the yarn onto it, following the unspooled yarn to the bag under a chair, and stuffed the ball and knitting into it. The fingers of her right hand felt odd, and she rubbed them with her thumb. "Oof," she said. Her heart was beating fast. "Oof," she said again, and put her hand to her forehead, which had begun to ache.

Connor said, "I was winding the yarn back on the ball, which had rolled away, and all of a sudden I got this headache."

"Jill," said Betsy, dropping Maddy's bag. "Jill!"

Jill started at the sound of her friend's voice. "What is it?" she said. "Oh my gosh, oh my gosh. Here, Betsy, come with me."

She helped Betsy get to her feet and hustled her off to the restroom, so she could wash her hands. Then she had Betsy wash them again. And again.

"Wow," said Betsy. "Wow." She splashed cold water on

her face, which was very pink, and dried it and her hands with paper towels. Her hands felt normal, but her pulse still seemed a bit rapid.

"What happened?" asked Jill. "What were you doing when you started feeling like this?"

"All I did was pick up Maddy's knitting and wrap loose yarn around the ball and put it in the bag. Then my fingers started tingling and my heart started beating a hundred miles an hour."

"Did you touch anything else? Drink something?"

"Nuh-uh. Wow. Whew! But I'm feeling better now. How's Connor? Can we get back to Connor?"

"Sure, let's do that."

When they came out of the restroom, they saw Connor, over his objections, being walked out to an emergency vehicle by the doctor. "I'm all right," he kept saying, "See? I'm feeling much better now."

But his face was still red, and he was walking with a stiff gait unlike his usual smooth one.

"Wait a minute," called Jill, and she ran to the bright green canvas bag into which Betsy had pushed Maddy's needlework. She picked it up carefully by its string handle. She brought it to the doctor, hanging it over her fingers, and said, "Maddy is dead, Connor is sick, and Betsy had a bad reaction, all because the three of them handled the contents of this bag. Give it to someone who can tell us what the problem with it is."

Chapter Ten

❖ ❖ ❖

CONNOR was treated and released the same day. "I haven't been taken that sick for a long time," he said, as he got into Betsy's car. "Do they know what did it to me?"

"No, not yet," said Betsy. "But they're pretty sure it's the yarn she was knitting with."

"The yarn? That's odd. Didn't you give the same yarn to everyone?"

"No, Bershada and I asked each one of the knitters what kind they wanted. Maddy's the only one who picked the dark blue merino. Maybe I'd better pull the rest of that yarn until we find out what's wrong with it."

"Do you think it could be the needles instead of the yarn?" Connor asked.

"Nnno," she drawled, thinking. "Everyone got the same size bamboo needles from the same box. Besides, it was the yarn you and I were handling, not the needles."

Connor nodded. "That's true. So yes, you should pull the merino."

The following Monday, the Bunch was in session, and the participants spent a few minutes talking about Maddy's strange passing. Betsy, as crack amateur sleuth, was asked for an opinion, but she said she didn't know what to think. Phil suggested it was a sudden allergy to wool brought on by all that knitting Maddy had done in aid of the auction, but his theory was voted down. No one else had any ideas, so the members dropped the subject and began working on needlework projects—any kind but knitting, as they'd all had their fill and more in the last few weeks.

Fulsome congratulations went around to all those who contributed: to Godwin, for the amazing price his knit leopard had brought; and again to Godwin, for winning a place among the honorees who had knit the most toys; to Betsy for contributing time, effort, and material to the auction; but most of all to Bershada, whose idea it was, and who ran the committee organized to pull it off.

Betsy said modestly she hadn't done all that much, Godwin smiled and allowed that the leopard had come out rather well, but Bershada just sat and raked in the accolades, secure in the knowledge that these people didn't know the half of it.

Just then the door chime broke into "I Want to Be Happy" and Jill came in. She was not a frequent attendee of the Monday Bunch anymore, with three young children and a part-time job at the police department (administrative assistant to the chief, a job she shared with another woman). She had her stitching with her and was brimming with grim news.

"What is it?" demanded Godwin before she had even said a word.

"The preliminary autopsy report on Maddy is back. It appears she was poisoned with nicotine."

Everyone at the table stared at her in surprise.

"Nicotine?" said Emily. "You mean she smoked herself to death?"

"No, nicotine was found on the yarn she was knitting with at the auction."

"Ick," said Emily. "I hate the smell of cigarettes. But how did it get from the yarn into her stomach?"

"It didn't go into her stomach. It went through her fingers into her bloodstream. You can absorb nicotine through the skin. When she handled the yarn while knitting, she absorbed a fatal dose."

"Then how come people who smoke cigarettes don't die from it getting on their fingers?" asked Phil. He looked around the table. "I smoked for over twenty years, and so did just about everyone I knew back in the day. Many's the time we stayed up all night, playing cards, talking, drinking beer, and smoking like chimneys. Didn't kill any of us. Not right then, I mean. Lung cancer might've got one or two of us, but I don't know, I haven't seen many of them in a long time." He sighed and looked a little sad about that.

Jill said, "I guess the paper wrapping protected your skin. Besides, tobacco leaves aren't pure nicotine, it takes a special laboratory process to extract the nicotine."

Betsy said, "You mean, nicotine all by itself is a poison?"

"That's right," replied Jill. "Someone poured pure liquid nicotine over the ball of yarn in Maddy's bag, and by handling it, she absorbed a lethal amount through the skin of her hands. It doesn't take much. It's an ingredient in insecticides; a squirt or two will kill a whole nest of yellow jackets. I know, I've done it."

"If liquid nicotine is so dangerous, why can you buy bottles of it in those e-cigarette stores?" asked Alice, a senior woman with a deep voice and rather a lot of chin. She was crocheting a fluffy blue prayer shawl for her church.

Godwin asked, surprised, "How do you know about bottles of nicotine?"

"There was a news segment about it back around Christmas. The bottles come in different sizes and different strengths. And they said even one small bottle can kill a child who drinks it—they come in tempting delicious flavors, apparently. I was quite appalled."

But Phil said, "I think those bottles aren't pure nicotine, they're diluted. And at least the smokers are not getting all that tar and other things you find in tobacco leaf. E-cigarettes are a lot safer than the real thing."

"No, they're not!" said Alice, surprised. "It's the nicotine that causes lung cancer."

"No, it's the tar," retorted Phil, equally surprised.

"I think it's the formaldehyde," volunteered Godwin.

"Formaldehyde!" said Doris. "In cigarettes?"

"Absolutely," said Godwin.

"What, do they embalm the tobacco leaves before they chop them into cigarettes?"

Godwin leaned sideways, laughing. "That's good, Dorie!"

"Surely you're joking; there isn't any formaldehyde in cigarettes," said Emily.

"Oh, there are all kinds of chemicals in cigarettes," said Godwin. "Nitrogen oxide, benzopyrene, hydrogen cyanide, and ammonia are just a few, besides formaldehyde."

Jill, meanwhile, had sat down at the table and brought out a project: a cross-stitched inspirational motto ornamented with a big, elaborate feather. It read, "She took a Leap of FAITH and grew her Wings on the way down." Done all in shades of blue, Jill had bought it in Betsy's shop as a kit.

"Has Joe Mickels stopped in to talk to you, Betsy?" she asked.

"Joe? Why on earth would he want to talk to me?"

"Didn't you hear what I said? The poison that killed poor Maddy was nicotine."

"What has that got to do with Joe Mickels?"

"Right around Christmas he bought a little chain of e-cigarette stores."

Betsy stared at her. "He did?"

Godwin said, "Why didn't we hear about it?"

Valentina said, "I heard he'd gotten into e-cigarettes, that he'd bought a store that sells them."

"Where did you hear that?" asked Jill.

"At the Leipold's store. Somebody was smoking one in there, said he'd bought the outfit to do it with at Joe's new store in Uptown." Uptown was an artsy neighborhood of Minneapolis famous for its night clubs, sophisticated shops, and ethnic restaurants.

"Oh my God," said Doris.

"But he wouldn't—he just wouldn't!" said Emily.

But Betsy was remembering some years back, when she and Jill stood in Joe's Excelsior office while he ranted viciously about another murdered woman, saying that if he'd known then what he knew now, he would have killed her himself. She looked at Jill, wondering if she was remembering that, too. But Jill had her deadpan cop face on, so Betsy couldn't tell what she was thinking.

"Wait a minute," said Phil. "I've looked at those bottles of nicotine they sell, and like Alice said, they all smell like candy or flowers, plus they look thick, like syrup. How could Maddy use yarn that smelled like strawberries and stuck to her fingers?"

"There!" said Emily. "See? There!"

"Why are you so hot to defend Joe Mickels?" asked Godwin. "He is not a nice man."

"He is a sad man. I think he's lonesome and doesn't know what to do about it."

"My goodness, Emily," said Alice. "Where on earth did you get an idea like that?"

"I saw him the other day—he didn't see me—just sitting in his car, and his face was sad, so sad. I almost went over to him, but he drove away. Honest, he was sad!"

"When was this?" Jill asked.

Emily thought briefly. "I'm not sure. Maybe a week ago? Or longer?"

"Before Harry Whiteside was murdered? Or after?"

Emily thought some more. "Before. I'm sure it was before."

"Maybe it was around the time he found out that Maddy

won the bidding war for that property on Water Street," suggested Godwin.

"I hope so," said Betsy. "Much better that he was sad, not angry."

There was a thoughtful silence.

Chapter Eleven

❖ ❖ ❖

"WELL, well, well," murmured Detective Sergeant Mike Malloy, looking over a photocopy of a single document laid in the center of his small desk in a back room of the Excelsior Police Department. He spoke to himself—the desk pushed up against his was unoccupied. Elton Marsh, the second investigator in the department, was taking a day off to attend a school concert his youngest daughter had a solo part in.

The document was a record of the sale of three e-cigarette stores to one Joseph Alan Mickels on receipt of "one dollar and other good and valuable considerations." Malloy had run across that phrasing before; it virtually always meant more money.

Malloy wasn't interested in how much more money; he was interested in the fact of the e-cigarettes. His fellow investigator was a smoker, and it had taken an order from the chief to get him to take a smoker's break outside the building. The problem now was, he was a heavy smoker and was frequently gone during the working day for five to ten minutes at a time. In Malloy's never humble opinion, he had just about gone from full-time to part-time employment and ought to be given a commensurate cut in pay.

Apparently the chief thought so, too, because the instant e-cigarettes appeared on the market, Elton had been persuaded to transfer his addiction to them and began smoking at his desk again. He and Malloy exchanged research on them, and Malloy was forced to admit that e-cigarettes were not a source of the tar that instigated lung cancer, and that what a "vaper" exhaled was merely scented water vapor.

"That's why we call it 'vaping,'" Elton had said smugly.

The only concession Malloy had managed to get from Elton was a switch from scented nicotine to the unscented variety. Filling the office with the smell of wintergreen or oranges was distracting and unprofessional, in Malloy's never, *ever* humble opinion.

Maddy O'Leary had been killed by nicotine. It had been absorbed through the skin on the palms and fingers of her hands—shocking to learn that nicotine could be absorbed through the skin. It could be absorbed quickly, too, judging by the way Connor Sullivan had gotten so doggone sick just from handling the yarn while helping clean up after the auction.

Nicotine is never a natural ingredient in yarn. So someone put it there. Who? And when? And why?

When investigating crimes against a person, Malloy knew you began with the victim. Why would someone have wanted Maddy O'Leary dead? She was a wealthy businesswoman, somewhere in her fifties—accounts differed as to her age. She was tall, five seven and a half, gray haired, with a robust build—one sixty-eight, the ME reported. She had been widowed after a brief marriage, had no children, no close relatives in the area.

Several people he'd talked to indicated she'd had a strong A-type personality that included a quick temper. She was the widow of a wealthy attorney and had immersed herself in business and become very successful at it.

Maddy's success came from her skill in real estate. She always appeared to know what the competition was up to and took quick action to counter them. She had a reputation for sharp business dealings but hadn't broken any laws—or at least was too sharp to be caught doing something illegal. She was not a drunk or a doper. Once a year she took a two-week vacation, but nobody knew where she went. Seven years ago she had left her Methodist church and formally become a Baptist. She was very generous toward her church and various charities, a surprising discovery few knew of, as she never spoke of it to anyone.

And she liked to knit. That last bit of information came from Betsy Devonshire, who said she had donated more knitted toys to that fatal auction event than anyone else. Who would have thought?

People were complicated. That's why Malloy preferred the kind of crime committed by professional—or at least semi-amateur—criminals. There, motives were clear and simple. Plus, it was relatively easy to convince a pro to confess or at least drop a dime on the perp. These amateurs lied when they didn't have to, or couldn't get their facts straight when they were trying to be truthful, or refused to learn the rules of the game. Malloy strayed from his train of thought. Funny how the expression "drop a dime"—to make a phone call offering a solid clue about the perpetrator of a crime—was still around, when public phones, which once charged a dime to make a call, now charged fifty cents if you could find one at all.

But back to the subject at hand. Who hated Maddy O'Leary enough to think up that ridiculous—and successful—plan to kill her?

Because it *was* ridiculous! Pouring a poison on knitting yarn so she'd absorb it through her skin! Why not just take a hunting rifle and ambush her from behind a tree, or use a handgun and shoot her from your car as she walked down the street? Or, like the unfortunate Harry Whiteside, lay in wait in his house to knock him on the head?

Say, could there be a connection between the two murders? O'Leary and Whiteside were bidding against each other—and Joe Mickels—for that property on Water Street. And Malloy's fellow investigators in Wayzata thought that maybe the mess in the Whiteside house wasn't what you'd expect a burglar to leave. It was more like vandalism; there was anger, even hatred, in the destruction inside that house.

Also, O'Leary hadn't paid off on her bid yet—she'd just won the war. Did her company inherit the right to buy the property? Or an heir? Or did the bidding reopen as a result of her death? Or, perhaps, was the property offered to the last person standing in the bidding war: Joe Mickels?

Mickels, notorious for his violent temper; Mickels, the recent purchaser of three e-cigarette stores. Hmmm . . .

Malloy reached for his phone.

Chapter Twelve

❖ ❖ ❖

Betsy was in her shop sighing over a bill that had come in, because it seemed to be charging her a whole lot of money for items she hadn't ordered—nor had they been delivered. Godwin was standing beside her making angry sounds.

"They did this once before, remember?" said Godwin. "There's another shop named Crewel World, in Iowa, and this vendor sent them an order we had made and billed us for it. This time they sent us a bill for some things they ordered. It's funny how they don't know that IA and MN are two different states."

"Maybe they think we're a chain, like McDonald's."

"Even so, if the Excelsior McDonald's orders a truckload of buns, I don't think the Hopkins McDonald's wants to pay for it. Give me that bill, I'll go call them."

"Thank you."

He was well into his tirade at the hapless accounts

manager and so didn't pay any attention to the door's "Hello, Dolly!" announcement of someone coming in.

Betsy looked up and saw it was Joe Mickels. His normal blustering demeanor was gone; he appeared uncomfortable and diffident. She had been wondering if he would dare stop in to talk to her. Apparently he did dare, but he didn't like it. Given their unhappy history, his attitude wasn't surprising.

Betsy put on her blandest expression and said, "Good afternoon, Mr. Mickels. How may I help you?"

He took a deep breath and walked to her desk, a solid chunk of a man, but not above five foot five, with a pigeon breast, a proud beak of a nose, nineteenth-century side-burns, and bushy eyebrows nearly hiding sharp blue eyes. Yet still she was struck by how much of a facade this bold front now appeared. Normally, he was strength and aggression to the bone.

"Good afternoon," he croaked quietly, then cleared his throat and tried again. "Good afternoon!" he barked asser-tively.

"Is there something I can do for you?" she asked.

"I hope so," he said, and it was a confession. "Sergeant Michael Malloy has been talking to me—almost accusing me."

"Of what, Mr. Mickels?" She was not surprised that Malloy had gotten around to Joe.

"You know, I think, that I own three e-cigarette stores."

"Yes, I had heard that."

"And you know Ms. O'Leary was poisoned to death with nicotine."

"Yes, I had heard that, too."

He drew a deep, angry breath through that nose. "Well?" he demanded.

"Well, what, Mr. Mickels?" She was having trouble hiding her smile.

And he realized that she was enjoying this. He turned on his heel and started for the door. Then, just as she began to regret baiting him, he thought better of it and turned back.

They said, simultaneously, "I'm sorry."

And they both grimaced.

She said, "Obviously you are here to ask me to get Mike Malloy off your back, either by providing you with an unbreakable alibi or by proving someone else guilty."

"Yes," he said, nodding, relieved. "I'm prepared to pay any expenses you may incur."

"That's generous of you. But please be aware that this . . . talent I have for discovering the truth behind a crime is just that: a search for the truth. If I agree to look into the case, it's not going to be entirely on your behalf. I'm not going to be out to clear you but to find out who murdered Maddy O'Leary."

"Sergeant Malloy thinks I also murdered Harry Whiteside. Will you investigate that, too?"

"I wondered if he'd roll that into the case, too," said Betsy. "He probably thinks it was an attempt to reopen the bidding on the Water Street property."

"Exactly," said Joe, nodding once, sharply. "It's not possible to do that, but it's an easy conclusion. I think he's not the only one thinking that's the case."

"I know he's not the only one," said Betsy. "I've heard it stated baldly right here in my shop."

Joe snorted. "I had better instruct my attorney to file for a change of venue as soon as I'm arrested!"

"Maybe it won't come to that," said Betsy. "Maybe Mike will find out what really happened, if it wasn't you. Maybe he'll discover Maddy and Harry are two different cases with two different murderers. They were each done in a different way, as if two different minds were at work on them."

"Do you think that's likely?" asked Joe.

"I think it's a valid theory. Harry was attacked in his home, his skull was fractured, and his house was burglarized. Maddy's knitting yarn was soaked in a poison she absorbed through her fingers, possibly by someone thinking her death might be ruled natural. That's two different mind-sets, don't you think?"

Joe thought about it. "That means two different murderers, which would mean two different motives."

"On the other hand, they were both into property—design, construction, rental."

But Joe had landed hard on her first theory. "Think about it. They moved in two different areas of that world. Maddy was into housing, Harry was into commercial and industrial buildings. There was some overlap, of course, but that's a lot of difference."

"So why did they both try to buy the Excelsior property?"

"Because they both planned to put retail on the ground floor and residential above. O'Leary was going to emphasize the retail end, Whiteside the residential. Me, I was going to have stores on the ground floor, business offices on the second, residential above that." He looked around the shop. "It's a common plan, business on the ground floor, residences above. What you've done here is like that. I'm just taking it a step further."

Actually, all Betsy had done was continue the setup she inherited from her sister: a two-story building with three apartments on the second floor—one lived in by herself—and three stores on the ground floor—one her own needle-work shop. Even the other two, a used-book store called ISBNs (pronounced "Iz-bins"), the other a deli whose name had remained Sol's through several owners, were in place when she came to Excelsior.

"Is it possible there's a fourth bidder waiting in the wings?" asked Betsy. "Someone who thought it necessary to get rid of Maddy and Harry but thinks he or she can outbid you?"

"I hadn't thought of that," said Joe, surprised.

"Maybe you should. Also, has anything threatening or dangerous happened to you recently? Something you might feel was a close call? Maybe the murderer is thinking he'll get rid of all three of you."

"No, of course not!" The thick eyebrows came down and gathered over his nose like thunderclouds over a mountain. "I don't like where you're going."

"Where I'm going is to look at alternatives to the theory that you murdered two people in order to gain ownership of a piece of property."

"And your theory is that there is a fourth person after the property who is willing to kill Harry, Maddy, *and me* to get it?" He snorted again. "Preposterous!"

"What's your theory?" Betsy shot back.

"I don't have a theory. That's why I'm here. You have a talent for helping people who've been falsely accused of a crime. I came here to hire you to work for me, proving to the satisfaction of the police—or a jury if it comes to that—that I have not murdered anyone. But if all you can offer is some ridiculous story of a fourth person who wants that Water Street property, then I withdraw my offer."

"Well, that's your choice," said Betsy with a good show of indifference.

Defeated, Joe turned and started for the door.

"Wait!" called Betsy.

He stopped and slowly turned back. And there again was that sad and baffled look.

"I spoke rashly just now. You must know you are a . . . difficult person for me to relate to, given all we've been through. But I don't think you are a murderer. I don't know if I can be of any real help to you. I'm willing to try. But you can't hire me. I don't take money for my efforts to clear people who've been mistakenly accused."

Joe stood silent for a long thirty seconds. Then he said, "All right. Go ahead with it." After a just-noticeable pause, he added, "Thank you."

Again he turned to the door.

Betsy called again, "Wait a minute. Maybe we should get right to it. Mike Malloy must have more than motive to be looking at you. For example, maybe you don't have a solid alibi for one or both murders?"

He said, "I don't think they know when nicotine was put on that yarn Maddy was using when she died. It could've been weeks ago."

"No, the window of opportunity is more or less a week. I didn't announce that champion knitters were picking their own yarn. And I didn't have the yarn and needles put into marked bags until near the auction."

"Still, you're talking about a week or so. I don't know how anyone could cover every minute of a whole week with alibis. I know I can't."

"Fair enough. What about the night Harry Whiteside was killed?"

"The night he was killed I went to a dinner meeting with a man I thought to hire to survey some land I bought up in Cass County. But he turned out to be a flake; he believes in extrasensory perception guiding his surveying. He told me he was in the process of moving from Chicago to Duluth, and now he's canceled his phone service, so I can't get hold of him. And he won't be getting in touch with me; I told him I wasn't going to hire him."

Betsy pursed her lips then said, "That's too bad."

"You think?" he growled. "If this was going to be easy I wouldn't have come to you." He turned away and reached for the door, but before opening it, he looked back at her and said, "You have no idea how hard it was for me to come in here." He left before she could think of a reply.

"ARE you serious?" demanded Godwin. "You are going to help that, that, that—?"

"I'm going to try. We've both known him for a long time. Years. He doesn't play nice, he's greedy, and he's bad tempered." She smiled. "Once, something set him off in front of me and he shouted words I haven't heard for a long time—from back when I dated a U.S. Navy bosun's mate."

The smile faded. "But I don't think Joe's a criminal, and I doubt he'd ever kill someone, especially in that sneaky way Maddy was killed. That's not his style at all."

"Yes, but from what you just said, that skull bashing poor Harry Whiteside got does sound a whole lot like him."

"Well . . . okay. Trashing someone's house sounds even more like him. If Harry walked in on him vandalizing the house . . . But think of this: Would he murder someone and then trash his house?"

"What, you think Harry's house was trashed *after* he was killed?"

Betsy suddenly realized she was thinking of the terrific mess left right here in her shop by the person who murdered her sister—and the fact that it was done after her murder. "I don't know that, either, not for sure. In fact, I don't know what was taken from his house." She frowned at her disorganized thinking. "Anyway, he has an alibi for Harry Whiteside's murder."

"He does?"

"Well, sort of. He was having dinner and a talk with someone he was thinking of hiring. But the man seems to have disappeared."

"In other words, no, he doesn't have an alibi for Harry's murder."

"No, he *sort of* has an alibi for Harry's murder. Plus, Joe Mickels must be eighty years old. Can you really see him trashing somebody's house and capping his efforts by beating the owner to death?"

"Well, okay, that's a good point. But what about Maddy's murder?"

"No, no alibi. He pointed out very sensibly that since

there's no firm day and time when the nicotine was put onto the yarn, any alibi he offers would be at best . . . spotty."

"But he has a motive for both murders."

"Well, yes, he does."

"And you agreed to help this man?"

Betsy sighed. "Yes, I did."

Chapter Thirteen

✦ ✦ ✦

LIKE many Baptist churches, Maddy's church—First Baptist of Minnetonka—was a modest white clapboard with a small steeple surmounted by a plain iron cross at the front of the roof. The windows, four on a side, had pointed arches, but the glass was plain gray. The small parking lot was crowded, and the street in front of the church was full of cars. Connor pulled into a space a block away, and he and Betsy walked back. It was raining, not hard but in that earnest, straight-down way that probably meant it was going to do it all day. There was no wind, no thunder and lightning.

"It's a *Schnurlregen*," said Connor, holding his big black umbrella so they could both huddle under it.

"What is?" asked Betsy.

"This kind of rain. Salzburg, Austria, is famous for this determined kind of heavy drizzle."

"*Schnurlregen*," said Betsy. "Very descriptive."

Betsy and Connor stopped inside the church to pull off identical raincoats. Under them, they were dressed alike in navy blue suits and white shirts—well, all right, he wore a shirt, she wore a blouse. He had a dark green tie; she had a modest white ruffle. At first they took a pew near the back of the church. A piano was playing a hymn very softly.

Despite all the cars and the smallness of the church, the pale oak pews were full but not packed. Connor nudged Betsy and nodded at the severely plain coffin up near the front. It rested on a wheeled bier and had a single bouquet of roses so dark a red they were nearly black.

After a few seconds Betsy realized the coffin was not wood but a heavy grade of tan cardboard. That's right, she thought, Maddy was going from here to a crematorium. It looked as if there was an aimless, widespread pattern of scribbles on the coffin—and it looked as if the man standing in front of the coffin was scribbling some more on it. Betsy was shocked—then she realized he was signing the coffin, the same way someone might sign a cast on a broken leg. Say, what a lovely idea! She stood and went forward. About to search her purse for a pen, she saw a cluster of Sharpie pens gathered around the bouquet to facilitate the writing.

She picked up a Sharpie. *I am grateful you brought your nimble fingers into my life*, she wrote. *God bless you. Betsy Devonshire.*

Connor took the pen from her. *You are at last in a place where there is nothing to try your patience*, he wrote, which Betsy thought was an impertinence, though it made her smile. She noticed he did not sign it.

They went back to their places. Betsy, unfamiliar with

Baptist churches, looked around. Plain off-white walls, no stained glass, no contrasting color anywhere. Up front was a vestigial altar with a bouquet of white lilies and a large black Bible on it. To the right was the upright piano whose notes they'd heard upon coming in. The pianist was a middle-aged woman with dark curling hair and an impressive bosom. She wore a long-sleeved gray knit dress with a black-on-white polka-dot scarf. Now she was playing a gentle version of "Nearer, My God, to Thee," and as Betsy tried to remember the words to it, she rolled it into another hymn Betsy did not recognize.

At ten thirty on the dot, the pastor, a rotund man with thinning dark hair and a pleasant face, came in from one side and took his place at the lectern on the left. He was wearing a charcoal black suit, white shirt, and dark maroon tie. A square of maroon silk handkerchief was peeking from his suit coat pocket.

"Good morning," he said. The piano player noticed his presence, stopped playing, and put her hands into her lap. "Good morning," he said again.

"Good morning," replied the congregation solidly.

"Welcome to a House of God, to a place of worship and praise. We have come here this morning to thank God that He led Maddy O'Leary to us, to praise God for her life, and to glorify God that she is now living in the perpetual sunlight of His eternal kingdom. Maddy was a faithful member of this church for nine years, a good Christian woman. But I suspect few of us really knew her. She kept herself to herself, and her charities, while many, were mostly anonymous. How many of you knew that our new piano was a gift from her?"

There was a murmur of surprise.

"Or that half the cost of our new roof came from her?"

More murmuring, louder.

"Maddy O'Leary was a God-fearing, intelligent, hard-working . . ." He paused for effect. "Difficult woman, who loved her fellow man, preferably at a distance."

There was surprised, agreeing laughter. "Amen," called someone.

"But she loved God and praised Him for sending His only begotten Son to us, to teach us how to live, to die for us, and to open the gates of heaven for us." He was getting into his preaching voice now, and electricity began to trickle into the room. "Let us praise Him!"

After a heartfelt invocation, he led them in singing "Face to Face with Christ, My Savior," a hymn Betsy was not familiar with. Connor, she noticed, seemed to know it. Or maybe, since he was holding an open hymnal, he could read music. He was always surprising her with a display of some skill or other she hadn't known he had.

When the pastor called on the congregation to speak about Maddy, only one person rose: Chaz Reynolds. Betsy hadn't realized he was there. He wore a dark brown suit with a dark brown shirt and black tie, and he went to the lectern with a deeply grave expression on his handsome face.

Betsy sat up straighter as he took hold with both hands and looked out at the congregation. "I don't think any of you know me," he began, "so I'm grateful you gave me this opportunity to speak. I had to come. I'm not even a Baptist, I'm a Lutheran. But I couldn't stay away!

"I worked for Maddy O'Leary for seven years. She took me on as a kind of office boy, taught me step-by-step how to collect rents, how to do basic repairs to kitchens and bathrooms, how to interview prospective tenants, how to evict tenants. I learned to keep records, fill out tax forms, make reports, do all the things necessary to keep her business running smoothly. She shouted at me—a lot—and praised me—not to my face, but to others. She raised my pay at least every year, upgraded my benefits, set me up with an investment program, and matched whatever I put into it. She gave me responsibilities and dared me not to live up to them. She made me a better man, faster than I thought possible." His voice was thickening and slowing. He stopped to swallow. "I loved her, though I never dared to tell her that. So I hope she can hear me tell her now." He looked upward. "I love you, Miss Maddy, and I miss you every day."

He tore himself away and stumbled back to his pew in front. Bershada was there, and she put an arm around his shoulders.

The pianist played a few bars, and the congregation broke into "Sweet, Sweet Spirit."

The pastor preached and offered more prayers, more hymns were sung, then he offered a blessing and said, "Because Ms. O'Leary is going from here to be cremated, and her ashes strewn in an undisclosed place, we ask that all who can please stay here for a luncheon prepared by the Ladies' Society. There will be a fifteen-minute break, then we will reconvene in the church basement. The stairs are forward and to your right, or if you want a breath of fresh air, there is another entrance around the east side toward the back. I hope to see all of you there."

Four people—two obviously from a funeral home—came to wheel the casket out while one more hymn was sung, and Betsy was reduced to tears, as always, by "Amazing Grace."

Chaz and his mother left without talking to anyone. Chaz was so obviously in distress that no one remarked harshly on his departure.

Many of the congregation chose to go outside into the open air, where, *Schnurlregen* be damned, it had stopped raining and sunlight was trying to break through the clouds. They stood around speaking in amazement of a fellow church member they only thought they knew.

The pastor joined the group. "You know, I didn't tell the whole story during the service," he said. "Ms. O'Leary helped build my discretionary fund to new heights so when members came to me with a financial emergency I would be better able to help them." He looked around the group. "Without naming any names, there are a number of you who needed your rent money or a mortgage payment made, or a month's worth of groceries, or a tooth cap replaced, or a plumbing bill paid that I was able to handle, thanks to Maddy."

An indignant man said, "Pastor, why in, uh, the heck didn't you say something about that a year or two ago? It would have been nice to know, y'know? So we could have thanked her while she was alive."

"Yes, it would have been nice and done her reputation a lot of good. But Ms. O'Leary gave me strict instructions not to say anything to anyone. I suspect it was because she didn't want to start a stampede of mendicants in her direction."

"Kind of sad she thought so poorly of us," remarked a woman.

"Well, now, think about it, Marcy," said another woman. "Suppose you knew there was a member of our church who was rich and very free and generous with her money. You recently had a big bump of a mortgage payment, didn't you? It hurt you, making that payment; you asked me to help you pray over it. Would you at least have thought of approaching her? Especially if you knew she had helped others?"

"No, of course not. Well, okay, maybe." Marcy laughed. "So all right, I might've joined the line with my hand out."

Her friend drew up her shoulders and confessed, "Me, too."

The group began to join the others going around the side of the little church toward the basement entrance.

"Is it true you don't know where her ashes are being strewn?" Betsy asked the pastor.

"She didn't want to tell anyone."

"Such a secretive woman!" said a man disapprovingly. "There's no reason for all that secrecy!"

"Does anyone know?" asked Betsy.

"I can give you the name of the funeral home," the pastor said. "I think they might know. But I'm sure they have been instructed not to give out that information."

"Thank you, Pastor," Betsy said. Shy, shy to the very end, she thought.

The luncheon was very like every church dinner Betsy had ever attended. The menu was fried and baked chicken, cole slaw, potato salad, baked beans with strips of bacon on top, dinner rolls, two kinds of Jell-O salad, and sheets of carrot cake studded with chopped nuts and little pieces of carrot and topped with cream cheese icing. Lemonade, milk, and coffee to drink. The meal was served buffet style; middle-aged women with hairnets handed out plates, silverware, and thick, soft paper napkins, and they brought out more food as needed.

The pastor offered a short blessing as the double line formed at the head of the long tables.

"Wow," said Betsy on the way home. "People sure are shocked at how they only thought they knew Maddy. Turns out her death is a serious loss to her church community. I wonder if that's so in other places."

"Didn't you say Bershada told you how Maddy would give her a check to cash so she could pass the money on anonymously to various charities? I suspect a lot of communities are going to be sad that Maddy is gone without ever knowing who she was."

As they drove up Highway 7, and nearly home, Connor asked, "Is there any reason you want to know where her ashes might be scattered?"

"I'm willing to ask anybody anything. There's got to be a key question in all this that will point me toward an answer. Who hated Harry strongly enough to physically attack him? Who was willing to play that sneaky, deadly trick on Maddy? Could it possibly be the same person? I don't really want to know where Maddy's ashes are going to end up. But I do want to know who she picked to do the scattering."

"I should think that information would be in her will," said Connor.

"No, wills sometimes are not even read until well after the funeral. They are mostly about the distribution of the decedent's property. Funeral arrangements generally have to be made before that. A 'living will' could have those instructions, I think. Or some kind of similar document." She frowned. "I should find out, because I need to ask someone to handle my instructions."

"What do you want that someone to do?" he asked.

"At present, you are that someone," she said. "And I want an Episcopalian church funeral, preceded by a wake at a funeral home. I keep meaning to find out if there's a space available next to the grave of my sister and her husband here in Excelsior, because if there is, I want to be put there. If not, cremate me and pour my ashes into Minnehaha Creek while a CD plays Bill Staines singing"—and she began to croon—"River, take me along, in your sunshine, sing me a song, ever moving, and winding and free; you rollin' old river, you changin' old river, let's you and me, river, run down to the sea.' Because the creek runs into the Mississippi, and it runs into the Gulf of Mexico."

She sat back with a sigh of contentment, thinking about little pebbles of bone carrying her spirit into the place all life began, the ocean.

HAVING delved all she could into Maddy's life, Betsy decided to switch direction and try to find out something about Harry Whiteside. She knew very little about him. She'd read the newspaper accounts, but in her experience, newspapers didn't always have complete or accurate information. She'd heard the gossip about the three-way struggle to buy the big property on Water Street. But a lot of gossip could be described as exaggerated and unsympathetic speculation, and in any case, it made two-dimensional caricatures of its subjects. The word *triangulate* appeared at the front of her mind. She needed another source, so maybe she could triangulate and from three flawed angles find information she could trust. So where else to look?

She turned to Whiteside's obituary in the *Star Tribune*. That at least would be a compassionate summary of his life.

There, as elsewhere, she learned that he was sixty-seven, the father of three children, all boys, all grown and married, with children of their own—and that he had two ex-wives. The children were all by his first wife. He had an MBA from the College (now University) of St. Thomas. He was the founder and CEO of Whiteside Design, Incorporated, the fourth-largest designer and builder of commercial property in the state.

He was to be interred in Lakeview Cemetery—where the elite were buried—on a date yet to be announced. Memorials were to be sent to the University of Minnesota.

The tone of the obituary was staid and respectful, without flowery or sorrowful prose. She wondered who had written it.

Now she felt prepared to talk to someone who knew Harry Whiteside personally. One of his children or ex-wives would be best to start. Bershada, who helped his second wife move out, could probably help her connect with the ex-wife. But Bershada was in Arkansas for the marriage of her youngest daughter and had apparently shut off her cell phone. Nor was she reading her e-mail. Both decisions were understandable; Bershada had talked several times about the "Bridezilla" her daughter Leeza had become, and about her overbearing and even bizarre behavior as the wedding date approached. Doubtless Bershada had her hands full with her large and sometimes volatile family's issues.

Then she remembered Phil's remark that Harry's downfall would be bankruptcy, not murder. What did Phil know about Harry?

She called him. Pleased to be consulted, he said, "I got a friend, he's a contractor. He says ol' Harry's a manipulator. He can be—excuse me, he used to be—your best friend when he was looking to hire you for a job he had pending. Saw you in a restaurant, he'd pay your tab. Out on the town, he'd buy you a drink—hell, two drinks. A real hail-fellow-well-met. See? Then you signed the contract and all of a sudden he was mad at everything you did. It wasn't good enough, it wasn't fast enough, you weren't working hard enough, he was losing money and it was your fault. He'd grind you down till you agreed to give him a discount. Once the job was done, he'd grudge that maybe you did all right, and in a few weeks he was fine with you, happy with the work you did, and if your paths crossed again, he'd shake your hand and offer to introduce you to someone he thought may be useful to you."

"What awful behavior!" said Betsy. "Do you think maybe he was bipolar? How did he stay in business behaving like that?"

"According to what I heard, when he was being nice, his deals were more than fair, and in the end he paid the amended amount in full and on time—which is not always the case with these big-time builders. Any contractor who could develop a tin ear to Harry's rants could make a living off him. But if enough people got tired of his methods, his business could suffer."

"This is wonderful information—thank you!"

"Hey, remember, this is all what they call hearsay. On the other hand, it's not just from my friend but a couple of his friends, too—during a late-night poker game when we were all half in the bag. Or is it still hearsay when it's from three drunk people?"

Betsy chuckled. "I think so. Still, this is very useful. You don't happen to know anything about his wives and children, do you?"

"'Wives'? What was he, a polygamist?"

"No, they were in succession; he married his second wife after divorcing his first one." She stopped short. "You know, I actually don't know if that's true. Maybe she died?"

"Sorry, I don't know, either."

"Well, do you know anything about his children? All I have is that there are three boys, all grown and married."

"'Fraid not. I guess that's what comes of him living on the other side of the lake. Like I told you, he owned a big architectural design company, and he had property all over the state. So this would be just another notch cut in the handle of his pistol."

Betsy said, "I wonder what will happen to it. I mean, who will come into possession?"

"If he left a will, you can find out."

"I can?"

"Sure, once it's filed, you can read it. Wills are public information."

"That's good to know. Where would I go to find it?"

"Now that I don't know. Call City Hall in Wayzata."

"Thanks, I will. You've been a great resource on this, and I'm grateful."

"You're welcome."

But the will hadn't been filed yet. So Betsy decided to run a Google search on Harry's sons. She went back to the obituary and found their names: Hamilton, Howard, and Hector. Whiteside surely wasn't a common surname. Or was it? Out of curiosity, she did another search and discovered about one person in twenty-five thousand is surnamed Whiteside. With that in mind, she searched the three sons by their first and last names and found links to three men named Hamilton Whiteside, two named Hector Whiteside, and five named Howard Whiteside. Five were businessmen, one was a builder, one was a hog farmer, one was an architect, and one was a college professor, but only four were of the right age to be Harry Whiteside's sons. One was a very old man and another perhaps of an age to be Harry's younger brother. None lived in Minnesota—was that a clue?

One of the Hamiltons and both the Hectors had contact information, and Betsy sent a brief e-mail to them, asking each if he was Harry Whiteside's son.

Now all she could do in that direction was wait, so she turned her attention back to Maddy O'Leary. Maddy was a longtime resident of Excelsior. Her life, like that of almost everyone in town, had been thoroughly sieved. Maddy, she knew, had begun her adult life as a legal secretary in a Minneapolis law firm specializing in real estate. She took classes and became a paralegal and a few years later caused a minor scandal when she married a senior partner in the firm—

who died after three months. Betsy held that thought out in front of her mind for a short while. What did her husband die of? She didn't know, but it couldn't have been something violent, or that fact would be prominent. Maddy wasn't left pregnant and never remarried.

Though her brief marriage left her well-off, she stayed with the law firm for a few years more, then began to buy distressed and/or repossessed properties, hiring people to rehab them, then selling some, keeping and renting others. Over time she moved from single-occupancy homes to duplexes and fourplexes and then to apartment buildings. As her holdings became more numerous and complex, she quit the law firm to focus on them. Gossip had it that nowadays some renters moved out when she took over a building because she was a harsh landlord, but she was never the subject of a successful tenant's lawsuit. When she sold a rental property, it was usually at a profit because of the upgrades she'd done. But a not inconsiderable part was because her tenants tended to be orderly. Betsy, who had twice suffered with difficult tenants, had often promised herself that she would ask Maddy her secret. Was it because she intensely interviewed prospective renters in order to screen out potential problems? If so, what did she ask them? How would she make that kind of interview legal? Or was her manner of supervising her properties such that she overawed her tenants? Betsy had never learned the art of overawing.

Or was it something else, something Betsy could emulate?

But Maddy had been abrupt to the point of rudeness to everyone, and Betsy had found herself shying away from asking her questions. Not that there was a lack of opportunity. Maddy bought a lot of yarn and other stitching materials in Betsy's shop. If she wanted something, she tended to buy it at once, only rarely waiting for a sale. Despite the amount of yarn and other items she purchased, she never asked for special consideration, such as a discount for buying in quantity. On the other hand, she was quick to return a product she found faulty or inappropriate for its intended use. Betsy was equally quick to make reimbursements, though she was careful not to overcompensate. As far as possible, she had wanted to keep both Maddy's custom and her respect.

She could remember only one time Maddy came into her shop in such good humor that Betsy dared to banter with her. It was the day Maddy had won the bidding war on the Water Street property.

"Hello, Betsy!" she had boomed in her loud voice, her eyes sparkling and her long skirts snapping in the speed of her stride.

"Well, something's made you cheerful this afternoon," Betsy had responded, surprised.

"I took down two people who were giving me grief," Maddy had said.

"Looks like they never laid a glove on you," Betsy had dared to say.

"Oh, metaphorically, I'm all over bruises," she had said, coming down to almost her usual brusque tone. "But unlike them, I'll be more than fine. I want three more skeins of that green Appleton wool I bought in here last week."

That was the only time she had been anything but abrupt. Too bad it was so shortly before her death; Betsy would have liked to look behind that shield to see what

Maddy was really like. And now it was particularly sad to learn there was another, softer, side to the woman. It appeared she gave generously but worked always in the background, not just at her church but in the toy auction. She knit more toys for it than any other person. But she had objected strenuously to Bershada's insistence that she sit in a place of honor for doing so.

I believe I was right, she was shy, thought Betsy now. Maddy hated being singled out, even for praise.

Betsy wondered what kind of childhood she had had.

But first, and more importantly, she wanted to find out if that gruff exterior and overweening ambition had created an enemy so angry that he—or she—had resorted to murder.

Chapter Fourteen

❖ ❖ ❖

I T was a slow time in the shop. Godwin had gone across the street to have lunch with Rafael in their condo. Betsy was at the big checkout desk writing checks for suppliers—and sighing over the numbers—when the door announced its opening with a bright chorus of "Anchors Aweigh." She looked up to see Detective Sergeant Mike Malloy coming in. Backward.

Actually, he had turned around to stare in bemusement at the door frame. He held the door open until the tune finished. Then he closed it and turned to see Betsy looking bemused at him.

"You don't know that melody?" she asked.

"Of course I do. Doesn't everybody? But you are going to get very tired of it after a few dozen repeats," he predicted.

"I won't have time to get tired of it. Godwin changes the music at least once a week. He's working his way down a very long list of titles."

Malloy looked back again at the door. "That's the Navy Hymn, isn't it," he said.

"No, the Navy Hymn is 'Eternal Father, Strong to Save.' What you just heard is a traditional Navy drinking song."

He looked at her. "You sure?"

She offered a snappy salute. "Ex–Navy WAVE here. I know at least two verses of 'Eternal Father.' I even know the countermelody to 'Anchors Aweigh.'" She would have sung it to him, but he didn't look interested. Instead, she asked, "How may I help you, Mike?"

"I'm here about the Maddy O'Leary case."

"I'll be glad to help any way I can."

He smiled his thin smile and came forward, a slim man of average height with a densely freckled face. His hair was a shade of tan, which happens to some redheads as they age. His light blue eyes were tired.

"I made a fresh pot of coffee less than half an hour ago," she said.

"Yes, thanks. Black."

"Have a seat." She gestured at the library table in the center of the room.

When she came out of the back, carrying two mugs, one of coffee and the other of an herbal tea, he was seated near the far end of one long side. On the table in front of him was a notepad with sewn-in pages and a fat ballpoint pen.

She put his coffee beside the notepad, put her own tea in front of a chair across from him, and sat down.

"Where do we begin?" she asked.

"Whose idea was this auction at Mount Calvary?"

"It was Bershada Reynolds's idea. I can't believe you don't already know that."

He nodded, but whether in agreement or not, she couldn't tell. "Who supplied the yarn for those little canvas bags?"

"I did. And the bags themselves, too." Surely he must have known that already, too. *Aha*, she thought, he's asking questions he knows the answers to in order to see how I tell the truth. Or don't. But that must be from habit; he knows me, and he knows I don't lie. She looked at him and smiled.

"What?" he said.

"Nothing," she replied. "Just recognizing your style of interrogation."

"This isn't an interrogation, it's an interview. I interrogate suspects, I interview witnesses."

"Noted, thanks. Next question."

"How did you select the yarn that went into the bags?"

"Bershada told me who the people were, and I asked them what kind of yarn they wanted."

"How far in advance of the auction did you pull the yarn?"

"About ten or twelve days."

"Was the yarn from your stock?"

"Yes. One person came in to look at what I had, and two people told me directly what they would like. Goddy, of course, picked his own yarn."

"Which way did Ms. O'Leary go?"

"She asked me if I had dark blue merino wool. I did, so I turned the skein into a ball—"

"What? Why?"

She turned away in her chair. "Those are skeins," she said, pointing to a basket full of fat ovals of yarn cinched in the middle by a broad paper wrapper. "It's how yarn comes, in skeins. I have a device that will turn a skein into a ball. It's easier to knit from a ball."

"So why don't they come already in balls?"

"Because balls roll away, and they unwind as they roll."

He wrote that down, paused, brightened, and said, "I remember how in old movies a man would sit with yarn kind of wrapped or draped around his wrists while a woman pulled it off in a single strand to make a ball." He held his hands about two feet apart, palms facing in.

Betsy nodded. "That's the traditional method. You can also drape it around the back of a chair, but my device is much faster. It depends on what the knitter is after, a quick ball of yarn or a chance to sit and talk with someone. Interestingly, it was also used as a safe kind of courtship. The man and woman could talk at length, but they couldn't get up to anything while his hands were engaged like that. Plus she got a ball of yarn with which to begin to knit him a pair of argyle socks."

"That's kind of nice," said Mike, nodding thoughtfully, and Betsy recalled he had two daughters of dating age. One of them was a knitter.

But the task of writing checks prodded, so she pushed forward. "What else do you want to know?"

"Where were the bags kept after you put the yarn in them?"

"I have a storage room in the basement."

"Is it locked?"

"No, but the front and back doors to this building are, as is the door to the basement."

"Who has the keys?"

"I have keys, my tenants have keys, Connor has keys, Godwin has keys. Only Godwin and I have the keys to the front and back door of the shop. We lend a key to the shop's front door to an employee who is coming in early, but only that one key. And we take it back when we come in. All the locks are dead bolts."

Mike, writing swiftly, nodded, then paused. "Your tenants have keys to the basement?"

Betsy nodded. "A washing machine and dryer are down there."

"Would they lend their keys to a friend?"

"Maybe. I ask them not to when I give them the keys, but you know how people are. The Pearsons, who have the front apartment, have a big family who drop by a lot, so it's likely their keys have been temporarily loaned out. It's even possible they've made copies for them." She frowned. "I should ask them about that."

"So getting at the bags of yarn might have been inconvenient for a non-tenant or non-employee, but not impossible."

"I would prefer difficult and complicated to inconvenient. But yes, not impossible."

"Did you see any evidence of tampering when you took the bags of yarn over to Mount Calvary?"

"I didn't take them over. Bershada came with another woman, and they took them out of the basement. Have you talked to her?"

"Not about that. When did the transfer take place?"

"The Wednesday before the Saturday auction."

"Did you see the bags in the basement at any time before that?"

"Probably. I mean I went down to the basement a few times between putting them down there and Bershada taking them away. I think I would have noticed if they'd been moved around or some were missing."

"Were they in a row on a shelf, or kept in a box, or what?"

"In a double row on a shelf. It was deep enough so the bags could line up two by two."

"But plainly visible to anyone going into that room," Mike said.

"Or just standing in the door, yes."

"Was Ms. O'Leary's yarn in the front row?"

Betsy thought. "I'm sorry, I don't remember. Godwin and I put the yarn and knitting needles in the bags and took them down."

"You didn't pack each bag yourself?"

"No. I had made a list of who got which ball of yarn. Goddy took the list, loaded the bags, and I took them downstairs. It didn't take long, but I remember waiting till after closing that day, so he wouldn't be thrown off stride by having to wait on a customer."

"Do you know of anyone involved in the auction who smokes e-cigarettes?"

Betsy shook her head. "No."

Mike sighed, made a note, sighed again, and closed his notebook. "Okay, thank you."

"I take it you're trying to clear Joe Mickels?"

"No, I'm trying to clear everyone else so I can arrest him." He stood, looked into her shocked eyes, and said with a straight face, "If you believe that, you're not half the sleuth I've taken you for."

Relieved, she laughed. "And sometimes I need to remind myself you're twice the investigator I used to take you for."

"SEE, I told you he's not the sharpest hook in the tackle box!" said Godwin.

"He was kidding, Goddy! Kidding! He's out to find the person who killed Maddy. Right now he thinks it might be Joe. So do you, remember?"

"Yeah, well, he hasn't had your experience with Joe, so what does he know?"

"He knows plenty—and he's had the training to see it properly. Plus, he has the backing of a very large set of scientific testing methods we have no access to. Let him do his thing."

"Yeah, okay, maybe you're right. But we'll do our thing, too, right?"

"Of course."

"So where do we go next, *kemo sabe*?"

"I want to talk to people who knew Mr. Whiteside and Ms. O'Leary."

"Looking for what they were like?"

"Looking for who hated them."

Chapter Fifteen

❖ ❖ ❖

LATER that day, Betsy wondered again what would happen to the property on Water Street. She called her attorney, Jim Penberthy, to ask.

"Real estate, especially commercial real estate, is not my area of expertise," he said. "I think the property belongs to Ms. O'Leary's estate. But let me check and I'll call you back."

Betsy returned to the struggle to assign her part-timers slots that met her needs and the desires of her employees. One never wanted to work on Wednesdays, another wanted to work only half days, and the third wanted to continue working even though she was two weeks overdue in her pregnancy.

So it was a relief to take a break when the phone rang. But it wasn't Penberthy. It was Bershada.

"Welcome home!" Betsy said. "How was the wedding?"

"Don't ask. And now Chaz is hanging around my house

making me crazy. I finally sent him to the store, but he'll be back in a few minutes. Will you please take him off my hands for a couple of hours? He would be wild to talk about Maddy with you, if you'd care to ask him."

"Yes, I'd like that very much. I was going to ask him to talk to me about her, if he would. What would be a good time?"

"Well, what are you doing this evening? Could your menu possibly stretch to a third person? Be warned, he eats like a horse."

"I think we're having beef stew. I'll call Connor and ask him and call you back."

Connor said he'd make biscuits to stretch the stew and prepare something with Jell-O to fill in the cracks. "Do you want me to make like a hoop and roll away after dinner?" he asked.

"No, please don't. You have a good ear for things; you might pick up something I miss." Betsy called Bershada back to say yes, and she said, "He's right here, talk to him."

In a few seconds a very pleasant man's voice came on the line. "Hello? Mom told me about you, but I don't think I've ever met you."

"Not formally," said Betsy, "but I saw you at Maddy's funeral and was impressed, plus I've often heard good things about you. Are you available to talk this evening? We'll feed you supper."

After a brief, surprised pause, he said, "Well, sure! Okay! What time?"

"About six thirty?"

"Okay. Thanks."

"Now, can I talk with your mother again?"

"Sure." His voice faded as he talked away from the phone. "Mom, she wants to talk to you some more."

In a few seconds Bershada came back on. "What is it?" she asked.

"You said you helped Harry Whiteside's second wife pack her clothes when she left him."

"Yes, I did."

"Were you and she friends?"

"Yes, she volunteered at libraries all over the nine counties that make up the Twin Cities, and the first time she came to Excelsior, we struck up a friendship. I didn't pry too much, and she liked that. But we talked about everything else. She was especially good with children, which was my area of expertise at the Excelsior library. She started coming regularly, and every time we'd wind up talking nineteen to the dozen, at work, over lunch, even sometimes over dinner. She was a kind woman, with a silly sense of humor the children loved."

"Did she talk about her husband?"

"Not at first. If I asked her about him, she'd say, 'Oh, he's so busy with work, I've almost forgotten what he looks like.' Or, 'I'm glad I've got my volunteer work. Harry doesn't want me to work for pay, and I'd go crazy just sitting at home, especially now all the boys are gone.'"

"So how did you find out she wanted to leave him?"

"She came to work with a bruise that went from just above her left eye nearly to her jawline. She'd tried to cover it up with makeup, but it wasn't just black and blue, it was swollen. I marched her into the ladies' room and ordered her to tell me what happened. She tried to say she'd fallen, but I could tell she was lying, and she started to cry. He didn't often hit her, but when he did, he'd do it where the bruise didn't show. And he was always telling her she was worthless and stupid—all the things that that kind of man does to his wife. She absolutely refused to make a police report, I think because she was afraid he might kill her. She said she'd been secretly saving money and had just barely enough for a bus ticket to Columbus, Georgia, where her sister lived. But this hit on her face was absolutely the last straw. I drove her home and helped her pack and took her to the station and sat with her until her bus was called. She wrote me a few weeks later, saying Harry had found out where she was and called, but her brother-in-law told him that if he came down there, he'd introduce him to his back-hoe in the east forty and nobody would ever see him again."

Bershada chuckled and said to Betsy, "He must have sounded very convincing, because Harry didn't even come down to contest the divorce."

"Do you still correspond with her?"

"We did for about eighteen months, then she wrote she was getting married and moving to Costa Rica, and that's the last I heard from her."

I T was just about closing time. Betsy was running the cash register and Godwin was cleaning the toilet when the phone rang.

"Crewel World, this is Betsy, how may I help you?" she said into the receiver.

"Betsy, this is Jim Penberthy. I was right about the Water Street property. The estate has possession of it—or rather the option to buy it. They can either proceed with the purchase, or they can offer the option to interested parties. But the original owner no longer has any ownership in it."

"Well, that's interesting. Thanks, Jim." So that at least removed one motive for Joe. Killing Maddy and Harry didn't give him the right to buy the Water Street property. It did, however, give him the opportunity, which he'd lost when Maddy won it in the original auction if her executor decided to put it out for bids.

CHAZ arrived about five minutes early at the downstairs entrance. Betsy opened the door to her apartment to wait for him.

He was as she remembered him, a little above medium height, slim, his face a masculine echo of his handsome mother's, and as dark complexioned. His hair was cropped short. He wore a dark red wool shirt under a light tan leather jacket, close-fitting jeans, and moccasins. An interesting touch was his pair of gold-rimmed spectacles—he hadn't worn glasses at the funeral or in the shop. They gleamed in the staircase lights, hiding his eyes.

"Ms. Devonshire?" he asked as he came up the last few steps into the broad hallway outside her door. His voice was the pleasant tenor she remembered from the funeral, unaccented.

"Yes, and thank you for agreeing to come."

"No problem."

She stepped back, gesturing for him to come inside.

Chapter Sixteen

◆ ◆ ◆

CHAZ paused in the entrance hallway to the Devonshire apartment. It was small, with a narrow door that was very probably a coat closet. A nice warm smell of beef stew, the kind with a mix of vegetables, was in the air. Beyond the closet door on his left was a galley kitchen, and in the kitchen stood a tall white man with graying hair, his two hands working in a big bowl. Facing Chaz was Betsy, a short, plumpish, middle-aged blonde with penetrating blue eyes. She was wearing a long blue skirt the color of her eyes and a pale ivory sweater in a complicated weave. She was smiling—she had a nice smile—and had her hand out, so he took it.

"Hello, Chaz," she said in a warm, pleasant voice. "I'm glad you could come."

"Hi, Betsy," he replied. "Offer to feed me, and I'll follow you anywhere."

She chuckled. "This way."

She turned and led him straight ahead to a wide, low-ceilinged living room. She let him pause for a few seconds to take his jacket off and look around the room.

The walls were painted a quiet mauve, and the carpet was a very pale cream, which Chaz thought daring. These people must rarely have visitors, especially children, over. On the wall to the right was a triple set of windows covered with drapes that were two shades darker than the carpet. Under the window was one of those cat beds that looked lined with sheepskin, and in the bed was a very large cat with tan and gray spots on its head and down its back. It regarded him with cool yellow eyes. A second cat bed, this one dark brown, was unoccupied.

Betsy came back from hanging up his jacket. "Would you care to sit down?" she asked. She went to stand beside a couch upholstered in narrow stripes of mauve, olive green, and cream with too many hand-stitched pillows on it. But it looked comfortable—and was, once he moved two pillows aside. *Why are women so nuts about pillows?* he wondered. "Thank you," he said. "This is a really nice place." Because apart from the pillows, it was.

"Thank you," Betsy said.

The tall man, who looked somewhere in middle age but was very fit, came into the living room from the other end of the kitchen. "Hello," he said, and Chaz stood up.

"Connor, this is Charles Reynolds, Bershada's son."

"Call me Chaz," Chaz said.

"Chaz," repeated Connor. "I'm Connor Sullivan. Nice to meet you." He came forward, and the two shook hands. "Dinner will be ready in about fifteen minutes."

"Great." Chaz sat back down. Betsy sat in the comfortable

chair positioned ninety degrees to the couch, and Connor sat at the other end of the couch.

Betsy's chair was an olive green wingback chair, low to the floor so it suited her petite stature. Behind the chair was a silver lamp with a flexible neck curved to look over the shoulder of someone sitting in it, and beside it was a small wooden folding frame holding a bag made of napless carpet. He'd seen those carried by his mother's stitching friends.

She sat back and said, "I think you may have important information to share with me. Your mother explained how I'm involved in trying to solve Maddy's murder?"

Her blunt question, coming in this comfortable place, struck him to the heart. Would he never even begin to heal? "Yes. I hope I can tell you something useful. But where do I begin?"

"I think by just talking about her. Her death hit you hard, I know. I'm so sorry that Maddy was taken like that, with no warning. But it's helpful that you agreed to talk with me about her. You probably knew her better than anyone. What was she like?"

"Well, like Pastor Woodruff said, she was a difficult person," he said, reluctantly admitting to an obvious fault, "especially at first. But she was totally amazing once you got to know her. She was strong and smart, and she taught me more about business than all my college courses put together."

"How long did you work for her?" asked Betsy, reaching sideways into that carpet bag, pulling out a long and narrow notepad. Where had he seen a pad like that? Oh, right, in a newspaper reporter's hand. Saves half a second when you don't have to come back across a wide notebook when taking notes. Interesting that she had figured that out, too. She opened the pad, pulled loose a pencil stuck crosswise into its middle, and scribbled something on an upper corner of the page—probably the date, or his name. Or both.

"Seven years, or close to it. I started out collecting rents and trying to talk tenants into using automatic withdrawal to pay rent. Our tenants are good people, most of them, just trying to get by or even move up a little. But sometimes . . . disorganized."

"Are you acting on behalf of Maddy's estate?"

Did she know this was an ardent desire of his, to remain involved in Maddy's business? Wait, she couldn't know. He said, "No, but I've got an appointment with her lawyer tomorrow. I thought it was about going over the books with him. Do you think—?"

"Think what?"

"That they'll let me continue to work with her properties?"

"I don't know. Would you want to do that?"

"I sure would. I really got to like the work. There was always something interesting going on, problems to solve, tenants and plumbers and glaziers and all to deal with, money to be collected, repairs to be made. She even taught me how to bypass locks some tenants would put on themselves. Plus—" He had to stop. How to explain?

Betsy said, "Plus it's a way of keeping her alive. I did the same thing with my shop. It was my sister's, and when she was murdered, it was a comfort to me to keep it going."

"You really do understand! Thank you!"

"You're welcome. How familiar are you with the way her business was run?"

He sank back. "Only with the rental stuff. She had all kinds of properties: houses, stores, apartment buildings, even a lumberyard." He shrugged. "And, of course, she was a real estate agent, too. I didn't know how big-time until I saw she was going after the Water Street property. That thing is going to cost millions to buy and build. Millions."

"Was she overextending herself to try for it?"

"Oh, I think she must've been, yes. Or, no. Well, maybe." He laughed at himself. "I really don't know. I thought I knew her business affairs pretty well, but I probably didn't."

"Was she secretive?"

He twisted his shoulders in discomfort. "Not exactly. People thought she was . . . blunt. And of course she was. She'd say right out what she thought about things, if she was willing to talk about them at all. If she didn't want to talk, she wouldn't say anything. Like, when I first started to work for her, I thought she owned a couple of houses and an apartment building on the north side of Minneapolis. Then I found out she owned a couple of houses in Uptown. And a store. Then more houses in south Minneapolis, a small lumberyard in Golden Valley—and a start-up construction company up halfway to Duluth. Whenever she widened my responsibilities, I'd find out she owned more property. The latest was I found she had this plan to build a multipurpose building in Excelsior. She never hinted at something, she'd just spring it on me." He shrugged, smiling wryly. "I think she liked to surprise me."

Betsy was busy writing all of this down. Then she looked up from her pad to ask Chaz another question. "She usually struck me as angry or impatient. Was she like that with you?"

"Oh yes," Chaz said. "That was her at her core. I think she was born mad." He grinned. "I got used to it. She barked a lot, but she never bit me."

"And she paid you well."

"Yes, she did. She even bragged about me, in her own way. 'At least Chaz doesn't shout at tenants for being late,' she'd say to a building manager she was about to fire. 'He's a chameleon, he knows how to get along with anyone, even me,' she'd say to someone asking how I kept on working for her."

"How do you know she said those things about you if she never said them to your face?"

"Sometimes she'd leave the door to her office open just a little bit. She never praised me to my face, but she did that eavesdropping-enabler thing enough times that I began to realize it was intentional."

His nose twitched. Was that the lovely smell of biscuits baking?

Betsy nodded, made a note, and said, "Now to the hard part: Did anyone you know truly hate her?"

Chaz laughed. "Oh God, yes. People she evicted would write terrible things about her on their Facebook accounts, or in anonymous letters, or even in spray paint on walls or the doors of their former houses or apartment buildings. People she outdid on business deals, too. Well, the business people didn't resort to spray paint. They'd sue. I think she kept one of her attorneys on speed dial."

"Did any of these people threaten her life?"

"Frequently." He smiled, remembering.

"How serious were these threats?"

"They were mostly just venting. Maddy didn't take them

seriously. Except some of the people who threatened to sue. She got right on those cases. Only one actually came to court while I worked for her, and she won that case." He snapped his fingers. "Like that."

"Did she ever sue anyone?"

Chaz nodded. "A couple of times, mostly small claims cases. One big one, but it got dismissed."

"Against anyone we know?"

Chaz looked uncomfortable. "Harry Whiteside," he admitted. "I think she was in the right, but Harry had a big-time law firm on his side, so she never had a chance. But at least she fought him to a draw."

"Now, let's turn my question around. Who was Maddy angry with? Was there anyone she hated?"

Chaz leaned back into the couch and fell silent. Betsy bit her tongue, and Connor, after a glance at her, followed suit.

"Oh God," sighed Chaz. "Harry came to Maddy's office a few days before he was killed. Now, he'd come before, just a few times, like less than once a year. I think there was bad blood between them going way back. Years before I came to work for her. I'm not sure what started it, or when, but whenever they communicated with each other, they tried to do it by letter or e-mail. If it was necessary for them to meet face-to-face, the temperature in the room would drop about thirty degrees when he walked in, and then the mercury would start to rise until they both came to a boil. Then the shouting would start. And a funny thing, she would meet him in the outer office where I could overhear at least the first part of their conversation. Maybe she wanted him to be aware there was an eyewitness."

"What would they argue about?"

"Deals they were making. She'd find a property she liked and then discover he was the one selling it. Or vice versa. Or she'd bid on a project and find herself dealing with him somehow, like maybe he was financing another part of the build, or bidding against her. She was always sure he was rooking her somehow, and he was sure she was doing the same. He'd swear to God that one day she'd regret ever knowing him, and she'd say that he was the one who'd be sorry, and when he left she'd sit in her office knitting ninety miles an hour until she cooled off."

"And this last time was different?"

He nodded. "It was like he was the one who won the bidding war. He was smirking and, and . . . well, it's hard to describe. He was standing like a winner. No, worse than that, like he was standing over her dead body and glad to be there."

"Do you think he'd found some kind of weakness in the deal?"

He sighed lightly. "Well . . . no, I don't think so. Oh, I don't know! Like he beat her in some other area. Yeah, like that."

"So this bidding war they got into wasn't just about acquiring the property."

"No, it was about 'doing' the other." He grimaced.

"Was she expecting him to come in that day?"

"Yeah, I think so. She didn't act surprised to see him. But the look in his eye—and the look in hers—made me break out in a sweat watching them, scared they'd lose it and she'd grab my laptop and smack him upside his head, or he'd knock her down. But neither one of them ever took that swing."

"What did he say that was different?"

"He said, 'Have you had your windows replaced yet?'"

"Had there been some windows broken in her properties?"

"Not that I knew of. But there must've been, because that's when I got scared she was going to pop him one."

"Does she have properties you're not aware of?"

Chaz stared at her, and suddenly she laughed. "Like you would know about some building you don't know about."

He nodded, grinning. "Yeah, like that." The grin faded. "On the other hand, if there was damage somewhere, I should've known. That was one of my jobs, arranging repairs. Or even doing them. I'm pretty good at replacing windows. Plumbing, not so much."

"So what do you think?"

"I think you're right, there's a piece of property I don't know about, that nobody is supposed to know about, but Harry found out. And it's damaged; someone broke some windows."

Connor asked, "Is it possible that Harry broke the windows?"

Chaz drew breath in through his teeth. "I hadn't thought of that! But no. I think she was so damn angry—surprised into anger—because he found out about this secret property."

Betsy frowned. "What kind of property could she own that she wanted kept secret?"

Chaz shrugged. "Beats me."

"Did he say where this property was? In the Twin Cities area?"

"No." Chaz shrugged. "But . . . I got the feeling it was out somewhere, maybe up north. Vacation property, maybe. Up at the lake."

Connor said, "Which lake?"

Betsy said, "In Minnesota, everyone who owns a cabin on one of our ten thousand lakes calls it 'the lake.' As in, 'We're going up to the lake this weekend.' The lake is never mentioned by name. Maybe to discourage drop-in visitors who'd want a free stay."

Connor laughed. "Very clever."

"*Row*," came a sound that could have been from a cat, except it was deep.

Chaz, looked around, startled, then saw the owner of the second cat bed, a Siamese, emerging from a back room. So it had been a cat's voice, after all. The cat, whose "points"—face, ears, legs, tail—were very dark, came to stand in front of Chaz. "*Arow*," it said again, more of a statement than an inquiry.

"That's Thai," said Betsy. "With a T-H. If you want to pet him, hold out your hand. He'll come and sniff your fingers, which is permission to stroke the top of his head."

"Huh," said Chaz, but he leaned forward experimentally, arm extended, fingers out.

The cat came near, lifted his small head, and sniffed, then presented his forehead. Chaz obediently stroked it a few times. The cat, satisfied, walked away toward the kitchen.

"What would have happened if I hadn't held out my hand?" Chaz wondered aloud.

Connor said, "He would have walked away—but a few minutes later he would have landed on your shoulders from behind the couch, just to see how high you'd jump and how loud you'd shout. He has a wicked sense of humor."

Chaz laughed. "I guess I should be grateful it's not that other cat who has a sense of humor."

"Indeed," said Connor, also laughing. "She currently weighs twenty pounds." He glanced at Betsy and said, "May I ask Chaz something?"

"Of course," Betsy said, looking a little surprised.

He turned back to Chaz. "This may seem like an odd question, but when you heard that Maddy had been murdered, whose name immediately jumped into your mind as the possible murderer?"

He said at once, "Harry Whiteside," then raised both hands, his gesture of frustration. "But of course he was already dead. Someone murdered him before he could murder her."

"Why did you think of Mr. Whiteside?" asked Betsy.

"Mostly because of that Water Street property. I remember he said, 'At least I made you pay more than you wanted, maybe more than it's worth.' Which might be true, I think he could have afforded the higher price better than she could. Still, he backed down first."

Betsy said, "So did Joe Mickels. Did you think of him, too, as a possible murderer?"

"No, not right away. He and Maddy had no relationship I knew of until this Water Street thing, but . . ."

"But what, Chaz?"

"Well, I'm sure Maddy was stretching herself pretty thin on this Water Street property. She had taken out mortgages on some of her buildings so she could keep up with the bidding, and she was angry about that. And that last confrontation, that was *serious*."

"Her behavior must have been disturbing. Did you ever think about quitting your job?"

"Yes, off and on. But never for long. She was honest—I know, I know, but she was. She wasn't out to cheat anyone, she just wanted a fair chance. She was the most . . . straightforward person I've ever known. She knew what she wanted and went for it." As he spoke, his tone grew warmer. "And she was interesting. She was complicated. She knew lots of things about lots of things. That sounds like Trivial Pursuit, doesn't it? But deeper than that, not trivia. Things like history, science, and art." His voice softened further. "She was a thinker. She challenged me to think, and I liked that." His throat filled, and it became hard for him to talk. He swallowed and tried to suck it up. "I loved working for her."

"That's wonderful, and it was brave of you to stand up among a gathering of strangers and say you loved her." Betsy made a note on her pad and asked, "How did Joe Mickels fit into the bidding war?"

"Well, I heard Mr. Mickels wanted that property, that he was a fanatic about it. But I'd also heard he was kind of a miser, so I think he was mad that the two of them kept bidding the price up. I'm pretty sure he knew Maddy and Harry were enemies—you couldn't get anywhere near them without learning that—but he didn't take sides or interfere between them that I knew of. He didn't egg them on." He stopped short, and added, "It would have been stupid to egg them on, as it would have just raised the price even more."

"Was he angry at them?"

Chaz nodded. "I think so—no, Maddy told me he was. He thought they were unbusinesslike, she said. Taking it personal, when this was a business deal—though it was personal with her, too. Maddy told me Joe had wanted a big building with his name on it for a long time. Years."

"That's true," said Betsy. "He tried to force me out of this building—he was my landlord back then and wanted everyone out so he could tear it down and put up the Mickels Building." She sighed. "I think all three of them were taking it personally, though perhaps not for the same reasons.

"You talked about her being angry. Was she capable of violence? Physical violence? Did you ever see her strike someone?"

"No, absolutely not. When she got really angry, it was mostly at herself, for losing her temper or making a mistake in managing or selling or flipping a property. She'd stomp around her office, and sometimes she'd throw something hard enough to break it, but it was her own something, and not just a stapler or a wastebasket. She might smash a valuable clock or vase, or she'd rip up a document, or, once, a nice wall calendar, the kind that comes from a museum, and then have to buy a replacement, and that would make her even madder. So then she'd sit down and knit. I was surprised at the way she'd knit, too, almost like she was mad at the yarn." He smiled and shook his head. "Knitting was her act of violence."

Connor said, "Maybe that's another reason she didn't want to be honored as the person who contributed the most knitted toys. It was a reminder of how often she was angry."

Betsy looked admiringly at him for his perceptive comment, and Chaz nodded over and over. He said, "Yes, that makes sense. On the other hand, I wonder if maybe she didn't see herself that way, not as an angry person, just as a person coping with a lot of stupid people and events."

Betsy smiled, made a note, and underlined it.

Then something in the kitchen dinged, and Connor said, "The biscuits are done. Let's eat."

Chapter Seventeen

❖ ❖ ❖

AFTER Chaz left, Connor said, "Well, what do you think?"

Betsy said, "I think he's a fine, intelligent young man who knows his own mind. Interesting how close he felt to Maddy. You saw how he's deeply grieved by her death."

"Do you think you have a better understanding of Maddy now?"

"I think so. Chaz is obviously biased, in that he liked and admired her, but he seems to have a good understanding of her difficult personality. What do you think?"

"I think she was a deeply flawed person," said Connor. "Problems with anger, first and most obviously, but also plagued by ambition and lack of empathy."

"I'm not so sure about the lack of empathy. She was exceptionally generous to various charities—you saw how she knitted more toys for that auction than anyone else. But I agree she was unhappy. Do you think she would have been happier if she'd had a better grasp on her anger issues or been better able to empathize with her business rivals?" asked Betsy.

"Maybe. But she wouldn't have been as successful in business. There's an element of ruthlessness in people who are successful, in any field. Don't you think?"

Betsy nodded. "Yes, I think that's true. Ambition has to sit in the driver's seat if a person's going to get good at something. Like you and ships, or me and my little shop." Emily was right: Betsy could sell it and never have to work again, but she remained determined to make it pay.

"You love your shop, but I think it's sleuthing that drives you," amended Connor. "But what do you think is sitting in Chaz's driver's seat?"

She looked at the closed door to the apartment, through which Chaz had exited a few minutes ago.

"I'm not sure."

GODWIN was feeling down. He and Rafael had gone out on his day off for an early spring game of golf, and while he hadn't lost his putting skills over the winter, his drive was yards shorter than usual. Now the two were cleaning and polishing their clubs in the kitchen of their condo.

Perhaps to distract him, Rafael asked, "Has Betsy been keeping you up to date on her investigation into the murders of Harry Whiteside and Maddy O'Leary?"

"She is trying to prove that Joe Mickels had nothing to do with them."

"And you believe Joe Mickels is guilty?"

"Yes. Yes, I do."

"Does she really believe he isn't guilty?"

"I don't know. It's hard to think so. I mean, he's such a terrible man!"

"So maybe what she'll prove is that he *is* guilty."

Godwin nodded as he rubbed hard at a grass stain in the grooves of his driver. It had turned out that way once before. "I'd like that." He put down the head of the club he'd inspected and sighed sadly at it. "I don't see what I'm doing differently in my driving," he complained to his partner.

"I noticed you were behind your usual distance," replied Rafael, putting his driver away and pulling out his chipping club. "But your stroke didn't seem any different."

"Yes, and my aim was good, the ball went right up the middle of the fairway—ah, mostly—but it was twenty, twenty-five yards shorter than usual."

Rafael stopped inspecting his club to look at his companion. "You are placing your feet correctly, so the ball is nearer your left foot?"

"Yes." Godwin wrapped his hands around the top of his driver, putting the club end on the floor next to an imaginary ball, feet apart, elbows straight, head down, knees slightly bent. He waggled his hands a little, preparing to lift the club.

"Ah, I see!" exclaimed Rafael.

"What? What am I doing wrong?"

Rafael moved to stand close behind Godwin and wrapped his arms around him, grasping Godwin's hands. He very slightly twisted Godwin's left hand clockwise. "There," he said. "Now, when you bring your arms back, and bend the wrists, you will find more power available on the down stroke from your left hand." But he did not step back.

"Is there something else?" asked Godwin.

Rafael said, his voice roughened, "I love you so very much, *mi gorrión*," which is Spanish for sparrow, his nickname for Godwin.

"Well, I love you, too, you know that." Godwin wriggled just a little, but still Rafael did not release him.

"I want you to marry me," said Rafael softly.

The wriggling stopped. "I—I—Do you mean that?"

"I do, with all my heart. Will you?"

"Oh, Rafael! Oh, my dear! Oh yes!" He twisted violently in Rafael's arms, so he could turn and face him. The golf club fell to the floor. "Oh, yes, yes, yes!" He was crying with joy and threw his arms around him. "Oh my God, I'm so very happy!"

"Then I am happy, too, *mi gorrión*. So very happy, too."

GODWIN, of course, wanted to plan the whole wedding out at once. Large or small (large), outdoors or in (in because it might rain), what each of them would wear (a black tuxedo for Rafael, a white one for Godwin), when (next June), how many to invite (hundreds, everyone they knew!), what to serve at the reception—

Here Rafael called a halt. "It is getting late, and you have filled my head to its capacity. I want to go on the Internet and see how that Davisson auction is doing, then do some more research on English coins. Or is the correct word *coinage*?"

"How can you talk about coins when we haven't decided on beef or chicken?"

"It doesn't matter. We could serve hamburgers, or shrimp salad, it doesn't matter. What matters is that we exchange rings and tell each other 'I do.' So which is it, coins or coinage?"

"Why are you asking me?"

"You have been speaking English longer than I have."

"So? Numismatists speak their own language. My second language is needlecraft."

Rafael laughed. "Well said, my dear. Now you also must find something to do that will unwind you enough for sleep. What will it be?"

"I don't know, all I can think about is— Wait, yes, I do. I've been neglecting my counted cross-stitch for knitting, so I think I'll get out that little bookmark I didn't finish in time last year." Godwin often stitched bookmarks as Christmas and birthday presents, working them between bigger projects all year long.

"That's better," said Rafael. And he went off to his office.

Though he did not display it, Rafael was elated over Godwin's acceptance of his proposal. He had begun to think such a wonderful thing as a lifetime partner was never to be his. Afraid his excitement would overwhelm him as it had Godwin, he determinedly set the subject aside and opened the locked cabinet where his collections—he had several—lay.

A numismatist is interested in money. Not as a medium of exchange, but as objects of beauty, markers of history, and items with a value outside—usually over—their face value. Rafael was a coin collector. Like most collectors, he had more than one interest, but he had focused hardest on one corner of the vast world of coins; in his case, medieval English hammered silver coins. Starting casually, but more ardently as time passed, he bought an Edward the Third here, a Richard the Lionheart there, a Henry the First, a Henry the Sixth, an Edward the Second. Eventually, he had a set that ran down six centuries, pausing at every reign, beginning in 1066 with the accession of William the Conqueror and ending in 1603 with the death of Elizabeth the First. The monarchs after her he considered less interesting.

Well, except Victoria, a remarkable woman who, like Elizabeth, gave her name to an era. He had a beautiful uncirculated crown coin from Victoria's reign, which he kept separate from the others, both because of the centuries-long gap between her and Elizabeth and because it was a "milled" coin, not a hammered one.

But now, having gone to coin shows at which the Minnesota coin dealer Lief Davisson had a booth, and seeing Davisson's remarkable offerings of British coins, both before and after the centuries covered in his own collection, he was thinking of expanding. He noted that if he went back just a few kings, from the Conqueror to his predecessor Harold the Second, then to Edward the Confessor, then to Harthacnut, then to Harold Harefoot, then Cnut, who became king in 1016; then forward beyond Elizabeth the First to the present queen, he would have a thousand years of English coins, a lovely round number.

To a collector, the hunt is even more engaging than the collection. Finishing a collection is satisfying, but it can be almost a letdown, too, and generally leads to the start of another, or at least endless upgrades of the individual coins. Here was a chance to build on a collection he had seemingly finished.

Toward his new goal, Rafael had signed on to an online auction Davisson was holding, hoping to win a good-looking Cnut he had on offer—and a superior Edward the Confessor. He booted up and went to the auction site.

There were excellent pictures of the many coins in the current auction, as well as the years they were minted (if known) and where. He scrolled down past the ancients to the medieval.

There he found coins dating back to before England was united into a single kingdom in the tenth century, back when kings had names like Sigehere and Egbert, and whose portraits were sometimes hard to identify as human. Reaching at last to England as a kingdom, Rafael found no one had raised his bid on the Edward. There was a Harold the Second being offered, but the portrait wasn't very good—Rafael insisted on good portraits—and besides, the price was already beyond what he was willing to pay.

Harold was king for less than a year before he was defeated at the Battle of Hastings in 1066, seriously altering the course of English history. Harold was a Scandinavian, and William the Conqueror, French—sort of. William was Duke of Normandy, a dukedom so named because it was settled by Northmen, or Vikings. So in a way, England ended up with Scandinavian rulers anyway, though by the eleventh century all of Normandy had become thoroughly French.

There was also a James the First, Elizabeth the First's successor, being auctioned. Among his few achievements,

James had introduced the custom of milled coins—made by a machine rather than struck by a hammer one by one, the blank round held on the die by a nervous apprentice. Just as you could tell a blacksmith by his burn scars, you could tell a medieval coiner by his crooked fingers.

Rafael found the coin uninspiring, perhaps in part because he found the king himself uninspiring. Okay, James had summoned the committee that wrote the King James Bible. But he also was responsible for the torture of witches and had a number of embarrassing personal defects.

Still, if Rafael wanted to complete the expansion, he was going to have to get a James the First. And then Charles the First, Cromwell (ugh!), Charles the Second, James the Second, William and Mary, Anne, George the First, Second, Third, and Fourth, William the Fourth, Victoria, Edward the Seventh, George the Fifth, Edward the Eighth, George the Sixth, then the current queen, Elizabeth the Second, the longest reigning monarch in English history. That admirable woman would put a nice finish to the collection. Eighteen coins—but all more common than the medieval ones, and getting more and more common as they approached the twentieth century.

Godwin had once asked Rafael how he kept track of all those kings and queens, and Rafael proudly recited a Victorian schoolboy's mnemonic rhyme that listed them from William the Conqueror to Victoria:

Willie, Willie, Harry, Stee—
Harry, Dick, John, Harry three,
One, two, three Neds, Richard two,
Harry four, five, six, then who?

Edward four, five, Dick the Bad,
Harries twain, Ned the Lad,
Mary, Bessie, James the Vain,
Charlie, Charlie, James again,
Bill and Mary, Anna Gloria,
Four Georges, William, then Victoria.

Then all he had to remember was Edward, George, Edward, George, and Elizabeth. But Rafael could not have told, for a million dollars, why he, a Spaniard by birth and an American by adoption, was so fascinated by British history.

Chapter Eighteen

◆ ◆ ◆

THE next morning, up in her apartment, Betsy found a reply to one of her e-mails. It was from a Howard Whiteside.

Hello, Ms. Devonshire, it began. *I am Harry Whiteside's oldest son. I am in Wayzata to make final arrangements of his estate, and to oversee the police investigation of my father's murder. I am the executor of his will. Are you a police detective? Your name is not familiar to me. Is this an interview we can conduct by e-mail? Or Skype? Or even old-fashioned telephone?*

But he did not give his phone number, so she e-mailed him back.

Hello, Mr. Whiteside, she typed. *I understand how busy you must be, and how sad an occasion this is for you, so thank you for your prompt reply. I am not associated with the police but an independent business owner who occasionally does private criminal investigations. I have been asked to look into a pair of murders that happened within a few days of each other in the area around*

Lake Minnetonka. One of them was your father's. It is possible that two different people are responsible but also possible that they are the work of a single individual. I would take it as a great personal favor if you would care to talk with me, however briefly.

She concluded by offering details about the shop she owned and giving the hours it was open and its phone number. She re-read the e-mail a couple of times, corrected a typo, and clicked Send.

When she went down to the shop fifteen minutes later, the phone was ringing.

"Crewel World, Betsy speaking, how may I help you?" she answered.

"Seriously? Cruel World?" demanded a man's voice, a light tenor with a little pleasant sand in it.

"Yessir. Perhaps you have the wrong number?"

"Are you Betsy Devonshire?" he asked.

"Yes, I am. Are you Howard Whiteside?"

"Yes. But Cruel World?"

"Oh my gosh, I didn't put the shop's name in my e-mail! It's crewel, C-R-E-W-E-L. It's a kind of needlework."

"Ah, I see. And you're also a private eye."

"No, I don't have a PI license."

A little sarcastically, "Oh, so you like to mix a little crime into your knitting."

"Sometimes. Reluctantly. It's a wild-card talent I often wish I didn't have. Murder is a very unhappy event."

"You got that right. Things are upside down around here, and I'm having all kinds of problems dealing with not just my father's business affairs but the fact that he was . . . murdered."

"It's an incredibly painful thing to have happen, I know.

116

My sister was murdered. The unfairness of it, the mess of trying to wind things up, the unexpectedness of it making your own life complicated—it's hard, very hard. I'm sorry this has happened to you."

There was a little pause, while he estimated the accuracy of that statement. Then, "So why are you poking your oar in?"

"Because someone has asked me to. As I said, it's something I have a talent for."

"I wish the local cops did. They're like from a comic book."

"Real cops are rarely from a comic book. I take it you're not happy with the official investigation?"

"I am not!"

"Why is that?"

"They all know who did this. They just lack the guts to go and arrest him!"

"Which 'him' are you talking about?"

"That jerkface from over your way: Joe Mickels."

"What makes you think that the police are ignoring evidence pointing to Mr. Mickels?"

"He had a motive, didn't he? He's rich, isn't he? He's not under arrest, is he? That triplet of facts speaks for itself."

"Maybe he's not under arrest because there's not enough evidence to make the case. Do you know of anyone else who was in opposition to your father? Because of something he might have done, or said?"

"No, of course not! My father was an honest business-man, well respected in his community."

"I see," said Betsy, and even as she spoke she could tell her doubts rang clear.

There was an icy pause. Then Howard Whiteside surprised her by saying, "All right, what I said is not exactly true. My father was a successful businessman, and successful businessmen have to step on toes now and then to make a buck. But I've been taught it's worse than rude to say something mean about someone who recently died. Plus, he's my father. Double-plus, who can I trust not to repeat anything I may say?"

"I understand, truly I do. All I can do is say that I'm trustworthy. I could give you some names of people to ask about me—but you don't know them any more than you know me."

"And so here we are, Mexican standoff—right?"

"All right," Betsy said, but doubtfully, because she was pretty sure that wasn't the definition of a Mexican standoff.

"Somebody's at the door. I'll call you back later." *Kuhlick.*

GODWIN was late. She wasn't too worried; sometimes he didn't show up quite on time—and he was always willing to stay a little late to compensate. When he finally came in that morning, he was grinning so broadly she began to be nervous for his mouth.

"Are you all right?" she asked.

"Yes, oh yes, I'm all right, I'm more than all right, I promised myself I wouldn't say anything until you asked, thank you for asking, I'm engaged!"

"Engaged? You mean to be married?" She was smiling herself.

Godwin was nodding over and over, short little nods, bob, bob, bob. He came and took her hands in his. "Isn't it wonderful? He asked me last night, just popped the question out of thin air! I couldn't believe it, I can't believe it, my face hurts from smiling, but I can't stop it, I'm engaged to the most wonderful man in the world!" He was dancing a kind of jig. His face was pink, his eyes shining. He had buttoned his shirt wrong. He'd missed a spot shaving.

She pulled him in for an embrace. "I'm so happy for you!" she said.

"We're going to be married in June next year, an indoor wedding. Will you be my matron of honor?"

"Hey, Goddy, are you sure?" Betsy looked flustered. "I mean . . . me? I'm not gay."

"Of course you. You're my best friend—except for Rafael, of course. And you're such a level head, maybe you can keep me from turning the wedding into a three-ring circus. I mean, I started planning last night, and I think Rafael is already scared. It's okay that you're not gay, nobody's perfect. Except Rafael, of course."

Moved to tears, Betsy hugged Godwin again. "Then of course I accept. I'm honored. You're the sweetest man I know. Except for Connor, of course."

He laughed, delighted, and did his famous "Singin' in the Rain" dance step, arms holding an invisible umbrella out in front of him, around the library table.

"I didn't get an e-mail about this, Goddy," she said when he'd made two circuits and stopped to breathe. "Who else have you told?"

"No one, I wanted you to be the first. Except Rafael told

his family last night. Or was it already early this morning there when it was last night here?"

"I'm sure they will be very pleased for him," said Betsy.

That dashed cold water on Godwin's ebullience. "Well . . . probably not. I'm pretty sure they've been holding on to the last shreds of hope that he would marry—not me, of course—and produce a son to carry on the family name. He's the only male of his generation, and they really do not want the name to die. They can trace their line back six hundred years, you know. And there are knights and earls and dukes and even a king or two in their lineage, I think. He doesn't care, he hardly talks about it, but it's terribly important to them."

"Oh dear."

"Do you know his grandmother actually suggested he marry a woman and keep a boyfriend on the side?"

Betsy nodded. "I think he mentioned that once, a long time ago."

"And she's the reasonable one."

"Oh *dear*! Maybe he shouldn't have said anything until after the wedding."

"I told him that, but he's got this honor thing going—can you imagine, honor among a family group like that?—and said it was the right thing to do."

"Well, it's his family, perhaps he knows best."

"We can only hope."

Apart from intermittent sighs and giggles on Godwin's part, the day went as usual. Howard Whiteside did not call back.

*   *   *

CONNOR and Betsy were preparing for supper. He was building a very elaborate omelet around a pair of pork chops, and she was setting the table. They were anticipating a quiet evening at home, so she put out the wineglasses.

"So Mr. Whiteside never called back," Connor called out from the galley kitchen.

"Well, he didn't say he'd call back today," she replied, inserting a napkin in an embroidered fabric napkin ring.

After they sat down, they used up the wine making first elaborate and then increasingly silly toasts to Godwin and Rafael and their amazing (probably) wedding.

They were just wrapping up dinner when the phone rang. Connor took the last of his wine in a single gulp ("And to their all-girl band," he said) and went to answer it.

"Hello?" he said, and after a pause, "Yes. Just a minute." He turned to Betsy, who was gathering up the dishes, and said, "It's for you. Hector Whiteside."

"You mean Howard," she said, coming to take the receiver from him.

"He says Hector."

"Hello?" she said into the receiver.

"Hello, Ms. Devonshire. Am I interrupting anything?"

The voice sounded different than Howard's, deeper, with a slight drawl. "Who is this?" she asked.

"I'm Heck Whiteside, Howard's brother."

"Oh, are you in town, too?"

"No, Howie called me. We agreed I might be the better one to talk to you. I'm flying out tonight, to Minneapolis."

"Just to talk to me? We're talking now, saving you a trip."

"I prefer face-to-face whenever possible. And I need to come anyway. Ham will fly in day after tomorrow."

"Ham? Oh, Hamilton."

"Yeah, cute nicknames we ended up with, Howie, Ham, Heck. Our parents obviously weren't thinking clearly when they named us."

Betsy chuckled politely, not sure whether the complaint was sincere. "I'd like to meet with one or all of you, if that's possible."

"It's possible, maybe. But I'm not sure if we can be of any help. We're not exactly a close family. Plus, I'm not sure Ham will go for this. But I'm with you; I think it might be a good idea."

"HAM, Heck, Howie," said Connor later from his side of the bed. "What a collection of names! How can parents do that to their children?"

"I don't know. Some of them aren't thinking of nicknames—I mean, Hamilton is a great American name, Hector a famous ancient Greek hero, Howard—Howard, hmmm, I don't know any famous Howards."

"There's Thomas Howard, a man famous in fifteenth-century England. His niece was Catherine Howard, who married Henry VIII, although that didn't turn out so well."

Betsy chuckled. "And on thinking further, there's Howard Hughes, Howard Hawks, and Ron Howard, from television and the movies. Or maybe Howie's named after a grandfather, or uncle. He's the oldest, so that's not unlikely. And then his parents went with that custom of giving each of their kids a name starting with the same letter of the alphabet."

"I see that none of the brothers live in Minnesota. What kind of information from them could be useful? What can they know about their father's business dealings?"

She said, "I want to know what kind of person Harry Whiteside was. I'm looking for the kind of personality that creates enemies. These three have probably known Harry Whiteside longer than anyone. I'm hoping they're perceptive and willing to be honest with me."

"Two—count 'em, two—big requests of this trio. I wish you luck."

"Thank you." And despite being excited at the prospect of really digging into Harry Whiteside's personality, Betsy quickly drifted off to sleep.

Chapter Nineteen

❖ ❖ ❖

"EVERYTHING is closed in London today," Connor remarked over breakfast Friday morning.

"What for, spring break?" Betsy replied, dipping into her Rice Krispies topped with canned peach slices.

"No, because it's Good Friday."

"I thought England was no longer a Christian country," she said, surprised.

"As long as the Church of England is the state religion and the queen is Defender of the Faith, schools and many stores close on Good Friday, Holy Saturday, and Easter Sunday."

"Wow," said Betsy, after a moment, because for all that America was a Christian country, stores were open the entire Easter weekend, at least in part.

"You're a Christian," he said.

"Is that a hint?" she asked, smiling.

"The weather report this morning is for unseasonably warm weather under clear skies."

"If we were to close Crewel World for religious reasons, we should go to church."

"I intend to, from twelve to three. The morning is for walking from Minnehaha Falls to the Mississippi and back again."

"I'm going to redesign the front window with Godwin to reflect summer patterns, and design the ad for the Big Bang July Sale. We've got to do something to recoup the bad sales we've suffered the past four months."

The first three months of any year at Crewel World were slow, but this year, for some reason, sales had been alarmingly poor. And despite the two good days of fourteen so far in April, they hadn't fully rebounded from the slump. Politicians had been insisting the economy was recovering, but evidence of it in Betsy's shop had been lagging. The fall and winter hadn't been too bad, but once Christmas was over, the bottom—while not exactly falling out—had been steadily drifting downward.

Easter was late this year, falling on April 16. Easter marked the start of spring, which generally brought in advance a noticeable uptick in sales. But that wasn't happening. Where was everyone? Had all of Betsy's customers moved south? It had been a hard winter, after all.

No, customers had been coming in, but fewer in number, and they just weren't spending as usual. Mrs. Hardy, for example, hadn't bought the materials for another pattern that would need expensive finishing.

When Betsy went down to open the store, she found Godwin impatiently waiting. "What's up?" she asked.

"Two things. First—" He held out his left hand. His

ring finger was newly graced with a fat gold ring set with a large, red cabochon stone.

"Oh my goodness!" said Betsy.

"I can't afford anything like this to give him for an engagement ring," he said a little sadly. Then he brightened. "Still . . . It's a real ruby!"

"It's beautiful, congratulations!" She took his left hand and looked more closely at it, a massive chunk of gold, elaborately worked in an antique design, and a startlingly large stone red as fresh blood. "Gosh, Goddy, I bet your hand will get tired carrying that thing around."

He smirked. "I'll have to start eating my Wheaties every morning."

"So, what's the other thing?"

"I've got a couple of ideas for the window."

"Good, let's get opened up and you can share them with me."

They turned on the lights, made an urn of coffee—Crewel World offered a free cup of coffee to any customer—and put on the electric kettle so there would be hot water for anyone who preferred tea. They put the start-up cash in the drawer, turned on the computer, and tuned the Bose radio to a soft jazz station. They did a walk-through to make sure the shelves were stocked and in order and dusted. Then, since the kettle hadn't started to sing, each pulled a Diet Pepsi from the little refrigerator in the back and sat down.

"So what's your idea?" asked Betsy. He had two, actually. One of them was a Fourth of July theme: "Skyrockets of happiness! Explosive bargains! Shooting star designers! Like that."

Betsy nodded. Little wonder Godwin had chosen something exuberant. "I like it, but we'll have to come up with another idea for after the Fourth."

"Well, yes, that's right. But that leads to my second idea. So we'll keep the Fourth and then have something else so the summer window doesn't start to look tired. I'm thinking we could call it Summer Under the Stars? Showcasing our best and most popular designers."

"Now that I like, it's a follow-on!" said Betsy. "Okay, let's start pulling patterns for the Fourth. There's that red, white, and blue butterfly, the eyeglasses case kit that's a flag, the patriotic Jim Shore angel, the E Pluribus Unum eagle."

"There's that sampler that says 'O Beautiful for Spacious Skies,'" said Godwin. "That needs to go in the window for sure. It's really pretty."

"And so for the Summer group, let's use Lizzie Kate's Sweet Summer booklet," said Betsy. "And keeping up the star theme, there's Flag of Stars from Bent Creek." That one was a simplified American flag made of red, white, and blue stars.

"Ooooh, good, we can feature that in the newsletter when we announce the Summer Under the Stars sale."

When Connor came in a little before noon, he found them at the long table scattered with patterns and models and notebooks covered with sketches. Betsy looked up to see he was smiling. "A nice walk?" she asked.

"A pretty walk and too early for mosquitoes," he said. "Now, can you abandon all this and come to church with me?"

"I would, but I can't. Mrs. Phillips called, and she wants to place a special order for a canvas."

"Goddy can take the order."

"Mrs. Phillips doesn't like Goddy," said Betsy, casting a compassionate look at Godwin, who raised his hands in a what-can-you-do gesture.

"You could tell her you won't serve her until she changes her attitude," said Connor.

"And end up like that bakery that refused to bake a wedding cake for a couple they disagreed with? Not a chance," said Betsy.

"Ah so," said Connor. "Sorry, fellow," he said to Godwin and, "See you later," to Betsy, and he went out. Mrs. Phillips was nearly eighty, hard to please, and chronically tardy. After she had finished placing her order, Betsy, fasting, spent the third hour in Excelsior's Trinity Church listening to readings and music until the lay reader declared, "It is finished."

GOOD Friday in the Christian religion memorializes a shocking, painful, sorrowful, "precious" event. But it's an event, something happening to make a big change in the world. "Sorrowing, sighing, bleeding, dying," predicts one of the Three Kings at Christmas.

Connor, usually not able to keep a Christian calendar while at sea, nevertheless often found himself during those years inquiring of God if He please could see Himself taking care of Captain Connor, his crew, and his ship when the seas were high, the sky dark, and the wind a massive, roiling presence. "O God, Thy sea is so great and my boat is so small," he often pointed out.

So now in safe harbor for good, he was glad of a church nearby where he could offer thanks for the fact that he had never been shipwrecked, or taken by pirates, or cheated by owners.

He and Betsy sat patiently through the reminder of the terrible three hours that Jesus had endured on the cross, and they came away mildly downhearted at the end.

He was glad that Betsy, this strong, warm comfort of his later years, would join him for part of it.

Of course, there was another big event coming, the polar opposite of Good Friday: Easter Sunday. But first, of course, there was Holy Saturday, a day the Christian world sat with its pensive head down, sorrowing, waiting. It's possibly the longest day of the religion for believers.

BETSY closed on time Saturday afternoon and shared a light supper with Connor. Then they shortened the wait for Sunday by setting off for Saint Mark's Episcopal Cathedral near downtown Minneapolis around seven ten, arriving just at seven forty to find parking already at a premium. It was a clear, chilly evening.

The church was unlit, but there were people, lots of people, gathered inside. And more coming.

It was dark out, or as dark as a big city gets at night. And dark inside. The big stained glass windows were barely visible shapes in the brick walls of the cathedral, the saints depicted indecipherable. Betsy and Connor found seats about halfway up the center aisle. An usher waiting at the door had given them, like everyone else, a slim, unlit taper with a cardboard collar and a bulletin with the order of the service printed in it, which they could not read in the dark.

At eight, a hush of garments was heard at the back, and heads turned as the congregation tried to make out who was gathering there and not coming forward. Then a click and a gout of yellow flame rose out of a pale stone about twice the size of a football, a stone that hadn't been there in the middle of the floor before. By its light people could be seen, perhaps a dozen of them, in ecclesiastical robes. One of them lit a long, fat candle at the flame and then from it, smaller candles young people in white albs were holding.

The acolytes came forward to light the tapers of the people in the back pew, who in turn lit the tapers of the people in front of them, who handed the flame forward until everyone had a lit candle, two hundred and more dots of yellow filling the nave with very soft, warm light.

Meanwhile, the Dean of the Cathedral was reciting, in a carrying voice, prayers about Christ passing from the darkness of death into the light. When everyone had a lit taper, a deacon raised the big candle and called, "The Light of Christ!" and the congregation, now reading from the bulletin by the light of the tapers, responded, "Thanks be to God!"

The group of priests, deacons, and acolytes at the west door started forward and up past the choir to the altar. As they processed, a member of the choir floated, a capella, something exotic and mournful in Latin. Gregorian chant, thought Connor, half closing his eyes in pleasure.

The hymn ended, and, having reached the altar, the

Dean turned to the congregation and proclaimed, "This is the night when Christ vanquished hell, broke the chains of death, and rose triumphant from the grave!"

Then a woman from the congregation made her way to the lectern on the left side and turned on a small reading lamp. She read from Genesis about Adam and Eve in the Garden. She was followed by three more lectors, all men, who read about Abraham, ordered and then stopped from sacrificing his son Isaac; then about the Jews crossing the Red Sea out of slavery in Egypt; and last, about Ezekiel telling of God turning from anger to bless his people.

The readings weren't long, but by the end Connor noticed his taper was becoming short, and he saw Betsy adjusting the collar on hers down to the very bottom.

The last reader was still making his way back to his pew when every light in the church came on, the organ blasted a mighty chord, and the Dean shouted above the uproar, "Alleluia, Christ is risen!"

The reader staggered in surprise, then laughed at himself and joined with everyone shouting in reply, "The Lord is risen indeed! Alleluia!"

And, accompanied by the organ, the choir broke into "Glory to God in the Highest."

Betsy's was not the quietest voice giving the reply, and Connor looked a little sideways at her. But she merely grinned back at him and blew out her taper, so he blew out his.

The candles on the altar were lit during all this, and there followed an Episcopal High Church Eucharist service, without a sermon, and with lots of familiar joyful and triumphant hymns. By ten o'clock it was over, and the altar crew stood at the door to shake the hands of the congregation as they left. Betsy noticed several women in large and elaborate hats. She turned to Connor. "I wish I had consulted with Cherie about an Easter bonnet for me."

"Please do next time," he replied. "I'd like to see you in one."

"You have to promise not to laugh."

"Oh, well, in that case, never mind."

They shook half a dozen hands and went out into the chilly night's nippy breeze to find Betsy's Buick. She wove it expertly through the crowd of departing vehicles, and they started up I-394 for home. While driving, Betsy remarked, "I've always felt a little sorry for people who celebrate Easter without suffering through Good Friday. You really need the contrast to get all the flavor."

"You wish they would just stay home and eat a marshmallow bunny instead?"

"No, it would be unkind to wish that. For a long while I was a Christmas and Easter Christian, myself. But it's much more thrilling to glory at someone rising from the grave when you first grieve at His dying."

"Kind of like celebrating spring without first suffering winter," agreed Connor.

"And Mardi Gras loses some of its meaning if you don't follow it with Lent."

"Well . . ." said Connor, "that's doing it backward. First the joy, then the repentance."

"I wonder if that's how the person who murdered Harry

Whiteside feels. Bang, slash, steal, wreck, then Harry walks in and the intruder smashes him on the head, in an exhilarating whirlwind of rage. But in his cooler moments the next day . . ."

"I hope so," said Connor grimly. "I truly hope so."

Chapter Twenty

❖ ❖ ❖

ONE of the rewards of going to the Easter Vigil service on Saturday night is that you can sleep late on Easter Sunday while still feeling virtuous. Connor and Betsy read and stitched through what was left of the morning, ate a debauched lunch of hard-boiled eggs and jelly beans, then spent the afternoon with Jill and Lars and their three young children. Lots of talk, a couple of silly board games, a walk along the lakeshore with Bjorn the big black Newfoundland, and a nap for the children. Dinner with them was ham, sweet potatoes, and Brussels sprouts, with creamed corn only for the adults and children who ate at least one brussels sprout (Einar was caught feeding his to Bjorn the dog and so was disqualified). Then they all watched *Easter Parade*, starring Fred Astaire and Judy Garland. Erik and Emma Beth thought the best part was Judy Garland walking down the street making a really horrible face.

*   *   *

ON Monday, Bershada came into Crewel World with
Alice. Both carried stitchery bags, ready for the weekly
Monday Bunch meeting.

Bershada was speaking. "Girl, you would not believe the
talking-to my aunt Sadie gave my daughter a month before the wedding! Backed her up against the wall! Put her
finger right up to her nose and said"—here Bershada's voice
changed to a thin old black woman's Southern drawl—
"'Ef you don' straighten up an' fly right, child, ain't nobody
comin' to this wedding, 'cause I'll call Pastor Rivers an' tell
him it's *off*!'" Bershada laughed. "And she could have done
it, too, because my daughter had moved the wedding from
her own church to Aunt Sadie's church because her own
church was 'too small, and not fancy enough.'" Bershada
had assumed a high, breathy voice with a nasty undertone
to it when quoting her daughter. Then she broke again into
laughter.

"Her own church is beautiful. Small, yes, but beautiful.
I grew up in that church—so did she. The pastor married
her father and me. He baptized her, and loves her like a
daughter. But the church was too small for my daughter's
big fat wedding."

Bershada threw a hand up in the air. "Children! Betsy,
you are so lucky you didn't have children! They break your
heart!"

Betsy smiled. There were days when she was sure Bershada was right, but today wasn't one of them, not after she
had spent a blissful Sunday afternoon and evening in the

company of the three Larson youngsters, who were sunny and charming the whole time. "In a week or two, you'll change your mind," she said.

"Humph," snorted Bershada, going to the library table. Alice trailed behind, her face sad. An elderly widow, she had lost her only child many years ago to a heart ailment.

Betsy said, "Bershada, I want to tell you that you have a remarkable son. I was so impressed with him at Maddy's funeral. And he was extremely helpful to me over supper the other night. I'm so glad you sent him to me."

Bershada sat down and pulled out her counted cross-stitch project of two kittens frolicking on a stack of books. "Yes, he's turning out to be my pride and joy. And I suppose in a month or two I'll forgive my daughter for her antics."

Alice said to Betsy in her deep voice, "So you are getting involved. On whose behalf?"

"Joe Mickels."

Alice blinked three times at Betsy, her mouth open in surprise. "Joe Mickels? Why, is he offering you half his kingdom?"

"No." Betsy smiled, taking a seat at the table. "What would I do with half a kingdom? What would half a queen look like?"

"Amateur night at the Gay Nineties?" suggested Godwin. The Gay Nineties was a downtown Minneapolis nightclub that offered a female impersonator competition once a month.

Betsy looked at him, laughing. "Hush, baby, we're trying to talk."

He sniffed and went back to pinning up some new needlepoint canvases on the set of hinged fabric "doors" hanging on a wall.

Alice said, "I assume Joe came to you because he feels he's a suspect in Maddy's death."

"And in Harry's."

"What, both of them?" said Alice.

"Mike Malloy thinks the two might be related."

"Ah, because of the property bidding war on Water Street."

"That's right."

Bershada said, "I should think Joe would be too busy coming up with a defense for when Mike arrests him to complain about his methods."

Betsy nodded, leaning sideways to pull out her current project: a counted cross-stitch pattern of nine young trees stitched in black and dark gray on white Aida fabric. She'd found the project for sale for two dollars in Leipold's eccentric shop on Water Street. The pattern, floss, and fabric were in a plastic bag, but without the original packaging, so there was no title or designer's name. One tree was finished, one was about half done, and one had just the back stitching. The rest was blank fabric. Stark and graceful, it was lovely. Mrs. Leipold said, "I hope you can finish it— and I hope you'll bring it back here when you do, because I'd like to buy it from you." Mrs. Leipold had a good eye for beauty but was not a stitcher.

Betsy bought it because she agreed it was beautiful, and she was working on it because, since the placement of Xs to indicate leaves was pretty much random, any mistakes she made were invisible. Usually counted cross-stitch made her tense; here she could relax.

Alice, preparing to continue her project of crocheting a prayer shawl for her church, arranged her yarn in her fingers and said, "I keep remembering what Emily said about seeing Joe just sitting in his car looking sad."

Betsy said, "You know, I think I saw that same sadness on his face when we talked. He's a hard man, but he seems pretty sure he's going to be arrested. And that may be making him sad."

"He shouldn't be sad, he should be scared," said Bershada. "Suppose he didn't murder Harry and Maddy. If someone else murdered both of them, then he may be next in line."

The thoughtful little silence that followed that statement was interrupted by the door's announcement of someone's entrance. Today Godwin had set it to play a chorus of "Mairzy Doats," which made Alice chuckle, since she remembered the silly song from her youth.

They all looked to see Jill Cross Larson come in. A tall, sturdy, beautiful woman with ash-blond hair and a Gibson Girl face, Jill worked in an admin capacity at the police department, where her husband was a sergeant. So they all were especially pleased to see her, because maybe she had news of the investigation.

"Good afternoon, everyone," she said after a pause, surprised at their intense interest in her arrival. Then she came to the table and sat down.

"What news?" demanded Godwin.

"About what?" she asked.

"The investigation into Maddy's murder, of course. Is Mike going to arrest Joe?"

"I don't think so, not right now." Everyone could see Jill was avoiding eye contact, uncomfortable with the topic.

"Do you know something we're not supposed to know?" asked Alice in her blunt way.

"No, of course not."

But as others arrived—Phil and Doris, Emily, Cherie, Valentina, Connor—they also asked. Jill, sensibly aware they hadn't already heard her uncomfortable reply, simply repeated it.

When the last arrival took his seat, Godwin said, "Let's all agree not to talk about Joe Mickels today."

"No, don't shut down the talk," objected Jill. "I just won't have anything to contribute."

"Why not?" asked Emily, pausing in the act of threading her needle. Unconsciously echoing Alice, she asked, "Do you know something we shouldn't find out?"

"No," said Jill. "But I have an 'in' with the police, so I shouldn't say something that might be misconstrued."

Betsy remembered a time when Jill had carelessly said something to her that broke a police department confidence and got them both in trouble as a result. Doubtless Jill remembered it, too.

To distract them from the topic, Jill said, "On the other hand, I'm dying to hear Goddy tell us why he is wearing a vulgarly large ring on the third finger of his left hand." Of course she already knew; Betsy had told her at the Easter Sunday dinner.

Godwin, delighted that someone had asked about his ring, came to the table to flash it at everyone. "I'm engaged!" he cried, rapturously. "Rafael asked, and he gave me this ring. It's a family heirloom!"

"Wonderful!" "Excellent!" "Congratulations!" "Brilliant!" "Good for the both of you!" went around the table.

"When's the happy event?" asked Alice.

"June. We haven't picked a site yet; all we know is that it won't be a church wedding and it will be indoors—I do not want to stand shivering in a downpour while we exchange vows and the cake gets washed away."

"That practically guarantees it will be a gorgeous day," said Doris, and the others agreed, laughing.

"You're all invited. We'll be sending a save-the-date postcard, of course. Meanwhile we're on the search for a venue we both like and will reserve the date for us." He pressed the back of his gold-heavy hand to his forehead. "So many details, so little time!" he sighed and went back to pinning up needlepoint canvases.

Doris said, "Goddy, you were such a help to me planning my wedding. Please let me help you plan yours in any way I can."

Godwin looked thoughtfully at her. His "help" for her wedding had been to make it bigger, less modest. Might hers, therefore, be to tone his down?

Betsy watched his face parade those thoughts across it.

"I think that's a lovely thing for you to do, Doris," she said. "I suspect Rafael might think so, too."

Amusement broke out on Godwin's face. "Oh, Betsy, you are so right! You should have seen Rafael's face when I talked about releasing a hundred doves dyed lavender! And so, Doris, I accept your offer. Let's you and me get together some evening soon."

"Just let me know when," Doris said, pleased.

"Isn't Goddy just the nicest person?" said Emily. "I'm so happy for him." She turned in her chair and smiled at him. He winked at her.

Then Betsy changed the subject. "Emily, did the refinance of your house go through?"

"Yes, it did. We decided to keep the mortgage payments the same size, but the house will be paid for six years sooner. We're so pleased!"

More congratulations passed around the table.

Betsy said quietly, "Bershada, I'd like to talk with you privately after this meeting, all right?"

Bershada said, "Of course."

Cherie asked, "Is your daughter safely away on her honeymoon, Bershada?"

"Yes, the long nightmare is over, thank God."

"Is she the last one?" asked Doris.

"The last daughter. There's still that one son. I'm holding on to hope that he'll find someone soon."

"Don't be too eager," advised Cherie, "you may not like the bride he picks, and daughter-in-law problems are particularly painful, because they last for years and years."

"Hmmm," said Bershada, who was currently suffering from a son-in-law problem.

Phil said, "Betsy, are you still convinced that Joe Mickels didn't murder Maddy?"

"I'm not 'convinced' of anything, except that this is Monday and you are sitting at this table," she said.

Doris reached over and pinched her husband on his ear. "Ouch!" he said.

"Yes, he's really here," she said. She looked at Betsy. "Shall I reach over and pinch you?"

"If you do, I'll reach over and pinch Jill, and who knows where that will lead?" teased Betsy.

Cherie said, "Let the blood sports begin!"

After the laughter, everyone settled into his or her projects for a while.

Valentina asked, "Does anyone know what will happen to the Water Street property now that Maddy is dead?"

Blank looks all around. Betsy held her tongue, but the others began to guess.

Alice said, "I think the fair thing to do is to open the bidding again. Start over."

Doris said, "No, I think they'll hand the deed to the second-highest bidder. That was Joe Mickels, wasn't it?"

"No, I heard Joe came in third; the second-highest bidder was Harry," said Alice.

"So then, since he's dead, too," said Phil, "Joe gets it."

"No, it should go to Harry's son—the one who's come to Wayzata to take over his father's business," said Cherie.

Godwin said from across the room, "Ask Betsy, she knows."

They all looked at Betsy. "Well, as a matter of fact, I did ask Jim Penberthy about it."

"What'd he say?" demanded Valentina. "Which one of us is right?"

"None of you. The right to buy the property belongs to Maddy's estate. The executor of her will can decide to pay the amount bid by Maddy for it, or he—or she, I don't know who it is—can put the option up for sale."

"What's the son's name?" asked Alice.

"What son? Maddy had a son?" said Valentina.

"No, I mean Harry Whiteside's son, the one come to town to clear up his father's affairs."

Phil said, "I'm not sure. Howard, I think."

"He's very upset with the investigation," said Connor. "Thinks there's a cover-up."

"A cover-up? In favor of who?" asked Phil. "Harry was the richest man in Wayzata, if not the county. On whose behalf would the cops do a cover-up?"

Godwin said, "Joe Mickels, of course. I bet Howard's angry because the cops haven't arrested Joe."

"Is Joe richer than Harry?" asked Connor.

"I don't know," said Betsy. "I don't think anyone but Joe knows how rich he is. He doesn't want it known. And I don't know how rich Harry was, for that matter."

"But Joe wouldn't carry any weight in Wayzata, would he?" asked Phil. "His home ground is over here, in Excelsior."

Betsy said, "He has an office in Excelsior, which is his official mailing address. I suspect he has other offices elsewhere."

"Why does he keep all these secrets?" asked Emily.

"I don't know that they're secrets," said Betsy. "He just doesn't advertise his wealth. People with a lot of money can be targets. If he needs to show the power of his wealth to gain something, he'll show it. But otherwise, he prefers to run quiet."

"Sort of like you," said Emily.

"*Me?*" Betsy stared at her.

"Sure. You have a lot of money, but you don't let it show."

"Emily, I am not rich!" Depending on how you defined rich, this was true.

"Sure you are. People say you could give this shop to Godwin for free and never have to work a day in your life ever again."

Godwin said, in perfect imitation of Betsy, "*Me?*"

"Sure, you. Who else would Betsy give it to?"

"Connor, of course," he said.

Connor said, "No, I'm done working for a living. I've got a fully funded pension and some modest investments that provide me rent, food, and the occasional new pair of shoes. I especially don't need to be sole proprietor of a small business that has recently decided to stay open late on Mondays."

Betsy said lightly, "Before we start a quarrel over who wants my business least, may I ask Emily who on earth told her these things?"

Emily blushed and looked down at her needlework. She mumbled, "I don't want to say."

There fell an uncomfortable silence, as several members of the group held the same opinion as Emily about Betsy's wealth but had never been rude enough to say so to her face.

Connor said, "Speaking of money, tell us, Bershada, how much money did the auction take in?"

"Our goal was twenty-five thousand dollars, and we raised thirty-six," said Bershada, chin lifted, eyes shining.

"Oooh, that's smashing!" cheered Godwin.

"Good for you!" agreed Cherie, and the others chimed in with congratulations.

Jill asked Betsy, "When is that Barbara Eyre trunk show going to come in?"

"I'm not sure. It got held up when the show was at Orts Galore in Cincinnati and a flood damaged the shop—and about a third of the canvases. Ms. Eyre is trying to restore some of them and add new ones to the collection. We're hoping to see it in about a month."

Cherie said, "I've heard you people use the word 'orts' before. What's an ort?"

"When you finish stitching with a length of floss," said Bershada. "The little end you snip off is an ort."

Emily said, "I collect mine in transparent Christmas ornaments. They look pretty on our tree, and remind me of finished projects."

The stitchers moved on to other topics and broke up around three thirty.

Bershada gave Betsy a few minutes to put her stitching away. Then she said, "What do you want to ask me about?"

"Maddy. How well did you know her?" Betsy picked up her long reporter's notebook.

Eyeing the notebook, Bershada said, "Not really well. I don't think anyone but Chaz knew her well. But I have—did know her for about seven years, maybe eight. Helen Fasciana started a book club, and Maddy was the third person to sign on. She had some excellent suggestions for what we should read, and she had interesting insights into the books, too. She was a very intelligent woman. But, she didn't like it when someone disagreed with her. We were all relieved when she dropped out after her first year."

"But you reconnected," suggested Betsy.

"Yes, we had become friends—of a sort. I wanted to stay in touch because of Chaz—he sometimes forms attachments to people who can hurt him. But I liked her for myself, too, because she had attitude, and I find people with attitude interesting. She wasn't cruel or dishonest. In fact, she was kind, in a sort of angry way. Always giving money to causes, usually anonymously. For example, the library—she'd write a check for a hundred dollars to me, tell me to cash it and give the money to them and not tell them where it came from. 'Here, take this,' she'd say, shoving a check at me. 'Give it to Trinity's food shelf.' Or, she'd say, 'Here, cash this, and give it to Temple Israel, they're raising money to send some young adults to Jerusalem.'" Bershada shrugged. "I think she didn't want to be thanked. Strange, strange lady."

"I got the impression that she was shy, that day she brought that last box of knit toys in here," said Betsy. "She didn't want people to look at her, put her forward, give her any attention. That's why she objected to your plan to put her in front of the auction room."

Bershada thought about that, then nodded. "It could be you're right. Does that put us any closer to finding her murderer?"

"Not really."

"You know, now you've put the word *shy* into my head, maybe another word for her is *defensive*. But I never heard her complain that someone was being cruel or unfair to her or that someone was angry with her—not murderously angry. Chaz says lots of people were angry with her for business reasons, and that Harry Whiteside was a particular thorn in her side. But is that a reason to kill her? She had no family, so there wasn't someone thinking he or she could inherit her money if only she'd die. Is any of this helpful?"

Betsy sighed. "Not in the way I was hoping."

Chapter Twenty-one

❖ ❖ ❖

I T took some arranging, but Hector Whiteside agreed to meet Betsy for lunch at Sol's the next day. The morning brought a rash of problems. The credit card reader worked only half the time, a customer brought in a painted canvas she'd obviously started and then pulled the stitches out and now she wanted a refund, two part timers called to say they couldn't work next week. Betsy left with a little sigh of relief. The delicatessen was next door to Crewel World, and Betsy went over a bit early so she could watch for him.

A few minutes after twelve a man in his early thirties came in. He was not quite six feet tall, stocky, with curly brown hair just barely covering a bald spot, a pleasant expression on his large, dark-eyed face, and a comfortable way of walking that indicated strength. This was a man who did not spend his workday at a desk. He was wearing a navy blue pullover and dress slacks. The collar of a light blue shirt grazed the sweater at its neck.

Betsy raised her hand, and he smiled affably and came to where she sat at the little table, one of three in the room. The chairs at the table had round wooden seats and wire legs and backs, a charming old-fashioned style, but Betsy wondered if the chair would hold his weight when he dropped onto it.

It did, and without protest. "Hello," the man said. "I'm Heck Whiteside, from Dallas." He did have a mild Texas accent.

"I'm Betsy Devonshire. I'm glad to meet you." She held out her hand, and he took it rather gingerly in his big, calloused one.

"I was shocked and sorry to hear about your father," she said.

"Thank you. But there's more than that with you, right?" he added. "You're interested in how it happened to him."

"And by whom, yes, you're right. I'm at the start of an investigation into your father's murder—into two murders, actually."

He studied her closely, leaning toward her, his mouth pulled a little sideways. Then he came to a conclusion. "You actually think you can find out who murdered my father."

"I think I can. I have done this sort of thing before."

"That's good. So, you have a license, a PI license?"

"No."

His eyes widened in surprise, then his whole face clenched, eyebrows pulling together and mouth pursed. "You're some kind of a goddamned amateur?"

"That's right. Didn't your brother tell you?"

He sat back, but his expression remained angry. "No."

"Nevertheless, I have solved several murders."

"How?" It was a demand.

"I don't understand the question." Was he looking for anecdotes?

"What are your methods? Do you kidnap a suspect and refuse to knit a sweater for him until he confesses?" Now he was teasing her, and not in a nice way.

Betsy held back the angry retort she wanted to make— she had come to this meeting already aggravated. But instead she took a breath and waited for her overheated blood to simmer down. Then she said, "I have been doing this for a number of years, and I have had the support of several current and former police investigators. I do not use force or deception or any illegal method. What I mostly do is talk to people. I look for motive and opportunity. Because I am not a professional, people tend to take me lightly and so give away more than they realize when I talk with them."

"What have I given away?" He was still annoyed but also clearly curious.

"Mostly that you are very angry about your father's death. That is both sad and understandable."

"Only mostly?" he said, eyebrows raised.

"Anger might—might—make you leap to conclusions. You and your brother want a fast, easy solution to this. Since it hasn't come, you and he both think the investigators are incompetent. I think that's why you agreed to talk with me, and why you are so disappointed to find that I'm an amateur, and worse, that I own a sweet little needlework shop. But I'm telling you that perhaps there is more to me than you think, and more to the situation with your father than you would like. Your anger and impatience won't change the facts."

"What are the facts?"

"I don't know all of them, or even most of them. But I want to find out. And I've been asked to find out."

"Who asked you?"

"Why do you want to know?"

"Ha, I bet it's that Mickels person."

"And if it is?"

Again he sat back, convinced and assured, smirking. "Then I won't talk to you. I think he killed my father, and now I think he's convinced you to help him get away with it."

"I think you'll regret that decision."

He leaned forward again and said softly, "I think I won't."

"Very well," said Betsy. She looked around and saw the current Sol—in Betsy's time there had been two previous owners of Sol's Deli, none authentically named Sol—behind the meat and cheese counter. He was looking at her. She called, "I'd like a tuna sandwich on whole wheat, small chips, and a big spear of kosher dill, to go." She looked at Heck. "You?"

And yet again that studying look. "All right," he said, his nod accepting her unspoken offer to pay. "I'll have a chicken on rye." He looked over at Sol and repeated his order, louder. "Chicken on rye! Lettuce and tomato! Mayo! Soup of the day!" He grinned at Betsy. "For here!"

Betsy paid for her meal and his and went back to her shop, her mood not improved by the encounter.

"Uh-oh," said Godwin on seeing her enter. Today the door was playing "With Her Head Tucked Underneath Her

Arm," and she grimaced instead of laughing at the music. "Not a good interview, I take it," he said.

"No, he's too angry to see I'm trying to help." She went to the library table and dumped her white sack on it. "Rats." She went into the back room to make herself a cup of black English tea, refilled the electric teakettle, and when she came back was surprised to see Heck Whiteside standing at the table.

"I'm not apologizing," he announced stiffly. "But hey, maybe I can tell you something useful and you can pass it on to someone competent." He smiled, recalling to her that affable look she'd noted when he first came into Sol's, though now she could recognize the snark behind it. "I'm not a badass," he continued. "I'm just angry. I've got things to do at home, but I can't leave till this is over."

He held up a white paper bag, a copy of the one in front of Betsy on the table. "Okay?" he asked.

"All right," she said, and gestured at a chair opposite the one she was about to sit in.

But before he could seat himself, she turned toward her store manager and said, "Godwin, this is Hector Whiteside, the youngest son of Harry Whiteside. Heck, this is my store manager, Godwin DuLac."

Godwin said neutrally and without moving, "How do you do?"

Hector replied in an echo of Godwin's tone, "How do you do?" and sat down.

"Mr. Whiteside," said Betsy, "would you like a cup of coffee or tea?"

"No, thank you," he replied, pulling a bottle of cranberry juice from his paper bag.

"Goddy, could you go back to the counted cross-stitch section and straighten out the Thanksgiving and Easter patterns?" Two customers from out of town had taken a special joy in finding patterns they hadn't seen before—and pulling them out of the slanted cabinets for closer looks, and dropping the ones they voted against on the floor. Or worse, stuffing them back into the slots any which way, out of order or even upside down. In the end, they hadn't bought enough to make up what it would cost Betsy in Godwin's wages to put them right again.

Betsy could have stayed after closing and done it herself, but she wanted to talk with Hector now, while he had come willingly to her—and she wanted to reassure him that no one would eavesdrop.

"What made you change your mind?" she asked Hector, opening her lunch bag.

He unwrapped a fat sandwich that dribbled shredded lettuce. "I decided to stop letting my anger run my mouth." He pulled a big, squat cardboard cup from his bag, lifted the white plastic lid, and released a gout of steam that smelled of ham and beans.

She pulled out her own sandwich and snack-size bag of chips. The sandwich was wrapped in translucent paper, the spear of pickle visible, laid diagonally on the bread.

"So, where do we start?" he asked, putting the sandwich down on his unfolded napkin and opening the glass bottle of juice.

"Tell me about your father. What was he like as a father? Were you close?"

"Depends on what you mean by close. He wasn't an absentee father."

"Well, did he take you to work with him when you got old enough?"

"Oh, hell, yes. Put all of us to work while we were still kids, gave us a little plastic bucket and had us picking up nails. He started in construction, was a foreman when I was in middle school. As we got older, we were treated like the rest of the help. He played some mean tricks, threatened to fire us three times a week—but never gave us that relief. By the time I started high school I could read a blueprint as well as anyone on the job, including him. All of us could, the three brothers. I liked it, Ham hated it, Howard started making his own blueprints in junior high. Howard's a designer and contractor, has his own company in Pennsylvania building warehouses and big-box stores. Dad tried to hire him to design the building right here in this town he was out to buy, but Howard turned him down."

"How did you find out about his plans?"

"Howard called me to warn me Dad wanted someone to help him with a building. I was primed to say no, but he never called."

"Were you disappointed?"

Heck thought about that briefly. "Kinda. Like the girl who doesn't want to go to the party but is sad she wasn't invited. Except I think I was more relieved. Dad always was a shouter, even to us as grown-ups."

"He must have been pretty confident he was going to win that bid if he contacted Howard ahead of time."

"He always thought he'd win—and he usually did. Dad was brilliant at acquiring property and making a profit on a build, but he was hell on wheels to work with. He used to knock me down when I made a mistake on the job, even after I was as tall as him. As soon as I graduated from college I moved to Texas, and this is the first time I've been back in Minnesota since then."

"You didn't come home for Christmas or Thanksgiving?"

"No. My wife included him on our Christmas newsletter list, but that was about it."

"Was he a crook?"

He grimaced at her plain speaking but then shook his head. "I don't think so. I'm sure he skated close to the line, and if he did cross it, I don't think it was deliberate. He was pretty sure people were out to 'do him,' as he put it, so he'd get mad, or excited, and push back, sometimes sneaky, sometimes hard, sometimes first. But his—and my—line of work is tough. It's not a place for the meek of the earth."

"How is your business doing?"

He paused to slurp a noisy spoonful of soup. "Okay. We're okay. Not that an infusion of cash wouldn't come in handy right now." He shrugged and admitted, "Damn handy."

"I suppose the lead investigator in Wayzata has checked your alibi?"

He put down his plastic soup spoon so firmly the handle cracked. "What kind of a question is that?"

"Come on, Heck, it's a question anyone with an IQ number above room temperature would ask. You could use the money, and you were not on loving terms with your father."

He said, just a little too casually, "So you actually think I flew up here one afternoon, murdered my father, and flew back the next morning."

"It's possible. Did you?"

"Hell, no!" He picked up his spoon, saw it was broken,

and put it down again. He said in an exasperated voice, as if he'd already said it several times before—as doubtless he had, to the Wayzata investigators—"I was, and am, working on a job, converting a high school building into condominiums. I talked with my foreman, an electrician, a plumber, and an interior designer, all of them on the day and into the evening that my father was murdered, went home to my wife, then first thing the next day I fired the plumber. Okay?"

Betsy, smiling, nodded. "Sounds good to me. Especially the plumber."

"Why the plumber?"

"Because he isn't a friend and so is not likely to lie for you."

The affable look settled again on his face. He nodded once. "Yeah, I see what you mean. And you're right, he was royally pissed."

"Who else was—to borrow your phrase—'royally pissed' at your father?"

"I don't know. I hadn't talked to Dad for three or four years, not a real conversation."

"You said your wife sent him a Christmas letter every year. Did he send one to you?"

"No. A card, yes, one of those commercially printed ones with a photograph of him smoking a cigar while seated in a big leather chair. Even his signature was printed. Two years in a row, the same card. They're cheaper if you order five hundred of them."

Betsy nodded. "Yes, I know. I order and send them to the suppliers and designers I like, and my most loyal mail-order customers."

Heck nodded. "We used to do something like that, but it got expensive, so we quit."

Betsy said, "Would your brother Howard perhaps know who had recently been caught up in some shenanigans or manipulations by your father?"

Hector thought about that while he ate his sandwich. Then he nodded. "Maybe, maybe." He gave her a wry smile. "We brothers don't talk to one another very much, either."

"Is Hamilton coming to Minnesota?"

"Yes, but I'm not sure when he's arriving."

"If Hamilton hated construction, what did he go into?"

"He first became a real estate agent down in Florida. The turnover down there is pretty brisk, you know."

"Yes?"

"They call it God's waiting room for a reason."

"Oh. Yes, I suppose that's right."

"Then after he married he went back to college and became a lawyer. He specializes in construction litigation."

"I'm not sure what a construction litigation lawyer does."

"You hire him after you move into your new building and the roof leaks or the windows fall out or the furnace sets your place on fire. He'll sue the builder for you." He raised his eyebrows significantly.

"So he, more than Howard, might know if your father had been subject to litigation that left him or a client angry."

"Maybe. Like I said, I don't know."

"Could you tell him and Howard that I'd like to talk to them? And that I don't bite?"

He chuckled, picked up the cardboard cup and drank a big mouthful of his soup. "Yes, I will do that."

"Do you smoke?"

He looked down at himself. "Why, do I smell like it?"

"No, but maybe you use e-cigarettes."

He nodded. "I've thought about trying them. But it was too hard to quit the real thing, and I suspect it would be just as hard to get out from under the vapor."

"How long had your father smoked cigars?"

"For as long as I can remember."

"How about Ham, or Howard?"

"I don't think so. No cigarettes, either, as far as I know. What's this interest in smoking?"

"I'm just poking around. I never know when an innocent question will give me a solid lead." Betsy had no reason to tell him she'd reconnected with a hospital pharmacist named Luci Zahray whose nickname was the Poison Lady. Luci had told her that boiling just three cigarettes in a small pot could extract enough nicotine to kill the average adult.

Chapter Twenty-two

❖ ❖ ❖

Doris sat at the dining room table in Rafael and Godwin's attractive condo overlooking Lake Minnetonka. Daylight savings time had been instituted, so instead of darkness, there was a deepening sunset washing over the lake. The view from the windows was to the north and east, so the sun was out of sight, but the colors were muted pastels with a bright flash here and there as a ray of sun caught a wave.

"The first thing you want to do is pick a venue," said Doris.

"No," said Rafael, "the first thing we must decide is how much we can afford to spend."

"If it were up to you alone," said Godwin, "we'd have a quick little ceremony down at the courthouse in Minneapolis and dine afterward at Subway."

"Actually, you are not far wrong," acknowledged Rafael.

"But if it were up to you, we'd have a destination wedding in Paris and a honeymoon in Barbados."

"Oooooh, Barbados," sighed Godwin. "But not Paris. Even your French is not up to their standards, and we'd waste too much time trying to get what we wanted—and end up in some dingy café full of cigarette smoke and cheap wine fumes."

"Are same-sex marriages legal in France?" asked Doris.

Godwin blinked. "You know, I have no idea."

"Yes, they are," said Rafael. "But I don't want to get married in France. Too close to Spain, and my family might choose to come and spoil things."

"You're right, you're right, you're absolutely right!" said Godwin with a shudder. "Nowhere in Europe, then." He looked at Doris expectantly.

"I suggest, since you want all of us to come, you plan on a wedding right here in Minnesota. You've already decided against a church wedding, so next you need to think about whether you want something formal, like in a ballroom setting, or something kitschy and fun like a resort, or something casual like a barbeque, or something truly unique and maybe a little edgy." Doris looked from one face to the other.

"Not edgy," said Godwin, and Rafael nodded. "I see lots of tables in a big room with a high ceiling and tall windows, dark blue tablecloths and silver candles and filmy blue curtains hanging from the ceiling—you know, looped up, with fairy lights inside them. Live music. Buffet dinner with at least three entrees for two hundred guests."

Rafael said, "I see forty guests at two long tables, white

tablecloths with little bouquets of flowers up and down them, and a little table for just the two of us, waiters serving game hens and a really nice cabernet wine."

Doris wrote all this down. "This is not going to be easy, is it?" she remarked dryly. "But you're talking reception. What about the ceremony? Do you know who should perform it?"

"It would be a hoot to get a rabbi, wouldn't it?" said Godwin. "Then I'd get to stamp on a glass at the end."

Doris said, "Be serious."

"All right, sorry. I don't know any judges, Raff, do you?"

"Well, one is a member of the coin club. His name is Franklin Noel. Do you remember him?"

Godwin thought. He'd been to a couple of meetings, trying to share Rafael's interest in numismatics. "What does he look like?"

Rafael pondered this, trying to pick his words carefully. "Tall, thin, very pale complexion, delicate bones in his face, an air of refinement. Wears a bow tie, and on him it looks good."

"Oh yes, I remember him! He'd be gorgeous presiding, don't you think? He's so classy, though, we'd better have a classy wedding."

"Would you mind a 'classy' wedding?" asked Rafael.

"I think it would be adorable!" He turned to Doris. "Write that down. A classy wedding, tuxedos all around. And Judge Noel presiding. He'll be perfect!"

"What if he says no?" asked Doris.

"Oh." Godwin looked crushed briefly, then brightened. "Then let's do it at a farm, in a barn, and have a hoedown reception!"

An hour later Doris went home. She had sixteen pages of notes and not one thing decided.

"I'm not strong enough to do this," she said to Phil. "Herding cats is nothing to those two, especially Goddy."

M ALLOY'S questions about how someone might gain access to the yarn that poisoned Maddy had made Betsy think. It wasn't just that some people had keys to her basement—who among them might have wanted Maddy dead? Plus, this person must have had access to nicotine. Did anyone she know meet all three conditions?

No.

Therefore, it was much more likely that the yarn was poisoned at Mount Calvary.

"Really?" said Connor when she shared this conclusion with him. "Maybe there's someone with a key you don't know about. Or, maybe there's someone with a motive you don't know about."

"Well . . . yes, that's true. I suppose I'm doing a sketchy investigation right now, looking for the obvious, hoping to get lucky and short-circuit a complex, lengthy investigation."

He nodded. They were sitting in the living room, having turned off the latest episode of something they'd been watching, finding the series had wandered into silly, stupid, even obscene territory. Their conversation was desultory, as each was focused on a needlework project.

Connor asked, "Do you still think Joe Mickels didn't commit the murders? Or should I say murder, as I suppose it's possible he only poisoned Maddy."

"I think that if I find out he murdered one of them, then he'll have murdered both of them. From what Jill told me of what Lars told her—third hand, I know—the house was trashed by an angry person, and Maddy was killed with nicotine. Joe has a terrible temper and owns stores that sell nicotine products."

"A 'perfect storm' for an investigator," said Connor.

"Maybe if I can establish a very narrow window for when the yarn could have been tampered with, and Joe can establish an alibi for that time, we'll be in good shape to bring it to Mike." She put her stitching down to think. "First, I have to find out if anyone's missing a key to the basement, or thinks it might have been copied, or will admit she—" (both of Betsy's current tenants were women) "—left the basement door unlocked."

"And that fact was somehow advertised," said Connor wryly.

"Well . . . yes, I guess so. But one thing at a time." She checked her watch. It was not quite 8 p.m. "I'll go ask right now."

She was back forty minutes later. "I'm going to have to come up with a different form of security!" she griped. "There are at least six keys missing, two of them basement keys. Whenever one of them loses a key, she goes next door and borrows the other's and makes a copy. Bad enough they're doing it with the basement keys, but three of them are to the back door! Now I have to have the whole place rekeyed. What's the matter with these people? Why didn't they come to me?"

"How old are they?" asked Connor, though he knew the answer.

"I'm not sure. Kit's probably twenty-four or twenty-five, and her husband's the same. Jenna's even younger, maybe twenty-two."

"In today's world, they are practically children, and so they act like it."

After a moment's reflection, she said, "You know, you're right. What were you doing at Kit's age?"

"At twenty-four? I was just promoted to second mate on a freighter operating in the Mediterranean. I'd been at sea for six years."

"Six—? Then when did you go to college?"

"At the same time, off and on. I got my degree mostly through correspondence courses. I think I spent less than a year actually on campus. I believe I've mentioned all the spare time a sailor has at sea. No lassies, no pub crawls, no rugby or football—pardon me, soccer—no bright city lights. So you have to do something to keep your brain from turning to pudding."

"And we think getting a degree via Internet courses is the newest thing."

"There is nothing new under the sun, *machree*."

THE next morning, Friday, down in the shop, Betsy called Kari Beckel at Mount Calvary, found she was on vacation, and so asked for Helen Bursar—who had an amazingly appropriate name. "I'd like to come and see you, today if possible," she said. "It's about Maddy O'Leary's death at the auction."

Helen, who with Kari ran the business side of the church, said, "I'm sorry, Ms. Devonshire, but I've got meetings scheduled all day today and into the evening."

"Could I buy you lunch?"

"Well, my brief lunch engagement was just canceled, so yes. But could you bring it here? I've only got half an hour, twelve thirty to one."

"Salad okay if it has chicken on top?"

"Fine. And thank you."

Helen Bursar's office was off the big round atrium that was the center of the church hall, behind the greeter's desk. Betsy carried an insulated bag just about big enough for two plates of Asian chicken salad in peanut sauce with crispy noodles on the side, and she'd brought a liter bottle of diet ginger ale as well.

In anticipation of her coming, Helen had cleared half her desk and pulled an armchair up to it. She was a small, thin woman with thick, dark, curly hair, pale skin, and hazel-green eyes. She was wearing a pale green wool dress with a silver brooch and dangly silver earrings, each with a violet iris on it.

"So nice to meet you, Ms. Devonshire," she said, standing and coming around her desk to hold out her hand. "Sergeant Larson has said nice things about you."

That's right, thought Betsy. Lars was a member of Mount Calvary Lutheran, though his wife, Jill, went to Trinity Episcopalian. "I'm glad to hear that," said Betsy. "You have an amazing musical program here, and such a beautiful church hall."

"Thank you," she said. "Now, won't you sit down and tell me why you need to talk with me?"

Betsy unzipped the insulated bag and brought out the covered plates. A delicious odor wafted from them. From her large purse, she brought out the ginger ale. "I hope you have cups or glasses. I forgot to bring them," she said.

Helen had coffee mugs on her credenza and, surprisingly, real silverware. "Those plastic forks are just not adequate, I find," she said. "So I borrowed these from our kitchen."

In another minute they were tasting the thin slices of chicken breast and crunchy greens. "This is good!" said Helen.

"I like the Wok," said Betsy. "Their food is delicious. Now, to business. You know Maddy O'Leary died right here in your atrium the Saturday of the auction. It turns out that someone poured pure nicotine onto the ball of knitting yarn that was in her bag. None of the other six knitters' yarn was poisoned, and each bag was marked with the user's name, so whoever did this was very likely after her.

"The yarn was poisoned long enough ahead of time that it had dried, so she didn't notice anything wrong with it. It's possible that the poison was put on it while the bags were stored in the basement of my shop, but there were several conditions necessary for that to happen. I am thinking it much more likely to have happened here."

Helen nodded while nibbling on a crisp noodle. "Sergeant Malloy was here yesterday. He seems to be thinking along the same lines you are."

"Where were the bags kept here at the church?"

Helen gestured toward the door to her office. "Here in the hall, right next door to me—it's a room where janitorial supplies are kept. We put the bags in there so they'd be handy on the day of the auction."

"Is that door kept locked?"

"Yes, always."

"Who has the key?"

"Our maintenance man has one, I have one, Kari has a master key that unlocks every door at Mount Calvary, Pastor Royale has another master key . . ." She paused, then nodded. "That's all." She gave a little start. "Oh, wait, that door was left unlocked from the day of the Lenten music performance, because we weren't sure when Ms. Reynolds was going to bring those bags over. And so of course it was still unlocked the day of the auction so the bags could be brought out for the seven people who'd be using them. That was such a clever idea, having those winning toy makers knitting up front during the auction."

"The door to the church hall wasn't locked when I came. Is it always unlocked?"

"During regular office hours, it is. Or when there are special events held here, like the Thursday before the auction. And we had a reception after the performance here in the hall."

"Did a lot of people come to that?"

"There were close to three hundred people in attendance."

Betsy said despairingly, "I don't suppose you kept a list of the people who bought tickets to the program."

"No, but while we don't have cameras in the church, we do in the atrium. Three of them."

Betsy's heart perked up. "Could I look at the videos?"

"I'm afraid not. Sergeant Malloy took them away with him."

"Did he look at them while he—and you—were here?"

"He started looking at one, just to see how clear the picture was. He said they were pretty good."

"Did they show anyone going into the room where the bags of yarn were being kept?"

"I didn't see that—but we only watched a few minutes of the video footage."

"Did you recognize anyone?"

"I sure did. A lot of the people who came are members of Mount Calvary."

"Do you know Joe Mickels?"

Helen thought about that for a few seconds. "He's not a member, is he?"

"I don't think so. But his appearance is distinctive: short, stout, white hair, big old-fashioned sideburns?"

"Oh yes, I saw him, on the video Sergeant Malloy was looking at. He froze the picture right about then and said he wanted to take the discs away. As evidence, he said."

"So," said Betsy, "things are looking dark for Joe."

Godwin stood silent, frowning.

They were in Crewel World. They should have been laughing and high-fiving each other, as the customer who had just left had spent nearly a thousand dollars on a hand-painted needlepoint canvas and the silks and wool necessary to stitch it. Instead they were baffled and having to rethink things.

"I think we should call Joe and warn him," said Godwin.

"It's probably too late for that," said Betsy.

The phone on the checkout desk rang, and she answered it. "Crewel World, Betsy speaking, how may I help you?"

"Is this Ms. Devonshire?" asked a man's voice.

"Yes?"

"I'm Nurse Amos Brighton, at Hennepin County Medical Center in Minneapolis. We have a patient here who has asked me to contact you on his behalf."

Betsy's first thought was a terrified, *It's Connor!* "Who—who is it asking for me?"

"His name is Joseph Alan Mickels. Do you know him?"

She pulled the phone away from her ear and stared at it.

Godwin asked, "What is it? What's the matter?"

She waved him off and said into the phone, "Yes, yes, I do. What happened? Why is he in the hospital?"

Godwin gasped and began waving a hand to draw her attention, which she ignored.

"He has suffered a gunshot wound."

"Oh my God! Is it serious? How did it happen?"

"What? What? What?" demanded Godwin, but she put up a shushing hand toward him.

"Are you a relative?" asked the nurse.

"No, just a friend."

"I'm afraid I can't discuss the details with you, in that case. You'll need to contact a relative."

"Can he have visitors?"

"Since he asked for you, yes, in perhaps another hour."

"Why did he ask for me, do you know?"

"No. I'm just the messenger."

"Well . . . thank you," Betsy said and hung up.

"What, what, what?" demanded Godwin.

"It's Joe. He's been shot. He's downtown at HCMC. No further details available."

"Joe? Oh, that's wonderful! I thought it was Connor!"

She sat down heavily behind the big desk and thrust her

fingers into her hair. "No, it's not wonderful! Don't you see? I think in my heart I wondered if maybe Joe did it, that he's a murderer. But I was wrong. Here's proof I was wrong."

"So what now?"

She leaped up. "What's the matter with me? I've got to go see him."

Chapter Twenty-three

❖ ❖ ❖

B ETSY took Highway 7 to I-494 to 394 downtown, frantically searched for and finally located a parking spot, then found her way to Joe's room in the hospital. But once there she had to wait until someone else finished talking with him. She strode impatiently up and down the hallway outside his room. Finally, she saw the door open and Mike Malloy come out looking angry. Well, sure: His case against Joe had just been blown away. He gave her a curt nod and strode off down the corridor.

She took a deep, calming breath and let it out, then took another. She felt the tension in her shoulders ease and opened the door. Joe's bed had lifted him to a sitting position. He was pale as a ghost, with dark shadows around his deep-set eyes. He seemed very interested in the pale green wall opposite his bed until she realized he wasn't really seeing it. He was taking rapid, shallow breaths.

He was wearing a hospital gown that draped over only

one shoulder. The other was covered with a thick bandage that ran far down his chest. The head of his bed was entirely surrounded by differently sized monitors clicking and beeping, reporting blood pressure, pulse, oxygen levels and God knew what other bodily functions. A kind of abstract metal tree rose over his bed, and from it three fat plastic bags hung, two clear and one dark red. Tubes ran down from them into his left arm and the back of his hand. A translucent tube of an alarmingly big diameter came out from the bandage and dripped a slobbery red into an oblong glass jar marked off in centimeters.

"Hello, Joe," she said softly, surprised into compassion.

"Huh. Took you . . . long enough," he muttered weakly.

"I came as quickly as I could. What on earth happened?"

"Visiting my e-cig store . . . in Uptown, a . . . bandit came in . . . shot me."

"Just like that? He just walked in and shot you?" She came closer to his bed.

"No, no, course not," Joe said, vaguely annoyed. "It was a stickup. I tell my employees to . . . just hand over the cash . . . when . . . armed robber comes in, don't . . . fight. So Liza put up hands, an' I put mine up . . . He took the cash, fired once in the ceiling, then . . . shot me."

"Why? Did he say anything?"

"Said, 'Oh, it's you . . . effer.'"

Effer? Then she realized he was using a euphemism for a very bad word. "So he recognized you, and shot you on purpose. Thank God you're not dead!"

He gathered himself and said, "If God was really on my side, he would've made the dickhead miss altogether." Joe smiled, just a little, at scoring a point. His face began to take on a look more like the fierce old eagle he normally resembled.

Betsy changed course. "I assume Sergeant Malloy was here to get a description of the robber."

Joe rasped, "Hell, no, this happened . . . Minneap'lis. Talked to Minneap'lis police. Mike came to see . . . 'f this man was after me." He glanced up at her, saw her incomprehension, and said, "Third one still standing."

"Oh, so he sees it, too. Harry, then Maddy, then you. What do you think?"

Joe sighed twice, then coughed very feebly, which clearly hurt him so badly that he laid a hand gently on the big bandage, and closed his eyes. After a few moments, he said, "Think . . . 'bout it. Someone so desperate . . . kill three people to get th' property? But . . . proves himself killer when . . . closes on't. Have to sell it to pay lawyer." Joe smirked crookedly. "Stupid."

Betsy should have thought of that. "You're right, of course. So why did he shoot you?"

Joe put his head back and closed his eyes. "I don't know."

"Did you recognize him?"

"Couldn't. Wore black nylon stocking over . . . head."

"Still, what did he look like? Was there anything familiar about him? Could he have been someone you know?"

Joe's eyes didn't open, and after a wait, Betsy began to think he'd fallen asleep. But then he said, softly, "Stocking mashed . . . face, crooked." But then he frowned, thinking. He continued, even more softly, "He didn't talk ghetto, but I think . . . Gotta peek at 's wrist, and t'skin . . . very dark.

So . . . maybe . . ." He did stop then, and his breathing gentled into sleep.

"Thanks, Joe. I'll let you rest now."

"So where did this happen?" asked Connor, who had come down to the shop after Godwin called him with the news, and waited there for her to return, appalled at this turn of events.

Betsy said, "At his store in Uptown."

"So not a high-crime area."

"No, not particularly."

Godwin put in, "A fun place to go for entertainment."

"Yes, I remember," said Connor, looking at Betsy with a smile. The two of them had gone to Uptown once for an Asian fusion dinner and salsa dancing.

Godwin said, "Um."

Betsy turned to him and said, "Something else?"

"Yes. Did you hear about Maddy's will?"

"No. I assumed she had one, but don't know its terms. I didn't know she had a will. What about it?"

"This is rumor, so if it's entirely true or not, I can't say. But I hear she left all or most of her property to Chaz Reynolds."

Betsy felt a great sinking of her heart. "Oh dear."

"What, aren't you happy for him?" asked Connor.

"Joe Mickels thinks the person who shot him was a black man."

"Stop it!" whispered Godwin, awed. "But wait, no, Betsy, not Bershada's boy! He wouldn't, he just wouldn't!"

Connor said, "This is very bad news—if it's true. I wonder if Mike knows yet."

"Who told you?" Betsy asked Godwin.

"Leona, over at the Barleywine. I went there for lunch."

"Who told her?"

Godwin was clearly surprised by the question. "I didn't think to ask," he said. "She said it like"—he paused, then made a pretty good attempt at imitating Leona's matter-of-fact voice—"'Chaz Reynolds is gonna party like it's nineteen ninety-nine. Maddy O'Leary left him all her worldly goods.' She didn't say it like it was a half-assed rumor but like it was really true. I said, 'Good for him, putting up with her for years like he did,' and she laughed and went to bring me my sandwich."

"I wonder where Leona got that piece of information," said Connor.

"I could call her and ask," said Betsy. Suiting action to words, she pulled out her cell phone, found the Barleywine number, and pressed Dial.

"Leona," she said a minute later, "how did you find out about Maddy's will?"

"By eavesdropping," said Leona. "Mike Malloy was in here with Chief Haugen yesterday, and when I brought their sandwiches I heard Mike say he had talked with Maddy's attorney, who said Chaz was the 'principal legatee' who got most of the property but hardly any of the money. The money is divided in half, one part going to the Golden Valley Humane Society and the other going to the First Baptist Church of Minnetonka." Leona chuckled. "It took me a minute to get the order right and then again when I was putting it on the table so I could overhear all the details."

"So pretty close to the horse's mouth," said Betsy. "Thanks, Leona."

"I've got a beer tasting coming up next month, on the fifteenth. Tell Connor to mark his calendar."

"Will do. Bye." Betsy hung up and relayed Leona's announcement about the beer tasting to Connor.

"Ah," he said, pleased. "I hope she's brewing that spring ale she had last year."

"Betsy," Godwin broke in, anxious to get back to the subject at hand, "are you seriously thinking that Chaz is a murderer?"

"I find it hard to think so—and I dread what Bershada is going to do if Malloy comes after him. But Malloy . . . I don't know. He liked Joe a whole lot for this, but now Joe's in the hospital, shot by someone who may only have been pretending to be a robber."

"Coincidences do happen, *machree*," Connor pointed out.

"Is it a coincidence that of the three bidders on a piece of property, two are dead and one is in the hospital with a bullet wound?" asked Betsy.

"Well," said Connor, "it rather depends on who winds up with the property. Is it some fourth person who was squeezed out of the bidding early on?"

Godwin said, "Also, each one of them was hurt in a different way. One was bashed on the head, one was poisoned by nicotine, one was shot. Is that how murderers work?"

"No," said Betsy thoughtfully. "I've read in several places that if criminals find a method that works, that's what they keep using. It's called an MO, modus operandi, and detectives use it to track career criminals."

"But on the other hand, it's kind of hard to think you're trying to track three different criminals," pointed out Connor.

Betsy threw her hands up in the air. "I know, I know," she said. "Is it one, two, or three people? This is really frustrating!"

Betsy decided she had to learn where someone could get nicotine. The most obvious way, of course, was to buy it in e-cigarette stores.

Connor volunteered to go out and gather information in one of those stores, and perhaps buy a sample or two of the nicotine mixture.

After he left, a woman came in to order finishing for her counted cross-stitch pattern, a "summer montage" that featured a slice of watermelon, a seashell, an ear of corn, a rose blossom, a birdhouse (with bird), a beehive, a straw hat, and other summery items in realistic colors set in squares and rectangles. The result was complex and attractive. It was one of a set of four montages—the others were autumn, winter, and spring. Mrs. Hardy had done the others; this was the last. Each had cost her a little over thirty dollars for the pattern, Aida fabric, and floss, but now, like the others, it was going to cost her nearly two hundred dollars to get it properly finished.

"You want it like the other three?" said Betsy, writing the order. "Washed and stretched, laced, plain three-quarter-inch white mat, two-inch-wide gold frame, right?"

"Yes," said Mrs. Hardy. "I get so many compliments on the spring one—just like I did for winter and autumn. I so appreciate your suggestion that I display just one at a time, so my eyes don't get tired of seeing them."

"You're welcome. This should be ready in three weeks. Any idea what your next project will be?"

"Godwin signed me up for that hardanger class you're offering. I've always wanted to try it. You do hardanger, don't you, Betsy?"

"I'm afraid not. I've taken three classes in it, and so far I've got one half finished bookmark and a strong determination not to try it anymore. But you do such beautiful, intricate counted cross-stitch, I'm sure you'll have no trouble with hardanger."

"Well, we'll see, we'll see."

A few hours later, she and Godwin were closing up shop when Connor entered. He had two small plastic bags hanging from one hand and was smiling.

Without saying a word, he upended the bags on the library table. Eight or nine bottles of different opaque colors with squeeze-nipple tops rolled out: orange, green, red, yellow. Godwin hastened to keep them herded together. Betsy stooped to pick up a midnight blue bottle that had gone off the edge of the table.

Blue Ox Vapor, the label read. On the side of the label was stacked a series: 0mg, 6mg, 11mg, 18mg, 24mg, each with a pale blue dot beside it. The 24mg dot had a black dash inked onto it.

"They come in different strengths," said Connor, seeing her looking at the list. "If you'll look at the others, you'll find one at thirty-six milligrams. That's the strongest blend you can buy. But hear this: That strongest mix would still be only two point four percent nicotine."

"That's all?" said Godwin, picking up the red bottle. "Not even a measly two and a half percent?" He put it down and picked up a yellow one. "Yeah, this one's thirty-six milligrams." He turned to Betsy. "Would that be strong enough to kill someone?"

"I don't know," said Betsy, and she asked Connor, "What did they tell you at the store where you bought this?"

Connor said, "When I bought the thirty-six milligram, the salesclerk warned me that if I spilled any on my hand I should wash it off right away. I asked what might happen if I didn't, and he said it would soak through my skin, and if I spilled a lot, like half the bottle, my fingers would start to tingle, and my heart would go flippity-flip, and I'd get a bad headache. I said, then what? I'd fall down dead? And he laughed and said not a chance. You can't buy a deadly dose of nicotine in a vape shop, he said."

"Well . . ." said Betsy. She put her hand out, fingers open, and waggled it back and forth. "I'm sure he's been told that. I'm also sure that if someone has a weak heart, he might be fatally stricken, or if a toddler drank a whole bottle, she might die." She put down the Blue Ox bottle and picked up two more. "Strawberry flavor," she read aloud, and she unscrewed the bottle to take a sniff. "Alice is right, this smells delicious," she noted with a grimace.

"Did Maddy have a weak heart?" asked Connor.

"I don't know—but I don't think so. She certainly never acted as if she was in fear that her heart was about to quit."

"You got that right," said Godwin with a grim smile.

"So we're back to Joe Mickels?" asked Connor.

"Why?" asked Betsy. "If a customer couldn't buy a lethal dose of nicotine, why would you think Joe could?"

"Isn't it possible he was mixing his own brand of vapor liquid? As a wholesale purchaser, doesn't he have access to things the general public doesn't, such as pure nicotine?"

"You ask good questions," said Betsy. "How about we do some research this evening to see if we can find answers?"

Godwin said, "I can do research, too, please?"

Betsy smiled at him. "All right, good idea. How about you and Rafael research Harry Whiteside from a business angle? How much was he worth? What properties and companies did he own or control? What did the people who worked with him think of him? But poke gently; don't step on anyone's toes, especially if they work for the Wayzata police."

Godwin snatched up a ballpoint from the checkout desk and began writing down Betsy's instructions: ". . . people who worked with him," he concluded, nodding. He looked up at Betsy. "And don't step on toes," he added with a grin.

Seeing a hint of mischief in his eyes, Betsy said, "Godwin, this is important. If you screw up—" She looked across at Connor. "If any of us screw up, we may irreparably harm innocent people."

"Yes, you're right, of course," said Godwin. "We'll be careful. I promise."

Chapter Twenty-four

◆ ◆ ◆

CHAZ was waiting at the door to Crewel World Monday morning. He was standing under a black umbrella—it was pouring rain—and was wearing a dark blue suit, dark red shirt, and silver tie.

Betsy unlocked the door and invited him in. "You look terrific!" she said.

"Thanks." He half closed his umbrella and shook it out the door, scattering redundant raindrops onto the sidewalk. He brought it back in and leaned it against the wall. "I've got a meeting with a lawyer this morning. I wanted to let you know, if you haven't heard already"—he grimaced against the probability that she had, given the reach of the Excelsior grapevine—"I'm inheriting a great deal of property from Maddy."

"Yes, I had heard. Not in any great detail, though," she hinted.

"Two large apartment buildings in Minneapolis," he

said, holding out one hand and pressing down on the fingers as he counted, "a corner grocery store with two apartments above it in Saint Paul, a building in Hopkins that's an empty store and a hair and nail salon on the first floor with four apartments on the second floor, two houses here in Excelsior, three houses in Wayzata, a dry cleaner and a lumberyard in Golden Valley, a gas station–mini mart in Minnetonka, and . . ." He had to pause and think. "That little set of three row houses over on North Water Street!" he concluded triumphantly.

"That's a lot of property, Chaz," Betsy said. "But they're spread out all over the place."

"Yes, I know," he said, "but I've already been managing most of them—some of them for a long while. I know the tenants, I know the problems—like the row houses need new roofs, and one of the apartment buildings has plumbing that seems to date back to the Civil War. And taxes? Whoosh! I've been telling Maddy we may have to raise the rents—I mean . . ." Suddenly, he looked near tears. "Dammit," he muttered as he struggled for control.

"Oh, Chaz, this must be at least as hard for you as it is good news." Betsy reached to touch him on the arm.

"Yes, it is. I mean, you're right. One part of me is celebrating because I'm actually rich, independently wealthy, and another part of me would give up any chance to own any of it if only Maddy would come storming into the office and chew me out for not getting the estimates for those roofs collected yet."

He drew a ragged breath. "But done's done. Mom said you wanted to ask me something."

Betsy turned away, pain gripping her heart. Chaz's distress

was palpable. How could she ask him a question that would add to it?

"What, what's the matter?" he asked. "Go ahead, tell me what it is. I have to get going. I have to be in that law office in forty-five minutes."

"All right." She turned back around. "Where were you on Friday afternoon?" The day Joe Mickels was shot.

"Oh jeez, you, too?" The words were jesting, but there was anger in his eyes.

"I guess the police have already asked you that."

"Damn straight." He took a calming breath. "Mom and I were on Skype with my sister Leeza, who is on her honeymoon in Key West."

Betsy was delighted and threw her arms around him. "Oh, that's so wonderful! Thank you!"

He didn't hug her back. "You're welcome. Now I gotta go." He made a sound that could have been a laugh, turned on his heel, scooped up his umbrella, and left.

Betsy called Excelsior's City Hall to see when she could get a peek at Maddy's will and was told it did not become public property until probate was complete, which would take at least four to six months, maybe longer.

A while later she sat down with Godwin at the library table. Betsy had her long notebook out, and Godwin had a small, fat spiral notebook in front of him. Each had a mug of tea.

"Okay, whatcha got?" asked Betsy.

"Harry Whiteside was a very rich man, his total worth somewhere around twenty-five or thirty million, maybe more. He owned property in four states, but primarily in Minnesota. He did big jobs and small ones. His last small one was at the University's hazardous waste disposal facility, replacing the pipes in the fire-extinguishing system. His last big one, which isn't finished, is building an industrial park up near Mille Lacs.

"He wasn't a crook—not legally. But there are people angry with him, some so angry that they've filed lawsuits against him. There have been four lawsuits in the past three years, and he won them all—he has a very good law firm on retainer. But his last lawsuit was a dilly."

"Who sued him?" asked Betsy.

"His son Howard."

Betsy stopped writing. "Howard? Are you sure?"

"Absolutely." Godwin handed over several multipage printouts and a screen shot.

It took Betsy, no economics whiz, a while studying the documents to understand what had happened. Harry had approached Howard to design an industrial park near Lake Mille Lacs in central Minnesota. Early in the negotiations, Harry asked Howard for some preliminary drawings. Howard complied—and Harry promptly turned them over to another contractor who signed a contract for thousands less than Howard was going to charge. The contractor's mistake was in making his plans too obviously derivative of Howard's drawings.

Howard saw the online advertising for the park and promptly sued. But Harry's law firm, through a feat of legerdemain Betsy couldn't quite understand, got the case dismissed "with prejudice," which meant Howard couldn't find another court to bring the suit in for essentially the same offense.

The screen shot was of an article from a Scranton, Pennsylvania, newspaper about an "outburst" in a courtroom where a hearing had begun in the lawsuit. Major fines were imposed on all parties, the heaviest on Howard and Harry Whiteside. "Objects were flung and a chair was broken," wrote the reporter.

"I'm surprised Hamilton and Hector didn't know about this," said Betsy.

"I guess if you move to different parts of the country and deliberately don't stay in touch, this sort of thing can happen. For example, the headline reads that the lawsuit was brought by Stonebridge Design, Incorporated. It's possible that the other two brothers didn't know Stonebridge was Howard Whiteside."

Betsy looked back into the papers. "Yes, Howard incorporated under that name only two years ago. So that would make it possible." She nodded to herself as she began to write a note. "It looks as if we have another motive for murder right here."

"So what did you and Connor find out?" Godwin asked.

"Even as the owner of an e-cigarette store, Joe couldn't buy pure nicotine. Only the factories that have a use for it, like making insecticides or bottling the flavored diluted nicotine, can buy the pure stuff. University medical departments and research labs can buy it, too. But not members of the general public, even if they sell vapor liquids. It's like buying cyanide or arsenic; you can do it, but you need a license, and a good enough reason to get a license, like working as a scientist in a research lab."

Business at Crewel World began its comeback that day. Seven customers came in that morning, five of them determined to buy something new, something complex, something challenging. Betsy and Godwin sold three hand-painted canvases to one regular, two to a man neither had ever seen before, and two to Jill Cross Larson. They sold two Dazor lights, four pairs of Gingher scissors, twenty-six cards of overdyed silk floss, three dozen skeins of cotton floss, six spools of Kreinik metallic, four packs of needles, three pairs of magnifying glasses, several yards of Aida cloth in eleven, fourteen, and eighteen count, and nearly a yard of Cashel linen. The rush of customers was so great that Betsy had had to call in a part-timer. By noon the cash drawer was plump and the charge card reader was, in Godwin's words, "smokin'!"

Bershada came in right at noon and said, "Betsy, may I take you to lunch?"

Godwin said, "Go, go, go! Milly's here, and I'm so pumped, I can handle anything."

"All right," Betsy said.

Bershada left her needlework bag under the library table, for when she'd return for the Monday Bunch meeting.

The rain had made the sunlight sparkle as if on a new-made world. The air was fresh and cool and smelled of new green growing things. Lake Minnetonka, across the street, twinkled blue and silver. A robin was in full song from near the top of a budding tree.

"Times like this, I forgive Minnesota for its winters," said Bershada as they crossed the street at Lake and Water—they were heading for the Barleywine.

They paused inside the door. Bershada had set a fast pace, and Betsy was a little winded. The place smelled strongly of beer (it was a microbrewery), cooked meats, fresh-baked bread, and steamed vegetables, with subtle undertones of herbs—Leona grew her own and used them generously in her recipes.

The floor was flagstone, a little uneven under their feet. A long bar to the left was made of dark carved wood. Behind it were slabs of clear glass, and behind them were the tall steel "kettles" that held the several brews. On the right were three booths left over from when the place was a simple country café, and at the back was a low counter and three stools; the Barleywine now had Wi-Fi for customers to use.

Bershada led the way to the back booth, slid in with a sigh, and said, "Chaz called me on his cell."

"Is he angry with me?" asked Betsy, sliding in across from her.

"I think he's not sure. He was upset. He thought you were on his side. I had a talk with him when he came home from court—did you know he's inherited about half of Maddy O'Leary's properties?"

"Yes, he was listing them for me this morning. Houses, businesses, all kinds of things. But he didn't say anything about money. Didn't she leave him any?"

"She didn't need to. Chaz has been putting money aside since he got a paper route in high school. The two of them were on the same page about money. You think Joe Mickels is a miser? Those two could give Joe Mickels lessons—and she gave him some good investment advice. She knew Chaz had more than enough to keep things going until his inheritance started paying off."

"Will they let Chaz continue managing her properties until the estate is settled?"

Bershada nodded. "Yes, and they'll pay Chaz a good salary."

"You said he's getting about half of her properties?"

"Yes, some of the rest are going to her church, some to other charities—who will probably sell them. It's a whole big business, managing properties, and it takes experience they probably don't have. The executors of her will—there are three of them, from a company with the super-imaginative name of Twin Cities Property Management, Incorporated—asked Chaz some questions. One question he couldn't answer, about a bill for window replacement in a cabin up in Pine County. Chaz knew nothing about a cabin, so he couldn't help them with that. He's wondering just how much property she died owning."

Betsy smiled. "Maybe it's half the homes in Duluth. It will be interesting to find out." Her smile faded. "Now for the hard question. Bershada, did Chaz think his race had anything to do with my asking for an alibi?"

Bershada bit her lower lip, then nodded, her eyes sad. "Yes, he took it as a sign of prejudice, which totally knocked him sideways, because he thought you and I were friends. I told him it wasn't prejudice at all, just your desire to get to the truth, but he doubts me."

"Oh gosh, the poor fellow! I couldn't believe Chaz

would do such a thing. It's just that Joe said he thinks the man who shot him was black, and the only black man I know who is in any way attached to this mess is Chaz."

Bershada asked sharply, "Is that true?"

"Yes. Don't you know I don't ask hard questions of people without a good reason?"

"I should know it, but I guess . . . But . . . You'd think this country would have gotten over that racist sickness a long time ago. We're way better than we used to be, but the virus remains, and it will ambush even me once in a while, often enough that I have to keep my guard up,"

Betsy looked sad now, too. "I'm a fixer—you know that. I see a problem, I want to find a solution. It frustrates me that I can't fix this one."

"You are fixing it, you and millions of others, all decent, caring people. I do my part by being decent and caring, too. In the words of the old song, 'We Shall Overcome.'"

Betsy reached out and took her friend's hand.

"Ahem," said someone, and they looked up to see a young man looking back at them, small notepad in hand. "Are you ready to order?"

They looked down at the neglected menus on the table—when had they been put there?

Bershada said, "I want that salad with little shrimps in it, vinegar and oil dressing. Diet Coke to drink."

Betsy said, "That sounds good, but I'd like an Arnie Palmer instead of a Coke."

The young man nodded, made a note, swooped up the menus, and walked away.

The two women looked at each other and laughed.

"Who needs menus when you come in here as often as

we do?" asked Bershada. Then she grew serious. "I know you're trying to prove Joe Mickels is not a murderer—"

Betsy drew a breath to disagree, but bit her tongue instead.

Bershada continued, "But if it wasn't Joe, then who do you think killed Maddy?"

"I don't know. Not Chaz, of course, I never thought him capable of murdering Maddy, but I'm glad he has a solid alibi."

"You seriously don't know who the murderer is?"

"I seriously do not."

O N Tuesday, Rafael and Godwin were in their living room overlooking beautiful Lake Minnetonka—but the view was lost on them. They were listening to their speakerphone setup. It was two in the afternoon, and Godwin had taken a late lunch to offer moral support to Rafael. The Davisson auction was in its final day, and numismatists from around the state were tuned in either by computer or phone. Davisson's actual building was small and remote, so this wasn't the kind of auction that had an auctioneer chanting for raises on bids.

Nevertheless, Rafael was deeply, intensely listening to a quiet voice calling out the raises as he heard them over the phone or read them on a computer screen.

The Cnut coin was next up for bids.

Rafael had rethought the Cnut coin and offered a bid forty dollars above the current bid of six hundred fifty dollars.

Godwin murmured, "Oooh, that's good, offering less than fifty more!"

The voice said, "We now have a bid of six hundred and ninety dollars." But a few seconds later, he said, "We now have a bid of seven hundred and sixty dollars."

Rafael made a face, raised his hands and his shoulders, shook his head, and then relaxed all over. He was done.

After about thirty seconds, the voice said, "Are there any more bids?" and soon after, "Sold for seven hundred and sixty dollars."

"Never mind," counseled Godwin, "there will be another Cnut, better and perhaps for less money."

"Next," said the voice on the speakerphone, "we have the Edward the Confessor penny, York mint, Extra Fine condition. Current bid is four hundred dollars." There was a pause that went on and on, and Rafael started to smile— the four-hundred-dollar bid was his.

But then the voice said, "We now have a bid for four hundred and fifty dollars."

"Ohhhhhh," groaned Godwin.

Rafael grimaced but said, "I'll bid five hundred dollars."

The voice said, "We now have a bid for five hundred dollars."

This time the silence went on for what seemed like several minutes but was just about thirty seconds.

The voice said, "Sold for five hundred dollars."

Godwin said, "Hurray! But you should have said four hundred and seventy-five, Rafael."

"No, because you saw what the forty-dollar raise did. Fifty dollars said I was *serious*."

Godwin shrugged. He didn't understand the subtleties of such things, but Rafael obviously did. Rafael hung up the phone and let out a long sigh.

"You aren't going to bid on the James?" Godwin asked.

"No, I'm spending too much as it is. I need to stop myself before I come up short on next month's association fee."

Rafael was by far the wealthier of the two men, so it was unlikely he could spend a few hundred on coins and be unable to pay May's association fee.

There was a delicate balance between the two on financial matters, because of the difference between their earnings. It was Godwin, with his substantial trust fund, who was currently making the mortgage payments on their condo. By expending a large chunk of money on something as important as their dwelling place, he felt less "kept" by Rafael, who bought most of the food—Godwin did most of the cooking—and paid for the condo's association fee and any upkeep, plus utilities, plus all their taxes and insurance, and took them on most of their vacations. Rafael came from wealth, managed his own investments, and was probably worth three or four times what Godwin was.

It was descriptive of their relationship that either felt free to call for an adjustment of this arrangement if he felt it was necessary.

BACK at work, Godwin found Betsy sorting through an order of floss. He stopped to admire Rainbow Gallery's new colors in the Treasure Braid line, Awesome Gold, Orange, and Pumpkin. Though it was spring outside, these autumn colors made his fingers itch to stitch something in the Halloween line—and actually, it was more than time to start a fall-themed project. Godwin liked complex needlepoint pieces, which took months to complete.

He picked up the Fyre Werks cards of floss in fluorescent autumn colors. Oh my, yes, it was time to pick something for autumn!

He went to the canvas doors hanging on the wall. Wasn't there something he'd pinned up just the other day? Ah yes, here it was, not a Halloween theme but a river-in-fall theme, with colorful trees reflected in the water, the bright reds and oranges mixed with green pine and blue water, and more subtle blending than is usual with needlepoint. Oh yes, this would keep his mind and fingers busy.

Then he looked at a lower corner of the taped canvas and yanked his hand away from the tacks holding it on to the door. Whoa! Nearly three hundred dollars! Even with his employee discount he'd have to give up a couple of outings and that fancy dinner he'd been planning if he were to buy this. Maybe he could find something similar in counted cross-stitch.

He turned away to find Connor looking at him. "Hi, Connor, is there something I can help you with?"

"I want to try to knit a Scottie dog using eyelash yarn. What do you think?"

Godwin considered this. "I love eyelash yarn, the cloud-like effect you get, like whatever you're knitting is set in a fog, all blurred edges. The problem is, sometimes you can't see your stitches after a couple of rows, and you end up knitting by feel. So when you put it down, you can't remember where you left off and you make mistakes. Of course, a lot of the time it doesn't matter, since you can't see the stitches anyway, so if you're doing straight stitch or knit one, purl one, that's okay. But I'd think after that marathon of knitting we did for the auction, you'd be off knitting."

"Yes, you'd think that. But in my case, you'd be wrong. So sell me some."

"Sure."

After the transaction was made, Connor took the little bag of floss and went to talk with Betsy, who was busy incorporating the new threads onto the appropriate spinner rack or into one of the little drawers of DMA and Anchor cotton floss.

"I did some more research on nicotine," he said to Betsy. "It's possible to extract it yourself from tobacco leaves, if you're a chemist with the right equipment. The liquid you get when you boil tobacco, as from a cigar or cigarettes, is deadly, but it's dark and has a very strong odor. You don't have to be in the southern United States to grow it; there are tobacco farmers in next-door Wisconsin, convenient if you want to slip into a field and steal a few leaves—which are enormous, by the way, as big as rhubarb leaves, though longer and narrower.

"You have to obtain a license to buy the pure stuff, and it's difficult to obtain. The University of Minnesota has one, though they were very reluctant to tell me what they use the nicotine for and not at all willing to part with even a small sample of it."

Then he changed the subject. "I'm on my way out to do a little grocery shopping. I'm thinking to fix a British-style curry for dinner, so I need a sharp-flavored apple and a box of golden raisins. Oh, and I love you."

"I love you, too. See if you can find a Honeycrisp apple. You'll have to buy one that comes from down under, as the local variety is long gone from the stores at this time of year. They don't keep, which is their only fault."

Chapter Twenty-five

❖ ❖ ❖

On Wednesday, Godwin came home from work to find Rafael sitting silent and motionless in semidarkness in the living room.

"What's the matter? What's happened?" he asked.

"My sister is on her way here from the airport—and she's very angry at me."

Godwin flipped the switch that turned on the lamps. "Your sister? Which one?"

"The oldest, Pilar." He leaned forward, hands over his face.

"Why is she angry?"

He straightened, dropped his hands to show Godwin his angry, depressed face. "Because, *mi gorrión*, I told her—I told the whole family—that we're getting married."

"Uh-oh." Godwin knew his partner's family, while not anti-gay generally, were rabidly anti-gay in Rafael's case. The last male twig on his family tree, he was considered the only hope of carrying on the family name. His grandmother had kindly suggested he marry a woman and keep a boy-friend on the side, just as her husband had kept a mistress— or two—on the side. She did not have to mention a certain oft-married but childless uncle with his one lifelong, very close male friend—or the spinster cousin with her series of roommates, all female.

So Rafael was not exactly an outlier; the gene was there. On the other hand, despite his family's record, he was not prepared to sacrifice some unfortunate woman's happiness on the altar of propriety, or himself for his family's desire to continue the name, and had told Godwin this.

"What's in a name?" said Rafael, plagiarizing shamelessly. "My sister has two sons and three daughters. They have the family's blood, so it's not as if it will vanish into the dustbin of history if I do not offer a son to the world."

"Wouldn't it be a hoot," said Godwin, seeking to lighten this depressing subject, "if you did marry and your wife had six daughters?"

For some reason, Rafael didn't think that was funny. "Then she would continue having children until there was a handsome, healthy son," he said, and Godwin thought he said it in all seriousness. "I would not sacrifice you for any-thing less."

Now, with his sister's visit imminent, he stood and said, "Prepare for fireworks, *mi gorrión*. She is a tiger when she is angry."

Godwin went into the kitchen to contemplate a din-ner menu. What would a very angry upper-class Spanish woman deign to eat? Especially if prepared by her brother's fiancé?

Godwin decided on a simple meal of tomato-basil soup, Cobb salad, and a grilled chicken breast sprinkled with herbs. And, if they were all still alive at the end of the meal, a lemon sorbet with wafer cookies.

The oven was hot, and he was rubbing the herbal mix into the meat, when the doorbell rang. Godwin heard the front door open. Rather than just press the intercom, Rafael had decided to go down and greet his sister at the main entrance, and escort her up to their apartment. That was probably a good idea, it would give Rafael a chance to gauge the strength of her anger.

A few minutes later, though the walls were thoroughly soundproofed, Godwin could hear a woman's penetrating voice coming up the hall. He couldn't understand the words, but he recognized the rhythms of Spanish speech. And the extra-rapid tempo made it clear that she was, in fact, angry. Very angry.

The door opened. *"Ni siquiera eres un verdadero hombre!"* she was shouting. Godwin's grasp of Spanish was poor, but after a few seconds he got *verdadero hombre*. Real man. Oh dear, this was not good. Was it himself or Rafael she was accusing of not being authentically male?

Rafael spoke gently to her, and Godwin put the chicken into the oven, washed his hands, and fearfully went into the well-appointed living room to see who he was up against.

First of all, she was beautiful. Slender and tall, nearly as tall as Rafael, with sleek black hair pulled back into a very large bun at the nape of her neck, she had white, flawless skin. Her huge dark eyes were lined with lots of false lashes, her full mouth was painted bright, shiny red, and her long, slender neck held her head high. She was wearing leggings and boots that barely covered her ankles, a close-fitting lightweight coat with a clever collar, and thin, tight gloves. Everything she had on was black, even her button earrings.

She was peeling off her gloves, and Rafael was standing behind her, waiting to help her off with her coat. When she shrugged it off her shoulders, the blouse under it was a soft black velvet that looked very simple but likely cost hundreds of dollars—Godwin had an eye for expensive clothing.

The entire time she had been looking at Godwin. At first, her magnificent dark eyes had widened as if in surprise, then narrowed.

Rafael, draping her coat over his forearm, said, "Pilar, this is Godwin DuLac, to whom I am engaged. Goddy, this is my big sister Pilar Gallardo."

If looks could kill, Godwin would have dropped to the hardwood floor. The woman's eyes glittered as they abruptly focused on the beautiful ruby ring that twinkled on Godwin's left hand.

She pointed to it like a vampire spying a crucifix. *"Como pudiste, Rafael! 'El Anillo de Soto' es un tesoro familiar, es invaluable, debe permanecer en la familia, en nuestra familia, no tienes derecho a dárselo a nadie!"*

Godwin looked helplessly at Rafael. He said, "She wonders how I dare give you a family heirloom, the Soto Ring." He said to her, gently, *"Es mio, Pilar, y ahora del hombre a quien amo."* To Godwin, he translated, "The ring is mine, and I have given it to the man I love."

"Que amas?" she shrieked. *"Es una locura! Esto no es normal! Vas a destruir el linaje de nuestra familia! Como vamos a explicarle esto a nuestras amistades?"*

Rafael said to Godwin, his voice still gentle, "She says I am insane and not normal, that what we are doing will destroy my family. She wonders how she will explain this to her friends."

Godwin felt his own anger rising. "Why does she have to explain anything to her friends? They are her friends, not ours! What do we care about them? It's our life, and we love each other."

Rafael nodded. "You are right." He turned back to his sister. *"Tú no tienes que explicarle nada a nadie, Pilar. Es mi vida, amo a Godwin, él me ama a mí, y vamos a casarnos."*

Eyes blazing, she shouted, *"Vas a matarla, a la Abuela, lo sabes, no?"*

Color was rising in Rafael's face. "This would kill our grandmother? She is stronger than either of us! She has survived worse, including her husband, including you, even including *your* husband!"

Surprisingly, Pilar replied in English. "I wish you dead! I wish I could kill you myself!" And she launched herself at Rafael, her fingers curved into claws. He threw up both arms to fend her off but staggered back under her weight, then sideways, falling into Godwin. She was screaming like a wildcat.

Godwin fell onto the floor, striking his head on a corner of the couch. Suddenly, his vision blurred and the sounds in the room grew softer. With an effort, he rolled onto his stomach and pulled himself free of the tangle that was Rafael and Pilar.

"Whoa," he murmured. "Wow. Man, oh, man." He staggered to his feet and looked back at the pair, wrapped around each other, striking at random, she screaming Spanish invective, he growling replies. Godwin went wobbling into the kitchen. He opened the refrigerator and got out a liter bottle of water, staggered back into the living room, unscrewing the cap as he went. The two siblings were shouting, screaming and hitting, kicking. Rolling, they thumped against the coffee table and the couch. There was a sound of fabric tearing.

Godwin coolly upended the bottle over the two of them. Two shouts rose up, different in timbre from what had been going on, and the couple broke apart.

Pilar shrieked, *"Estas loco!? Que estas pensando!?"*

"Well done, *mi gorrión*!" shouted Rafael, getting to his feet, as water rolled past his ears. He glanced with indifference at Pilar, struggling to her knees. His nose and cheek were bleeding, and his shirt was torn at the collar. He came to shake Godwin's hand but winced when Godwin squeezed back, pulling his hand free to look with a grimace at a deep scratch on it.

Then he went to his sister, stooped, and put his hands under her shoulders to lift her to her feet. There was a red mark on her forehead, and her bun had come undone, spilling her long hair down her back. She brushed down her leggings and looked with dismay at the tear in the side seam of her velvet top.

"We have not put our hands on each other for long time," she said in English.

"It was rude of you to speak Spanish in front of someone who could not understand you," he said.

"Is that why you tear my clothes?"

"I was trying to get your fingernails out of my eyes."

"Ha! I wish I had blinded you! You are too stupid! You are not thinking——" Out of vocabulary, she lapsed into

Spanish. *"Tu deber es primero con la familia, y asegurarte de que nuestro apellido continúe, nos estas quitando oportunidades para el futuro! Porque no haces lo que dice la Abuela? Cásate con una mujer, ten un hijo, y él podrá continuar el apellido!"*

Rafael turned to appeal to Godwin. "She says my grandmother is anxious that I marry a woman long enough to sire a son, so that the family name can continue."

Pilar said, *"Si, si. Y divorciate despues si quieres, pero ten ese hijo."*

"Then," translated Rafael, "I may divorce her if I wish, but sire that boy!"

"Yes, yes," said Pilar, "have that boy!"

"What's it to you?" Godwin asked her. "Don't you have any boys of your own?"

"I have two boys." She held up two fingers. "Two. But the *importante* boy must come from him," she added, pointing to Rafael.

"Why?"

"Family," she said, opening her arms wide, then raising and lowering them, to encompass the world. "Family is everything. The name is everything. Our family name is *everything*."

"We are a family," said Godwin, going to put an arm around Rafael.

"No, no, no!" said Pilar, waving a hand as if to erase what she was seeing. "That is crazy—*loco*—to think that!"

"Pilar, Pilar, enough," said Rafael. "You are tired from your long airplane ride. You are tired from striking me in the face. Your hair has fallen down."

"Eeee!" she said in a squeaky voice. She reached to the

back of her head to gather her long crow black locks, twisting them around her hand and expertly tying them into a knot at the back of her head, tucking the ends inside it.

"Listen to me," said Rafael. "Take your suitcase to our guest room and change out of that destroyed shirt. There is a bathroom at the back of the bedroom you can use to clean up. I will also clean my face and change my shirt, which you have torn. Meanwhile, Godwin will salvage what he can of dinner—"

Godwin made a squeaky noise of his own and ran for the kitchen, which was just starting to fill with the scent of overcooked meat.

He heard Rafael say in the living room, "We will eat a little something, and then maybe we can talk like civilized people. Okay?"

"Show me this guest room," she said in a wounded, imperious manner.

THE chicken was beyond repair, so Godwin discarded it. Everyone's appetite was already dampened, so the soup, salad, a crispy loaf of French bread, and the lemon sorbet with wafer cookies was about all anyone wanted. More than enough; not even half of it was eaten.

The conversation was in English, desultory and quiet, and after they'd finished with their meal, Godwin took the dishes into the kitchen to be put into the dishwasher. With an ear cocked for sounds of combat coming from the living room, he put the dishwashing pellets into the cups and started the cycle. He went into the living room to find brother and sister sitting quietly, Pilar on the couch and Rafael in an easy chair watching darkness overtake the big, beautiful lake out the window.

"Is a silly name for a lake, no?" said Pilar. "Min-ee-tunk-a."

"It's Minnetonka, an Indian name," said Godwin. "It means Big Water."

"Is the biggest lake in this state?"

"No, it's number nine, or maybe ten, I forget. There are many lakes in Minnesota. Our license plates brag that there are ten thousand, but actually there are way more than that."

"Your license plates lie?" she said, amusement in her voice.

"No, long ago they made a guess, picked a big number, and now are stuck with it. That's my theory, anyhow."

"There are new lakes forming and old lakes dying all the time," said Rafael. "It is impossible to keep track. But that is not why you are here, to count our lakes. You have made your demand, and I have declined to obey. We are at an impasse."

"What is this 'impasse'?"

"*Punto muerto*," said Rafael.

"No, no, no," said Pilar, with a triumphant smile. "I have arrange things at home for you. Consuela Montserrat is your bride."

"What? What are you saying?" demanded Rafael.

Pilar continued as if he hasn't spoken. "You remember her, she was best friends with our cousin Maria Eugenia. Very nice woman, her years are but twenty, she is pretty, she look like her mama, she have six brothers, so you see she is perfect! And when I go home, I shall . . ." She paused to translate her Spanish thoughts to English. "I shall *release* the news that you are promise to, to *diarios*—the media!" She produced the word with an effort of thought, pleased to have succeeded. "The TV, the radio, the newspapers, no? Yes! Then you *must* marry her."

Rafael said nothing, but when Godwin looked at him, it was as if his partner had turned into a pale marble statue.

So Godwin spoke for him. "You can't do that!"

"No?" she said, pleased. "You jus' watch me, buster!"

Godwin burst into laughter.

Insulted, she retreated again into Spanish. "*Rafael*," she began, rolling the *R* until it screamed for mercy, "*Rafael, se nota que no estás pensando con claridad! Eres un irresponsable, y por lo visto necesitas que te recuerde cuál es tu deber ante la familia! Tú bien sabes que es tú responsabilidad que la línea familiar continúe de manera honorable, decente y bajo la Ley de la Iglesia.*"

Rafael grew serious, leaning forward out of the chair. "You will not do this thing," he said to his sister in a voice made of icicles. "You will not arrange my life for me."

"You cannot stop me unless you kill me!"

Rafael looked about to rise, and for just an instant Pilar looked frightened, as if she'd gone a step too far and he might indeed reach for her with murder in his heart.

But he spoke calmly, although there were razors in his voice, "If one word of my engagement to anyone but Godwin DuLac reaches the media, I will make a release of my own, of a set of e-mails I received from your Franco."

"What has my husband to do with this?" she said with disdain.

"We used to be friends, Franco and I, before he understood I am gay. He was then, and remains, unfaithful to you."

"So?" she said, but less certain.

"So not long ago he was very close to a certain woman, and still may be. He bragged about her to me. He sent me a picture of the two of them smiling at me. She is called Si-Si, do you know of her?"

All the color drained from Pilar's face.

"I see you do. She is notorious, is she not? Franco is like many men of our class, who marry for advantage, not love. But this, this is too much; she is promiscuous to an infamous degree, she discolors all she touches." He looked at Godwin. "Is 'discolors' the correct word?"

"I think the word you want is 'taints.'"

Rafael looked at his sister. Now she was the one sitting pale and frozen. "I think we have again reached a *punto muerto.*"

Chapter Twenty-six

❖ ❖ ❖

T HAT same evening, Betsy called Mike Malloy at home.
"May I ask a favor?" she asked.

"Tell me why I should do you a favor," he growled.

"Having a hard week?" she asked.

"All my weeks are hard. What's making this one hard is that Joe Mickels's alibi turned up."

"You mean the man he was interviewing for a job?"

"That's the one. Wayzata PD found him up in Duluth. He agrees he went to a late dinner with Joe, didn't like the terms of employment he was offered, and turned him down."

"Well, that's good, that's progress!" Then she remembered he liked Joe a whole lot for the murder of Harry Whiteside. "Still . . ." she said.

"What do you want?"

"I understand you've got some video of the reception over at Mount Calvary, and Joe's on it."

"Can't *nobody* keep their mouths shut anymore?" he complained, intentionally colloquial.

"Apparently not. But is it true? You actually saw Joe there and going into the janitor's closet where the bags were kept?"

"In the video footage he's there, all right."

"But not going into the closet."

"You can't see the closet on the camera. He was near it, going toward it, we got that much."

"Mike, can I watch the videos?"

"What for?"

"I want to see who else was near that closet door. Have you watched all three of them?"

"Of course I have."

"Did you see anyone else on the footage who is significant to the case?"

"Sure, I did. Chaz and Bershada Reynolds were there; both the Larsons, Jill and Lars. My wife and oldest daughter were there. Sergeant Larabee of Wayzata PD was there. Hell, Harry Whiteside was there."

"Harry was there?"

"Sure, why not? He came to all kinds of events. Looking for more clients. Letting people see him talking to important clients. You know, being a big shot. Showing the flag."

"I don't remember seeing him around," said Betsy, who went to a number of "events" herself. Then she had a second thought. "Well, I might have. I didn't know him and I don't remember anyone introducing him to me. Unless he wore a name tag, I wouldn't have recognized him if he stood right beside me."

"I didn't see you on the videos at Mount Calvary," Mike said.

"That's because I wasn't there," said Betsy. "I was doing taxes. But what I want to ask is, may I come over to the station and borrow those discs?"

"No, you may not. But you can come over and watch them at the department."

"When?"

"How about right now?"

He was being sarcastic, but she decided to take him at his word. "Thank you, I'll meet you over there shortly."

It was a little after six when Betsy drove up to the little brick and white stone building that was Excelsior's Police Department.

Betsy went into the air lock that was the entrance to the station. She got out her cell and called Mike. "I'm out front," she said.

"I'll be right there," he said.

A minute later, Mike came up to the thick glass that looked into the station and pressed or levered something that made a door to the inside open with a clack. Betsy went through, and Mike escorted her to his little office with the twin desks pushed up against each other. There was no one at the other desk.

"Where's Elton?" asked Betsy.

"Home eating dinner," said Mike.

"Mike, I'm sorry to get you out like this. But you offered, and I'm grateful you agreed to let me see the recordings."

Mike said, reluctantly, "Well, sometimes you come up with things, I have to admit."

On Mike's desk was an old gray laptop computer, and beside it were three dark brown plastic computer disc cases. One was open, and a disc was shoved halfway into the side of his keyboard.

Mike sat down on the office chair behind his desk, gesturing at the armless wooden chair next to it.

Betsy pulled it around to sit next to Mike. He pushed the disc the rest of the way in. The computer gulped and twinkled and displayed a menu with only one item on it. Mike moved his mouse to bring a fat arrow to the item and clicked on it.

His computer grumbled and hummed, and suddenly they were looking at the big rotunda that was Mount Calvary's church hall. There were six or seven people there, nicely dressed for church in light spring coats, all adults. Along a far wall was a long table with a white tablecloth on it, ornamented with two punch bowls, one full of something orange, the other full of something pink. Between the punch bowls were various platters displaying very small crustless sandwiches, crackers with dabs of cheese topped with slices of something dark, probably olives, and small cookies. Plastic glasses rose in towers behind the punch bowls, and while Betsy watched, two women came to dip ladles into the bowls.

Meanwhile, the room was filling up. Betsy leaned forward. She saw Joe accepting a clear plastic cup of orange punch and one of the little sandwiches, tucking a tiny napkin into a curled little finger. He wandered off around the room. She followed him until he went out of camera range.

She recognized several of her favorite customers, then Jill and Lars, without the children.

"There's Harry," said Mike, touching the screen.

"Where?" she asked, leaning forward.

"There," he said, touching the screen again. Harry Whiteside, tall and silver haired, in a dark topcoat, turned away from the camera then turned back. He seemed to be looking for someone. Then he wandered out of the camera's range.

He looks like Heck, she thought.

The room became increasingly crowded, and it was harder to pick out individual faces. She thought she saw Alice, but the figure turned away and didn't reappear.

The recording lasted a little over an hour, the crowd thinning slowly at first, then more rapidly. By the time it was down to the cleanup crew, it suddenly cut off.

"Seen enough?" asked Mike, pushing a button to expel the disc.

"Does one of them show the door to the janitor's closet?" she asked.

He rattled his way among the plastic boxes and picked one. "None show the closet door," he said, "but this one comes closest."

He popped the disc into the computer, which grumbled again, and suddenly the church hall was back on Mike's computer screen.

Mike touched a spot on the screen. "The door is just about two, two and a half feet from here, this way." He moved his finger out and up off the screen.

Betsy studied the screen and located herself in the scene. "Yes," she said, "right over there is Kari's office." She touched the screen up and to the left of where Mike had touched it.

She focused in on that part of the screen and just watched. Alice came near it, Joe came near it, Harry came near it, several other people Betsy recognized came near it. Harry came back a second time, went off camera in its direction for a short time, perhaps fifteen seconds, then came back. He was smiling, as if someone had told him a cruel but funny joke. Then Joe came back, thrust a hand into his pocket, and went off camera and was gone longer, nearly half a minute. When he came back he looked around as if for spying eyes.

Uh-oh, thought Betsy.

Then Alice came back. Betsy saw her reaching out, as if for a doorknob, as she went off camera in the direction of the janitor's closet. She backed away from it, frowned at it, then turned and walked away.

"It seems to me," said Betsy, "that Alice is behaving as suspiciously as Joe or Harry."

"Harry's dead, and Alice has no motive I've been able to find."

"Hmmm," said Betsy, and she went home discouraged.

W HEN Betsy came down the next morning a few minutes before opening-up time, she found the shop lit and dusted, smelling of fresh coffee, the teakettle singing to itself in an undertone. Godwin was sitting at the little round table in the back of the shop, a cup of tea in front of him. He was looking very pensive.

Betsy made a very sweet and milky cup of coffee for herself and came to sit across from him.

"What's on your mind?" she asked.

"Oh . . ." he began, then sighed.

She asked, alarmed, "Is the marriage off?"

"Oh yes," he said but not unhappily, and she took a drink of coffee, unable to reply.

"Oh," he said, looking at her, "not our marriage, the other one, the one his family arranged for him in Spain, to a woman named Montserrat—isn't that a Spanish mountain?"

"Goddy!"

"All right, all right. Let's see, where to start. When we drove Pilar to the airport to wait for a plane that will begin her journey home, she and Rafael talked. She had to change in Chicago, I think. She wasn't angry anymore."

"No, sweetie, that's the end of the story, not the beginning. Who is Pilar?"

"She's Raf's big sister. She came on behalf of the family, I think. Trying to talk him out of marrying me."

"Was she difficult?"

"Difficult?" He raised pale eyebrows at her, making his light blue eyes open very wide. "Oh, Betsy, 'difficult' is entirely too mild a word to describe her. She was a screaming harridan. She actually attacked Rafael, knocked him down, tore his clothing half off him, tried to scratch his eyes out."

"Are you serious?"

He nodded, frowning painfully at the memory. "Knocked me down, too. Collateral damage, but still. Gave me a knot on my head." He touched a place above his left ear tenderly. "It was a total war. She frightened me to *death*! I managed to crawl away, then actually had to pour cold water on her to make her let go of Rafael."

Betsy felt uncertain laughter start to bubble up and severely choked it down, sending down a big swallow of coffee to drown it. "What about this woman, Montserrat?"

"Apparently Pilar thought that if she announced their engagement in the papers, Rafael and this woman's engagement, he would be shamed into going to Spain and marrying her."

"She *announced* it? Before she *talked* to him?"

"No, it hadn't actually been announced; she just told us her plans. Thought the fix was in because she—or maybe the whole family—did apparently get the unfortunate woman to agree to marry him. She's supposed to be very pretty, and she's got six brothers."

"What does six—oh."

Godwin nodded, now amused himself. "They really, really want Rafael to father a boy, to carry on the family name. Do you think there's a title in his family somewhere? Maybe if enough people die childless, Raf can be Sir Rafael. Maybe that's what's got them so excited. Rafael was instructed to take back the ring from me and to be sure to wear it when appearing before his grandmother at home in Spain." Godwin straightened in his chair and flourished his left hand, which twinkled. "*Which* he is not going to do!"

"So how did he persuade Pilar to abandon this plan and go home by herself?"

Godwin looked uncomfortable. "Blackmail," he said.

"He is going to blackmail his *grandmother*?"

"Oh no, she is halfway already to being on his side; says after he fathers a boy, he can divorce the Montserrat and come back to me. Or he can stay married to her and keep me like a mistress on the side. Whichever."

"Oh, Goddy!"

"Not to worry, he refused absolutely. Said he would not do that to an innocent woman. Or me."

"So who is he blackmailing?"

"Pilar. Her husband is some kind of rutting pig, and he's not at all faithful to Pilar—which amazes me, seeing how beautiful *and* how vicious she is. Anyway, he had a clandestine affair with a notorious woman—and made the mistake of bragging to Rafael about it—sent pictures and everything. Rafael said he would release Francisco's e-mails to the media the day after she releases the news of his engagement to the mountain." Godwin smiled, an ugly smile, and hid it behind his cup of tea.

"Oh, Goddy! But wait, if she's notorious, isn't everyone already aware of it?"

"Raf told me that it's like the English royals and Hollywood stars back in the day. People around them knew, but not the public. It was never in the papers."

"And Rafael has threatened to tell the papers."

"Yes. I know, it's all too, too utterly shabby!" He frowned unhappily. "Needs must," he mumbled.

"But it's over, right? She's going home and will not do anything further."

"It looks that way. But I hate what Raf had to do. I hate it."

"Poor fellow." She reached for his hand, and found it cold. "Come on, let's take your mind off it by opening up."

An hour later, checking her e-mail, she found a message from Heck Whiteside.

Ham's in town. He has agreed to talk to you if Howie and I come along. We want you to come to our father's house in Wayzata. The address is 1250 Lakeview Street, and we're meeting there at eight o'clock tonight to talk about an estate sale. Ham says he'll give you half an hour, so don't be late.

It was signed, *Heck.*

"Should I go?" Betsy asked, in succession, Connor, Godwin, Jill, and Mike Malloy.

All said she should go, even Mike. And all, even Mike, asked for a report of the conversation.

Chapter Twenty-seven

◆ ◆ ◆

WAYZATA is a beautiful little town, though its Indian name is not spelled the way it is pronounced: Why-zet-ah. Its main street, unlike Excelsior's, runs along the lakefront, and its shops along the inshore side are attractive and upscale. Behind the main street, the land rises in steps, and those homes lucky enough to face the lake are beautiful and costly, without being overbearing, vainglorious mansions.

It was dark when Betsy arrived at the late Harry Whiteside's house, on a big corner lot up three "steps" from the lakefront, too dark to see anything other than that the house itself was white stucco and at least two stories tall.

The driveway started at the back of the lot and curved around to a broad parking area. There were three outsize vehicles taking up all the space, so Betsy pulled beyond them to find another space set forward in front of a two-car garage.

She got out and went back to a broad front porch—well, a back porch, really, since the front must face the lake. The porch was as broad as the house and marked with arched stucco pillars.

She rang the doorbell. The chimes inside were three deep notes, *ding, dang, dong.*

The door, made of polished vertical boards with a little window guarded by wrought-iron filigree, was promptly opened by Heck. "Well, howdy, Ms. Devonshire, glad you could make it!" he said, his Texas accent a little more on display than it was during their conversation at her shop. He was wearing a red and gray plaid flannel shirt of western design, plain jeans, and old cowboy boots. Betsy suspected his wardrobe choice was an overreaction to being away from home, like an American discovering patriotism while in France.

"I'm glad you offered me this opportunity to meet all three of you," said Betsy, coming into the house. They were in a roomy reception area with tile paving and a small wrought-iron chandelier overhead.

Heck came around behind her to help her off with her white cloth coat. He hung it in the coat closet and gestured at her to precede him through a big, gourmet eat-in kitchen into the living room. There she stopped in her tracks. An even more beautiful room!

It was big, and done all in shades of gray. The floor was shining wood stained dark gray, the square-cut couch was light gray, as was the severely modern occasional chair, and the walls were a medium gray. Very light and filmy silvery gray curtains were pulled back from the gigantic square of glass that was the wall facing the lake. Beside the one window was a huge square of plywood covering what was undoubtedly a twin opening now lacking glass.

In front of the couch, which faced the windows, was a highly polished chrome coffee table. It and the couch rested on a big rug woven in a geometric pattern of dark taupe and white. To the right, suspended on the wall, was a long gas fireplace with a surround of small rectangular stones a darker shade of gray than the walls. Tiny yellow flames danced through black gravel down its length, and hanging above it were two large framed architectural drawings of commercial buildings on pale gray paper. On the left side, the entire wall was a floor-to-ceiling bookcase made of matte black metal. The books in it provided touches of color. Small lights on the ceiling spotlighted the bookshelves, the coffee table, and the architectural drawings.

As Betsy stepped farther into the room, she glanced back the way she'd come and saw on the wall a large Impressionistic painting of Marilyn Monroe's head, done in shades of black, gray, and white, except for her lips, which were a brilliant red.

"Wow!" said Betsy, turning back around slowly to take a second look. Someone had paid a professional interior designer a lot of money to put together this room. Outside the front window the land fell away. There were a few mature trees in black silhouette flanking the window, and houses with glowing windows were down the hill. The main feature in view was the dark, restless surface of the lake, and the darker sky with clouds moving swiftly across a half-moon high in it. The view was wonderful, in tune with the room's message of masculinity, power, and money.

"You like it?" asked one of the other two men standing

near the windows. He was just a little taller than Heck, slimmer, older. He and the other man, even taller and very skinny, but not so much older, had dark hair and features very much like Heck's. Clearly, the men were his two brothers, Howard and Hamilton.

"Impressive," said Betsy.

"But perhaps lacking a woman's touch," said the thinnest brother with a wry smile. He was wearing a dark blue suit with a faint pinstripe and a dark tie, also pinstripe, but from side to side. A short glass, half full of whiskey-colored liquid and ice, was in one hand.

"I'm Hamilton Whiteside," he said.

"I'm Howard," said the other, who was wearing a very thick brown pullover and brown corduroy trousers. He held an identical glass in his hand.

"The house is for sale, of course," said Hamilton.

"Would you like to make an offer?" asked Howard, only half seriously.

Betsy laughed. "No, I don't think so. For one thing, it's not my style. For another, I don't think I could afford it."

"Come over, sit down," invited Hamilton, gesturing at the couch. "Would you like something to drink? We have beer, wine, gin, scotch, Campari, and—" He glanced at Heck.

"Diet Coke, and something called 'spicy ginger ale.'"

"The ginger ale, please," said Betsy, hoping it was what she thought it might be, and in any case thinking it was the best of the choices.

So she took the tall, ice-filled glass of the pale stuff when Heck brought it to her, and she smiled. "Thank you," she said, and she took a taste. It was what she hoped; she recognized the taste, not too sweet and very gingery. "I'll come to your estate sale to buy all of this you have." Betsy had found WBC Craft Sodas at a now-closed craft beer store in Saint Louis Park and was sadly disappointed when she couldn't find the Spicy Ginger variety she'd quickly come to love anywhere else she looked.

"There's a whole case of it back beside the refrigerator," said Heck.

"I'll take it."

"Write that down," said Hamilton to Howard, gravely.

Betsy drank some more, then realized a silence had fallen. They were waiting for her.

"Ah," she said, looking for a coaster on which to place her sweating glass.

"Just put it on the table," said Heck. "It can take it."

She obeyed, then went into her purse for her long, narrow notepad and a pencil—ballpoint pens sometimes failed her when she was trying to get something down on paper quickly.

She looked up and around at the three of them, all still standing, and got up to go to the egg-shaped occasional chair, which was under the window. She moved it near the coffee table and sat down. It was surprisingly comfortable. "Will you all sit?" she asked.

"Sure," said Heck quickly, and they moved to the couch. It was more than long enough to hold the three of them.

"I'm interested in the kind of person your father was," she began. "Howard, you're the oldest; presumably you knew him best. He was a very successful businessman. But what was he like as a man? What were his hobbies? Did he fish? Play golf? Own a motorcycle?"

"He liked to fish," said Howard. "When he was a kid, he

used to spend summers with his grandparents up somewhere in Pine County in a cabin on Pine Lake—imaginative
names you people have for landmarks. He took me up
there a couple of times to see the old place, which was about
the size of this room and had a roof that was missing half its
shingles. It actually had an outhouse, which he thought was
a fine feature." He made a sideways mouth at the memory.

Hamilton said, "I remember that! Somebody else owned
it, and he wanted to buy it from them and restore it. But
they wouldn't sell it. He kept raising his bid for it, but
they had hopes some company was going to build a lodge
up there and refused to sell it to Dad."

Heck said, amused, "An outhouse? An actual two-holer?"

Howard said, "Yes, and he was going to *keep the outhouse*.
Wanted us to go on vacation up there. Said roughing it
would be good for us, because it was good for him." He
shook his head.

Betsy hid a smile behind her glass of ginger ale, and
took a drink.

Hamilton said, "I saw where the hopeful owner finally
died, but now someone else has it and tore down the old
place to build a new cabin on it. So I guess we can be grateful we dodged that bullet."

Betsy asked, "Did your father know who the newest
owner is, the one who built a new cabin?"

Ham looked thoughtful. "I don't think so—I never
asked him."

"Could it have been Maddy O'Leary?"

"Why Maddy O'Leary?" asked Hamilton. "Who is she?"

"She and a man named Joe Mickels were bidding on the

Excelsior property," said Heck. "And you know Dad when someone was trying to keep him from something."

The brothers looked at one another. Then Howard said slowly, "If Dad thought someone bought that cabin in order to keep him from having it . . . Especially someone he was already quarreling with."

The others drew long faces at the thought. But Heck said, "There's no way to know that, is there?"

Hamilton said, "Sure there is. A search of listings of property owners on Pine Lake would tell you that. The county—and I'll bet you a dollar it's Pine County—would give you the names. Easy peasy." He said to Betsy, "They call me Ham."

Betsy made a note. Then she said, "What do you think was your father's strongest personal strength, Howard?"

"Tenacity," said Howard at once. "He tried for years to acquire that rotten old cabin. Said his grandfather built it with his own hands. And call me Howie."

"Fine, Howie. Was he friendly? Honest? Temperamental?" At that last word, all three stirred. Howie snorted and hid his mouth with his hand.

"Easily stirred to anger?" suggested Betsy, and this time all three of them snorted. She made a note. "Is it possible he poisoned Maddy O'Leary?"

"Hey, no, no, no," said Howie, surprised at her. "Where'd you get an idea like that?"

"It's Dad who was murdered," said Heck, equally surprised.

"She's also been murdered," said Howie.

"And you think our father killed her?" Ham's tone was incredulous.

"No, the cops think Joe did it," said Howie. He was looking quizzically at her.

"I was originally thinking there was one murderer who killed both Maddy and Harry," said Betsy. "And that still may be the case. But Joe has an alibi for your father's murder. I'm looking for someone else who was angry with him."

"You've come to the wrong source," said Heck. "None of us knows diddly about who Dad was dealing with currently."

"Now hold on," said Ham. "If you're looking for who was tight around the jaws, get a list of who he was doing business with, and you'll have a list of who was mad at him."

"Well," said Betsy, "he dealt recently with Howie."

"He asked me to help him design a building he wanted to put up in Excelsior," said Howie. "I turned him down. No fight, no quarrel, I just said no."

"I'm talking about before that, the time your father took elements of an industrial park design you started doing for him and hired someone else to execute a new design based on your drawings. And you sued him for doing that."

"What are you—how do you—where did you—?"

"Do you deny that you are Stonebridge Design?" asked Betsy.

"Uh-oh," said Ham in an amused voice.

"So you knew about it?" Betsy asked him.

"A chair thrown at the judge in his courtroom? Yes, I'd read the story. But I didn't know that was you, Howie—or Dad. But I should have; it sounds a whole lot like him. And you." Ham was smiling broadly.

"That's enough!" said Heck. "This is serious."

Everyone looked at Howie, whose face had gone red with fury. He took a long, noisy breath through his nose, then said, "Yes, that was me. I couldn't believe that a dad would do that to his own son."

"Not all dads," said Ham. "Not even most dads. But our dad? Sure, why not?"

Betsy said, "I know Heck has an alibi for the night your father was murdered. Do the rest of you?"

"Now she sounds like a cop," said Ham, amused. "And yes, I have an alibi. I was in my office at home researching some upcoming litigation—which I should be home doing more of right now—while my wife kept freshening my coffee mug."

Ham, Heck, and Betsy looked at Howie. He threw up his brown-sweatered arms and tried to make a joke of it. "Well, how the hell was I to know I'd need an alibi?" he demanded. When they didn't laugh, he continued, "If I'd known, I'd have stayed at home! But I had a fight with Abby, and I went out for a drive, stayed out all night."

"Did you go to a hotel?" asked Heck. "Or to a friend's house?"

"It was three o'clock in the morning before I cooled off enough to think about finding a place to bed down. I looked like a bum—I'd been working in the yard, I was all over dirt and blisters, I didn't want to show my face anywhere. So I went to the work site and slept in my car, went home around eight to find Abby sick with worry, and we made up." He shrugged. "We hadn't had a fight like that for years."

"So the investigators here in Wayzata wonder if you picked that fight," said Betsy.

Howie stared at her with respect. "Their very words," he said.

"If he didn't want to show his dirty face at a hotel," suggested Heck, "then why would he show it on an airline?"

"If we're talking premeditated," said Ham, "you stash a change of clothing in your trunk beforehand, clean up in the airport bathroom. Then change back and roll on the floor of the parking garage before you go home."

"What are you trying to do to me?" Howie shouted at Ham. "Get me hanged?"

"Minnesota doesn't have the death penalty," said Betsy.

He turned an angry face to her, then suddenly laughed, a harsh, ugly sound. "This is stupid!" he shouted. "You're all stupid! I didn't murder my father!" He made a sound dangerously near a sob. "I never killed any human being in my life!" He turned away from them all. "I'm not staying here for this! She's not a cop, she can't arrest me! I think we're done." He gestured at Betsy. "It's over. This was a mistake, agreeing to talk to her. We're done, you're done, all right? Heck, show her out!"

"Hold on, pardner, hold on just one minute," said Heck. "Ham didn't mean anything—right, Ham?"

"That's right," said Ham, with a placating smile. "No reason to fly off the handle. I apologize. We've got a problem here, and we need to work together to solve it. I don't think you murdered Dad, all right? Seriously, I don't."

"Me, neither," said Heck. He looked to Betsy for an agreeing comment.

But Betsy didn't give him one, instead drank some more ginger ale. "What time did you leave the house after the argument?" she asked Howie.

"Answer her," warned Ham when Howie appeared about to explode again. Ham was looking very lawyerly.

Howie blew out the big breath he'd taken in order to resume shouting. He took a lesser one. "All right, all right, let me think." He turned to look at the long line of little flames in the fireplace. "It was almost dark. I remember being surprised by that. I was working outside and didn't realize how dark it was getting—you know how that happens."

Ham and Heck made soft sounds of agreement

"The argument started at a late dinnertime—she'd called me in about four times before I *did* come in, and I came to the table looking like the wrath of God, and she told me to at least go wash my hands. But dammit, I was hungry and I grabbed a chicken leg—and she knocked it out of my hand. I was pissed. I picked it up off the floor and took a bite, and she yanked it out of my hand and threw it in the garbage, and we were off to the races, the kids crying and hiding in their rooms, me totally out of control." He took a breath and blew it out through pursed lips. "So I don't know, it was probably after eight when I stomped out." He looked at Betsy. "Okay?"

She said, "Your home is in the Eastern time zone, so here in the Midwest it would be after seven. You'd need time to clean up, get to the airport, get a ticket, fly to Minneapolis, then get from the airport to Wayzata. The medical examiner has set the time of death somewhere around eight thirty, give or take forty minutes. So . . . you're okay, if she's right—and you're right—about the time." She wrote briefly in her notebook.

"There, see?" said Heck, grinning. "See?"

"All right, all right, you're right, I guess," said Howie, looking a little ashamed of himself. "But dammit . . ."

"Yes, you are right," said Betsy. She had let this get out of hand because she had underestimated how volatile one of them might become when he realized he was suspected of murder.

She said, "I'd like to shift focus from you back to your father. He seems to have been quick to anger, willing to use physical force."

"That's him exactly," agreed Howie, and the other two nodded.

"But what about more subtle ways of aggression?" she asked.

"I don't understand the question," said Howie. "Subtle aggression? Is that like when a person hugs you to death?"

"I'm thinking practical jokes—like he did to you, Heck, when you were a kid on the job."

The men's almost identical puzzled expressions cleared up.

"Oh, that," said Heck. "Is a practical joke a kind of aggression?"

"Of course it is," Betsy said. "You make a fool of someone, he may laugh, but he feels injured. You're showing him you're smarter than he is, more clever."

"I think almost everyone working on a building site plays practical jokes," said Howie.

"So do soldiers, so do cops, so do cowboys," said Heck. "It's part of the rough-and-ready mentality, I think."

"Attorneys as well," put in Ham. "Only ours are sneakier, of course. Sometimes a victim never realizes he's been played."

"But did Harry like practical jokes played on him?"

"Now, that's a whole different story," said Heck. "He'd lay for anyone who pulled one on him. Didn't find them funny the least little bit."

"That's right," said Howie, nodding.

"But he liked to play them," said Betsy.

"Sure he did," said Howie. "All his life, and some of them were damn mean. But so what?"

Ham said, "She's thinking about that woman, what's her name, O'Leary, Maddy O'Leary. Someone sneaked poison onto her knitting yarn, remember? A really filthy practical joke. And Harry was very angry that she outbid him. And if she'd already done him out of the cabin . . ."

"No, no," said Heck. "She died from that poisoned yarn. That's not exactly a little ol' practical joke. And anyway, she died *after* Dad."

"The trap was laid before Harry was killed," said Betsy, and a silence fell.

Finally, Heck murmured, "Well, damn."

But that was it; without saying a word, the trio seemed to draw together, to make a pact to say nothing more. The man, after all, was their father. Betsy tried to ask a few more questions, but she got monosyllables in return.

"Maybe we had better wrap this up," Betsy said at last. "I am grateful to all three of you for allowing me to come here and talk with you. I hope there are no hard feelings and that you'll allow me to contact one or more of you if I have additional questions."

There was a little murmur of reluctant agreement, and Betsy collected their current contact information.

She thanked them again.

Heck walked her through the beautiful kitchen, retrieved

and helped her on with her coat, but when he opened the door, rain was falling in a steady patter.

"Oh, rats," sighed Betsy. "I knew I should have worn my raincoat."

"Where's your car?" asked Heck, peering out into the rain past the three SUVs.

"Over past the end of the porch," said Betsy, gesturing. "In front of the garage."

"Oh, well, come on, there's a door to the outside through the garage. I'll let you out there. Less of a hike."

"Thanks," said Betsy.

A sudden silence fell as they came back into the living room. Heck smirked at his brothers and said, "Raining. Letting her out through the garage."

He hustled her across the room, out a dark gray door, into a hallway. Betsy got a glimpse of an office through an open door halfway along, then reached for a doorknob at the end of the corridor.

"Wait!" ordered Heck. "It's dark and there's a step down." He went around her to open the door.

"Ow!" He went into a dark space beyond the door, and a second later a pair of overhead lights came on, and she saw him grasping his right hand. A tiny trickle of blood was just barely visible through his left fingers.

"What happened?" Betsy asked.

"That damn door bit me!" He was smiling, but it was a painful smile.

He'd gone down a step, and Betsy saw a big concrete block a couple of inches below the threshold. Betsy looked at the door, which was standing open. It looked uninjured.

Heck said, "Here, let me look at that doorknob." He

bent down to examine it. "Looks like there's a screw loose," he said. "And I don't mean in me."

Betsy came for a look. There was a small, dark stain on the underside of the bright brass knob, on the area where it fastened to the flange that came through the door latch. It was partly covered by fresh blood, and the flat head of a screw was standing up a fraction of an inch through it.

"I'd better fix that before it gets someone else," said Heck.

"It already has," said Betsy. "And I think we'd better leave it alone. The police need to be called right away."

"They do? Why?"

"Because that dark stain already on the screw is probably blood, and I think it was left there by the murderer."

Chapter Twenty-eight

❖ ❖ ❖

A T breakfast the next morning, Connor asked, "So the police investigator wasn't as excited about the bloody doorknob as you were?"

"No, but he did take samples."

"What are they expecting to find?"

"Probably that Harry Whiteside cut his hand on the knob."

"But you don't think so."

"I think if Harry cut his hand, he would have cleaned himself up, then wiped the knob, then fixed the loose screw. That house was immaculate, everything in order, no books stacked on tables or the floor, no dishes in the sink, nothing dirty or dusty. The kind of person who likes cleanliness and order is not going to leave a hazard like that doorknob unrepaired. It's my opinion that the murderer cut his hand going out the door. I did persuade the investigator to look around the garage for more blood traces. I looked, too, and didn't find any.

"But you see, I don't think they'll get any usable evidence from the blood they did find at all. Heck Whiteside also cut his hand on that door, so the blood sample is mixed, and DNA testing won't prove anything useful." She looked down at her two soft-boiled eggs in the little blue dish. "Rats," she mumbled.

Downstairs, she found Godwin just starting to open up. He was unusually quiet, and she let him go unquestioned until at last, the opening up finished, she asked, "Something on your mind, Goddy?"

"Well, yes. But, there is, um . . . but . . ."

"Oh dear. What now?"

"Well, I don't know which one of them had this brainstorm, Raf or Pilar, but they talked about it on the way to the airport, and most of it was in Spanish, and it was late when we got back, and I sort of forgot about it until this morning. So I remembered and asked. And so now he's told me what they think they've cooked up. And I don't know if I like it. I mean, maybe it's all right, but I never did think I'd be a parent one day." He went to the library table and dropped into a chair with a sigh.

She joined him there and said, "A parent? I don't understand. You mean he got talked back into doing that? He will after all go ahead with the plan and marry Ms. Montserrat, and try to get custody of the child when they divorce?"

"No, he's not going to marry Ms. Mountain."

"Who, then? And what if it's a girl?"

"We talked about that, earlier, that he might have to

breed a long string of girl babies before they got to a boy. But no, that's not the plan at all."

"Then I really don't understand."

"We'll still get married. But then . . . things like in vitro and, and a surrogate." Godwin drew up his shoulders, his face showing his distaste for the idea. "Because the way he and his family think, it has to be his biological son, not an adopted child. And so, of course, we will be the ones to raise it."

Betsy sat staring at him while the silence went on and on. He just stared at the collection of stitching tools in a bin in the center of the table.

Finally, she said, "What are you going to do?"

"I don't know. Rafael's halfway to being pleased with the idea; he thinks it's clever. But somehow the idea of me being a daddy—well, it just never occurred to me. I knew a long time ago that I wouldn't ever . . . you know, with a *girl*, so I just accepted that to be the way it was. And I put a brave, bad face on it, because after all, babies are loud and messy, and you're up all night and ishy *diapers* and icky *potty training* and crying for no reason and *expensive* . . . so I told myself that was okay for some but not for me. Besides, I wasn't ever going to be old enough to be a *father*. Fathers are old, and I'm always so . . . *young*." He looked at her, his expression so pitiful and yearning that her heart turned over.

"And now, the man you love is suggesting the two of you do this thing that will upset that applecart," she said. "What did you say to Rafael when he told you?"

"I hugged him so he wouldn't see the look on my face and said I had to get to work early. I've been here for nearly an hour. I'm trying to think, and I can't think. What can I say to him?"

Betsy took several minutes to gather her thoughts. "First of all, you mustn't lie to him. You have to talk to him, tell him you have deep reservations about this plan. You could begin by saying you don't think you'd be any good at parenting—"

"Well, I wouldn't! I mean, look at me! I'm frivolous! I'm vain! I like pretty clothes and nice vacations and everything neat and clean, sweet and peaceful. Except at parties, I like loud parties and drinking too much and then sleeping till noon the next day. You can't do that with a baby!"

"It wouldn't stay a baby forever, you know. They grow up quicker than you think. But then, of course, you're faced with new problems: dating, and driving, and getting into a good college."

Godwin's eyes widened. "Oh my God, you're right! Suppose he drops out of school, takes drugs, and falls in love with absolutely the wrong person?"

"Suppose she's a girl, this child of yours?"

He waved that off with one hand. "No, not likely. There's something they can do, some processing of the sperm that makes it extremely likely it will be a boy."

"What if he's gay?"

Godwin stared at her, then bloomed all over. "Wouldn't that be the biggest hoot in the *world*?" He laughed. "I don't think dear Pilar thought about *that*!"

Then he sobered. "So you think I should tell Rafael what I think."

"I think you must, because you are not to go into this unwillingly. Remember how your father reacted to learning you were gay? Think how this child will react to a father who dislikes him for a reason he cannot understand?"

Godwin's mouth fell open, then his face crumpled. He jumped to his feet and ran into the back room. Betsy heard the bathroom door slam. She went there but heard noisy weeping and retreated. Neither of Godwin's parents spoke to him, hadn't seen or communicated with him in any manner since he was fourteen and they'd thrown him out into the street.

She had cut him to the quick with that single careless remark.

She felt tears of her own beginning, but the front door began to play "Yes! We Have No Bananas," and Jill came into the shop with the children, Emma Beth, Airy, and Einar. The children ran to her for hugs and loud greetings—she was Emma's godmother and informal aunt to them all.

But Jill saw something in Betsy's face and said, "What's wrong?"

"It's Godwin. He's in a real pickle, and I don't know what to tell him."

"Get the coloring books," ordered Jill, and Betsy went into a bottom drawer of the checkout desk for the big plastic box of crayons and three coloring books.

In another minute the children were settled at the library table telling stories about the pages they were coloring—or scribbling over, in Einar's case—while Betsy drew Jill out of earshot and swiftly gave a condensed version of Godwin's predicament.

"Where is he now?"

Betsy grimaced. "In the bathroom, crying his eyes out. It's my fault. I brought up his parents, who didn't want him once they learned he was gay. If he is burdened with a child he doesn't want . . ."

Jill nodded. "That wasn't a very clever thing to say."

"I agree, I should have thought harder before I spoke. But on the other hand, he needs to really think this through before agreeing to help Rafael raise a child. He thinks children are pretty awful."

"Does he? Does he really?"

"Well, he said so, in so many words, just a few minutes ago."

"Hmmmm," said Jill. "Watch the children for me." She walked into the back room.

Betsy went out front and found Einar, already bored with his coloring book, beginning to scrawl on the table.

"Here now, sweetie," said Betsy, taking the crayon from his hand. "I have a different job for you."

Einar puckered up as if to cry and reached for his crayon, but Betsy lifted it higher. "Would you like to pop bubbles?"

"Bubbles!" shouted the child.

"No, not really bubbles," said Betsy. "This is something different." She went to her desk and opened a middle drawer. Under a clipboard was a length of bubble wrap.

"Yay!" cheered Airy—his real name was Erik, but Emma Beth had called him Airy when they were both very young, and the nickname stuck.

"Awww, baby stuff!" scoffed Emma Beth and went back to coloring a crowned frog in her book. She was very good, even adding shading to the frog's foreleg.

"No, it isn't!" shouted Airy. "Me, me, give me some bubbles to pop!"

So Betsy cut the piece into two unequal pieces and gave the bigger to Airy, who immediately began to pop his between thumb and forefinger. Einar watched him for a few seconds, then began popping his own piece. It took him under a minute to master the technique, and then, successful, he growled a low, dirty laugh, "Hurrr, hurrr, hurrr."

Betsy stared at him, amazed. She'd never heard such a sound from a little child before. It was practically a baritone.

"Isn't he just the cutest thing?" said Emma Beth without looking up from her book, obviously quoting some adult.

"Remarkable," said Betsy.

Snap, *crackle*, *pop*, went Airy's plastic wrap. He was an expert at popping the wrap.

Pop . . . *pop* . . . *pop, pop* . . . *pop*, went Einar's. "Hurrr, hurrr, hurrr."

Betsy retreated to the other side of the box shelves that divided the shop in half. There she found Jill and Godwin seated at the little round table, talking in low voices.

"Oh!" Betsy said. "Excuse me!"

"It's all right," said Godwin, offering her a watery smile. "We're just talking. I think . . . I think I'm starting to understand what I'm going to do."

Betsy looked at Jill, who smiled and nodded. "It's going to be all right. Goddy is a good man; he's just a little frightened at all this happening so fast. It was thoughtless of Rafael to make an agreement with Pilar without consulting him first. But it will go much slower now; these things take time, lots of time. And he'll have all the time he needs to think about it, talk about it, make sure he knows what he wants, and what Rafael wants, and that they're on the same page."

"Oh, Jill, you're so *wise*, so *sensible*, I just love you to *death*!" said Godwin.

There came the angry wail of a small child, and Jill got up to go see what atrocity had occurred in the front of the store. Her mere appearance stopped the wail in its tracks.

"Wow," said Godwin, looking through the opening at her. He said to Betsy, "Do you think she'll give Rafael and me lessons?"

THAT crisis over, Betsy told him about her adventure with the Whiteside brothers last night. She sighed a bit over the unfairness of discovering the tiny sample of blood only after it had been hopelessly mixed with Heck's. "I'm as sure as I can be that the first drop of blood was left by the murderer, but now there's no way to prove that."

"Somebody, probably you, will think of something else that will break this case wide open," Godwin predicted.

But it was Jill who lifted her spirits when she said, "They can test mixed DNA samples. They do it all the time; they just separate them. That's how I knew my second child would be a boy."

"What do you mean?"

"I mean a baby's DNA gets into the mother from the womb through the umbilical cord. She's sending oxygen and food to the baby, and the baby is sending fragments of itself to the mother. A blood test will pick up those fragments, and a technician can separate the DNA in them from the mother's DNA."

Betsy said, in a very quiet voice, "Really?"

"Google it. DNA technology is galloping headlong down the road, past what you're wishing it might do. They've been doing it for years."

Betsy went to her computer and asked her search engine to tell her if it was possible to separate mixed DNA samples. Indeed, yes, said several sites, though sometimes in language that gave new meaning to the term "scientific explanation": The terminology used in some of the scientific abstracts she read—"loci," "contributor genotypes," "biostatical software"—was enough to give her a headache.

Jill, reading over Betsy's shoulder, said, "See? In a case like Wayzata's, only two samples are in the mix, none of it fragmentary or degraded. That means it'll be relatively simple to separate them. And since one of them is Heck Whiteside, who is currently present and can give a fresh sample, it'll be even easier, using one they pull from him for comparison."

Betsy began to smile. "God bless the scientists who keep getting better and better at using DNA," she said. "Do you think it would be interfering if I called Detective Larabee and told him about these advances in DNA testing?"

"Oh yes, I think it would. He's better educated about DNA than you and I are. I would be very surprised if he isn't well aware of the separation technique."

"Then he'll be able to test that second sample of DNA against all the suspects in Harry's murder."

"I'm absolutely sure he'll do that," said Jill.

*　　*　　*

JILL had been gone for about forty-five minutes, having left with one hand holding a fistful of beautiful Silk and Ivory floss in a small plastic bag, when the door began to play "Yes! We Have No Bananas" and Joe Mickels came in. He was looking triumphant, and he said to Betsy, "You're fired!"

Godwin scolded, "Who do you think you are, Donald Trump?"

Mickels frowned at Godwin, then laughed, a sound rarely heard. Certainly neither Betsy nor Godwin had heard it before.

"Whatever is the matter with you, Joe?" Betsy asked.

"They arrested the man who shot me!" said Joe.

"Not Chaz, surely!" exclaimed Betsy.

"No, o' course not! I never thought it was him. It's Herman Glass. He used to be a tenant of mine. He's a student at Rasmussen College, and to finance his education he was selling drugs out of his apartment. When I found out about it, he asked me to give him a break, so I didn't call the cops on him, I just evicted him. He called me names anyway. Then he decided selling drugs wasn't his forte, so he started pulling stickups. When he walked into one of my stores and saw me there, he took advantage of the opportunity and shot me."

"The dastard!" said Godwin.

Joe turned and looked at him. "What did you say?"

"Dastard."

"What is that, a ladylike version of bastard?"

"No, it's a word of its own, dates way, way back, medieval. It means a contemptible, sneaky coward."

"Dastard," repeated Joe, trying it out on his tongue.

"Dastard," agreed Godwin. He had a curious fondness for old-fashioned words—and old-fashioned music, and cartoons, and radio shows, too.

Joe turned back to Betsy. "But that's not what I'm here about. They found the man I had dinner with the night Whiteside was killed, so I've got an alibi for his murder, so I don't need your help anymore."

"What about for Maddy?"

He shrugged. "They'd have to prove I had access to pure nicotine, and they can't, because I don't. QED, I'm in the clear."

Betsy nodded. "Very well, I won't spend any more time trying to prove you didn't kill Maddy O'Leary."

He turned serious, even morose. "I take it you will bill me for your expenses?"

"I don't charge for my investigative services. I thought we were clear on that."

He brightened. "Yes, you did say that, didn't you? I'm glad to have that confirmed. Good day to you."

He turned and stumped out.

"Not a 'thank you' in a carload," remarked Godwin. "But maybe we should be grateful he didn't poke you in the eye with a sharp stick."

BETSY took the cordless shop phone into the back room and called Bershada. "Is Chaz there by some chance?"

"No, why?"

"Because apparently there's a cabin up on Pine Lake in Pine County that might have had its windows broken by a vandal. I'm wondering if that cabin belonged to Maddy. Does Chaz have access to a complete listing of her holdings?"

"I think he does, or knows how to get one, at least. A cabin up in Pine County, you say?"

"On property that used to belong to Harry Whiteside's grandparents." ·

"Oh my Lord! Where did you find out—never mind! I'll ask him and call you back."

"Thanks, Bershada."

S ERGEANT Frank Larabee wrote up an order directing the Hennepin County medical examiner to take a sample from the body of Harry Whiteside suitable for DNA testing. He also ordered samples to be taken from Hamilton Whiteside and from the Merry Maid woman who cleaned Harry's house and from Harry's friend Martin LeBeau (who had dined with Harry the week he died), and for all samples to be compared to the separated DNA samples taken off the doorknob shank in Harry's house. All had denied cutting a finger while in the house, but the blood sample was very small, and it was possible they hadn't noticed. Or they were lying.

Meanwhile, Sergeant Larabee was rounding up files on known burglars active in the Wayzata area and checking their alibis. Someone had injured his or her finger on that loose screw, not badly, but enough to have left a usable sample of blood behind. He had a hunch that it was Heck's brother Howard who cut himself walking out after slamming his father on the head and breaking one of the big front windows (not in order to get in, just in a fit of anger, or maybe to make the police think that was how a thief got in), turning over chairs and tables, and maybe stealing a few things from the house—there wasn't any inventory available to prove that—to make it look like the work of a burglar. Howard had his father's temper, and there were years of quarrels between them—that business of the dismissed lawsuit still rankled. Howard had tried to shrug it off as water over the dam when Larabee spoke to him, but it hadn't been difficult to see the anger still smoking in Howard's closed fists and tight vocal cords. And he didn't have an alibi worth spit.

Larabee was pretty sure he'd be able to arrest Howard Whiteside as soon as the results came back.

He was about to close up shop when his phone rang.

"Larabee," he said on picking up.

"Sergeant Larabee, this is Betsy Devonshire—"

"Oh jeez, what is it now?"

"Have you had that mixed blood sample separated and tested?"

"It's being done. But I'm not going to share the results with you."

"That's fine. I'm sure you're being very thorough and testing every possible person who might have been in that house."

"You got that right."

"Including Maddy O'Leary."

"Maddy—? What makes you think I should test a dead woman's DNA?"

"She wasn't dead when Mr. Whiteside was killed."

"Ms. Devonshire, I'd really appreciate it if you wouldn't call me up to tell me how to do my job." He hung up on her.

What a crazy, interfering, ignorant woman! Not only wasn't she a cop, she wasn't even a licensed private investigator!

He finished locking the files away and went off to spend ninety minutes in the gym, fifteen minutes of which he'd spend looking at himself in the big mirror in various poses. His chest was coming along well, but he needed to do something to tighten those glutes.

WHEN Betsy closed shop and went upstairs that evening, Connor wordlessly indicated she should go look in the dining nook.

Standing proudly in the center of the round table was a bouquet of two dozen roses, with an additional half-bushel of baby's breath and some kind of large-leaf foliage. The roses were the large, pale ivory kind with deep pink edges to their petals. Best of all, they were the scented variety, filling the air with a heavenly odor.

"What's the occasion?" Betsy asked, flashing a delighted smile at him.

"They're not from me," he said. "But there's a card."

Betsy approached and found a small card tucked in among the blooms. She opened the tiny envelope and read the message inside: *Thank you for your efforts on my behalf. Joe Mickels.*

Betsy laughed. "Goddy was wrong. He does know how to say thank you."

Chapter Twenty-nine

❖ ❖ ❖

"So, you're off the hook, right?" said Connor over supper. They had had to move the rose bouquet to the living room; it was so large that it impeded sight lines, even the placement of dinnerware. Connor had actually had to go over to Leipold's for an especially large vase.

"I suppose I am. So why don't I feel like it?"

"I don't know. Why don't you?"

"I think because I have a theory about what happened. But I don't have any proof. It makes me uncomfortable, not having proof."

"You're saying that for your own peace of mind, you need to continue sleuthing."

She sighed. "Yes, I guess that's what I'm saying."

"All right, it's your decision, and I understand what's driving you. Do you want to tell me whom you suspect?"

"N-no, I don't think so. Without proof it's just a theory."

"I'm not going to find myself in a scenario where you're dead and I don't know whom to blame?"

She laughed. "No, absolutely no danger of that."

"I'm glad to hear it. What do you want to do next?"

"I need to find out how someone on my list of suspects got hold of pure nicotine. It's not easy to come by. But it doesn't take a large quantity, so suppose I really, really wanted just a little, a couple of teaspoons or a tablespoon of it. Where would I have to go?"

"Contact the people who produce it, I suppose. Where does it come from?"

"Well, from tobacco, of course." She held up both hands. "I know, that isn't what you're asking. It comes from laboratories, from chemical factories. I'll have to do a search to see if I can find someone who works in the manufacturing end willing to talk to me."

It seemed startlingly easy at first. There was actually a company in Minnesota that advertised it made and sold nicotine (among other things)—and its factory was in Minnetonka, right up the road. But when she tried to phone them the next morning, their phone number had been disconnected, and Google Maps seemed never to have heard of them. They'd gone quietly out of business, leaving no forwarding address.

So she backed up and called an e-cigarette store. Where did they get the "juice" they sold? That led her to a distributor. Several distributors, actually; but at first her questions seemed to lead them to think she was an undercover activist, and they refused to give her any information.

Her line of questioning became more polished as she

went along—she'd even connected with a laboratory that made nicotine for commercial use, but they didn't want to tell her anything about it. Then, finally, a distributor gave her the name and phone number of the public affairs officer in a chemical company in Virginia—of course, prime tobacco country.

Jill had once told Betsy she'd make a good con woman because she was a good liar. So, since her various approaches to the truth weren't working, she decided to lie.

There were several female crime fiction authors in the Twin Cities area. Betsy picked one, and when she got the PR fellow on the line, she introduced herself as that person. She continued, "I'm writing a mystery in which my victim is killed when her husband pours a little liquid nicotine on her favorite sweater. She absorbs it through her skin."

"Say, that's pretty mean," the man responded.

"You bet. But would it work?"

"Oh, sure."

"Good. But I've been having trouble finding out how he might get hold of the stuff without leaving a trail. Retail and wholesale e-cigarette dealers only get the mixes, and the strongest mix is still only three percent. What kind of job or occupation can I give my murderer that will allow him to get hold of one hundred percent nicotine?"

"He could be a chemist, of course. But that's a little obvious for your purposes, right?"

"Yes, that's right. I've discovered that when a medical examiner conducts the initial test for drugs on a body, nicotine is one of the basics. That surprised me."

"It surprises me, too. Well, okay, in order not to leave a

trail, he's going to have to steal it, unless he takes classes in chemistry at a university under a fake name."

"No, I think stealing it is best—fastest, anyway."

"Sure, I get it. Maybe he's a painter and gets a job painting the walls of a factory where they manufacture the vapor mixes." The man seemed to be getting into the spirit of Betsy's quest. It was surprising how many people had a trace of the criminal in them. Probably not a good thing, except for the bottom line of mystery authors.

"Have you handled pure nicotine yourself?" asked Betsy.

"Oh yes. Not often, but yes. You have to be careful; it doesn't take a lot to make someone damn sick."

"So my idea of putting it on an article of clothing is good."

"It would have to be something that comes into direct contact with the skin, and for a prolonged period of time. That sweater idea is good. Underwear might be better. Gloves would be good, too. Where are you calling from?"

"Minnesota."

"Oh yeah, a land of winter sports. Pour it onto her socks, send her skiing, find her body on the slopes." He really was getting into this.

"Is there a tobacco smell she might notice?"

"No, it's just about odorless. Colorless, too."

"The stuff you buy for e-cigarettes seems to be like syrup," said Betsy.

"That's an additive to make it burn. And another to make it smell good. Nicotine is only a little thicker than water. But it oxidizes fairly rapidly, so your killer would have to do it so it dries not more than a day or two before

your victim puts the socks on. Oh, and here's an idea: Have
your murderer be a maintenance man, working in a lab. He
could find an almost-empty bottle of the stuff in a waste-
paper basket."

"Scary to think someone would just toss a bottle away
without at least rinsing it."

"It's illegal to pour it down a drain. Much better to put
it in a landfill."

And on that note, Betsy thanked him and hung up before he could ask her to send him a copy of the book when
it came out.

She barely had time to serve a customer who wanted to
buy the magnificent counted cross-stitch Eagle Owl pattern from Riolis, when the phone rang.

"Wow, you really are a sleuth!" Chaz exclaimed when she
answered. His previous anger toward her seemed to have
disappeared. Betsy thanked her stars for Bershada, who obviously had been able to calm his resentment over being
thought a suspect.

"Why, did she own a cabin up on Pine Lake?"

"She sure did! Bought it five years ago from a party
named Makepeace. It had a raggedy old cabin on it, which
she tore down and replaced with a log house. All modern
conveniences, plus a river rock fireplace. It's on the shore of
Pine Lake, so she built a little boathouse that you can paddle your canoe right into. And it was vandalized back in
February, windows broken, couple cans of paint emptied
into it. Froze the pipes, which broke the toilet. Over fifteen
thousand dollars in damage."

"Can you find out if there was an owner named Whiteside, back in the fifties?"

"Oh my God. You're thinking—oh my God. No, I don't believe it."

"But you'll find out for me?"

"Yes, but you're wrong, Betsy."

"For your sake, I hope I am."

Betsy was restless in bed Sunday night. Some fragment of information was nagging at her, and though she chased it all over her brain, she couldn't catch up and get hold of it. "Laboratory," she murmured to herself. And, "Landfill." She finally fell into an uneasy slumber and dreamed all night of houses on fire. She woke up from a dream of someone setting fire to the back door of her own building and causing major smoke damage to the contents of her shop. The dream was so vivid she went all over the apartment, sniffing for evidence of smoke, thinking something must have triggered those dreams. But there was nothing but clean air.

So she pulled on her swimsuit and some clothes on over it, grabbed a change of underwear, and went off to water aerobics.

Over time, people had dropped out of the Early Bird class at the Golden Valley Courage Center and new ones came in, the instructors changed, even the kind of aerobics changed. Tabata was now all the rage, with its twenty seconds of action and ten seconds of "rest" (marked by gentler movements, not standing still). Yet it still all took place in the very large, heated, Olympic-size pool, with its flat platforms at increasing depths, under a pair of enormous glass windows with a stained glass pattern that looked like a map of several rivers converging here and there.

Betsy had been going to this aerobics class for years. It started at six thirty and went for an hour, which made it perfect for people with day jobs. Oddly, most of the current participants were senior citizens. Connor had joined her for a few classes then decided he preferred to sleep in and get up only in time to have her breakfast cooking when she got back home.

A Russian immigrant, Michael, with a hearing problem and not much command of English, was a newer member of the class. He had multiple physical problems as well and often just stood in one place, clumsily shuffling his feet and feebly moving his arms while everyone else was doing cross-country ski or jumping jack movements back and forth across the pool.

On the other hand, another newcomer, Sarah, was tall, young, and strong. Betsy was jealous of her ability to move swiftly and smoothly through the water while Betsy puffed and struggled.

An old, familiar, and much-liked couple, Peter and Ingrid, were no longer members of the class. Peter had had a stroke, and Ingrid dropped out to care for him; Betsy missed them both.

But there remained the heated water and the movements, and focusing on those elements gave her a break from everything else.

A small whiteboard was fastened to a section of wall between the windows. There was a new riddle written on it for each day's class. Today's was: *What happens when you don't pay your exorcist?* As usual, the answer was not written on the board, and Betsy spent several minutes trying to think what it might be.

Samantha—Sam—was running the class today. She was a new instructor, not fond of Tabata, and her method was to get a movement started and then let it run awhile—other people who taught the class switched off very frequently, not letting the muscles settle into a routine. But Sam liked to give each set of muscles a thorough workout. Once she picked up the rhythm, Betsy's mind was free to work on the riddle.

And suddenly, she knew the answer and laughed out loud. Lifeguard Amy had earlier acknowledged she knew the answer, so when Betsy arrived at Amy's side of the pool, she gave her guess, and Amy said, "Correct!"

Perhaps it was the mental exercise of the riddle, or the oxygenation of her brain from vigorous exercise, but on her drive home, Betsy thought she understood at last what her dreams had tried to tell her last night. Her shop didn't have those pipes that carried water that sprayed during a fire. A serious fire would have destroyed her whole building. But the University of Minnesota's waste-handling building did. Their pipes had needed replacement. And Harry Whiteside had contracted to replace them.

To Betsy's mind, that was a very large clue.

She got home to find Connor preparing to pour pancake batter into a heated pan as soon as she opened the door. A few minutes later, while sitting at the table, she was putting butter and syrup on those very pancakes. "What happens if you neglect to pay your exorcist?" she asked Connor as she tucked into her breakfast.

"I don't know, what?"

"Think about it."

"You've the devil to pay?" he guessed.

She laughed. "Good guess, but no."

He sat down to his own breakfast, and silence fell for a few minutes. Then he began to laugh. "You get repossessed?"

She laughed back at him. "That's right!" After breakfast, Betsy retreated to the bedroom to change into her work clothes. She put on a two-piece suit in a medium yellow that had very faint patterns of large pink flowers woven into it. She wore yellow heels with it that were more comfortable than they looked.

Connor approved. "You look like a morning in spring."

"Thank you. Connor, could you do something for me?"

"Anything, *machree*." The English spelling of an Irish word that means "my heart," it was his favorite nickname for her.

"I need to visit the hazardous waste disposal building on the U of M campus. But I need an excuse."

"And you think I might come up with one?"

"Well, can you?"

"Not off the top of my head. What's there for you to see or find out?"

Armed with her fresh insight, she was not willing to explain her theory.

"Does Mike Malloy know about this?" he asked.

"No—well, I don't know. I haven't said anything to him."

"Why not?"

"Well . . . I guess the thing is, I want to do this myself."

"My dear, dear heart," he said, coming to take her by the elbows. "'Pride goeth before a fall.' It seems to me you either have to lie—which is never a good thing to do to innocent bystanders in a criminal investigation—or tell the truth and be rebuffed. I suggest you take the third choice, the high road, and talk to Mike."

"But he—he doesn't like me."

"That's not true. He respects you, but you make him nervous. He wishes you'd stay out of his business, or at least get a license. You're a wild card, and law enforcement officials don't like wild cards. When you do things that break open a case, he probably has a hard time explaining you to the chief, to prosecuting attorneys, to defense attorneys, to judges, maybe even to his wife." He was smiling warmly at her, and her heart turned over—who else in the whole world could criticize her, warn her, advise her all in a couple of sentences, and make her like it?

She put her arms around him, and he took her in a warm embrace. They stood that way for a couple of minutes, until the threat of tears went away, and she stepped back.

"I'll call Mike today," she said.

Chapter Thirty

❖ ❖ ❖

"GOOD morning, Mike," said Betsy on the phone. "What do you want now?"

"I have an idea, but I need your help."

"What kind of help?" he asked, warily.

"I think I know who killed Maddy O'Leary."

"Yeah? Who?"

"Harry Whiteside."

"Harry Whiteside? But that's not possible! He died before she did!"

"Yes, but that yarn was poisoned before he died. He was at Mount Calvary's Lenten service—or at least at the reception afterward—and he approached the closet where the knitting bags were being kept. And he hated Maddy, had hated her for a long time. He saw an opportunity to get at her, an opportunity he was sure was safe—"

"What are you talking about, what was safe?"

"A chance to get hold of a deadly poison without having to buy it. A chance theft no one would think to blame him for. He did some work at the University's hazardous waste disposal building."

"And this has something to do with his work at the hazardous waste place?"

"It could."

"How?"

"One of the last jobs Harry did was to replace the pipes in their fire-extinguishing system. So he was there. The term 'hazardous waste' can cover things like poisons used in laboratory research testing, which they do a lot of at our university. You can't pour radioactive material or plague germs or poisons down the sink. You need that kind of waste professionally handled; that's what places like that are for. The question is, could someone just passing through get hold of a dollop of something he could use to kill?"

"Hmmmmm."

"Right."

"So maybe I should go have a look at this place," said Mike.

"And you'll take me with you."

"The hell I will!"

"Mike, I brought this to you. I think I deserve a reward for that."

"I'll send you a dollar in the mail. Two dollars if it plays out."

"You want me to go over there by myself?"

"You wouldn't get past the receptionist, probably."

"All right, you're probably right. So please? Didn't you say yourself I sometimes see things other people miss?"

There was a long silence, followed by a heavy sigh. "I'll call you back."

"Thank you very much." *It'll probably take him an hour to think of a way to tell me to butt out*, she thought, disgruntled.

"Anything else?" he asked in a sarcastic voice.

"Um . . . actually, yes."

"What is it?"

"Do you know if Sergeant Larabee has gotten the results of that DNA test he was running on the blood found on the doorknob at Harry Whiteside's house?"

"Yes, no matches."

"What? None at all?" Betsy was incredulous. How could she have been so wrong?

"That's what he says. Why, whose did you think it would match?"

"Maddy O'Leary's."

There was a silence of several seconds. "Mike?" she asked.

"I'm here. Why in the *hell* do you think that blood would be Maddy's?"

"Well, I'll tell you," she said, and she did. Then the penny dropped—as her father, who was British-American, would put it, meaning she saw the whole picture. "He didn't test her DNA, did he?" she asked.

"No. I saw the report, and no, he didn't. I'll give him a call later today."

"What's the matter?" asked Godwin, when she'd hung up.

"Oh, that dreadful man!"

"Who, Mike? I've already told you he's hopeless!"

"No, not Mike, that detective over in Wayzata, Larabee. Mike's going to talk to him. I hope he can get results. The other thing is, there's a place I want to visit, over at the U, but I can't think of an excuse to get in there, and Mike doesn't want to take me." *Jeepers*, Betsy thought, *I sound like a spoiled nine-year-old who's been told she can't go to the zoo.*

"Never mind," she said aloud. "I'll find a way. I just need to practice a little patience. Tell me, what's going on with you and Rafael?"

"So," he said, drawing out the word, "I screwed my courage to the sticking place—isn't Shakespeare wonderful?—and told him I had made up my mind a long time ago that I wasn't the parenting kind and the idea of taking on a baby scared me witless."

"Uh-oh," said Betsy. "What did he say?"

"He said he felt just the same way! Isn't that amazing? I was so shocked!"

"So you're not going to go through with it."

"Oh, but that's not decided yet for sure."

"What?"

"Well . . . you see, the more we talked about what a bad idea it was, the less of a bad idea it seemed. There are nurses and nannies and babysitters in the world, and when kids get older, they're in school all day, and there are even boarding schools where they go all the school year. So it's not like a twenty-four-seven job, is it? Rafael says that when he was a little boy, he saw his parents for about twenty minutes a day, sometimes less, until they sent him to a boarding school when he was eight and then to a prep school and then college, and he only came home for Easter and Christmas. And even then he saw more of his grandmama than his parents. He says he's surprised he can remember what they looked like, though I think he's joking."

"So it's back on again."

"Well . . . maybe."

"What do his parents say about this plan to use a surrogate to have a child?"

"Not a thing. They're dead. They died in a plane crash
when he was twenty-three."

"Oh, that's sad."

"So maybe ours'll be one of those angelic kids, and if so,
we're thinking maybe not a boarding school."

"You are? That's good." Rafael would be the strict parent, and Godwin would be the indulgent parent, and the
thought of Godwin being indulgent with a toddler made
her smile for the rest of the morning.

"LARABEE."

"Frank, this is Mike Malloy."

"Say, little buddy, how's life over on the wrong side of
the lake?"

"Not good. I read that report you copied to me on the
DNA results from the Whiteside house."

"Yeah, looks like we're back to square one on that case.
Too bad. I was betting on a match with Howard Whiteside."

"Why didn't you order up a test on Maddy O'Leary?"

"In case you didn't hear, the lady is dead."

"The ME stores samples from murder victims, and
there's more than enough for a DNA sample to be taken."

"The lady had no reason to be in that house."

"I have information that would indicate otherwise."

"What information is that?"

Mike started to explain but hadn't said more than three sentences before he was interrupted. "That damn amateur you got over there planted that idea in your head, right?"

"That damn amateur, as you call her, has broken more than a few cases. She may be wrong, but her reasoning is solid. I think you—"

"I don't give a rat's ass what you think! We're doin' just fine without your help, especially if it comes secondhand from some old spinster seamstress who sells silk thread for a living!" And crash went the phone in Mike's ear.

SHE was barely through with the turkey salad Godwin had brought her for lunch when the phone rang.

"Crewel World, Betsy speaking, how may I help you?"

"It's the Safety and Environmental Protection Facility," said Mike.

"What is?"

"The hazardous waste disposal plant on the campus."

"Oh. And, am I coming with you to tour it?"

"Yes, I'll pick you up tomorrow morning, nine o'clock sharp. Don't dress froufrou, and don't ask any questions without asking me first."

After a startled pause, Betsy said meekly, "All right."

OVER supper that evening, Connor was pleased that his advice to contact Mike Malloy had worked out well. But he was a little more concerned about Godwin's talk about having an angelic baby. "No matter how angelic," he said, "there are times when you'd cheerfully leave them in a basket at the side door of an ophanage."

Betsy wan't sure what Mike meant by not dressing froufrou. She contemplated the contents of her closet the next morning before picking a dark green lightweight wool dress with a modest hemline and filling its décolletage with a green and tan silk scarf. She put on gold earrings and a little gold watch and slipped into low-heeled tan shoes, transferring her notepad, wallet, lipstick, comb, cell phone, and other items to a matching tan purse that hung from her shoulder. She almost decided against perfume but thought she needed the reassurance of just a trace of good oldfashioned Chanel No. 5.

Connor said, "You look good enough to hire."

"Thank you," she said, smiling gently at him, and went downstairs.

The day was bright and cloudless, but the temperature hovered at sixty-eight. Of course, it was early, and the forecast was for it to rise to seventy-five.

Mike was very prompt. He drove up in a big old sedan that wasn't marked as a squad car, though it had the complex regalia inside—except there was no shotgun attached to the dash.

"Does this belong to the Excelsior Police?" asked Betsy, letting herself into the front passenger seat.

"Yes," said Mike in a tone that discouraged further inquiry. He pulled away from the curb, went up Lake Street to cross at the asterisk of streets, and then turned onto Highway 7 headed east.

"The man in charge of the facility is Dr. George Seely— a PhD doctor, of law. He's an adjunct instructor at the law school, but his primary job is director of the Safety and Environmental Protection Facility. The building is on the campus across from the University's TCF Bank Stadium."

"All right," said Betsy, getting out her notebook and beginning to write. "Did you ask him about Harry Whiteside?"

"Yes, and as a matter of fact, Dr. Seely knew Harry personally. They started pre-law school together. But Harry dropped out and went into engineering."

"Is that how Harry got the job of repairing the fire control system?"

"I don't know; we didn't get that far. I do know that Harry was in and out of the facility for over a week back in early March."

"Does Dr. Seely know you're bringing me along?"

"I told him I might bring someone with me, but that's all."

They got off the highway at University Avenue and went over to Twenty-third, around the stadium, and pulled up in front of a good-size, new-looking brick building with no windows.

Dr. Seely was evidently looking for their arrival, because he came out and leaned down to speak to Betsy, who rolled down her window. Mike produced his ID and badge, which Dr. Seely looked at for several seconds, though he did not take hold of it. He was a very tall man, with keen, dark brown eyes and a lot of nose. His iron gray hair grew down over his ears. He wore a pale blue dress shirt with the sleeves turned back and crisp black trousers.

"You'll need a special pass to park here or you'll get a ticket," he said, handing Betsy a red and white striped card about the size of an iPhone. She gave it to Mike, who put his badge away and hung the card from his rearview mirror.

Then they both got out of the car and followed Dr. Seely to the deeply inset entrance on a corner of the building. Seely had to press a card against a box on the wall to gain entrance.

He led them down a severely plain corridor with a high ceiling, past an office with a big window, to another door, and this time he had to slide a card down a slot to make the door unlock.

Then they were in a very large, oddly shaped room that looked kind of like a factory, only with no machinery, all hard surfaces. Paths were marked with narrow stripes of white paint on the gray concrete floor. Overhead were pipes: boxy green pipes, fat yellow round pipes, narrower red pipes, very narrow pipes in tan and black.

The air smelled faintly of . . . something. A kind of chemical odor, as if it had passed through a number of extremely efficient filters before being allowed in.

Off to the left was a room set with big panes of glass, and inside were three or four people at consoles facing the glass. The rest of the room was studded with big, sturdy-looking red metal doors. The whole place looked very clean.

Dr. Seely gestured at the doors and said, "We sort the incoming material according to kind—the really dangerous stuff goes into one of those rooms to be unpacked, which room depending on what kind of hazard it presents. Some materials, for example, react badly to moisture in the air. Some are dangerous to breathe."

Mike said, "I hope the people who work here are very picky about what they're doing."

"I try to make it so," Dr. Seely replied, smiling.

"What kind of hazardous material do you handle?"

"Anything, really. Disease germs, outdated prescription medicines, poisons, even small amounts of radioactive material. We have this whole building all to ourselves. It's an interesting job, and quite safe, if you're very careful."

"So, how do you dispose of such dangerous substances?"

"We sort it, seal it in drums, and send it to a special kind of incinerator that burns very hot, destroying everything, even the drums themselves."

"With extra-good scrubbers on the smokestacks," suggested Mike.

"Yes, indeed."

"Interesting that you knew Harry Whiteside from years back," Mike went on. "I'd like to talk to you about him."

Dr. Seely started to say something, then changed his mind and asked instead, "What's your interest in Harry?"

"I'm investigating a murder, and it's just barely possible that Harry is involved in it."

"Indeed? I thought it would be Harry's murder you were interested in."

"No, his murder is being handled by the Wayzata police. This is a second murder, of a woman, that happened around the same time. She was bidding against Harry for some property. Did Harry happen to mention to you anything about this bidding war?"

Frowning, Dr. Seely shook his head. "We didn't discuss business, except in very general terms."

"How did you come to hire him?"

"As I told you on the phone, we became friends here at

the U when we were both pre-law students. I went on to get my JD, and he got a master's in architectural design. We stayed in touch, but only casually—he was a difficult person, you see. I found him . . . manipulative and sometimes bad tempered. But he was also very amusing, witty, fun to be around.

"Well, as it happens, we ran across each other at a Golden Gophers basketball game back in February, and he mentioned that he'd installed a sprinkler system in a warehouse and his foreman—his *former* foreman, that is—had ordered half again the number of pipes needed for the job. Funny how that sort of thing can happen, his having extra pipes and us needing them."

"He didn't by chance know about your need for pipes before he told you this story?"

"Oh no, not at all. He told me the story first, and I said how interesting that was, because we needed new pipes to replace some corroded ones in our building. I suggested that perhaps the University could buy them from him at a discount, him being an alum, you see. Because most of the building and repair on campus is done by employees of the university. And he seemed open to that. Sometimes, though, we farm out a job, and it turned out that we needed to farm out this one. So I told him never mind and explained why, and he asked if he could submit a bid. I said he could, and I recommended his company, and he put in a nice, low bid and got the job."

"Was his work satisfactory?"

"Oh yes. But I'd forgotten what a son of a bitch he could be." Seely shook his head. "He complained the whole time because he had to carry an ID card and swipe a pass card every time he came in. 'You'd think you're storing nitro-glycerin in here,' he said." Seely winked. "I didn't tell him we had a package of bubonic plague germs on the counter right under where he was complaining to me about our stringent security methods."

"Where in the building did the pipes get replaced?" asked Mike.

"Come on, I'll show you."

He led them past two very large doors beyond the glass room. They led into yet another big room, and at the far end of it a sliding door was raised. Betsy could see the back end of the trailer of a semi truck up against it. Parked near the trailer's back end was a bright yellow forklift truck.

"We're about to send out a shipment to be incinerated," Seely said.

"Where's the incinerator?" asked Mike.

"This shipment's going to Saint Louis."

"Kind of far from here, isn't that?"

"Well, there aren't many of those incinerators in the country, and the one that's nearer, in Illinois, is backed up. Believe me, things are packed very thoroughly. Our pack-aging can survive even a rollover."

"Good to know," observed Mike.

"Come on. The pipes were replaced in here, where we pack things up."

He led them through a door high and wide enough to easily accommodate the forklift. In the first room—there was a second room beyond it, where Betsy could see row upon row of big blue barrels—was a small enclosure with a big metal hood over it. "We open some packages in there," he said. "The ventilation system sucks up vapors very efficiently." He made a gesture that took in the whole room. "This is where Harry did his work for us."

Betsy looked up but didn't see any new pipes. Dr. Seely saw her looking and said, "He painted them to match." The room's ceiling had the same complement of many colored pipes as the other.

Its walls were lined on three sides by a deep shelf about waist high. On the shelf were shoebox-size packages wrapped in brown paper and a few open boxes holding small bottles in Ziploc bags.

Curious, Betsy dared approach the shelf—though she stopped short when she saw that each wrapped package had a big black-and-white HAZARDOUS MATERIAL sticker on it. She came back to stand near Mike. This was a dangerous place.

"It's safe to go for a look," said Seely, amused. "Just don't open anything."

"Don't even touch it," warned Mike.

Betsy went closer and saw that most of the bottles in the open boxes looked like prescription bottles, though one had a chemical formula on it: HCN.

Mike, who had come along with her, said, "What's HCN?"

"That's cyanide," said Seely.

"Whoa!" said Mike.

Someone with a sense of humor had put a green Mr. Yuk sticker on it, next to the skull and crossbones sticker.

"Do you get a lot of poisons?" asked Betsy, and Mike cleared his throat warningly.

Seely nodded. "We got a lot of everything. Mostly outdated medicines, though. When you think how much prescription medicines cost, it breaks my heart to see how much of it gets thrown away."

"I assume you keep careful track of things like that," said Mike. "I mean, someone could come by and just pick up a bottle of outdated penicillin and take it home with him."

"It would have to be someone who works here," said Seely. "We don't allow non-employees to wander around unaccompanied. And look at this." He went to the counter and pulled a two-page packing slip from one of the open boxes, one white and one yellow, "See, the sender writes down what's in the packet and how many bottles of it there are. And our packer checks it off, making sure the bottle matches the description and that the number of bottles is correct."

But Betsy had got the bit between her teeth, and she pressed, "Does anyone ever make a mistake? I mean, the shipper writes down three bottles and there are only two in the box?"

Seely gave Betsy a long look.

But Mike said, "That's a good question."

"Okay, sometimes—*not often*—mistakes are made," he said. He repeated it. "Not often, you understand."

Betsy and Mike nodded.

"How does it happen when it does?" Mike asked.

"The guy packing things up over in the lab—this is the lowest-grade job a grad student can have, you understand—goes to pack up three bottles and can only find two, and he'll scratch a line through the three and write two and initial the change. Or someone here, unpacking, finds two bottles and the invoice says three. It could be just a case of bad handwriting—a two looking like a three—but it could be a bottle got misplaced, or the chemist decided he needed one and took it back. Now my guy is supposed to call the lab and run down the person who did up the package, but it's time to quit and he's tired, so he'll draw that line through the number himself and make the three a two. It can happen. But you've got something specific on your mind. What do you think went missing from here?"

Betsy looked at Mike, who said, "A bottle of nicotine."

"OKAY, it's a possibility," said Malloy in the car on their way back to Excelsior, "but how do we prove it?"

"You'll have to go back through those packing slips," said Betsy. "That card Doctor Seely swiped coming in, he told us it tracks him, records the day and time every time he passes through. He said everyone, employee, subcontractor, everyone has to use that tracking card. You heard him tell us that Harry complained about having to swipe a card every time he came in. So you look through the packing slips that came in on the days he was here and see if there's not one for nicotine that has a line through the number of bottles."

"Do you know how much time that will take me? They must get dozens at least every day."

"I'll do it. Get me access, a search warrant, whatever it takes. I'm way long overdue for a vacation, Mike. Hire me and I'll spend it at the Safety and Environmental Protection building. I'm sure I'm right."

"And so what if you are? We don't need to do this, you know. Every possible suspect has been cleared; no one's in danger of arrest. According to you—and I agree with you—the likely perp is dead."

"But people will talk if this isn't cleared up. They're already talking. Half the town thinks Joe's gotten away with murder; the other half thinks Chaz did it. This can destroy their lives. You can't let this go, Mike. You can't."

B ACK in his little office in Excelsior, Mike called Wayzata PD and asked to speak to the chief of detectives, Andy Taylor—and yes, he took a lot of hazing over his name, thanks to the old *Andy Griffith Show* that featured a small-town sheriff with the same name.

"I've got a little problem I'm hoping you can help me solve," Mike said after the usual introductions and pleasantries were exchanged.

"What's your little problem?" asked Captain Taylor.

"The investigator in charge of the Harry Whiteside case was given a piece of information, and because it came from a private citizen over here in Excelsior, he's dismissed it. Even after I suggested he follow up on it, he has taken no action. Now I'm well aware that we cops don't like interference in a case—"

"You got that right, for sure," interrupted Taylor, who did not sound the least little bit like his far friendlier TV namesake.

"On the other hand," Mike went on, "Larabee is stymied, and it's possible he's ignoring a very solid lead."

"Well, what is it?"

"That he should have the DNA of Maddy O'Leary compared to that blood sample collected at the Whiteside house." Mike explained Betsy's—and his own—reasoning for doing so.

"So why has he turned it down?"

"Because the suggestion first came from, as he puts it, an old spinster seamstress."

"Are you talking about that woman, Devonshire, who owns a needlework shop over in Excelsior?"

"Yes, sir, I am."

"Damn nosey parker interfering amateur."

"Yes, sir, that describes her pretty well. The problem is, she's right a lot of the time."

"Yeah, that's the word I've gotten about her. Not from my juice monkey, of course."

"Juice monkey?"

"Larabee. He's a weight lifter, and he's bulked up so fast the past year or so I suspect he's using steroids. Sometimes called juice."

"Ah, juice monkey. Now I see."

"And I've noticed that steroid use shrinks the brain while it swells the abs. Okay, I'll order that test. And thank you, Sergeant Malloy, for calling this to my attention. I'll let you know if it checks out."

"Thank you, Captain."

Chapter Thirty-one

❖ ❖ ❖

A WEEK later, Mike got a forwarded e-mail with an attachment originated by the undergrad the University had hired to comb through the file of packing slips at the Safety and Environmental Protection Facility.

Is this what you're looking for? the young woman had asked Dr. Seely.

And, sure enough, the attachment was a color copy of the yellow packing slip used by the University. It showed that three one-ounce bottles of nicotine—two full, one reduced to .63 ounces—were sent to be safely disposed of, but the numeral 3 had a diagonal line drawn through its box and the numeral 2 written in beside it. The box was further crowded by an illegible scribble meant to be someone's initials.

The date on the slip indicated that the box had been packed on March 9 of this year and opened at the facility on March 11.

Harry Whiteside had worked at the facility from March 7 through March 17.

Mike called Dr. Seely.

"I was about to call you," Dr. Seely said. "I checked the security records, and Mr. Whiteside was here the day the packing slip was changed. Moreover, no one I've spoken to can identify the initials on the changed slip."

Mike would have preferred to check out the initials himself, but considering the careful attitude of Dr. Seely, that would be duplicating an already thorough effort.

So as far as he was concerned, Harry Whiteside was guilty of the murder of Maddy O'Leary. He went into his computer and pulled up the file on the case and added a brief note to Dr. Seely's report, printed out the whole thing, and hand carried it down the hall to Chief Haugen's office.

Chief Haugen was a tall man nearing fifty, thickening in the waist. A square-faced towhead with very chilly light gray eyes, his blond hair was almost unobtrusively turning white. He was taciturn by nature, and he merely nodded at Mike coming into his office.

Mike said, "Good afternoon, sir," and put the report on the chief's desk.

"He was a quick study," said Mike, after Chief Haugen read the report. "It only took four days for Harry to discover the weak spot in the control system that made it possible for him to take a little bottle of nicotine without being detected."

"But did he take it?" asked the chief. "Has the stolen bottle been found in the vicinity of Harry Whiteside?"

"No, and we won't find it," said Mike. "Anyone with a

room-temperature IQ would know to get rid of it in a way that it would never be found. Anyway, if you think a search should be made, the person to ask is Sergeant Larabee of Wayzata PD. It's his case. I hope you don't want me to ask him, because he blew up all over me when I suggested he have Maddy O'Leary's DNA compared to the blood sample sorted out from the mix found on that doorknob. I had to go over his head to their chief of detectives, Taylor, and ask him to order it. I almost think Larabee's madder at me because they found a match than he'd be if they didn't."

"What made you think to suggest Maddy O'Leary's DNA might be in the Whiteside house?"

Mike fell silent for a few seconds. Then, because the chief was amazingly perceptive and Mike was basically honest, he said, "A private citizen talked to me about it."

"Is she a resident of Excelsior?"

Mike sighed. "Yeah, she is." Haugen kept looking at him, so he reluctantly continued. "This woman found out that Harry Whiteside got a job replacing some pipes in the hazardous waste disposal building on the U campus. Harry and Maddy O'Leary have been at loggerheads for years, and when she got in ahead of him on the Water Street property, he was over-the-top pissed. At that hazardous waste building he saw a banquet of poisons just sitting there waiting for him to select one. So he decided he didn't have to share the world with her anymore and acquired some liquid nicotine, which he poured onto some yarn she was going to knit in public at that toy auction."

"That's this woman's theory."

"Well, yeah. But the evidence supports it."

"Is she the same person you took with you to that hazardous waste facility? And who suggested that we check the packing slips?"

"Well, I was already thinking we should do that."

"That was your thinking."

"Yessir." Then he added hastily, "But I'll admit she thought of it, too. Actually, maybe she thought of it first."

"And you think maybe I should call a news conference and explain all this to reporters, making the two of us look like fools who needed the help of this amateur to solve a murder."

"Yessir, except you can leave out the part about us looking like fools by leaving out her role. That's what I'd suggest. Sir."

"Why should we do this? Why not just say the case is closed?"

"Because there's gossip all over town that maybe Mr. Mickels or Mr. Reynolds got away with murder, and I think it's irresponsible of us to allow that if there's any way to clear them."

"Uh-huh, you were thinking that."

"Well, she's thinking that, too. And, okay, she told me I should think of it. But it's true, I had someone tell me to my face it's a shame we haven't arrested Mr. Mickels."

"And you agree with her conclusions."

"Well, I've come to the same ones."

"With her help."

"Ah, well, yes."

"Maybe I should let you go and hire her instead."

Mike forced a chuckle and said, "You can make the offer, but she won't even get a PI license. So no way will she agree to carry a badge." Then he offered his best crooked smile to show he knew they were both joking.

But it was also true. No way would she make it as a cop.

And a good thing. He and Elton had had enough trouble with Jill Cross Larson when she was a sergeant on the force; there was no way Elton could endure working with a crazy lady like Betsy Devonshire. Yes, she was a very clever lady, and sometimes a big help on a difficult case, but Betsy Devonshire was the proof that clinched his argument that females didn't belong as cops. She didn't think like a cop, and she didn't like the rules and restraints they worked under. Much better, to his way of thinking, that she stay in that needlework shop of hers and be free to only poke her oar in once in a widely separated while.

Betsy Devonshire, PI? That might be helpful, if only because the training would teach her the rules she would nevertheless continue to ignore. Detective Sergeant Betsy Devonshire? As if!

IN what had become a required ritual at the end of each case, Betsy Devonshire sat at the head of the library table in Crewel World while the Monday Bunch surrounded her, and Godwin sat at the foot.

"All right, girl," said Bershada. "Give."

"First of all, neither Chaz nor Joe had anything to do with these two deaths."

"We knew that!" said Bershada.

"About Chaz, yes," said Godwin. "About Joe, not so much."

"So who did murder them?" asked Phil. "Did the same person do both of them in?"

"Of course not!" said Valentina. "Don't you remember that there were two very different methods? One was, like, break in, break things, break the man's skull; the other was sneaky. That *must* mean two different murderers."

"Now, not necessarily," said Alice. "It could have been that the murderer needed different methods because the victims were so different."

Jill said, "Perhaps if we just sit quietly, Betsy will tell us how it happened."

The others gave abashed laughs, then fell silent and looked at Betsy.

She said, "There's going to be a joint news conference tomorrow morning over in Wayzata, with Detective Sergeants Mike Malloy and Frank Larabee speaking, with backup from Chief Haugen and Chief Weil. They are going to announce that they are 'satisfied' they have identified the murderers of Maddy O'Leary and Harry Whiteside—and it's each of them. Maddy murdered Harry, and Harry murdered Maddy."

There was a stunned silence around the table.

"I don't see how," said Emily. "How could Mr. Whiteside murder Maddy after he was already dead?"

"He poured the nicotine onto Maddy's yarn while it—and he—was at the music reception at Mount Calvary in the afternoon. Then he went home and surprised Maddy vandalizing his house, and she killed him."

"*Maddy* was the one who burglarized him?" asked Valentina.

"Why?" asked Emily. "She wasn't poor; she didn't need any of his stuff."

"I'm sure it will transpire that she took nothing. She

was exacting revenge for his vandalizing her cabin up in Pine County."

Blank looks all around. Finally Doris ventured, "What cabin?"

"That cabin was the precipitating—if precipitating is the word I'm after—" She paused, then nodded, deciding it was, and continued. "Maddy and Harry have been at odds for a long time. They often ended up bidding on the same job or piece of property. Harry was richer, but Maddy was more clever—or at least less willing to aggravate and provoke the people she was working with. They might have gone on like that for years. But then Maddy found a piece of property for sale up in Pine County. It was on a lake that wasn't already surrounded by cabins, so it was nice and private. There was a raggedy old cabin already on the property, which she tore down and replaced with a beautiful one with indoor plumbing and electrical wiring.

"The problem was, that property and primitive cabin was originally owned by Harry's grandparents, and he had happy memories of summers spent up there. His plan was to buy and restore the cabin, complete with kerosene lamps and an outhouse. He tried for years to get it, without success—but Maddy happened to be up there a few years ago when the owner died suddenly, and his family immediately put it on the market. She snapped it up. People wondering where she went for her annual two weeks' vacation should have looked at lakeside rental cabins.

"Harry thought she deliberately outmaneuvered him to deny him his grandparents' land, but I can't find any evidence of that. Still, she was probably pleased when he accused her of it.

"Then, when she outbid him on the Water Street property, he totally lost his temper, went up there, and smashed the windows of her cabin. Chaz remembers Harry asking her about repairing some broken windows. He knew of no broken windows in her rental property and was surprised at her furious reaction. Harry was letting her know he was responsible for the damage to the cabin. So she went to his Wayzata home and began breaking things."

"How did she get in?"

"Talk to Chaz; he'll tell you about how she taught him to bypass locks a tenant would put on without permission."

"Why would he need to do that?" asked Emily, diverted.

Bershada said, "Chaz told me that sometimes people move out without leaving the keys. Sometimes they don't want their landlords to investigate because they're doing something illegal in their unit."

Betsy said, "My problem is tenants making copies of their keys and handing them out to unauthorized people.

"But the point is, Maddy knew how to bypass locks." Betsy made a sad face. "I've seen Harry's place; it's gorgeous and very expensively decorated. She could have done—she may have done thousands of dollars of damage very easily.

"But Harry walked in on her while she was there. And a very short fight ensued. Maddy wasn't injured. She probably had something in her hands she was using to break things and she struck him on the head with it. I don't know if she meant to kill him; it's possible she hit him in self-defense. But whatever, she left him dead on his kitchen floor."

Jill said, "And you know she's the one who did this—how?"

"She came in here the Friday before the auction with more knitted toys, remember?"

They all nodded.

"And she had a Band-Aid on her finger."

Godwin said, "Yes! I remember because the Band-Aid was red, white, and blue, and I'd set the door to play 'Hail to the Chief.'"

Betsy said, "And whoever murdered Harry cut her finger on a projecting screw on a doorknob. A DNA test proved the blood left on the screw belonged to Maddy. That test proved she was in his house and there is no way on earth he would invite her to come for a visit. So why was she in there?"

Betsy sighed. "But Harry had already poisoned her yarn with nicotine he stole from the University's hazardous waste disposal facility when he went there to repair their fire-extinguishing system."

"Mmmm-mmmm-mmmm," said Bershada. "Nasty. Serious anger problems in both of them."

Phil said, "But at least the anger was limited in its direction: strictly at each other."

"The really hot anger was," said Betsy, "but both of them were well-known for shouting at other people, some of whom didn't deserve it. All three of Harry's sons, for example, moved out of state to get away from him. And poor Chaz put up with an awful lot from Maddy, some of whose tenants would move out when they heard she'd bought their apartment building. Harry and Maddy were both accomplished, talented people, but they were by no means governed by sweetness and light."

"Awwww," said Cherie, "I was kind of hoping we'd hear

from you that there were going to be people arrested and sent to jail. Instead, we get . . . nothing."

"We got plenty!" disagreed Phil. "We got a neat little package of two mean people destroying each other and no innocent bystanders killed in the process. Well . . ." he conceded, "Joe Mickels is still standing."

"He's going to get his Mickels Building at last," said Emily. "Good for him. Now maybe he won't be sad anymore."

"Let's begin again," said Doris to Godwin and Rafael. They were in the pair's condo and had just finished a light supper of poached salmon and vegetable soup, served with wine. "How much do you want to spend on this wedding?"

"I don't think we ought to start with a budget," said Godwin. "I think we should decide what we want and find a way to pay for it."

"Well, I think we should have a budget," interjected Rafael. "Some weddings cost tens of thousands of dollars, which I think is ridiculous. Is the object of this ceremony to see how ostentatious—is that the correct word?—we can be? Or is it to celebrate the legal joining of our lives while our friends celebrate, too?"

"The legal joining of our lives," sighed Godwin. "What a sweet way you put it, Rafael."

"So of course we will do it in the presence of God and the company we invite, and so it should be beautiful. There should be flowers and perhaps balloons, and bright colors, and good food. And we will wear something appropriate—yes? Or festive. Which do you prefer, *mi gorrión?*"

"If it is to be formal, we should wear tuxedos. If you want to go festive, we could wear bullfighter costumes—"

"Not bullfighter costumes, because we are not bullfighters. No costumes. We are not making believe; we are Rafael and Godwin, two real men doing a real thing."

Doris hastily drew a line through something she had written. "I think tuxedos are nice, unless you want to go full formal and wear tails."

"Tails?" said Rafael.

"It's very formal menswear," said Doris. "White shirt and tie, white vest, black trousers, and a coat that has a back that is very long and split in half at the bottom. Orchestra conductors wear them. The outfit probably has some other name, but I've always heard it called tails. Of course, if you want to go that far, then you have to get married in the evening, as it is incorrect to wear tails during the day."

Godwin stared at her admiringly. "How clever of you to know that!"

"I've been studying up on weddings. Miss Manners has been very useful."

"I think we want an afternoon wedding," said Rafael. "So tuxedos, all right?"

"All right," said Godwin. "But maybe with rainbow cummerbunds?" He made a gesture indicating the size and location of a cummerbund.

Doris laughed. "That sounds like fun."

"And my tuxedo black, Raff's white?"

Rafael nodded. "But then I want my . . . my cummerbund to be lavender."

"Yes!" cheered Godwin. "And matching bow ties, lavender for you and rainbow for me!"

Doris made some more notes. "Now," she said, "about location. The wedding's a little more than a year away, so it's possible not all the good places are taken."

"We want it indoors—remember?" said Godwin.

"I remember. Did you know you could use the Minneapolis Institute of Art?"

"Wow, that would be fabulous." He turned to Rafael. "Just imagine a photo of the two of us at the top of those stairs leading up to the old entrance. Do a video, starting long-distance, from the bottom and gradually coming up and up, closer and closer . . ." His eyes closed, and he smiled.

"In the rain," Rafael said.

"Oh. Well, we could shoot that on another day, when it's not raining, unless it's not raining on our day. Still . . ." He looked at Doris. "Where else?"

"Well, there's Loews Minneapolis Hotel downtown. Their Stone Arch Ballroom has seventeen-foot-high ceilings and can seat four hundred, and they have other, smaller rooms. And an on-site catering service that can do plain or fancy. I didn't ask for a quote, but they sound pricey. But for real extravagance, there's the Saint Paul Hotel. Beautiful location, however."

Doris named several other places, from an arboretum to a retired railroad station. Then she said, "Look, I'm not a professional. I don't want to plan your wedding for you, just help you make important decisions, tell you what your options might be. What I think you should do is contact a professional wedding planner. Sunrise Styling looks great, judging from their web site, and they specialize in gay and lesbian weddings. Ariane Criger is another. They have venues, catering, photographers, everything at their fingertips. I want to stay involved, help you make decisions—keep you, Goddy, from sitting up the night before dyeing white doves lavender; and you, Rafael, from holding the reception at McDonald's. Does that sound good?"

"No lavender doves?" sniffed Godwin, pretending to be heartbroken.

"No Quarter Pounders?" mourned Rafael—then he laughed. "All right, Dorita, you are to accompany us to our planning sessions and wear a big hat with a long pin in it, so you can prick us in our backsides when we start failing to do this properly."

Doris's eyes shone. "You two are so wonderful!" she said.

JOE Mickels sat up late in his modest Excelsior office. He was calculating the value of assets he could draw money from, considering the disposition of other assets, moving money into accessible accounts. Those people running Maddy's estate would have no wish to involve themselves in the complex and time-consuming building project over on Water Street, so they would—probably fairly quickly—put the option to buy on the market. And he was not going to be caught short again.

He could see it in his mind's eye, rising above the surrounding buildings. Maybe copper clad—or was that too ostentatious for little old Excelsior? But not plain glass; he wanted something ornate. And over the main entrance a massive granite lintel with letters cut deep: THE MICKELS BUILDING.

He was no longer feeling his age. He felt young and vigorous and energetic. Maybe he should invite Betsy Devonshire to the grand opening.

IT was close to bedtime. Connor was in the bathroom, brushing his teeth. Betsy was in bed but reading—rereading, actually—Jerome K. Jerome's famous comic novel, *Three Men in a Boat.* A best seller over a hundred years ago, it was still very funny. Betsy was making the bed jiggle with her chuckles when Connor crawled in beside her.

"*Machree,*" he said, "I have something to ask you. Something important."

Betsy immediately put the book down. "What is it?"

"All this talk of marriage has reminded me that I haven't asked you to marry me for several months. So I ask again: Will you marry me?"

"Oh, Connor . . ."

"Is it because you don't love me enough?"

"I love you with all my heart, you know that."

"Then what's holding you back?"

"I've tried marrying, twice. And failed at it both times."

"You haven't tried it with me."

"You've tried it before. And it didn't work."

"I think my marriage failed because I was so often and for so long at sea. But I'm home from the sea now."

"I think my marriages failed because I'm lousy at picking men to marry."

Connor looked so stricken that she said at once, "Don't you see? That's why I haven't married you! I love you, I love who you are, where you came from, what you can do, everything about you! I love having you in my life; you are very good to me and for me. But I'm scared. I don't trust my own judgment. I'd be devastated if you left me. And for some stupid reason, I'm scared witless that if we marry, you'll leave me. And I couldn't bear that, I couldn't!" She felt herself beginning to weep and started to turn away.

But he gathered her into his arms. "Oh, my dearest darling, my own heart, how could I leave you? You are everything to me." He began to kiss her gently, stroking her face, her hair, her back, then more ardently, insistently . . .

Later, all tension gone, she purred, "You are such a comfort to me."

"And you to me. So let's make a bargain. If I am still here a year from now, and you are still with me, then we will reopen the question. Until then, I will not ask you again. All right?"

"All right." A year. In a year, surely she would know.

"Sophie" Knitted
Amigurumi Cat Pattern

Designed by Diane Davis

"Sophie" is a fluffy little avalanche of white with a patch-work of gray and tan on her ear, back, and tail. She'll be great company while you're reading one of the Needlecraft Mysteries by Monica Ferris!

FINISHED SIZE:
   Approx. 7" long by 3" wide

MATERIALS REQUIRED:
   Worsted weight yarn—approx. 65 yards in Main Color
      (MC), 10-15 yards in Gray (A) and Tan or Gold (B)
   Satin ribbon for collar (approx 9")
   Embroidery floss or yarn for embroidering face
      (Optional: Small plastic cat eyes and nose)
   Stuffing material

"Sophie" Knitted Amigurumi Cat Pattern

Size 3 double pointed needles
Plastic needlepoint or darning needle

ABBREVIATIONS:

CO: Cast on
K: Knit
P: Purl
M1: Make 1 stitch
M1K1: Make 1, Knit 1
skpo: Slip 1 stitch as if to knit, knit 1 stitch, pass the
    slipped stitch over
K2 tog: Knit 2 stitches together
w&t: Wrap and turn
PU: Pick up
dpn: Double pointed needle

SPECIAL STITCHES USED:

M1—Used to increase stitches. Make 1 stitch, lift
    right leg of the stitch in the row below the next
    stitch to be worked and place it on the left needle,
    then work it as a normal knit stitch.

W&T—Used in short rows to avoid "holes" in your
    work. When knitting, knit required stitches, pass
    yarn to the front, slip next stitch to the right
    needle, pass yarn to the back, slip stitch back to left
    needle and turn your work. When purling, pass
    yarn to the back, slip next stitch to the right
    needle, pass yarn to the front, slip stitch back to the
    left needle and turn your work.

"Sophie" Knitted Amigurumi Cat Pattern

Double Knitting—In this pattern, we'll use double knitting to combine all of the stitches onto one dpn before binding off. However, instead of using separate strands of yarn for front and back layers, we're going to use just one strand of MC, switching to B when we reach the left ear. *Purl one stitch from the rear needle, knit one from the front, continuing in the same pattern across the needles.* When you reach the B stitches, let MC trail out between the MC and B stitches (you'll need it again when you're ready to bind off). Continue in B for remainder of row until all stitches are on one dpn.

HINTS FOR COLOR WORK (INTARSIA) KNITTING:

- When switching from one color to another, wrap the two strands around each other to minimize holes or gaps between color patches.

- When knitting intarsia in the round, there are many times when your working yarn will end up at the wrong end of the patch you're knitting. When this happens, knit up to the color change, slip stitches to be knitted from one needle to the other and turn your work. (These spots are noted in the pattern instructions.) Pick up the working yarn and purl back across the stitches, then turn your work again and slip the purled stitches back to the right needle. Carry your MC behind the stitches and continue with your next color.

BODY
CO 26 st in MC, divide between 3 dpns (10 st on dpn1, 8 st each on dpn2 and dpn3). Connect in the round, making sure your stitches are not twisted.

Rounds 1–2: K all

Round 3: Dpn1—K3, M1 K4, M1, K3 (12 st); Dpn2 & Dpn3—K2, M1, K4, M1, K2 (10 st on each)

Round 4: Dpn1—K4 in MC, attach color A and K3, attach color B and K2, MC K3; Dpn2 & Dpn3: K all in MC

Round 5: Dpn1—K3 in MC, slip next 6 st, turn, P3 in B, P3 in A, turn and slip those 6 st back to working needle, K3 in MC; Dpn2 & Dpn3: K all in MC

Round 6: Dpn1—K4 in MC, K2 in A, K2 in MC, K3 in B, K1 in MC; Dpn2 & Dpn3: K all in MC

Round 7: Dpn1—K4 in MC, slip next 7 st, turn, P5 in B, P2 in A, turn and slip those 7 st back to working needle, K1 in MC; Dpn2 & Dpn3: K all in MC

Round 8: Dpn1—K2 in MC, K5 in B, K3 in A, K2 in MC; Dpn2 & Dpn3: K all in MC

Round 9: Dpn1—K3 in MC, slip next 7 st, turn, P5 in B, P2 in A, turn and slip those 7 st back to working needle, K2 in MC; Dpn2 & Dpn3: K all in MC

"Sophie" Knitted Amigurumi Cat Pattern

Round 10: Dpn1—K3 in MC, K3 in A, K4 in B, K2 in MC; Dpn2 & Dpn3: K all in MC

Round 11: Dpn1—K3 in MC, slip next 7 st, turn, P5 in B, P2 in A, turn and slip those 7 st back to working needle, K2 in MC; Dpn2 & Dpn3: K all in MC

Round 12: Dpn1—K3 in MC, K3 in B, K4 in A, K2 in MC; Dpn2 & Dpn3: K all in MC

Round 13: Dpn1—K3 in MC, slip next 7 st, turn, P5 in B, P2 in A, turn and slip those 7 st back to working needle, K2 in MC; Dpn2 & Dpn3: K all in MC

Round 14–16: Dpn1—K all in MC; Dpn2 & Dpn3: K all in MC

Round 17: Dpn1—K5 in MC, K2 in B, K5 in MC; Dpn2 & Dpn3: K all in MC

Round 18: Dpn1—K4 in MC, K4 in B, K4 in MC; Dpn2 & Dpn3: K all in MC

Round 19: Dpn1—K4 in MC, K5 in B, K3 in MC; Dpn2 & Dpn3: K all in MC

Round 20: Dpn1—K4 in MC, K5 in A, K3 in MC; Dpn2 & Dpn3: K all in MC

Round 21: Dpn1—K4 in MC, slip next 5 st, turn, P5 in A, turn and slip those 5 st back to working needle, K3 in MC; Dpn2 & Dpn3: K all in MC

"Sophie" Knitted Amigurumi Cat Pattern

Round 22: Dpn1—K5 in MC, K3 in A, K4 in MC; Dpn2 & Dpn3: K all in MC

Round 23: K all in MC

NOTE: Knit rounds 24–28 in MC****

Round 24: K3, skpo, *K6, skpo* 3 times, K3 (28 st)

Round 25: K3, skpo, *K5, skpo* 3 times, K2 (24 st)

Round 26: K3, skpo, *K4, skpo* 3 times, K1 (20 st)

Round 27: K3, skpo, *K3, skpo* 3 times (16 st)

Round 28: K3, skpo, K2, skpo, K2, skpo, K2, slip last stitch, pass over 1st stitch in the round (12 st)

Round 29: In Color A: K2, skpo, K1, skpo, K1, skpo, K1, slip last stitch, pass over 1st stitch in the round (8 st)

TAIL
Continue with the 8 stitches on the dpns

Round 1: K all in A

Round 2–16: All 3 colors should be trailing out the hole where the tail will be. For the remaining rows, hold together two of the strands for one round, and change combinations for each round.

"Sophie" Knitted Amigurumi Cat Pattern

Round 17: *K2 tog* in A only, repeat from * 3 times. Cut a length of yarn and thread a plastic darning needle. Pass stitches from needles to the yarn and pull tight to close the end of the tail. Fasten off and weave ends down inside tail. (Tail doesn't need additional stuffing.)

PAWS (TWO)
CO 10 st in MC, divide between 2 dpns to give paws a flatter look. Connect in the round, making sure your stitches are not twisted.

Rounds 1–15: K all

Round 16: Skpo, K1, skpo twice, K1, skpo. Cut a length of yarn and thread a plastic darning needle. Pass stitches from needles to the yarn and pull tight to close the end of the paw. Fasten off. Stuff lightly to within a ½" from the closed end of the paw and shape paws around your thumb, giving them a slight downward curve. Sew paws to underside of body approx. 8–10 rows from neck opening. After paws are attached, stuff body to desired fluffiness.

HEAD/CHEST
Determine center of front neck opening, count 8 stitches to the right. This is where you will begin picking up stitches for the Head/Chest section. Pick up 26 stitches around the neck opening, moving clockwise as you look at the opening. Distribute the stitches on 3 dpns with 8 st each on left and right front sides (dpn1 on the right as you look at the

opening, dpn 2 on the left) and 10 stitches on dpn3 across the back of the neck opening. Knit all of the stitches on dpn 1 (K8), which will bring you to the center of the neck opening, and begin the short rows. (The short row section will only be worked across dpn1 and dpn2.)

Rows 1&2: Dpn2: K2, w&t, P2; Dpn1: P2, w&t, K2

Rows 3&4: Dpn2: K3, w&t, P3; Dpn1: P3, w&t, K3

Rows 5&6: Dpn2: K4, w&t, P4; Dpn1: P4, w&t, K4

Rows 7&8: Dpn 2: K5, w&t, P5; Dpn 1: P5, w&t, K5

Rows 9&10, 11&12, 13&14**:
Continue adding a stitch each pair of rows until all 8 stitches on each dpn are wrapped and turned.

Row 14—Note: You will end the 14th Row at the center of the chest, then K the next 8 stitches on dpn2 to make the front rows even on both sides. Transfer 1 st from the ends of dpn1 and dpn2 to dpn 3, giving you 7 st on dpn1 & dpn 2, and 12 on dpn3.

Round 15: Begin knitting in rounds, starting with dpn3. Dpn3: K11 in MC, K1 in B (beginning of color work for ear section); Dpn1: K1 in B, K6 in MC; Dpn2: K7 in MC

Round 16: Dpn3: K10 in MC, K2 in B; Dpn1: K2 in B, K5 in MC; Dpn2: K7 in MC

"Sophie" Knitted Amigurumi Cat Pattern

Round 17: Dpn3: K9 in MC, K3 in B; Dpn1: K3 in B, K4 in MC; Dpn2: K7 in MC

Round 18: Dpn3: K8 in MC, K4 in B; Dpn1: K4 in B, K3 in MC; Dpn2: K7 in MC

Round 19: Dpn3: K7 in MC, K5 in B; Dpn1: K5 in B, K2 in MC; Dpn2: K7 in MC

Round 20: Dpn3: K6 in MC, K6 in B; Dpn1: K6 in B, slip last st on dpn1, K first st on dpn2 in MC and psso, K6 in MC (7 st on dpn1); Dpn2: K6 in MC (25 st)

Round 21: Dpn3: K6 in MC, K6 in B; Dpn1: K7 in B; Dpn2: K6 in MC (25 st)

NOTE: At this point you will need to stop and stitch the facial features and stuff the head and chest before seaming the top. Don't forget to add a few whiskers!

Round 22: There are now 13 stitches on dpns1 & 2, and 12 stitches on dpn3. Turn work so that dpn3 is closest to you, and hold the front needles parallel to it. Starting with the first st on dpn2, double knit the front and back stitches (P st from dpn1 & 2, K st from dpn3), alternating until all stitches are on one needle. (1st 6 from each dpn will be in MC, remaining 7 will be in B).

Row 23: Turn work so the back of the neck is closest to you. K2tog, binding off the row as you go. Fasten off and weave in ends.

FINISHING TOUCHES:

- Stitch along where ears meet the head and over the top seam between the ears to give them more definition. Tie off at back of head and weave ends in.

- Tuck tail around the side of the body and stitch if desired, or let it hang naturally.

- Add a "collar" of satin ribbon with a bell or charm on it for a sophisticated touch.